1984

Michael A. Faleth
410 Grover Street
Joliet, Illinois

THE COLLECTED STORIES

OF

Ben Hecht

THE
COLLECTED
STORIES
OF
Ben Hecht

PREFACED BY

Some Introductory Thoughts

BY THE AUTHOR

Grosset & Dunlap

PUBLISHERS
NEW YORK, N. Y.

BY ARRANGEMENT WITH CROWN PUBLISHERS
PRINTED IN THE UNITED STATES OF AMERICA

For

DAVID LEBESON

who was killed fighting the Germans

Some Introductory Thoughts

READERS are a much odder tribe than writers. They are much more fretful and egotistic.

The vainest of writers will often pause and ponder whether he knows anything about writing. No such humble moments afflict a reader. The reader knows everything—that is, about writing.

I imagine this is as it should be. It would be disastrous if a critic ever had any doubts about his opinions. He would cease to be a critic instanter and become something else, perhaps an artist, or worse—a man out of a job.

A reader is a critic with a very fine and important job—to please himself. It is, however, his job, not mine.

The stories that fill this book will undoubtedly fail to please a great many readers. I shall identify them in advance and thus save us both an unprofitable meeting.

Those readers who are fond of reading things that bore them, under the delusion that boredom is the mark of high class art, will find little profit in me. I have never tried to wheedle myself into their parvenu libraries by pulling a long face and putting lead in my sentences.

Those readers who pleasure themselves with reading things they can't quite understand so that they may seem to others smarter than they are will find no comfort in me; although I am not completely positive on this point. I may be given to occasional lapses of intelligibility and whilom rhetorical flights that wind up in a fog bank—for I began life as a poet. But such misty patches are infrequent in my prose and provide small manna for the enigma fanciers.

Those readers who like to read about very dull people who do and say and think very dull things under the delusion that they, the readers, are coming to grips with Real Life by such slumming, will waste their time on me.

I have my periods of dullness, but they are not deliberate. I was weaned on The Arabian Nights and Dickens—both of whom taught me that a man who aspires to dullness is following a line of least resistance.

Those readers who admire Slices of Raw Life—real human beings lying inanimately on a fictional platter like a collection of rutabagas and pineapples, will be irked by my opposite offerings.

I have disliked always stories in which, right bang in front of you, nothing happens. And I have disliked always stories which have for their plots the opening of a door, or the creaking of a rocker or somebody sighing at a soda fountain.

And I have disliked always stories that tried to make me feel what a subtle fellow I was to understand them. There is at present a rash of this pretentious and inept vignette-fiction—and all of it as subtle as a bad shave.

Those readers who fancy what they like to call a chaste style and demand that a love story or a great adventure be told in words that would not embarrass a tomato-can label, will find me not their dish at all. For I am, and always have been, a very clever fellow with words.

I have been often fiercely challenged by readers as being insincere and superficial because I was fond of adding wit to my lucubrations and sticking a verbal feather in the hats of my characters. I can understand their challenge well enough. People who sweat when they think and to whom an idea comes with all the impact of a toothache, refuse to believe that gayety and not pain may be the mark of intellect.

Those readers with bobby-socks minds who like to read only celebrities will automatically skip me, so I need not address them.

I have, alas, never been a celebrity. I have had a good mead of admirers, and my files bulge with enough flattering communiqués to keep me soothed for the rest of my life. But I have never yet won to that unreasoning and uncritical back-slapping that makes a celebrity—and leaves everybody happy to be seen shaking hands with him or his works.

I have in the above paragraphs dismissed quite a bag of readers, and my publisher who is investing his money in the production of this volume may wonder with a twinge whether there are any left. God knows. However, under the assumption that there are, I shall address my remaining comments to them.

The stories they will read in this volume were written out of a greater variety of moods than it is customary for one writer to have. This variety in my work, and the contradictions it involves, have inspired one critic of parts to identify me as a schizophrenic or split personality. As an authority on schizophrenia I can easily deny this.

There is a basic and never varying reason behind all my short story writing. It is this—I write to cheer myself up. I know the world well and it fills me with an ugly mood. The stupidity of humans and their horrid incompetence toward life is a theme with which I have wrestled in many of my books.

My short stories are my chief social effort to escape the gloomy pits of information in my mind.

One does this by entering the happy storehouse of the imagination. Here is a world not yet gone to pot, here are people and events still as dreamy and charming as filled the days of one's innocence. Sitting down to write of them, I enjoy myself.

Yet in my stories, after they are written, I find always that I have actually invented nothing, that the people I have written about are actually people I have known, and that the anecdotes in which I wrap them up are truly adventures which have befallen me or those around me at some time.

It becomes obvious to me, then, that the only fictional thing' in my stories is my point of view. My point of view in most of my stories is that of a child who finds the world full of exuberant and engrossing matters, who dramatizes what he sees so he may enjoy it more, and who asks as a reward for his labors only the illusion that existence is a fine thing.

If you read the stories in this book, however, you will notice that my innocence and gayety are not constantly present. The folly and poison of life manage to unhorse my sturdiest efforts at cheer. I am full of contempts that my wit and Arabian-Nights plots do not entirely conceal.

And try as I may to cheer myself up with spanking tales and a jolly point of view, a moan lurks in the corners of many of my tales.

I apologize for this unseemly sound. It belongs in me and not my tales. For I have had always a picture of myself as a story teller. I have seen myself like those sunny and cackling fellows who once upon a time stood on the street corners of Bagdad and unfolded tales to the harassed citizens who paused to listen—and fling grateful kopecks at their feet.

BEN HECHT

Nyack, N. Y.,
April, 1945.

Contents

ix

Contents

THE COLLECTED STORIES

OF

Ben Hecht

Concerning a Woman of Sin

EVERY YEAR or so a new conqueror appears in Hollywood and, seizing it by the tail, swings it around his head. And for the year or so this conqueror rides a gold elephant to work and lives on a dream boat.

Sometimes there are two, three or four conquerors in Hollywood all at the same time and all swinging it around their heads. On such occasions the hostesses, bartenders and publicity departments of the cinema capital break down and the neighboring spas become crowded with convalescents.

This story is the account of one such conqueror who, singlehanded, sent the mightiest of Hollywood to Arrowhead Lake and Palm Springs to recover from the tumult of her conquest. Jerome B. Cobb, head of the great Empire Studios, was one of these many refugees. The top Pharaoh was accompanied by two nurses and an osteopath who toiled for several weeks to bring Mr. Cobb back to sanity, or what passes for sanity in the Cobb cosmos. An entourage of important Nobles kept Mr. Cobb company taking hot mud baths and trying to shake the impact of Daisy Marcher out of their nervous systems.

But before I can start this account of Daisy Marcher's conquest of Hollywood it will be wise to explain a few things about the movie capital. It has been my experience that it is best to approach a tale of Cinemaland like an anthropologist and discuss the odd tribal customs of the place so that the reader will be partly persuaded at least that one is not writing with an opium pipe in one hand. I will confine these preliminaries only to that phase of the movies which makes possible the unnerving advent of a Daisy Marcher.

In Hollywood a movie star receives from $100,000 to $150,000 for acting in a single picture. This chore occupies about ten weeks of the star's time, which means, on a basis of an eight-hour day, that the star receives roughly from $5 to $7 a minute for acting. This includes the many minutes (more than two-thirds of them) during which the star lies dormant in the dressing room; also the many minutes in which the star gets mad and won't act at all; likewise the many minutes during which the star is kept from the full practice of his or her art by infidelity, amnesia or a hangover.

Similar pots of gold are handed over to the top writers and directors of movies who are sometimes incapacitated for whole weeks at a time (while on salary) by being unable to think at all. But whether they are thinking or merely sitting staring at the wall these artists receive from $4 to $6 a minute. In fact, there is no one connected with the artistic side of movie-making—not excluding somebody called the producer who usually just comes along for the ride—who does not receive some staggering sum for his participation.

There are many reasons why we movie makers are so prodigiously rewarded for tasks that might well come under the head of trivia. I will skip most of them as having nothing to do with Daisy Marcher and offer only the one that is pertinent—the Hollywood Agent. Foremost in the forces that have skyrocketed the earnings of the movie artist has been this peculiar sleight-of-hand worker.

His emergence on the Hollywood scene some twenty years ago was occasioned by the fact that most of the movie artists were unable to add or subtract and also needed someone to look up telephone numbers for them. From these humble beginnings the agent (the Great Agent) has risen to breath-taking heights. Although on the surface he has remained a stylish sort of mendicant hunting handouts for his finicky clientele, actually he has become one of the major headaches in the movie industry—and as such stands shoulder to shoulder with its leading Pharaohs.

The Great Agent has under his wing today bevies of stars and geniuses whose venality he has inflamed (a not difficult task) with purring tales of their worth. The peddling of these treasure troves is the simplest part of his labors. For it was the agent who first uncovered the Basic Principle of Hollywood. This is that the Pharaohs who run the studios measure their own greatness by the amount of money they are able to spend. There is, in fact, no other activity open to them. The Pharaoh who can spend the most money on stars and geniuses becomes automatically the most dazzling figure in the cinema capital. Thus the competition to run the studios into bankruptcy is an extremely hot one. That all the studios are not quickly ruined by these royal extravagances is due to a single factor out of their control.

The popularity of the movies has become almost equal to that of sex. And as in the case of the latter enterprise, no amount of extravagance, disappointment or mismanagement seems able to impair the success of the studio product.

Such a situation has enabled the agent to mature from a menial who originally looked up telephone numbers for his clients to a Power who thinks in them.

Yet nobody in Hollywood, least of all the movie artists whose incomes he has tripled, has ever a happy word for this magician. The industry regards him as a combination beggar and pirate who divides his time between harassing the Pharaohs for alms when they have no need of him and scuttling their studios when they have. And his clients are inclined to think of him as a quisling bent on selling them out to the Bosses and solely responsible for their decline in public favor.

Burdened by these calumnies, with a status wavering between that of a White Slaver and a crooked Senator, the Great Agent has nonetheless found a certain sweetness in his toil. For today he is richer than any one of his illustrious clients. He, too, is one of the conquerors of Hollywood, albeit a minor one. And the Pharaohs themselves, though they howl behind his back that he is a parasite and a highwayman, must greet him with the hand of royal fellowship.

Orlando Higgens, who is the villain of my story, has been my Hollywood agent for seventeen years. His depredations as my representative have been, however, modest ones. It was as Daisy Marcher's agent that Orlando succeeded in almost wrecking Hollywood. And, as Orlando himself says, if that be villainy, make the most of it.

Whatever other achievements I may have in Hollywood, Orlando is my true bid for fame. It was I who started him as an agent. He was originally a tall, scatterbrained and explosive financier, at least financier was what he called himself when I first met him in his twenty-fourth year. It developed his claim to the title of financier was based on a mania for borrowing money. Orlando was no sponger but at twenty-four he had been unable to figure out any other way of making his "million or two," except by raising it in small sums from former fraternity brothers who had gone to work. Men without vision, he called them.

We were sitting in my house one evening seventeen years ago discussing a trip around the world on a chartered yacht that Orlando had planned—to involve twenty-five congenial souls at $10,000 apiece, which would nicely cover all expenses—including his own salary as financier. Somehow during this discussion Orlando stole an unpublished manuscript of mine from my desk. Five days later he wired me from Hollywood asking me to wire him back immediately $1,500 as his ten percent of its sale money. He had disposed of my manuscript (a foul one) to a movie studio. This was Orlando's first taste of porch climbing.

How it befell that my friend whose chief characteristics were an inability to tell the truth on any subject, an evasiveness worthy of a bank embezzler and a childlike abhorrence of all toil—how it befell that so giddy and incompetent a character could rise to the heights of Orlando Higgens, Inc., is a matter I will skip. For like most Hollywood facts the rise of Orlando Higgens belongs more to the field of magic than biography. I give you merely Orlando in all his grandeur just as mythology gave us Minerva who jumped fully dressed out of Jupiter's head. To cap the mystery, I will add that seventeen years of Huge Deals and Masterly Manipulations had in no way changed my friend. He was as incompetent, evasive and irresponsible a character as head of Orlando Higgens, Inc., as he had been in his lowlier days. Apparently his inability to remember anything—an inability bordering on amnesia—his habit of lying about everything to everybody and his chronic state of confusion were the very talents that had brought him success. These and possibly the fact that he was one of the nicest men I have ever known.

I was sitting in Orlando's office on one of those glaring Hollywood afternoons when everything, including your own soul, seems made out of shiny new stucco, when the telephone rang and Orlando's fourth secretary (there were six in all) informed him that a Miss Daisy Marcher wished to speak to him.

"Who the hell is Daisy Marcher?" Orlando inquired peevishly.

"She's an author," the secretary said.

"For God's sake," Orlando yelled, "do I have to talk to every half-witted author who calls up? Tell her I'm busy."

He hung up and beamed at me.

"You used to like authors," I said, "before they made you rich."

"Before they drove me crazy," said Orlando. "I loved 'em, seventeen years ago. But I swear to you the way I feel now about authors I can't read a book any more. I know them too well. Talk about hams!" He shuddered. "Authors are worse than boy sopranos."

The phone rang. There were five differently colored instruments on Orlando's fifteen-foot Italian antique desk and each had a different ring. After seven years Orlando was still unable to tell which ring belonged to which phone. He picked up two at a time and called out in a clipped efficient voice, "Hello. Who is it?"

"Mr. Sylvester for Mr. Higgens," Secretary Number Two answered on one of the phones. Orlando winked at me.

"This is going to be fun," he whispered. "*That* fathead!"

"Hello Syl," he chuckled into the phone, "nothing doing at Fox. Nope. No dice . . . Yep. I'll hop right on it. O.K. Goo'bye. Right . . . Goo'bye. What's that? No, Zanuck read it personally and thinks it stinks . . . Yep. Will do. Goo'bye."

Orlando hung up and cackled happily, as he always did when any of his clients were in despair.

"I can't sell that big know-it-all for peanuts," he grinned. "Did you read that last book of his? It turned my stomach."

"What's happened to Sylvester?" I asked. "He was pretty hot a while ago."

"Well, he ain't hot now," said Orlando with a snort.

One of the phones rang.

"Did I tell you Chick is in the conference room?" Orlando continued. "He moved in two days ago with a case of Scotch. Great fella." He looked proudly at the leather-panelled door of the conference room and chuckled.

"I thought Chick was directing the Dietrich picture," I said.

"He is," Orlando beamed. "But he said he hit a snag and is going to drink himself out of it. Nobody knows where he is, so don't say a word." A larkish light filled Orlando's eyes and he murmured in an awed voice, "It's costing Empire a mint of money. If they don't find him by tomorrow they may even have to call the picture off."

I picked up the ringing telephone.

"Miss Daisy Marcher wishes to speak to Mr. Higgens," said Secretary Five.

"It's Daisy again," I said. Orlando's face reddened and he seized the instrument.

"What the hell is this?" he demanded. "I've got five secretaries" (he had six) "to see that I'm not disturbed. So they all keep bothering me. I told you to tell her I'm busy."

"We've told her that seven times," said Secretary Five. "I've hung up on her myself three times in succession and she keeps calling right back and asking to speak to you, as if nothing had happened."

"What do you know?" An admiring light came into Orlando's eyes. "A nut, huh?"

"I'm afraid so," said the secretary.

"Put her on," said Orlando.

"Is this Mr. Higgens?" a purring voice inquired.

"Yes, this is he," said Orlando.

"This is Daisy Marcher," the voice continued. "I would have called you up sooner but I have been ill with a fever and I could not get out of bed. Today is my first day up."

"Is that so?" Orlando beamed. "And how do you feel now, Miss Marcher?"

"Oh, I feel all right now," said Miss Marcher, "as long as I keep my muffler on around my neck."

"Well, thanks for letting me know about your health," Orlando chuckled. "Anything else on your mind?"

"Oh, yes," said Miss Marcher. "I am getting very impatient to know if you have sold my motion picture drama. That is why I called."

Orlando winked at me and whispered, "Some goddam foreigner. Probably a Hindu."

"What is the name of the drama?" he spoke into the phone.

"It is called *A Woman of Sin*," Miss Marcher said.

Orlando winced.

"Let you know tomorrow how it's coming along," he said.

"You've had it already two weeks," said Miss Marcher, "and I can't understand why it should take so long to sell."

"Oh, is it that good?" Orlando beamed.

"Yes indeed," said Miss Marcher. "I consider it the best motion picture drama that has ever been written."

"You don't say," Orlando purred. "Well, when you get your strength back drop in and we'll have a drink."

"Thank you very much," said Miss Marcher, "but I don't drink—ever."

"What, a great author like you doesn't drink! I can't believe it!" Orlando chuckled. "I bet you're soused to the gills right now."

"I think you are a horrid man," said the gentle voice, "an utterly nasty man and I am sorry I selected you to be my agent."

There was a bang. Miss Marcher had hung up. Orlando sat glaring at the instrument. Miss Betha Flannigan entered and walked to her desk in the corner. As Secretary Number One, Miss Flannigan shared the Higgens sanctum.

"What the hell do you mean by letting half-wits like that send us scripts?" Orlando demanded of her. "Did you hear that title? *A Woman of Sin!* My God, are we sending out junk like that!"

The round-faced Miss Flannigan, who had no idea of what Mr. Higgens was talking, answered soothingly.

"I'll have it checked right away."

"Fire that manuscript right back at her as fast as you can," Orlando growled. "*A Woman of Sin*. It turns your stomach—just the title."

"I'll double check," said Miss Flannigan firmly.

A phone rang.

"That's your private phone," said Miss Flannigan.

Orlando paled. Only his current sweethearts and his most important clients were permitted to call on this number. Any one of them meant trouble. He picked up the instrument and spoke guiltily into it. "Hello." A voice rumbled back. "Right," Orlando answered with a snap. "Will do. Yep. Immediately. Yep. Is that so? Will do. Take care of it right away."

He hung up with relief.

"That was Chick," he said.

"I thought he was in the conference room," I said.

"He is." Orlando stood up glaring at the leather-panelled door. "He called from there. He says he's dying and I should get him a doctor. Come on, let's go to lunch."

"Shall I send for a doctor?" Miss Flannigan asked.

"Good God, no," Orlando said. "And don't stay out for lunch so long because I get all mixed up when you're away."

It was four o'clock when we returned. I had decided to spend the rest of the day on Orlando's office divan, it being the coolest place in town. Orlando entered his office with a business-like "What's new?" to Miss Flannigan.

"Mr. Chick Howser has left," she said. He looked disappointedly at the leather-panelled door. It was open. "Paramount called," Miss Flannigan continued, "and Mr. Goldwyn wants you to call him immediately on your return. Mr. Zanuck says he'll see you at 2 A.M. in his office. And Mr. Blue called."

"Freddie Blue, eh?" said Orlando with a frown. "Hm. No likee."

Freddie Blue was part of Jerome B. Cobb's hierarchy. There were several figures closer to the throne of the Pharaoh but Freddie was Shock Troops.

"Get me Blue," said Orlando. "Something's up. They probably found out about Chick camping here. Am I going to get hell! How did he sound, Flannigan?"

"Very eager," said the secretary. "He's on the wire now."

"Hello," Orlando chirped heartily. "Freddie? How's the world's greatest ladies' man? . . . Never mind. I've heard plenty . . . Fine . . . Great . . . Listen, how about a hearts game tonight? . . . Okeydoke.

Tomorrow's a date . . . What's new, Freddie? . . . What! What's that!" Orlando's eyes opened wide. "You don't say! Glad to hear it. She's a great girl. Brilliant as hell. Sure, we're handling Daisy. Been keeping her under cover for months, sort of coaching her. Yep! Right. Get hold of her immediately. Call you right back . . . Yep . . . Yep . . . Goo'bye."

He hung up.

"Well, I'll be damned," he said blankly and turned to Miss Flannigan. "Get hold of that half-wit what's-her-name—that Hindu or whatever she is."

"Daisy Marcher," Miss Flannigan suggested.

"That's right," said Orlando. "I'm kind of stunned. Empire is buying *A Woman of Sin*. Can you beat that!"

Miss Flannigan spoke into her private phone, an ordinary black one. "Have Mr. Horowitz contact Daisy Marcher right away," she said. "Mr. Higgens wants to speak to her personally. It's important."

I didn't know as I dozed off on the divan that one of the greatest calamities ever to threaten Hollywood had been officially launched.

Orlando arrived at my hotel shortly after midnight. I was just leaving my room. The producer of the picture on which I was working had decided we needed a new ending. He was waiting in the studio for me with the director, and my presence there was a matter of life and death, he insisted.

"Forget about Walter," said Orlando when I started to explain. I'm in a hell of a pickle. In fact, I've been going crazy all day."

We started out of the hotel together.

"I can't find that half-wit Daisy Marcher," said Orlando. "I've called seven hundred people. Nobody ever heard of her. And Empire's gone nuts about *A Woman of Sin*. Stark, raving nuts. Freddie Blue been hounding me to close the deal. And Mike Devlin's been hounding me too."

I was impressed. Mike Devlin was Mr. Cobb's royal right hand. He had in his youth gone nine rounds with Jack Johnson and then retired from the ring and cast his lot with the motion picture industry, beginning as a masseur. How so honest and humanly worthy a character as Mike Devlin had ever climbed the shenanigan heights of Hollywood was always a mystery to me. It may have been with his fists.

"I'd like to read that script," I said.

"So would I," said Orlando. "There isn't a copy in the office. It got sent over to Empire by some mistake. Some bumble-head put the wrong script in an envelope. I'm going to fire half the staff tomorrow. You can't run a business that way."

"A fascinating situation," I said, "genius rising above the handicaps of an agent."

"Genius, my eye!" Orlando snorted. "J. B. Cobb's gone crazy—that's all there is to it."

"What's he got to do with it?" I asked.

"He read it," Orlando said. "That's part of the whole mistake. Once you start a mistake it keeps on. That damn script got on his desk, somehow." He chuckled. "The title must have attracted him."

The thought of Mr. Cobb reading a manuscript was truly astonishing. Mr. Cobb never read manuscripts nor concerned himself with any of the details of movie-making. It was his function to preserve a fresh, unused mind so as to be able to harass all the Nobles under him when they did wrong. Nobody could harass Mr. Cobb for the reason that he never did anything. And there was no questioning his genius because he was getting constantly richer and more powerful.

"He read it," Orlando repeated, "and it went to his head like a shot of hop. I'm betting that script is pure drivel."

Jerome B. Cobb was standing on the curb outside the hotel waiting for his palanquin. Two Wazirs were in attendance. Mr. Cobb looked at me coldly but his heavy face lighted at the sight of Orlando Higgens.

"I want to talk to you, my boy," he smiled.

The two Wazirs immediately hailed Orlando with shouts of camaraderie.

"You have done a lot of things I haven't approved of," the Pharaoh began in measured tones, "such as selling me material which was nothing but low grade rubbish. And holding me up for it."

"Oh, come now, J. B.," Orlando protested. "In the first place I didn't sell it to you. I sold it to Empire."

"I am Empire." Mr. Cobb quivered and then controlled himself. "Now please don't interrupt me because I am going to say something of importance to you. I consider that you have finally redeemed yourself in my eyes by sending us this new story."

"*A Woman of Sin,*" Orlando beamed.

"I will be frank with you," said Mr. Cobb. "I read the story myself, busy though I am. And I'm glad I did. Because God knows it might have slipped by us. My boy, I consider that story not only a great masterpiece but one of the greatest pieces of box office entertainment we have ever made. I'm going to shoot it without a single change and I am going to make it an all-star production."

"I'm glad you like it," Orlando purred.

"Like it!" Mr. Cobb raised his voice to a shout. "I'm crazy about it! By God, it's what this country needs—a great sex story." The Pharaoh turned a stony face suddenly on Orlando.

"I want that deal closed by tomorrow at ten," he said, "and if you try any Orlando Higgens tricks with any other studios, I'll ruin you. I'm telling you openly and aboveboard."

"What the hell you talking about?" Orlando said peevishly. "I would have closed the deal today except for that damned writer."

"What writer?" Mr. Cobb demanded darkly. His thought was unused to delving this low in the movie business.

"Daisy Marcher," said Orlando.

"What's the matter with her?" asked Mr. Cobb.

"She's asking too much money," said Orlando. "And I simply don't want to stick Empire. It's bad business for me in the long run, J. B. I've been arguing my head off with her."

"How much does she want?" Mr. Cobb asked coldly.

"It's preposterous," Orlando feinted, "but I can't budge her."

"How much?" Mr. Cobb shouted.

"Seventy-five thousand dollars," said Orlando in a contrite voice. "And frankly, J. B., I don't think that script is worth it. No script is."

"It's a deal," said Mr. Cobb quietly. He turned to one of the Wazirs. "Get Blue on the phone immediately and tell him that seventy-five thousand dollars is the price we will pay for *A Woman of Sin*."

He held out his hand to Orlando.

"We'll shake hands on it like old friends," Mr. Cobb smiled, "and remember we got witnesses."

Orlando's phantom bonanza fascinated me and I hurried to his office as soon as I could get off the set on which our new ending was being shot. It was noon. I found the three outer Higgens salons in turmoil. Phones were ringing and voices barking in all corners.

Orlando was pacing in his sanctum, his coat off, his suspenders moist and a gleam on his face.

"I haven't slept a wink," he greeted me.

"Find her?" I asked.

"No. I sicked a detective agency on her at seven this morning," he grinned.

"How about the Screen Writers' Guild?" I suggested.

"Those fatheads," Orlando sneered. "They never heard of her. I've been tracking her down from every angle. She's a myth, that's all."

"How about telling Freddie Blue the truth?" I said.

Orlando laughed contemptuously.

"For one thing they'd never believe me," he said. "They'd think I was trying to pull something crooked. Besides," he added, "I haven't got her signed up yet."

"Mr. Cobb on the phone," Miss Flannigan announced. "The green one."

"Hello, J. B.," Orlando began quickly. "Listen, I've been talking to Miss Marcher half the night like a Dutch uncle. But I can't get her to see it our way . . . Yep. Yep. . . . Nope . . . Nope. . . . Listen, J. B., she absolutely refuses to sign any contract that doesn't give her a percentage of the gross over and above the seventy-five grand. . . . Yep. Right." Orlando raised his voice to a righteous scream. "I told her it was absolute lunacy," he cried, "and that I thought she was behaving like an absolute stinker." His wrath subsided as he listened with a business-like frown to Mr. Cobb's bellows. When he spoke again it was in a sad voice. "That's exactly what I've been begging her to do, J. B.," he cooed, "go over and talk it out with you. And that you were the fairest man in Hollywood. But she spit in my eye and told me to go to hell and we *both* almost lost her. . . . Nope. Nope. Listen, J. B., all I know is that she just simply won't go see anybody connected with a studio. She hates movie executives or something. It must be some kind of a curious quirk."

Orlando listened with a suffering expression. Then he spoke again. "J. B., honestly I'm going nuts with this," he said. "These goddam writers drive you crazy . . . What? How much? . . . Now wait a minute, J. B. I can't stick you like that. I'll try my damnedest to get it for the seventy-five grand like we agreed and shook hands on. Yep. Right. I'll tell her. Will do. Call you back."

Orlando hung up the instrument and sat looking moodily at a Picasso on the wall.

"This damn business really exhausts you," he said and added thoughtfully after a breather, "He offers one hundred thousand and will go higher."

"How long can you keep this up?" I asked.

"Frankly, I don't know." A grin brightened Orlando's face. "But I've got an idea! Flannigan, get me Freddie Blue." He sat humming and staring at me with a larkish beam. "You know, this is a very interesting situation," he said.

"Mr. Blue is on the red phone," Miss Flannigan announced.

"Freddie," Orlando cried. "Listen, honeyboy, you've got to help me.

Yep, I've talked to J. B. But I want you to do this for him and me both. I want Empire to put out a story that they're buying *A Woman of Sin* . . . I know it's against the rules but it's our only hope. If that silly fathead Marcher sees her name in the papers it'll soften her up . . . No, use psychology, Freddie—it won't make her worse! I tell you I know her like a book. She's fame-hungry. It'll show her you people are sincere. . . . O.K. Thanks. That's a pal. . . . Right. Yep. Absolutely. Call you back."

Orlando hung up and beamed.

"That'll smoke her out," he said. "Come on, let's go swimming. It's hot as hell." He turned to Miss Flannigan. "You know where to find me if that hambo Marcher turns up."

"This is a great town," said Orlando happily as we drove to the beach, "the only place left where a fella can use his wits."

The movie columns the next morning carried enfevered accounts of Empire's new project—the production of the screen drama *A Woman of Sin*, considered by Mr. Cobb the greatest study of human emotions ever attempted by the cinema. The picture was going to be blessed with an all-star cast. At the tail end of the publicity stories, which recounted mainly the brilliance of Jerome B. Cobb as a master showman, was a single line identifying the author of the screen drama as a newcomer named Daisy Marcher. This was an unusual break for Orlando, for it is rarely that a writer, unless he is adept at blowing his own horn, figures in the symphony of adulation that cinema critics offer to the industry.

I reached the Higgens office at two o'clock. Orlando was having lunch at his desk.

"Kind of exciting, eh?" he beamed at me.

"Daisy turned up yet?" I asked.

"Nope." Orlando chewed thoughtfully on his food. "I've got a theory she's dropped dead somewhere."

"Mr. Cobb is on the phone," said Miss Flannigan, "the blue one."

"Tell him I'm in conference with Miss Marcher," said Orlando. He resumed his thoughtful chewing.

"What makes you think Daisy dropped dead?" I asked.

"Drink," said Orlando. "She was drunk as a coot when she called me. You remember. And she said she's been laid up with a cold. Well, you take a lush like that and give her influenza, and they never recover. Flannigan, get me all the obituary columns for the last four days. I want to look them over." Orlando beamed at me. "That's irony, isn't it?" he chuckled. "To end up in a drunkard's grave, with fame and fortune as your pall bearers. Real irony. Make a great movie."

Orlando kept on chewing. The phone rang.

"Miss Daisy Marcher to see you," Miss Flannigan announced and her voice had dropped a little of its coolness.

Orlando turned and stared at her.

"No kiddin'," he said softly. "Where is she?"

"In the waiting room with Mr. Horowitz," said Miss Flannigan.

"Have her come right in—and be sure she's alone," Orlando ordered. "It smoked her out, just as I figured it would. They're all hams, drunk or sober."

He had no more than finished this statement when the door started opening. The three of us looked expectantly. It seemed to open rather mysteriously.

"Come in, come right in," Orlando called in a saccharine voice.

A child with blond hair falling over her shoulders appeared. It was an unusually small child. It wore a sort of Scotch dress about a foot long and its legs seemed bare to the waist. On the top of its head stood a large, pink hair ribbon. The tot regarded us with a pair of frowning and unwavering eyes.

"What do *you* want?" Orlando asked peevishly.

"I'm Miss Marcher," said the child in a slightly awed voice.

"Well, tell your mother to come in and you wait outside like a good little girl." Orlando smiled winningly. But his nerves were jangled. Turning to his secretary, he added, "Damn it, Flannigan, can't I have this office run the way I want to? How many more secretaries do I need?"

"I have no mother," said the little visitor. "I am an orphan." She looked about her solemnly and inquired, "Which one of you is Mr. Orlando Higgens?"

"I am Mr. Higgens," said Orlando slowly. "Why?"

"Is that so?" said the child. "Oh dear, oh dear—that's too bad."

"It is, eh?" said Orlando testily.

"Yes, it is, indeed," said the child whose tones had now become firmer. "Because I don't think I'm going to like you."

"Why not?" I asked, always interested in character analysis of Orlando.

The little visitor flashed a smile at me.

"Because he has red-rimmed eyes," she said, "and an insincere look."

Orlando was staring with his mouth open. Repartee failed him.

"So you're Daisy Marcher?" he asked finally.

The child nodded.

"Well, that's very interesting." Orlando leered at the tot. "And I suppose you're also the author of *A Woman of Sin*."

"Yes, I am," said the child. "Indeed I am."

"You're nuts!" Orlando exploded and leaped to his feet. "Do you know what happens to little girls who tell lies—dirty, rotten lies?"

Daisy sniffed.

"Oh, don't be silly," she said. "I can't bear silly men."

"God Almighty!" Orlando cried. "What is this? Is this a gag or something! This is the damnedest, most idiotic thing that ever happened!"

"I wouldn't swear in front of the child," Miss Flannigan said.

"You keep out of this," Orlando roared.

"Oh, I don't mind at all," Daisy's gentle voice stopped him. "I am used to profanity. People always swear at me."

"I'll betchya," said Orlando witheringly.

"Especially if they got red-rimmed eyes," said Daisy.

Orlando pulled himself together.

"Listen," he said haughtily, "I am not in the habit of quarreling with babies."

He walked around the table and, lifting Daisy to its top, stood looking fiercely into her eyes.

"What I want to know is," he continued coldly, "are you actually the author of *A Woman of Sin*? Cross your heart and hope to die."

Daisy solemnly crossed her heart and answered,

"Hope to die. Yes, I am."

"Yes, you are what?" Orlando was not to be taken in by half oaths.

"I am the author of *A Woman of Sin*," said Daisy, "hope to die."

There was a hush in the office. Miss Flannigan tittered. No one spoke. The little visitor remained on the table top swinging her legs and fluttering her eyelids. She seemed very happy now. Orlando broke the silence.

"That hair ribbon is what kills me," he said hoarsely. "Take it off."

"What for?" Daisy asked.

"It gets me nervous," said Orlando.

"Oh, but it makes me look taller," Daisy smiled. "My mother gave it to me."

"Oh," Orlando snapped. "I thought you said you didn't have a mother."

"On her deathbed," said Daisy demurely, "when I was a little girl."

"Listen"—Orlando's voice was firm and he seized the tot by her pipestem arms—"I want the truth. About everything. You're an orphan, eh?"

"Yes," said Daisy. "My father ran away with another woman who afterward stabbed him to death in a saloon brawl. And my mother hanged herself because of a broken heart."

"I thought you said she died in bed," Orlando snarled.

"Oh, yes," Daisy agreed. "They cut her down and she lingered because her neck hadn't been broken. Only twisted."

The child swung her legs over the table edge and sighed, "I've been through a lot."

"Never mind about that," said Orlando peevishly. "Where do you live?"

"Oh, in the hills," Daisy waved a little hand. "I like the wilderness."

"I suppose you live in the hills all alone," Orlando sneered, "like a hermit."

"Not altogether," said Daisy. "Because my grandmother is there."

"Now we're getting somewhere." Orlando beamed at me. "What's your grandmother's name and what's the address?"

Daisy frowned and was silent.

"You're just wasting my time, damn it," Orlando cried. "Where does your grandmother live?"

"It wouldn't do you much good to meet her," said Daisy softly.

"Why not?" Orlando demanded.

"Because she's an Indian," said Daisy, "and like most Indians she doesn't care to talk very much. She goes for a whole year sometimes without saying a single word. Her name is Minitonka. And she's very old. A hundred and ten, I think, anyway. So you see you will be wasting your time talking to her."

Orlando listened spellbound.

"Jee-rusalem!" he cried. "You're the damnedest liar I ever met!"

The child started climbing breathlessly down from the table.

"How dare you!" she cried. "After I crossed my heart and hoped to die and everything, and now you call me a liar!"

"Shut up or I'll spank you!" Orlando's face was red.

"Why, of all the nasty men I ever met"—Daisy screamed and started for the door.

"No, you don't!" Orlando grabbed her. "Come on, Flannigan. We're taking this brat home and finding out the truth about her if I have to skin her alive."

We learned a number of things in the next hour.

Daisy Marcher lived in a modest apartment over a grocery store with a stout and amazingly coy mother, who had never hanged herself. Daisy's critical sense had apparently invented the hanging. There was no grandmoher and there were no Indians. Daisy's father, whose picture was shown us, had been a Methodist clergyman until he succumbed to pneumonia during her teething period. The mother, an expert knitter (she knitted calmly during the entire conference), had supported herself and her precocious baby by supplying several local knitting goods counters with a steady line of sweaters and socks. The mother's name was Lillian Egelhofer. Daisy Marcher was a *nom de plume*. The child was nine years old and had always been called Mildred. There was no question of the authenticity of *A Woman of Sin*. Mrs. Egelhofer had seen her child put the story down page by page and had not added or removed a word—only corrected the spelling.

"The child will simply not learn to spell," the mother explained with a martyrish sigh, "although I've told her it would be a great help to her career. Haven't I, darling?"

"Oh, mother! For Heaven's sake!" said the child, doubling up as if with a cramp.

Mrs. Egelhofer fed herself a large chocolate cream out of a half-emptied box and settled her billowy figure more comfortably into the chair.

"Sugar deficiency," she explained in a sad voice. "The doctor says I must watch out for it." She munched the chocolate cream like a Spartan. "Well," she resumed, her needles flying, "those are all the facts I can think of about little Mildred. Unless you care to have me tell you about her aura. I'm very susceptible to auras and have made quite a study of them. Hers changes from a delicate yellow to a sort of magenta."

Little Mildred made a noise in the back of her throat like a tiger on the flanks of a bullock.

"Come here, darling," said Mrs. Egelhofer, "and let me fix your hair ribbon. These gentlemen will think you're a little street Arab."

"Mother!" Daisy exploded. "This is too much!" Her little face could not do justice to the look of murder in her eyes.

"Why, babykins," Mrs. Egelhofer extended a plump hand full of knitting needles, "where are your manners?" She looked at her child with a reproving but tender smile and in her distraction connected with another chocolate cream.

"Stop it! Stop it! Stop it!" Daisy cried through clenched teeth and threw herself face downward on the couch. It appeared for the moment that the child had burst into tears. But this was erroneous. Daisy wasn't crying. She was biting the cushion under her face.

"An uncontrollable temper," said Mrs. Egelhofer. "Her father, you know, was just like that. Dark purple, most of the time. I always felt that it was his aura that killed him. Not pneumonia at all."

"Flannigan," said Orlando, watching the child tearing the pillow with her teeth, "take Daisy into the other room. She's only disturbing her mother."

"Oh, thank you," said Mrs. Egelhofer, "but I'm used to her."

She bit into the medicinal chocolate cream.

"I want to talk business," Orlando said confidentially.

Daisy sat up.

"Oh, no you don't," she cried. "Oh, I should say not. I don't leave my mother alone with you. You'll cheat her."

"Do what the gentleman says." Mrs. Egelhofer smiled archly at her little girl.

"Go on, get out!" Orlando stood up and mopped his neck.

"Don't strike her," said Mrs. Egelhofer faintly.

"I'm not going to strike her," said Orlando peevishly. "I'm going to take her and throw her into that other room—from here."

Daisy got to her feet and looked up at him thoughtfully . . . Then, holding her head high, she walked proudly and slowly out of the room.

"Get in there with her, Flannigan," Orlando ordered, "and keep the door bolted."

"She needs a firm hand," Mrs. Egelhofer sighed and continued her knitting. "Would you be kind enough to bring me a glass of water? These scenes are really bad for me. My heart, you know." She smiled sadly.

I fetched the water. Orlando outlined his plan. It was very simple. It involved the mother giving him power of attorney for herself and the guardianship of Mildred Egelhofer alias Daisy Marcher for one year. In return she would receive $125,000 minus the ten per cent commission. Orlando paused a moment and then added that there would be another ten per cent reduction to cover the expenses of the baby's keep. Mrs. Egelhofer continued knitting calmly.

"Oh, I don't know, really, if it will do any good," she sighed. "You know, I've worked so hard."

"It will be roughly a hundred thousand dollars," said Orlando soothingly, "after the necessary deductions."

Mrs. Egelhofer nodded. There seemed to be little difference to her between $100,000 and $125,000.

"Oh, I'm not thinking of that," she said. "I was just worrying about little Mildred. After all, she's my first concern. And all that money going to her. It may spoil her character entirely. She's so simple and unassuming now."

"The money is not going to her," Orlando said firmly. "It's going to you. It's your money to do what you want with. It would be criminal to hand over that money to a crack-brained infant like that."

"Poor babykins," Mrs. Egelhofer sighed. "I hate to deprive her of it. But I'll be able to do so much for her. After all, she needs an older head."

"Done and done," Orlando snapped and then explained the second phase of the situation. This was the need for complete secrecy. No one must find out that a child of nine was the author of *A Woman of Sin*.

"You see it's this way," Orlando said candidly. "Empire is going to sink two million dollars into this picture. Maybe more before they're through. And they're going to advertise it as the most sophisticated sex drama ever filmed. That's the angle they bought it on. In fact"—a hysterical light came into Orlando's eyes for a moment—"Mr. Cobb himself told me he considered it the most penetrating study of human passions ever attempted on the screen."

Mrs. Egelhofer nodded over her knitting with motherly pride.

"And if it was found out," continued Orlando, "that a child of nine —a mere baby—had written it, by God it would not only ruin Empire but give the whole movie industry a black eye. Oh, boy!" he added and looked mistily out of the window.

"Oh, yes, I know," said Mrs. Egelhofer. "The public is very fickle."

"That's right," said Orlando. "In putting over this deal for you I'm taking a terrific gamble. Do you know, for instance, what would happen to me if Empire found out about her?" He pointed to the bolted door. "I'd be lynched. I mean it. Lynched, by God!"

Orlando drew a deep breath and went on brightly. "The only way to avoid that sort of thing is to have Daisy put in my charge. I'll provide a fine home for her—and keep her locked in it—till after the picture is released. Of course, you can come to visit her whenever you want."

"Well," said Mrs. Egelhofer with a sigh, "I've got a bad back." She groaned by way of illustration. "It's very difficult for me to get around."

"You mean you won't let her go?" Orlando demanded.

"Oh, no," Mrs. Egelhofer sighed again, "you can have Mildred. I wouldn't think of standing in her way. And I know you'll be sweet to her. But couldn't we arrange it so that if the child gets lonely for her mother you can bring her to me at the seashore? You see, I want to go away and try to recover. I've been through a lot, you know."

"Will do!" Orlando snapped. "It's a deal!"

He walked to the bedroom door.

"O.K., Flannigan," he called, "you can let her out."

The door opened. Daisy was sitting in a large chair with her nude legs thrust rigidly in front of her.

"I heard every word you said," she announced.

"That's a lie," said Miss Flannigan, "we couldn't hear a thing."

"*You* couldn't," Daisy sneered, "but I heard him cheating my mother plain as anything."

"Come on, we're going," said Orlando happily. "Never mind taking any of her clothes along. We don't want her looking like a circus freak."

Daisy stood up.

"Am I going with you?" she asked softly, ignoring the insult.

"Yep," said Orlando.

The child dropped to her hands and knees and removed a pile of True Confession and True Love Stories magazines from under the bed.

"Let's hurry up," she said.

There were a score of telephone messages waiting in the office, most of them from Jerome B. Cobb.

"Get J. B.," Orlando ordered, "and then lock her up in the conference room. Go on, baby," he beamed on the authoress.

"I don't have to go home any more?" Daisy asked slowly.

"Not for a whole year," said Orlando.

With a cry of joy the child went skipping after Miss Flannigan toward the conference room.

"I want you to be a witness to this conversation," Orlando grinned at me as he held the phone. "You'd better take notes. Because it may be very important—afterwards."

"Hello, J. B.," he said heartily into the instrument. "Well, it's in the bag. All settled. Yep. Yep. Nope. No royalties. I put it over for you. I had to practically blackjack her. Just a hundred and twenty-five thousand flat, payable on signing the contract."

There was a slight rumble over the wire.

"Can't help it, J. B.," Orlando spoke up firmly, "she won't consider taking it in three payments. And, by the way, I'm signing the contracts for her. She's given me power of attorney."

There was a larger rumble over the wire.

"Listen," said Orlando, "I can't perform miracles. She simply refuses to see you or any other movie executives. Even talk to them on the phone. It's got something to do with psychoanalysis . . . Oh, didn't I tell you before? She's going to one. She's suffering from some kind of a shock, I guess . . . Yep. Yep. That's what makes her a genius."

Orlando listened and yepped happily for several minutes.

"That's fine," he resumed. "And now that you've agreed on the deal and everything's settled I want to go on record with something, J. B. And please don't interrupt me. I want to say frankly to you that I've read that script and I think it's pure rubbish. Worst I ever sold you. It could only have been written by a half-wit or some child of nine."

Orlando listened to Mr. Cobb's shout with a happy smile.

"I'm not trying to double-cross you, J. B.," he resumed. "I'm just trying to be honest, for once in my life."

The Cobb roars crackled out of the instrument.

"All right, I'm crazy," Orlando agreed cheerily. "But I just want to go on record that in my opinion *A Woman of Sin* is a piece of unadulterated childish rubbish and should never be made by a grown-up company."

Orlando jerked his ear from the receiver and sat staring blandly at the instrument as it threatened to explode in his hand.

"O. K.," he resumed in a contrite voice, "maybe I'm wrong. No, I don't pretend to know as much as you, J. B. And if I haven't convinced you that only a child could have written that script, I'm willing to take your money. No, I'm not against your making great pictures. . . . No, J. B., I gotta be honest, it didn't make me cry when I read it . . . It did, eh? How about Mike Devlin, did he cry too? Is that so? Well, maybe I'm wrong . . . Listen, I'm an agent, not a genius."

His voice grew crisp.

"Yep. Tomorrow morning at ten. Bring all the contracts over. Yep. Okeydoke. Ten o'clock. *Be* there. Right. Will do! Call you back."

Orlando hung up the phone and, leaning back in his papal chair, laughed until the tears came from his eyes.

"The picture of Jerome B. Cobb crying over that brat's script is worth anything that happens," he said. "God, I love this town."

II

Considering that Orlando Higgens, Inc., was less than two miles removed from the Empire Studios and that some thirty Higgens employees were more or less involved in the Daisy Marcher secret, you would naturally conclude that the whole thing would be out of the bag in a day or two. This is a conclusion, however, based on logic and rationality, neither of which attitudes will get you far as a Hollywood historian. For the cinema capital has a psychology of its own—as illusive as a frog's dream and as capricious as a June bride.

I will not go into the matter further than to explain how so elephantine a conspiracy as launched by Orlando Higgens could thrive undetected practically in the open. The basic reason is that nobody believes anything in Hollywood. The rest of the world may be skeptical about Hollywood stories, but Hollywood itself is far beyond that. It unblushingly knows itself for a liar and behaves accordingly, ignoring anything short of murder, open rape or other well-proved major world events.

Scandal and fantasy are not cake in movieland but daily bread. The place is a wilderness of tall tales and Sinbad anecdotes. A hundred publicity departments work twenty-four hours a day pumping insanities out of the industry for world consumption. Thousands of eccentric movie artists are continually engaged in eccentric marriages and divorces, feuds and public fandangos. Cyrano, Munchausen and Prester John—Cagliostro, Aladdin and the Mad Mullah—were they all to drive into Hollywood at once, would soon be lost in the shuffle. In a week the gossips would be wondering whatever had become of them. And in two weeks they would have formed themselves into a little foreign colony to which no one paid any attention.

There was a second factor that helped keep Orlando's secret hidden practically under everybody's nose. In Hollywood the Pharaohs and their Nobles are a sacred institution. They do not mingle except among themselves. They will unbend on occasions to listen to flattery from lowly sources but the discourse of such fortunate satellites must be brief and ecstatic. There are no hardy couriers to bear evil tidings to the royal ears. They live and thrive, incommunicado, like the happy Kings in Mother Goose.

It was thus that Orlando was able to become the guardian of Daisy Marcher, to board and room her in his hotel, to ride her to his office every morning (as befell later) and to continue in his desperate deception of Jerome B. Cobb and his myrmidons without discovery.

I was myself amazed.

Daisy remained in the hotel only for a brief time. Three nurses, hired by Orlando to watch his little client when he was too busy with other business, resigned in the first three days. Daisy refused to be treated as a parasite. She insisted on continuing with her literary career.

"Well, you can do your writing in this hotel suite," said Orlando. "It's a beautiful place. And when you get tired you can use the pool and learn how to swim."

"I don't want to swim," said Daisy, "and I can't write in a place like this. I want to write in your office."

Orlando was eating ice cream with his little client during this discussion.

"Okeydoke," he beamed at her. "I'll have everything fixed up for you in the conference room."

"And nobody can come in except me," said Daisy.

"Nobody," Orlando nodded, "unless you want them. It'll be your studio. But you've got to stay there. No monkey business."

After this Daisy rode to work with Orlando every morning and locked herself away in the conference room for the rest of the day. Within two weeks the whole thing had become a matter of routine to the Higgens organization.

The contracts were signed and Mr. Cobb, laying aside his Pharaoh mantle, busied himself personally with his chef d'œuvre. His work consisted of hourly conferences with the heads of his publicity department, for Mr. Cobb felt that his moods as an artist were a matter of great public interest. The great Empire studios buzzed with the magnitude of the event and the Nobles sweated loyally to make certain that Mr. Cobb's achievement would be worthy of his position.

There was only one disturbing element for Mr. Cobb. This was the continued absence of Daisy Marcher from the arena of his labors. J. B., who had never felt the existence, let alone the need, of an author, conceived an odd longing for Miss Marcher. He spoke of her frequently and it was obvious that her indifference to his favors had impressed him as much as her great work.

"She's an unusual type for a writer," he explained to his publicity heads, "the kind that you read about. She lives in her dreams and refuses to come out into the world. I understand that—and respect it."

And Mr. Cobb wooed this fellow dreamer daily in the press. His publicity department filled the movie columns with copy relating the depth and beauty of Daisy Marcher's mind. She was—one columnist friend of Mr. Cobb informed seven million readers of her syndicated articles—the first great dramatic talent to write directly for the motion pictures. Another proclaimed her as the greatest sex psychologist since Havelock Ellis. A number of literary figures, expensively employed by Mr. Cobb, read her screen play and likened it in print to Dostoevsky and Joseph Conrad and some of the more sophisticated ones to Balzac and Bernard Shaw. I am not being redundant. This is actually what happened, for literary figures in Hollywood (as literary figures everywhere else, for that matter) are unselfish in their admiration of the Boss' Mind.

Mr. Cobb's hopes of endearing himself to the exclusive Daisy Marcher by allowing her to share his press campaign had an unhappy effect on Orlando. He was reminded every morning of the volcano on which he was sitting and his digestion suffered—for part of the day. But Orlando found a use for the Empire fanfare of Marcher publicity. He was able to keep his child authoress reasonably contented by reading the stories to her at night.

I was busy for two weeks attending a life-and-death rewrite matter on location. The new ending I had written for our picture had necessitated a new beginning. I called on Orlando immediately on my return. He was bland and untroubled. He assured me that everything was hunky-dory and that Daisy was an interesting child and was getting along nicely.

"I've changed her a little," he said, "so she don't look so much like a baby cooch dancer. We've had a barrel of fun."

Daisy came out of her atelier holding some newspapers in her hands. She *was* somewhat changed. The hair ribbon was gone and the hair itself had been reasonably cut. Her dress came below the knees and she had on long stockings.

"Looks a little older and a little fatter, don't you think?" Orlando chuckled.

"I'd still take her for about nine," I said.

"Yes," said Orlando, "but not a young nine."

Daisy greeted me happily.

"What do you want now?" Orlando glowered at her but there was a chumminess in his voice.

"I want to know," said Daisy, "who puts all these things in the papers about me."

"Why, I do, honey," said Orlando tenderly. Daisy climbed up on his lap and kissed him.

"You're wonderful," she said.

"How about my red-rimmed eyes," Orlando asked, "huh?"

"Oh, those," said Daisy, "they're getting better."

I was impressed by the fact that in some curious way the master-mind of Higgens, Inc., and Daisy Marcher seemed twins, mentally and spiritually.

"I would like you to put something else in the papers," Daisy pursued.

"A real ham," Orlando chuckled proudly. "What's biting you now?"

"I'm tired of reading about *A Woman of Sin*," Daisy pouted. "I would like to read about *The Sea of Blood*."

"What the hell is that?" Orlando's eyes widened.

"Oh, for heaven's sake," Daisy scowled. "I've told you and told you a hundred times. That's the screen drama I'm writing about those pirates I told you about. And it's half finished, too."

A phone rang. Miss Flannigan announced, "There's a Mr. Moriarity to see you."

Daisy slipped to the floor and ogled the door excitedly.

"Oh, he's come!" she panted. "Oh, goody, goody! Oh, my, isn't that wonderful?"

"Who the hell is Moriarity?" Orlando demanded.

"You'll see. Just wait." The little authoress started jumping up and down. "Tell him to come in right away, Miss Flannigan. Oh dear, this is very nice. Now I can finish *The Sea of Blood*. He knows all about pirates."

"He's on his way," said Miss Flannigan coolly.

The door opened slowly as it had done on a certain afternoon some weeks ago and there appeared on the threshhold a figure almost as startling as had presented itself on that other time. It was a small fat boy in tight knee pants with legs protruding at a remarkable angle like a pair of props. He was wearing a sort of pancake hat and holding a large ice cream cone in his hand.

"Is this Moriarity?" Orlando asked. Daisy was too blissful to speak. She nodded.

"Yes, I'm Moriarity," the fat boy squeaked.

"Come on in," said Orlando and Moriarity advanced two paces before his valor gave out. He covered his confusion by concentrating on the ice cream cone.

"What's your first name?" Orlando asked.

"They call me Captain," said Moriarity. "Hello, Daisy. I got your letter and I come over soon as I can. First I come over to your mother and she told me here."

"How is her mother?" Orlando asked.

"Knittin'," said Moriarity.

"Come on in here," said Daisy. She had skipped over and seized Moriarity's unoccupied hand. "We're going to work in here. And you can bring your boats. There's plenty of room and a sink even."

"I can only stay a couple hours," said Moriarity, "then I gotta go home. But I'll come back and bring my boats."

The two children vanished into the conference room.

"Kind o' cute," said Orlando, beaming.

A phone rang.

"It's Mr. Cobb," said Miss Flannigan; "the white one."

"Hello, J. B.," Orlando greeted him, "how's everything coming along? . . . Oh, is that so? Start Wednesday, eh? Well, here's hoping." Orlando nodded and yepped for several minutes. He resumed suddenly, "Listen, J. B., you know I'm on your side. I've been breaking my neck to get Miss Marcher to see it your way. I told her straight I considered her absolutely psychopathic for behaving the way she is. She owes it to you to attend the studio party in her honor. Listen, we're absolutely together on that, J. B." There was a pause and more yepping. Orlando resumed, this time in a hurt voice, "I give you my word of honor I've done everything humanly possible. Do you know what happened? Last night I went so far as to threaten to kidnap her and drag her over to you by main force. She lit out and grabbed a midnight train . . . Oh, I don't know. She'll be back. Just one of her huffs. . . . Okeydoke. I'll keep plugging, J. B. Will do. And good luck to you."

Orlando hung up and shuddered.

"This is getting a little complicated," he said. "They start shooting Wednesday."

I asked him if he were worried. The larkish light returned to his eyes.

"Uh, uh," he said, "nothing will happen. These sort of things always blow over."

A Woman of Sin was finished on schedule. I sat with Orlando and a group of Empire Nobles in the projection room and watched a first rough cut run off. It was as daffy a piece of cinema claptrap as I had ever seen. It had cost two million and it was acted almost entirely by stars earning from $4 to $7 a minute. It related the woes of a beautiful Girl of the People who sought happiness through four different society

men, all stars, and ended by dedicating her broken heart to the Red
Cross. Here in the great struggle between Democracy and the Nazi
philosophy she met a patriotic doctor—the only nonstar in the picture
—with whom at last she found true happiness as an ambulance driver.

When the lights went up, I beheld Jerome B. Cobb in a back seat.
His eyes were streaming with tears. He was too overcome to speak but
handed Orlando a sheaf of publicity matter. *A Woman of Sin* had
been seen in its first rough cut by nine of the nation's leading cinema
critics and acclaimed by all of them as Hollywood's finest and most
sophisticated sex drama. These opinions were already in print awaiting
the monster advertising campaign.

"The picture," said Mr. Cobb, who had finally stopped sobbing,
"will be released in two months—just in time for Christmas week. It
is my present to the thinking people of America."

"Great idea," said Orlando and then looked thoughtful. The
Pharaoh's eyes were regarding him with the hunger of the artist before
his wet canvas. Orlando was always at his worst in a projection room.
"I can't help it," he had often apologized to his clients. "I guess I'm
not a judge of movies. I hate 'em too much."

"Well, J. B.," he continued in a strained voice, "it's quite a picture.
Lots of stuff in it. Ought to go big. But do you think you can get those
sex scenes by the Hays office?"

"What sex scenes?" Mr. Cobb cried.

"Well, for instance, the one where she leaves her first husband's
bed and rushes in her nightgown to the arms of her lover," said
Orlando, "and gets into bed with him because it's raining."

"Only a pervert would notice that," said Mr. Cobb and stalked out.
Seven train bearers followed him, all drying their eyes and all disdain-
ing to say "good afternoon" to Orlando.

I was sound asleep a week later when my phone rang. It was almost
noon and the caller was Orlando. He spoke in a throbbing sort of voice
and said he had to see me at once. I asked, for what reason.

"I can't tell you over the phone," Orlando throbbed, "but you'd
better shoot over right away. Don't stop for anything, for God's sake."

There were four people in the office when I got there. Two of them,
Miss Flannigan and Daisy Marcher, were crying. Moriarity, the fat boy,
was sitting in a chair, his hands folded in his lap like a neutral, and
his splayed legs dangling. Orlando's face was mottled.

"There's hell to pay," he greeted me hoarsely.

"What's happened?" I asked.

"That big know-it-all, Flannigan." He glared at her.

"I tell you I didn't mail that script out," Miss Flannigan interrupted tearfully. "She mailed it herself."

Orlando continued in a relentless voice.

"Flannigan, that big know-it-all, mailed a copy of *The Sea of Blood* to Jerome Cobb, personally. With Daisy Marcher's name on the envelope so he would be sure to open it and read it. His favorite writer, for God's sake."

"I didn't!" Miss Flannigan threw herself on the couch and wept.

"Who did then?" Orlando cried. "I've watched Daisy like a hawk. Ever since I read that pirate hog wash I've been worried something like this might happen. I haven't taken my eyes off her." His face grew redder. "The damnedest drivel I ever read," he went on as if fascinated by the horror of his tale. "A hundred and thirty duels to the death in the first twenty pages. And fifteen women have their heads cut off, including five harmless old ladies. And the hero, singlehanded, captures a whole fleet of ships. He stabs seventy-five sailors to death in the battle all alone. And for a finish, guess what? They hang a whole town. Two thousand men, women and children get hanged and then they set fire to them. Everybody gets hanged—God knows why!"

"Didn't Cobb like the script?" I asked.

"He threw a fit." Orlando glared at the phone. "He hollered for two hours. I told him it was a practical joke—some sorehead writer trying to get back at Miss Marcher."

At this point Daisy flung herself to the floor and sobbed aloud.

"Go on, cry," Orlando sneered. "I ought to break your neck. Why didn't you stick to sex? Why'd you have to show what an ignoramus you are by writing about pirates?"

He had entered the conference room as he talked and started hurling various sailing-ship models across the office.

Moriarity began to scream.

"Get these goddam things out of here," Orlando roared.

Moriarity slid from his chair and, still sobbing, started moving cautiously across the room.

"You little sneak!"—Light struck Orlando—"You did it! You sent that script out, didn't you?"

Moriarity made a bolt for it but Orlando thrust out a long leg and tripped him. The fat boy sprawled on his face and let go an ear-splitting bellow.

"You've killed him," cried Miss Flannigan.

"Shut up," Orlando shouted, "or I will!" He lifted Moriarity to his feet. "Come on clean, you little tub-o'-guts, you sent it out, didn't you?" He shook the fat boy by his shoulders.

"Only a carbon copy," Moriarity wailed.

"That's right, that's right!" Daisy screamed. She was crying savagely. "I never let anybody have the original one. I keep it myself. So there! You horrible monster, you!"

"You sex maniac!" Orlando glared at the smeared face of the little authoress. "Gimme that original, do you hear! And I want the original copy of *A Woman of Sin* or I'll break your neck."

"I'll break your neck, you!" Daisy jumped up and down and rushed for a lamp base. It was too heavy to lift. She continued screaming as she tugged at it, "You can't have it. You can't have *A Woman of Sin* either. I wrote it and it's mine. Nobody can have it. Stand back or I'll kill you."

This was evidently out of *The Sea of Blood*. Unable to take the lamp base with her, she rushed at Orlando unarmed and started kicking his shins and trying to bite him. There was a considerable racket in the room but the noise was not loud enough to mute the voice that spoke from the open doorway.

"What are you running here, a madhouse?" said Jerome B. Cobb. "What's the idea of beating up children in the middle of the day?"

Orlando turned but his eyes were not for Cobb. They rested on the persons of Freddie Blue and Mike Devlin who stood behind the Pharaoh and, staring at the scene, were ominously still.

"Come in, come right in," said Orlando and waved his arms at the bleating Moriarity and the attacking Daisy. "My sister's kids. They've been raising hell."

He pulled himself out of range of Daisy's teeth and mopped the back of his neck.

"I came over," said Mr. Cobb, whose patriarchal soul appeared revolted by the scene, "because I want to track down personally the dirty crook who wrote this dreadful thing." He waved a manila envelope in the air. "This thing called *The Sea of Blood*."

"You give me that," cried Daisy and made a jump for the envelope.

"Go away, little girl," Mr. Cobb said sternly. "Go to your mother!"

"Gimme that!" Daisy yelled again and kicked Mr. Cobb.

"Where are your manners?" Mr. Cobb shouted. He glared at Orlando. "For God's sake, get these children out of here. I want to talk to you."

"Hold it, chief," Freddie Blue broke his silence. "Let 'em stay."

"Don't be a stinker, Freddie," Orlando whispered desperately.

Freddie Blue, a dapper, lean-faced little man with cold grey eyes and a thin grey mouth, kneeled on one leg and confronted the little authoress.

"What's your name, little girl?" he asked soothingly.

"Daisy Marcher," she gurgled through her teeth, "and I want my story back from that fat man over there."

At the name, Jerome B. Cobb clapped his hand to the side of his head. He looked down at the disordered tot and asked in an abstracted voice, "What do you mean, your name is Daisy Marcher? What are you talking about?"

"Hold it, chief," Freddie fastened his eyes on Orlando. "There's something pretty fishy around here."

The blood was out of Mr. Cobb's face and with it the organ-like voice of the Pharaoh ebbed to a whisper.

"What are you trying to tell me?" he inquired and his eyes rolled toward Orlando. He moved vaguely toward a chair and sat down. It was obvious his mind had stopped working for the moment.

"Little girl," Freddie Blue resumed in a seductive voice that seemed to fascinate Daisy, "did you really write *The Sea of Blood*?"

"Yes, I did," Daisy answered. "I did so, absolutely."

"I helped her," Moriarity spoke up with sudden pride. "But I got to go home now. My ma's waiting."

Mike Devlin, a stocky and powerful figure, closed the door and placed himself in front of it, barring the little fat boy's way like an ogre in a Walt Disney picture. Moriarity began to bellow. Mr. Cobb was wiping his grey face with a handkerchief that smelled of violets.

"Can you prove you wrote that story?" the unctuous Freddie Blue pursued and patted Daisy's head tenderly.

"What are ye askin' questions for?" Mike Devlin's gravelly voice sounded from the door. "You heard what she was sayin' when we came in. She's got the original copy. That one we got is only a carbon. I noticed that when I was reading it."

"Yes, I heard her," said Freddie Blue softly. "I also heard her say she had the original copy of something else."

He pursed his thin mouth. No one spoke.

"If you'll just let me handle this," Orlando finally said in a down-to-earth voice, "everything will be okeydoke. My word on it."

Mr. Cobb's eyes had been devouring Daisy for several minutes. He managed now to pull them away from her and look at Orlando. The sight of Orlando brought him roaring to his feet. He shook a finger wildly at Orlando.

"This man," he shouted, "is trying to put something over. Something so dirty and cheap I refuse to believe it. I refuse to believe that any human being could sink so low as this man!"

"Hold it, chief," Freddie Blue said quietly. He was still kneeling in front of Daisy. Orlando frowned and kicked one of the sailing-ship models across the room.

"Is there any other Daisy Marcher besides you?" Freddie Blue asked.

"No, there is not," Daisy cried. "I'm the only one."

"Holy God!" Mr. Devlin growled from the door. "Go on, Freddie —ask her and get it over with."

"Have you ever written any other screen play than *The Sea of Blood*?" Freddie Blue pursued softly and patted the little golden head with a gentle hand.

"Yes, I did, I should say I did," Daisy answered.

"What was the name of that other screen play?" Freddie Blue continued his gentle quiz.

"*A Woman of Sin,*" said Daisy. "It's been in all the papers every day. *A Woman of Sin*. So there!"

Freddie Blue stood up and looked intently into Orlando's eyes.

"Is that true?" he asked.

"Listen, fellas." Orlando hopped to a seat on his table. "You come barging in here like a pack of hoodlums and frightening the wits out of that poor baby."

"You ain't said if it's true yet," Mike Devlin growled and his jaw muscles began working.

"For God's sake," Orlando yelled, "it isn't going to do any good to start getting tough about it! You'll spill *all* the beans then. I've broken my neck trying to protect you fellas from the beginning."

A cry came from Jerome B. Cobb but there were no words. His hand moved furtively to his bosom and rested over his heart. He closed his eyes and leaned back in his chair.

"Get Mr. Cobb some water," Mike Devlin growled.

Miss Flannigan hurried out.

"Never mind me," Mr. Cobb moaned. "The company . . . the company."

Orlando ignored this seeming deathbed interruption.

"Listen, let's get everything straight," he said. "I begged J. B. not to buy that story. I pleaded with him. I told him it was pure childish tripe. But he wouldn't listen. I went on record that only a half-witted baby could have written it."

Miss Flannigan had returned with the water. Mr. Cobb pushed her aside and leaped to his feet like a Lazarus on springs.

"You scum!" His roar filled the room and he moved slowly toward Orlando. "You grave robber! Taking advantage of my friendship!"

"Nobody took advantage of you," Orlando shouted. "You took advantage of yourself like you always do, goddam it!"

"Shut up!" The Pharaoh's organ voice opened two more stops, "You have ruined me! For what? Why? Tell me why! Using a dirty child to make a dirty penny."

"Hold it, chief," Freddie Blue interrupted. "She's the author of our biggest epic. There's no sense in antagonizing her."

Mr. Cobb reeled. He clapped a hand against the side of his head again. His other hand reached out blindly for a chair.

"It's a lie! It's a rotten lie!" he shouted. "She never wrote it. I don't believe it! This innocent child write that thing! Never! Mike—call the police!"

Mr. Cobb had come close to Orlando but there were no blows struck. And Orlando at this minute did a curious thing. He laughed— not hysterically nor mockingly. He laughed with a sound of honest if somewhat childish relief. And he sat down calmly behind his fifteen-foot antique desk.

"Call the police," Orlando said aloofly. "Do anything you want. I'm washed up on this. You boys have got the ball."

The ironing out of the Daisy Marcher imbroglio took a full fifteen hours and was accomplished in Jerome B. Cobb's secret office, the one to be entered through a sliding panel. It was tastily furnished and had no telephones.

Until eleven that night there were present Mr. Cobb, his two Nobles, three lawyers from the legal department famed for their loyalty to the company, Orlando and myself. I had been invited as an accomplice. Daisy, under the guard of Mr. Cobb's sister-in-law—a Mrs. Sophia Cobb—was forced to cool her heels in one of the conference chambers adjoining the Pharaoh's main sanctum. Mrs. Sophia Cobb was a tall woman with a square face set in an expression of aversion, an expression she may well have caught from anyone around her. I felt sorry for Daisy as we left her to this monitor.

I also felt sorry for Mr. Cobb. The spectacle of a man face to face with the incontrovertible proofs of his own idiocy is never a pleasant one, however idiotic the victim. But my sorrow was more or less flitting. Mr. Cobb, confronted by the fact that he was an imbecile and that he had mistaken the droolings of a nine-year-old child for Art of the highest water, revealed himself a man of great resource. He pointed out in an oration lasting three hours that he had taken the cheap nonsense of this horrid child, Daisy Marcher, and converted it by his own genius into a powerful motion picture. He defied anyone to deny this. He defied anyone to deny the fact that he had been suspicious of that manuscript from the moment he clapped eyes on it. But somehow, by a miracle for which he was ready to thank God, this childish nonsense had struck a creative chord in his bosom. He had toiled—nobody would ever know how hard he had toiled—and created an adult Academy Award picture out of absolutely nothing.

These thumping lies were received with clucks of wonder by the three loyal barristers. Freddie Blue kept himself in a state of suspended animation during this rebuilding of the Pharaoh, by the Pharaoh for the Pharaoh. Mike Devlin scowled as if these revelations of human mendacity were too much for him. I felt he was thinking of happier days in the ring. As for Orlando, my friend conducted himself like a veritable craven. He bore out each and every one of the Pharaoh's idiotic statements and professed himself solemnly amazed at what J. B. had managed to make out of the sow's ear he had sold him.

"He turned a debacle into victory," said Orlando, beaming on everybody.

I decided that sorrow for Mr. Cobb was an emotion wasted.

After Jerome B. Cobb's summing up of his own genius the meeting took up more general topics. It was decided that the good of the industry required the suppression of the fact that a nine-year-old child had written Empire's two-million-dollar drama of human emotions—already advertised in all the magazines as Hollywood's Top Art Film.

"Exactly what I've been doing right along, hiding that fact," Orlando chirped. The group ignored him.

"We could explain to the public that I actually wrote it," said Mr. Cobb, "but I don't want to figure personally in the matter. It has always been my policy to work behind the scenes. I don't want to start hogging credit and setting a bad example for everybody."

He looked sternly at Freddie Blue and Mike Devlin.

"Well," said Freddie Blue, "it wouldn't help the situation to advertise you as Daisy Marcher's collaborator."

Mrs. Egelhofer, summoned from her seashore retreat, arrived at this point. She had left in a hurry and forgotten to bring her knitting, which seemed to rob her of her personality and her wits. She was touchingly pleased to see Orlando and hoped in a quavering voice that nothing had happened to her child. She was certain it had. She didn't want anyone to keep anything from her. The truth was better than the terrible suspense under which she had been laboring ever since the telephone had wakened her.

"There's nothing to worry about," Orlando assured her. "Daisy's in the next room and she's in fine health."

Mrs. Egelhofer trembled and sat down. Her mother's heart was not entirely convinced. It was explained to her that she would have to sign some papers transferring the guardianship of Daisy Marcher from Orlando Higgens to Jerome B. Cobb. Mrs. Egelhofer was unexpectedly stubborn.

"But I don't know any Mr. Cobb," she fluttered. "I can't just give my little girl away to anybody."

"For God's sake," Mike Devlin growled, "you gave the kid to that guy"—he pointed at Orlando—"and for all you knew he might have been a burglar."

"Oh, no," said Mrs. Egelhofer, "his aura was quite good. Very good. That gentleman's aura"—she looked critically at Mr. Cobb—"is quite something else. Dark green. I don't like it."

"Mr. Cobb's aura is all right when he's feeling better," said Mike Devlin and it was explained to the perturbed mother just who Jerome B. Cobb was. The Pharaoh himself sat down next to her and took her plump hand in his.

"My dear young lady," he said soothingly, "I want to place the little girl in the best private school in southern California. And more than that. I am sending my own sister-in-law to live with her. She is a grand woman and understands children better than any of us. They're a hobby with her. In such a school, under the guidance of great teachers, who knows but what the child will have a chance to amount to something."

"I don't think any more fame would be good for her," Mrs. Egelhofer demurred. "At her age, too. She's had quite enough, don't you think?"

"I'm talking about real, human education," said Mr. Cobb, "something that will make a human being out of her and not just a—a movie writer."

Mrs. Egelhofer sighed.

"I don't know," she said. "It's all so queer and yet so heartbreaking. My little girl has been taken from me again."

Ten minutes later the papers were signed and Daisy was brought in. It was 1:00 A.M. but the little authoress was as alert as at any high noon.

"My poor darling," Mrs. Egelhofer said, holding out her arms.

"What are you doing here?" Daisy asked and backed away.

"I came here to rescue you," said Mrs. Egelhofer, putting a handkerchief to her eyes. She recovered a smile. "Let me be the one to break the news to her." She looked wistfully at the group. "Babykins, you are going to have a new father."

"Who?" said Daisy impassively.

"That gentleman over there." Mrs. Egelhofer indicated the Pharaoh. Daisy made a noise as of dice rattling in the back of her throat. The open-mouthed stares of the group in no way embarrassed her. She looked from one face to the other and said, "Why him?"

"Darling," said Mrs. Egelhofer, "Mother knows best."

Daisy turned and started for the door but Orlando grabbed her. He held her by the shoulder, pretending to pat it.

"Well, as I see it," said Orlando, "the whole thing depends on my little friend Daisy here. If she'll keep quiet, you're O.K. If she won't— well, that's another situation."

"Come here, little girl." Mr. Cobb smiled sourly at the child.

Daisy made no move.

"Of course she won't say anything," Mr. Cobb went on. "Why should she? She isn't a crook like you, Higgens. She's an honest, decent, sweet little girl."

Daisy was silent. Orlando shrugged his shoulders.

"O.K.," he said. "If you want to take a chance, that's all right with me. But I don't feel it's straight thinking."

Something seemed to give way in Mr. Cobb.

"Get out of here, you crook!" he shouted. "Get out of here and never darken this door again or I'll throw you out of the window with my own hands."

"Hold it, chief," said Freddie Blue. "Let's see what Higgens has to suggest."

"I don't give a damn what he's got to suggest," Mr. Cobb tried to scream but his voice broke and both his eyes appeared to fill with red tears.

"Take it easy, J. B.," Mike Devlin growled.

"I have this to suggest," said Orlando as if there had been no interruptions. "I suggest that you buy *The Sea of Blood* and produce it. With a few rewrites, of course. And also that you take an option on any other works from Miss Marcher's pen. She's going to be a great name in pictures after *A Woman of Sin* and all the ballyhoo you've given her. The critics are nuts about her. I think you're damned short-sighted if you don't cash in on all this."

He turned amiably to his little client.

"How about it, honey?" he asked. "You'll keep quiet if they do that, won't you?" He looked happily at Mr. Cobb. "Frankly, I wouldn't blame her if she blabbed her head off if you let her down now."

The room was silent.

"A Daisy Marcher picture every year," Orlando continued, beaming at his little client. "Each one a super-special. And your name in lights —same billing as the star or director. What do you say, Daisy?"

"Oh, yes," said Daisy, "I would like that very much. If I can work with the Captain."

"Who's that?" Freddie Blue asked softly.

"Moriarity," said Orlando. "You met him in my office."

"Holy God!" Mike Devlin groaned. "Did he help her write *A Woman of Sin?*"

"No, he did not," said Daisy. "I wrote that all by myself."

Mike Devlin sighed with relief.

"Well, gentlemen," said Orlando, a jolly note in his voice, "is it a deal? Same price as *A Woman of Sin* for the next two. And a slight increase on the two thereafter. We can figure all that out later."

Mr. Cobb said nothing. His eyes were closed. Freddie Blue was likewise silent. Mike Devlin alone spoke. A faint grin was around his fighter's mouth. I could see he admired Orlando Higgens almost as much as I did.

"It's a deal," said Mr. Devlin.

It thus befell that Daisy Marcher was whisked off to a private school in southern California, her little arms loaded with papers, among them contracts for *The Sea of Blood* and for her next four pictures. Mrs. Sophia Cobb sat in the drawing room facing her, but all the distaste that lady could summon into her square face was not enough to flicker one of Daisy's eyelids.

No sooner had the train started than Daisy had asked for a table. When they were passing the town of Azusa the little authoress was already sitting hunched over it, her tongue protruding from the corner of her mouth, and a fierce light in her eyes. She was writing Picture Number Three.

Mr. Cobb, accompanied by his entire court, several nurses and a special osteopath, rushed off to the mud baths at Arrowhead Lake. Here the Pharaoh and his Nobles lay basking for several weeks. They took short walks and discussed the state of J. B.'s health. It did not seem to be improving. The Pharaoh lay on his sun porch and grew greyer. He complained of pains around the heart. Mike Devlin summoned a specialist from Hollywood. The Empire publicity department sent three movie columnists down with the doctor. The specialist was glum. J. B. had been doing too much. He couldn't say what might happen.

His face gaunt, with the marks of dissolution plainly on him and a tall glass of milk at his side, Jerome B. Cobb unbosomed himself to the movie columnists in what he termed his first personal interview. "And maybe my last," he smiled wanly.

"Movie-making is more than a job," he said slowly. "It's a man's whole life. It's not earning money or fame that counts. It's bringing beauty and pleasure to a sorely troubled world.

"We who make movies"—the Pharaoh's eyes brightened for a moment with memories—"are on a battle front day and night. Sometimes we fall—and others take our place and carry on. And we are forgotten. But as long as there is life left in us—we must keep the show going with everything we've got."

Jerome B. Cobb closed his eyes. The movie columnists were deeply moved. They rose and tiptoed out of the sun room.

Mr. Cobb's recovery amazed his Nobles. The very next morning he was up at dawn packing his own suitcase and touching his toes fifteen times. He tarried only long enough for a final massage and then, gathering his court about him, whizzed back to Hollywood, refreshed for the great problem of movie-making.

A Woman of Sin, written by Daisy Marcher, the new Balzac of the screen, was released the week before Christmas. It grossed four and a half million dollars.

Miracle of the Fifteen Murderers

THERE is always an aura of mystery to the conclaves of medical men. One may wonder whether the secrecy with which the fraternity surrounds its gathering is designed to keep the layman from discovering how much it knows or how much it doesn't know. Either knowledge would be unnerving to that immemorial guinea pig who submits himself to the abracadabras of chemicals, scalpels and incantations under the delusion he is being cured rather than explored.

Among the most mysterious of medical get-togethers in this generation have been those held in New York City by a group of eminent doctors calling themselves the X Club. Every three months this little band of healers have hied them to the Walton Hotel overlooking the East River and, behind locked doors and beyond the eye of even medical journalism, engaged themselves in unknown emprise lasting till dawn.

What the devil had been going on in these conclaves for twenty years no one knew, not even the ubiquitous head of the American Medical Association, nor yet any of the colleagues, wives, friends or dependents of the X Club's members. The talent for secrecy is highly developed among doctors who, even with nothing to conceal, are often as close mouthed as old-fashioned bomb throwers on their way to a rendezvous.

How then do I know the story of these long-guarded sessions? The answer is—the war. The war has put an end to them, as it has to nearly all mysteries other than its own. The world, engaged in reexamining its manners and its soul, has closed the door on minor adventure. Nine of the fifteen medical sages who comprised the X Club are in uniform and preside over combat zone hospitals. Deficiencies of age and health have kept the others at home—with increased labors.

"Considering that we have disbanded," Dr. Alex Hume said to me at dinner one evening, "and that it is unlikely we shall ever assemble again, I see no reason for preserving our secret. Yours is a childish and romantic mind, and may be revolted by the story I tell you. You will undoubtedly translate the whole thing into some sort of diabolical tale and miss the deep human and scientific import of the X Club. But I am not the one to reform the art of fiction, which must substitute sentimentality for truth and Cinderella for Galileo."

And so on. I will skip the rest of my friend's all-knowing prelude. You may have read Dr. Hume's various books, dealing with the horseplay of the subconscious. If you have, you know this bald-headed master mind well enough. If not, take my word for it he is a genius. There is nobody I know more adept at prancing around in the solar plexus swamps out of which most of the world's incompetence and confusion appear to rise. He has, too, if there is any doubt about his great talent, the sneer and chuckle which are the war whoop of the super-psychologist. His face is round and his mouth is pursed in a chronic grimace of disbelief and contradiction. You can't help such an expression once you have discovered what a scurvy and detestable morass is the soul of man. Like most subterranean workers, my friend is almost as blind as a bat behind his heavy glasses. And like many leading psychiatrists, he favors the short and balloon-like physique of Napoleon.

The last dramatic meeting of the X Club was held on a rainy March night. Despite the hostile weather, all fifteen of its members attended, for there was an added lure to this gathering. A new member was to be inducted into the society.

Dr. Hume was assigned to prepare the neophyte for his debut. And it was in the wake of the round-faced soul fixer that Dr. Samuel Warner entered the sanctum of the X Club.

Dr. Warner was unusually young for a medical genius—that is, a recognized one. And he had never received a fuller recognition of his wizardry with saw, axe and punch hole than his election as a member of the X Club. For the fourteen older men who had invited him to be one of them were leaders in their various fields. They were the medical peerage. This does not mean necessarily that any layman had ever heard of them. Eminence in the medical profession is as showy at best as a sprig of edelweiss on a mountain top. The war, which offers its magic billboards for the vanities of small souls and transmutes the hunger for publicity into sacrificial and patriotic ardors, has not yet disturbed the anonymity of the great medicos. They have moved their bushels to the front lines and are busy under them spreading their learning among the wounded.

The new member was a tense and good-looking man with the fever of hard work glowing in his steady dark eyes. His wide mouth smiled quickly and abstractedly, as is often the case with surgeons who train their reactions not to interfere with their concentration.

Having exchanged greetings with the eminent club members, who included half of his living medical heroes, Dr. Warner seated himself in a corner and quietly refused a highball, a cocktail, and a slug of brandy. His face remained tense, his athletic body straight in its chair as if it were poised for a sprint rather than a meeting.

At nine o'clock Dr. William Tick ordered an end to all the guzzling and declared the fifty-third meeting of the X Club in session. The venerable diagnostician placed himself behind a table at the end of the ornate hotel room and glared at the group ranged in front of him.

Dr. Tick had divided his seventy-five years equally between practicing the art of medicine and doing his best to stamp it out—such, at least, was the impression of the thousands of students who had been submitted to his irascible guidance. As Professor of Internal Medicine at a great Eastern medical school, Dr. Tick had favored the education-by-insult theory of pedagogy. There were eminent doctors who still winced when they recalled some of old bilious-eyed, arthritic, stooped Tick's appraisals of their budding talents, and who still shuddered at the memory of his medical philosophy.

"Medicine," Dr. Tick had confided to flock after flock of students, "is a noble dream and at the same time the most ancient expression of error and idiocy known to man. Solving the mysteries of heaven has not given birth to as many abortive findings as has the quest into the mysteries of the human body. When you think of yourselves as scientists, I want you always to remember everything you learn from me will probably be regarded tomorrow as the naïve confusions of a pack of medical aborigines. Despite all our toil and progress, the art of medicine still falls somewhere between trout casting and spook writing."

"There are two handicaps to the practice of medicine," Tick had repeated tenaciously through forty years of teaching. "The first is the eternal charlatanism of the patient who is full of fake diseases and phantom agonies. The second is the basic incompetence of the human mind, medical or otherwise, to observe without prejudice, acquire information without becoming too smug to use it intelligently, and most of all, to apply its wisdom without vanity."

From behind his table Old Tick's eyes glared at the present group of "incompetents" until a full classroom silence had arrived, and then turned to the tense, good-looking face of Dr. Warner.

"We have a new medical genius with us tonight," he began, "one I well remember in his pre-wizard days. A hyper-thyroid with kidney disfunction indicated. But not without a trace of talent. For your benefit, Sam, I will state the meaning and purpose of our organization."

"I have already done that," said Dr. Hume, "rather thoroughly."

"Dr. Hume's explanations to you," Tick continued coldly, "if they are of a kind with his printed works, have most certainly left you dazed if not dazzled."

"I understood him quite well," Warner said.

"Nonsense," Old Tick said. "You always had a soft spot for psychiatry and I always warned you against it. Psychiatry is a plot against medicine."

You may be sure that Dr. Hume smiled archly at this.

"You will allow me," Tick went on, "to clarify whatever the learned Hume has been trying to tell you."

"Well, if you want to waste time." The new member smiled nervously and mopped his neck with a handkerchief.

Dr. Frank Rosson, the portly and distinguished gynecologist, chuckled. "Tick's going good tonight," he whispered to Hume.

"Senility inflamed by sadism," said Hume.

"Dr. Warner," the pedagogue continued, "the members of the X Club have a single and interesting purpose in their meeting. They come together every three months to confess to some murder any of them may have committed since our last assembly.

"I am referring, of course, to medical murder. Although it would be a relief to hear any one of us confess to a murder performed out of passion rather than stupidity. Indeed, Dr. Warner, if you have killed a wife or polished off an uncle recently, and would care to unbosom yourself, we will listen respectfully. It is understood that nothing you say will be brought to the attention of the police or the A.M.A."

Old Tick's eyes paused to study the growing tension in the new member's face.

"I am sure you have not slain any of your relatives," he sighed, "or that you will ever do so except in the line of duty.

"The learned Hume," he went on, "has undoubtedly explained these forums to you on the psychiatric basis that confession is good for the soul. This is nonsense. We are not here to ease our souls but to improve them. Our real purpose is scientific. Since we dare not admit our mistakes to the public and since we are too great and learned to be criticized by the untutored laity and since such inhuman perfection as that to which we pretend is not good for our weak and human natures, we have formed this society. It is the only medical organization in the world where the members boast only of their mistakes.

"And now"—Tick beamed on the neophyte—"allow me to define what we consider a real, fine professional murder. It is the killing of a human being who has trustingly placed himself in a doctor's hands. Mind you, the death of a patient does not in itself spell murder. We are concerned only with those cases in which the doctor by a wrong diagnosis or by demonstrably wrong medication or operative procedure has killed off a patient who, without the aforesaid doctor's attention, would have continued to live and prosper."

"Hume explained all this to me," the new member muttered impatiently, and then raised his voice. "I appreciate that this is my first meeting and that I might learn more from my distinguished colleagues by listening than by talking. But I have something rather important to say."

"A murder?" Tick asked.

"Yes," said the new member.

The old professor nodded.

"Very good," he said. "And we shall be glad to listen to you. But we have several murderers in the docket ahead of you."

The new member was silent and remained sitting bolt-upright in his chair. It was at this point that several, including Hume, noticed there was something more than stage fright in the young surgeon's tension. The certainty filled the room that Sam Warner had come to his first meeting of the X Club with something violent and mysterious boiling in him.

Dr. Philip Kurtiff, the eminent neurologist, put his hand on Warner's arm and said quietly, "There's no reason to feel badly about anything you're going to tell us. We're all pretty good medical men and we've all done worse—whatever it is."

"If you please," Old Tick demanded, "we will have silence. This is not a sanatorium for doctors with guilt complexes. It is a clinic for error. And we will continue to conduct it in an orderly, scientific fashion. If you want to hold Sam Warner's hand, Kurtiff, that's your privilege. But do it in silence."

He beamed suddenly at the new member.

"I confess," he went on, "that I'm as curious as anybody to hear how so great a know-it-all as our young friend Dr. Warner could have killed off one of his customers. But our curiosity will have to wait. Since five of you were absent from our last gathering, I think that the confessions of Dr. James Sweeney should be repeated for your benefit."

Dr. Sweeney stood up and turned his lugubrious face and shining eyes to the five absentees.

"Well," he said in his preoccupied monotone, "I told it once, but I'll tell it again. I sent a patient to my X-ray room to have a fluoroscopy done. My assistant gave him a barium meal to drink and put him under the fluoroscope. I walked in a minute later, and when I saw the patient under the ray I observed to my assistant, Dr. Kroch, that it was amazing and that I had never seen anything like it. Kroch was too overcome to bear me out. What I saw was that the patient's entire gastro-intestinal tract from the esophagus down was apparently made out of stone. And as I studied this phenomenon, I noticed it was becoming clearer and sharper. The most disturbing factor in the situation was that we both knew there was nothing to be done. Dr. Kroch, in fact, showed definite signs of hysteria. Even while we were studying him the patient showed symptoms of death. Shortly afterward he became moribund and fell to the floor."

"Well, I'll be damned," several of the absentees cried in unison, Dr. Kurtiff adding, "What the hell was it?"

"It was simple," said Sweeney. "The bottom of the glass out of which the patient had drunk his barium meal was caked solid. We had filled him up with plaster of Paris. I fancy the pressure caused an instantaneous coronary attack."

"Good Lord!" the new member said. "How did it get into the glass?"

"Through some pharmaceutical error," said Sweeney mildly.

"What, if anything, was the matter with the patient before he adventured into your office?" Dr. Kurtiff inquired.

"The autopsy revealed chiefly a solidified gastro-intestinal tract," said Sweeney. "But I think from several indications that there may have been a little tendency to pyloric spasm which caused the belching for which he was referred to me."

"A rather literary murder," said Old Tick. "A sort of Pygmalion in reverse."

The old professor paused and fastened his red-rimmed eyes on Warner.

"By the way, before we proceed," he said, "I think it is time to tell you the full name of our club. Our full name is the X Marks the Spot Club. We prefer, of course, to use the abbreviated title as being a bit more social-sounding."

"Of course," said the new member, whose face now appeared to be getting redder.

"And now," announced Old Tick, consulting a scribbled piece of paper, "our first case on tonight's docket will be Dr. Wendell Davis."

There was silence as the elegant stomach specialist stood up. Davis was a doctor who took his manner as seriously as his medicine. Tall, solidly built, gray-haired and beautifully barbered, his face was without expression—a large, pink mask that no patient, however ill and agonized, had ever seen disturbed.

"I was called late last summer to the home of a workingman," he began. "Senator Bell had given a picnic for some of his poorer constituency. As a result of this event, the three children of a steamfitter named Horowitz were brought down with food poisoning. They had overeaten at the picnic. The Senator, as host, felt responsible, and I went to the Horowitz home at his earnest solicitation. I found two of the children very sick and vomiting considerably. They were nine and eleven. The mother gave me a list of the various foods all three of them had eaten. It was staggering. I gave them a good dose of castor oil.

"The third child, aged seven, was not as ill as the other two. He looked pale, had a slight fever, felt some nausea—but was not vomiting. It seemed obvious that he too was poisoned, but to a lesser degree. Accordingly I prescribed an equal dose of castor oil for the youngest child —just to be on the safe side.

"I was called by the father in the middle of the night. He was alarmed over the condition of the seven-year-old. He reported that the other two children were much improved. I told him not to worry, that the youngest had been a little late in developing food poisoning but would unquestionably be better in the morning, and that his cure was as certain as his sister's and brother's. When I hung up I felt quite pleased with myself for having anticipated the youngest one's condition and prescribed the castor oil prophylactically. I arrived at the Horowitz home at noon the next day and found the two older children practically recovered. The seven-year-old, however, appeared to be very sick indeed. They had been trying to reach me since breakfast. The child had 105° temperature. It was dehydrated, the eyes sunken and circled, the expression pinched, the nostrils dilated, the lips cyanotic and the skin cold and clammy."

Dr. Davis paused. Dr. Milton Morris, the renowned lung specialist, spoke.

"It died within a few hours?" he asked.

Dr. Davis nodded.

"Well," Dr. Morris said quietly, "it seems pretty obvious. The child was suffering from acute appendicitis when you first saw it. The castor oil ruptured its appendix. By the time you got around to looking at it again peritonitis had set in."

"Yes," said Dr. Davis slowly, "that's exactly what happened."

"Murder by castor oil," Old Tick cackled. "I have a memo from Dr. Kenneth Wood. Dr. Wood has the floor."

The noted Scotch surgeon, famed in his college days as an Olympic Games athlete, stood up. He was still a man of prowess, large-handed, heavy-shouldered, and with the purr of masculine strength in his soft voice.

"I don't know what kind of a murder you can call this," Dr. Wood smiled at his colleagues.

"Murder by butchery is the usual title," Tick said.

"No, I doubt that," Dr. Morris protested. "Ken's too skillful to cut off anybody's leg by mistake."

"I guess you'll have to call it just plain murder by stupidity," Dr. Wood said softly.

Old Tick cackled.

"If you'd paid a little more attention to diagnosis than to shot putting you wouldn't be killing off such hordes of patients," he said.

"This is my first report in three years," Wood answered modestly. "And I've been operating at the rate of four or five daily, including holidays."

"My dear Kenneth," Dr. Hume said, "every surgeon is entitled to one murder in three years. A phenomenal record, in fact—when you consider the temptations."

"Proceed with the crime," Tick said.

"Well"—the strong-looking surgeon turned to his hospital colleague, the new member—"you know how it is with these acute gall bladders, Sam."

Warner nodded abstractedly.

Dr. Wood went on.

"Brought in late at night. In extreme pain. I examined her. Found the pain in the right upper quadrant of the abdomen. It radiated to the back and right shoulder. Completely characteristic of gall bladder. I gave her opiates. They had no effect on her, which, as you know, backs up any gall bladder diagnosis. Opiates never touch the gall bladder."

"We know that," said the new member nervously.

"Excuse me," Dr. Wood smiled. "I want to get all the points down carefully. Well, I gave her some nitro-glycerine to lessen the pain then. Her temperature was 101. By morning the pain was so severe that it seemed certain the gall bladder had perforated. I operated. There was nothing wrong with her damn gall bladder. She died an hour later."

"What did the autopsy show?" Dr. Sweeney asked.

"Wait a minute," Wood answered. "You're supposed to figure it out, aren't you? Come on—you tell me what was the matter with her."

"Did you take her history?" Dr. Kurtiff asked after a pause.

"No," Wood answered.

"Aha!" Tick snorted. "There you have it! Blind man's buff again."

"It was an emergency." Wood looked flushed. "And it seemed an obvious case. I've had hundreds of them."

"The facts seem to be as follows," Tick spoke up. "Dr. Wood murdered a woman because he misunderstood the source of a pain. We have, then, a very simple problem. What besides the gall bladder can produce the sort of pain that eminent surgeon has described?"

"Heart," Dr. Morris answered quickly.

"You're getting warm," said Wood.

"Before operating on anyone with so acute a pain, and in the absence of any medical history," Tick went on, "I would most certainly have looked at the heart."

"Well, you'd have done right," said Wood quietly. "The autopsy showed an infraction of the descending branch of the right coronary artery."

"Murder by a sophomore," Old Tick pronounced wrathfully.

"The first and last," said Wood quietly. "There won't be any more heart-case mistakes in my hospital."

"Good, good," Old Tick said. "And now, gentlemen, the crimes reported thus far have been too infantile for discussion. We have learned nothing from them other than that science and stupidity go hand in hand, a fact already too well known to us. However, we have with us tonight a young but extremely talented wielder of the medical saws. And I can, from long acquaintance with this same gentleman, assure you that if he has done a murder it is bound to be what some of my female students would call 'a honey.' He has been sitting here for the last hour, fidgeting like a true criminal, sweating with guilt and a desire to tell all. Gentlemen, I give you our new and youngest culprit, Dr. Samuel Warner."

Dr. Warner faced his fourteen eminent colleagues with a sudden excitement in his manner. The older men regarded him quietly and with various degrees of irritation. They knew without further corroboration than his manner that this medico was full of untenable theories and half-baked medical discoveries. They had been full of such things themselves once. And they settled back to enjoy themselves. There is nothing as pleasing to a graying medicine man as the opportunity of slapping a dunce-cap on the young of science. Old Tick, surveying his colleagues, grinned. They had all acquired the look of pedagogues holding a switch behind their backs.

Dr. Warner mopped his neck with his wet handkerchief and smiled knowingly at the medical peerage. What he knew was that this same critical and suspicious attention would have been offered him were he there to recite the tale of some miraculous cure rather than a murder.

"I'll give you this case in some detail," he said, "because I think it contains as interesting a problem as you can find in practice."

Dr. Rosson, the gynecologist, grunted, but said nothing.

"The patient was a young man, or rather a boy," Warner went on eagerly. "He was seventeen, and amazingly talented. In fact, about the most remarkable young man I've ever met. He wrote poetry. That's how I happened to meet him. I read one of his poems in a magazine, and, by God, it was so impressive I wrote him a letter."

Dr. Kurtiff frowned at this unmedical behavior.

"Rhymed poetry?" Dr. Wood asked, with a wink at Old Tick.

"Yes," said Warner. "I read all his manuscripts. They were sort of revolutionary. His poetry was a cry against injustice. Every kind of injustice. Bitter and burning."

"Wait a minute," Dr. Rosson said. "The new member seems to have some misconception of our function. We are not a literary society, Warner."

"I know that," said Warner, working his jaw muscles and smiling lifelessly.

"And before you get started," Dr. Hume grinned, "no bragging. You can do your bragging at the annual surgeons' convention."

"Gentlemen," Warner said, "I have no intention of bragging. I'll stick to murder, I assure you. And as bad a one as you've ever heard."

"Good," Dr. Kurtiff said. "Go on. And take it easy and don't break down."

"I won't break down," Warner said. "Don't worry. Well, the patient was sick for two weeks before I was called."

"I thought you were his friend," Dr. Davis said.

"I was," Warner answered. "But he didn't believe in doctors."

"No faith in them, eh?" Old Tick cackled. "Brilliant boy."

"He was," said Warner eagerly. "I felt upset when I came and saw how sick he was. I had him moved to a hospital at once."

"Oh, a rich poet," Dr. Sweeney said.

"No," said Warner. "I paid his expenses. And I spent all the time I could with him. The sickness had started with a severe pain on the left side of the abdomen. He was going to call me, but the pain subsided after three days so the patient thought he was well. But it came back after two days and he began running a temperature. He developed diarrhea. There was pus and blood, but no amoeba or pathogenic bacteria when he finally sent for me. After the pathology reports I made a diagnosis of ulcerative colitis. The pain being on the left side ruled out the appendix. I put the patient on sulfaguanidin and unconcentrated liver extract and gave him a high protein diet—chiefly milk. Despite this treatment and constant observation the patient got worse. He developed generalized abdominal tenderness, both direct and rebound, and rigidity of the entire left rectus muscle. After two weeks of careful treatment the patient died."

"And the autopsy showed you'd been wrong?" Dr. Wood asked.

"I didn't make an autopsy," said Warner. "The boy's parents had perfect faith in me. As did the boy. They both believed I was doing everything possible to save his life."

"Then how do you know you were wrong in your diagnosis?" Dr. Hume asked.

"By the simple fact," said Warner irritably, "that the patient died instead of being cured. When he died I knew I had killed him by a faulty diagnosis."

"A logical conclusion," said Dr. Sweeney. "Pointless medication is no alibi."

"Well, gentlemen," Old Tick cackled from behind his table, "our talented new member has obviously polished off a great poet and close personal friend. Indictments of his diagnosis are now in order."

But no one spoke. Doctors have a sense for things unseen and complications unstated. And nearly all the fourteen looking at Warner felt there was something hidden. The surgeon's tension, his elation and its overtone of mockery, convinced them there was something untold in the story of the dead poet. They approached the problem cautiously.

"How long ago did the patient die?" Dr. Rosson asked.

"Last Wednesday," said Warner. "Why?"

"What hospital?" asked Davis.

"St. Michael's," said Warner.

"You say the parents had faith in you," said Kurtiff, "and still have. Yet you seem curiously worried about something. Has there been any inquiry by the police?"

"No," said Warner. "I committed the perfect crime. The police haven't even heard of it. And even my victim died full of gratitude."

He beamed at the room. "Listen," he went on, "even you people may not be able to disprove my diagnosis."

This brash challenge irritated a number of the members.

"I don't think it will be very difficult to knock out your diagnosis," said Dr. Morris.

"There's a catch to it," said Wood slowly, his eyes boring at Warner.

"The only catch there is," said Warner quickly, "is the complexity of the case. You gentlemen evidently prefer the simpler malpractice type of crime, such as I've listened to tonight."

There was a pause, and then Dr. Davis inquired in a soothing voice, "You described an acute onset of pain before the diarrhea, didn't you?"

"That's right," said Warner.

"Well," Davis continued coolly, "the temporary relief of symptoms and their recurrence within a few days sounds superficially like ulcers —except for one point."

"I disagree," Dr. Sweeney said softly. "Dr. Warner's diagnosis is a piece of blundering stupidity. The symptoms he has presented have nothing to do with ulcerative colitis."

Warner flushed and his jaw muscles moved angrily.

"Would you mind backing up your insults with a bit of science?" he said.

"Very easily done," Sweeney answered calmly. "The late onset of diarrhea and fever you describe rules out ulcerative colitis in ninety-nine cases out of a hundred. What do you think, Dr. Tick?"

"No ulcers," said Tick, his eyes studying Warner.

"You mentioned a general tenderness of the abdomen as one of the last symptoms," said Dr. Davis smoothly.

"That's right," said Warner.

"Well, if you have described the case accurately," Davis continued, "there is one obvious fact revealed. The general tenderness points to a peritonitis."

"How about a twisted gut?" Dr. Wood asked. "That could produce the symptoms described."

"No," said Dr. Rosson. "A vulvulus means gangrene and death in three days. Warner says he attended him for two weeks and that the patient was sick for two weeks before he was called. The length of the illness rules out intussusception, vulvulus and intestinal tumor."

"There's one other thing," Dr. Morris said. "A left-sided appendix."

"That's out, too," Dr. Wood said quickly. "The first symptom of a left-sided appendix would not be the acute pain described by Warner."

"The only thing we have determined," said Dr. Sweeney, "is a perforation other than ulcer. Why not go on with that?"

"Yes," said Dr. Morris. "Ulcerative colitis is out of the question, considering the course taken by the disease. I'm sure we're dealing with another type of perforation."

"The next question," announced Old Tick, "is, what made the perforation?"

Dr. Warner mopped his face with his wet handkerchief and said softly, "I never thought of an object perforation."

"You should have," Dr. Kurtiff smiled.

"Come, come," Old Tick interrupted. "Let's not wander. What caused the perforation?"

"He was seventeen," Kurtiff answered, "and too old to be swallowing pins."

"Unless," said Dr. Hume, "he had a taste for pins. Did the patient want to live, Warner?"

"He wanted to live," said Warner grimly, "more than anybody I ever knew."

"I think we can ignore the suicide theory," said Dr. Kurtiff. "I am certain we are dealing with a perforation of the intestines and not of the subconscious."

"Well," Dr. Wood said, "it couldn't have been a chicken bone. A chicken bone would have stuck in the esophagus and never got through to the stomach."

"There you are, Warner," Old Tick said. "We've narrowed it down. The spreading tenderness you described means a spreading infection. The course taken by the disease means a perforation other than ulcerous. And a perforation of that type means an object swallowed. We have ruled out pins and chicken bones. Which leaves us with only one other normal guess."

"A fish bone," said Dr. Sweeney.

"Exactly," said Tick.

Warner stood listening tensely to the voices affirming the diagnosis. Tick delivered ·the verdict.

"I think we are all agreed," he said, "that Sam Warner killed his patient by treating him for ulcerative colitis when an operation removing an abscessed fish bone would have saved his life."

Warner moved quickly across the room to the closet where he had hung his hat and coat.

"Where you going?" Dr. Wood called after him. "We've just started the meeting."

Warner was putting on his coat and grinning.

"I haven't got much time," he said, "but I want to thank all of you for your diagnoses. You were right about there being a catch to the case. The catch is that my patient is still alive. I've been treating him for ulcerative colitis for two weeks and I realized this afternoon that I had wrongly diagnosed the case—and that he would be dead in twenty-four hours unless I could find out what really was the matter with him."

Warner was in the doorway, his eyes glittering.

"Thanks again, gentlemen, for the consultation and your diagnosis," he said. "It will enable me to save my patient's life."

A half hour later the members of the X Club stood grouped in one of the operating rooms of St. Michael's Hospital. They were different-looking men than had been playing a medical Halloween in the Walton Hotel. There is a change that comes over doctors when they face disease. The oldest and the weariest of them draw vigor from a crisis. The shamble leaves them and it is the straight back of the champion that enters the operating room. Confronting the problem of life and death, the tired, red-rimmed eyes become full of greatness and even beauty.

On the operating table lay the naked body of a Negro boy. Dr. Warner in his surgical whites stood over him, waiting. The anesthetist finally nodded. The dark skin had turned ashen, and the fevered young Negro lay unconscious.

The fourteen X Club members watched Warner operate. Wood nodded approvingly at his speed. Rosson cleared his throat to say something, but the swift-moving hands of the surgeon held him silent. No one spoke. The minutes passed. The nurses quietly handed instruments to the surgeon. Blood spattered their hands.

Fourteen great medical men stared hopefully at the pinched and unconscious face of a colored boy who had swallowed a fish bone. No king or pope ever lay in travail with more medical genius holding its breath around him.

Suddenly the perspiring surgeon raised something aloft in his gloved fingers.

"Wash this off," he muttered to the nurse, "and show it to the gentlemen."

He busied himself placing drains in the abscessed cavity and then powdered some sulfanilamide into the opened abdomen to kill the infection.

Old Tick stepped forward and took the object from the nurse's hand.

"A fish bone," he said.

The X Club gathered around it as if it were a treasure indescribable.

"The removal of this small object," Tick cackled softly, "will enable the patient to continue writing poetry denouncing the greeds and horrors of our world."

That, in effect, was the story Hume told me, plus the epilogue of the Negro poet's recovery three weeks later. We had long finished dinner and it was late night when we stepped into the war-dimmed streets of New York. The headlines on the newsstands had changed in size only. They were larger in honor of the larger slaughters they heralded.

Looking at them you could see the death-strewn wastes of battles. But another picture came to my mind—a picture that had in it the hope of a better world. It was the hospital room in which fifteen famed and learned heroes stood battling for the life of a Negro boy who had swallowed a fish bone.

Remember Thy Creator

Remember now thy Creator in the days of thy youth, while the evil days come not, nor the years draw nigh. . . .

GOD HAD had a bad night with Nebula 19. That orderly womb of space had launched a trio of premature planets into the Infinite. Scorning all the delicate relationships of form and movement with which God had carefully nursed the Nebula, these three brothers of Chaos had galloped off without orbit or chemical conscience and threatened a goodly section of the Heavens with disaster.

Not only God but His Host had labored to avert a thousand collisions. Certain rarely used Forces had been hurried into the erratic paths of the three runaway bombs of matter. Not until after a score of His worlds had been shattered had God finally trapped the anarchists and destroyed them.

The Angel Michael, who had remained at God's side during the entire disturbance, listened now to the Deity's account of the matter and held his tongue. He was sad that so many of God's most obedient creatures had been forced to share the inevitable doom of anarchy. There was one planet in particular whose coloring and complex movement the Angel Michael had always deeply admired. He had tried to influence it out of its orbit, and so save it from the three brothers of Chaos. But it had remained faithful to its laws, and been shattered into a long spray of mist, which was still falling dismally down the chutes of space.

God looked at His grieving angel, and then at the dismally falling mists that were the funeral plumes of His most amiable worlds.

"What happened last night," God continued calmly, "has turned My Mind to certain elemental problems. I am reminded that the great law of My existence is that I and I alone am mystery, and that there are no mysteries beyond Me."

The Angel Michael nodded. He was always a little surprised when God grew garrulous, for his own wisdom, which was practically infinite, told him that to know was to be silent.

"Yet we saw last night," pursued God, "how mysteries may evolve from that which is simple, and how Chaos, My ancient enemy, still lurks within the perfect laws of matter. It will not happen again for a very long time," God added thoughtfully, thinking of certain readjustments. "Nevertheless . . . it seems to Me I have not come to grips with the actual problem of this vestigial Chaos that haunts My existence. . . ."

Presently He spoke again.

". . . that bit of moon dust," He said suddenly, "that you visited not so long ago. I'm thinking of it."

"The Earth," said the Angel Michael, and shuddered.

"I am not reconciled," said God, "to the fact that matter should speak, that dust should dream, and that atoms should think. It seems to Me that in the evolution of Dust into Thought there is a certain anarchy to which I have not given enough attention. Of course the Thought that has evolved itself out of these audible and contemplative atoms of mankind has been too absurd to consider seriously. Yet consider it I must," He concluded, "for it is there that Chaos lurks."

"You investigated the Earth some time ago," said the Angel Michael softly.

"Yes," said God, "I sent a Son there."

"You wish to call Yourself to its attention again?" asked Michael, whose quasi-omniscience told him that dark and difficult labors were coming nearer.

"Yes . . . No . . . Wait . . ."

God paused and brought the Earth close to His eyes.

"Before I can command their minds, which give off such an ever-darkening cloud of error, I must study them more closely. I know the fire out of which they are made. I must know the smoke that rises from this fire.

"Go there," He said to the Angel Michael, "and find out the secrets of their thought. Study everything that lies in their minds, however absurd or futile it may seem. Bring Me back the full history of their Thought."

The Angel Michael spread his wings, hovered for an instant over the vaults of space, and then vanished.

There were many things that occupied God during the Angel Michael's absence, but for the most part He delegated their doing to His Host. He vanished into one of the Voids. Which one of these Voids God had sought out none could tell, since they all appeared equally non-existent. Thus when the Angel Michael finally returned and sought them out for some news of God, they could give him no definite information.

The Angels Azriel and Malliol, among the wisest of the Host, bade Michael rest, for he appeared greatly cast down and there was that in his eyes which disturbed them. In reply to their most subtle questions, however, all that the Angel Michael would say of his absence was that he had been among men. How this could have disturbed one accustomed to walking into the engulfing fires of newly hatched stars, none could conceive. But Azriel and Malliol, who had once been to Earth on a confusing errand, nodded and tried to explain to the others of the Host that there were matters on Earth undreamed of in Heaven.

"As for God," said the Angel Malliol, "He has not shown himself since you left His side. I should advise you to remain with us."

But the Angel Michael shook his head at this excellent advice and wandered off. Placing himself on the rim of Infinity, the Angel Michael moved disconsolately from one Void to another, peering into their Nothingness and murmuring stubbornly the name of God. He continued his search outside the Nowheres of Infinity until he found himself shivering before so dark and deep a pit of non-existence that his heart grew small and his eyes felt all light falling from them.

God emerged. He regarded Michael with the frown of One disturbed at labors.

"What are you doing here?" asked God.

"I have returned," said the Angel Michael.

"I know," said God, "but why do you haunt the Brink, as I have forbidden?"

"I was waiting for You," persisted Michael as he followed God into the more familiar corridors of Infinity. "I have strange things to relate."

The Deity regarded the darkened, desperate face of His favorite Angel.

Michael was silent.

"You were gone some time," said God.

Michael nodded.

"Did it take so long for you to understand the History of Human Thought?" pursued God.

"It has no history," said the Angel slowly.

God continued to look at Michael, in whose eyes an abstraction remained. What, He thought, has become of Michael's serenity and of that lovely glow of humility and irony that had set his face apart and made it the cleverest in Heaven?

"So you found that human Thought has no history?" God repeated in His kindest voice.

Michael smiled.

"It has a certain capricious record," the Angel answered, "but it is less a matter of history than a chemical chart."

The Angel Michael paused.

"A synthesis of all animal movement reduced to nothing and yet existing in a sort of dream," he added. "If you wish, I shall explain."

God nodded indulgently.

"In the Thought of Man," said the Angel Michael eagerly, "I found the spread of a bird's wing, the quick and subtle dive into sea caverns of a fish, and the thrust of a tiger's claw. I found, too, the lumbering shadows of ancient monsters and the terror of ice."

God noted the elation in Michael's voice and remained silent.

"This Thought," the Angel Michael went on, unaware of God's scrutiny, "is a shadow of a thousand and one shapes cast by the little surface of existence on which they move. And this shadow is, mysteriously, able to create other shadows that are cast by Nothing into Nowhere. This process is called Logic. Lost in these shadows, they love each other and slay each other and stagger grotesquely and vociferously back to the dust they are. This staggering and the cries that accompany it they call History. For their Thought is more a record, very brief, of phantoms that have led them into never-ending battles. As hunger leads the animals to tear one another's throat for good, so does Thought prey upon Thought; so does one dream devour another, and all this devouring of dreams by dreams is attended by fearful and constant massacres. This never-ending warfare of their dreams they consider their spiritual existence, and point proudly to all their thousand monuments of bloodshed as proof of this same spirituality. They are disdainful of their physical sides, which they use only for the more peaceful business of living. They raise their monuments, it would seem, only to that which destroys them."

"You sound bewildered, Michael," said God, "but continue. Something may occur to Me."

"If I am bewildered," said the Angel Michael, "it is because human Thought is difficult for divinity to understand."

"You found it so," said God slowly, for this statement was offensive to Him.

"Yes," said the Angel Michael, defiantly. "There is in this Thought a contradiction that startled me. For unlike our Thought, it knows nothing. Yet it thinks. It is the tongue of an animal wagging idiotically out of a cave filled with horrible bones. Yet it whispers of matters not in the chemistry of those bones."

Michael paused and stared into Space.

"They dream," he continued, "yet their most delicate dreams echo with bestial howls and their most beastly utterances seem lit with fairy-tale lanterns. They think of things they are unable to believe. And they believe in things they are unable to think about. This is their Religion. They pursue in the Nowhere of their brains new names for that which is eternally hidden from them. This is their Science. They are able to uncover a few of the mysteries. But as each mystery is uncovered they bury it in an equally mysterious darkness that prevents them from ever understanding what they know. And in their curious lust to be greater than they are, they are continually reducing each other to endless piles of corpses. This is their Politics.

"They flounder and stagger," said the Angel Michael, "in the increasing mists of their minds and live and die in the deepening shadows of their reason. And blind, they talk of light; ignorant, they scream of wisdom; monstrous, they weep like Angels; devoured by the maggot of mortality, they laugh like Gods. That is how it is," concluded Michael and fell silent, wondering at his own garrulity.

"I have not been idle," said God.

"You knew what I had to tell You?" asked Michael.

"I know more," said God. "You are correct when you report there is no history to human Thought. For that which has no Law to guide it has neither past nor future. It is unpredictable and can be measured only by its own shifting fallacies. As the fire is lost in its smoke, so are My Laws hidden in this effluvium of Thought given off by the perfection of matter."

"It will be difficult to introduce form into that which is less than a shadow," said the Angel.

"It has always been difficult," said God softly. He moved His hand across Space. "This was extremely difficult," He said and smiled. "In a little while the confusion you noticed on that planet will be over. Their Thought will bow to Me."

"Will it be Thought then?" asked the Angel Michael.

"It will be part of Me," said God. "It will contain the predictable and regulated overtones of matter. It will be the intelligent tongue of the atoms. It will speak with understanding and it will know itself as the shadowed particles of My will."

Once more the Angel Michael stared sadly into Space.

"Where is the Dove?" God asked when He looked at Michael again.

"It flew past a minute ago," said the Angel, and his eyes followed a silver thread of light that led beyond Infinity into the Void.

"We are going there together," said God. "Come."

The Angel Michael stood once more on the Brink and once more peered into the terrifying Nothingness of the Void.

"Am I going with You?" he asked.

"Yes," said God.

"What will happen in there?" the Angel asked.

"You will lose your wings," said God. "You will lose all radiance, beauty, and wisdom. And when you are reduced to the status of a human being I shall make you small and the Dove will carry you to Earth. You will be My messenger and truth-teller. You will grow up and you will overthrow the anarchy of the Earth and lead the disorganized smoke of its Thought to My feet. You will be My redeemer."

"Will I be black or white?" asked the Angel Michael.

"White," said God.

The Angel nodded.

"Will I be of any use in the guise of a human?" he asked.

"The truth has its own power," said God.

Again Michael nodded.

"Shall we go in?" he asked softly as he peered beyond the Brink, and his heart shivered at the touch of Nothingness. He started forward. God touched his shoulder.

"Wait," said God. "You are the fairest of the Host. There is none to take your place at My side."

The Angel Michael looked into Nothingness and then raised his eyes calmly to God.

"I am already changed," he said.

"You desire to leave Heaven," said God.

"Yes," said Michael.

"Your brother Lucifer—" began God, and paused. After a time He asked: "Is there revolt in your heart?"

"No," said Michael, "there is no revolt in me."

God held the Angel Michael's eyes with a terrible scrutiny. Michael felt his heart shrink and the recesses of his soul tremble at this look. But he remained upright and his own eyes refused to close.

"There is no revolt in me," he repeated softly. "There is a memory of Earth. I desire to help them."

"Come," said God and stepped into the Void.

The Angel Michael's eyes now filled with tears, and everywhere around him he heard a sound of lamentation. Turning, he beheld the Heavenly Host swarming like a great cloud below him and sorrowing for his pain. He heard Azriel call his name and cry to him to stay. And other voices sought him and covered his heart with their love. But he turned his head away and entered the unimaginable Space where nothing existed.

For some moments his radiant figure remained in the darkness, bold and glittering like a phantom struggling in the nets of night. Then a lightning smote him, and without pain but with a sigh which drifted out of the Void and echoed through all the Heavens he vanished. The Angel Michael was no more.

God emerged. The Dove sat on His shoulder and in the palm of His hand He bore tenderly a tiny creature. As He moved toward the space in which hung the Earth, He spoke softly.

"You will give My truth to them, Michael," He said. "You will speak to the anarchy of their Thought. You will have no other powers than the knowledge of the Truth. You will pit that against My enemy. You will enter his mind with My love and breathe into his mind the truth of My glory. And in a little way at first, but later more and more, you will bring him to his knees with the understanding of My plan and the knowledge of My mystery."

As God moved, around Him crowded the silent Host. God's eyes remained on the thing in His palm.

"You were more dear to Me," said God, "than the Son I sent to them before, for I was more used to you, and yours was the proudest and cleverest of My souls. You were always gallant and without fear," said God, "and you are the first who has ever stood beside Me in the Void. Michael, Michael"—God's voice grew soft—"who are they that you love them so? Who are they that you vanished unafraid?"

The faces of the Host now crowded boldly to the edge of God's hand and looked into its palm. The tiny creature who lay there seemed too ridiculous for their attention. So absurd and ugly an object had never been known in Heaven before. Yet as they looked, this writhing bit of matter opened its eyes and in their straight blue stare they beheld the Angel Michael.

"It is a child, new born," said God.

"Michael, Michael," the Angels wept.

The child moved in the palm of God.

"Michael, where are you?" wept the Angels.

The child raised its tiny hands with fingers too weak to open and its little mouth uttered a delicate and humorous sound.

"He is saying good-by," said God.

He gave the tiny creature to the Dove.

"Remain with him," said God. "If he sorrows too much or longs for Me, be at his side."

On a spring morning an old woman named Sarah opened the doors of the Good Samaritan Home for Children, which is one of the less ambitious buildings of the City of New York. The morning was still wet with dawn. A breeze moved over the pavements. The old woman Sarah, whose eyes were dim and whose body was without sap, stood on the threshold alone in the half-light like a little bent tree whose tired roots remember the morning. Her work-curled hands fluttered in aimless truant gestures against the heavy folds of her work dress. She looked gravely at the new color of the day, and in her face, reshaped by age and toil, a little light appeared to be glowing as if the dawn had kindled her nose and cheeks. She regarded the familiar street with so deep a smile of gratitude that all its colors, dews, smells, and sounds seemed to be radiating from her. Then she became again old Sarah, the scrubwoman, and, fetching her dented pails out of the vestibule, dropped to her knees with the agility of an acrobat and began on her tasks. These were each dawn to clean with chemicals and water the brass plate under the doors of the Good Samaritan Home and to remove thoroughly all the bits of leaves, dust, and scribble of disquiet that had accumulated on the Home's stone stairs since the preceding daybreak.

As she began with the rubbing of the wet powder over the brass plate, her eyes fell on a large basket a few feet away. The basket was on the top step. Old Sarah disliked matters that interfered with her work, for in many years her work had achieved a rhythm much stronger than her will. Her battered hands plying brush and cloth as she moved back and forth on her knees were almost as aloof and persistent as the beat of her heart. They continued to move, rub, rinse, polish, and dry the brass threshold like a pair of ancient grenadiers faithful to their posts though a thousand baskets beckoned. It was only when her task brought her a few feet nearer that old Sarah paused, while wringing out her scrub rag, and looked into the basket. A smile puckered her face as if a strong light had hit her eyes. There was a baby in the basket.

She wiped her hand on her dress and lifted the small blanket covering the infant. Her eyes brightened with glee as she studied this basketed visitor at the doors of the Good Samaritan Home. It was a well-formed and amiable visitor, waving curved arms and clenched fists and beating with curled legs on the air. Then its face, staring intently up at the entranced old Sarah, began to glow much like her own—and it laughed. This laugh, which had no sound but consisted of a remarkable twisting of mouth and cheeks, tightening of eyes, and frantic waving of all its movable parts, so overcame Sarah that she too began to wave her hands, still holding the scrub rag, and to guffaw like an old witch over a kettle. The laughter of the scrublady contained an amazing variety of sounds, including cat-calls and Indian war whoops. She laughed at this marvelous comedian in the basket until her throat ached and her eyes overran. Then she reached her hand to its neck, where a card was tied like a tag on a package of groceries. She read the card and wiped her eyes and her face continued to beam as if it would explode again. The card read:

"Michael."

"Ho, ho kok, kaka kak!" said old Sarah. "Mikil, Mikil!" (making the name rhyme with pickle). "Ho keek, keek keek. So dat's who you been, huh. You little devil, you. I fix you. Ho kak, kak kak," and she dug her fist into his stomach as if intending to disembowel him. However, she was only tickling Michael to see him laugh again, which he did. For five minutes old Sarah remained on her knees beside the basket, cackling and whooping in the dawn, her eyes swimming with bliss at every grimace and movement of her entertainer. She continued to kneel and peer into the basket, surrounded by her pails, brushes, rags, soaps, and cans, and to clap her hands and wave them in the air and roll her body back and forth like a Hindu dancer —until she noticed that her scrub rag, hanging from an infatuated hand, had been dripping all the while on the infant. She fell excitedly to wiping the dirt-spattered legs, spitting on her fingers to rub them clean. The reappearance of the pink skin under her efforts squeezed old Sarah's heart as if it, too, were a sponge at work.

Looking up for a moment, like a pirate from his treasure chest, old Sarah grew very angry at an intruder. A white dove had perched on the basket's rim and was blowing itself up like a balloon and emitting strangled noises.

"Shoo, go way," she commanded and made a swipe at the bird with her wet cloth. The Dove hopped out of danger, and continued to balloon its throat and to gurgle excitedly. It occurred to Sarah, who was quick to understand certain of the simpler things in life, that this pretty bird meant no harm to the one in the basket.

"All right," she said with a series of kek-kek-keks, "don't you *scheiss* on him, you doity boid," and shook her fist crazily over Michael's unwinking face.

Her eyes turned nervously to the still unshining brass floor plate. A panic sent her crawling on her knees to its clouded surface and she fell vigorously to scrubbing. As she scrubbed and rinsed and re-rinsed her rags, she continued to beam at the basket, clucking hilariously at its occupant, winking as she caught his moving stare and waving her brush and rag for his delight. Ever and anon she wagged her finger warningly at the white Dove still perched on the basket edge.

"Ka ke ke ke," said old Sarah to the infant, attacking the brass with great swoops. "Just a minute. Don't start hollerin', you crazy. I fix you. Kok, keek, keek, keek. You stay there, you little devil."

When the brass was shining as brightly as it had shone every dawn for seventy years, Sarah crawled back to the basket. She hoisted the visitor out and stood up with him. She became silent as she held him against her old body. Looking down at his widely opened eyes, she grew bewildered as if a sudden social embarrassment were at work on her tongue. So soft and warm did this prince of entertainers feel through the heavy cloth of her dress, so delicious and wondrously ornamental did he seem, that old Sarah felt like apologizing for holding him. Her face grew stern with fright and she stood cringing for several moments, like some wizened little embezzler halted by the shout of invisible police.

Then very fiercely she opened the tall doors of the Good Samaritan Home and, with a last guilty look at the still unwashed stone steps, entered the building. Michael lay in one of her arms. From the other hand dangled her scrub pail, which like a scepter she was loath to lay down.

The officials who had allowed old Sarah and her morning's loot to enter the superintendent's office, after a great to-do that involved waking a lot of dozing dignity, were kindly people, but they all began explaining to the old scrublady that the Home was now overcrowded, its endowment already overtaxed, all its orderlies, nurses, doctors, and teachers overworked. Having informed Sarah of their dilemma, they debated among themselves while she stood nailed to the carpet and clinging to Michael, glowering as if before a jury of executioners.

Then one of the officials, a bearded, rheumy old gentleman whose name was Dr. Rufus, came forward and had a long look at Sarah's find. He inspected it professionally, holding Michael by one foot, his head a-dangle, and pinching his skin, slapping his behind, and ogling the inside of his mouth. With a final wallop across Michael's reddened buttocks, Dr. Rufus returned him to Sarah. The amazing child had given forth not a sound during these indignities. Dr. Rufus stood nodding his head in thought and chewing on a mustache that obscured most of his mouth. He was a frosty-mannered and slightly doddering savant who seemed, for the last ten years, to have held himself together with a snarl, a sneer, and a disgust for his fellowmen.

"Fine specimen," said Dr. Rufus to the other officials present. "Excellent disposition. No blemish inside or out. It's too bad he has to grow any older. He's perfect now."

"Our problem remains the same," said Mr. Jorgenson, who was the Superintendent of the Home, "whether he's perfect or not."

Dr. Rufus turned his short square of red whisker at the superintendent and thrust it forward as if it were a battering ram.

"The hell you say!" he snorted. "If you gentlemen will permit me, I will settle this problem for you and you can go back to your work of pretending to be Good Samaritans spending other people's money—with a clear conscience."

"There's no occasion for anyone to be insulting," said Superintendent Jorgenson with a look to Sarah.

"Poppycock," said Michael's red-haired champion. "Listen to me. Old Sarah has been working in this black hole since she was old enough to blow soap bubbles. She has scrubbed the floors of this miserable den of charity for seventy years. Seventy years," Dr. Rufus repeated with a powerful sneer. "I remember old Sarah scrubbing away when she was about the age of that young gentleman in her arms. The long and short of it is," went on Dr. Rufus, to all the faces confronting him, "that old Sarah has found gold while scrubbing. And the gold belongs to her."

He poked the old scrublady in the ribs and winked at her.

"It's yours, Sarah," said Dr. Rufus. "The findings of this muddled group of Samaritans is that you keep the little bastard, feed him, wash him, wipe him, and to hell with that pail of slops for the rest of your life. Here"—he stepped forward—"give me that."

Sarah sidestepped his grab for her scrubbing pail.

"Naw," she said, "that's mine. I take him to my room. I got the steps to finish. Come on." This was added to Michael. Still carrying her loot and her ballast of a pail, old Sarah stamped out of the office. Scorning as always the elevators, the ancient scrublady hurried Michael up three flights to his new home, which was a corner of the cot she had occupied for forty years. Here she placed the infant, and then fell to her knees, which was an all too easy gesture for her. She looked furtively at the door to make certain it was shut. Cackling quietly to herself she leaned forward and began kissing the infant's hands. A curious noise interrupted her. The white Dove was pecking at the single window of her cubby-hole room.

"Shoo!" cried Sarah. "Go way!"

Then she returned to the child's hands.

Michael for twelve years was Sarah's son. As she had beamed on him kneeling beside his basket, so the old scrublady continued to beam on him through each hour of these twelve years.

She grew deaf, distorted, and a little unreasonable and seemed to acquire with age an unseemly speed in her movements. By the time Michael had grown old enough to observe such matters, she had taken to sprinting and darting about in a manner disturbing to the decorum of the Good Samaritan Home. In this Home, Charity wore its never-varying air of kindliness and its pastry smile, and moved as if someone were lying ill in an adjoining room. Old Sarah offered a continued offense to this Mysterious Personage lying in state somewhere on the premises. Here, where Virtue tiptoed about as self-consciously as a villain entering a forbidden parlor; where orphans, always fresh from barber shop, bath, or organ recital, moved in solemn little chorus formations up and down the stairways of philanthropy—amid all this paralysis of Good Deeds, which appeared to have stiffened even the chairs, couches, and beds of the Institution—old Sarah pranced like a withered and tottering Mother of Fauns.

It was a mystery to all but Dr. Rufus how someone like Sarah, who had known nothing of life, could love it so. Her constantly clattering pails interrupted conferences, lectures, and even religious services. She charged through these events like some soapy piston. Her increasing disdain for her superiors not only astonished them but left them impotent. Old Sarah had once been so humble that the most minor of officials was able to strike her dumb with awe, and the slightest of greetings had set her to curtsying like a demented courtier. Now she had become apparently oblivious of all command.

She seemed, in her own mind at least, to have taken possession of the Home. All humans appeared to be losing daily their importance to old Sarah. They became, and this sometimes angered them, part of the furniture that obstructed her duty—which was to clean, to scrub, to rinse, and re-rinse her rags, and remove from floors, stairs, wood, stone, and linoleum all marks of human occupancy. But there was more to it than cleaning. A rhythm and a significance had come into old Sarah's battle with dirt, as if she were obliterating a trail.

This she did with such a high air of devotion, with so gamin-like and helter-skelter an indifference for the rest of the world, that the orphans marching from barber shop and organ recital began to look on the old scrublady as a creature out of a fairy-tale, a grandma Cinderella on her way with pails and scrub brushes to the Ball.

In vain the Officials introduced new and rival scrubladies. Unable to dislodge Sarah from her knees, to which position they had assigned her in her girlhood, they went about trying, like European statesmen, to parcel away the homeland of her dripping brushes. Driven from one stairway by such interlopers, routed from another floor by a whole cordon of rivals, old Sarah would reappear crawling like a wily turtle down unsuspected spurs of the never-obliterated trail.

Wherever feet had left tracks, there old Sarah appeared with the flourish of an acrobat, with the pomp of a Mardi Gras and the right-eousness of a jury; and there, banging away with her brushes and rags like some Paderewski valorously smiting the keys of an instrument dearer than life, the shrinking witchlike little figure filled her soul with a music inaudible to others.

When Michael became of an age to be of help to his guardian, which was shortly after his first birthday, scandal shook the Institution. Nurses and orderlies came knocking on Superintendent Jorgenson's door with the news that old Sarah had gone completely mad.

Superintendent Jorgenson quickly left his desk and made for Hall 3, where the organ recitals took place. There he saw Sarah with her pails, brushes, cans, and rags, but now with another addition to her flotilla. This was Michael, a diaper trailing from his loins, and gliding, stomach to the wet floor, on a large cake of soap. Old Sarah, on hands and knees, was whooping after him.

Superintendent Jorgenson, shaken by the spectacle, dashed forward and laid hands on her two dented pails. He handed them to an assistant, and they were whisked out of the hall.

"That's enough of this!" he cried. "You're mad! You're crazy! You're out of your head. A crazy one. Do you understand me?"

But the superintendent, howling and illustrating his ideas with forefingers whirling at his temples, seemed the crazy one and not old Sarah. She stood staring with dignity and, as his shouts and gestures continued, her ·crinkled eyes filled with contempt. Michael had come crawling to her feet and sat, with his rump full of soap suds, clinging to her large comedian's shoes.

Dr. Rufus left the group of officials in the hall. When he returned in a few minutes, the superintendent's voice, a bit hoarsened, was still offering evidences of old Sarah's lunacy. Dr. Rufus held the two pails in one hand and a scrub brush in the other. Old Sarah received her possessions back in silence. She hoisted the equally silent Michael from the wet floor, and holding him face down in the crook of her strong arm as if he were a more precious bundle of rags, the while her pails, brushes, cans, and cloths loaded her other side, she marched out of Hall 3.

If not for Dr. Rufus's defense, old Sarah would have been routed from her domain, then and there, forever. The defense, conducted in Superintendent Jorgenson's office, lasted an hour. The old doctor, whom Jorgenson considered fully as mad in his own way as Sarah, was nevertheless a difficult man to best in any argument. His thirty years of service to the orphans who had enjoyed the haircut of the Samaritan Home, his curiously high standing with the board of trustees, his uncontrollable temper, which he swung like a fire pot around his head—all combined to leave him the victor on any debating field. But this time his victory was not entirely a complete one. Although he fought valiantly for Sarah's right to scrub where she liked and to employ any assistant she chose, the official contention was a trifle too much for him. This contention had it that the spectacle of Sarah and the naked brat wallowing about on the floor under the eyes of any visitors was belittling to the Institution. Despite the noise of his rebuttals, Dr. Rufus gave ground before this charge. He agreed to a compromise. Sarah was to be allowed to wallow and scrub to her heart's content on the fourth floor only.

It developed that Sarah had no snobbish feelings about first, second, third, or fourth floors. She agreed curtly to confine herself to the last on condition she be allowed to do the front steps as always. As this task took place during an hour when her new co-worker was still asleep, the point was yielded.

Thereafter old Sarah scrubbed only the fourth floor, which, in addition to a long corridor, offered a dozen sleeping rooms of nurses and orderlies for her brushes. And Michael remained at her side. For many months he was more a hindrance than a help to old Sarah, overturning pails of water on both of them, choking on pieces of soap furtively crammed into his mouth, and vanishing like a lost ball under beds, out of which darkness the busy Sarah wasted a great deal of time retrieving him. But after his second birthday, which had sent him to the hospital for a week with an attack of indigestion, Michael developed talents that infatuated his guardian. Suddenly he had blossomed into a chubby miniature of her. He not only crowed like her but had learned to stagger rather than walk and to hurl himself like an acrobat at the pail handles and scrub cloths. He also scrubbed and rinsed and re-rinsed and dried and polished as ably, if a little more slowly, than his ancient colleague. She assigned him whole patches of floor and baseboard and important sectors of corridor. Over these, little Michael, crowing and cackling with a delight that never failed to transport old Sarah, moved with pails larger than himself and cleaned with a devotion amazing in a two-year-old.

In the three years that followed, the irascible Dr. Rufus often pondered on what Michael's future would be. Old Sarah had apparently settled this in her mind, which even Dr. Rufus was beginning to feel was a little warped. She considered Michael's career firmly launched. He would remain at her side, scrubbing away with more and more agility. He would move forever as she had moved, on knees growing stronger, his head down, bringing a clean look to wood, stone, marble, and linoleum.

Dr. Rufus, despite his cynicism toward the world, felt that Sarah's conception of Michael's life was too one-sided.

"I know of nothing better or more honorable than scrubbing," said Dr. Rufus kindly. "There is no human activity that does less harm and no other of which you can say it leaves the world a little better each day than it found it. Yet there is in our Michael's head a force that scrubbing alone will never develop."

"He gotta go to school?" asked Sarah, in whose cubby-hole of a room this conference was being held. She looked proudly at Michael busy on the fire-escape outside the window. But while she beamed on him, a sigh came from her heart and she turned little trembling eyes to the doctor. She had had a vision of Michael full of the importance and learning to be found in school. But in the midst of this vision her heart tugged frightenedly at this educated Michael's frock coat, and her eyes stared helplessly at his savant's silk hat.

"I'll teach him myself," said Dr. Rufus. "I'll see to it, by God, that he learns enough to keep him from remaining an idiot and not enough to turn him into a fool. I'm against one entire educational system," he added, scowling at Sarah, "for the incontrovertible reason that it has never educated anybody. All it does is hatch more and more chicken minds and send them cackling and overrunning the world with their confounded chicken-headed theories. God Almighty! After three thousand years of injecting education into our bloodstream, show me one honest heart!"

As if in answer to the old physician's cynical cry, Michael appeared on the window ledge. His face was smudged almost beyond recognition. His clothing was torn and fluttering in wisps from his behind. Beside him, ballooning its throat and gurgling, was the white Dove.

"Dat crazy boid!" cried Sarah. "Shoo! Get out, you!"

She flung her arms in its direction, but the Dove continued to stand where it was and gurgle.

Michael, however, fell into the room, picked himself up, and marched to Sarah's side. He climbed into her lap, balanced himself on her thighs, crouched down for a moment, and then leaped. He landed on all fours, his forehead banging against the floor.

"He'll kill himself," said Dr. Rufus.

Sarah chuckled.

"He's gonna be a fine joomper," she said.

"I think he's hurt." Dr. Rufus leaned forward.

"Leab him alone," said old Sarah authoritatively; "joomping don't hoit nobody. I got boomped lots of times." And she laughed like a parrot screeching and slapped both her knees furiously with her hands.

Michael sat up, holding his forehead. He was silent. Old Sarah left her chair suddenly and crawled to his side. Her work-battered hands touched the bruised skin.

"It'll go way," she said, staring into Michael's eyes to see if there were tears. "Hoits always goes away."

Dr. Rufus educated Michael by reading books to him and holding forth, once they were read, on their asininity and the asininity of all writers and all existence.

During the day, Michael remained at Sarah's side, so content at his continual water hauling, scrubbing, polishing, and drying that the Officials of the Home came to regard him as a harmless little lunatic. He was seldom seen by the other orphans, except during organ recitals and the religious services, which Superintendent Jorgenson insisted, despite the boy's seeming idiocy, he attend. When not at work during the day, Michael played on the fire-escape. Here, racing up and down, he had adventures, full of the lonely glamour of childhood. And between falls and contusions he was very happy.

At night he lay on the cot with Sarah, while she slept with her wrinkled, shrunken, and muscular arm flung across him, and listened to the red-bearded Rufus. The doctor was never tired of filling the cubby-hole room with endless tales of human conquest, human travail, human disasters and progress, all bespeaking, according to him, the ineradicable backwardness of the human race.

"I want you to remember history, son, as I have told it to you. And never mind trying to learn dates of battles and the names of battle leaders. To hell with that and to hell with your learning the Causes of Wars. They're all alike, all battles, all dates, all leaders, all causes, and all wars. From the first breaking of heads in the jungles of China, where our idiotic race seems to have originated—yes, we're all Chinamen—to the present bombing of children and old ladies in the streets of Spain—they're all alike. I don't care, son, who wanted what, or what was called right and what was called wrong. All these wars I've told you about were all fought in the same fog of human stupidity. Animals kill for hunger. That's why we call them animals. But we members of the human race kill for no reason. That's why we are called reasonable beings. It's all an endless futile struggle, son, to locate the meaning of ourselves.

"I have it figured out, Michael, in my own way. We are all of one blood—we humans. The blood of the race is an ocean divided into a billion little cups, like you and me, son. We're divided, but we're all one ocean, and we have a tide in us that is run by the moon and the stars, as the ancients once said. And they said more science when they said that than has come out of all the Galileos and Darwins since that time. When we crawled out of the sea and fastened ourselves on the first stones of the earth, we took the sea with us. That's obvious to me, son. The sea continued to wash away inside us, washing against our stomachs and our hearts. It remained running through us in little pipes we call arteries. What I say, son, is that there's an ocean in us that can be charted and that responds to the movements of all Nature around and above us. But that's not all of us. There's another element in us that didn't come out of the sea. There's a wind that blows over this blood ocean, that beats it with hurricanes and bedevils it with whirlpools. This wind is our thought. God knows where it came from, and what makes it blow. Son, all we know is that a wind blows and the ocean is never at rest."

Each night as Michael lay beside the peacefully sleeping Sarah, Dr. Rufus elaborated on this theme, adding historical facts to it, peopling it with fish and monsters and crustaceans, and finding in the records of history, science, and art a multitude of illustrations. But there was another education that Michael was experiencing, which, more than all the roaring of the Red Beard, was shaping his life. This was love. With all the violence of his child's heart he loved old Sarah and Dr. Rufus and even the cynical fairytales that the angry physician brought trooping around his bed.

There was no memory in him of any previous Michael, and no knowledge remained in his head of the long ride from Heaven under the wings of the white Dove. He was not yet aware that God had sent him to redeem the world. But there had grown in his heart by the time he was seven a tenderness that set him apart from the normal ways of life.

He grew taller, and his face took on a curious look that bore out a legend in the Home that he was more than half mad. It was the fierce and concentrated caress to be found in the face of a mother leaning in the night over the crib of a fevered child. It was a look that was to bring great trouble into his life, and seemed even in his childhood a magnet for misunderstanding and growing enmity. But in this expression, that was beginning to disquiet even Dr. Rufus, there was nothing mysterious. It was the gleam old Sarah had turned on the dawn as she emerged to scrub the brass plate on the morning that Michael lay kicking in the basket. It was a look that radiated a dream. And as he grew older, it was a look that searched for Sarah—for old Sarah died when he was twelve, and left him this look as her only heritage, the look that through terror, abuse, and despair kept seeking her sweet, half-mad smile in the confusion and glower of all the world's faces.

Sarah's dying took three days. During these days Michael moved on his knees alone down the fourth-floor corridor and in and out of the many rooms to be cleaned. He could feel in his heart the aching tissues of his old friend and the familiar face stared continually up at him out of the cleaned patches of flooring, as if it were her cheeks that were shining in the polished wood, marble, stone, and linoleum. Through all his life Michael was never to see anything shining but he saw old Sarah in it.

At night he remained in a corner of their cubby-hole room and watched Dr. Rufus come puttering in in night robe and slippers, feel her pulse, put his trembling bony hand to her forehead, stick lozenges on her tongue, sink to his knees and hold his ear cocked against her heart like a robin listening for a vanishing worm. On the third night, the Red Beard beckoned Michael to its side.

"Not much longer," he said and stared at the boy.

Sarah opened her eyes and beamed at Michael as she had beamed over the edge of the wicker basket in which she had found him.

"We neber found out who your mudder was," said old Sarah with a foolish and triumphant wink at the doctor.

"You were my mother," said Michael.

"Me?" said Sarah as her eyes rolled weakly.

"Be a good boy," said Sarah.

Michael nodded.

"Keep everything clean," said Sarah.

Michael's eyes smiled at her.

"Thash right," Sarah whispered, her speech seeming to grow a little drunken. "I ain't 'fraid. Kek, kek, ke . . . heh heh." Her cackle grew far away. "Mikil," she smiled, "gib me a kiss like a good lil fella. Yeh. Mikil, gib me a kiss."

Old Sarah raised her arms, dropped them tiredly around Michael's lowered head, and died.

And when he stood in the chapel at the coffin, Michael still felt his lips on her forehead. Her voice cried in his heart as if not Sarah but all of life were still asking for this kiss.

The services were brief. Superintendent Jorgenson, despite the glowering of Dr. Rufus, spoke of Sarah's loyalty. He informed the freshly haircutted orphans assembled that Sarah, whose antics had long been a legend, had been found as an infant on the doorstep of the Home that was burying her. She had set a good example, said the superintendent. God, he said, would now reward her for her great loyalty. God would take her to His merciful bosom and bless her. Throughout this talk, Superintendent Jorgenson continued to wipe his eyes, remove and replace his spectacles, and sniffle shamelessly. An orphan at the organ began to play, and a choir of orphans began to sing over the witchlike body in the coffin. This ended the services, and the coffin was carried out of the chapel.

Dr. Rufus and Michael rode in the single car that followed the hearse. Later they stood in the autumn afternoon and watched the coffin lowered into the earth. Michael looked at the bottom of the grave. He felt suddenly that he was standing on the edge of the world peering into a pit of Nothingness. Life was vanishing into this pit. The pain of the Nothingness into which old Sarah and her thousand and one cakes of soap, her rags and cans and brushes and cackles and Indian war whoops had disappeared, tore his heart. Death ached in his veins, and life sobbed beside him at the edge of the world.

When he rose to his feet, his eyes were wide and quiet. He walked away from the covered grave with the frightened bent little figure of his mother clinging to his hand. When she could no longer walk he lifted her in his arms. And when her body began to shiver in the autumn wind, he placed her in his heart and continued to walk, but a little more slowly, for he was burdened.

Michael went to live with Dr. Rufus in an impressive-looking old stone house.

The physician, now turned seventy, had announced his retirement from the Good Samaritan Home. He complained violently to all who would listen that senility had marked him, and that his body was unfit for any future social uses. But since he complained only to fellow-physicians, who, perhaps out of a mutual protective code, have a way of ignoring one another's diseases, Dr. Rufus's claims to invalidism went without investigation. He was given a farewell dinner by his colleagues, toasted, sung, and placed half drunken into an automobile. Michael was beside him.

Standing before the impressive relic of yesterday's grandeur that was his home, the red-bearded Rufus waved his arms, and talked to Michael.

"Here it is," he said, "my tomb. Not a tomb like Sarah's where you can lie, son, in dignified dissolution, one with the happily rotting contents of the earth. But a tomb to breathe in, groan in, wait in. A tomb for the living. A vestibule for the worms. I know whereof I speak, son. Disease is in me. Each of my joints is inflamed like a drunkard's nose. I'm doomed. I've outlived my carcass. Have you ever seen a beetle trying to shed its old frock coat? That's me, son. I'll be crawling into one of the beds in this house and I'll lie there for years trying to wriggle out of a dead shell . . . while those wisenheimers, the doctors, stand around chanting like a Greek chorus: 'He's got arthritis, poor old Rufus.' "

The Red Beard sat down on the steps and took Michael's hand.

"I'm an angry man," it proclaimed loudly to the boy. "In a few months that's all that will be left of me—my anger propped up on a pillow. Prometheus chained to a handful of chicken feathers, while the devil wrestles for his soul. That's what our old friend arthritis does for you, stretches you out, turns you to stone and blinds you."

Michael shivered in the cool night and squeezed the doctor's hand. The hand seemed to be leading him to Sarah.

"Don't contradict me," bawled the Red Beard, "and I'll tell you something more; something I couldn't tell you about while that crazy grasshopper of a Sarah was alive. For we must never offend the happy with our wisdom. There is no God. Not for today at least. We have elbowed Him off the stage, shoved Him into the wings, saying: 'We are the show. We are the Plot. We are the Main Characters. Keep off the stage until we get done with our parts!'

"So that," continued Dr. Rufus, "is where God is at the moment— in the wings. And we occupy the night alone. We investigate ourselves, our grass glades, our internal and external atoms, without that bewildering Hosanna in our ears. In the end it is nothing but a heroic form of self-torture. For who are we?" The old doctor raised his voice angrily. "Who are we? Looking for our meaning like a monkey snatching at his face in a mirror."

Michael clung to his hand. As long as he held this hand he seemed to be near Sarah.

"We are the glory of God in exile," he said softly.

Dr. Rufus looked at the boy beside him.

"Who told you that?" he demanded.

"I don't know," said Michael, "but sometimes I feel that people don't belong in the world, but in Heaven. They're crippled angels, and have to wear shoes, and God's looking for them."

Dr. Rufus began to whoop and slap his thighs, reminding Michael of the way Sarah used to carry on when she was happy.

"Looking for us, is He?" The old man laughed in the dawn. "Well, He'd better look for Himself. We're here. But where is He? Listen, son, if there's a God, He's somewhere inside us—modestly concealed like a bright penny in some vest pocket. And if there's a Purpose in our crawling out of the hot primeval ooze and wrestling ourselves into the shape of man, that purpose is inside us."

"No," the boy answered, shivering. "It's in God. There is nothing in us but God's breath."

"Holy jumpin' mackerel!" said Dr. Rufus and stared at the boy beside him. "Where did you pick up that lingo?"

Michael's glowing eyes looked back at him.

"Either I'm drunker than I thought," said Dr. Rufus, "or there's something wrong with your face. And your hands," he added, lowering his eyes. "What have you turned so white for, Michael? Are you frightened?"

"No," whispered Michael.

"Here, let me see that hand," said Dr. Rufus with sudden professional calm. He picked up Michael's small hand and held it close to his eyes, turning it over and studying it. "Curious loss of pigmentation," he muttered. "What are you staring at, Michael? What's in your mind?"

"The glory of God," said Michael.

A heavy frown filled the doctor's face. He tugged at his red beard.

"Well, I'll be goddamned," he muttered finally. "You bring a boy up on a diet of pure science, and he ends up having hallucinations. The duck's egg in the eagle's nest"—he smiled at Michael—"or is it the eagle's egg under the duck's tail? Who knows?"

Dr. Rufus rumpled Michael's hair and slapped playfully at his cheeks.

"Wake up, son," he smiled. "Duck or eagle, I'm taking care of you my way. And I don't want to hear any more about God or Purpose out of either of us. We'll stick to facts. And the facts are that we didn't fall from Heaven, but rose out of the Sea. Our bodies are still full of gills and sea water and third eyes and second noses and dead muscles and a hundred vestigial organs in which our Past stares out of us as out of a taxidermist's window. We're full of jungle shadows, and our art and reason and even the music we make are the ferment of chemicals that haven't changed since the earliest days of chlorophyll and haemoglobin. We have an inch or two of brain more than the rest of Nature, that's all. But don't overestimate the human brain, son. The brain is only one among a hundred thousand muscles. The muscle that thinks."

Dr. Rufus looked up and smiled wearily.

"You see those stars?" he said. "Far away, aren't they? We've thrown rope ladders out to all the mysteries and kept climbing—out of one darkness into another. But we won't climb any more tonight. Come on —we march into the tomb." He grinned, turning toward the house. "Give me your shoulder, son. My legs are creaking like a baby's rattle."

In the house of four floors in which Michael found his new home were two servants and the doctor's sister, Margaret Rufus. The two servants were a married couple, and reminded Michael of a pair of mice peering around doorways. Miss Rufus seemed oddly related to them, as if they had all once belonged to the same litter. But where the eyes of the two servants were gray and veiled, those of Miss Rufus were black and full of anger that was something like the doctor's. But Michael did not notice this too much. He saw a thin woman with a bluish face that never smiled.

During the first month Michael, who was burdened, remained unaware that this bluish face hated him. He continued to live in the protection of his memories, and around him the echo of the rattle and bang of old Sarah's scrub pails continued to make fairytale music. In vain Miss Rufus's heart cast its shadow where he walked, laughed, or slept. He continued to smile at her with that unawareness which is infuriating to all neurotic spirits. Her scrawny face, thin-featured and thin-skinned, as if life were the flimsiest of veils, returned his smiles with an increasing anger. Michael then began to feel the darkness of her heart, and he thought childishly that she was troubled, but it did not occur to him yet that he was the one who troubled her.

His attention was taken up chiefly by the doctor, who had begun to make good his prophecy of falling ill. The doctor grew stiff in his movements, and pain often brought a deeper rage into his face. Michael haunted his friend's side, his heart heavy, eager to run errands, to talk or laugh or listen to the sick man's fierce protests against his own body.

"I've hit a reef in that blood ocean I told you about, son," he growled. "I'm banging to pieces on a reef."

But Dr. Rufus remained alive. He did not die but launched into a slow retreat, with all guns blazing. He retreated first out of the streets, into a wheel chair; and then up the stairs, into a bed. Here he lay finally, unable to move his legs or turn his body, and the doctors, as he had prophesied, decided that he had arthritis. They puttered with the fires in his joints, and discussed tirelessly the meaning and causes of the calcification process that now began to turn their patient half to stone. The old serving couple nursed and fed him. Visitors arrived with bits of gossip, which, like their sickroom gifts, they left uselessly behind. It was understood that Dr. Rufus had come to the end of his retreat. Here in this bed, where he had been born, the red beard would remain jutting from the pillow until death came to pluck it.

In the midst of these changes, the undying red-bearded face continued, undaunted, to talk. Michael remained beside it, listening as he used to do in Sarah's cubby-hole room, sometimes holding onto the doctor's hand. Soon his friend began to grow blind, and whenever he was tired of speaking, Michael read aloud to him from books and newspapers. This reading was often interrupted, as the things that Michael read set off angers in his listener's still turbulent brain.

"This man Hitler," he said one afternoon, when Michael had been reading to him of Germany's annexation of Austria, "is an ancient and honorable phenomenon proving that Evolution works both ways, up and down, except when it works around. Its chief direction is a cockeyed circle and the zigzag of a drunk making for home. As . . . witness the free swimming water bugs who have lapsed into barnacles. . . . And the once liberty-loving bacteria that have turned into parasites. And then, there is the other type of progress—forward in no direction. The narwhal who sports a single tooth eight feet long, for instance, and he himself only a scant fifteen. There's no sense to this tooth. It has no function that a decent-sized molar couldn't fulfill as well. And there's as little sense to the extra armorage of the hedgehog, or the overthickened skins of the saurians, or the extra fol-de-rols of structure in the shell animals. They don't need them. They don't use them. These things hatch and grow as part of the Vanity of Evolution, who seems to be a carpenter with too many tools, and without lights. For there's many a bug and quadruped who's worked himself into a cul-de-sac, and vanished.

"In man too there's the same sprinting in the wrong direction, the same lapsing mentally from eagle to lizard, and the same growing of spurious tusks and landing head down in the swamps again.

"Yes . . . this Hitler-hatching is one of our oldest habits. It's the empty flourish of Ego. It's the Ego without an Art to dissipate itself in, the dream that escapes the personality of the dreamer, and enters the psychic bedrooms of his neighbors. We all have dream-ideas of this or that, but we hold them in check either by art or learning or by the cautious desire for anonymity that keeps most of the world sane. But when the idea becomes greater than the man in whom it hatched—like the dream of nobility in a paperhanger—history appears. And history is always bad.

"For there's small profit to us in studying the Hitlers. Now if we could learn what it is that improves mankind and advances the evolution of our monkey-brain a notch! But it's always easier to see the forces that foul the human mind, and to trace its lapses. In men like Hitler it is the same werewolf facts that always operate. *Quos Deus vult perdere, prius dementat*—excuse the reference to God. These facts are the phosphorescence of defeat. They come limping out of every debacle to haunt the victors. By the time humanity, justice, and sanity have triumphed, it is always over a wasteland. . . . And it's there the Germans will end—on the manure pile that waits for all mania."

Further and further away from Sarah the hand he held tried to lead Michael. Perhaps the doctor felt the weight of this small hand in his own, felt it tugging backward.

"There is too much love in you, Michael," he would say, as a prologue to his discourses. "You embrace life too tenderly. Put away that embrace, son. Examine what's around you. I know how pretty the birds, the trees, and the flowers are. But those things are only life. Man's sky is his mind. And it's a sky you can't lie under dreaming. It's a sky that's got to be rebuilt. Torn away and built over until it's large and fair enough for man."

Even when Michael was silent and held the hand gently, the tired face in the bed would grow truculent and rumble such complaints.

"Why is it that, after listening to me so long, you remain Michael? Your silence contradicts me, and the tone of your voice, when you speak, is too gentle, as if you were humoring the vagaries of a blind man's mind, and forgiving them."

At first he had spoken kindly in this way, and Michael understood humbly that this was a remnant of Sarah's love that was still left in this world. No matter how Dr. Rufus attacked the light he saw in his pupil's heart, blowing on it with all the winds of his disillusion, Michael knew that he did not want to blow out this light . . . but somehow to increase it.

But as the illness encroached further with its fearful pangs into the victim's every limb and vital organ and, for a long time seemingly, everywhere but into his mind, the complaints grew more frequent and bitter, and Michael felt in his friend an increasing antagonism. Their battle grew more open.

There was another, more human, reason for the doctor's bitterness against the boy to whom from childhood he had given a strange love, and the fruits of all his knowledge. Abandoned by the world now, and brooding about it as do all martyrs, Dr. Rufus was hurt by Michael's evident ingratitude, and the boy's apparent desire to leave him. This ingratitude was proved by Michael's frequent and increasing absences from his bedside.

Behind these absences was the dark story of Miss Rufus's ill-treatment and finally her torture of the boy Michael. No sooner had the doctor retired to his bed of slow death than she had decreed that the boy should eat in the kitchen. He was forbidden the important rooms of the house. Soon other restrictions were built around him. He was locked in his bedroom at nine in the evening. The books the doctor had given him were removed from the shelves near his bed, and he was allowed no lights. Later, the carpet was removed from his room, the chairs carted away, his blankets reduced to a single bit of torn matting, and sheets and pillow-cases were no longer allowed him. Day by day, these hardships and indignities multiplied, pouring from the spinster's heart, as if, no longer sterile, it had become wildly blooming, but with weeds and cactus growths that sought to choke the soul of the child who had come into the house.

Soon she began to slap and pummel the boy, her hands seeming to grow drunken with the punishment they adminstered. The fair face that had known only Sarah's loving eyes and the caress of her work-battered hand felt a mania of hate tearing and gouging at its beauty. As Miss Rufus grew more assured of her brother's blindness, the savagery of her beatings increased. Michael's face often showed great swellings and bruises.

Still he did not inform Dr. Rufus against his sister. It was only when she, with new cunning, began to lock him away from the sufferer in the sickroom, that Michael desired to cry out to his friend that he did not mean to hurt him. But he continued to keep secret the sister's hatred, because he felt that to reveal these things would bring needless pain to the helpless man.

For five years, he, who had been loved more perfectly by Sarah than an angel is in Heaven, lived by the side of this hatred. During these years, Michael's look never changed. He was looking for Sarah, and despite the blackness of the hate that confronted him, he found her. He saw Sarah's little eyes staring into his own to see if there were tears, as she used to do whenever he fell and bumped himself—and he did not cry out. Still the poem that had been his childhood remained secure in his heart. And presently he was able to see Sarah's eyes in everything. He found her in the pain that lay under the blackness in Miss Rufus. He found her in the fear, hidden away like a criminal, out of which arose the ugliness of this aging woman.

As his goodness grew strengthened, the truculence and enmity of the doctor increased against it. When he was seventeen, Michael knew that the Red Beard looked on him angrily, as at a stranger rather than a son and pupil. The rumbling voice had ceased its wandering discourses, and now came to grips only with Michael; at him the brain launched itself, wrestling subtly and wildly with his soul.

"You offend me, Michael," he would say.

"How?" the boy would plead.

"Your brain hides from me. It lurks at the feet of some Jesus like a dog that's crawled back to his master. There's something comes out of you, an attitude like a priest's robe, that shames me and makes me seem small. My thinking seems small beside your silence."

The doctor was at this time in hideous pain. Under the coverlet drawn tight to his chin, his chest heaved as if it were signaling desperately for help. The skin of his face was covered with a granite gloss, and his voice broke in its hollow rumblings.

The boy, his face full of love, would place his hand on the hot forehead and smile intently into the blinded face.

"Your hand is cool," Dr. Rufus would mutter. "It has a healer's touch." And he would add: "Do your hands turn white as they used to?"

"Yes," Michael would say.

"And you feel a power inside you?" he would ask.

"Yes," Michael whispered.

"Take your hands away," the doctor growled then. "I prefer pain to mystery."

Or: "When you touched me you seemed far away," said the doctor. "Where were you?"

It was useless to evade.

"Why are you silent?" the invalid would rage, in his weak voice.

"I am trying to remember something," Michael faltered. "Someone who is trying to speak to me . . . someone I once knew. . . ." He had heard, as if he were dreaming, the lamentations of strange beings in strange places, voices weeping and calling for him: "Michael, where are you? Michael . . . Michael, come back."

"Hallucinations," muttered the Red Beard.

"I don't know, I don't know," Michael pleaded.

"Hallucinations," the Red Beard repeated, and its laugh was more dreadful than its cries. "You have the religious mind. It's amusing to me to know that all my work in behalf of reason has turned you into a crystal-gazer. That's what the religious mind does . . . looks into itself as if it were a crystal globe, instead of looking out, like a prisoner. . . ."

In the silence that followed, Michael felt the doctor's fierceness. And he, who had not wept at all at Miss Rufus's persecutions, now wept in the night for all the love that had faded from his world. Now it was only Sarah's hand he held when he slept in his room for a few hours. And only her work-battered fingers that touched lovingly in his dreams the bruised skin of his face.

"It goes away, Mikil," she whispered, staring into Michael's eyes to see if there were tears. "Hoits always goes away."

Another Presence, perhaps not much more real, but dear and familiar, consoled him in his room. It startled him sometimes, and then made him smile. It was the Dove, gurgling. The Dove appeared sometimes on the ledge of his opened window, and Michael, looking at it through the tears in his eyes, saw it shining and unbearably white. It was the same dove he had known as a child, making the same quaint noises with his throat. But now, in its presence, a wild thought cried out in him sometimes that there was a power in him to heal all that suffered. The whiteness of his hands seemed to grow whiter, and a voice, soundless and far away, spoke inside him.

One day the weeping boy turned away from the delightful sound that was the throat of a dove gurgling. Cowering, he hid from the Voice inside him that would have spoken. He thought of the tortured one dying slowly in the room near by, and an impulse came to him to deny what was in himself, and affirm what was in the doctor. He felt he had failed in allegiance to his friend, and he decided to confess to him, hoping that the dying Brain on the pillow would exorcise God.

"And so . . ." the doctor catechized, with a remembered kindness in his voice, "when you are silent, you do know what it is you think about?"

"God," said Michael softly.

There was a pause so long that Michael began to hope the doctor hadn't heard him.

"And who is that?" the Red Beard inquired.

"I don't know," said Michael.

"Where is He?" persisted the Red Beard. "Is He in Heaven?"

"Perhaps," said Michael softly.

"Come now." Dr. Rufus raised his voice. "There must be something more to God than a hole in your head that contains neither words nor ideas. Don't be so shy with your God, Michael. I want to hear about Him."

"I see Him in the world," said Michael slowly.

"That's better." The Red Beard smiled. "Once we've located God we can discuss Him. In just what portion of the world do you see Him, Michael? In the history of man?"

"No," said Michael, "not there."

"Where then?" the Red Beard demanded.

"In beauty," said Michael.

"That needs another secondary definition," said the doctor. "What do you consider beautiful?"

"It's hard to pick out separate things," said Michael, "as if you asked what waves in the sea were beautiful."

The Red Beard chuckled weakly.

"I understand," it said. "So you've discovered God in the fields, hills, and streams. In birds flying, flowers nodding, animals running, and the whole gamut of terrestrial color and grace. And you've decided that this dream of beauty around us is God, eh?"

"Yes," said Michael. "Beauty is our dream, but it is God's reality."

"How many madmen have said that," the voice rumbled wistfully from the pillow, "and how many scientists have confirmed it!

"Yes," continued Dr. Rufus, "our scientists after measuring the world have found the same surplus that spells God. The same too much and too intricate and too useless that proclaims a Divine and Artistic hand in its manufacture. Beauty is again God's calling card at the laboratory bench as it was at the altar. We've wrestled a lot of new statistics out of the Heavens and the Earth, but no new philosophy. Our scientists add a new alto to the Magnificat at eventide.

"'In the world,' they say, 'where every bit of fuzz on a bug's leg is usually so purposeful, what of that extra cosmos of beauty that has no purpose? Well,' they say, 'it has a purpose. Its purpose is to turn our souls to God.'"

Dr. Rufus paused.

"Is that what you think?" he asked.

"Yes," said Michael.

"So looking on Nature, you see God," Dr. Rufus said more loudly. "You see in Beauty evidences of a Divine breath superior to ours, eh? Well, Michael, I see something else."

"What do you see?" asked Michael.

"I see that there is no Beauty," said the Red Beard. "Like the word God, the word Beauty is a name that reveals not our souls but our ignorance. I want to discuss this with you, Michael, because I lie here thinking about it. I'll grant you this: there's nothing nimbler than God. You'd think that when Reason first shooed Him away from his Magician's Table and stripped Him of His Miracles and booted Him out of the entire history of man, He would retire in good order. But no. He leaves the little domain of Psychology and takes possession of Chemistry, Astronomy, the Quantum Theory, and all the test tubes of Science. Our scientists, uncovering one by one the secrets of existence, end up with bent knee before the daffodil and the dinosaur. God exchanges His white whiskers for an X. There's a promotion! Instead of being the soul of bad reasoning and childish thinking, He becomes now the soul of Beauty. The Pan X. Having nothing else to think about, Michael, I've been thinking that the fear of God will never quit men's minds until they either lose or understand their love of Beauty.

"I am blind," the voice on the pillow resumed, "and I spend a lot of time remembering the look of things and thinking of their beauty, and wondering what made them so. And it may be only a blind man's revenge that makes me discover now that there was no beauty. But I doubt this. I prefer to think it is an answer that has come to me, a large answer. It's an answer that I'll give you, Michael. You will use it as an exorcism to drive God out of the hills and flowers and to remove His breath from the whole of Nature. And don't cry out in your heart to 'get thee behind me.' It's not evil—what I tell you, Michael. It's loyalty to a race you belong to—the race of the brain. It's the little muscle that thinks against all the lightnings of Heaven. You come on my side, Michael."

Michael shivered and covered his face and shook his head desperately, as if he were struggling to drop out of it the light that continued to glow faintly and terrifyingly in all the crevices of his being.

"You seem more friendly now," said the Red Beard. "I don't feel you trying to shame me with that silence of yours. You seem very close, Michael. Let me feel your hands."

Michael leaned over and touched the blind forehead.

"It isn't cool," smiled the Red Beard. "It doesn't feel like a healer's hand, but hot and bedeviled like the inside of my head. Well, that makes our little discussion easier. I'll tell you about my Answer. It's this:

"I say, Michael, that there is no face of God in the beauty of the world and the Heavens. There's only our own face in it. We consider the phenomena of life beautiful because they are the multitudinous homelands we've left behind. We're not exiles from God's glory, as you once told me, Michael. We're exiles from Nature.

"Beauty is our memory of beasts and houses we've outgrown. Our aesthetic sense applauds the beauty of stars, hills, grasses, wings spread, flowers blooming, and the sea glittering with its half-foliage denizens, because these things are our biologic memories. Our aesthetic sense is a salute to our past. It isn't God we see, or Beauty, but a memory of self in the surviving crucible of the world. Things too dimly remembered to call brother, we call Beauty. We were once birds and fishes and crustaceans. And we still look at the treetop with the heart of a bird. We stare at the sea with the heart of a fish. We admire the sun with the heart of an amoeba and we look into caves with the heart of a lizard. Just as the village of our childhood glows with mysterious charm when we return to it, so the colors of the sea fascinate the gills still inside us when we look at them. We call our Mother beautiful because she bore us. Color and shape and movement and odor are similarly lovely to our senses because they were once the wombs we moved in. They are our ancestors, and we hail them as far back as they reach with that dispersed and sublimated self-love we have for the greatness of our fore-bears.

"But proof," smiled the Red Beard. "Every idea must have a toe to pirouette on. How do we prove that Beauty isn't Beauty? How do we prove that Beauty isn't the largess of God, but the romanticized history of evolution? Well"—the voice appeared to be growing childlike and losing its rumble—"let us apply the theory of relativity to it. If relativity works for the stars, it should work for the color of an apple blossom. For instance, it's conceivable that all the orderly world with all its color and movement and surplus of pure entertainment would not stir a single sigh in a Martian. Or in any other form of life evolved out of any other planet. For such an organism as might visit us would have been created in a world of fire, and come to life out of a heat wave of at least 2000 degrees Centigrade.

"Now imagine such a connoisseur from the Milky Way looking at our world. He would see no beauty in grass, birds, hills, sea, or flowers, for the good reason that he had not derived from them. The sight of our colors and shapes would touch off no nostalgic memories in him, nor fill him with that vestigial sense of triumph over Nature which is our Aesthetic Sense.

"The Martian, having triumphed over Flame, would undoubtedly consider ashes more beautiful than verdure and sigh more tenderly over melting rocks than leaping brooks. He would hear a hymn to himself out of the scarified tissues of his Martian landscape. And all that we think beautiful would be meaningless to him. And all that we hold ugly would be the wonders of God to him."

The tired voice trailed off.

"Go on," it whispered presently, "go to bed and say your prayers."

Sobbing wretchedly, the boy threw himself across the feet of the figure of stone.

But the man who had already spoken his swan song with his last strength, in torment, did not console him for his treason.

"There's something about you, Michael," he sighed, "something about you . . . something that washes my words away. It bothers me when you stay near me. It bothers me." The voice sank. "Don't bother me, Michael," it sighed.

One more year Michael's servitude continued. For one more year he attempted to repay his debt—and Sarah's—to Dr. Rufus. In that year a last change came into the illness. Pain, unspeakable and beyond bear-

ing, attacked the old doctor. Other doctors came and decided that his
eyes should be removed. They had turned to stone and were causing
pain by their pressure on nerves and brain. This measure Dr. Rufus
refused.

"No, gentlemen," the weary tongue jested, "I prefer the cadaver intact. My stone eyes lend a certain dignity to the ensemble."

In vain they pleaded, and tried to administer sedatives for his agony.
The stone man refused. For him, he said, there would be no mor-
phine at the end, and no religion, only the comfort of his thought.
Reason had been his flag, and he would fly it to the end.

Michael stood in the doorway, listening. Perhaps this was Dr.
Rufus's final taunt to Michael.

From that time on, silence fell in the sickroom. The silence
deepened with the passing months. The mania of pain ruled the
house.

Now it was Michael who nursed Dr. Rufus. The old serving couple,
frightened, were no longer to be seen in his room. They clung to their
quarters unless evoked by the sister's bells. No guests came. Alone,
Michael bore the burden of the man who was slow to die, the burden
of the madwoman, and the burden of the silence, which might have
been sweet with the service of his willing heart. The tired boy, from
whose form all buoyancy and strength had disappeared, no longer took
the time to walk in the streets, but remained for months inside the
house. At night, often hungry, he lay awake full of a sense of mount-
ing event, and the silence around him was like the approach of a
stealthy crime.

Michael grew thin. His body, which had grown strong under en-
couragement and love, was wasted, and his face was hollow-eyed and
old with the weight on his mind. Still the extraordinary beauty of his
face did not diminish, and it was this beauty that brought his final
sorrow in this house to the innocent boy.

One day, returning to Dr. Rufus's room after a brief absence, he saw
an unaccustomed sight. This was Miss Rufus, who, though she had seen
Michael daily, had not visited her brother in many weeks. A change
had come into Miss Rufus's hatred of Michael recently, one he could
not have defined.

Long ago, in seeking a reason for her loathing of the child, the
ugly spinster had found and confided one to the servants. This was that
Michael, with his orphan's haircut, had been the spawn of love, the repulsive symbol of a sin committed by some woman in the dark of a

lover's arms. For this she had tortured him, her hysteria fed daily by the fear that Michael would inform against her to her brother. But she had realized long since, through vigilance and spying, that he would not betray her. Now it was she who accused.

In this change that had come into her mania of late, Michael had become no longer the symbol of love, but love itself. Her thin-breasted body and withering arms had felt the sweetness of the tall boy, and her entire being had launched itself at him as at a robber come to steal her single treasure—the hatred by which she kept herself strong enough to live without life. Now she called him a monster, she raved that he was full of dreaded powers and monstrous secrets, and even his smiling was a mask for hidden danger.

"You are being accused, Michael," Dr. Rufus greeted him in an unfamiliar voice—a voice that spoke unctuously out of a personality that had escaped all pain.

"Speak your complaints, Margaret," he added to his sister.

In a rasping voice that spread into the air the horror of her hidden life, Miss Rufus spoke of Michael's persecutions. She raved of his plotting against her, watching her through keyholes while she was undressing. . . .

"And worse, worse!" she screamed, unable to find words for her crazed meanings. At last the shrill voice collapsed into its culminating sobs.

"Delusions of persecution," said Dr. Rufus in a voice more pleasant than when he had used it professionally, and he continued: "You are charged, Michael, with being part of the madness of my sister, Margaret. What have you to say?"

The voice waited, and then resumed, with a chuckle.

"Ah, he preserves his divine silence. He stands and radiates. Very good. We'll make a note of it. He offers radiation as a defense."

Again the voice chuckled.

"The charge stands as follows," it said. "Your radiation, Michael, or as you call it, the Glory of God, drives people mad. The divine presence does not heal but disorders. That cool sweet love you exude, Michael, falls on the human mind like an evil dew out of mystery and poisons it."

"I've tried to keep him out," Miss Rufus wailed, "but he sees through doors and walls."

"Let me speak for us, Sister," the voice silenced her. "The truth is, Michael, that I've lain here with your secret for a long time. My mind wrenched it out of your silence and radiation. The truth is," repeated the voice, rising with anger, "that you are God. You are God, Michael. Look at him carefully, Sister, with your two eyes that stick out like toads ready to jump. He is God."

"No, no!" the woman screamed. "He's the Devil. The peeping Devil. The Devil with an angel's face."

"Well said," the voice on the pillow attempted to chuckle. "God and the Devil are a pair of interchangeable masks. And now, Michael, my own complaint. Are you following the proceedings? Answer me."

"Yes," said Michael.

"When I thought you were Michael I loved you," the voice went on. "Then I found out who you were and I hated you. And in hating you I, too, have stepped a little out of line. A little out of line," the voice rumbled wistfully. "But if you think I'm mad, Michael, you're wrong. You're wrong," it cried suddenly. "I'm crippled, paralyzed, blind, half turned to stone, withered to a handful of pipe stems, brittle with disease and tormented by the nails being driven into my brain and the nails through my hands and feet, Michael. And nails through my heart and groin. And with all this nailing going on I have to retreat somewhere to think. I retreat to the last little perch. I become a bird on a twig, twittering crazily at the destruction below. But be patient with my twittering. My mind is still in it. Do you hear my mind, Michael, behind my words—above agony and sitting in judgment on God?"

"Yes," said Michael.

"Thank you," said the voice. "Then it's understood that I'm mad, but not too mad. It's understood that I'm a little Argument that won't give in, a little bird chirping on a tomb. It's understood further that my sister Margaret and I are human beings—we belong to that plague that speaks and thinks and dreams. We give off the stink of humanity—cruelty and unreason and despair. And we ask you, Michael, to remove your light from this house. We refuse the light, whatever it is and wherever it comes from. Because it doesn't come from where it should—from the Hell of the human mind. We refuse to live by any other light than that. You are judged and dismissed, Michael."

The voice grew hoarsened.

"You will leave this house," it said. "Get out with your angel face. We don't want it hovering . . . the old jackal of Divinity that haunts the death beds . . . waiting for the soul to be tossed to it. . . . I am going to die without falling into God's arms, Michael. You will not shine on me, O Spirit. . . ."

The Red Beard continued to tremble as the mouth became silent. Michael waited. The two figures in the shadowed room seemed locked in some tormented embrace, each so sad he could feel the same wail of tears in their throats.

At last Michael came and kissed the motionless forehead on the pillow.

"Good-by," he said softly.

Still he waited.

"Why must I go?" he thought. But the words he had heard pushed him from the bedside and moved him across the room. Here he remained in the darkened doorway. He stood, thinking of the life begun in a basket on the steps of the orphanage, and knew it was finished. There was the cry in his heart that rises from all endings, the good-by of days that all too suddenly become the Past, and leave us exiled and forlorn in a new, strange hour.

A voice came from the pillow.

"Michael," it called faintly, "Michael, are you gone?"

"No," said Michael. Tears fell from his eyes.

"I see a light," the voice on the pillow whispered. "Take it away . . . take the last light away."

Michael smiled at the madman.

"I will always love you," he said.

He moved away and when he was in the hall he heard a new sound from the pillow. The voice wept.

Michael walked from the house weeping, for he had been cast out. In the streets his eyes searched the night sky as he moved. The night sky grew large with his loneliness. So vast a darkness to cover so little a thing as his heart, he thought—so deep and far-away a mystery to haunt eyes so small as these looking up.

Michael stood on a dark and empty road beside the cemetery where Sarah was. Behind him lay a waste of land, and before him the trees where the dead lay. But it seemed to him that he was standing on a little bridge between Heaven and Earth, and that the way back for him was easy.

He walked under the trees where the dead lay, and stopped to look at the white stones that marked their homes in the earth. And it seemed to him as if a voice were calling to him to come back.

The moon on these white stones spelled out names and figures and words, and Michael thought, not of the dead who lay beneath them, but of the living still further from him who must come this way, of the dreams and powers and agonies that must speak finally only from a white stone.

"Michael," the Voice called, "Michael. You cannot see Me, though I am close to you, and My arms are around you. I am He, Michael, for whom you once toiled. You were My friend, Michael. Remember now that I sent you to this little place where you stand. Remember, Michael."

Michael remembered. He continued walking, and came to the grave that was Sarah's. The little white stone leaned erratically over the grass as if the careening soul of the old scrublady were in it. Michael stood remembering vividly all the tones and movements that had been hers, and a tenderness for the half-crazed smile overcame him, as if it were crying eagerly for him to bring it back to life.

Many voices came to him now. They seemed to surround him, clamoring joyously and calling out his name, calling to him to remember.

Michael remembered. Many were the memories that came crowding around him on the little bridge between Earth and Heaven where he stood. The sky came close to him, as if the rope ladder that Dr. Rufus used to speak of had been let down. And names he had never known were known to him, and the stars were near. But stronger than all was the memory of Sarah.

He beheld her in himself as in a mirror, and before his mirror she postured and cackled and banged away with her pails and brushes. But as he looked closer into this mirror, her image became silent and the careening little body stood motionless. Michael looked into the eyes that were gone from the world and at the half-crazed smile that was nowhere except in this mirror. He saw not only Sarah but his love for her, as if it, too, were in this mirror, standing like a child with its hand in her work-battered fist. They were waiting, both of them, for him to speak.

"Mother, Mother!" he cried, and cast himself on the grave.

He had chosen Sarah's world.

He was glad.

"In the hearts of the living," he thought, "the dead have their little extra hour of life." He would not have deprived Sarah of this hour. And though he no longer understood the true bliss of the eternity he had forfeited, he remembered still the truth about himself, and knew that he would never go back to Heaven.

The sound of the Dove came to him.

And, looking at the familiar bird on a tree branch close to him, at last Michael knew. Human he was, only that God's truth was in him, and this, the white friend that had first danced on his foundling's basket, was truly God's spirit, and it was his mission to carry God's message throughout the world.

Soundless and far away, the Voice now came to him.

"Go and tell them, Michael. When you speak My name, I shall be there beside you. I will be there as a light for your eyes and a whiteness on your hands. You will not be afraid, Michael, for My light will lead you. My truth will make a road for you. I am God. Go now, Michael, and bring Me the world."

But as he walked away, Michael's eyes were wide and thoughtful. There was no exultation in them but a question and much sadness. His heart did not exult with the memory of the Dove. It lay in the grave with Sarah, and beside Dr. Rufus moaning in his head.

When it was morning, Michael found himself on the outskirts of a small town, watching a little army of men raising a circus tent in a meadow full of daisies, butterflies, and the chirping of frogs. A ring of circus wagons painted red and gold enclosed one end of the field.

The summer dawn was a-scurry with exuberant figures. Tall blue painted poles rose magically out of the daisy patches. Ropes fluttered, pulleys creaked, and, to the accompaniment of shouts and of sledge hammers ringing, and a roar and whinny of hidden animals, a great spread of wrinkled canvas rose like a giant bird and became a circus tent, scalloped and minareted. Michael watched with delight. Everything around him hinted of gaieties, and the rough, unshaven figures assembling this toy world in the summer meadow reminded him of old Sarah as they dashed about with hammers, poles, and ropes.

As he stood enthralled by this little world that seemed to be hatching out of the daisies and the long grass, he heard a voice calling insistently. He turned and saw a preposterous-looking man standing in the doorway of one of the red and gold wagon trucks. The man was thin as a beanpole and naked to the waist. He looked like a huge insect with a gaunt human head attached to it. Michael stared at him and, never having been to a circus, was unaware he was being addressed by one of its Artists.

"Hey, you," called the man, shaking a finger, "what are you doing?"

"Nothing," said Michael, trying not to stare too much at the gruesome body. "I was just watching." And he began to move away, but the man laughed, and said: "What's the matter? You scared of me, kid? Come in here and give us a hand. Nobody's gonna eat you up."

Michael entered the wagon. The interior was a dark little house crowded with cots, chairs, a table, and innumerable chests. There was a little window with curtains. And there were three other figures. One, a huge creature who dwarfed everything around him, was sitting on the edge of a cot, his chin in his palms, and staring like a half-asleep monster out of the curtained window.

"Make yourself at home," the beanpole man was chuckling, as Michael, open-mouthed, stared at this and that. "We got some work for you. We're short-handed and want somebody to carry our stuff to the sideshow tent. We'll show you where. But first meet Mr. Henry Marblehead, better known as the Giant Munso—the tallest man in the world. What's your name, kid?"

"Michael," said Michael and smiled.

"O.K., Mike," said the Giant Munso in a soft boyish voice as if someone else had climbed up into his monster's head and were speaking for him. The huge man reminded Michael suddenly of a gangling, loose-skinned little chicken just hatched—and wondrously enlarged.

"And this," said the beanpole, "is Captain Achilles."

A midget, with a round baby head and a face puckered as if it were about to cry, bowed like a courtier and then extended a puny hand.

"Allow me," continued the beanpole, who appeared to be enjoying their visitor's wide-eyed interest, "Dr. Holmes, the India Rubber man— a fascinating creature made of rubber bands instead of flesh. Snap him, if you wanna, kid."

A man with a pirate's mustache sat up from under the covers of a cot.

"What's transpiring?" he inquired dazedly.

"I've got us a valet," said the beanpole.

"How do you do, sir," said the India Rubber man and Michael saw that his naked body was tattooed so completely that he seemed clothed in a tapestry.

"I'm Philo, the Human Skeleton, as you have no doubt observed by this time," said the beanpole. "And now to your duties, kid. We want all this truck removed to the sideshow tent. And when you've done with your interesting chores, young fella, breakfast will be ready for you in the cook tent. Just follow your nose."

It was thus Michael joined the circus. For several weeks, as the painted wagons rumbled from town to town, and the blue and white tents rose in various summer meadows, Michael remained more a spectator than a participant. He watched the performances, the crowds, and the animals with undiminished excitement. He ran errands, was hustled about by acrobats and bareback riders, and slept at night in the wagon occupied by four freaks. But gradually he seemed to enter the mind of the circus, and he began to feel the painstaking and concentrated little talents out of which rose the daily illusion of glitter and gaiety.

It was in his relationship with the four strange men in the little dark house of the circus wagon that the major change occurred. In the mornings Michael still served them as he had on the first day—carrying their trappings to the sideshow tent. The afternoons he spent tidying up the wagon interior. But after their evening exhibitions, which were concluded long before the Main Performance, the four freaks would return to their wagon and stretch themselves in the grass around it. Michael would then talk to them as the music of the circus band came muffled from the lighted tent and filled the summer night with its dancing far-away sounds. He talked softly, and at first inspired no more than awe for his quiet eloquence and remarkable erudition. He discussed with Dr. Rufus's words as much as his own the activities everywhere in the world, explaining the tawdry secrets behind the bombast of the world's leaders. But in explaining these matters there was a gentleness in his voice, like a deeper vocabulary, that made even Dr. Rufus's philosophies sound mysteriously tender.

His four friends stretched on the grass grew nightly more eager for his talk. In his absence they took to strutting about with brooding philosophical looks on their odd faces. They grew proud of the things Michael had put into their heads, and looked down from their sideshow platform, like sages, on the pathos of the uninformed.

In the second month of his travels, Michael emerged from the status of mere philosopher. The Giant Munso became ill. A physician was called, and the tallest man in the world was pronounced in grave danger. He lay doubled up on his long cot, groaning through the afternoon and complaining of frightful pains in his groin. His large loose-fleshed face rolled on the pillow. That night, when the other three crowded into the wagon, Michael was absent. The freaks wondered at this, for Munso had always been kind to him. And now Munso kept calling his name like a frightened child. A great gloom lay on the three friends watching him. Each knew that the giant quivering on the cot was dying. Several years ago, there had been another giant among them who had lain just this way, doubled up and gray with pain. And though three doctors had attended him, he had died, refusing to leave the circus wagon. The band had played just as it was playing tonight, and this other giant had sat up and listened to it for a moment with a sudden childish smile on his huge face and then fallen back dead.

Michael appeared in the doorway, and the three heads turned miserably to him. He came to the cot and stood looking down on the enormous figure.

The Giant Munso opened his eyes and paused in his groaning as he saw Michael. The others also looked at Michael with a silence that became like fear. They saw a light in his face and on his hands.

Michael, looking into the pain-filled eyes of the stricken giant, kept smiling, for in these eyes he saw Sarah. He felt her withered muscular arm flung again across his neck as he slept. A great love seized Michael, and he felt that his heart, glowing with power, was in his hands; that his heart was his to give away. He placed his hands on the giant's head and continued to smile. This perplexed and pitiful giant seemed to Michael all he loved in the world, and his hands caressed the huge head as tenderly as if it were the little fledgling out of a chicken egg it had once seemed to him. And his eyes, smiling as over a crib, begged for an answer, as if they were saying aloud: "Deep inside you, little giant, lies the secret of life—the child love for the works of God. Love life, little giant. Be grateful. The night is your mother, and all that lies hidden in the dark loves you."

The look of pain and perplexity passed from the giant's eyes and he smiled at Michael.

It was thus the miracle was done. In the little dark house of the circus wagon the four freaks sat in silence and looked at Michael with fear. Munso, the world's tallest man, felt no more pain and his face was no longer gray. He placed his feet on the floor and straightened till his head touched the ceiling.

"I feel all right," he said in his soft, boyish voice. "I feel mighty good."

Captain Achilles, the midget, climbed like a distracted infant into the vacant cot and began slapping one little fist into the other palm, which was his way of expressing wonder. And Dr. Holmes, who was made of rubber bands and tattooed like a human mosaic, pointed silently to the wagon window, in which perched a white Dove, gurgling. Somehow the white Dove was even more frightening than this strange Michael whose hands had turned so white as they rested on the stricken Munso's head. Philo, the Human Skeleton, covered his face in panic.

Michael spoke.

"It is the Spirit of God," he said.

The Dove fluttered to his hand and couched itself in his palm.

"He has spoken to me," said Michael, "and I know the Truth. It is simple. I will tell it to you. But you must not repeat it, yet. You must only dream of it and let it fill your hearts a little more each day."

As the four freaks listened, the Dove in Michael's hand began to shine with an unbearable light and for a moment all of them felt that the entire night had burst into a single flame and devoured the earth. When they opened their eyes again, the Dove was gone.

Michael spoke to them until the dawn came. He told them it was his mission to redeem the world. He spoke of a Soul that was greater than the souls of men, of life and its meaning, and of the mystery of God.

All night long the freaks clamored to hear about Heaven, and if they were going there immediately when they died.

"I don't know," Michael said at first, unhappily—for it seemed to him there was a greater Truth than the tinseled Heaven for which they longed.

"I think we are the leaves on His Tree, and fall to make room for other leaves. Only the Tree that produces and destroys us is divine. We must resign ourselves to the mystery of the tree trunk, and the hidden roots that lend us life, and not try to see too much. That is the way God wishes it. He wishes us to live on this Tree, and shine in the sun as part of His mystery."

"But we die just the same?" asked Dr. Holmes.

"We die knowing we please God by being part of His plan," Michael said.

"It's hard to understand—if there is no Heaven," said Philo sadly.

"Maybe we're not smart enough to understand yet," said Captain Achilles.

"You don't have to understand," said the Giant Munso, who had just been saved.

But the others kept asking questions, and searching Michael's eyes, which grew sad and far away.

"Maybe we express ourselves too crudely," Dr. Holmes said, calling the attention of the others to Michael's darkened face.

"Yes, we ought to do a lot of reading," piped Captain Achilles, anxiously, "and then we'd understand better."

In the end Michael, smiling suddenly, promised them the eternity for which they asked. He was young, and he was not sure of his words yet, and the Truth told him that it was better not to be too wise. For the wisest thing a man can do is dream, and dreams have no words. This he told them.

"Dreams," he said, "are the mists of Heaven brightening our souls for a moment. Some day," he said, "we shall be overcome by these mists, and instead of falling like leaves from the Tree, we shall remain eternally green, and rest like a crown on God's head."

When he had promised them this, the freaks were happy, and wished to know shyly if, when they went to Heaven, they would still be freaks.

Michael comforted them on this score.

And now they were excited by their new religion.

"What shall we do?" they cried, crowding around him.

"Love God, and you will know how to pray to Him," he said.

And he told them the following story:

"There was once such a good heart in a boy who had been born without the gift of speech. His parents were pious people, but as their child grew up they were ashamed to bring him into church because he was unable to speak. As he grew older his parents saw, too, that he was a backward boy without much sense in him and their shame in their misfortune increased. But their son was unaware of the trouble he caused them, for they were not bad parents. Left to himself, he learned happily a few simple and foolish things. Among the foolish things that he learned was how to play on a little fife made out of a willow-tree twig. It had three holes in it and he could blow three notes out of it as if he were a bird.

"One Easter Day the parents, seeing their son running about like a pagan when everybody else was off to church, decided to smooth his hair and wash his face and take him with them. They thought that perhaps his dumbness wouldn't be noticed by their neighbors while they were rejoicing so ardently over the Resurrection.

"So their son sat between them in the church, awed and thrilled by his first visit, and listened breathlessly to the choir and the priest and the exultant praying of the flock. And all this pleased him so that he reached into his pocket for his fife to play his three bird notes on— because he was unable to make any other sound. His father, seeing what he intended, grew angry and slapped his hand. The boy sat still for a time, but again the rapture of the prayers excited him and made him want to join in. And again he half drew his fife from his pocket. This time his mother slapped his hand and whispered fiercely to him to behave. Once more the boy sat silent and quivering. But the voices of the choir chanting of God's glory overcame him a third time and a third time he started to draw his fife from his pocket. His parents grew scarlet with shame, for the antics of their son had attracted attention. Fearful of offending both God and their neighbors, they rose piously. They seized their stupid son by his hands and started to lead him with flushed and apologetic faces from the church.

"And as they walked up the aisle a strange thing happened. A sound came piping out of their son's pocket. It grew louder. Its three notes trilled and rose above the choir voices and filled the church with sweeter sound than had ever before been heard in it. And the boy, afraid to move because of the disturbance his foolish fife was making in his pocket, stood still and stared around full of terror. But this time no one slapped his hand. His parents sank to their knees in the aisle, and all the devout and more gifted people thronged toward him and kneeled in silence as his willow-tree fife continued to trill its woodland hosannas from his pocket."

The four freaks wept at the miracle concerning one who was so like themselves. They assured Michael that they would know how to pray. They would pray humbly, like freaks.

"And God will love us, just as the public loves us, because we perform before them as freaks," Captain Achilles piped.

"If we pretended we were better than we are, God wouldn't love us," Dr. Holmes said thoughtfully.

Before the dawn came, they wished to know from their friend, the new Redeemer, how they would know when the world had been redeemed.

Michael explained to them as follows:

"There was once long ago," said Michael, "a great rabbi who was renowned among all the sad Jews of the world as one of their holiest men. When he was old he traveled to Jerusalem to look before he died on the place where God had once been kind to the Jews.

"While he was sitting at twilight in a room overlooking the lost wonderland of his race, a strange thing happened in Jerusalem. A madman, seizing a shofar, which is the ram's horn the Jews blow from their altar, ran to the top of the Mount of Olives and blew wild and terrifying blasts on it. The shofar calls echoed in the streets below, and the Jews, hearing the holy horn sounding, grew blissful and rushed out of their houses, crying that the Messiah had come at last and that the day of Redemption was here.

"As they rushed singing and rejoicing through the streets, they passed under the window of the holy rabbi, and cried out to him to join them quickly, for the Messiah was calling from a hilltop.

"The old rabbi opened his window as they shouted and sang in a frenzy below. Then he smiled and silenced them for a moment with his hand.

" 'Go back to your homes, my children,' he said, 'and wait a little longer. It is not the Messiah come nor Redemption calling.' The holy man pointed outside his window.

" 'Look at that little bird on the tree,' said the holy man. 'The little bird is not singing.'

"And he closed his window and went back to studying his holy books."

For several days the Giant Munso, Captain Achilles, Dr. Holmes, and Philo went about in a trance, and wherever Michael moved, these four were beside him. Alone, on the platform in the sideshow with the country folk gaping up as the barker described their remarkable abnormalities, Michael's disciples smiled giddily and went through their little routines as bewilderedly as amateurs. For their heads were in their promised Heaven.

This greatness, still extending their thought as they moved among others, brought smiles to the circus people. The sight of the midget at the long table in the cook tent closing his eyes and moving his lips in prayer as each dish was handed him began to stir chuckles. And Philo, the Human Skeleton, stealthily slipping notes into their hands reading, "Join Us and Be Saved," was also diverting. And for several weeks as the circus traveled among the prairie towns, there were only these smiles and good-natured comment among the performers. For these talented folk who could fly, tumble, balance, and caper in a hundred ways were fond of the freaks and had always treated them with a pleasant half-mocking deference that was part of the circus code.

But when the constant breakfast, lunch, and supper praying of the midget and the increasing flood of salvation notes from the Human Skeleton were climaxed by certain antics of the Giant Munso, a feeling of disquiet came to the circus people. Munso, who towered three feet above the tallest of them, took to extending his huge hands over their heads as they passed him, and uttering blessings. Finally Dr. Holmes completed their misgivings. The India Rubber man, heretofore esteemed for his wit and sarcasm, appeared one Sunday dressed in a frock coat with a priest's collar and his pockets filled with enormous quantities of feathers. These he threw by the handfuls at all he met, crying out that they were the Feathers of the Dove and that whoso wore one would be possessed of the Spirit of God.

The feeling that all four of their freaks had gone mad took hold of the circus people, and their smiles and banter gave place to irritation and then fear. Michael, who might have saved his four friends, for he was a sane and observant youth, had been too busy with his mission to notice the increasing anger of the artists and canvas workers. And when he did finally see the unhappy change that had come over his little world, it was too late to act.

By this time his four disciples, completely vanquished by his continued discourses, had disobeyed even his most important admonition. They had added to their other curious behavior the announcement that their valet Michael was the Saviour, and that God had visited them in their wagon in the form of a Dove and had filled their souls with light.

The sense that madness was among them began to unnerve the acrobats and tumblers, and so compact is the mind of the circus that its growing panic was felt in the animal cages. The cats took to roaring, the three elephants grew restive and pulled their stakes out of the ground at night, and even the horses leaped and bucked in the ring during their performances. These disturbances grew worse, and the circus, which had played happily in the summer meadows before Michael's arrival, became full of angers and plots and threats. One night while the management, consisting of two sawdust veterans who had trouped shows for a generation, was discussing possible ways of coping with the lunacy that had overtaken their freaks, a final and unforgivable event happened. Captain Achilles rose from his toy chair on the sideshow platform and addressed the astonished villagers gathered in the tent to behold the Wondrous Freaks of Nature. He cried out in a piping voice that Salvation was at hand for all who would listen and, falling to his tiny knees, raised his head in passionate prayer. The Giant Munso, seeing this happen, also forgot himself and began casting benedictions over the heads of the audience. In vain the barker's voice rose in its rhythmic twang of phrases. Philo, the Human Skeleton, attired only in his pleated silken trunks, was on his feet bawling that Michael was the Son of God, and Dr. Holmes, who had been snapping his rubber skin for the edification of a group before his section of the platform, reached for his frock coat hanging on a hook behind him and began throwing feathers.

After the performance, the circus management visited the wagon occupied by the four freaks and Michael. The four were given a week's salary and asked to leave the organization. Michael, who had received no salary for his many labors, was called a hoodlum and ordered never to show his face again. Carrying their bundles, Michael and his disciples walked from the circus lot through muttering and menacing groups of those who had been their friends. The four freaks held their heads high. But Michael was sad and tears were in his eyes. For he knew this was only the beginning of his wretchedness.

In the hotel room where they arrived an hour later Dr. Holmes ordered up food and drink. Michael was unable to eat. He sat slumped in a chair and watched the others gloomily. No word was said. But when the meal was done, Dr. Holmes stood up and tapped his spoon against a glass. He made a speech.

"Gentlemen," he said, "we are the friends of God's Son."

"Yes, sir," Captain Achilles piped and beat his tiny fist into his palm. "We are the Four Apostles."

"We have followed Him where others cast Him out," continued the India Rubber man. "If He had wanted to He could have destroyed that tent and scattered that circus to the winds. But His heart is kind and He would rather pick up His Cross and walk away than cause any inconvenience. Am I right?"

The Giant Munso nodded his head.

"No use making trouble," he said softly.

"Now I want to ask Him Who we know is the Son of God, just what are His plans," concluded the India Rubber man.

"I haven't any," Michael said truthfully.

The four looked at him in silence.

Then Captain Achilles spoke.

"Yes, You have," he piped. "You ain't gonna let a lot of circus hoodlums get You down."

Philo left the table and came to Michael.

"You're in the dumps," he said softly, "which is only natural, considering the blindness and injustice of our fellowmen. But God's truth is in You. You can't say it ain't."

"You can't deny it," shrilled Captain Achilles.

"We saw it. We heard it. We know it," they all cried.

The midget climbed up into the giant's palm and leaned against his chin.

"We'll all go out in the streets together," said the India Rubber man, "and speak to the people."

"Not us, but Michael," said the giant.

"But we'll be there to draw the crowds."

"We'll give a free show."

"He needs us, just like we need Him," piped Achilles.

Philo raised his voice.

"What You got to tell the people, Michael, is this. You'll say:

'Looka here, folks, these were born wrong outside, but you folks are freaks inside. That's the Truth of God.' And that's where we come in."

"The Truth of God," spoke the giant. "I felt it. I was dying, and it cured me!"

"I was blind," Dr. Holmes cried. "All I did was cover myself with the false glory of worldly beauty—tattooed from head to foot—a living, breathing symbol of the world's vanity, Dr. Holmes, the golden calf himself! And then I saw the Dove!"

The freaks jumped up and down around Michael, calling his name, repeating their hackneyed phrases of salvation, urging him onward, to the cross if necessary, and crying out that they would stand by him to the end.

In their midst, Michael pondered on how to bring God's message to the world.

The next night Michael spoke for the first time to the world. It was a little world, gathered on a street corner to see the four circus freaks performing free of charge. The crowd laughed and applauded good-naturedly at the show.

When Michael stepped forward and began to talk, they listened, at first in curiosity, and then in silence. A great eloquence was on Michael's tongue this night. Though he spoke of God, he seemed like no minister of the gospel they had heard, but a poet making words come to life in the night street.

The simple rhythm and the insight of his thought stirred something deeper in his listeners than they usually brought into the streets with them. They stood a long time, moved by this strange emotion inside them and by the smiling, glowing face of the pale boy who spoke.

Throughout Michael's talk, the freaks too remained devoutly silent, proud of his gift and of his beauty too. To help detain the crowd, they had struck postures: Captain Achilles still smaller on his little knees; Philo, who imagined himself a symbol of mankind's distortion, holding piously a posture with his legs around his neck. Dr. Holmes held a torch aloft and let the light flicker over Michael's face. The Giant Munso stood behind Michael like a mystic bulwark. But the freaks went unnoticed.

Michael told the stilled crowd something different from what the freaks had suggested. It was a simple parable of a traveler who had found a field so beautiful that he paused to admire it. As the traveler stood thrilled by the beauty of this field, said Michael, he saw that the beauty came from wondrous stones that dotted it. These stones were radiant with many colors, and the traveler looking at them grew more and more filled with delight. He raised his voice and other men appeared. All came running into the field and all looked and saw the beauty of the stones and were overjoyed. For a long time this group of men stood thrilled and full of pleasure for the beauty around them.

Then the first man, overcome by the radiance of a particular stone, approached it and knelt before it. He picked it up, holding it in his hands that he might be closer to its beauty and feel it actually against him. At first the stone weighed little but as he continued to walk in the field, exulting over his possession, its weight increased. Finally it was so heavy he began to stagger and sweat under its burden. He could no longer look at the other many beautiful stones, so busy was he carrying his one prize and so exhausted did he become clinging to it.

Looking around after a long time he beheld a curious sight. The other men, like himself, had also each picked up a stone and, like himself, each was staggering and sweating under his burden. This angered the first man, who began to shout that all the others were foolish to pick up the stones they had, since his was the most beautiful that had been in the field and the only one worth picking up. Shouts answered him. All the burdened men cried out he was mad, and each announced that the stone he held clutched to his bosom was the only thing of beauty that had been in the field. Soon after this they all lost their tempers and began to hit each other with the stones they were carrying. Although exhausted by the growing weight of these stones, they found enough strength to wield them as weapons. And soon all the stones that had lain in the field as objects of breath-taking beauty had become dreadful things with which the travelers, panting and bellowing, slew each other. And as each man killed he cried out he was wiser than the others, and as each man died he lamented that all wisdom and beauty perished with him.

It was thus, said Michael, that man had turned the world of nature into a battleground for insanity and greed of ego he called wisdom.

"Return to the field," said Michael, in so strange a voice that many of his listeners felt tears. "Return to the field. Put down your stones."

This was the first of his talks to the world. There were many more. Week after week Michael and his four friends traveled from town to town. He spoke sometimes with humor and brought laughter from the little crowds on the street corners. And at times his voice sounded so fresh and childlike that women wept without hearing what it was he said but feeling that someone tender and innocent was asking for their love.

One evening when he had told again of the travelers in the field and asked his listeners to put down their stones, he was sought out as he walked back to the country rooming house with his four friends. A man seated in the rear of a large and shining automobile, driven by a uniformed chauffeur, called to him. Michael stepped into the road as the car stopped.

"I would like to talk to you, if you could spare a few minutes," this man said graciously.

"Certainly," said Michael.

"I'll take you where you're going—you and your friends," the man offered.

Michael called to the four, who came running, the Giant Munso carrying Captain Achilles under his arm. They stepped into the car, Munso doubling up to keep from sticking his head through its top. On the way, their new acquaintance said he had listened to Michael's talk and that he had never heard so moving and beautiful a sermon.

"You've got the gift," he said, smiling. "No ranting, no bad style. But something spoken from the heart that's beautiful. . . . It got me, young man."

The stranger reminded Michael of Dr. Rufus. He had the same stern and superior face, though without a beard, and the same almost coquettish charm behind the sternness and superiority. He was asking Michael questions as to who he was, where he came from, and what he hoped to do. Michael stared at him, thinking of Dr. Rufus. A pang passed through his heart and, looking at the man with eyes full of remembrance, he answered his questions simply, as if he had become again a child being catechized by his old teacher.

In return the man had given his own name, George Griswald. Pronouncing it, he paused to see if it was known to any of his odd passengers. But all five went on looking at him as if he had spoken no name.

"You'll call me George," he continued, "and I'll call you Michael, and neither of us will have any other names."

As they rode to the rooming house where Michael and his followers shared a single room, as they had once shared the circus wagon, Mr. Griswald laid a plan before Michael. The world, he said, was exactly as Michael said it was. And what it needed was exactly the message Michael was preaching, whether it was God's or man's. And what Michael needed was this world to preach to, not just a few handfuls of it on a small-town street corner.

"I can get you a great audience," said Mr. Griswald, "a great mass of human beings. And you can talk to them, night after night. And thousands will come from all over the country to listen. That's the way you'll be able to save them."

"Save them?" Michael repeated and looked confused.

"Bring them to God," said Mr. Griswald. "You tell me He has spoken to you. And your friends here have seen Him. Is that true? Or is it a parable? Something you've made up to explain some inner truth?"

"It's true," said Michael. "He has spoken to me."

"Well and good," said Mr. Griswald. His fingers trembled as he rested them on the arm of this tall, glowing boy. "I believe you."

The automobile had stopped near a sagging wooden house.

"Here's where we stay," said Michael.

"Just a minute." Mr. Griswald drew a deep breath. "I want to finish with my plan.

"I want you to come to Hegemish, inside of two weeks," said Mr. Griswald. "That's a town two hundred miles from here, or thereabouts. I'll have everything ready for you. I'll put on an advertising campaign, put up a tent large enough to hold thousands. Will you speak to them?"

"Yes," said Michael.

"There are a lot of poor bewildered people in Hegemish," said Mr. Griswald, "whom your words will straighten out. That's what you want, isn't it? To tell people they belong to God? And to tell them who and what God is?"

"Yes," said Michael.

"Well and done," said Mr. Griswald, and mopped his head with a large clean handkerchief. "I'll expect you in Hegemish on the nineteenth. Do you give me your word, you'll be there on that date?"

"Yes," said Michael.

"It's hardly a word any man can doubt," smiled Mr. Griswald, "since it comes from God."

Michael shook hands with his new friend after he had stepped out of the car. For a moment, as his hand rested in Mr. Griswald's, something cold touched his heart and he stared intently into the man's eyes. They were frightened and kindly and returned Michael's look with so pleading an air that he smiled.

"Thanks," said Mr. Griswald.

"What for?" asked Michael.

"For smiling at me," said his new friend.

In the days that followed, Michael continued to preach. During this time, his friends rejoiced at the good fortune that was coming to them all. But Michael knew only that the way was dark. Each time he had spoken, and each time he had felt love for the faces raised to him, and made them the promises he felt they longed for, he had felt the truth grow less. At last it seemed to him that when he stood alone, and tried to remember the divine message, it was only Sarah he remembered. Then he refreshed his spirit, not by contact with God, but with Sarah.

"I loved her," he said to himself, walking alone in the night, "because she was close to God. He tells me this now, but I knew it by myself then. She was close to God because she was such an unprotesting bit of life. The street she walked in was all the world she needed for walking. And in her purity she made a delight even of the toil that had been assigned her. She delighted in her movement beside the scrub pail as a bird might be glad to fly. She found success in the polish of a floor. And without dreams or thoughts she was able to embrace life and love it. There was no hardship or injustice for her, because, like a child, she played a game in which hardship and injustice were her favorite companions, her familiars to be loved. They could not make her see with their eyes. She saw only with her own, which were full of simplicity, and loved that which she should have hated, and embraced that which sought to ruin her. . . . Yet she told me something more than that. She told me that there is a golden age in the heart, that there is a fairytale world in which life smiles forever like a happy visitor— a fairytale that lies under the feet of Miss Rufus and the rest of them— nearly all of them. Under their feet and trampled away. . . ."

He stood in a dark street and looked up at the white leaf of dawn falling idly from the night. "What of them . . . ?" he asked himself. "What of all those who have trampled too much and buried Sarah too deep in themselves? How am I to talk to them?"

It was of Sarah he decided he would talk to the people in Hegemish.

On the night of the eighteenth Michael and his friends boarded a train that would bring them into Hegemish before dawn. They had learned that Hegemish was a town where steel was made.

It was still dark when Michael and his companions got off the train at Hegemish, where his first tabernacle waited. Dr. Holmes had sent a telegram to Mr. Griswald telling the hour of their arrival, and he hurried with Philo now from the station to look for the automobile they expected. Michael, flanked by Captain Achilles and the Giant Munso, sat on the platform, his feet on the railroad tracks, and listened to the train roar become a whisper. The night, routed by the train, returned. Silence and darkness rode the tracks, but the breast of the coming day was to be seen beyond the moon. There seemed nothing more wonderful in the world to the young Michael as he sat on the platform than to sit this way in a strange place and smell the dark prairies and watch the dawn restore the world.

Three men appeared behind Michael. One of them spoke softly.

"Are you Michael the Evangelist?" he asked.

"Yes," said Michael.

"Come along," said the figure. The Giant Munso rose with Captain Achilles under his arm.

"Not you," said the figure, "just the Evangelist. The man of God." Michael smiled at the giant.

"You wait here," he said, and two of the men took him by the arms.

"Did Mr. Griswald send you?" Michael asked as he walked between them.

"Yeah," said one of them.

In the early gloom Michael saw that the three men were stocky and heavy-faced. Two of them were scarred. He heard Dr. Holmes calling his name in the distance.

"They're calling me," said Michael.

"Never mind," one of the men muttered and his fingers tightened on Michael's arm.

"Where are you taking me?" asked Michael.

"Shut up, you fink," the other man answered.

A fist struck Michael's face. He would have fallen but the hands on his arms kept him erect. Blood began to come from his nose.

"Keep your stinkin' trap shut and come along," a voice spoke in his ear.

Dizzied from the blow, Michael continued to walk as best he could. One of the men began to talk in a hoarsened voice.

"So you're gonna preach here, huh?" he said. "You're gonna set the workers right about God, eh? Well, try preachin' to this."

A fist struck him again, filling his head with sparks. A sting remained in his eye, and the side of his face grew slowly numb.

"You lousy strikebreaker," went on the hoarsened voice, "you and your fink God. Go on, yell for your bodyguard now, And your God, too."

"What have I done?" asked Michael, blood streaming from his nose and from cuts over his eye. He felt choked and blinded.

"He don't know what he's done," sneered the voice. "He's innocent. He's a man of God."

"Listen, you sonofabitch," another of the three spoke. "Griswald brought you here to break the strike in his steel mills—and paid you plenty. So don't start claimin' you don't know what it's all about."

"A Judas, that's what you are," said the first man. "A God-damn Judas. Comin' here to hop up the hunky workers with a lot of God talk. And take their fight out of them. I suppose you didn't know that, you fink!"

"I didn't know," began Michael and a fist struck his nose, again. He sagged between the two men holding him and heard a voice saying faintly:

"You know now, you louse. And you're gonna do no preachin' in Hegemish . . . after we get through."

Another blow struck Michael's mouth. A fist in his groin made him sag and scream. A third blow on his ear deafened him. He pitched forward, but a hand seized the collar of his coat and held him up with his head hanging. For several minutes Michael remained aware of fists beating at his face. He could hear and see nothing, but in the darkness that tasted of his own blood the blows continued. He dropped to his hands and knees. A foot smashed his fingers. Another foot stamped his face into the earth and a heel ground itself deep into his cheek.

The day was bright when Michael opened his eyes but he saw only a mist. He tried to rise but he could only crawl a few feet and then collapse. His right hand was crushed and he knew he was covered with blood. The blows seemed still to be echoing in his face. Each pulse of his blood tore at his eyes and ears.

An hour later Michael woke again. This time he saw figures around him, and with a childish moan he tried to hide his face in his arms. He heard Dr. Holmes's voice calling his name and through his swollen mouth he answered faintly: "Run away. Run away."

As he lay trying to understand through the battering in his head where he was, arms lifted him into a bed.

Michael lay in a hospital for two days. On the third morning he sat up. His eyes were swollen and patches of gauze covered most of his face. Two of his fingers were in splints. The door of his room opened and Captain Achilles looked in from under the doorknob. Michael saw the tiny figure and tried to smile. The midget gestured excitedly into the hall, and his three companions appeared. They walked cautiously to the bed. The eyes of the Giant Munso were reddened and his mouth hung loosely open. They stood beside Michael's bed in a long silence till Captain Achilles began to weep.

"Are you all right?" Philo asked.

Michael nodded.

"Never mind speaking," Dr. Holmes whispered quickly. "Come on." He prodded the giant, and to Michael he added in a low voice: "We'll be outside."

The four tiptoed out of the room and returned to the wicker couch in the corridor where they had been sitting for three days.

At the end of the week, Michael left his bed. His swollen and discolored face still pained, and occasional lightnings danced in his head, but he was whole and able to walk and speak. His four friends led him to an automobile waiting outside the hospital. Their eyes were full of pity, and a desperate friendliness was in their silence. But Michael, smiling at them, understood that they were confused. They had spoken to him of how the police were working to find the men who had attacked him, and of Mr. Griswald's great concern for his recovery. But of what was most in their minds they had said nothing. Michael knew that though they loved him and looked on his battered face with anguish, he had grown dim in their souls as a champion. Pity was a difficult emotion for these freaks who were Michael's disciples. As they rode, Captain Achilles finally spoke this disillusion.

"You should have smited them all," the midget piped, banging his fist into his palm. "You shouldn't have let them do that."

The automobile turned in at the opened gate of a tall ornamental iron fence, and followed a graveled lane flanked by boxed hedges. It wound through an area of lawn and gardens and stopped before the tall doors of a large house made of white stone.

"We got to wait outside," said Dr. Holmes. "He said he wants to see you alone first."

Michael was admitted through the tall doors. He was led up a curving flight of heavily carpeted stairs, down a stone-walled corridor hung with tapestries, and into a towering wood-paneled room. The room was full of books, and its floor was covered with glowing carpets. The late afternoon sun came dimly in through heavy red curtains over its windows. In this great and heavy room, Mr. Griswald appeared less a myth and more the prosperous owner of steel mills that he was.

Michael silenced this gentleman's greetings, his pained expressions of sympathy, and his profuse apologies by telling him he would not preach in Hegemish. Michael had figured out something during his days in the hospital. This was that, if he told the workers Sarah's message, of her love of life and simple-hearted abnegation, and if they believed it, it would be used against them. It would be used by Mr. Griswald and others to make their lives still harder, and to deprive them of more things.

In vain the capitalist pleaded, telling Michael he would be safe now, speaking of police protection, and of the tabernacle that would be more crowded now that the papers were full of news about Michael. In vain he apologized for not having told Michael of the strike, which was unimportant, he said. What was important, he cried out, was that there was something wrong with the world. A devil was loose in men, a devil of strife, people killing each other for ideals and ideas, and making the world a frightening place to live in!

The stern superior-looking man humiliated himself before the youth with the deep smile on his bruised face.

"Forget me," he said, "forget the strikers. Remember only that you've got something we all need. Not only your words, Michael, and your uncommon beauty, but I saw your spirit come over that crowd like an angel's wing."

Michael looked at him, knowing that even though he told the truth, he lied. He explained to Mr. Griswald that he would never preach any more, not in Hegemish or anywhere else.

The millionaire blurted out, in seeming sincerity:

"But your sermon, Michael—the sermon about the stones. Surely it can't hurt anybody if you preach that. It's true, Michael, it's so deeply true that it's haunted me every day since I heard it."

"You've got the biggest stone," said Michael. "Lay it down first."

"I can't," said Mr. Griswald, touching Michael's arm with trembling fingers. "Listen to me—please. I believe in you—just as those four freaks do. You can add me to them—the freak of a Rich Man who believes in God and His messenger. I swear on my soul, Michael, I believe the Truth of God is in you and there's some sort of divinity in your spirit. . . . Now listen, if you don't want to preach in the tent I've put up, well and good. But you've got to preach. You'll go somewhere else and preach."

"No," said Michael, "not here or anywhere again."

The steelmaker stared at him.

"You'll keep God's voice silent?" he said softly.

"Yes," said Michael, "God's truth is only one of the beautiful stones in the field we stand in. It is one of the heaviest and largest to pick up and it makes one of the most powerful weapons with which men kill each other."

Michael raised his head and stared at the carved wooden ceiling that stretched coffin-like over the handsome room. His bruised face and swollen eyes were full of passion. He spoke to God.

"I have a memory," he said, "of having heard somewhere that the Thought of Man is Your enemy, and that it has brought chaos into the world You created so well. I can see how true this is. I can see also what endless trouble this Thought must continue to bring into Your universe, where everything else is so serene and obedient. For this Thought is a smoke that cannot be chained. It will escape from the strongest dungeons of Your will. It will trickle out of the deepest disasters with which even You can smite it. And if with Your power You destroy not only Thought but its possessors, if You slay every human who walks the Earth, it will continue to coil and uncoil in the heads of dogs and birds, of simians and other forms that will continue to take Man's place in soil, water, and air. And if You destroy not only Man but his home, if You reduce to a funeral plume of dust the planet on which we live, our Thought will still hover in the particles that remain to darken the winds of space. It will not die.

"But if You want it otherwise, it is not I who will help You.

"For Your truth is of no use to men. I have no wish to preach it to them. As death puts an end to their lives, Your wisdom puts an end to their minds. And I have seen that it is not we who are Your enemies but You who are ours. For I have seen that those who have hated men the most and warred the most violently against their dreaming and thinking have been always such humans as have had a little of Your light in their souls.

"I have no wish to preach the wisdom You have given me," Michael said, and closed his eyes, "because I like better the fragment of wisdom, the shred of cunning, we have won for ourselves out of so much disaster. And because there is no reason for us to worship You, since You are interested only in our bodies and never in our souls.

"The bird at sunrise may sing to You," said Michael, "but we do not step into light and space when we leave our bed in the morning. We do not enter a universe perfectly made for us. We awake into a world created by our own Thought. Miseries and injustices dawn for us with each sunrise and no light floods our spirit as the day brightens. Our Thought has built for us only darkness and phantoms. But if You would have it otherwise, I will not help You.

"If I did what You have asked me to do," went on Michael more softly, "I would end perhaps as another of Your redeemers once ended —in agony on a Cross. And I would be remembered as a Son of God who had suffered and died a miserable human death in order to call men's attention to Your truth, Your glory, and Your mastery over Man.

"I am not afraid of being Your redeemer and of dying on a Cross. But in the world where I live Your Cross is a little one and to die on it is a little death.

"For if You want Crosses, look down, O God, not on any son but on man writhing atop the world, and hear his cries of pain going up without end. Look on him hanging a little space above the beast's lair, nailed to time by his philosophies and crowned by his thorny dreams.

"I do not understand the mystery of his suffering," said Michael after a pause, "or the goal of his Thought. But my heart leads me to his side in the darkness and I throw away the truth You have placed in me. I will never preach Your word or dream of You again. And if You would find me, come into the darkness where I live. And if you would see a Cross, come into that world beyond the bird song where Your enemy hangs."

Michael walked from the wood-paneled room, leaving the rich man for the moment paler because of the blasphemy he had heard. Outside he met his four friends. He said nothing to them. They rode to police headquarters. There he was shown the men who had beaten him into unconsciousness. Their faces were bruised almost as much as his own. One of them, under police beating, had confessed. But Michael lied to the police. He said his assailants were much taller and in no way resembled the three being held. After some discussion the police released the three men. Michael waited for them outside the station. Leaving his friends with instructions to meet him later, he walked with the three bruised faces.

The three sluggers looked suspiciously at their victim. Their swollen faces waited sullenly for some trick from this battered youth who again walked between two of them. Nothing was said until they had gone several blocks. Then one of the men muttered something.

"Here's where we get off," Michael heard him say.

"May I come inside with you?" asked Michael.

"Come along," the man said curtly.

Michael entered a saloon. Clusters of silent angry men stood at a long bar. They were the striking workers from the steel mills and, like all workers, looked ominous in their idle postures. The interior of the saloon was dim and smelled as if it were a cavern in the sour, wet earth. The workers looked at Michael. Despite the swollen face they recognized him as the man of God brought by their arch-enemy Griswald, to break their strike o' here," a voice spoke softly from the bar.

e want in here, you punk?" another voice growled.

sluggers answered for Michael.

w," he said, pausing at the bar, "he keeps folla-ing us."

around, eh?" A beer-drinker stared at the three.

another of the sluggers, and then, with a look at Mich... .. "Not him. The cops."

The three ordered beer. Then one turned and suddenly seized Michael by both lapels and held him helpless with one hand as if he were going to punch him with the other.

"What do you want?" he demanded.

"I want to talk to you," said Michael. "I'm sorry they beat you."

The bar was silent. The angry workers sipped their mugs of beer.

"Cut out the Christ stuff," said the bruised slugger. "It don't go." He looked up and down the bar for corroboration and repeated loudly: "It don't go."

Michael nodded.

"I know," he said. "Could I have some beer?" he added to the bartender. He was served a glass mug of beer as the strikers stood watching him with their unwavering silence and anger.

Michael raised the mug.

"Here's to your strike," he said. "I hope you win."

He drank alone.

"What I wanted to say," said Michael, smiling, "is that God isn't on your side. That's one of the reasons I quit Him."

"Oh, you've quit Him?" sneered the slugger who had seized Michael by the lapels.

"Yes," he said and finished his beer. His face grew flushed.

"God doesn't know the difference between the poor and rich," Michael went on, "or between right and wrong or the good and the bad. He doesn't care about men's souls and the ideas in men's heads. I'm not preaching to you or anybody else again. But I wanted to tell you this. I want to tell you what He told me—that He hates you all."

Michael asked for another mug of beer. It was handed to him and he gulped it down. He felt happier when he looked at his listeners again.

"He wanted me to do something," said Michael.

"You mean God?" inquired one of the strikers suddenly.

"Yes," said Michael, "God."

"I see," said the striker and spat slowly and thoughtfully.

"He wanted me to do something," repeated Michael. "Not just beat your strike. But beat you. Everybody. Hand you all over to Him, like a boxful of bugs. The whole race. I didn't want to do that. That's why I quit."

Michael smiled dizzily at the blurred faces along the bar. They had moved toward him. Some of them were spitting and some were frowning violently. But Michael remained unaware of the wave of indignation he had stirred along the bar by his words. He turned to the three sluggers.

"You beat me up," he said softly to them, "but you were really beating someone else. You were beating God. And you were doing right. That's why I lied to the police. Keep on beating Him."

Michael smiled again at all the frowning faces.

"I am not a Saviour," he said, "I'm a man. And I love men. I love you all."

Michael extended his unbroken left hand for the sluggers to shake. One of them took it and pulled him to the door.

"Outside," he whispered in Michael's ear, "before somebody starts pasting you again. You're drunk."

"Good-by," said Michael in the swinging door, and waved at the dim, odorous barroom. "Don't forget me, I'm your friend, Lucifer."

He laughed and was pushed into the street. Inside, the steel strikers stood silent and angry. The bartender, wiping the place where Michael had left his beer mugs, spoke.

"That's the yellowest preacher I ever heard," he said.

The sluggers ordered more beer. They were silent. They thought the preacher had gone mad from the blows they had given him.

Michael met his four friends. He talked to them for an hour, persuading them to go back to the circus. They finally agreed and all of them thought, like the sluggers, that the beating had driven Michael crazy.

Sitting together in the day coach of the train, the four friends were silent at first. Then Dr. Holmes removed some feathers from his pocket and began dropping them listlessly to the floor.

"Cut it out," said Philo, the Human Skeleton; "no use getting the conductor sore at us, now," he added practically.

"He threw us down," said Dr. Holmes, "a fine Saviour."

There was silence.

"Not very much like the former Saviour," Dr. Holmes resumed. "The former Saviour didn't take a runout powder."

Captain Achilles puckered his face.

"I wonder what he'll do about the Dove?" he piped. "That bird's gonna hand him a lot of trouble, whether he likes it or not."

The Giant Munso, hunched in his seat, sniffled and looked out of the window. Tears clouded his pale blue eyes.

"I got an idea," said Philo, "that the bird was an optical illusion."

"It was the Holy Ghost," shrilled the midget. "Let's be careful what we say about it."

"He sold us out," said Dr. Holmes, still dropping feathers. "He was scared, that's all."

"Who sold us out?" demanded Captain Achilles.

"Michael," said the India Rubber man.

"Oh, all right," said the midget with relief, "just don't say anything against the Dove. We don't want any wrecks on this train."

"I don't know," said Philo, slowly. "I keep wondering. His last words were there is a God but He's no good."

"That's not a new philosophy," said Dr. Holmes in a lofty tone.

"It's a shame," said Captain Achilles. "I would have stuck to him to the crucifixion."

The midget paused and then added in a frightened voice: "Maybe that was the crucifixion we seen."

There was silence as the train chattered on through the prairie. The Giant Munso wept with his face turned from his friends. Tears seemed to be coming out of his skin as well as his eyes.

"We ought to figure out what happened," the midget resumed. "We were the Four Apostles. And we ought to know what happened—in case somebody asks us."

"Nobody's going to ask us," Dr. Holmes muttered.

"You can't tell," said Philo.

"I say he was crucified," piped Captain Achilles.

"I take it you are speaking figuratively," said Dr. Holmes.

"Who crucified him?" demanded Philo.

"He did himself," cried the midget shrilly. "He crucified himself. I seen him! I seen him!"

Philo pushed the tiny man off his feet against the plush seat and spoke, ignoring the midget's exultation.

"He told me once," said Philo slowly, "he told me he had a feeling he was born in Heaven and brought to earth by that Dove."

"He told you that, eh?" Dr. Holmes snorted, and slapped his hands free of the last of his feathers. "Well, if I were you, I'd forget it."

"Why should he lie?" persisted Philo.

"Listen," said Dr. Holmes, "he lied to one of us. Because he told me his mother was a scrublady in New York. Now, I ask you, which of those two statements sounds like a lie? What did he tell you about where he was born, Captain?"

The midget jumped to his feet on the seat.

"He told me his father was a famous doctor worth millions of dollars," he piped.

Dr. Holmes snorted again.

"That's one of the troubles with religious-minded people," he said. "They always lie like hell."

"He sold out to the Devil," Captain Achilles piped, "and crucified himself for good measure. That's the long and short of it."

"Shut up," said Dr. Holmes. "I want to think this through."

The apostles sat in silence. The memory of Michael's battered face as they had looked on it the morning he was found in the ditch haunted them. And the thought came to them that they had not been the apostles of a messenger from God but the friends of a poor, weak boy. At length Philo spoke.

"I think the story is," he said, "that we all lost our heads. That's what people expect of freaks, anyway. So they'll forget it."

The Giant Munso continued to weep and sniffle as the train entered the night.

Michael's life after his last sermon contained only a single miracle and that was the miracle of his survival through the years of pain and misfortune that followed.

After he left Hegemish, Michael found work in a steel mill in South Chicago. Here he spent several years in the furnace rooms. His body, never powerful, grew gaunt and dry with the blasting heat of the furnace pits and crucibles.

In South Chicago, where he was unknown as an evangelist, he made a few friends, and this was a recompense for the daydream that he had resolutely put away from him. Daily he moved only among these poor people, and what he saw filled and overfilled his heart with a great kindness and pity. It was this love that burned away the last shreds of the Angel Michael in him and that made him each day weaker and more human. In this love, all the powers he might have nursed as his heritage from Heaven disappeared.

Seven years of toil in the glare and burn of the furnace pits removed all of Michael's youth. He was turned into one of those gaunt hungry-eyed workers under whose strong muscles a perpetual weariness lies. This weariness finally dropped him exhausted out of the ranks of the laboring ones, like some over-used animal that had shed its vigor, and he wandered off. He moved through the snow, rain, and sun of the Middle West, helping out on farms and sleeping often in fields and under trees.

At times, lonely and hungry, he sat beside a dusty road and watched birds move in the summer sky, and wondered if the Dove would ever appear again. When he found himself looking eagerly at the birds he became shamefaced, and tried to keep certain thoughts out of his head. These thoughts were about his having been a Divine messenger and having heard God's voice. Although these things seemed to him still to have actually occurred, he began to attribute their seeming occurrence to something wrong in his head. Remembering the Voice that had spoken to him, he would smile sheepishly. And if there were people around him he would smile at them quickly, hoping they would be unable to detect what he thought.

One day, after two years of wandering, Michael came on the circus he had known as a boy. It was a summer afternoon and the meadow was alive with the familiar sounds and movements of the toy world he had once known. He watched the people crowding the scalloped and minareted tent, their faces already happy with the promised wonders. He walked into the sideshow tent, wondering if his friends Philo, the Giant Munso, Dr. Holmes, and Captain Achilles would still be sitting on the platform. He saw a midget and an India Rubber man and a giant, but they were strangers. At first he was depressed. Then he felt relieved, for he would not have known what to say to the four freaks who had been his apostles—except that he had been a bigger freak than any of them.

At night when the tents were being struck, Michael offered himself to the boss canvasman as an experienced hand. He was hired. Thereafter he worked in the circus as a razorback and traveled with it, as he had once done, from meadow to meadow. None of the few who had known him recognized him, for he had changed greatly from the tall glowing youth who had once brought God into their midst.

An hour of happiness came to Michael. He fell in love with one of the pretty girls who rode the horses. Her name was Josephine de Ballo. This young girl, walking at night with Michael and listening to the softness of his voice, and looking a great deal into his gentle eyes, fell in love with him—as she knew she should not have done. For, belonging to the lowliest of the circus personnel, he was no one for an aspiring young equestrienne to marry. Yet there was no resisting this sad and curious man who loved her, and who seemed as happy as a child at her side. And Josephine, who had always had an easy heart to give, gave it to Michael and overwhelmed him.

Some months later Michael's wife became pregnant and was forced to quit her work. She and Michael left the circus, and Michael, still happy, still full of gratitude for this hour of dream and sweetness that had finally come to him, grew ambitious. He found work as a waiter and kitchen helper in a country hotel. His child was born in an unpainted little wooden house on the edge of the village where he worked. It was a beautiful and healthy son. Michael's face grew smiling. He smiled on the world through the months that followed, and an endless springtime was in his eyes. One day he brought his wife to the photographer's gallery in the hotel where he served and Josephine beamed over his son as he held them both in his arms and was photographed. This was the only gift Michael was able to give his wife, for there was hardly enough money for them to live on, and never any left over for gifts or pleasures. But it seemed to Michael they needed none of these and that his wife and son were enough riches and entertainment for any man. Josephine talked sometimes of returning to the circus, but her figure had changed and idleness had taken away her girlhood ambitions. She continued to love Michael and her child, who was more beautiful than any infant she had ever seen pictured. This was truer than mothers' opinions usually are, for young Michael, as he took to walking and chattering, was as radiant as an angel. Unlike his father, whose hair was black, young Michael had blond clinging curls. He filled the days and nights with a marvelous excitement for his parents. For though she had given up her ambitions to become an equestrienne, Josephine grew very ambitious for her son. When he was two, she began training him to walk on his hands. He learned to tumble and to sit on a trapeze that Michael had rigged for him over the vegetable garden. Here he swung and yelled and tumbled, and Josephine, watching him, heard the faraway music of the circus she loved, and Michael dreamed of him growing up strong and agile and never having to feel the blast of the furnace pits or the humiliation of the waiter's apron.

Then tragedy struck the house in which the little family lived. When he was three, little Michael was run over while playing in the road. An automobile hit him. He was carried into the house by a policeman. He breathed for an hour, although his ribs were broken and his head crushed, and blood kept pouring from his mouth. Then he died, and Michael, who had come rushing home in his waiter's apron, wept. Josephine sat white and mute. She wept only when they lowered the little box containing her son into the ground. Here she remained kneeling, and tears shook her body. There was no comfort in Michael's arms. She raised her face to the chilly morning sky and began to pray wildly through her sobbing. She prayed to God to take her little Michael in His arms, to see that he was happy and to preserve his soul forever.

Michael, her husband, looked at her in silence as she prayed. He tried to join her, but as he raised his head to the sky, a blankness came into his heart. Bewildered, he ran over the words of prayer he knew, looking for some he could utter. But he was unable to pray. Dim thoughts peered into his mind, and he grew confused. He fell forward on the fresh grave and buried his cheek in the newly turned earth and muttered the name of his son over and over into the ground.

Michael returned to his work as waiter and kitchen helper. His heart hung like a stone from his throat, but he smiled at the travelers around the dining-room tables and took their orders, and later washed the dishes they had emptied. There were a few who knew of his loss, and for a week or two were kind and soft-spoken with him. But after a short time they forgot and became unaware of the grief that hung in his throat. Soon no one knew his life was darkened, and he moved without the aid of human understanding through the painful days and nights.

But the tragedy had not ended for him. One day in the early spring when he came home from his work, he found the little wooden house empty. He waited till late at night for Josephine, thinking she had gone to visit somewhere. As the night deepened, Michael grew frightened and was going to run to the police, when he saw an envelope on Josephine's pillow. He opened it and read a letter she had written, saying she was going back to the circus and couldn't live with him any more because her heart was empty and their lives were too dull.

"Although I love you still," the letter read, "I can't stand to be buried alive like a nobody. It is driving me crazy, and when I look into the future, that drives me crazy too. You will be better off without me, in the long run. I will always remember you and little Michael and, oh, please forgive me. I can't help it. . . ."

Michael put the letter in his coat and it stayed there for several months. He read it two or three times a day as he continued to wait on tables and clean dishes, and again as he lay alone in the bed his wife had left. So deep was the pain he felt that he did not speak of it, even to himself. He felt as if something had been amputated from him, and he woke in the night crying. His tears wet the pillow on which his wife's head had lain, and when the darkness and the silence became unbearable he spoke her name softly, over and over. This would soothe him and he would fall asleep, as if her name, like a mother's hand, had taken the fright from his heart.

No curse ever came from Michael. His pain was as much for the pretty girl into whose life he had brought so much sorrow and trouble as for himself. He took to walking in the country roads at night, remembering their hours of sweetness together. His eyes stared at the star-brimming vaults over his head as he walked, and some of the heroic thoughts he had had as a boy returned to him. But he was diffident about thinking them, for they reminded him of matters too strange now and too dim to pursue.

One night Michael failed to turn back in his walking. He walked on into a field where he lay down and slept. And in the morning he was again a wanderer. From this morning on, luck seemed always against him, and his mind, inuring itself to misfortune, grew emptier and emptier of the Michaels he had been. Such jobs as he found he lost quickly, for the times had grown worse and the world of the workers appeared to be growing smaller, like the pond in which the ugly duckling swam.

At times, sitting around wood fires with other wanderers and looking into the night grown deep and large above him, Michael would remember some elation that had been his, and he would speak in turn to the disinherited ones around the little wood fires. But words were unable to unlock the hiding place into which Michael, his vision, and his youth had disappeared.

The New War came. This war, so long foreseen and so wildly babbled about by the terrified nation, swept up millions of men; cleaned, shaved, and dressed them in its insignia; and set them across the Pacific. Michael was among those who marched, drilled, and ended up lying in tropic trenches, cursing with fever and vermin, and heroically firing their guns and trotting bravely forward into death.

During this time no thought at all came to his head, but his heart surged with a desperate reawakening of the love he had felt long ago. His heart embraced his comrades as they lay cursing under the heavy blankets of sun, fever-ridden and with an incorrigible snarl and laugh for all that touched them—even death. They were of the same men he had known in the mills and in his wanderings, but here around him they no longer seemed the casual, drifting figures of those other days. They were men concentrated into a single mood. This mood was not of war or courage or anger against an enemy, but a simpler mood of manhood. They seemed, now that they lay fevered, cursing, and dying, to have for the first time become men, who had been only strangers and exiles before.

Michael was gassed in one of the attacks. A fire burned in his lungs and throat. He was carried into the trenches taken by his comrades. Later he was removed to a hospital. This time there were no bruises to be seen on him but inside, invisible, his organs were shattered with poison. He spewed and screamed through nights that lit and relit themselves like flames in his tissues. But though he burned through months he was not consumed.

After a year he came out of a hospital in New York, pronounced cured, and for another year he crawled about the streets, a yellowed shrunken man clinging to the fringes of life. He slept in verminous beds, found food in charity wagons and on fly-covered saloon bars. But he was not consumed. Life trickled and then once more began to pulse hopefully in his maimed tissues. Michael resumed his wandering, working in factories, restaurants, and among cattle on farm lands. Wherever he went now, he heard the rumblings of deeds to come. The great and scattered body of labor was threatening to raise its fist.

When he was forty-two, Michael came back to New York, still spewing and coughing at night, but darkened by sun and wind. One evening, walking the city streets in the rain, he saw a familiar face. He stopped in the crowd, looked long at the face, and then followed it. It was painted but gaunt almost as his own and its eyes were ugly with a rim of charcoal. He came next to the face and said softly: "Josephine."

The face looked at him and its voice simpered: "Hello," and the charcoaled eyes smiled coyly.

"Come along, big boy," it said. "Let's get out of this damn rain."

"Josie," he whispered, "I'm Michael."

The face grew pale under its paint and Michael took the arm of the woman who had been his wife and walked on in the crowd with her.

"I got no place to take you," said Michael. "Where do you live?"

Josephine pointed to the west of the city.

The rain fell on the crowd in which they walked, and in the wet twilight the city opened the huge umbrella of its lights. They entered the house in which Josie said she lived, and she whispered to him as they went in—as if it were a matter of great importance: "My name ain't Josie in here. It's Belle. I had to change it because they got two Josies already. We'll go upstairs," said Josie. "Maybe she won't see us."

"Who won't?" asked Michael, staring at her.

"Madam Hattie," said Josie, as she led him up a worn stairway. "I work here. It's a house, you know."

Michael nodded.

"She's pretty mean," said Josie, looking back at him and smiling with her mouth twitching.

In a dim lace-curtained bedroom that looked out on an alley, Michael and the woman who had been his wife lay on the sagging white iron bed. Michael held the yellow curls against his bosom. They reminded him in a hideous way of the little Michael's head he had buried. Josephine tried to talk, and Michael thought of questions to ask. But neither of them had any words. They lay clinging to each other in their wet clothes. The poison in Michael's tissues began to burn him. He coughed, and Josephine begged him not to make any noise. After a long silence, this woman, who had been so pretty and whom Michael kept seeing in the photograph he had once had taken of him and her and his son all beaming at one another, began to cry. As she wept she made a heavy frightened sound that was like a wail, half agonized and half idiotic.

Michael started coughing, and his coughing and Josephine's wailing brought the dreaded Madam Hattie to the door. This was a fat-shouldered creature with dulled black eyes. She stood looking at the two figures clinging together on the bed and demanded to know what in hell was going on. Josephine sat up and ended her wailing as quickly as if she had been only pretending her distress.

"He's an old friend," she began.

Madam Hattie interrupted viciously.

"If he ain't got any money he gets out," she said. "We ain't running no charity institution."

Michael would have argued, but a man with even fatter shoulders and duller eyes than Madam Hattie's appeared behind her. Josie whispered to him quickly to go away. Michael tried to take her in his arms again. But she jumped from him and stood screaming harshly for him to get out. Curses and foul words came from her twitching mouth.

Michael returned to the rain, but he was changed. He looked at the crowded street with rage in his heart. He was not angry at the faces he saw or at the eyes that looked curiously at his blazing expression as they passed. But at something else, something much littler and yet looming behind the crowd—at a Thought, an Idea, a Scheme, which seemed to him suddenly hideous. He walked slowly, and the towers that lined the streets became to him caverns in which a monster lurked. Although he had known misfortune and injustice all his life, he had never cried back at them before. Now the years of misery and the memories of his pain all seemed to explode in his soul.

He felt the face of the painted street woman, who had once been so sweet, wailing against his broken and poisoned bosom. And her wail and his own pain rose in him like a battle cry. He looked up desperately at the monster he had seen in the gleaming towers of the city. Why should this monster, coiling like a lighted dragon over the heads of the crowd, remain unchallenged? There was another monster in his heart and in the hearts of those like him—the monster of pain, dark and hidden. Michael's heart opened and this long cowering beast emerged.

From this hour Michael became one of those who met secretly in halls, basements, and barns; who plotted and organized and inflamed one another with angry and prophetic words. He was never among the leaders but among those who listened and followed. But his set face, his wild smile, his curious concentration, as if he himself were a bullet aimed at that monster in the towers, won him a little place in the Revolution. He commanded a group of men when the first barricades went up. Again he lay under clouds of gas and the whine of shell, and again he fought. Desperate and heroic men fought beside him. Towers were tumbled, streets blasted, and fires lighted in many proud sectors of the Republic. For a year the Revolution ripped at the fabric of a society grown hateful and too painful to those who lay at its bottom. Driven from town to town by superior armies, Michael's cause stumbled into disaster. It went down, blasted by too many guns, and those who survived its last defeat were hunted.

Michael had not believed, despite all he had seen, that men could be so cruel as were these who came now in pursuit of his scattered comrades. Gone were the easy-spoken rulers of the democracy, and in their place angry and implacable minds scurried like hounds through the nation, leaping at the throat of every contradiction and every lingering hope. Michael, who had dreamed to make the world a better place, found himself unforgiven for his dream. He hid himself, and hid what was harder to hide, the very color and smell of his mind, from these hounds. And again, despite the poison still burning in his tissues and the despair emptying his heart of all hope, he survived.

He resumed his life of wandering, finding small tasks that kept him fed. He was now nearing fifty, and no longer tall or straight. His body was bent, his hair whitened. He coughed at night and felt his tissues grow weaker with the fire that never quitted them. He became silent, and for a few years longer kept himself alive with the aid of the government that had risen triumphantly over the barricades. This government was proud to take care of its citizens, and when citizen Michael, shuffling wearily from street to street, was called to its attention, it provided him with employment. He was given a flashlight, a stool to sit on, and a large empty warehouse to watch each night.

Now there was no more left of Michael than of a machine long dismantled, rusted, and discarded. Yet as he sat on his night watchman's stool, his flashlight on his withered thighs, there was one thing still Michael that remained and that had never changed. This was the look old Sarah had left him as a heritage.

Though his mind had long ago grown clumsy with disuse and disease, and what had once been the remainder of his wisdom had become as tattered as his clothes, this look of tenderness remained fixed as a star in his eyes. His eyes had always smiled on other eyes, and when Michael had lost the words with which to speak their meaning, they had spoken in their smile, saying always, life is sweet somewhere in the dark.

Toward the last of his life, his bad health almost entirely dimmed his perceptions and there came to his wrinkled face the same half-crazed smile Sarah had turned on him in his childhood. He came to work with the night, holding a flashlight in his hand. Coughing, he made the rounds of the empty warehouse, sending his light into its unoccupied shadows, and returned to sit on his stool in the doorway. Sometimes men older but no more battered than himself would join him and talk. Listening to them relate their tales of misfortune, and recite their own little tattered hopes for tomorrow, Michael would smile at them and feel a warmth in his tired body. Though he no longer knew himself, he still knew life; and the less he became, the deeper grew the warmth of his heart in which he rested.

In the third year of his employment by the government of hounds, Michael caught a cold. He continued, however, walking through the shadows of the empty warehouse, fearful of losing his job if he stayed away. One night he collapsed. He was found in the morning lying on the floor, fevered and too weak to move. As he lay on the hard boards he remembered fists that had once battered him, gas and bullets and hungers that had continued this battering, and he sighed for fear this heat now in his head would be the last blow. He desired to live. When he was taken to the crowded ward of the city's largest hospital, where others like himself lay spent and fevered, he still desired to live.

On a bed surrounded by men moaning with pain and crying in delirium lay Michael, who had once been an Angel and who had been sent by God to redeem the world. He lay with his face shrunken, and whimpered in his fever like a little dog run over and left in the middle of the road.

His fever increased, and the interne who made the rounds of the hospital wards reported that the patient in Bed 9 would die in a day or so. This report occasioned no stir in the hospital. There was no little group of relatives pacing and chattering at the end of the corridor and waiting for the dreaded news. There were no friends to hear it over the telephone. The nurses passed with a perfunctory look at the chart that hung on Bed 9, and on which every two hours the thermometer and pulse readings appeared like the nearing footsteps of death.

Michael, unknown and unmourned, lay dying in the epidemic ward of this overcrowded hospital. Nurse, interne, doctor, and orderly who looked casually at him saw no more than an old man with a bad medical history, as Michael's gas-shattered tissues and the many years of malnutrition were called; an old man such as must always be dying some time. They noticed the fear of death in his eyes, and the night nurse, who despite her youth was used to this look, wondered, as she always did when she saw it, why people so shattered and friendless should be so frightened to die. What was there that could be worse than the darkness of their lives, thought this young nurse, and why did they want to hang on to nothing? It was true, they sometimes sighed when Death came, as if they realized in their last minutes the mistake they had made by living and desiring to live. And probably this white-haired old man, whimpering in his fever, would also sigh when his only remaining friend appeared.

The night nurse smoothed the pillows under Michael's burning head and looked over at the other beds in the ward. How alike they all were, she thought, all these half-dead brought in from the streets. Here in the ward their empty lives more than their disease made a circle around their beds, and they lay exposed in their loneliness— as unvisited as fish pulled out of some far-away sea. She wondered, as she marked another footstep on the chart, how long it would be before she would have to remake this bed. Then she straightened and listened calmly for a moment to the whimpering and moaning in the dimly lighted ward. It was like standing in a graveyard, she thought, listening to the dead going home.

The night nurse walked slowly out of the ward and closed the door on these little last sounds of life, and Michael, who lay near a window, continued his dying, as nameless and unattended as the grave into which he would soon disappear.

But there were eyes that watched. God looked through the window and searched for the Angel Michael whom He had loved. At His side were the two who had taken Michael's place—the Angels Malliol and Azriel.

"He is in here," said God, holding the epidemic ward of the hospital before their eyes, "but which of them is he? Their voices are all the same and their faces are like brothers', and they are without names."

The Angel Malliol pointed to one who tossed unshaven on a pillow.

"No," said God, "there will be something in his eyes by which to recognize him." Then He added softly: "There he is by the window."

The Angels Malliol and Azriel looked at a battered face with whitened hair.

"The one who has become silent?" asked Malliol.

"Yes," said God, "he is Michael."

"He is dead," whispered the Angel Azriel.

"No," said God, "he is listening to his brothers moaning. Look how tender his eyes are. There is a dream in his head. He hears someone laughing. An old woman's laughter is in his ears. And he sees her. He imagines she is in the room and he watches her move on her hands and knees from bed to bed."

"What is she doing?" asked the Angel Malliol.

"Scrubbing," said God. "She scrubs the floor and Michael watches her."

God was silent.

"He dies looking at her," He spoke at length, "he dies without asking for Me. Michael, Michael, turn your eyes to Me."

"He keeps smiling," said the Angel Malliol softly.

"Because he dreams," said God. And suddenly a great compassion came into His voice.

"He dies as My enemy," God spoke, "smiling and unregenerate. Look at him who was once so radiant. Now shrunken and miserable, discarded and unknown. All the terrors of life have burned in his soul. All the pain of unreason and injustice has ached in his heart. He has feasted only on defeat. Wounds and sorrow have tormented him. And now he lies among faces like his own. He whom I sent as a Redeemer dies as the lowliest and most forgotten of men. No eyes weep for him. No songs will be born for him. He will be buried and he will vanish and there will be none to speak his name and none will know that he was one apart and that My Truth was in him.

"Yes," said God, "he failed Me. He betrayed Me and blasphemed against Me. Yet My heart softens. For hidden in his blasphemy there are love and courage. Look how his eyes refuse to lift to Me but continue to smile on the world. Look how this man tormented and crucified by life still turns to it with love.

"O suffering one," said God softly, "for whom do you suffer? What gain is there in your agony? My Angel, once so wise, where is your wisdom?"

"He moans again," said the Angel Azriel.

Tears clouded the eyes of the Angel Malliol.

"I loved him," he said.

"I too," said God.

There was a pause, and then God spoke so sadly that a mist filled the hearts of the Angels.

"I remember," said God, "the hour of his betrayal when he threw away the truth I had placed in him and ceased to be My Son. And bade Me, if I wanted to see him again, come look for him in the darkness, hanging on a Cross as My enemy. There is that darkness, there that Cross, and there he hangs. My light is nowhere round him. And yet something dim glows about his head. It is the light of humanity."

"I can see no light," whispered the Angel Azriel.

"Nor I," said Malliol, looking eagerly.

"It is too feeble for your eyes," said God. And His own eyes wandered from Michael.

"Look," He went on, "this light is everywhere over the earth. A wretched little glitter such as hovers on Michael's head. Look, above the blaspheming of Me and tormenting of one another, this sad little light is everywhere."

"He once spoke of their souls," said the Angel Malliol.

"How long, Michael," God said softly, "how long, little man who has forsaken Me, how long will you stay on your Cross?"

God was silent.

"A long time," He said then more softly, "even as we reckon time. Ah, Michael, there is none who watches you but Me, and none to weep over you but the Angels. And you have not lived as I ordered or died as I desired. And none in the world is the better for your living or the wiser for your dying. None in the world.

"But I, Michael, hear a prayer and see a light, and I turn to all those on the Cross beside you, to all those who have left Me. I speak to you a last time out of My love. Michael, I have seen your Cross in the darkness. Michael, I shall watch that never-empty cross you have shown Me. I shall listen without anger to the blasphemies that rise from it. And I shall wait for a face to glow in the darkness.

"Only now, Michael, remember Me once, for I too am part of the wisdom you sought. I am a little part of Chaos. Michael, hear Me, you have not died in vain."

In the dimly lighted ward, the burning head of Michael heard a sound. His eyes turned to the window, and on the ledge outside he saw a white Dove. A faint gurgle came from its throat. He stared bewilderedly. As the Dove cooed, words came into his head, familiar and far away. He could not distinguish them. His fever converted them into echoes and caused them to sound as vague as music. But he kept staring at the white Dove outside the window whose whiteness seemed to fill the night. He smiled at the little throat ballooning with its curious gurgle of greeting and lamentation.

"Little Dove," said Michael, "it is cold outside."

Then he closed his eyes and died.

The Mystery of the Fabulous Laundryman

I WILL WRITE this story out as it was told to me with the hope that you will believe it, as did I, listening to the bibulous and rococo verbiage of Mr. Dick McCarey.

In the days when I was a newspaperman such a tale as my friend McCarey unleashed between his first and fifteenth drinks in that buzzing Harlem speakeasy would have sent me bouncing into the night to run it down, nor would I have rested till the last detail had been garnered and verified and the whole thing blazoned across a front page. (A statement, this, which such of my erstwhile editors as happen upon these words may very likely challenge with snorts. But what newspaperman, having quit that daft profession, does not remember himself as one of its heroes? And this is not so much a boast as an obeisance to a lost and glamorous vocation.)

The braves of the press today seem to me a less gaudy lot than those I once knew as colleagues. But that is perhaps due to the romanticism which distance and a thousand lies throw upon the past. This McCarey, however, who will in a moment take the floor, is of that species which rather egotistically I choose to fancy extinct. He is of that tribe that once practiced journalism as if it were Holy Orders.

Mr. McCarey was sitting by himself in a corner of the noisy, foggy barroom when I spied him this night and he was a man full of truculence and contempt, as I expected him to be although I hadn't seen him for a year.

"Hello," I said, "how's Parnell this evening?"

Mr. McCarey looked up and from the fact that his eyes failed to blaze at the name Parnell I knew that the highball before him was his first. For my friend McCarey, despite a dourness and cynicism derived from twenty years of newspaper work, is one who, having a sufficient number of drinks under his belt, will never fail to rise and do battle in behalf of that last most confused and ineffectual Irish patriot, Mr. Parnell.

Mr. McCarey grinned and beckoned me to sit opposite him.

"What are you doing in this foul town?" he said, laboring as always under the delusion that I was, despite five years' residence in Manhattan, an alien. But this was a rather general attitude held by Mr. McCarey toward men and women encountered in the secret barrooms that were his stamping ground—that they were all aliens, all wanderers with their hearts in faraway places. Such noble and romantic concepts are peculiar to the colleagues of my past.

"Still in search of fame and fortune," I answered him.

"Oho!" said Mr. McCarey and sneered.

His voice will bear mentioning that you may hear him. It was a husky, rushing voice whose most characteristic tones were those of boundless and derogatory anger. He spoke chiefly in sneers but the sneers, these, not of small frustration but of a large and tumultuous romanticism which found the world too dingy for its practice.

Then, looking me slowly up and down, Mr. McCarey remarked, "Same old suit of clothes, eh?"

I nodded and this brief confession of my unimproved estates appeared to lighten the McCarey mood. His swollen but still boyish face relaxed, his lip uncurled and his Celtic eye softened.

"How's the world been treating you?" I said.

"The world," said Mr. McCarey with an angry squint, "has seen fit to harass and bedevil me beyond the power of speech. You are looking upon a man who is one of the foul favorites of misfortune."

Turning his squint on the bartender some thirty feet to the leeward, Mr. McCarey cried out, "Here, you foul Corsican. Another glass of that peculiar liquor."

"I'll have one too," I said.

Mr. McCarey held up two fingers and the barkeep nodded.

"You are looking upon a man," then resumed Mr. McCarey, seemingly entranced by this locution, "who is one of the darlings of disaster."

He laughed cruelly as if he were a merciless spectator of his own distress and fell silent, making faces the while of deep inner meditation.

"What," I inquired, "is the general cause of your depression—women, debts or the ennui of a noble soul?"

"The cause of my depression," said Mr. McCarey, "is a laundryman. Oh, what a laundryman!" The Celtic eyes fluttered and a sigh shook the McCarey frame from head to foot. "You are looking upon a man," he added, falling after a pause into his favorite rodomontade, "who bears in his bosom a secret so fabulous, so heartbreaking as to render him speechless. Speechless!" he repeated loudly, and favored the coterie of drinkers draped around the bar in front of us with a carnivorous glare.

"Let's get out of this fish trap," he said after having sneered and squinted separately at a dozen of the customers. "Hey, you peculiar Aztec!" This brought the waiter. "Rechnung, bitte. Verstehen sie? The bill," he added, translating contemptuously. "Here are your thirty pieces of silver," he said with a high aversion for the whole transaction. "Count them, ingrate." To me he said, "Come on."

I started for the door but Mr. McCarey moved in an arc and, with an unexpected list, tacked into an unoccupied corner. Here, overturning a chair and kicking it savagely out of his path, he sat down in another.

"Ober kellner!" he bawled. "Hey, you foul Swiss! Some service here. If you please!"

Mr. McCarey would have fought for Parnell now.

"This place," he confided abruptly to me, "has one asset which distinguishes it among its horrible ilk. It is the watering trough of that foulest of all bipeds, Monsoor Gavin, my esteemed city editor."

"What paper are you on now?" I asked.

"None," said Mr. McCarey loudly. "I have tonight severed my association with the depraved press and as soon as Monsoor Gavin sticks his snout into this tallyho I am going to cool him off and lay him to rest."

Mr. McCarey, despite his scowl, seemed appeased by this pronouncement. He smiled sullenly and, ogling the doorway through which his enemy was to appear, lifted his glass and seemed to drink not his liquor but his foe's very blood.

"I would like to tell you about this laundryman," he said. "One reason being that it is slowly driving me mad. And the other being that Monsoor Gavin is a toad among toads, a snake and a varlet whom it will give me a great pleasure to betray. Foully."

This last word was a happy mouthful.

"The laundryman's name was Meyer," he went on. "What was that name that Mary Queen of Scots had written on her heart?"

"Calais," I said.

"Calais," repeated Mr. McCarey. "Well, the name Meyer is written on my heart. Meyer the laundryman."

Again Mr. McCarey laughed cruelly as if there were within him a Greek chorus cued to deride his hurt whenever he expressed it. Having ended his laughter, however, he looked at me with so sad and appealing an eye that I nodded sympathetically.

"May the angels guard his sleep," he said.

"Is this laundryman dead?" I asked.

"Yes, thank God," said Mr. McCarey. "Dead and under a slab in Potter's Field."

"What happened to him?" I asked.

"Words fail me," said Mr. McCarey and his eye, the one that wasn't squinting, clouded with tears. He swallowed his fifth drink in silence and then tossed his head in the manner of a bull entering the arena and glared about him.

"It's a foul world," he said.

"Let's hear," I insisted.

"Well, I can't tell you everything," he said. "My lips are sealed regarding certain matters. I'm sorry."

Mr. McCarey assumed the look of a sibyl and for several minutes he gazed at me darkly.

"I can tell you this much," he said finally, "Meyer died on a hot night a month ago, shot through the head twice. And his right hand chopped off at the wrist, for good measure. But I don't want you to misunderstand me. I am not one who sits in mourning for Meyer's death. It's his living, his ten years over the washtub in Harlem, that unnerves me when I think of it."

Mr. McCarey grew grave and squinted with both eyes.

"I can tell you this much," he said. "He was a short, thin old man with a thoughtful face and a weak chin. He came to Harlem ten years ago and moved into one of those putrid tenements on Troop Street— a hovel reeking with poverty and disaster. That's the kind of a home Meyer moved into," grinned Mr. McCarey as if in derision of his literary flourishes, "one of those edifices that seem built out of sweat and refuse. He took a single room, renting it off a monstrous wench named Mrs. Maum. An oily, sweating behemoth in a wrapper who tipped the scales at 314 pounds. One of those female hippogriffs that seem to thrive best, peculiarly enough, in districts where food and space are scarcest."

Another drink was directed with grace and thoughtfulness down the McCarey gullet.

"Meyer moved in with this unsightly piece of tenement fauna," he went on, "and started taking in washing. Yes, he pursued his career as a laundryman in the basement. You know what he did? He went around all day, soliciting customers. And then on the next day he presided at the tubs. Nobody ever looked at him or spoke to him. He just shuffled back and forth fetching his wash and carrying it in a basket—

on his head, by God. On his head in a basket," repeated Mr. McCarey. "Tie that!"

I nodded blankly at this challenge.

"Tie that," insisted Mr. McCarey, full of an odd excitement.

i changed my tactics and this time shook my head in impotence and Mr. McCarey was appeased.

"I thought so," he said and looked grim. "It's a foul world," he added, "full of horrible and fantastic things."

Again there was silence during which Mr. McCarey communed and debated the ways of life and washed down the secret results of his cerebration with another highball.

"Well, there's no use in hiding anything," he resumed. "Anyway I can tell you this much. This foul dinosaur, Madam Maum, was a widow with a weazened and half-idiot babe in arms, when Meyer moved in. And what attracted her beautiful ferret's eyes was the fact that Meyer spent all his hard-earned nickels buying new bolts for his door, putting steel bars across his windows and boarding himself in like some daffy old boy with a nightmare on his heels."

Mr. McCarey paused to ogle the door and his thoughts shifted angrily.

"Monsoor Gavin," he said, "is overdue. His dog sled is usually along by this time."

"What's wrong with the Monsoor?" I asked.

"Very, very many things," said Mr. McCarey. "He is a skulking ape that it will afford me considerable pleasure to cool off in seventeen shades of lavender. That's as much as I can say now."

True to his word Mr. McCarey lapsed again and fell to making menacing faces at his liquor glass. Then he laughed cruelly and said with a growl:

"He didn't have a friend. Not a friend."

"Who?" I asked.

"Meyer. Meyer," said Mr. McCarey. "Meyer, this fabulous laundry-man. Not a human soul to talk to. Not one human being to take his hand."

"And why should they do that?" I asked.

"Because," said Mr. McCarey, "he was the loneliest, saddest creature alive in the world. What a life for him!"

"Who?" I asked.

And my friend McCarey shut his eyes and laughed with greater cruelty than ever this evening.

"There are some thing that can't be told," he said. "But this much I can tell you. He was up at dawn, washing in the tubs. In the afternoon he tottered through the streets, that foul basket on his head. He always showed up at six in a cigar store a block away and bought a package of cigarettes. One package a day. And then home and to bed and asleep behind his bolts and bars by eight."

"Not a very interesting regime," I said.

"Is that so?" said Mr. McCarey, ogling me as if I had been transformed into the mysterious foe, Monsoor Gavin himself. "Is that so!" he repeated. "Well, I beg to differ."

Rebuked, I beat to the leeward and inquired casually, "What happened to Meyer?"

"All these peculiar didoes on the part of this laundryman," said Mr. McCarey, "stirred the female curiosity of that horrible creature Mrs. Maum, who began to set her cap for Meyer. And there," he deflected himself with a snarl, "there you have the eternal feminine. Love coming to bud among the ashcans. Cupid bombarding this hippogriff with a battering-ram. This dismal squaw used to lie in wait for Meyer as he came shuffling home, puffing on a cigarette. Ready to make wassail she was. Primed for the kill, her five chins and three stomachs jiggling seductively. What a foul Cleopatra! But Meyer was proof against these blandishments. He chose to ignore them. He said good evening to her and so much for romance. But, mark you, there was a woman scorned and roundly."

"Come," I said quietly, "who was this Meyer?"

But Mr. McCarey appeared not to hear this question which had begun to aggravate me. A smoky look was on his face.

"Imagine this man," said Mr. McCarey, "living like that for ten years. Friendless and chained to a washtub like a Carthaginian slave. All sorts of fantastic things happened in the world during these ten years but none of them as fantastic as this that I'm telling you—Meyer at the washtubs. Meyer with a basket on his head. And nothing as heartbreaking. What a laundryman!"

I settled back in my chair, deciding on silence and indifference as the most effective measures. But Mr. McCarey was walking the ways of his secret and had no eyes for my tactics. He drank with dignity as I kept silent, and appeared to be toasting the dead and gone hero of his tale.

"Monsoor Gavin," he said, setting the glass on the table with ominous poise, "has heard that I am lying in wait for him and is shunning this horrible rendezvous like a plague spot."

"Let's hear of Meyer's death," I said.

"On a hot night," said Mr. McCarey wit han unexpected rush of words, "full of that summer steam which the dwellings of the poor begin to exhale no sooner does the foul sun go down; and in a darkness mixed with dust, cinders and disease that turned the shadows into pumice stones; amid these wretched and famine-haunted scenes Meyer was done to death and his right hand chopped off.

"I can tell you this much and no more," Mr. McCarey squinted cautiously at me. "The police arrived at ten o'clock and found Meyer's room locked, the doors bolted from the inside, mind you. The windows barred. The street agog with the news that there had been a murder done. Mrs. Maum, that dismal squaw, had heard two shots and come wallowing out of the house like a square rigger with her mouth full of screams. The foul police whacked away trying to get into Meyer's room and couldn't. They were thwarted. They brought axes and battered down the wretched door and there was Meyer, murdered and mutilated on the floor."

Mr. McCarey grew wistful. He lit a cigarette with a great deal of grace. And he stared morosely into the foggy air of the speakeasy, shaking his head and heaving three separate sighs.

"Let me tell you one thing," he said. "I have always looked on Gavin as a man of parts. He may be a rat and a varlet, as you say, but he knows more about the newspaper business in his little finger than all the foul geniuses on Park Row put together. But despite all this dazzling cunning which I am ready to admit in fairness, this Gavin has the heart of a snake. He is a craven and yellow thing that crawls. That's a very fair picture of the man."

"I've never met him," I said.

"He's a wizard," said Mr. McCarey. "Although I'm going to tear his heart out and stuff it like an olive, I give him his due. Let me tell you something."

Mr. McCarey wagged a wild forefinger under my nose.

"This bulletin of Meyer's death dropped on Gavin's desk was no more than two lines long," he said. "A stupid laundryman done to death in a tenement. One of those dull, poverty-ridden crimes. A bubble coming up from some dismal sewer revealing for the moment that there is life in those stale waters. That's all the bulletin showed. But not to Monsoor Gavin. Monsoor Gavin called me over and, with that peculiar sneer with which he addresses his betters, pointed at this dull, stupid announcement that some totally unimportant human being named Meyer had been snuffed out in some wretched hovel in Troop

Street and said to me, 'There's something in this. There's more in this than meets the eye.' So much for Monsoor Gavin's cunning."

Again my friend scowled and, ogling the door, dramed his foe's life-blood from his glass.

"Let me tell you another thing," he said and spat. "Lieutenant Neidlinger of the Harlem police is a bird of a similar ilk. A species of double-dealing cringing officialdom that I will cool off and lay to rest before yonder sun has set."

Mr. McCarey chuckled.

"What did you find when you got to Troop Street?" I asked.

"The usual blather," snarled Mr. McCarey. "Lieutenant Neidlinger was all agog when I descended on this tenement. He was hovering about the premises and perspiring like an African bride. I tackled him for the facts about this dull, stupid crime and he at once unburdened his vulgar heart to me. There was some wretched mystery about the business that filled this pretzel-headed police official full of confusion and alarm.

" 'Item one,' said this peculiar fellow, 'how had the desperado responsible for Meyer's death gained entrance into this laundryman's stronghold? Item two, having gained said entrance and committed the bloody deed, how had the same desperado made his exit, leaving every door bolted on the inside and the windows barred? Item three, the dastardly criminal could have pot-shotted Meyer from the street but how could he have chopped off his hand without coming inside the room? Item four, why had this peculiar assailant removed Meyer's hand and whisked it away?' All these nuances were rattling around inside that vast, empty policeman's skull on this hot night.

" 'There's some mystery here,' he said.

" 'We'll discuss that later,' said I. 'First I want to take a look at this dull corpse of a laundryman.' "

Mr. McCarey began to weave over the table and turn suddenly from left to right as if facing his enemies.

"Who was this Meyer?" I asked again and more soothingly than ever.

My friend was drifting through mists. Once more I could feel him walking the ways of his secret. He was beyond the prod of questions.

"I knew him at once," said Mr. McCarey. "I can tell you so much. I knew him. I took one look and I knew him. And I grabbed this dithering cop and fastened myself like a foul burr to his coat tails. I gave him no rest. I heckled and bedeviled him until he was panting like one of those horrible little Pomeranians. I drove him out of his mind.

I dragged that dizzy Teuton up and down this Pomander Walk where Meyer had lived. We pumped and blasted and burrowed, but not a ray of light. Nothing. There was less to find out about this strange laundry-man than if he had never lived. He was a man with no more substance than a shadow on a screen. He was Meyer Nobody. We had at his customers. He was Meyer Nobody to them.

"And all the time this dull fellow Neidlinger kept mumbling, 'Why did he bar the windows and bolt the doors for ten years and how did they get away after killing him?'

" 'Because,' your oratrix replied, 'he was afraid. Because there was some peculiar nightmare on his heels.' And I kept prodding this dismal bloodhound to redouble his efforts. To no avail."

"But you knew all the time," I said.

"Yes," said my friend and snarled.

"Who?"

Mr. McCarey stared at me. In the long pause that followed it became apparent that what kept my friend silent was neither drink nor reticence but a great desire not to cry. A series of symptoms showed that Mr. McCarey was overcoming the womanish crisis that held him spellbound. He brought his glazed eyes slowly back to reality until they encountered his cigarette, which hung in his fingers and trembled. He then carried this cigarette, which he held like the Prince of Wales, to his mouth and maneuvered it promptly back toward the table.

"We won't go into that now," he said. "This little thin, thoughtful-faced old man with a weak chin who slaved over a washtub for ten years kept his strange mouth shut and ended up cornered in his tenement fortress, murdered and wallowing in his own gore with his right hand chopped off."

I realized that Mr. McCarey's great secret was out on its feet but still fighting, and I summoned patience into my voice.

"Did they solve it?" I asked.

"All I am privileged to tell you," said Mr. McCarey, "is Yes."

His voice had thickened and grown angrier.

"But that worm of a man, Monsoor Gavin, writhes on the hook of his own cowardice. That foul Corsican trembles lest he hit a sunken road. He refuses to print it. Lieutenant Neidlinger refuses to open his dull mouth. He skulks in the bush. Three dithering cops who know what I know have been transferred and promoted and are full of a craven, foolish silence. You are looking upon a man," Mr. McCarey burst out, "who is slowly wilting under the bludgeonings of a conspiracy greater than St. Bartholomew's Eve."

"How did they solve it?" I asked, closing in on Mr. McCarey.

"By following Mrs. Maum," said he. "By shadowing that barely animate and faintly human mass of tissue to an office on Forty-ninth Street."

Mr. McCarey communicated with the waiter, ordered more drinks and issued a confused command that Monsoor Gavin immediately on his appearance should be haled before us for summary justice.

"What was she doing in Forty-ninth Street?" I asked.

"Who?" asked Mr. McCarey.

"La Maum," I said.

"Oh, that foul wench," said Mr. McCarey and spat.

"Yes," I persisted.

"My lips are sealed on that subject," said McCarey. "All I can tell you is that she went to collect the wages of her sin. She journeyed to Forty-ninth Street in quest of her share of the blood money. You see, it was she who had baffled that master mind, Lieutenant Neidlinger. It was this abnormal trollop that had hoisted her idiot boy in through the transom, barely large enough for a cat to crawl through, to bolt the doors inside after the murderers had left. This wizened and backward stripling had crawled in and out of the transom like some trained lizard."

"Why did she want the doors bolted from the inside?" I asked.

"For no reason," said Mr. McCarey, "just a foolish, silly female ambition to create mystery. She derived some species of deformed pleasure from her son's didoes in and out of that transom. But they had nothing to do with the case, per se. This dithering pachyderm of a female Macbeth had been hired only to get Meyer to unbolt his doors to the murderers. This she did by cooing outside his portal for an hour."

"Were they caught?" I asked, still closing in.

"No," said Mr. McCarey. "A thousand times, No. We followed Mrs. Maum into that Forty-ninth Street office but the dastardly crew we were after were wigwagged by some peculiar outpost—and escaped. Leaving behind," Mr. McCarey's eyes both squinted and his voice grew harsher, "leaving behind a package in the safe containing Meyer's right hand. It was addressed and ready to be mailed."

"To whom?" I asked.

Mr. McCarey was silent.

"To whom?" I persisted.

"To a man named Stalin in Moscow, Russia," he said. "It was being sent him with its fingerprints intact to verify the report already over the cables." "Who was Meyer?" I asked and this time with my hand on the McCarey arm.

He was silent again, his eyes glaring. I waited.

"Will you believe me when I tell you?" said Mr. McCarey softly and pulled his head erect with a lurch. "Or will you join this foul conspiracy against truth and justice led by Monsoor Gavin and his peculiar myrmidons? Will you believe me if I tell you I've got all the facts of this fabulous crime?"

"I will," I said.

"This laundryman," said Mr. McCarey in a soft voice, "was the Czar of Russia."

I regarded Mr. McCarey calmly.

"Nikolai the Second," he said with dignity, in a sad croak. Then he went on in a mumble, "Escaped from his executioners in Siberia in 1918. Shipped across the world, his royal mind fogged by the tragedy of his murdered kin. But enough of his brain left to know he was hunted and that murder waited for him around every corner on the globe. So he drifted into Harlem as a little laundryman with a Jewish name."

Mr. McCarey slowly folded up over his fifteenth drink and allowed his head to hang and his eyes to close.

"The Czar of all the Russias," he whispered.

I kept my hand on his arm.

"You said you knew the minute you saw him," I said.

"Yes."

"How?"

The McCarey heart came charging out of its torpor.

"How did I know?" he said. "Because when I looked down on this dead laundryman I saw a cross in his left hand. A Muscovite cross. And a look on that dead face I'll never forget. It was the look of a noble, graceful, royal soul. There were some people who knew who was on the middle cross." Mr. McCarey sneered, his face thrust close to mine. "They could tell by a light that hovered peculiarly in the air. There was a light on this laundryman—this Meyer. This little dead Meyer."

"What did Neidlinger say?" I asked.

But the McCarey was in the mists. Tears were slipping down his stiffened cheeks and his head was wagging loosely over the table.

A short, gray-haired man appeared beside him. He had a red, excited face and a pair of black bristling eyebrows. He began shaking the McCarey shoulder.

"Wake up, you lout," said this man. "Come on, quit your stalling, you lousy drunken bum."

Mr. McCarey opened one angry eye.

"Monsoor Gavin," he said and tried to rise, "you foul Armenian!"

"Pull yourself together," said Monsoor Gavin and stood trembling with an excitement even greater than Mr. McCarey's had been. Mr. McCarey slowly opened a second eye, glared and emitted a carnivorous snarl.

"I'm going to stuff your heart," he said, "like a foul olive."

The fearless Monsoor with the red face ignored this promise and hoisted the McCarey to his feet. He was pushing at him from behind with eager, almost frantic, gestures and steering him for the door.

"Pull yourself together," he whispered fiercely into the McCarey ear. He turned to me. "No, I can handle him. I don't need you." To Mr. McCarey he added, giving that brave a final shove toward the door, "You're going home and pack. I got it all fixed up. The boss has agreed. Do you hear me? Agreed, by God! You're leaving in the morning for Moscow."

The Adventures of Professor Emmett

THERE WAS a certain moodiness to Gifford Emmett which he had picked up somehow while acquiring human shape in his mother's belly and which caused him to enter the world with a special lack of equipment for living in it. What he lacked chiefly was the desire to become a human being. Life sometimes produces these reluctant blood-streams which, like backwaters without beat or destination, remain morbidly outside the traffic of existence.

Gifford Emmett spent his thirty-six years of life in a subtle campaign to return to his mother's womb. Though he matured physically, and his mind developed far enough beyond its fetal stage to earn him a full professorship at a university, Gifford actually never existed. He merely imitated the ways of life as one might the manners of a repugnant country. Like an exile in an undesired land, his soul retained nostalgic recollections. It yearned for its larval state, and all its subsequent stages seemed full of alarms and discomforts.

You will understand this matter better, perhaps, if you look back on your own birthday. Few of us arrive in the world with any real conviction or even positive attitude. We are inclined to squander our time in the womb, only to be dislodged at the last moment, and in many cases evicted. And with many of us, thus driven from our only Eden, there is a tendency to turn our tiny, half-simian backs on the world into which we are ejected. Even the best of us who later grow to assertive manhood come out protesting furiously at the miserable change of fortunes the forceps have to offer. Once out, we signal our despair with heartbreaking noise, or we lie stunned and unbelieving of the nasty trick that has been played on us by our mother's suddenly hostile muscles.

Our infancy is as much a time of readjustment as of education. During the first wretched months of our existence, we must inure ourselves to the repulsive oddity of a cradle vastly too large for us. We have been dethroned and our soul is full of complaints. As the days pass, however, we are wooed and purred into certain revaluations. We are kissed and fondled and made the focal point of this new and inferior existence into which we have blundered. A new if lesser ego is offered us. We are loaded with despot scepters and bedazzled with tyrant crowns. Whereupon, slowly and with many a night of sad weeping, which I myself can well remember, we reconcile ourselves to our second nests, and say farewell forever to our original dream of perfect living.

No such time of reconciliation or farewell, however, came to Gifford Emmett. The reasons for this I shall do my best to reveal.

Little Gifford was born on a December morning of the year 1902, in an old brick house that stood in the second nicest residential section of a small Wisconsin town. At the moment, the town was covered with snow, and in its streets lonely figures, booted and mittened, were prowling about in a blizzard. Under the cold beat of the wind, the Emmett house stood quilted and turreted with snow, its windows and doors half obliterated. In a bedroom too cold either for amour or for its public sequel, Mrs. Emmett lay doing her best to persuade little Gifford to take his place in a larger world.

After some seven violent hours, Mrs. Emmett finally triumphed, and little Gifford appeared, refusing to breathe or offer any tell-tale signs of life. His efforts to outwit the new and the horrible by a possum-like unconsciousness availed him nothing. The family doctor, a canny old gentleman aware of the ruses of the newborn, belabored little Gifford's bottom with a stout palm. Then he shook and rattled him about as if he were no more than a dollar alarm clock to be jarred into ticking. Eventually a tiny moan rewarded the scientist's work, and Gifford Emmett was declared officially in the land of the living.

At this vital and sensitive moment, a disastrous thing happened. The street door of the Emmett house was flung open, and eleven adolescents ranging in age from twelve to sixteen entered as if they were the spirit of the blizzard outside. They came in howling and prancing and fell to rolling on the floor and assaulting each other with snowballs scraped from each other's shoes and hair. Five of these arrivals were the moaning little Gifford's brothers and sisters. The other six were a species of local self-elected orphans who preferred the Emmett home to their own as an arena for feats of strength and budding musical talents.

The opening of the Emmett street door let in a wintry blast that scampered icily up the stairs and into the accouchement chamber. And since none of the eleven arrivals could find time to close the door, the wintry blast grew wintrier. It swirled and steamed up the stairs, and little Gifford, but recently induced to breathe, found himself swept by such frigid currents that he turned instantly blue and began to shake as if with palsy. He wailed once and then fell into that stoical, powerless silence that marked his demeanor for life.

There is no doubt but that little Gifford's aversion to life was fully developed when the forceps seized him. The opening of the door, the wintry blasts, the horrifying shouts of laughter, and the sounds of furniture toppling were merely details that instantly and forever verified his already full-blown conviction that he had been cast out of the best of all possible worlds into a nowhere.

Biologically, the facts are that little Gifford was the fruit of an unexpected and autumnal flicker of parenthood. Mrs. Emmett had conceived in her forty-third year, to the disquiet of her husband, himself nearing sixty. And though little Gifford had emerged a fine infant, with a full quota of appendages, it is fairly good science to conclude that he had been put together a little tiredly. The elderly genes and chromosomes laboring at his fashioning had sighed at their work. And that cymbal crash of life that inspires the newborn to shed its larval soul fell on tired ears with little Gifford, if he heard it at all.

Whatever world he had been born into, it is likely that Gifford would have bloomed as a psychosis rather than a sultan. Still the Emmett home did have its share in the non-development of little Gifford's human side. There was no room or role for this laggard little guest in the firmly established hullabaloo of mixed quarters, juvenile sports, and endless riotings that were the routine of this Wisconsin ménage. Gifford had arrived too late to be of any use or interest to anybody. For his mother, no new activities focused on his crib. His father instituted no new regime for his sake. Nobody breathed or kissed or fondled an ego into his consciousness. His brothers and sisters regarded him with the perfunctory interest they had for all creatures who fitted into neither football squads nor wrestling tournaments, to say nothing of moonlight singing.

And from his first weeks little Gifford exhibited the detachment of one who knows himself an interloper. He allowed himself quietly to be stowed away in attics and back bedrooms and other distant culs-de-sac where the banjo and piano banging and other alarums of adolescence could not reach to break his hypothetical slumbers. He suffered sudden drafts, hunger, and terror, without even the little comment at his command. And during such naps as he was able to steal amid the hurly-burly of the household, he dreamed happily of that land of warmth and plenty from which, like a peri, he had been expelled.

And so Gifford grew into a sober and unprotesting infant, well shapen but enigmatic. Soon he shuffled about on hands and knees, doing his best to avoid flying missiles, charging feet, and other hazards of life. He had no interest in living, but his intelligence had not yet encompassed the idea of suicide. In his second winter, he seemed to all the Emmetts but one a model child. He had by that time completely abandoned his small struggle to become part of life. No music or laughter could lure him now from his seclusion. He haunted the unwanted corners of the house, sitting on the floor and staring tirelessly into space with a sort of Oriental calm. When summer came, he crawled into the currant patch behind the house, and lay in the cool dirt under the bushes. His mother, busy with stretching Mr. Emmett's weekly pay check (he was a chemist in the town's bottle works) over the seven days, smiled gratefully on his seeming ability to amuse himself. She misunderstood entirely the moods that sent him crawling under beds and into airless closets. There were times, however, when Gifford's eyes, looking intently at her, startled her and made her wonder if anything was wrong with him. It appeared to her then that the child Gifford looked at her with a most curious and desperate concentration, as if he were weaving a spell. Drawing him to her, she would ask kindly at such times what her little man wanted. But Gifford kept his secret.

The lone Emmett to whom Gifford seemed something less than a model child was Edward, the father. When Gifford was a few weeks old, Edward Emmett perceived that his son hated him. Mr. Emmett said nothing about it. He had long ago been elbowed out of any vital existence by his brood and their satellites, and converted into a fluttering, negligible shade of parenthood who continued to drop lamb chops and fried potatoes on the Emmett table from his little perch as a bottle maker. This history had conditioned him to keep his thoughts to himself.

When the curious fact that Gifford fell into a fit whenever his father approached him began to be generally noticed, a number of theories sprang up as to its cause. Mr. Emmett defended himself vigorously against charges of clumsiness and unfriendliness. But Mrs. Emmett had still another theory that left him silent. His wife was of the opinion that the little creature objected to the smell of chemicals always arising from Mr. Emmett's person. And her husband recalled that Lily, as a bride, had once burst into tears over some chlorine gas lingering in his mustache, and concluded that Gifford had inherited from his mother this unreasonable distaste for antiseptic odors. Mr. Emmett took to bathing and cologning himself like a stage beauty, but, sweetened though he was, his effect on his son remained unchanged. The otherwise placid infant continued to have convulsions at the sight of him.

Such, without going any further into the matter, was Professor Emmett's childhood. Ignored by his brothers and sisters, misunderstood by his mother, and mysteriously outraged by the male collaborator of his being, Gifford tottered about at the age of three like a little ghost whom every dawn threatened to dissipate. At four he took to running away from home and hiding beneath neighborhood verandas, from under which he was dragged weeping at the frustration of his plans. At five he became a moody survivor of a vanished era, for his brothers and sisters and their hallooing intimates were then scattering to work and to college. Gifford haunted the once gay household like a little beggar poking around in the wake of a carnival. In the summertime, shooed out of the house to get some air, he spent long hours under the currant bushes, inert and moody.

It was in this retreat that Gifford, at six, discovered surprisingly a world that fascinated him. This was the world of insects. His child eyes became aware of ants and spiders, wasps, butterflies, grasshoppers, and earthworms. Lying on his stomach, chin cupped in his hands, Gifford would remain absorbed for hours by the busy ways of this wonderfully unhuman population. He began to see in the seemingly aimless careenings of these, his first friends, certain patterns of conduct. These minute creatures, in whose midst he sprawled like a Gulliver, became significant and interesting to him as human beings had never been, and he watched them as if they were tiny letters spelling out a new and breathless tale.

Through long summer hours he would lie this way, and sometimes, lured by these Pied Pipers of the garden, he followed them to sit like a guest on the thresholds of their curious homes. He learned many things. He became aware of the mother love of the beetle, of the precision and cruelty of the spider, and of the marauderies of the wasps. He grew to know the little wind lanterns of the glow-worm. The large head of the grasshopper, like that of a tissue-paper horse, became as familiar to him as if it spoke. The beetle, senile and saucer-eyed, and the paunchy spider, with its crown of legs, waiting owlishly in its hazy net, were his comrades. None of these diminutive ogres frightened him. Their ominous caricature of human limb and feature pleased him like a set of strange toys. He never tired of watching this little universe crawl and fly and dart, weave its homes and struggle murderously for its food.

Unguided by books, he created for himself a childish version of all he saw. The dark leafy tunnels of the overhanging currant bushes became a fairyland where eccentric-looking heroes performed for him. Dragons and helmeted knights battled on their twig arenas. Hobgoblins hung by invisible threads. Miniature witches leaped through the air, and the eyes of genii gleamed out of tiny holes in the ground. Troubadours, transported by summer, played their violins, and little scarecrow kings teetered on the berry clusters. The ants seemed to him like beaded acrobats of the grass blades. And over the bushes the darning needles fired arrows at the sun, and the butterflies swayed like tiny flags.

Like his friends, Gifford prepared himself for the winter months. He erected an insect zoo in his room. Glass jars containing ants and spiders, wasps, beetles, and flies, crowded his bureau top and his window sills. When the cold days came, Gifford tended his charges anxiously. He fed them and invented diversions for their welfare. He constructed exercise yards for them out of shoe boxes and built rickety mansions of mosquito netting. For the ants he modeled special hills of dirt so that they might not grow homesick.

It seemed unnatural to Mrs. Emmett that anyone should be interested exclusively in bugs. But her efforts to lure her child away were unavailing. It was the despised Mr. Emmett, whom Gifford still hated, but in an inactive fashion now, who rescued his son from the shadows of ignorance that seemed to be permanently enclosing him. Mr. Emmett understood that Gifford was a scientist. He was proud to have handed on to his son his own interest in this profound side of life. Diffidently, Mr. Emmett sat with his son and imparted to him his own theory of education.

"If you will go to Bible class and pay attention to your teacher in school," he said, "you will be allowed to study what you like when you grow up. I can't explain why it is, but you must study about angels and presidents before you can study about bugs. But I can promise you that after you've gone to school a long time, you'll be able to return to insects, and nobody will bother you."

Lured by the promise of this reward, Gifford submitted himself to the educational system. And long after Mr. Emmett's death, the prophecy he had made came true. At thirty-four, Gifford Emmett was raised to a full professorship in the university he had entered as a gloomy, gangling youth. Jars filled with insects, and elaborate cages teeming with his beloved coleoptera and arachnids, crowded his bachelor apartment just as they had his childhood bedroom. And for several hours a week, as Professor of Entomology, he lectured happily on the secrets of that Kingdom of the Little which he had first discovered under the currant bushes.

In leaping thus from the seven-year-old Gifford to the tall, thin, dark-haired, and goggle-eyed savant of thirty-four, I have omitted little of his life that calls for chronicling. During these missing decades Gifford was engaged chiefly in the moody but ungraphic business of receding from the world. He continued to hold himself like a by-stander on the outskirts of its charms, its follies, and its adventures. He read tirelessly and studied deeply, and his mind evolved within the egg of inaction. It was a curious mind full of wit and learning. But it revealed itself to no one. .

He had matured without tasting anything of life. Now he thrived like some specimen in a bottle, detached from his species and forgetful of them. Only one thing occasionally disturbed him. This was a periodic lapse into melancholia. The desire to die seized him each year of his life, and stretched him weeping and inanimate in his bed. These melancholic fits lasted usually through the week of his birthday. He suffered then from a sense of suffocation. The chill and contemptuous wit of his mind turned to fog. He lay staring at unbearable walls and listening to sounds of a life that tortured him. However, he always recovered quickly, and resumed his reading and his friendless ways of living as if nothing had interrupted them.

There are some of us, many more than are usually counted, who do not grow up at all. Life is unable to alter these little ones among us despite the plant-like increase of their bodies. In them the child persists not as a dim imprisoned ghost, but as a face always visible. All the trappings of age, its wrinkles, its wisdom, and its very largeness, seem like misfit clothes in which these children must stagger grotesquely about. And no matter what their lives or passions may be, there remains stamped on their reluctant adulthood the bewitched and pathetic contour of innocence.

Professor Emmett was one of these nursery lingerers. His face glowed as if it were a shell that had never known wind or sun. So gentle and disarming did the smallest of his gestures seem that there was hardly a female student but felt an impulse to mother him. Men were equally charmed by his staccato wit and child-like simplicity. But Professor Emmett, who, if you looked closely, was still the little Gifford busy with his currant-bush comrades, evaded any intimacies.

In his thirty-fifth year, however, an adventure and a relationship befell him. And with it my tale of Professor Emmett's Homeric adventures in a sense begins.

Myra McKillup entered Gifford Emmett's life at that precise moment when he had decided to quit it. The melancholia that had assailed Gifford since his boyhood had subsided in his thirties. Now as he was approaching thirty-five it returned. Animation once more left him. Mysterious tears coursed out of his soul and overran his cheeks.

Of the diseases that touch the hearts of others, those of the subconscious are certainly the least. It is difficult to take seriously the nightmares which these oddly afflicted ones seem to parade as pets. We are inclined to regard them as impostors rather than martyrs. The fact that these impostors frequently leap from windows, hurl themselves under trains, thrust their heads into gas ovens, or blow out their brains is not enough to convince us of their reality. Their deaths come too late to impress us with their diseases. Even those who weep at the bier of the neurotic are inclined to withhold their sympathy for the secret agony that sent him to the undertaker's.

Thus, though I have come to a moment in my hero's life that might well call for a little tenderness from any reader, I feel it better to deal unemotionally with the matter. Of objective griefs such as we fancy drive folk to their deaths Gifford had no more than any of the grasshoppers he tended in their bottles. No amorous or professional entanglements beset him. No frustrations sawed at his nerves. Around him lay a little world of flattery, and he had no dreaded tomorrows awaiting him. Yet with all this well-being at his fingertips, Gifford sat ready to die. And if the reader will not cry over the fact he must at least believe it, and not assert that Gifford was behaving absurdly, as wives have been known to remark of husbands just before the latter leaped out of windows.

For a half-hour Professor Emmett sat inert and befogged. He held in his hand a small bottle of chemical which he was about to drink. Outside, it was a lavish spring morning. The windows of his study were open and through them came the shout of early vernal winds, colors, and odors. But this lean, goggle-eyed man remained insensible. Insensible, too, he stayed before another phenomenon. His spiders, hatched on this spring morning, had climbed the towering bamboo stalks provided for them and were escaping through the open windows, afloat on their silken rockets. Unmindful of this long-awaited spectacle, Professor Emmett blankly regarded the poison in his hand. Like any of his brothers in their bottles, he too sat separated from life by walls that obscured its breath. No tragic thoughts were in his head, and his reason for dying was no more than an oppression that called for death as thirst calls for water.

Occupied thus with the vague gesture which in a moment would bring about his dissolution, Gifford was unaware of a visitor until she had come close to him and removed the open bottle from his mouth. He looked up and saw dimly a dark-haired young woman with large, trembling eyes. And at this moment Gifford was overcome with a misunderstanding of Myra McKillup that precipitated his first romance.

He saw her, this sad man pulled back to life, as a creature full of calm, beauty, and goddess-like radiance. A measure of his misunderstanding may be seen in the fact that Miss McKillup was a thin girl, undersized and meatless except for her breasts. These were not large, but, landscaped as they were by famine, they seemed plenty.

Because Gifford's desire to die had been only a temporary one he felt a surge of gratitude for this student who had entered his study by mistake, as she explained. Part of the need he immediately felt for her was probably due to her seeming to his bewitched senses a maternal figure. She had brought him to life, like a secondary mother, and Gifford's long campaign to re-enter his mother's womb transferred itself, a little more practically, to Miss McKillup. He stared at her from that first day with timorous, incestuous eyes, and she seemed to him a human being cast in a tender and superior mold.

This concept too was as completely unrelated to any image of the young woman as his first physical estimate. In addition to being as unmotherly as a hop-toad, Miss McKillup was actually a flibberty nerve-racking creature with a touch of pituitary emaciation. She owned a mind much like a sieve, through which her twenty-five years of life had passed leaving behind a froth of hysteria. She was an unstable and muddle-headed girl. She had a thin, forward-thrusting face like a bird's, bony hands, and a talent for breathlessness. She considered herself a superior person, for no reason that I can determine. It may be she fancied herself more sensitive than most people, and regarded her inability to talk rationally on any subject as a measure of some kind of mysticism rather than stupidity. She inhabited every cliché like an Archimedes yelling "Eureka." She was a-swoon with economics, art, and a bit of biology. There are whole continents of such women, who seem to feel that they master any subject they take up merely by sighing on it. Attracted by an idea, they belabor it with gasps and tremors as if they were coaxing it into bed with them. Usually, to do them justice, there is some sort of male attached to the idea.

Miss McKillup was of this inarticulate and oracular run of femininity. She was enrolled in a post-graduate journalism course under the not entirely erroneous impression that she belonged on a newspaper—as some kind of critic. Perhaps there was nothing more the matter with her than a need for seeming more intelligent than she was, which so often turns people into fools. Or perhaps she sought to reveal a beauty of soul as a lure for the opposite sex, there being little other bait at her disposal. Unsavory-looking girls often go in for this sort of spiritual cosmetics and flit about with over-rouged ideas and insane-looking mental coiffures.

I intend, however, to run no magnifying glass over Myra. That Gifford should have fallen in love with this lady at first sight and beheld her as a Demeter full blown with the blessings of the earth is a matter between him and his subconscious. My hero, who had never once felt the stirring of libido, was overcome suddenly by a mating instinct as implacable as it was mistaken. This movement of sap in Gifford, however, expressed itself only in a desire to talk. And the professor's many admirers looked on with surprise as their good savant devoted himself to addressing incessantly on the most abstruse of topics a young woman whom they knew to be as rattle-brained as a mongoose.

The curious couple was to be seen haunting all the lonely places that neighbored the university. Pale with long confinement in its bottle, the soul of Professor Emmett emerged and fluttered moth-like before the light it fancied lay in Miss McKillup's eyes. It filled the night with the colors of its wit and wisdom, for it is the habit of long-locked-away lovers to create themselves first before they fall to sighing for another.

It would be cruel to say that Myra understood nothing of what Gifford revealed to her during these trysts. Women usually understand what is said to them in courtship, but their listening has so much more coquetry than scholarship in it that the most Socratic of dialogues turn to valentines under their applause. Yet it is only fair to point out that if Myra listened with other organs than were meant for words to the wisdom of Professor Emmett, the latter was, in a sense, not speaking to her at all. She had accidentally removed the top of the bottle and the professor was emerging genie-fashion.

Gifford began his love-making with an attack on life. His aversion for living had spun many dark ideas in his head. His wooing of Miss McKillup consisted, to the end, of an effort to convince her of the infamy and absurdity of human existence.

For their first tryst, Miss McKillup had guided the professor to a little hilltop overgrown with tall grasses. This was the evening of Gifford's rescue from death. He had clung all day to Miss McKillup, allowing her to cool his head with icy towels and to induce him to eat. Still shaken by the double experience of attempting death and of discovering the first woman he had ever found tolerable, Gifford sat moodily on the hilltop. Now his melancholia thawed into phrase. The shawl of pain lifted from his senses and he spoke coolly and lucidly to his companion.

"I have always hated life," said Gifford, "and have found human existence a sort of calamity."

"You say human existence," said Miss McKillup with the air of a philosopher. "Is there any other?"

Gifford's romance almost collapsed under this insensate question. He looked coldly at the young woman.

"Human existence," he said, "is the least of the phenomena of Nature. The most rudimentary thinker must see us as a needle in a haystack. The history of the human race from its first grunt to its last sigh will be hardly more than a footnote to the story of life. We are less than a chirp in Bedlam."

"I know," said Miss McKillup sadly, "but don't you think there's some God who is aware of us, or some force?"

"God is aware of us only if He is a microscope," said Gifford, "or unbalanced. Our species will have come and gone too quickly to interest any sane Super-Intelligence."

Miss McKillup sighed and her face became full of compassion for the littleness of man.

"I've often wondered," she said, "what the end of our race would be. Whether the insects would finally vanquish us—or what?"

"The insects are not interested in us," said Gifford irritably. "We are too vague and unimportant in the scheme of things to attract their attention. They bite us purely by accident. As for vanquishing us, nothing could be further from their thoughts. It is rarely that one species vanquishes another. The mind of the earth which we call Nature is so exquisitely balanced a pendulum of creation and destruction that even the most foolish of its children are able to survive."

Miss McKillup looked wistfully at the stars as if she were saying farewell to them.

"It is not the insects who will nibble our species into extinction," announced Gifford. "Our fate is more tragic than that. Man will be one of the few suicides in Evolution."

After a silence during which he continued to stare abstractedly at her knees, Gifford informed Miss McKillup that the dissolution of the human race already cast its shadow into our day. Thought, like a Walpurgis Night, was descending on man and the time was nearing when he would vanish on all the broomsticks of his philosophies. Luckily Miss McKillup was more stirred by his attentions than his assertions, or she might have become sincerely depressed.

Gifford launched into his first courtship essay. The human mind, he said, began very slowly. It took a long time to improve on its first growls. Why it began at all is a mystery. All we can be sure of is that it was intended as a serviceable bit of plasm. Let us say a sixth sense—a sense of knowing. Nature is full of similar compensating gifts for those of her children unable to run, fly, dig, smell, see, or hear too well. Each of these possesses the gift of some ruse by which it can outwit its enemies sufficiently for survival, like the spider's sting, or the glue arrows of the soldier ant.

Miss McKillup, listening, was surprised to find so much violence in this gentle and child-like man. Nevertheless, it pleased her, for it gave her a duty. She would make this morbid but delightful scholar change his opinions about life, which she was certain he would do under the influence of a little sweetness.

"For a long time," Gifford spoke up again, "the human mind fulfilled its simple destiny. It enabled us to outwit our better-equipped enemies. Primitive man was a very fortunate animal. But we are in no way related to him. We have been whisked out of Nature into the Alice-in-Wonderland realm of thought. Our mind has hatched a universe. It has projected a world of phantoms on the screen of our senses. We inhabit this world. We crawl on our animal legs into a mirror."

"Please go on," said Miss McKillup throatily.

Gifford remained silent.

After a pause Miss McKillup added wistfully, "I want to hear."

"I think you will understand me better," he resumed, "if I discuss the human mind merely as a parasite."

"Yes," said Miss McKillup breathlessly, "oh, yes. It will be much easier for me. Although everything you say is marvelously clear. Marvelously!"

Gifford nodded and waited for her to find a more comfortable piece of ground. She selected a place near his ankles and, lying down again, this time on her stomach, raised her face eagerly.

"The parasite mind," said Gifford, "is already nibbling at the biologic sanity of the species. Most of modern medicine is the record of the mind's ability to cripple the body. Modern history also has become a record of mental aberration on a grand scale. Intellectual quibbles now breed our wars. It's not difficult to foresee a world locked in a death struggle over theories for its improvement.

"But," mused Gifford, "I don't think the species will destroy itself in this coming struggle of Tweedledee and Tweedledum."

Miss McKillup sighed like a harp that is being plucked. All the same, the dissolution of the race disturbed her much less than the appearance of a slight flush in the professor's cheeks.

"It's so warm," she said softly. "Wouldn't you rather take your coat off?"

"Thank you," said Gifford mechanically and removed it.

"And your waistcoat," Miss McKillup insisted. This too was removed.

"No," Gifford resumed as she loosened his tie, "it will not be the war of man against man that will bury us in the grave of the dodo bird. Man against himself will be our finish. Not an honorable death, mind you, on the field of battle, but a gruesome suicide in the loneliness of the night, is the fate that awaits us. This suicide has begun. Thought has already crippled our nature. Our efforts to live by our ideas as if they were our bloodstream have rotted away half our health.

"Just look at us today," Gifford cried out to the seemingly fascinated young woman beside him, "us creatures who call ourselves the top of Evolution. Lords of the world, indeed! Why, the humblest beetle might laugh at us if it had time for the study of nonsense."

Gifford paused and stared at the night over the hilltop. How pleasant it was to speak thoughts, even the sullenest! He breathed excitedly. A new and exhilarating argument against life had just occurred to him.

"Our senses," he announced, "are caught in a net of reason. There's hardly a single thing we feel but we must busy ourselves misunderstanding or improving it. All our animal desires must crawl around on the flypaper of our mind and either die there or drag out an enfeebled existence breathing the poison of our ideals. All the magnificent functions of Nature are becoming confused in us. We can't sleep. Eating gets to be more and more complicated. Sex has become full of hazards and confusions. Morality and poetry have so bewildered the spinal cord that it has forgotten how to signal for a blood supply.

"Yes," cried Gifford triumphantly, "our search for the Ideal has converted our glandular system into a rubbish heap! Unable to transmute us into angels, our minds have turned us into invalids. Our last stand will be in the laboratories—as patients. Our scientists will toil away desperately at extricating our organs from the octopus of the mind. But I'm certain they won't succeed."

After a pause, during which he noticed with some surprise that Miss McKillup's head was now resting in his lap, Gifford continued.

"Have you ever noticed how the spider captures and destroys the powerful locust that leaps accidentally into its net?" he asked.

"No," Miss McKillup said, and sighed.

"The legs of the locust," explained Gifford, "are strong enough to kick the silken snare to shreds. But, as the spider stays out of reach, invisible to the procrastinating locust, it remains busy at work. It envelops the struggling bit of life in a flow of almost invisible thread. Round and round the locust the spider spins its delicate strait-jacket. Finally the locust is unable to move. Then our spider leisurely drains it of its blood, and the locust shell is left hanging in a net to rattle in the wind. We will end in a similar way. Enveloped by thought spun around us, our species will finally wither away to a few last neurotic husks, and then hang motionless in the web."

A little later the two strolled down the hill to the university, Miss McKillup clinging to Gifford's arm. She was pleased with what she called their first heart to heart talk, for she saw that it had made Professor Emmett extremely happy. He smiled when he said good-night to her, and she watched him walk off with a youthful spring in his long legs, trailing his coat and vest like a workman come home from a picnic.

A number of similar trysts followed, which I might report. But I shall hold myself down to the account of only one more. This took place a week later.

After they had dined together one evening, Miss McKillup—she was known to Professor Emmett as Myra now—guided him to a new rostrum, a little wooded river bank remembered from a previous love affair with a member of the university rowing crew. But Gifford ignored the loveliness of the spot, as he did for the most part the presence of his companion. For he was still too selfish in his pleasure to notice any contributing factors.

Just the same, he spent the first few minutes fidgeting and silent. This was because he suffered as always from the result of too much expectation. It takes time to adjust oneself to the reality of a Miss McKillup when one has walked with Dante's Beatrice all day.

Miss McKillup—Myra—did not allow herself to become discouraged by this ominous beginning. She smiled breathlessly as they sat in the little grotto once sacred to Venus and an oarsman.

"I've been looking forward so all day to this," she said. "I've lost interest in everything else in the world—except listening to you."

Gifford blushed, being unused to such bouquets. He remained silent and listened to the frogs and crickets singing everywhere in the spring night.

"I feel," went on Myra, "I feel as if we had known each other a long time. A terribly long time. I suppose that's because I can't remember ever having had any thoughts except those you've given me."

"The frogs sound very musical, don't they?" said Gifford.

"Divine," said Myra quickly.

"But it's a horrible music to others," Gifford said.

"Others?" cried Myra and looked around in alarm.

"I mean the insects," said Gifford. "Whenever I hear a frog I can almost feel the terror of the coleoptera and arachnids."

"Nature," said Myra, "is cruel, isn't it?"

"No," said Gifford. "That's a most ridiculous misconception. There's no cruelty in Nature. There are only necessity and precision. No animal tortures another animal. The frog devouring the spider acts out of an instinct shared by the spider. It is their stomachs and not their souls that are thrilled by murder."

"I hadn't thought of that," said Myra soothingly.

"Nature," said Gifford, "is a banquet board at which the feasters and the feast are one. This was shown to me once when I watched a praying mantis eat a grasshopper. The grasshopper had caught a caterpillar a moment before. It continued undisturbed to eat this caterpillar while the praying mantis munched on its own legs. Not until the mantis sank its teeth into the grasshopper's digestive organs did the latter abandon its own feast."

"It's all so frightening." Myra shivered.

"To me," said Gifford, "it is merely sane. I find our own species vastly more terrible than the mantis, the spider, and the humble caterpillar. Our mind is supposed to have improved on the manners of Nature. But if you examine our activities you will find that the mind has done little more with our animal criminality than rationalize its crimes. It has added to the simple murder-politic inherent in Nature the genius for depriving the victim not only of his life but of his good repute. There's no monster, in Nature, whose fangs are as cruel as our ideas."

"We are all animals in exile," said Myra with a shiver.

Gifford thought it astonishing that she should not only understand him but share his point of view. He was also surprised that this young woman's head in his lap failed to check the flow of his thought, but somehow increased his desire to communicate his ideas to her. Despite a slight numbness in his thigh, he permitted her to remain pillowed there.

"I'm afraid it's going to rain," said Gifford.

"Oh, no," Myra sighed, "I'm sure it won't."

"There's no question of it," said Gifford firmly. "I've been watching that spider." He pointed to a bush overhead. "She refuses to repair her web. When the spider refuses to reweave her web at night it's always a sign of rain."

"And yet," sighed Myra, "man believes himself the only thinking animal."

"He is," Gifford corrected her. "Spiders don't think. Nor do the bees or the ants. It's true some entomologists presume to see in the precision of insect life human motivations such as love, hate, ambition, or sacrifice. This is ridiculous. Take the case of the Clotho moth. This moth, who sews so wonderful a nest for her children, fills it also with materials out of which they will be able to weave their first spring frocks. Without these they would die of cold. Having laid out this wardrobe, the Clotho moth finishes her work of nest building by plugging up the last little hole in it with her own body. She dies with her wings spread as a barrier against her children's enemies. She might seem to be the most infatuated of Nature's mothers. Yet to call her a mother at all is to libel her. For the moth is unaware of what is in her eggs. She never lives to see them hatch. It is absurd to imagine that love for these never-to-be-seen moth infants animates her. They are, in fact, not her children but her ghosts. They are her future shapes. It is life she perpetuates. She is as devoid of personality as the wind that rocks her tiny body. Her loving and thinking are both done for her by a never-blundering hypnosis we must call instinct."

Gifford paused and looked lovingly at the night, and Myra wondered why he was trembling.

"How wise the insects are," he said softly. "Their learning is so great and their joy of life so intense it seems almost inconceivable that they have not evolved that foolish talent for comment which would

destroy their Eden. How enviable their world is. . . . The bee, for instance, so industrious, and yet as devoted to capering and singing as any
drunken troubadour. You might," he added wistfully, "call the bee a
hymn to life."

He addressed the girl tenderly.

"You never see an insect becoming irrational or insane, do you,
Myra? The reason for this, you see, is that her talent is not her own.
It belongs to her species, and she can neither improve on it nor discard
it. She feels the pleasure of living, but she has no ego with which to
distort or exaggerate it. And so she doesn't confuse either herself or her
species.

"For instance, the cicada is like some wonderful fiddler. When it
emerges from the earth in the spring, it is overcome by the marvel of
sun and air, and it strikes up a tune, playing on its wing with its saw-
toothed right leg. But luckily it is stone deaf and doesn't hear its own
paean to the spring. If it did, it might become a musician and cease to
be an insect. It would devote all its instincts to music and disintegrate
as a cicada."

Myra opened her eyes and smiled.

"You know," she said, "you have made me realize how much
greater our spirit is than our so-called intelligence."

Gifford hoped she was using the word "spirit" in the right sense,
but was fearful of inquiring. In a moment, however, he forgot completely the presence of his companion despite the fact that both his
legs had now turned numb under the weight of her head. He sat looking happily at the scenery of the night. The rain was coming. Its smell
arrived first. He smiled at the wise spider idling on the verbena leaf.
The dark about him trembled as if awaiting a visitor. The leaves were
stirring with the new pressure of the air. The night was full of microscopic traffic as his old friends fled for shelter or emerged to flit and
dive in the film of moisture hanging everywhere. He remembered that
in his childhood he had lain often under the bushes waiting for the
soft explosion of the rain.

"It's amazing," said Myra, who had reached the collaborative stage
of female pursuit, "but sometimes when you talk I almost feel that
you're not really a member of our species, but an ant or a beetle or
something."

Afraid that she had disparaged her admirer, Myra presently
amended this.

"I mean with a soul of course."

But Gifford was flattered.

"It's hard to tell what we are," he smiled. "We have only our mind to figure with—and it's difficult to think out any of the mysteries of which we are only so small a part."

Myra had no such difficulty.

"I believe in the transmigration of souls," she said, throwing back her head.

"Fairytales," said Gifford, after a pause, "are likely to contain just as much truth as science. For, whatever Truth is, it seems to express itself as much in fantasies as in facts. Every movement of our mind is inspired by the Truth that exists forever outside it. Who knows but we will yet discover that our myths are the real science and that science is the only myth?"

"Then you do believe in soul transmigration!" Myra cried. "You do! Please don't deny it!"

"I never deny anything," Gifford said patiently. "All thought is the shadow of some truth we cannot understand. And since we can't ever see the Truth, I think it wise to study all the shadows it casts and to discount none of them."

"How wonderful that we should both believe in soul transmigration!" Myra chanted.

This was too much for Gifford.

"I don't know anything about soul transmigration," he said a little angrily. Then he added, more for the sake of politeness:

"However, Nature is so economical, it may be she uses her forces over and over. Perhaps she does this with the spirit of life, and perhaps this life force continues like a never-broken thread on which she strings the endless little brittle beads of our bodies."

"Oh, to come back to life again as a bird!" cried Myra, carried away by what she felt to be their mutual understanding. "Oh, to fly, to sing, to—"

"It would be terrible for the bird," Gifford interrupted in alarm. "A bird with a human soul in it, even the remains of such a soul, would be a most ridiculous and incompetent fowl. I can't bear to think of anything in Nature so handicapped."

The rain came. A mist and an odor trickled into the little clearing. The roof of leaves resounded with the rain clamor.

Gifford was silent. It occurred to Myra that he was a very strange man. She sat up and looked at him. He was sitting, ears cocked to the wild hum of the rain. She watched his dark unflickering eyes and wondered what they were seeking in the night. He seemed to have fallen into a trance. She touched his hand to waken him, but his curious expression remained unchanged. The round black eyes protruded, empty and sage-like. The thin lips were curled inward over the teeth. The entire face glistened with so mad a preoccupation that Myra shivered. Gifford's face seemed for an instant like something brittle rising out of the grass and regarding the night with an ominous and secret understanding.

"What are you thinking?" Myra asked softly.

"Nothing," Gifford answered. "I wasn't thinking."

Myra drew nearer to his side.

"How foolish people seem in the rain," said Gifford suddenly, "as if rain were no longer meant for them. They've left the breast of Nature."

"Is there no way back for us?" asked Myra. "I mean, for those who understand?"

"No," said Gifford, "we're on our way somewhere else."

After its first gusts, the rain dwindled. Myra decided that the climax of their tryst had been passed.

They walked back arm in arm to the university. On this night Gifford was too preoccupied to smile when he left her.

After Myra McKillup had listened to Professor Emmett for a month she put an end to his talk by marrying him. There is no need to go into the tender and unscrupulous progressions at the end of which our hero found himself before the altar. He was a little amazed and considerably bewildered. After having been blessed by the minister and kissed by the bride, Gifford suddenly asserted himself. He refused to go on a honeymoon.

He announced, a little tardily, that he had been looking forward to these three summer months as a perfect time to investigate the stomach of the termite. He was determined, Gifford firmly told his bride on their way home, to solve the riddle of the parasites that inhabited this wood-devouring insect's stomach. It was these parasites that provided the termite, to Gifford's never-ending amazement, with a digestive apparatus omitted by Nature in its construction.

Seated in his apartment, now newly curtained and groomed out of recognition, Gifford did his best to explain the intricacies of the problem to his bride. And technical though this problem was, I feel its details are entitled to the precedence given them by the bridegroom. His investigations into the termite's digestive phenomena, started on the day of his marriage, were to mean more to him than the pathetic relationship into which he had been whisked. They were to outlast this union and even himself, and they were—in these pages at least—to place his name on the small scroll of heroes. I shall therefore join Gifford Emmett in elbowing aside his marital duties in favor of the colony of termites to which he hurried right after the wedding ceremony.

Gifford's interest in the parasites that served the termite in the place of digestive organs antedated by many years his wooing of Myra McKillup. He had, as he explained soothingly to Myra, often watched these microscopic mills at work. The parasites and not the insect converted into a nutritive pulp the otherwise fatal wood cellulose it consumed. It was indeed odd that the termite, considered by scientists the most essential mouth in Nature, should be lacking in its own digestive equipment. For it was the termite whose unique and diminutive jaws were the pestles that ground death into life. They transmuted the cadavers of trees into that womb of nitrate which is earth. Without this spectacular work done by the termites, as Gifford had often informed his students, the world would have hardened into a vitrified and unproductive crust long ago. The mundane detail that in their heroic task as earth-makers the termites also nibbled away a few wooden houses seemed to Gifford hardly worthy of consideration. The termites were of vastly more importance to the world than the handful of people they inconvenienced. Yet for this vast and scientific task, Nature had devised an incomplete tool. The stomach of the termite was incapable of the miracle assigned it. Its labor was contracted out to parasites.

Concerning this, Gifford had a theory which he admitted (to his petulant bride) was more romantic than scientific. He sometimes thought that the very importance of the task had inspired Nature to divide its execution so mysteriously. Thus, if something disastrous happened to the termites as a species, the parasites, much more invulnerable, would survive to seek out another ally within which to carry on the great work.

But the greatest riddle to him (Gifford also confided to Myra) was that of the parasite's genesis in the insect's stomach. For the termite was born innocent of them. They showed up later, a work-crew arriving as if by magic to take up the business of converting the earth's dead wood into life-giving soil. On the death of the termite they departed. Gifford was determined to uncover the secret of the parasites' arrival.

Two theories attracted him. Either the newly born termites acquired their work-crew from the excrement of their older fellows, on which they fed and which served as a transport service for the parasites; or the termites were part of a double birth phenomenon truly unique in Nature. It was possible that they were born with parasite eggs already in their useless stomachs and that these eggs contained their supplementary selves.

Myra was left during the long days of her honeymoon to contemplate these matters and a few others even more disturbing. But for Gifford his parasite hunt was the happier side of marriage. He secured the help of Professor Gerald Canning, an accomplished biological chemist, with whom he spent the greater part of his honeymoon.

But Gifford's home life can no longer be ignored. Even Gifford was becoming aware of certain challenging factors in it. The first and most disturbing of these was that in marrying the provocative Miss McKillup he had suddenly found himself locked away with a companion to whom he was totally unable to talk.

The explanation for this evaded our confused bridegroom. Like so many men Gifford had been lured into wedlock not by a woman but by a superior version of himself risen genie-fashion out of his bottled existence. It was, in a sense, himself he had married. He had taken a witty and exuberant Professor Emmett to the altar, and apparently left him there.

This hidden and evanescent self, which the most unlikely of women are able to evoke in us, is one of the chief causes of marital disaster. Its disappearance at the first breakfast table gives the groom the uneasy impression that he is bewitched. The phenomenon occurs most often to unsexual men in whom the mating instinct gives birth to personality rather than desire. Enchanted by their vivified personalities, these bridegrooms collapse like a jack-in-the-box at the first conjugal caress. The superiority born during their courtship is almost instantly deflated in the marriage bed. The former lover full of dreams and rhetoric vanishes like an impostor. There is left an inferior and useless husband.

Gifford was thus stranded. The situation of the incompetent male has long been a comic fixture. But it inspires less laughter today than in heartier times. There is a phase of sex of which the world is becoming sadly more and more aware. It is the fact that the generative organs have a deeper capacity for giving pain than pleasure. Normality, pleasing and diverting though it be, rarely lifts the soul higher than the bedposts. Abnormality, however, can plunge it down into Hell.

It is perhaps to insure our survival as a species—as Gifford might have explained it—that Nature places such a penalty on the absence of sex in us, and invests its lack with such irrational agonies and confusions. Though love, to the male, is usually a minor diversion, his inability to love becomes an entire career. It became, and quickly, the whole consideration of the loveless Emmett household.

The issue, at the beginning, was not of Gifford's making. Although cast down by his lack as a husband, Gifford was inclined to regard the matter in its perspective. It had no bearing on his labors of dissecting the termite stomach, which he considered his real lifework. The absence of any sensual interest in Miss McKillup came as no surprise to him. Neither she nor any other woman had stirred even so much as curiosity in his head. He would have been as much astounded at any evidence of passion in himself as if he had grown horns. Accordingly he had weathered the first nights with more distaste than panic and hurried off to his termite colony with the childish hope that his incompetence would soon turn his bride's attention to other matters.

Although innocent, he had brought to his nuptial couch a curious sex lore gained from watching through a magnifying glass the libidinous moments in the lives of his spiders, beetles, and ants. His shyness before the swooning Myra was a little complicated by these memories of cohabitings studied since his boyhood. The hundred fierce little dramas of insect amour, whose details he had fully recorded in notebooks, bewildered him on his own bridal night as much as the memories of any rake. There was one scene in particular that kept recurring to him during his first days as a groom. It was the mating of a praying mantis observed seven times enlarged under his glass.

He had come upon the affaire mantis just as the female, lean and spectral, had permitted the woefully lesser male on her back. He had watched the tall and dreadful bride turn her serpent head and begin slowly munching on the passionately employed lover. The Romeo's head, wings, legs, and torso had disappeared under the razor-edged jaws of his mate. Yet this headless, legless, armless, but still enfevered swain had continued at his devotions. There had remained of him finally little more than a sexual organ. This, still alert and full of lubricity had concluded by itself the act of love.

Gifford's imagination fastened on this spectacle the moment Myra emerged from her dressing-room in a creamy, green-dappled negligee with flaring sleeves, and held out her arms to him. The costume had instantly reminded Gifford of the hieratic and macabre wings of the mantis used by that ogress to bewitch her prey. He had said nothing of this to Myra. He felt during the following days, however, that he would be unable to embrace her as his wife as long as she reminded him, by coloration and gesture, of that cannibal insect.

On the fifth day of his marriage Gifford stopped on his way home from Professor Canning's laboratory to buy Myra a blue unpatterned negligee with tight sleeves. Myra, whose sex lore had not been acquired through a magnifying glass, accepted the gift without understanding. She kissed her husband gratefully, but appeared that night in the creamy, green-dappled, mandarin-sleeved transparency which she believed to be extremely seductive. Gifford shuddered, broke into a cold sweat, and clung fearfully to his own bed. After some minor caresses Myra retired to her pillows. She lay for a long time considering the various courses open to her in this combat with Gifford's virginity.

Left alone during the day, Myra preoccupied herself with what now appeared to her a tragic matter. She went over in her mind her own experiences. Though limited to the oarsman and a youthful cousin seduced during her own adolescence, these had left her with a workman-like knowledge of sex. She was also well read on the subject. Her thirst for wisdom of every sort had led her to devour numerous books on sexual abnormalities. Like most young women of the time she had substituted Freud for Browning and was as versed in the horrors of love-making as her sisters had once been in its poetry. But Myra's mind being a sieve, neither her experience nor her reading availed her. Her therapy was reduced to clumsy attempts at rape. All this rough-and-tumble wantonness failed to help the bridegroom. The impression only deepened in Gifford that if there ever was a praying mantis, here was one in his bed.

My attitude toward Myra is, perhaps, unfair. It occurs to me that the ex-Miss McKillup was a young woman lacking in malice or any of the villainies of temperament that wives so often bring as their sole dowries to marriage. She was neither possessive nor given to that home-wrecking preoccupation with her mirror which vainer faces, or prettier ones, adopt as a career. Her heart was kind, and her delusions of being a superior woman were for the most part harmless and inarticulate. She felt deeply on the subject of the professor's prestige and future, and was awed, as she should have been, by his talents. And no one could have asked of Gifford's wife a more hopeful scientific prognosis for his single but vital failing.

Yet with all these qualities I am inclined to accept Gifford's first nuptial glimpse of her as a praying mantis. She would devour him a little more subtly than that rapier-bodied, balloon-winged horror of the insect world. But devour him in the end she would. Stupidity is the cannibalism of the female. It is able, no less than razor-edged teeth, to devour men of talent.

Gifford Emmett did not live long enough to be either devoured or uncolored by the commonplaceness of the woman he had married. He underwent, however, some preliminary fading, just as Myra exhibited that first blossoming of a vocabulary enlarged by his phrases which would have resulted in time in that pathetic common denominator that Strindberg has named "the marriage likeness."

During this first and only year, however, Myra was too busy in other spell-weaving directions to have any influence on Gifford as a mind and an entomologist. She had fallen to work during the first flush of their honeymoon on turning Gifford into a male—which, by the way, is about the only thing women can't turn us into. They can clip our wings and turn us into barnyard companions. Or dip our sandals in the glue of their devotion and turn us into domestic statuary. But men they cannot make of us. It seems a pity, too, that the alchemists who are able to transmute us into the gold of husbandhood can do so little about the simple backwardness of our glands. But the truth is that perhaps the only medicine that fails utterly as a cure for male impotence is a woman. Exercise, a change of diet, an ocean trip, diathermy, a confession to the police, a rise in the stock market—these are among the numerous therapies for a shy libido. At least they are harmless. But the female rampant as a panacea is not only useless but as menacing as the unrestricted sale of arsenic. In her avid arms, impotency, a minor disease if there ever was one, turns into lunacy.

Not that there was any hope for Gifford's insufficiency. My poor hero was as lost to the joys of sex as any parthenogenic worm. His spinal cord was as detached from the signaling female as if it were a-flutter in the wind.

Yet, there is this point—before his marriage Gifford had not suffered from his missing libido. He had been, I admit, the victim of a melancholia that had led him unassisted to the portals of death. But it was a poetical and uncrystallized melancholia. Neither a doting wife nor, later, medical science, had stripped him of his toga as a philosopher. Had he died at that time he would have been buried with his soul intact. It was a serpent's trick to give him of the apple to eat and to send him cowering and outcast to his grave.

Gifford's cowering began in the third month of his marriage. Before that time he worked feverishly over his termites. He filled scores of notebooks. He sought to hide his unserviceable masculinity in other industries. But there is no concealment for a man who has found a part of himself ridiculous. The canker will eat away his conquests, and his one little useless organ, like a worm, will devour his greatness.

Finding himself night after night stretched beside a woman, and always as futile and absurd as if he were a bit of rotten cork, Gifford began to lose his character. The mornings found him more and more morose. He arrived at the laboratory with a clouded eye. Week by week the talents he had developed came to seem less than those he had been born without.

His impotence finally spread to the ants. He was as unable to deal satisfactorily with the termites as with Myra. Soon he was no longer able to eat properly. A tremor made his delicate research work impossible. Sleep withheld itself. Nightmares rode his bed. He grew gaunt and a little stooped. A harried look gleamed from his eyes. His desire to become a male, and his increasing psychic efforts toward that end, had been received apparently as a declaration of war by his well-armed subconscious. A conflict had started in Gifford, and his organs became a befogged battleground. He sat around twitching and bedeviled with the echoes of this hidden warfare.

In the fourth month Myra insisted that he consult a psychoanalyst. It was only fair to both of them, Myra argued, that he turn to science, since love had failed. Gifford resisted. His soul rebelled against this picture of itself being stripped like an onion in an analyst's office. His wisdom shuddered before the thought of being treated as if it were the layers of a disease. How foolish it seemed to him then to reduce the jewels of the mind and all its talents to the symptomatology of inert glands, to make of himself an enemy and harry himself like a traitor. But, as Myra pointed out, he *was* his enemy. His mind, brilliant though it was, must be regarded as the foe of Nature. And Gifford hung his head as his theories came home to roost. He saw himself as among the pioneers of disintegration. He was tasting the future of the species which must end, as he had prophesied, in the laboratory as patients. And so Gifford Emmett and all his wisdom and talents went to the doctor.

There has been in my generation such a blathering on the subject of psychiatry and its capricious twin—psychoanalysis—that I hesitate before this last phase of Gifford's life. I have no desire to reshuffle those new terminologies by which medicine has crept another millimeter into the vast dark of the human being. But this is hardly a time to desert my hero. And if we both sound a little befuddled, there is no help for it. The science of charting our subconscious—that secondary bloodstream that flows through us without arteries or tissues to mark its course—is a work so in its infancy that all who discuss it must sound in some way infantile.

The notion that it is possible to reshape our souls and play shoe-maker to our tattered egos is perhaps the most ambitious project since the Tower of Babel. And at present at least its success looks as dubious. Its artisans are already screaming at one another in languages nobody can understand. But this may be only the disorder that attends the launching of all great tasks and not the confusion that marks their collapse.

I am not certain but, standing beside my hero in his travail, I am inclined to believe the former as the truth. In a time to come these Maestros of the Spirit Ducts may be able to reset a psychosis as easily as they do a bone. Chants, rituals, sesames may be discovered which, better than the scourges of our ancestors, will be able to drive the unwanted devils of Neurosis from their lurking places. A race of Mood Surgeons will attend our gall bladders, and medical Dostoievskys will operate on our dreams to cure us of such ills as stem from them. It may even become known and proved in the time that I foresee that all ailments, including the ravages of bacteria, and the accidents by which we break our necks, are no more than visitations hatched by our wills. And it may even be that on that day when Disease and Death have been identified as the effluvia of disordered Thought, we will seek for immortality on the analyst's couch.

There is of course nothing new to this theory except that it has come to be regarded by organized medicine a little more as science than imbecility. How sensible this change of attitude is, only the layman will eventually be able to say, for he is, in medicine as in politics, ultimately the proof of the pudding. The prognostications that doctors have to make concerning their own business, their judgments of what is science and what is quackery, can be more or less dismissed, historically.

In fact one would think that, confronted by a history so dubious as their own, so full of greed, bigotry, and organized outcries against every bit of medical fact that has been uncovered, its present custodians might feel hesitant about coming again to final conclusions. They have only to look in the dusty corners of the centuries to see them full of pale savants groping for mysteries beyond the purgatives and operating tables of their day, and discovering these mysteries, only to be ridiculed and cast out by Contemporary Medicine.

The biologist and his little umbrella-carrier, the doctor, have always been slow to yield the small ground they have won for the ever-befogged and uncharted spaces of the New—first asepsis, then endocrinology, now psychiatry. The sons of Hippocrates struggled violently enough against their elevation from barbers to medicos. How much more will they battle against a fate that now asks of them that they be geniuses!

The case of Gifford Emmett will, in a way, bear out what sanity there is in their aversion to psychoanalysis, and mine—not to mention the cases of my friends, who, with the aid of these present-day soul searchers, are committing everywhere around me a sort of intellectual hara-kiri in their efforts to outwit their ills. The condition of these friends—my contemporary neurotics—seems to me truly as pathetic as was that of the ancient lepers whom science sought to cure by the application of hot irons to the afflicted parts.

Our current lepers have their attention now scientifically directed to the obscene and idiotic waywardness of their souls. The rubbish heaps of their subconscious are turned over for their dazed inspection. Their wounds thus uncovered, and their hideous diseases thus exposed, they are handed diplomas that entitle them to cure themselves. Having given them a bad name, the scientist in charge washes his hands of them. It is presumed that, once a patient has located the sickening part of himself, he will vomit it out or rid himself of it elsewhere by virtue of some spiritual physic of which the doctor has no knowledge, but which he is sure exists in the pharmacopoeia of the patient. Thus the new therapy is placed in the hands of quacks and amateurs, for what else is a layman and particularly a diseased one? It is no wonder that most of these pathetically combined doctor-patients are bundled off to asylums to scream away their convalescence, or, more therapeutically, to put a bullet through their brains.

Dr. Oliver Jerome, the soul searcher into whose office Gifford was piloted by Myra, was an extremely talented man with an instinct for spiritual anatomy that soon won his patients. Gifford was immediately attracted by this new lens under which he was placed. His own keenness grasped quickly the manner of its operation. And instead of the repugnance he had anticipated, he felt himself being drawn into that friendship for the dark-eyed, placid-faced Dr. Jerome which is the first step of the "cure."

The human being has a remarkable and tireless gift for loving himself, or at least for being fascinated by himself, and he will fasten his gratitude on anyone who assists him in this direction. Within a week Gifford felt deeply attached to his ally—the analyst. The quiet-spoken, unemotional questioner seemed to him both guide and matchmaker. The analyst's eye that looked on human sins as if they were blood cells removed Gifford's social sensitiveness. He was able to experience the thrill of encountering the unknown in himself without embarrassment. He became oddly pleased to discover that his soul was as full of intrigue as a nest of spies and that the Gifford Emmett he had known was a sort of Character-President who had achieved office through the political chicanery of his subconscious.

This first uncovering of self is usually a delight to the neurotic. He embraces with elation the new features revealed, and sees in their often horrid and despicable aspect the mystic charm of kinship that our own always has for us. For a time he is actually happy to meet the disheveled Cromwells of his underworld, and he feels himself, giddily, as full of local color as a slum. Later, when this colony of gangsters and perverts on whom he opened a door loses its novelty, his elation is likely to give way to disgust. On his return to his capitol, the patient grows haunted by the chicanery and lawlessness of his own government. And sometimes in his disgust he abdicates.

This, briefly, was the history of Gifford's analysis. During the first days spent with the analyst, he fumbled nervously with his memories. In the second week, Gifford was in full cry after his past. Dr. Jerome, delighted by the eagerness and intelligence of his patient, explained they were trying to discover the origin of his aversion to sex. It was necessary to locate the exact moment in which the patient had decided on the criminal career of impotency.

Gifford offered his theory of the praying mantis, and related excitedly the many points in common which he had detected between that baleful insect and his wife. Dr. Jerome listened patiently to these somewhat lyric comparisons and then informed Gifford that the mantis religiosa was only a ruse to distract him from the deeper, darker truth of his ailment. Guiding him past the mantis, Dr. Jerome led his patient inexorably back to the scene of his crime. This turned out to be the wind-swept room in the Wisconsin home in which Gifford Emmett had been born. On the way back to this room poor Gifford ran the gamut of father-hatred and mother-fixation and a score of other criminal selves. Each day he was whisked along these byways and sent stumbling further into his past, until he arrived before the true and implacable enemy of his life. This was the tiny emerging infant that had, after a fashion, gladdened the Emmett home one snow-bound morning.

Dr. Jerome, aided by Gifford's memory of family tales, discovered that the little visitor had wanted none of this world. Spanked into existence, the indignant tot had devoted the rest of his life to a kind of suicide. Unable to get back into the womb for whose warmth he yearned, little Gifford had compromised on an aversion to all life outside it. Dr. Jerome was certain that if not for the currant bushes his patient would have willed himself into some form of idiocy. Gifford pathetically agreed that his learning was no more than a ruse by which he had evaded the world of reality. He agreed that his philosophy of hatred of humanity was the flowering of his original aversion to the doctor's forceps. As for his sexual impotence, Gifford saw that it was part of his fixed decision to remain, as much as was possible under the adverse conditions of maturity, a child in the womb. He was a little confused by Dr. Jerome's added hint that his frigidity toward Myra involved also a fear of committing incest.

In the seventh month of the analysis, Gifford was in full possession of his criminal history. His elation over his unknown selves had long since left him. He had returned to his capitol, and there he sat brooding and helpless. He mastered the conception of himself as an intricate and tireless suicide, and there he halted. He understood that his cure lay in his ability to dispatch his infant nemesis with some mystic *coup de grâce*. But how does one destroy one's oldest self? And with what weapons can one attack that which is deeper than the mind?

Gifford retired into himself and remained there with a futile, moody smile signaling defeat from his lips. His wisdom, silent since the first hour of his marriage, reasserted itself. It considered the quality and strength of his enemy. It measured him by all the science at his command and it came to certain conclusions.

I shall report Gifford's words on this subject because they were the last movement of his human-bound mind. Myra heard them excitedly, for she hoped that the analysis was bearing fruit. She was unaware that Gifford had risen finally from his analyst's couch only to speak his epitaph.

"I should like to believe," said Gifford, sitting with Myra in their lonely home, "that it is possible to re-educate the human soul. But I doubt whether even Dr. Jerome has been able to convince himself of this. For how can one re-educate the soul when it is obvious that it is impossible to educate it at all in the first place? The womb, alas, is the only university from which we may graduate with honors. The rest of our schooling adds hardly a credit to our standing. For the life particles of which we have been compounded have completed their studies before Nature entrusts us to the world. They have even completed our particular design. Our glands contain the full album of our photographs. The amount of our hair, its situation and duration, our height, weight, and coloring; our capacities for love and hate and even the nature of those who are to stir our emotions—all these are written in our embryos. The strength of our muscles and length of our bones, the very bent of our talents—whether we shall sing or be mute, whether we shall think brilliantly or dully or not at all; our politics and hobbies, in fact, are assigned us in the womb. Our thousand moods as well as many of our physical mannerisms are all predetermined for us by the quality of our thyroid, pituitary, adrenal, pineal, and other bits of tissue. We can move only in the directions charted for us in these glands. The distances we may cover are also fixed. We are, in the main, as predetermined as the insects—but less perfectly so. For there is left for us a small margin of chance and an even smaller one of effort. Within this little margin we are permitted to rattle around like peas in a pod. It is this pathetic movement we call our individualism, free will, divine independence, and so on.

"Seeing ourselves complete this way when we are born, with our destiny inscribed in every gland, I can't understand Dr. Jerome's theory that we are capable of rewriting our fate—that is, if he has such a theory.

"I am afraid," said Gifford, "that my cure lies in a more practical rebirth than our psychiatrist has to offer."

A look of torment came into his eyes and he muttered almost inaudibly: "It's not pleasant to be a human being."

Myra squeezed his hand tenderly, but Gifford continued to look fixedly at his shoes.

"Dr. Jerome's science is not impressive," he said at length. "But for that matter no science is very impressive. If you look back on what the Mind has thought since its first known statement, there's only one thing worth noting. This is the fact that its thinking invariably turns out to have been comic. Today's truth becomes tomorrow's jest. The Mind is always a hero to its own generation and usually a clown to the following. It is well to remember that we are in the midst of a constant yesterday of folly.

"The tale of who and what we are," Gifford said sadly, "is the tale told by a Peeping Tom flitting from one keyhole to another. Our knowledge is full of scandal and rumor, but none of it has seen the face of life or looked even for an instant into its eyes."

Gifford finished and stood up. He smiled for a moment on the alien woman whom he had married, and then went to his room. In the morning Gifford Emmett was found dead. Beside him was the bottle which Myra had taken a year before from his lips. It was empty. Myra, who had come into the room to waken Gifford, stood looking at his body with more amazement than grief. It was curled up, the knees clutched against the chin, and the head tucked down in a sightless and yet pleasant-seeming sleep.

II

Now that we know that the spirit of the tree returns to the earth, to be born again as loam, mushroom, or forget-me-not; now that we have discovered that when sea-water dies, algae appear to breathe back to it those very chemicals that had fled its dead and mighty cheek; now that we have mastered, however vaguely, the fact that all matter is a transitory display of eternal energy, and that there is no destruction but only renewal, it will be an aborigine of a reader, indeed, who sneers with incredulity at the bewildering fate that turned Gifford Emmett into an ant.

I say bewildering because, despite the assurances of science, there are some things I don't understand about it. I understand fully that the human spirit is chemically related to the sap of the vegetable and the whinny of the Unicorn and shares their fate. All that lives must ride and bob along on the same curving but unbroken seminal river. The headwaters of this eternal stream are unknown, and the Sea of Death into which it empties is another vast and unknown place. We know only the little landscape between that we call Nature. Having completed our brief excursion on this bright river, we very likely become part of some piece of legerdemain such as the sun performs on the sea. We, too, are probably lifted out of the Sea of Death and precipitated again into the hidden headwaters. And I can understand fully that this evaporation must be a fine democratic sight—that a man, a crocodile, and a gnat all evaporate, as it were, together into one great mystic cloud. And out of this far-away womb we come tumbling out again in an anonymous and intermingled cloudburst, hailstorm, or drizzle. We are returned to life as capriciously as weather. And out of this reservoir of vibrations or, at best, a sort of laboratory mist, we must not expect to emerge in the guise we entered. This would indeed be preposterous. We are re-costumed for our new excursions out of a most chaotic wardrobe. And it is our fate that any cap fits, whether it be a rooster's comb or a bishop's miter.

Of these matters I am fully cognizant and I can thus understand Gifford's reappearance as an ant. I could, if I wished to devote more space to the problem, explain it in considerable detail. But still one phase of it bewilders me. This bewilderment does not lie in the fact that Gifford became an ant but that he remained a human being. There I am a little at sea as an explainer.

I can only state categorically that Gifford's soul passed unchanged into the newly laid egg of a termite in the low Sierras to the southwest of the Republic. What the psychic and intellectual points were that made the new-laid termite still Professor Emmett, I shall eschew for the time being. Also, if there is something more mysterious in Gifford's appearance as a California termite than as a Wisconsin infant—in itself a very mysterious matter if you stop to think of it—it is an increase of mystery on which we had all better turn our backs if we wish to avoid too much confusion.

The egg out of which Gifford emerged was one of some fifty thousand that waited constantly, mob-fashion, for egress from the belly of the termite Queen. It was the habit of this ovarian monster to pump some five to ten thousand of her children daily into the royal bed. Each of these remarkable litters contained, in a ratio deemed proper, supplies of workers, nurses, agriculturalists, soldiers, and lovers. (Since Darwin and all the succeeding biologists have failed to explain the phenomenon of an ant hatching a social system, I shall also ignore the explanation. It is obvious that Nature is not only a scientist but a magician too, and, if she chose, cows would give birth to guinea-hens and Minervas to tree-toads.)

Gifford arrived in the contingent of lovers. He was born a male with the single destiny of cohabitation. All other insect learning would be denied him. He would be unable to forage for food. He would lack all equipment for toiling and fighting. Sex would be his lone talent, his delirious and solitary objective.

In the beginning the Gifford Emmett who lay curled in this tiny egg was scarcely any more related in character than in size to his preceding status. There was no more in this egg than a flickering consciousness of previous human estate.

For many days after he was born the new Gifford lay sightless, tiny, and content to be a grub. His human intelligence was the most delicate of obstructions to the perfect passage of time as the insect knows it. It existed like a bubble against which the great chemical currents of insect life swept and whirled. But, bubble though it was, they failed to dislodge or shatter it. The bubble persisted and within it, as within a secondary body, Gifford's human soul grew stronger.

When he had reached his third instar, having shed his chitinous exterior three times, and acquired the wings that identified him as one of the male reproductives of the kingdom, the human Gifford awoke sufficiently to become aware of his status and surroundings. But he experienced no shock, for what his mind saw appeared to him only the most fascinating of dreams. And, as one accepts in a dream the strange clothing and abortive geographies of the wandering Personality, Gifford accepted with no sense of panic his dwindled guise and amazing habitat. His dream of being an ant pleased him—though not entirely. He would have preferred in his dream to have been an early paleontologic insect with a wing-spread of two feet, and he made an effort to re-transform himself into such a redoubtable coleopteran. But while he could see himself as an elephantine gnat of some sort, the dream ant remained.

By the time of his fourth instar, Gifford had given up his efforts to alter the time and condition of his dream self. He devoted himself amiably to the study of this little phantom. Yet if it were an escape dream, why had he invented himself as a sexual ant? Here, Gifford thought, was something that would tax the psychiatrist's dream-book lore a bit.

He contemplated other things, among them the lineage of his dream figure. It had descended unchanged from lower Oligocene Tertiary times—as was evidenced by its identical amber-imbedded ancestors still in his college laboratory. It stood to reason, likewise, that the activities of the colony in which he lay maturing had also never changed since that far-away time. The government of which he was now a subject had not found it necessary to pass a new law for a million or more years. It had achieved social perfection when man was still lost in the anarchy-ridden debut of his evolution. This pleased Gifford and he was proud to be a member of a kingdom so hoary and glamorous.

In his sixth instar, curiosity beset Gifford. His dream seemed to him too static. He desired adventures. He was accordingly pleased to notice that his termite self was moving about. But even as he nodded with approval (an inward nod which the nonvertebrate termite in no way shared) he became aware of dangers now besetting this sightless and winged dream self. He recalled with a touch of fright that the status of the alate in the termite colony was a most precarious one. For this alate, who alone of all the castes in the kingdom was designed for love, inspired revulsion and rage wherever he appeared. Unequipped for foraging for food himself, he was ignored by the busy workers, who seemed intent on providing food for all mouths but his own. In fact these toilers seemed full of contempt for him and for all his sexual brothers, who lay about dreaming of their coming hour of love in the spring. And the soldiers too exhibited toward him the warrior's distaste for the sybarite. They were constantly decapitating and dismembering the defenseless, half-starved Romeos of his caste, tearing off their wings in what seemed to Gifford nothing more than the sadism of morality.

Wisely, Gifford accepted the fate of his kind in the kingdom, a sort of leper's fate. He must hide away from every one of his fellows, steal his food at the risk of his life, tremble before every clanking troop of warriors that passed, and lead a bedeviled existence that was truly heart-breaking—all this because for one hour in spring he was to enjoy the pleasures of love. It would seem that the State, jealous of its metro-nomic soul, resented even that exercise of individualism which insured its continuance.

Undeterred by the dangers that beset him, Gifford continued to study the swarming life around him. He saw the workers toiling at their thousand tasks, keeping the ventilator corridors in repair, hurrying down the spiral roads with food for the combination store- and furnace-rooms. He could feel the warmth rising from the decomposing provi-sions and calculated quickly that winter lay outside.

In addition to the multiple domestic tasks of feeding, cleaning, airing, heating, storing, nursing, and all that occupied the kingdom, there was the constant work of battle. Troops of soldiers were con-tinually a-rush to the outer gates of the kingdom, for here the enemy everlastingly threatened. The black and red ants, scenting the stores of foodstuffs and hungering for the soft bellies of the termites, were forever hurling themselves into the kingdom and advancing down the ventilator roads.

Gifford watched a number of battles. He saw the warrior ants march in formation to meet the enemy, and take their stand like a praetorian guard barring the way of conquest. These armored bullies, whom Gifford had come to hate because of their wanton and vicious manner toward his own daydreaming caste, now became heroes whom even the alates must admire.

He had watched angrily these idling guardsmen standing about so overarmored that they were unable to feed themselves. A sycophantic worker class not only brought them viands but stuffed them in their mouths while these robots stood glowering like visored knights with iron-gloved hands clutching halberds that could never be laid down. But when the tocsin sounded in the termite land, and the alarm of the enemy at the gates was spread through the kingdom by the soldiers, and the corridors echoed with the beating of warrior helmets against enameled walls, Gifford, flattened against a ceiling, would see a rally and a march forward that were unforgettable.

The several battles Gifford witnessed were beyond anything he knew in the history of human heroism. He learned now that the courage of the termite warriors actually modeled their figures from birth, for they wore no armor on their backs. Since they would never turn tail to the enemy, no wasteful protection covered their rears, which were as vulnerable as the bellies of moths.

Calmly and precisely the soldiers advanced to meet the dreaded enemy now streaming down a ventilator corridor. Arrived in one of the vast chambers through which the zigzagging roads of the kingdom ran, the halberdiers would spread into a double-rank formation. Thus they stood barring the way into the interior. The enemy, usually sharp-fanged black ants, came rushing forward. They charged like a mass of little black bulls. Swifter than the termites, their armor more supple, they came in a deadly rain upon the defenders, whom they often outnumbered a thousand to one. Motionless against this tide of shields and sabers, the termite soldiers stood swinging their mace-like claws into the bodies of the swarming enemy. They fought erect. As long as possible, with their legs interlocked, they stood barring the way into the heart of the kingdom. On their courage depended all that was termite. Once past this barrier, the enemy would swarm triumphantly down all the roads of the kingdom, devouring the stores, the workers, and bursting into the royal chamber in murderous waves. Here, with the last of the royal guardsmen destroyed, the feast of the King and Queen would end their conquest. And the vandals who had found a kingdom would leave behind them a tomb in which not a tentacle was left moving.

This knowledge was in the halberds of the termite warriors. They fought on fiercely, piling the dead around them in great heaps. But from the top of these heaps, as from a thousand towers, the enemy continued to hurl himself in ever-increasing numbers. Losing ground, the beleaguered warriors sounded the signal for the reserves. The signal, like a high bugle note, drifted down all the roads of the kingdom, and in answer to it the waiting reservists moved forward. This signal was not only the warriors' cry for help but also their swan song. The reserves arrived, rank on rank of unarmored workers. With their arrival the termite warriors moved forward into the charging enemy. They had saved for this moment their last store of prowess. Erect and implacable, they held off the fanged host, and behind them the reserves worked desperately. They sealed the passage into the kingdom.

Pumping glue and plaster out of their bodies, they walled off the battlefield. The road to life thus cut off for them, the termite warriors gathered themselves into a last phalanx. Left sealed in with the enemy, they were torn to bits by the thwarted hordes.

Gifford watched and admired these constant Thermopylaes. He grew to feel a regard for the clanking militarists in whom burned this great mood of valor and sacrifice which seemed to him a little nobler than his own dream of a spring cohabitation.

And still the half-delusion that these were all fantasies parading in his human sleep held Gifford's mind calm. The delusion remained until his seventh instar. On that day, full grown and finally winged, Gifford tasted for the first time the whole horror of finding himself an ant. His awakening occurred in the following manner. Moving furtively along the deep corridors, he had made his way through encampments of warriors and caravans of workers toward the place he knew existed somewhere in the kingdom and which he had not sufficiently observed in his first metamorphosis. This was the royal chamber of the Queen, where he discovered himself standing presently.

At first his human mind was fascinated by what he saw. But as he stood watching the hailstorm of termite life heroically brought forth in her bed, realization smote him. He became wildly aware that he was not dreaming this sight, that he lay in no bed of his own, hatching fantasies out of his subconscious. This tiny deviled termite standing on the Queen's threshold was himself. These pin-point features, this drop of matter was Gifford Emmett. His human mind was attached like some incredible fungus to an insect. It existed within its tiny structure. It was he, Gifford, who was the dream. And it was the ant who was reality.

With this knowledge, horror streamed through Gifford's mind. Despair erased for a time all his thought. His soul sought to hurl itself out of this minute and suffocating world in which it was trapped. But the insect in which it had its spurious seat clung to it with the clutch of doom. He sought to cry out and like some insect Samson to wreck the pillars of his prison and bring the kingdom crashing down on him and all its subjects. But no sound came from him and, though his mind vaulted, his midge of a body remained motionless. And he realized that he had no powers of expression other than those of an alate. His soul, complete with all its human senses, was not only without face but without talent of utterance.

Recovering slowly from this shock, Gifford found himself clinging to the wall of the great royal gallery and, philosopher that he was, he presently concluded that his condition and new environment were of minor importance.

There were many dead thinkers, mused Gifford, shaken but heroic, who occupied an even smaller space in the world than he did at this moment. And what, he argued, was the human body compared to the operation of reason but a cloud to the sun?

From this it will be seen that Gifford's former notions about the horror of Thought underwent a most thoughtless change no sooner than he had discovered that it was his only human possession. He clung to reason now like a survivor to a wrecked homeland. Despite his former infatuation for bugs of all kinds he refused to consider himself one, now that so ideal an opportunity offered. It was no doubt odd that Gifford, having become one of Nature's superior children this way, should cast his lot so loyally with a species he had always derided. But we are, perhaps, none of us ever ready to be what we dream.

His mind careening in the rapids of these revelations, Gifford opened his eyes again to the monster mother on her couch. Monster was a poor word, he mused, shuddering at what he saw. The termite Queen was no new sight to him, but it was one thing to have studied her as a scientist and another to look on her as one's progenitor. This new view held Gifford spellbound and nauseated. Two thousand times bulkier than any of her children, for she was six inches long, three inches tall, and as many thick, the Queen lay motionless like the figure of Mother Earth at the core of the world. Her great saucer eyes were sightless. Her legs hung from her as useless as feather fans. She was neither animal nor insect but a fount of life—a God-like ovary that hatched by itself an entire race. For there were no other mothers in her world. Within the great clay ball swarming with myriads of her progeny, she alone gave birth.

In the chamber all about her, several thousand soldiers stood guard. They were picked troops, taller and more unwieldy-looking than those of the corridor encampments. They stood immobile, as the workers fed them. A stream of caterers also attended the Queen. Her gigantic face, gray and bloated and lost in a spermatic dream, swarmed with subjects bearing food. These kept her mouth constantly filled, stuffing its monster jaws with cellulose pulp, dung, and the mangled bodies of her own children. She munched constantly as she lay. Another stream of attendants presided over her continuous accouchements. As the eggs issued from her in an unbroken larval ribbon, the medical caste hurried them off to the nurseries of the kingdom.

And Gifford, watching the horrid manner of his birth, saw too the ugly mechanics of his conception. He saw the pallid King, half the size of his consort, come dragging himself like some sack of concupiscence to the royal bed. The movement of this gouty Lothario made him more horrible-seeming than his inert mate. This, like the Queen, was no longer an insect but a mass of seed, an ugly and bloated servant of Nature, servile with lust. His very eyes were distended with sperm. Pale, crippled, and unrecognizable as one of his family, he dragged his volcanic loins toward his immobile bride. Slowly he mounted her and Gifford beheld the disemboweling deed of creation.

The cordon of warriors also looked on. Dwarfed by the occupants of the royal bed, they seemed like homunculi defending a throne. They watched the deed with awe, for it was the holiness of the kingdom, the chant to creation. There was no other sire in the land and no other such deed anywhere. The writhing Monarch astride the Queen was her single lover. From his loins poured the immortality of the colony.

The thought came to Gifford that this ritual before him was his own future. He had been born to breast the thousands of hazards of death that lay on the way to the insect throne. If he survived them, he too would become a king. Even now these were the precarious hours of his apprenticeship. And hours even more laden with death awaited him. He would be among the thousands of kingly aspirants who swarmed out of the termite fortress into the world of spring. There in the open, he would seize on a mate. Around the multitude of bedazzled lovers that coupled in the maddening light of life, all Nature would be waiting, ready to devour. Lizards, spiders, black ants, frogs, everything that crawled or leaped or flew, would swoop upon the orgiastic nuptials and dine on them.

But there would be a few who survived. These would drag themselves wingless and exhausted into some burrow to found a new kingdom, to copulate endlessly, to hatch new myriads of workers, lovers, and soldiers, to grow into twin monsters of lubricity. Gifford, watching the bloated Monarch and his insatiable Queen, turned his thought coldly against such a future. His human aversion to sex was multiplied a thousandfold.

He left the royal chamber. Weak with hunger, he crept through a crack into an abandoned room recently the scene of some mighty battle. Around him he saw the disfigured warrior bodies all fallen forward on their faces, and the enemy dead. Gifford paused and feasted.

When it had gorged itself with its first full meal in weeks, Gifford's alate self started forward. It moved slowly, for it was burdened with food. Gifford's mind grew alarmed. He knew the fate that awaited the lethargic insect, and he turned his thought for the first time to the control of the alate's movements. For several minutes Gifford saw that both he and the alate continued to crawl slowly toward the distant corridors filled with clanking soldiers and inimical workers. But as he exerted what he hoped were hypnotic powers, the insect stopped moving. He remained uncertain whether his will had curbed the termite, or some tropism. Nevertheless, a sense of triumph came over him as the insect crept into a niche, where, safe from all dangers, it fell asleep.

At least, he exulted, he, Gifford, would not have to submit to being dragged about willy-nilly by an ant. He could bend it, evidently, to his own desires, even though the process by which he was able to dominate the insect seemed not only mysterious to Gifford but at variance with his learning as an entomologist. But whatever the situation was between himself and his ant self, he would soon determine it, Gifford assured himself. No entomologist had ever been so ideally equipped and situated for research.

Now there were other, more pressing, matters. These were his Thoughts. Like Robinson Crusoe's few possessions salvaged from the shipwreck, they must first be put in order.

He had just learned that he was an ant, and had survived the shock. Now he had to admit he was Gifford. For proof, he had been calling himself by that name. And otherwise, too, as far as he could make out, he was everything he had been before, even, he sighed mentally, to the point of being Myra's husband. Regarded externally, it is true, he seemed no more than an ant, but, observed from within, his learning, sense of personality, and human consciousness were intact as Gifford Emmett.

This raised the question—and one that might fascinate any psychologist, Gifford thought—of what constituted a man. Were he to crawl in his present guise before any group of scientists and address them to the effect that the human body was an unwieldy and superfluous masquerade, Gifford doubted whether a single one of the scientists would remain long enough to hear him out. And those who didn't bolt would identify him as a mass hallucination perhaps, and hurry off to some other scientist, maybe Dr. Jerome, to be cured of delusions.

On the whole, after musing for some time, Gifford was glad that the structure of the termite was too rudimentary to permit of speech.

Not that he feared he would drive any of his former colleagues into any serious aberrations. Considering the shocks he himself had just survived, the sanity of his former species seemed to him well-nigh indomitable. Besides, Gifford was too well aware of the propensity of orthodox science for ruling out unruly facts from their organized learning—thus making man's reason doubly safe.

But why, mused Gifford, when they had so much prettier theologies, should he attempt to substitute the promise of anthood for that of Heaven, if indeed such a metempsychosis as his own were the rule, and not the exception? (Since his courtship, Gifford disliked the word transmigration.)

This left him all alone with his immediate problem. This problem was to ponder, first, the generality of man's survival, then its relation to his own specific rebirth, and, finally, to compute, if possible, the various eventualities before him.

He eliminated as unimportant any question of the generality of rebirth. The immortality of the human soul was, after all, the most ancient of theories, and, *ipso facto*, he considered it proven.

As for his own rising from the grave as an ant rather than an angel, this was a more intricate idea. For one thing, it left him at least no closer to the bosom of God than he had been as a university professor. Then, it had not enlarged his wisdom according to the popular theory, but neither had it removed such enlightenment as he had, for which he found himself now wonderfully grateful.

In fact, closing his mind to any disputation for a moment, Gifford for the first time in his two lives repeated slowly and gently the words of a voluntary prayer. He pleaded with the Lord to accept a humble ant and open His arms to its wandering soul. And from this deed he learned the power of prayer as a bulwark against the extremely unusual.

At this point, although it was a far cry from his own Bible school Deity to the Hindu, his scientific mind obliged Gifford to take such a leap. He recognized in this older myth of the genus Homo a perfectly serviceable theory, according to which he was now scheduled for numerous incarnations. Death after death would probably be his, and also life after life. He would persist through these as Vishnu, Krishna . . . or, far more likely, he corrected himself, once he was through with the ant, as a moth, a lizard, and so on.

And here the disquieting question offered itself to Professor Emmett in all its darkness and bedevilment. Why, *why*, had he survived as Gifford Emmett? What possible purpose could Nature have had in fashioning an ant man?

The answer was inescapable. Professor Emmett found himself with no choice but to admit that something must have gone amiss with his death and the mechanics of his survival. He was no soul at all pursuing its normal orbit after death. He was a mistake. Owing to some aberration of Nature, he had entered this termite stage as Professor Emmett instead of arriving incognito as the pure spirit of life. Death had obviously blundered and forgotten to strip him of his useless human consciousness. He was at large in the Unknown as an interloper.

And now he faced the prospect of being doomed to exist—as a Professor Emmett forgotten by Nature—through an eternity of anthills and birds' nests and fish hatcheries. He might even find himself meditating amid the electrons of inorganic matter and forced to lie about for aeons as a stone. This thought that he was ordained to travel through the wonders of Nature like some perpetual tourist grew stronger in Gifford. Just as he had been born unfit for his former world, he had been reborn unfit for the Unknown. Gifford asked himself sadly if there was any profound and secret reason for his having been appointed eternal freak. Perhaps there was some pattern in his mismaking, some plot of which he was a mysterious part?

At this point, remarkable doings aroused Gifford from his scientific inquiry. A great commotion filled the kingdom. Gifford entered the senses of his termite self, now astir, the better to understand what was going on. A series of astonishing impressions smote him. Although blind, the alate was capable of a curious kind of sight. It saw reality as an inward dream. No objects existed for it, but it was as full of visions as a saint. Gifford applied himself eagerly to its sensory fibers as to a series of microscopes. Although still unable to translate most of its sensations into human understanding, he knew enough now to realize that the tiny body in which he resided was leaping about in a state of mingled exultation and panic.

A great noise filled the kingdom. From everywhere came the whistle of ants and a ghostly shout of song. The towering corridors were full of rout and revelry. Masses of ants appeared singing and leaping and rolling wantonly over each other. The once orderly roads had become the arenas of a Bacchanal.

Gifford moved forward into the hullabaloo. He saw the alate was no longer in any danger. Its status had changed. Bedeviled since birth, it was suddenly cock-o'-the-walk. And Gifford knew that the festival of Priapus had begun in the dark of the termite kingdom. The dreaded warriors greeted him with whistles of joy. They beat their helmets against the walls, and their cruel halberds had become castanets and tambourines. They had become an orchestra playing for his delight. Above the chant pouring from a million ant throats they sounded their delirious and compelling drum-beats. Gifford stood on his hindmost legs and danced.

Everywhere crowding all the roads the termites were dancing. They stood upright, swaying to the banging of the soldier drums. Now another wilder element entered the festival. A wind appeared, swirling and beating against the walls. Gifford perceived that the wind came from the swiftly moving wings of the alates. Above the heads of the mobs these males and females were now fluttering and leaping, heedless of everything but the joy of flight. They spun and dived into the press of orchestras and dancers, overturning whole ranks of them and scattering them fearlessly. And as he danced and hurtled with the rest, Gifford became aware that he was being fed. Honey-tasting morsels were being pushed into his mouth, and his head was covered with tidbits as with garlands. Food rained down on him from everywhere. The armored bullies ran beside him, clearing the way for him. Garlanded and serenaded and preceded by hordes of dancers, the males and females were being escorted to their hour of love.

Swaying, chanting, and with a bullet-like urge in his heart, Gifford reeled along as part of the insect hallelujah. The writhing and screaming processions were moving toward some holy place that signaled from somewhere, and the subterranean kingdom was a single cry and its myriads were a single wave.

Suddenly the whirling spokes of some magical illumination overwhelmed Gifford. The chant around him was drowned by roars of light and sound that lifted him on their reverberations and tossed him headlong. The rush of the lovers out of the bowels of the kingdom to the couch of the sun was on. The exultation of air and light swept away all the memories of that dark termite land, and the alates, wings spread, were flashing toward its gates.

Gifford's mind removed itself from his insect self. He went to work again as a hypnotist. Desperately he exerted his will. He had set his mind implacably against any future that led to the royal bedroom. His human aversion to sex now gripped his insect self with a violence not to be denied. As he neared the little disk of sky at the end of the termite road, he struggled to command the clamorous instincts of his tiny body. Violently his mind proclaimed that he was not destined to couple with any of these million Myras, or to expire, still throbbing with pleasure, on a lizard's tongue.

The moment of exodus arrived. As out of a thousand rifle mouths the alates vaulted into space. Puff after puff of wings burst from the kingdom and remained like madly waving ribbons of smoke. Gifford was among them. He guided his insect self, however, to a leaf-shadowed twig. He knew that there would be neither bride nor enemy in the dark. And from his perch, he witnessed the prenuptial flight of his fellows. He saw that even the soldiers and workers had emerged to watch the spectacle. These stood thronged about the many gates of the kingdom, as the once despised lovers filled the bright spring air with the fiery prelude of their passion. Gifford's insect self trembled, but Gifford held it firmly in the shadow.

Looking at the world above him, he perceived a mass of forms whirling around as if caught in some overwhelming spout of sun and air. And from these insect jets came the bellow of bulls and the bugles of the chanticleer. The dance in the sun and air continued for a long time. Then, having saluted the mystery of space, the lovers sought out one another. They embraced in mid-air. Gently they exchanged caresses, as yet too overcome by this first taste of pleasure to dream of more. Clinging together, legs and wings locked in a first innocent kiss, the lovers drifted downward, seeking a couch. And Gifford saw that their couch was the frog's toothless mouth and the spider's glue-dipped web.

Blinded to all but their dream of pleasure, the lovers died in droves. Shining-backed bugs leaped at the double morsels. The air and the earth became thick with murderers come to the carnival. Here and there a pair of lovers escaped for a moment the gulp of the wedding guests. They lay coupled and creating. And when the moment dreamed of through the dark year was done, they threw aside their wings and started off for immortality. But the locust and the cicada came to bar their way. The killer flies swooped into the grass jungles after them. The snails and the earthworms closed the roads.

Gifford watched this scene of bliss and death until the grass grew still and the hum of slaughter was ended. Seemingly all the lovers had been destroyed. But he knew that somewhere the road to immortality had been left open. He thought of the two or three royal couples, attended by the souls of the slain multitude, crawling into the earth to continue the everlasting kingdom of the termites. And his one-time admiration for the nobility and cunning of the insect cosmos fell from Gifford as if only now that he was an ant had he become a man alive with human ego.

A contempt came to him for the manner in which Nature had just now handed on the termite scepter. The few alates who had survived to become Kings and Queens had earned their royalty neither by merit of their own nor by the operation of any law. Caprice alone had planted the crown of survival on them. And though he had always been aware of this lack of individuality in Nature, the fact seemed now outrageous to Gifford's mind.

Gifford recalled that in his human days he had been full of admiration for the Perfect State in which the termites and so many other insect species existed. But viewed now from within, this Perfect State seemed to Gifford a challenging and empty structure. There was, he mused, something revolting about the egomania of Nature, who, like some tireless dictator, demanded a kingdom of sleepwalkers to hymn her glories and never their own.

The perfection of Nature, thought Gifford, is made out of the imperfection of her subjects. The lower the slave the finer the state, was the secret of her ideality. The beautiful government of which he had been a part existed at the expense of a million individuals who had no existence at all. Their life and death were a command performance. And he thought of his termite brothers as somnambulists trapped in a monotonous dream. All experience was denied them, even that of age. They were permitted to learn nothing, for the wisdom of the tiniest grub and that of the hoariest grandfather were identical. They lived and died under a hypnosis that prevented them from ever changing or bettering the world into which they had been summoned. Their valor, industry, sacrifice, and even love-making were grimaces of obedience, and submission was their only genius.

It was a form of genius that occurred often among men, as a degenerative process. Whole nations of humans became capable of stripping their minds of all individual existence. Unquestioning and prostrate before Authority, their souls, identical and callous as so many beetle backs, offered the rhythm of their servitude as their greatness.

Those human groups like the Germans, the Italians, and the Japanese, thought Gifford, who seek for strength in the destruction of the individual, are operated by some dark and ancient ideal of Nature's. The lust for mass power is stronger in them than the dream of human development. By depriving the individual of a soul they are able to create an external and hypnotic soul called the State. Neither truth nor justice nor the graces of intellect become then the goal of the individual in it. But an ant-like metronomic existence allures these citizens. Their glory lies in being able to become by the surrender of self something more powerful and glamorous than lay in these scattered and struggling selves. These ego-castraters are the turncoats of evolution and they betray humanity back to its pathetic beginnings.

"I wish," added Gifford sadly, "that I had concerned myself a little more with the politics of the world when I was a human part of it. For I see now that politics is not the history of governments but the broad currents of biology. I was extremely stupid in admiring the spider and the termite above Lucifer and Prometheus."

In the midst of his musings Gifford became aware that he was crawling somewhat uncertainly down the tree in which he had been roosting. He quickly placed his Thought within his alate self and looked on the outdoors for the first time as an insect. What he saw bewildered him. He was plunging through ravines and craters which he recognized, after some hesitation, as the bark of a tree trunk. Monsters beset his way and, holding his breath, Gifford careened to the ground. Arrived at the foot of the tree, Gifford felt that he had been suddenly translated to the dead and awesome caverns of the moon. Around him loomed shapes of infernal size and strangeness. Monstrous scimitars waved over his head which, with difficulty, he remembered were grass blades. Above the grass, the leaves of bushes floated like vast domes. As from the floor of an abyss, Gifford looked up at a gargoyle world.

Around him, as he crawled, rose the scream and roar of enemy figures too gigantic for his vision to encompass. Disaster echoed everywhere. Every bit of stone was a mountain inhabited by ogres and every hollow was a chamber of death. Of all that moved, he alone was without size. And Gifford perceived that to an ant Nature was a storm blowing and a sky falling. Weaving onward, Gifford held his breath as if in the midst of panic. No one thing threatened, no visible fate pursued, but he was part of some general rout going on all around him. His ant was fleeing aimlessly from life, scaling crags and tumbling into pits, scampering up waving roads that ended in nowhere and toppling from these spiraled highways, moving ever without destination like some pilgrim lost in chaos.

Then suddenly Gifford halted. He felt a warmth within his body. And his ant self remained motionless in this bedlam as if before a friendly hearthstone. The warmth was some sort of signal. Gifford recognized it presently as the rays of the termite kingdom beckoning. Flattened against the earth, Gifford refused to move. The belly of a spider like a great cloud passed over him. He watched the forest of its legs drift away. Huge and jagged shapes leaped from the abyss with the noise of thunderclaps. Meteor bodies flashed beyond the leaf domes and vanished. He beheld horned creatures of incalculable lengths sliding down mountainsides toward him. Great heads protruded hissing and slimy from the earth, and Gifford stared into the chimera faces of the worms. In the midst of this paean of destruction the ant remained crouched as at some fireside.

Then it resumed its movement. But now it had discovered a road. Gifford realized that it had located the rays of the termite kingdom. He thought, rushing forward now, that here lay the secret of the homing instinct in nature's children. The air was honeycombed with radioactive currents. Placing themselves on these as on invisible rails, the unerring travelers of the sea, land, and air were able to return to their homes and homelands. It was obvious, mused Gifford, that this electric spoor was exuded by every species and that the seemingly trackless wastes of air contained a wonderfully organized system of vibrating streets. But this problem, which would have fascinated him in his human guise, occupied him only a moment in his present travels. He thought instead of the fate that awaited him on re-entering the termite kingdom. The warriors were undoubtedly still hovering about its gates, for it was their custom to assassinate such useless stragglers as returned unwedded from the field of love. Exerting his will, Gifford halted the termite and led it to the top of a vast stone. Here, he reasoned, it would be safe from its subterranean enemies. On this stone, with the warmth no longer in its body, Gifford's alate self submitted to his commands and lay motionless.

When he had rested on this stone for a long time, Gifford heard a sound different from all the noises around him. It was a muffled and continuous note, rhythmic as a purr. As he listened, Gifford grew frightened. This surprised him, for, being ringed everywhere as he was with the faces of death, why should he conceive of a sound coming from somewhere within the earth as unusually terrible? Surely there were no gradations to doom, argued Gifford against the terror-inspiring purr that filled his senses.

"It is not the ant who is frightened, but I," continued Gifford. "It lies with its wings folded like the toga of a Stoic. No hero was ever so calm in the face of disaster or so unperturbed before its many hideous heralds. Surely, I am as good a philosopher as an ant."

Thus, gathering courage from the termite's example, Gifford's mind grew calmer, though the horrible sound continued to come from somewhere in the earth.

"And of what," pursued Gifford, "have I to be frightened? If I am to be slain as an alate, I shall obviously make my reappearance in some other form. And no guise into which I am translated could be so distasteful and unflattering as this over-sexed little somnambulist I now inhabit. My efforts to keep this priapic midge alive are absurd and short-sighted. Certainly there must be something more for me in Infinity than a post-graduate course in entomology."

Now entirely calmed by his musings, Gifford settled himself to wait for whatever doom lay in this ominous sound beneath him. But no monster came protruding from the earth or creeping over the edge of the rock. And as the sound continued, Gifford tried to locate and identify it.

"It is evidently something in the earth," he thought, "some monster of terrific proportions creeping along. Its eyes will be white, for it will be earth-blind. It will have a remarkably long and armored snout with which to dig and it will be possessed of countless shovel-like claws. And like all subterranean creatures it will smell disgustingly. But what monster is there," Gifford pondered, "that can creep through stone? For this noise is immediately under me. I can feel the vibrations of the creature's travels in this rock. I know of no animal or ogre who can crawl through the interior of rocks."

An enormous shape suddenly appeared and loomed on the stone. A vulture had alighted beside the professor. He stared at the arrival, pleased to be a morsel too insignificant for its powerful beak. The vulture was evidently resting, for its lidless eyes seemed full of weariness. Then, without warning, something astonishing happened to Professor Emmett's winged rock-mate. Gifford saw its legs disappear into the rock, and a moment later it had vanished entirely. It had fallen into the stone as if into a drum. There was a wild flapping of wings, and after some moments the vulture lifted itself out of this unexpected trap in a billow of dust. Without pausing to examine anything, the bird beat its way off toward the clouds.

Professor Emmett looked bewilderedly at the place where the vulture had stood, asking himself what sort of stone was this that collapsed under a bird's weight. Moving toward the hole, which was still smoking with dust, he beheld a sight incredible to his human senses. A multitude of termites was in the heart of the rock. Spread symmetrically before him like the spokes of a wheel, the insects were feasting. He watched the wheel turn and the stone disappear slowly before it, vanishing grain by grain into the bellies of the termites. They were eating their way into the rocky core of a mountainside, and Gifford realized that this was the monster at whose purring he had been eavesdropping.

Looking further into the stone he saw that this wheel was only a segment of the monster. There were other wheels turning. A series of circular tapeworms was moving like cogs of destruction within the flinty mountain base. Gifford looked up at the mountainside. The thought came to him that this whole towering and bouldered land-scape was a shell similar to the rock through which the vulture's feet had plunged. And he remained for some time lost in wonder.

"I have come on a new species of termite," he reasoned, "that is able to penetrate rock as easily as its brothers penetrate wood. It is evident that these rock-eaters have evolved a new race of parasites as their digestive equipment, and that these hardier occupants of their stomachs are able to convert particles of stone into a nutritive pulp. Since nothing is impossible to the chemical genius of the insects, I must accept without further quibble the fact that they have mastered the secret of extracting nitrogen from a completely inorganic form of matter. As Newton said, one must not ask unfair questions of Nature. One must study her secrets not as if they were miracles but as the simple, visible links of a hidden chain."

Fortunately Gifford was able to bolster up his unbelievable obser-vation with the memory that there were certain ants that had always been able to penetrate but not digest limestone. These ants were equipped with small tanks of formic acid that acted as a solvent. How-ever, no species of ant had ever before been able to turn a whole moun-tain into a shell from top to bottom—a soufflé of earth and granite whose very existence would presently be threatened.

If this were to be the case—and he feared it would be—Gifford knew that it was a climax which was to be postponed. In the first place the ants were not likely to reveal their presence to their enemies, and in the second place they would be sure to devour the landscape com-pletely before allowing any avalanche to interfere with their meal.

Pleased to be the first man in the field to view such a phenomenon, Gifford started on a tour of inspection.

"One can't help admiring the little beggars," he mused to himself as he toiled upward from rock to rock, listening always to the purr beneath him. "They know to a fraction the amount of material to remove without collapsing the structure they disembowel. This ability to calculate swiftly and with the most delicate precision the various stresses of a mountainside, the different pressures of its boulders, forests, and rivers, is an instinct containing in it information beyond all the engineering data known to man. Such a talent would be com-parable in man to the ability for measuring the weights, distances, and constituents of the stars merely by looking on them with the naked eye."

This was backsliding toward his older attitudes, and Gifford knew it. And he knew, even in the midst of that vacillation so comically typical of the scholar, that there were greater duties before him than that problematical report to a scientific commission with which his fancy kept toying. What this tremendous adventure was to be, he did not know as yet.

Here, half-way up the mountain, he made another scientific discovery. He was resting from his labors on a high rock covered with frost, but the alate was apparently undisturbed by the chill of his lofty roost. Gifford couldn't help marveling, for the termites of every known species perished in a temperature below fifty degrees. This astounding fact, and his present certainty that the whole mountain, from peak to base, was alive with the insects, led to only one conclusion. The termites were engaged in some sudden evolutionary spurt. They had not only acquired new talents—for eating stone, resisting cold, and so on—but they had obviously increased fantastically their rate of reproduction. (Any numerical estimate was impracticable.)

Gifford paused at this point in his musings and observed that a storm was gathering around the mountain peak. He noted also that the purring within its heart had ceased. Full of apprehension, Gifford watched the black clouds massing and hurrying forward like armadas. Great gusts of wind came from their careening hulls and then the rain leaped down. Thunder crashed and the lightning brandished its quicksilver knives over the mountain peak and hurled its broken spears into its forests.

Gifford waited wretchedly. The mountain was quivering all about him. With each thundercrash it seemed to breathe and swell as if it were coming to life. Under the beat of wind and rain its sides shivered like rattled drumtops, and a rumble issued from its heart that drowned the noises of the storm. The din from the earth increased and the pulsing of the mountain grew wilder.

Then Gifford saw the mountain vanish. Bellowing and screaming, the great hill turned to dust. Its boulders exploded, its ravines and gullies opened into great umbrellas of dust. The mountain roared in the darkness. Cavernous night filled the air. Through the darkness Gifford beheld the forests raining out of the sky. Trees were shooting past him. Like a great rocket that had burst in midair, the mountain plunged out in every direction and collapsed in a thousand avalanches. Gifford leaped to a falling bush. Tossed far into the air by winds and gases, the bush parachuted to the earth. It lay on the edge of the smoking shattered mountain base.

Gifford looked out at the disaster. The rain had ceased. A cloud of vultures was drifting toward the mountain corpse. Looking into the great pile of wreckage extending for miles, Gifford saw that all that had lived in this mountain had been destroyed. The fish in its streams, the animals, large and small, who had haunted its forests, and great colonies of birds had all perished. All had been crushed and entombed, all but the voracious little wheels that had devoured the great hill. These still lived. Gifford saw the termite regiments racing undisturbed through the mountain remains, like vandals abandoning a razed and alien house.

Then suddenly Gifford realized the full import of what he had beheld. He had seen a new war lord launch a world conquest. The vision of all the cities of the earth devoured by termites came to Gifford as he lay staring at the mountain corpse. It was the insects who had conquered the Greeks (despite his argument to Myra), for that valiant race had degenerated through malaria. But how much greater a conquest this would be than all the plagues and epidemics of the past! These termites, whose numbers were already incalculable, would multiply within a year into great moving deserts of destruction. They would spread like a quicksand. As the mountain had fallen, so would all the steel and stone towers, all the homes and factories topple. The structures of the world would become a dust drifting away.

Gifford pondered the vision of civilization ravaged. Man would be stripped of all his inventions. All his refuges, instruments and machines, all his books and his seven-league boots would end in the bellies of the termites, ground to dung by a horde of parasites. The great human house of toys would be devoured and man would be left like an infant, naked and resourceless, on the inhospitable doorstep of Nature.

For a time Gifford lay motionless with his vision. He thought of the shout of panic as the first great structure toppled in the cities, carrying millions to their deaths. He imagined then the next inevitable downfall—civilization collapsing like a row of dominoes; art, beauty, and achievement vanishing in a rain of dust and splinters.

How long, he wondered, would it be before all man's systems of philosophy were swept from his soul as he returned again to the caves and campfires? How long before all wisdom and delicacy of spirit would be outlawed as incompetence? A month, a year, at most a handful of years, and power would be seized by sinew and sadism. And would the spectacle of man struggling in the savage state for which he had so vaingloriously unfitted himself be his final deathbed scene? Would he be able to repeat the great conquest of his near ape ancestors and come marching triumphantly out of the jungle mists once more? No, thought Gifford, he is a poor creature now, incapable of defending himself against the climate alone. The sun, moon, wind, rain, and snow would do for him without any other enemy's helping.

And Gifford thought of what a tragic little rabble of bad spearsmen all the politicians, preachers, industrialists, poets, and philosophers would make. How quickly Nature would close in on this child who had bartered his animal birthright for a fragment of soul.

There would be a battle against the ants, of course, before all this came to pass, for the human species was not without weapons and courage. It would mobilize all the chemicals in the world, and fall upon the termites with poison and fire. But all this would be futile against the overwhelming numbers of termites that Gifford foresaw at their present rate of increase. Also, the chemicals would give out, for the manufacturing plants would be destroyed. And, courageous though man might be, the ant was possessed of a heroism beyond his. Death had no meaning for the ant, for it was only a cell that died. The termites would attack as a single monster, invulnerable and immortal. Villages, farms, and cities would disappear—a scattered rubble heap of a decomposing species.

Here the thought that had been haunting him came into Gifford's mind like a thunderclap. It occurred to him that he could save the world. He could carry news of the coming conquerors to the scientific outposts of the race, and give man time to prepare for the termite raid. He could, somehow or other, guide an army into this unpopulated land where the conquerors were still hatching. Attacked quickly here in the desert, the termites could be destroyed. The entire mountain range which they now inhabited could be blown up, the surrounding desert irrigated with poisons, and the human race saved.

"I could save the world," Gifford repeated to himself, and lay staring as if under a spell. Then he began irrationally to move. For several minutes he darted about, climbing through the branches of a tree.

"I could save the world," he kept repeating as he climbed the tall tree. Arrived on its uppermost leaf, he hung from its pointed tip and was silent as he looked at the sky.

"I could save the world," he resumed finally. "I can save the entire world of Thought. It is something I must consider. A few hours ago I was full of sentimental memories of the human race. I felt indignant at Nature and her hordes of somnambulistic children. But let me think now of man. Where is his worth? For instance, is there a single thought worth saving? Is there one dream or scheme that has not brought misery to the species? Where in all its history is there an idea that, once launched, has not crippled and tormented it? What have its philoso-

phies and religions been in the end but the means for the creation of
new victims? And what is the mind of man, seen as a whole, other
than the ghost of his fangs still tearing at the throat of life?"

And, looking back into the world, Gifford denounced it from his
high leaf as an ugly place.

"Ah," he said, "if only thought were perfect, or half as perfect as
anti-thought; if the human mind were not so eager to surrender its
little handful of questing words to every charlatan who crossed its
path!

"Unreasoning, malformed world," he cried, "world that fills its
governments with witless, howling tyrants, that is forever driving
reason into caves and placing ogres on its thrones, what is there in such
a world to save?

"Remorseless and inhuman world, that postures like a parson and
roars like a beast, wherefore save this world? Intolerant, cowardly
world, that mangles its weak and spits upon its poor, what is there in
such a world worth preserving?

"Wherefore save this world," Gifford cried to himself, "that has
from age to age torn at its brother's face? This mocking, gall-souled
race that denies solace to itself, that allows itself to be everlastingly con-
scripted into the vile armies of unreason, what is there in its soul
worth the preserving? Stupid and clamorous race that can be bled of
all honor so easily by any mountebank and brought crawling on its
belly to cheer at every crucifixion—it will be well for itself to end. For
what is there to rescue," demanded Gifford, "what is there to man but a
little mask, a bit of silly lace that covers the tiger's eyes, a dainty little
glove that hangs tattered from tiger claws?

"I shall stay here," pronounced Gifford, "and wait till all the pretense and vileness that has come to be called civilization shall have
achieved the honest pattern of termite dung. And from some place
astride a grain of sand I shall witness the extinction of the human race
with the equanimity that befits an ant."

Gifford was silent. The matter was ended. Within the body of this
termite high up in a tree, the fate of man had been decided. Let the
termites multiply and devour man—his soul and his works. Gifford
would not move from his leaf.

A little awed by the situation, Gifford decided to put the whole
matter out of his mind and devote himself to the business of being an
ant. And returning to his termite's senses, Gifford observed the scene.
He noted that the sky and the leaf were of equal size, and that the
tree in which he roosted was like a limitless sea whose waves roared

and tumbled beyond the rim of the world. Thus occupied with the cosmos of an ant, Gifford suddenly heard a faint voice, a little sound of words that rose from his innermost self. It was his own voice, coming out of a buried self, that spoke. The humanity he had condemned was speaking in him, as if lingering in the court of his mind to whisper against the verdict it had heard.

We have not done so badly, it said, not if you care to look at us a little more closely. Considering everything, we have not done so badly. Before you condemn us, look on us again. Not on our pomp and murder, not on our governments and gibbets, nor racks nor righteousness. But look deeper and beyond these. The list of human evils is long and humanity's record of honor is small and scattered. But it is worthy of survival.

Gifford listened to the voice of the world he had found intolerable during his residence in it, and a sadness overcame him.

Consider, it went on softly, consider who we are, and the darkness out of which our mind was born. Consider how ancient the beast is beside the little furrow of thought that has come to mark its brow. Though we have in our ignorance spilled a great deal of blood, we have also wrested a little wisdom out of the dark. In the midst of our lusts and bigotries we have found time to draw maps of the heavens, to examine the roots of plants, to peer through microscopes at our bacterial forefathers, and to pry open a fraction or two the doors of mystery.

And listening to this cajoling voice in him, Gifford beheld slowly another vision of humanity. He looked at its science. Behind the political diseases of its centuries, hidden in the ugly shadows of its religions and conquests, he beheld the isolate mind of man—a never-dying light that gleamed through the ogreish history of the race. How valiantly it twinkled even in the darkest corners, how steadfastly it shone out of the ever-dreadful shadows! No wind had ever blown it out. No tyrant with whip and sword and exile but had left it glowing more brightly.

Consider, he mused, how great was the ignorance with which we were born and how many priests and captains have held us forever chained in this ignorance. Though we have come forward only a small way, it is a noble inch we have moved.

There are a few, continued Gifford, who do not merit my judgment. They are those who have preferred the search for truth to the banners of tyrants. They are the few who devoted themselves to something other than the making of crowns for bigotry and hysteria. Amid all the great hunger for applause and power which has wrecked each age, there have been always these humble ones.

And Gifford thought of the scientists, of the eyes that had kept everlastingly peering out of the human shambles at the ways of the moon, the sun, the stars, winds, birds, beasts, and all the elements and exudations of Nature. Even in the day when piety was feeding infants to the god Moloch there had been eyes to look beyond the fires of sacrifice at the meaning of the heavens.

And Gifford recalled these immemorial heroes of the mind whose names were written on the small scroll of wisdom. Where the many others had butchered and lusted and left behind the gaudy, vanishing tracks of conquest, these few had toiled and died and left only some tiny fact to mark the small road of learning. But how much brighter this little way shone than all the tracks of glory. And how much sweeter was the fame of these everlasting little plodders than that written on the arches of Triumph. Their names were inscribed on bugs and insects, on the skeletons of sea monsters and on the petals of flowers and the sacs, vesicles, and fibers of all physiology. Atoms and gases kept their memory green, and in every chemical and computation their laurels bloomed. They had striven for truth and not for greatness; died in poverty but bequeathed riches. And their honest names, unknown to the changing crowd, had found immortality in a spider's genus or a bit of human tissue.

And how far and tirelessly, Gifford thought, these had journeyed in their quest of truth, dissecting the eyes of butterflies and weighing the flaming bodies of the stars, ever a-tinker with mice and lichens, sea bottoms and cloud tops, and pursuing God or Nature into the invisible and marching on with their mathematical lanterns where there was neither light nor matter to guide them.

These are the mind of man, thought Gifford; these are the law-givers and the rulers of the world. These are the soul of the race. All the rest is a froth of hunger and ego, lust and lies and actors sick with the need of applause. The light of these remains to deny the most abominable darkness. I have judged wrongly. That grim and suffering face of humanity that finds solace in torturing its fellows is not to be judged, for it is only the rudimentary face of man. The list of human evils is long and the record of human honor small and scattered. But it is worthy of survival.

Having come to this conclusion, Gifford trembled on his leaf and began to glow with excitement.

It is possible, he thought, that I am not a freak but a Messiah and that I have been appointed to save the human race from extinction.

That is, if there is a God it may well be that I am a Saviour, and that . . . But here Gifford paused and frowned at his own musings.

Such a theory is nonsense, he resumed coldly. It would seem that whoever allies himself too fully on any side, be it even that of reason, becomes forthwith full of the rankest delusions in its behalf. Obviously, if there was a God who had selected me to be His Saviour, He would now invest me with some sort of divine power, or some sense of His existence other than this worrisome quibble at present in my mind. At least He would not rely on an ant to rescue Mankind, if such a rescue was His intention.

Perhaps, added Gifford, I should pray. Whether I am a Saviour or not, it can do no harm.

And Gifford prayed for some metamorphosis which would enable him to speak and enlighten the race as to its impending doom. Trembling within his ant body, he tried to make the prayer sound as unselfish as he could. He murmured humbly that he was content to be an ant but that his desire to serve God's will made him long for increased measurements and some means, denied to the hymenoptera, of expressing God's word to the human race. Nothing came of his prayers, and Gifford found himself convinced neither one way nor the other by their failure.

The history of God, Gifford remembered, as written by His most infatuated admirers, reveals Him as too busy to give more than a glance at any of His problems. He has never asserted Himself in other than an incalculable way. He smiles out of Infinity like a coquette, and turns His back on anyone smitten by His light. As a result His messiahs usually end up in bonfires, crucifixions, or as mince-meat.

"Whether or not I am part of some divine pattern for the saving of mankind," Gifford smiled, "of all messiahs, false or true, I am surely the most pitiful and futile to look at."

These confusions finally passed from Gifford's mind, and the decision he had made sent him helter-skelter down the tree. During his descent he kept looking about him with his human senses and wondering where he was.

"It is going to be very difficult fulfilling my mission," thought Gifford, "with or without divine assistance. And until I receive some revelation I will approach the career of Saviour as scientifically as I can. This desert around me may be part of Africa, Asia, or America. It is too bad I am such a poor geologist. Professor Wallachek could have told at a glance where he was. My ignorance is unbecoming both to a scientist and to a Messiah. However, I will not waste time bemoaning it. My first problem, wherever I am, is to find some human habitation and then figure out some means of attracting human attention and imparting my Message to human intelligence." And without further debate Gifford started forth.

For forty days and forty nights he continued to dart aimlessly over desert sand and hills. The bewildered but obedient ant plunged about this way and that, and no Saviour of mankind ever turned so many circles as did this termite. During this time Gifford was tempted often to give up his search and abandon the human race to its doom.

"It would be so much easier to be a Messiah," he mused wearily as he pursued his desperate journeyings, "if there were a God." And he paused time and again to pray, excusing the vagueness of his supplication by thinking: "If my piety is uncertain, it is not nearly so uncertain as God's interest in me. However, I should be a fool if I ignored altogether the possibility that I am a Messiah. In the midst of so many miraculous events as have befallen me, prayer is not entirely out of place.

"It will be easier to persuade Americans to save humanity than it would be to interest other nations in such a project," mused Gifford, "for Americans are about the only people left still amiable enough to be interested in preserving the race rather than in exterminating it."

On the fortieth morning Gifford emerged from the wilderness. He came upon a road. Urging the bedraggled ant to its edge, he surveyed the enormous stretch of concrete. The perfection of this road, the symmetry of its seams and smoothness of its surface, gave him a feeling that he was in his native land. A few minutes later an automobile swept by and he recognized it as American. At least his mission lay in a familiar country.

For several hours Gifford remained thus at the edge of the road, while a half-dozen dust-caked American automobiles appeared and vanished. The sight of the doomed but heedless human beings in them filled him with a sense of compassion. Gone now were all the doubts that had assailed him during his wanderings in the desert. Instead, his mind was full of plans. Foremost was the decision to go to Washington and reveal his news. Since the destruction of the termites would undoubtedly be a Federal project, much time would be saved in bringing the menace to the attention of the White House itself.

Gifford thought hopefully of the Chief Executive, famed for having surrounded himself with men of vision. Surely, he jested to keep his courage up, there would be no difficulty in adding an ant to the Cabinet, particularly in these times of social experiment. As each car passed, he looked desperately up at it.

"It is too much to expect," he decided presently, "that any of them will stop to give me a lift." And he began to crawl along the road.

Hour after hour he crawled, until, finding himself lying flattened against the hot concrete and no longer moving, Gifford realized that the inevitable had happened. His ant body had collapsed. Gifford remembered its hysterical scramble through the desert with death everlastingly looming and roaring around it, and was not astonished at its exhaustion. The termite, like a toy wound up, had run its course. His will was no longer able to budge that spent creature.

"How pathetic it seems," thought Gifford, "that the fate of the human species should depend on the fragile legs of an ant. For without its body to transport me I am powerless."

Studying his alate self closely, he saw it still breathed. The only thing left to do, he thought, was to signal some passing car. And Gifford's soul took its position on the road's edge and fell to sending out thought waves at each speeding vehicle. Toward nightfall the miracle happened. The despairing ant saw a car come to a halt in front of him. It was a lowly and battered conveyance, snorting as if in the last stages of mechanical existence. Smoke poured from its hood, and its doors were tied shut with pieces of cord. It had broken down, and its driver had alighted and started repairing the engine. There were two elderly women in the back seat. Gifford crawled slowly toward the car, mounted the hot wheels, and deposited himself on one of the four shoes. Here he lay listening eagerly to the conversation of the travelers. He learned that he was in the State of California, route 9, spur 52; and that the mountains some thirty miles to the south were called the Navajo range.

As these were the hills in which the termite hordes were toiling, Gifford memorized the information carefully. Eventually he heard the sound of the motor and the rush of wind and knew his journey of salvation had begun again.

During this journey Gifford changed automobiles a number of times. Hitch-hiking from tourist camp to tourist camp, he remained loyal to his mission. Daily he listened to groups of mindless people debating the ways of the world, and in the nights, as he lay tiny in the dark, he was shaken with doubts as to this civilization he was so desperately intent on saving from the termites' bellies. And though he saw that his fellow-travelers were as untouched by the three thousand years of science, art, and philosophy to which they were the heirs as if they had doffed only yesterday their nose rings and skirt feathers, and that if every statue, painting, book, idea, and instrument of learning were to disappear from the earth overnight these people would experience no more sense of loss than a backward child for a school that had burned down, he kept alive his ideal.

"I am riding to the rescue not of humanity but of a few of its dreams," thought Gifford. "I must bear this in mind lest everything I see and hear disillusion me and turn me back. It is a pity in a way that to save so little that is good so much that is stupid must be allowed to flourish. But a Messiah cannot afford to be critical."

On the afternoon of the eleventh day Gifford arrived in the city of Washington, which he found full of alarums. Crawling to a news-stand, he learned that the hysterical aspect of the capital was due to five recent attempts on the life of the President, all within the past ten days. The government, as a result, was full of panic, and the press was lucratively occupied with the horrors of the would-be assassinations. Gifford read a more or less cool account of the events in a Republican (anti-administration) newspaper. The criminals, this gazette reported, had all been captured. Four of them were men, and the fifth a scullery maid in the White House. The latter had poured a bottle of arsenic into the President's soup, endangering not only his life but the lives of his entire family. The others had concentrated on shooting and hurling bombs.

Under questioning, the five were revealed to be suffering from what several psychiatrists (Republican) identified as a New Deal psychosis. All five of them considered themselves in the light of saviours. The scullery maid submitted in defense of her action that she had heard on excellent authority that the President intended to close all the churches and banish all the priests, as had been done in Russia. She had acted solely in the interests of the Church, and felt certain that if she were executed for her so-called crime God would receive her with grateful arms as a valiant foe of the present administration.

One of the bomb throwers, a professor of economics at a boys' prep school, had acted out of the delusion that the President had tried several times to break into his study and set fire to it. And on two different occasions he had, in the nick of time, discovered fires lighted by the President in the main dormitory. He regarded his deed not only as one of self-defense but one in defense of many thousands of lives.

"I have nothing more to say," he declared, "except to express my regret that the pyromaniac President is still alive, and, what is worse, at large."

The third would-be murderer, a sergeant of police, appeared to be suffering from a misinterpretation of the finest Republican thought. He had read hundreds of editorials proclaiming that the President was seeking unscrupulously to retain his power by drugging the lower classes. The sergeant had conceived the idea that the nation's Chief Executive was head of a gigantic dope ring and engaged in distributing narcotics to a demoralized Republic. He had accordingly sought to remove him. From his cell this zealot called indignantly on other patriots to rally to the rescue of their country. Otherwise, he announced, the United States was doomed to share the fate of a drug-ridden China.

The other two assailants refused to give any reason for their attempts to shoot down the Chief Executive. Informed that they would be tried for high treason, the penalty for which might be death, they answered proudly that Germans knew how to die in defense of their Fatherland.

Gifford digested these matters and all their sidelights from the journals. He realized he had come to Washington at a difficult time, for with all these attempts on his life the President was bound to feel a certain prejudice against any Saviour, however authentic. Just the same, that afternoon Gifford crawled down the policed and deserted street leading to the White House. Undeterred, he scurried up the wide steps and entered the Mansion. The vestibule too was crowded with Secret Service men. Lingering among them, he learned that the President was in his study upstairs preparing his message to Congress. Gifford zigzagged up the steps, located the study door by the presence of four armed guards, and entered through a tiny space over the threshold. A few minutes later, Gifford, from behind a towering ink-well, looked out upon the face of the Chief Executive, who sat in his shirtsleeves. He had a faraway look in his eyes and was chewing on a pencil.

Gifford observed that there were three other figures in the study. Two were obviously guards, for they remained stiffly looking out of the windows. The third was evidently someone very close to the President, for, like his Chief, he also was in shirtsleeves. After a period of silence, this friend of the President spoke.

"It isn't necessary to finish the message today," he said. "You've got a whole week."

The Chief Executive nodded. He addressed the two guards and Gifford was surprised by his whimsical tones.

"Any more assassins lurking about?" he inquired.

The guards answered solemnly that the coast was clear.

"It's damned hard trying to write with a lot of hecklers around," pursued the President.

"Hecklers!" cried his friend. "That's a fine name for those murderers."

"They didn't murder anybody," said the President amiably. "I guess, along with my other shortcomings, I'm a pretty bad target."

"Listen," said the friend, "I'm dead set against joking on this subject. And, what's more, I'm not going to let you pull any grandstand plays about those assassins. There's going to be no humorous attitude or official clemency. If you let them off easy, it'll just encourage every poisoned mind in the country to take a shot at you."

"That would be a lot of shooting," the President chuckled. Then he added: "How do you like this paragraph?" And he started reading from the penciled manuscript on his desk.

"We must bear in mind," he read, "when we listen to our great industrialists proclaim that they are motivated only by an interest in the welfare of the working classes, that these same gentlemen achieved their high estates by a complete indifference to the welfare of these same working classes." The President smiled apologetically. "That's all I wrote today," he said. "And I guess we better get fixed up for dinner."

"O.K.," said the friend, and turning to the guards at the windows he ordered them to remain at their posts until they were relieved in the morning.

"I don't think that's necessary," the President objected.

"There's no telling what some poisoned mind will do next," his friend insisted. "One of them might hide himself in your study and lay for you."

"Take it easy, boys," the President said.

Gifford watched the President and his friend leave. He had long before decided on his method of communicating his information, but he waited now patiently behind the inkwell. Knowing the literary obsession of the President, Gifford was fearful that he might return for another bout with his Congressional message. Accordingly he allowed hours to pass.

At one o'clock Gifford moved. He crawled quickly up the inkwell. On its edge the ant paused. Gifford urged it on but it remained obdurate. It refused to plunge into the ink. This unexpected mutiny delayed Gifford a half-hour. At the end of that time his will overcame the termite's reluctance and the insect, quivering for a last second on the edge of the inkwell, dropped into its black contents. A moment later Gifford came crawling out of the well. He moved with difficulty, being half choked and blinded with the ink. Down the side of the inkstand he crept and on toward the President's message. Here Gifford pressed his belly firmly against the paper and began to write. The writing required a score of trips to the inkwell and constant use of his human will. At the end of his labors, however, he had completed the first of a series of carefully contemplated messages to the President. In a wavering thick script, full of erratic deviation caused by the termite's inability to move in a straight line, Gifford had spelled out with his belly the first words of his Message: *Beware the Ants!* The warning covered the entire page of the manuscript.

When it was done the ant sank into a stupor, and Gifford waited for the dawn. He was not worried, for he felt that with practice his ant body would improve as an amanuensis. He felt certain, too, that despite its present exhaustion the ant would survive the hardships of composition.

The President entered his study at eight o'clock in the morning. He greeted the guards amiably and sat down before his desk. Gifford, who had stationed himself under a blotter edge, watched eagerly. He saw the President glance at his manuscript and start to sharpen a pencil and then pause and stare.

"Mr. Sykes," said the President sharply. "Come here, please."

Mr. Sykes came to the desk.

"Who wrote this on my manuscript?" the President asked quietly.

"I don't know." Mr. Sykes frowned. "There's been nobody in this room since you left."

The other guard came to the desk.

"Are you sure of that?" asked the President.

"Absolutely," said both guards.

"If you didn't write this, and there's been nobody in this room since I left . . ." began the Chief Executive, but gave up the logic of his case with a thoughtful "Never mind."

"Thank you, just the same," he added abstractedly.

The incident made a small stir in the White House. The President's friend pointed out that there could be only two explanations: either the guards had dozed off, permitting some vandal to enter the room and deface the manuscript; or one of them or both of them had done it themselves in a fit of aberration.

"It goes to show," said the friend, "that we can't be too careful. Even the White House is overrun with poisoned minds. I'll have those two guards questioned by a psychiatrist at once."

The President worked until late on his manuscript. When he left, it remained on the desk. But four new figures stayed behind this time to watch the premises. They had been carefully selected from the Secret Service ranks by the friend himself. Their instructions were not to leave their posts at the windows and door for any reason, except to apprehend an intruder.

"Nobody moves," repeated the friend. "We don't want suspicion falling on any of you four. Just keep away from that desk and keep your eyes open."

The following morning there was a greater stir in the White House. For the President had found on sitting down to his desk that his manuscript had been defaced once more. Across its top page was a wavering scrawl as if some infant or idiot had trailed an ink-dipped match over it. The scrawl read: *Termites now eat stone.*

A number of officials were instantly summoned. The four guards were removed to military headquarters. Here they were grilled by the Secret Service head, flanked by two psychiatrists. They persisted, however, in their original statement. None of them had moved from his post and no intruder had entered the study.

This absurd but mysterious sabotaging of the President's manuscript appeared to all concerned as something sinister. It was regarded as the beginning of a sixth plot against the President's life. Investigations were started within the White House. Every inmate and every inch of space were gone over by squads of detectives. After several conferences, the President stated, late in the afternoon, that he had something more important to do than chase a will-o'-the-wisp. He settled down again to the writing of his Congressional message. It was eight o'clock when he quit his desk. Six men remained behind, among them the Secret Service chief himself. Guards had been placed outside the windows, and at every door of the Mansion. The garden shrubbery was jammed with detectives. The President himself took the further precaution of placing his unfinished manuscript in a desk drawer.

"I don't think," he smiled on the group guarding the room, "that we'll have any more trouble with that scribbler."

The next morning the Chief Executive entered his study at the unusual hour of six. He was accompanied by his friend and an unknown man whom Gifford designated as his Chief of Staff. The guards and their leader greeted the President with smiles, and the latter was pleased to be able to report that there had been no vandalism during the night. The President unlocked the drawer of his desk and removed his manuscript. A frown came over his face as, without comment, he pointed to the ruined top page.

Scrawled in smaller letters that wavered less than those of the previous messages were the startling words: *Civilization in danger. New ants coming. Eat stone. Trillions. If think mankind worth saving hurry up.*

Several hours later the President, his Chief of Staff, his Secret Service head, and various wise men from the Military Intelligence Department were still in conference. A clue had been discovered and the best analytic brains of the nation were wrestling with its significance. Traces of ink had been found in the keyhole of the drawer in which the manuscript had been locked.

The men confronted by the mystery were all agreed on one theory. This was that some mechanism involving perhaps radio-activity and controlled from some point outside the White House had been used. The motive, it was decided, was a plot against the sanity of the President.

"But I am not at all likely to go insane," the President protested. "And besides, most of the Opposition think I am already crazy."

"The Opposition," his friend answered, "has underestimated you for eight years. Let us not underestimate them."

"What's more," said the President, "I am convinced that no mechanism is being used."

Pressed for further opinions, the Chief Executive remained glum for a space.

"I would dislike this to get out," he finally offered with a sigh, "but there is such a thing as Revelation."

The friend was the first to speak in the silence that followed.

"Well," he said, "the plot is working."

"What plot?" demanded the President.

"You can see the effect of such a notion on the country," explained the friend firmly. "They're bound to crucify you for it."

"Me?" cried the President. "Crucify me for what?"

"For thinking that God is writing you letters," cried the friend.

"I have not referred to God or made any statement involving Him in this mystery," said the President coldly.

"Indeed," said the friend and lit a fresh cigar, "you said it was Revelation. And who else can make revelations besides God?"

"I don't know," said the President.

Although every effort was made to keep the bizarre events of the President's study hidden from the world, news of the White House mystery spread. It was garbled news, to be sure. The rumor that billowed through the nation concerned itself with the uncovering of some monstrous plot against the President's life.

In Republican circles, the tale ran that several members of his Cabinet had turned on the President, as in the case of Julius Caesar, and had tried to stab him as he was taking a walk. Another rumor swept through brokerage firms and other strongholds of conservative thought. This had it that the White House had been undermined, and numerous caches of dynamite discovered. These rumors and others reached the editorial desks of a thousand newspapers and set a thousand editors bristling with expectancy. By nightfall the reports had reached such proportions that a new and corollary whisper became current. This was that the President was dead. Oddly enough, gossip agreed he had been strangled by a close friend while in the White House study. The New Dealers, however, were in a plot to keep the news from the country in order to insure, for a while at least, the continuation of their policies.

Despite the absurdity of this last rumor, it had gained such circulation by midnight that the press took to clamoring through its representatives in Washington for the President to show himself and be photographed then and there—if he was alive.

This the President, ever ready to outwit the Republican press, was glad to do. At twelve-thirty he appeared in one of the larger drawing-rooms, and allowed a dozen photographers to take flashlight pictures of him. He was in evening dress, having been to a state dinner. Of the curious matters that had thrown the Secret Service and Military Intelligence into so obvious a panic, he refused, however, to make any explanation.

"If anything of any importance happens to me or to the country," the President smiled, "I or my survivors will inform the press immediately. Let me assure you, though, that nobody has shot at me, tried to poison me or blow me up for five whole days, and that if this armistice continues I shall have my message to Congress done on schedule."

The journalists were quick to note that the White House was a veritable encampment of generals, detectives, and bodyguards, and that the rugged face of the Executive was pale, and his large eyes far away. Leaving, they spoke to one another furtively of these impressions, and of the grave and ominous events that were obviously in the offing.

Some of them doubted that they would ever take the President's picture again, and decided secretly to save the plates of these "last" ones.

The President's mind, so apparently elsewhere, had actually been fastened on the scene in his study upstairs. Here some twenty-five officials, scientists, and Secret Service operatives were assembled. They were standing in a regularly spaced circle around the room and their eyes were intent on the President's still unfinished message to Congress, which lay exposed on the desk. There was no light in the room other than that of the moon in the windows.

The twenty-five vigilantes were armed with various devices as well as weapons. The army had brought over its most recent radio-activity detectors. Three of the scientists present were world-famous psychiatrists on the *qui vive* for evidence of mass hypnosis.

At last the President hurried upstairs. A dozen guards made way for him. He entered the study as smiling and eager as a boy finally arrived at a circus.

"Well, gentlemen," he blurted out, "any more messages?"

There was a stir in the unlit room. The officials in charge assured him nothing had happened and urged him to leave the premises. They hinted that danger lay in the room and that the conspirators had most obviously planned some final *coup* for this night.

"Well, if you don't want me to go insane," smiled the President, "you'd better let me hang around here. After all, it's my study and it's my writing that somebody is defacing and it's to me that the warning about those ants is being given. I'll just sit here and wait with the rest of you."

The Secret Service chief explained that they had decided to make everything as easy as possible for the villain controlling the radio writing, as the mysterious warnings were now termed. Therefore the vigil would be kept in the dark. All the conditions prevailing at the times of the previous defacements would be duplicated. No one was to go near the desk. The President's message was to lie exposed as it had on the first night. And nothing was to be done to prevent the scrawling of the gibberish. However, a new type of radio-active camera had been trained on the desk. This camera, able to photograph in the dark, was even now taking pictures of what was going on on the desk.

"We are remaining here until dawn," concluded the Secret Service chief.

"So am I," whispered the President, and there was a note of glee in his voice.

Silence had been agreed upon, and the occupants of the room remained without sound. The white page of the manuscript on the desk shone faintly in the dark. Every half-hour the President's friend tiptoed over to examine it, and returned to whisper that nothing had happened yet.

At five o'clock in the morning the Secret Service chief rose from his chair. Dawn was coming.

"Nothing," repeated the friend, after a trip to the desk. He moved toward the President, who had dozed off in his chair.

Alarm was in his voice as he asked: "Are you all right?"

Immediately five Secret Service men turned their flashlights on the Chief Executive. The silence became suddenly full of hissing breaths and a hum of awe and consternation. The voice of the President's friend rose sharply.

"Nobody move," it ordered. "Everybody stay just where they are. I'll take care of him!"

"Take care of whom?" muttered the President, opening his eyes.

"You," said the friend. "Be still, please."

"Lights!" the Chief of Staff demanded.

The study became bright with electricity. The twenty-five figures stood staring excitedly at the Chief Executive.

Rubbing his eyes, the President looked about him and demanded nervously: "What's happened?"

"It's on your shirt front," said the friend hoarsely.

"What's on my shirt front?" the President began, and looked down. "I'm sorry," he added after a pause, "I can't read at this angle."

"It's a message in ink scrawled on your shirt front," repeated the friend.

"I know that," the President answered irritably. "The point is, what does it say?"

The friend looked at him strangely.

"Don't you know?" he asked.

"I told you I can't read it," said the President. "I'm no contortionist."

"Do you have to read it?" said the friend meaningfully.

The President burst into a guffaw.

"Are you suggesting," he managed to say presently, "that I have been writing on my own shirt front?"

"You have had access to it," began the friend, but the President interrupted him.

"Listen," he said in a low but vibrant voice, "use your head. Why would I write a message on my shirt front? Why would I try to confuse the country with that kind of shenanigans?"

"There's some ink on your collar!" cried out the Secret Service chief, who had been examining the President closely during this discussion.

"There are some ink blots on the third bookshelf!" spoke a detective, who, among others, had been combing the room, inch by inch.

"Will somebody kindly read what *is* written on me," demanded the President, "or must I undress?"

The Chief of Staff stepped forward and saluted.

"It's the same general type of message, sir," he said. "It reads as follows: 'Hurry, hurry, Mt. Navajo, route 9-52, or world lost. Send ant expert. Hurry. Consult atlas.'"

"There's some more of it on the back of his collar," the Secret Service head spoke up.

The President grinned.

"Well, that exonerates me," he said. "I'm no good at writing with the back of my head. What does the collar say?"

"It reads," said the Secret Service chief, "'Can't keep this up much longer. Hurry, for God's sake.'"

"Well," said the President, "the whole thing sounds very impressive to me. This makes the fourth warning about ants. Did anybody ever hear of ants that could eat stone and steel?"

A psychiatrist present who had studied entomology smiled at this absurd layman's question.

"There is no such ant," he stated with scientific finality. "The thing is a hoax from beginning to end."

"I see," said the President and added: "Did anybody see anybody writing on me?"

The Secret Service chief replied nervously after a pause.

"No," he said, "but we expect a number of arrests within the next few hours."

"Mt. Navajo, Mt. Navajo," muttered the President. "Sounds like the Southwest."

He walked toward the bookshelves, where an officer guarded the new ink blots.

"Keep away from those books!" cried the friend and several others.

"Gentlemen," said the President, "if we are to be afraid of books, we may as well resign as human beings."

The room remained silent as the President removed an atlas.

The vigil keepers watched him as he turned the pages of the large, heavy volume. At length the President spoke.

"Here's a Navajo mountain range," he began and then paused, open-mouthed.

"Quick, somebody come here," he whispered.

"What is it?" cried the friend, and the Secret Service men drew out their revolvers and stood in a ring about the Chief Executive.

"An ant," said the President softly. "Somebody pick it up." Both his own hands were occupied. "Look. It's sitting on the Navajo mountains."

The Secret Service chief reached for the volume. By a slight miscalculation the President removed his hands from it before any others received it, and the book fell and slammed shut as it hit the floor. The Secret Service chief picked it up.

"Page two hundred and sixty," said the President.

The atlas was carried to the President's desk and opened. Page two hundred and sixty revealed a detail map of lower California.

And on the map near the Navajo mountain range lay splattered a blot of ink. The squashed remains of an insect protruded from it.

"Was that ink there when you looked at it first?" asked the Secret Service chief.

"No," said the President softly, "there was only an ant."

Two days later, the first telegraphed report from the Federal Mount Navajo Investigation Committee arrived on the President's desk. It read: "Fifty thousand men needed here at once to fight new species stone-eating termite. Termites already undermined several hills and moving northward in incalculable numbers. Will devour nation if not stopped here. Scientific survey of situation follows."

Of the remarkable battle that took place in the Navajo Hills between man and the termites I have little new to add. The two-thousand-mile ditch dug around the enemy's domain and filled with two-thirds of the nation's supply of petroleum appears to have checked, for the time at least, the termite conquest.

As for Gifford Emmett, of him there is no further record. After several conferences between the President and his advisers it was decided that no reference be made to the blot of ink on the atlas page. The President made a brief address to his Cabinet on his reasons for silence.

"Whoever that Saviour was who came to the rescue of mankind," said the President, "it will be best, I feel certain, to let him die unhonored and unsung. For history shows that only confusion arises from the worship of God's emissaries. We are in the midst of too much confusion today to add to our troubles the hysterias and dissensions which this miraculous ant would bring to our nation and perhaps to the world. If it is God who saved the race, let Him be content that it is saved. And if it is God who sent a Son to us in the guise of an ant, we may well believe He did it in order that we might ignore the Messiah. The Almighty could not very well have sent us a more inconsequential Saviour and one calling more for our indifference—if He desired any practical results. A gnat or a microbe would have been physically incapable of the Divine warning given us. I say, therefore, that we should continue to worship God's previous representatives without adding an ant to the galaxy."

Thus Gifford Emmett's cross was oblivion, which he may well have preferred. I am moved, however, to add an epitaph to the blot of ink that lies in the President's atlas. Of this little blot of ink I write:

Here lies one who hated life, who shuddered before the scurvy inhumanity of the world, who considered with revulsion the record of its endless injustice and triumphant cruelty.

Here lies one whose soul was wasted by the stupidity and barbarism of his fellows, and whose mind, looking out upon the earth, saw it overrun by the inane, the unscrupulous, the aberrant, and the sadistic children of the beast.

Yet here in this little blot of ink lies one who in all that he hated beheld the bright and beleaguered face of tomorrow and died full of hope.

Café Sinister

ALWAYS IN A CAFE of elegance where the elite come to advertise their boredom I feel the promise of sinister events. My years as a newspaperman still make me think of the fashionable and the famous in terms of derogatory headlines. I never enter one of these hothouse roosts without feeling immediately that around me are the important scandals of tomorrow.

Here they sit—in the ornate anteroom of suicide, bankruptcy and blackmail—a-glitter with the spoils of life including that last most dangerous treasure—ennui. You would never fancy that these toy-faced heroes and heroines of the city's night were anything but what they seem—a group of beribboned insomnia victims come to stare at one another and exchange yawns. But this is a deception. For in these moribund huddles sit beauty, talent and wealth. And, however bored they seem, you may be sure that where such sit there is always devil's music playing nearby.

I have a friend, Dr. Mortimer Briggs, who is a Harun-al Rashid sort of psychiatrist. He is given to wandering the city after midnight and peering into its psychoses and, perhaps, looking for customers. This soul-gazer assures me that his favorite haunt, El Granada café, is the most clinical spot in town, and I have taken to haunting it with him. My interest is chiefly Morty, who is a witty and instructive companion and who has the gift of making the dullest people blossom into werewolves and moon monsters—a side of psychiatry that has always pleased me.

In El Granada after midnight, says Morty, assemble the daemon-driven of the town—the rich, the brilliant and the beautiful. The rich, he tells me, have warped souls—all of them—as a result of exercising their egos rather than their wits. As for their playfellows—the men and women of the arts—these are in an even worse situation. For only successful geniuses can afford to bask in El Granada, and medically, says Morty, there is nothing as troublesome to genius as success. It substitutes press notices for dreams and cocktail parties for the pursuit of beauty. Fame, holds Morty, is a sort of mummy case in which the creative talents of yesterday lie in state and glitter with mania.

As for beauty, my friend's theory is that all the lovely ladies who bloom nightly in El Granada are more phantom than female. They are, he says, shallow and dangerous. They are designed, like mirages, only to stir hunger and arouse the imagination and they have no food to offer either.

In the months we have been squatting almost nightly in El Granada, that ornamental cauldron has yielded the press four suicides, one murder, fifteen divorces and innumerable lesser items involving bigamy, treason and embezzlement. None of these events actually happened in El Granada, but its violent actors were all recruited from its yawning tables.

It was while sitting with Doctor Morty in this Pandora's box of a café one night that I witnessed the debut of the Baron Corfus, and with it the opening scene of a drama as fantastic as any in the Arabian Nights, and one that fulfilled in abundance its promise of sinister events.

There was no hint of macabre enterprise about the tall, pottery-faced gentleman who made his first entrance that night. It was midnight—an hour in which El Granada is so crowded with men and women of distinction that it is practically impossible for anyone to achieve the slightest attention.

The arrival of an elegant-looking elderly man wearing a camellia in his lapel and accompanied by a beautiful girl in camellia-studded furs is a matter of no more import to El Granada at midnight than the squeezing of two more shoppers into a subway train during the rush hour. The fact that Ganzo, the headwaiter, himself conducted the pair to a reserved table was no clue to the importance of the newcomers. It indicated that a $20 bill had changed hands. The presence at the newcomer's side of so fetching a companion was also an indication of nothing. Fetching companions in El Granada may mean anything from another $20 bill to a major disaster. You can tell nothing by looking at them. They are a bland and radiant lot who manage to exchange their characters for a coiffure when they come to El Granada.

Thus it was that the Baron Corfus and his companion created no ripples with their entrance. I remember well, however, that Morty was quick to bag the newcomer.

"Never saw him before," he said, "and the girl is new, too."

"Not bad looking," I said. You have to be modest in your opinions in front of Morty or he explodes. Psychiatry is basically the science of contradiction.

"Strip her, scrub her face and comb her hair out," said Morty, "and you have a slight case of pituitary emaciation plus a bit of Narcism."

"She still looks like Salome to me," I said. "Do you think that red hair is real?"

"The hair is real," the great scientist admitted grudgingly, "but the eyes are of glass. The man is vastly more interesting."

"He looks well preserved," I said.

"To the contrary," said Morty happily, "he is in the last stages of disintegration. A well-dressed case of cachexia always looks like a visiting diplomat." Morty mopped his face with one of his many handkerchiefs. Though not a fat man—as psychiatrists go—he was in a constant perspiration, and regardless of the temperature seemed always either to be choking to death or about to be laid low by the heat. He performed this mopping operation with quick and furtive gestures as if he expected nobody to notice the oddity.

"Besides," he went on, "that man has too much poise unless it's arteriosclerosis. By God"—Morty changed handkerchiefs—"a very curious fellow—that fellow."

I shall describe the new arrival as I saw him this first time. He was a man so imbedded in an attitude that his age seemed a mystery. The attitude was one of charm and aloofness. The gray face with its long jaws, its thin lips, its enamelled gloss, was raised as if it were in the midst of some performance. He had metallic gray hair that was curled tightly on his skull and seemed to have been polished rather than combed. But the man's eyes were his chief attraction. They were almost tightly shut. The eyelids were lowered as if against a glare and the eyes were reduced to two glittering lines—like the dashes in a code.

"I'd say he was almost blind," Morty went on slowly, "and the squint is a ruse for increasing his small vision. Or else—"

"Or else, what?" I asked, humbly.

"Or else," said Morty, happily, "he's as mad as a hatter. A man closes his eyes like that for one reason, usually. He doesn't want to be seen. I call them ostricho-maniacs." Morty considered this a joke.

"That's a hell of a theory about a gentleman who seeks out a spotlight like El Granada," I said.

"It's his soul, not his camellia, that's in hiding," Morty answered.

The music resumed. El Granada was filling up for the night, which meant that the fashionable and the famous were being reduced to sardine-like postures that made drinking, talking or eating well-nigh impossible. Dancers inched about on the small floor. The service grew panicky, breathing difficult; elbows sent glasses toppling; the crash of dishes sliding from overcrowded trays punctuated the South American melodies; table hoppers tripped over furs strewing the floor; the dancers, diners, waiters, bus boys and bandsmen became wedged together in an immovable mass. And in the midst of these intolerable discomforts the clientele of El Granada sat with mysterious satisfaction as if they had finally achieved the best of all possible worlds.

Baron Corfus had added himself to this ensemble as if it were his natural element. At one-thirty the newcomer rose to leave. Morty and I automatically called it a night. Together with some twenty other frolickers bored to a point of nervous collapse, we squeezed our way out of El Granada. I wondered idly as we stepped into the life-restoring street who the elderly glassy-faced dandy in front of us was and what type of insomnia had brought him to our roost.

An elegant automobile drew up to the curb. The Baron handed Ivan, the doorman, a five-dollar bill for his single bow and entered the car with his lovely redhead.

"A very strange fellow," said Morty. "I hope we see more of him."

We did. In the weeks that followed El Granada had produced a new diversion for us—a mystery man.

Mystery is not a thing that happens quickly. It is the negative side of events, the blank curtain concealing drama. You must look at this curtain a long time before even becoming aware that it is hanging in front of you. Having located it, however, you have a front seat at the greatest show on earth—the Unknown.

The Baron Corfus—headwaiter Ganzo had supplied his name—became our show—more Morty's than mine. For while I was content to enjoy knowing nothing and imagining everything, like any good mystery fan, Morty was busy with solutions. The trail, said Morty, after several weeks of studying furtively our camellia-tipped dandy, offered several scents. For one thing, the unvarying midnight entrance and the unvarying departure at exactly 1:30 A.M. was the sort of cere-monial behavior, said Morty, that revealed mania. Since my friend managed to discover lunacy in practically everybody who came under his scientific eye, I was not too impressed.

"The difference in this case," said Morty, "is that here we have lunacy in action. We are all lunatics, but inert ones. Psychic duds, so to speak. But the Baron's mania is up to something. It's performing for us. It's plotting away every night."

"Plotting what?" I asked modestly.

"That, I don't know," beamed my Sherlock, "but I will soon. All we know now is that the Baron arrives here with ceremonial regularity on the stroke of midnight with a beautiful young lady in whom he has no interest and we have also the fact that our Baron, a tireless exhibitionist, nevertheless refuses to commune with any of the customers here."

We had both observed that our mystery man had frozen off a dozen neighborly attempts at conversation. I attributed this to jealousy of his companion.

"Nonsense," Morty answered in a smacking voice that made me wonder if any of his neurotics ever jumped up from the analyst's couch and took a poke at him. "Definitely the Baron is not jealous. He's just busy and doesn't care to be interrupted."

"Busy doing what?" I asked, humbly.

"Hiding," said Morty, "and plotting."

It was I who first noticed, a few evenings later, that the Baron had a different young woman with him. This was not as easy an observation to make as it might seem. For the new siren was out of the same bandbox as her predecessor. In fact, all the young women who come to El Granada look sufficiently alike to line up at the sound of a music cue into a perfectly matched chorus. The Baron's new lady friend, in addition to wearing the same camellia-studded furs, the same fingernails and the same fixed glow of an enchanted window dummy—was also a redhead.

"Well, we've got a new clue," I said. "We've found out that the Baron has a redhead fetish."

"A putrid deduction," said Morty. "A man who keeps his eyes shut isn't going in for color fetishes. The redhead is a coincidence. Or perhaps a drug on the market." But I could see that Morty was not too impressed by this notion.

A young naval lieutenant squeezed into a chair at our table. This was Dickie Malchen, one of our night-life alumni who had wheedled his way into the landlocked sector of the Navy.

"Hiya," said Dickie, "I'm on leave again. First free breath in five weeks. Ever been in Washington in the summer?" The young mariner shuddered. "There's nothing worse on earth than that Navy Building."

"War is war," I offered. I had never liked Dickie. He was of the tribe of rich young men who go in for a career of billboard love affairs. El Granada has a large complement of these Romeos who, lacking all other enterprise, devote themselves to the pursuit of ladies. The pursuit seldom goes beyond a jog-trot but even at this pace the night club Isoldes are easily lassoed. The goal of both sexes being identical—to achieve mention in the gossip columns as often as possible—little time is wasted outside the limelight.

There was actually nothing objectionable about Dickie, but for that matter there is nothing objectionable about stewed calf eyes, a delicacy also on tap at El Granada. As for the amount of damage he did as a Don Juan, I imagine that Dickie was as harmless in his amours as in his new calling of war.

"The old hunting grounds," our lieutenant said sentimentally, turning a flaccid face on the clientele.

"How do they look after the terrors of Washington?" I asked. Dickie always appreciated minor insults.

"Better than ever," he laughed, still sweeping the horizon with an expert eye. His attention came to halt. "At least," he went on, "I know now what I'm fighting for."

"And what's that?" I asked.

"That redhead," said Dickie softly. "Holy hat! That's an item! Who is the graveyard with her?"

I gave the Baron's name.

"Never heard of him," said Dickie. Since Dickie had heard of every dubious character in the world, this was flat ostracism. "Corfus—Corfus," he repeated. "A phony."

Morty beamed and was about to say, "Out of the mouths of babes," but I forestalled him.

"Ever seen the girl?" I asked.

Dickie sipped his drink and was thoughtful. One had the impression of a young man peering into a myriad of hotel rooms.

"Uh, uh," he said moodily, "but it's my dish. I think I'll go over and cheer the poor little thing up. I never could stand to see redheads wasted."

"You won't get very far," I said. "The Baron is a seclusive type. He shuns people."

"My dish," Dickie repeated softly and stood up. "Watch me. The Navy never misses."

We watched and were astonished. Lieutenant Malchen stood in front of the Baron's table smiling and speaking easily. The Baron arose, smiled and bowed. Whereupon the beautiful redhead stepped from behind the table and in a twinkling our lieutenant and the Baron's prize were on the dance floor locked in a sort of rigor mortis. I watched Dickie and noted that he had not lost his cunning as a ballroom artist. He still favored the strangle hold for waltzes and the bear hug for all other rhythms.

Morty nudged me.

"That bears it out," he said.

"Bears what out, oracle?" I asked.

"My first diagnosis—that the Baron doesn't give a hoot in hell about redheads." Morty mopped his seething brows. "He hasn't opened his eyes, turned his head or stolen a single peek at the blitzkrieg on the dance floor."

Twenty minutes later, Dickie returned the rumpled beauty to her perch beside the Baron, and sat down next to her. There was a small group of tax-tortured citizens at our own table discussing the future of the world. This vital topic, however, failed to hold my attention. I waited for the Navy to bring us tidings of Baron Corfus. And while waiting, I noted with some surprise that our Don Juan apparently had lost interest in his redheaded quarry. Both he and the "dish" sat unaware of each other, listening open-mouthed to the elegant Baron.

At 1:35 Dickie returned from the vestibule and joined us. The tax-debating society had moved on to the Stock Club for inspiration and Morty and I were alone.

"Holy hat!" said Dickie. "What a guy! The most exciting old polly-wog I ever listened to."

"How'd you get in?" I asked.

"Oh, that," Dickie grinned. "Just pulled the old gag. Introduced my-self and told the old boy I'd made a fifty-dollar bet with you gentlemen that I could prevail on him to let me dance with the lovely young lady at his side. It worked like a charm. The thing that helped was that the old boy knows you and doesn't like you. Uh, uh—not for apples."

"Knows who?" I asked.

"The doctor," said Dickie. Morty beamed. "He hates psychiatry," Dickie went on, "if that's of any interest to you."

"Of the deepest," said Morty.

"What did he talk about?" I asked as Dickie sunk his nose into a wine glass.

"Terrific." He looked up. "Biggest authority on Nazis in the world. He knows them all—Goebbels, Goering, Hitler. All the big shots. He's been at their homes. My God, I never heard anything so fascinating."

"As for instance," I prodded.

"Oh, well," said Dickie, "an absolutely inside track on all those boys. Don't you think that's pretty interesting? By God, I do. You know—who loves who and what those goddamn Nazis say when they let their hair down."

Here at least was an answer to the Baron's fascination for the two redheads. Our mystery man was full of intimate tidbits concerning the nature of the enemy and apparently had bowled over Dickie as well with tales of the home life of Germany's boogiemen.

"Holy hat!" Dickie jumped up suddenly. "I forgot to get her telephone number. I'm slipping."

"Sit down; she'll be back tomorrow night," I promised. "What did she have to say about his nibs while you were dancing?"

"Not a talking type," said Dickie, with a soulful look toward the vestibule, "but quite a dish, eh? Looks a little like Evie, wouldn't you say?"

"Which one was Evie?" I asked.

"That beautiful redhead that ditched me for the movies last year," said Dickie, "just as I was recovering from the big thing with Miss Colligan. God, I had a terrible time. I find 'em and Hollywood grabs 'em."

"Was Miss Colligan another of your conquests?" Morty asked, shyly.

"I was cut to ribbons," Dickie sighed. "God, I would have married that girl—if she'd waited."

"What was the color of Miss Colligan's hair?" Morty inquired, archly.

"Red," said Dickie. "Most beautiful redhead I ever met. Well, you can't have everything. Be seein' you." Dickie started squeezing his way toward another part of the room.

"Well," said Morty, "we've found out one impressive clue. The Baron knows who I am and dislikes me. I think that's vital information."

"For your press book, perhaps," I said. "Personally, I am more interested in his being so close to the great Nazis."

"Lies, all lies," said Morty. "He doesn't know any Nazis. He never met Goebbels or Hitler. He's merely taking advantage of the ingénue American interest in backstairs tittle-tattle to put something over. His dislike of me proves that absolutely."

"You're sending up bubbles," I said. "I don't follow you."

"My dear friend," Morty beamed, "the man's up to something and he's terrified I'll see through him. All lunatics feel that way about me."

Morty let his face drip in exultation.

"They're telepathic," he went on. "They can sense a brain piercing through their hocus-pocus. That's what ails the Baron. He knows I've got his compulsion neurosis by the tail and that I'm likely to see where it's going—any minute."

Highly pleased with himself, the moist thinker forgot it was his turn as guest at our table and picked up the check.

Thus our mystery remained for a week. The only progress made was by Dickie Malchen, whose relationship with the redhead had already borne fruit in the gossip columns. I had hoped the lieutenant would play go-between and get us a bid backstage of our mystery. Nothing of the sort happened. The only news that Dickie brought us of the Baron was of his remarkable collection of paintings and of his aversion for Morty.

"I suggested we all get together," said Dickie, "but he can't stand psychiatrists. You ain't mad, are you, Doc?" And Dickie winked at me.

"Not in the least." Morty also winked at me. "Nobody loves a nosey psychiatrist."

Dickie chortled and squeezed off toward the dance floor.

It was the next night that the curtain at which we had been staring so long began finally to rise. It did not rise far, but enough to give us our first glimpse of the design of the hidden stage. The design was Uncle Albert Malchen, Dickie's most renowned relative.

The honorable and disintegrating Albert was rarely seen in such gaudy dens as El Granada. He belonged to an era that had come to a full stop with the diabolic invention of the income tax; an era, also, that had regarded sin as a very important matter worthy of secret mansions, secret yachts and posthumous autobiographies. Uncle Albert, having squandered millions on amour, was averse surely to seeing it knocked down nightly in the open market for a single magnum of champagne, which may have accounted, in part, for his absence from such haunts as ours.

His appearance on this night sent a ripple through the blaring room, for Mr. Malchen was more than a celebrity come to be seen holding hands with another celebrity. He was a legend stepped out of ancient Wall Street deals and international love scandals—a gentleman as archaic as the Devil in red tights—and the flesh-pots curtsied nostalgically to him. Beholding him, the clientele of El Granada remembered tales of chateaus on beaches, mountain tops and boulevards, recalled Rembrandts and Raphaels showered on strumpets, wheat markets cornered and somebody shooting somebody else on the opening night of the Opera.

The lieutenant piloted this white-mustachioed, red-faced legend through the crowded room. He held it tenderly by the elbow and a look of extreme piety was on him as if he were guiding an abbot to his prayers. The two, uncle and nephew, stopped in front of the table of our camellia-studded Baron. Introductions took place and chairs were adjusted.

"Well, my friend," Morty scowled, "at least the first part of the mystery is cleared up. We can dismiss the Titian sirens from here in."

He mopped his face frantically.

"We're a pair of idiots," he resumed. "Good Lord, imagine my not seeing through the whole thing in a minute. It makes me sick."

"But you did see through it," I comforted the scientist.

"Only as far as Dickie," Morty frowned. "I saw that the redheads were a bait set out for our naval hero. And I saw that the Baron had gone to considerable research for a foreigner to establish the fact that Dickie had a fetish for red-haired ladies. But I didn't think beyond Dickie to Uncle Albert."

"You're quite right," I said. "It looks pretty obvious. Our Baron snagged Dickie with a redhead. And then used Dickie as bait for Uncle Albert. And Uncle Albert is now going to be taken for something neat and considerable."

The Baron and Mr. Malchen were conversing amiably against the padded satin wall. Mr. Malchen's red rubbery face was full of a sort of roguish good humor of the old school. He appeared to be urging something on the Baron and the Baron with much charm appeared to be refusing whatever it was.

"One thing confuses me," Morty spoke up suddenly. "There doesn't seem anything mad about the whole business. And there should be. There should be something very definitely maniacal going on. And there isn't. It's all too stupidly logical."

Morty glared at our Baron as at a mendacious patient.

"We are being misled," he sighed. "If that man's a swindler, I'm a chiropodist." And Morty sat glaring at the Baron indignantly.

Our mystery was being seated when we reached our El Granada roost the next night.

"I wonder what the next step is," I said as Ganzo with tip-dizzied tenderness guided the Baron and the redhead to the padded wall.

"The next step involves us," said Morty in a whisper; "the fellow is beaming at us like a brother Elk."

I turned and saw this remarkable sight. Baron Corfus was smiling unmistakably in our direction, and Ganzo was moving toward our table.

"The gentleman over there," said Ganzo, "Baron Corfus, asks if you care to join him as his guests."

"We'd be delighted," said Morty softly.

Ganzo bowed and smiled like a good fairy whose work is done. We squeezed our way to the Baron's side.

His voice fitted him like another camellia. It was softly accented and full of good humor, the voice of a man of wit who has learned English where it is spoken only by the most elegant of people.

"I feel we are old friends," he said after the introductions to the red-haired Miss Annabella Wilkerson were done and we had all sat down. "Your faces have the quality of long companionship. I am certain that mine must be equally familiar to you."

This was not bad as a dig at our weeks of scrutiny.

"Yes," said Morty. "We've been interested in each other for some time. In fact, my friend and I have been happily mystified since your first appearance."

I thought this a little crude but the Baron was delighted.

"I didn't know psychiatrists were ever mystified," he said. "I thought people were an open book to them—a rather ugly book."

"Open," said Morty, kittenishly, "but hard to read halfway across a room."

The Baron nodded and failed to look wary. His eyes continued to glitter through their slits with a sort of gayety that confused me. But not Morty. Morty apparently understood this symptom thoroughly. He seemed, in fact, full of a friskiness that matched the Baron's and I was reminded of two fighters who square off with a grin on their mugs, each equally certain of himself. We ordered wine and I tackled the red-haired Miss Wilkerson with a few opening remarks about Dickie.

"Oh, really now," Miss Wilkerson answered in a swooning southern voice, "all Navy men are alike, don't you think? Ah don' mean anything disrespeckful tawed the Navy, but they ah so Navy, wouldn't you say?"

The Baron smiled at her without mockery.

"I find this place very interesting," he resumed, "and also a little sad."

"Why sad?" I asked and earned a mysterious kick under the table from Morty.

"It is sad when you see how little riches have come to mean," said the Baron. "And how small a thing luxury has become. Hardly more than this." He nodded wistfully at El Granada, and continued, "Luxury was once the goal of all intelligent human beings. Now we are all a little ashamed of it and actually frightened of its fine clothes and pleasant hours. It's a pity that the dream of luxury has been frightened out of the world."

"It will not be luxury that's removed from the world"—Morty

mopped his face and kept peeking like a schoolboy from behind his handkerchief—"but only its present formula—a great deal for a very few. This is being altered into another formula, a little for everybody."

"I wonder," said the Baron, "if useless things can be rationed or idleness evenly distributed. It is doubtful."

"Why did you ask us over?" Morty asked suddenly, and I was glad to see that the boys had come to an end of their sparring.

"The scientist is always direct," the Baron smiled. "Here is our wine. Shall we drink first?"

The lovely Miss Wilkerson cooed over the bubbles.

"Ah just adaw champagne," she said. "It relaxes yaw mind. It really does."

The Baron raised his glass to her.

"To you," he said, "for being so beautiful."

"Thank you." Miss Wilkerson widened her eyes at all of us.

Our host said, smiling at Morty, "I asked you over because your deep interest in me made me think you might enjoy the only small gift I have to offer—that of the raconteur."

"I knew that," said Morty smugly. "I knew you had something to tell us."

"Perhaps you even knew what it was," the Baron smiled.

"Whatever it is," beamed Morty, mopping his face and peeking excitedly, "I'm sure it will be very persuasive."

"You mean untruthful," the Baron said.

"I never discuss psychopathology with laymen," Morty lied pompously. "If you want to tell me a story, go ahead. I can take it."

A waiter appeared bearing a telephone instrument which he plugged in.

"We have your number now," the waiter said.

"Excuse me." The Baron smiled at us and spoke into the instrument. "Hello. Is that Emil? Emil, this is Corfus. Do you remember that time I told you I expected the gentlemen. . . . Ah. . . . They are? . . . Please, I will speak to the lieutenant."

The Baron sighed and looked at Morty.

"I have done a very stupid thing," he said. "I thought my appointment was for one-thirty rather than midnight. Isn't that what I told you, Miss Wilkerson?"

"Yes," she nodded earnestly. "Ah understood it was one-thirty. Ah remember distinctly. . . ."

"I'm afraid we are wrong," he smiled. "You must explain to me, Doctor, how it is that one's memory can be so accurate, so vivid and accurate about the past and so completely worthless on matters of the present."

"Perhaps the present is of no interest to you," Morty cooed. I knew he had spotted the shaking of the Baron's hand and the tension in the slitted eyes.

"Hello," our host spoke into the phone, "Lieutenant? . . . Oh, I'm so very sorry, Lieutenant. I had an impression that we were to meet after the café. . . . Oh, really? . . . Yes, I recall now. In fact, I've been uncertain for fifteen minutes. Please convey to your uncle my deepest regrets and ask him if he will be kind enough to look at the paintings. I will be over very soon. Tell him the data is on my desk. . . . Oh, he is? I am delighted."

The Baron's breath caught in a curious gasp and the shaking of the hand holding the instrument increased.

"Then there is no need for me to rush," he resumed. "And how are you, Lieutenant? We missed you this evening—in more ways than one. Yes, she is here. Would you care to speak to her?"

He handed the phone to Miss Wilkerson. Morty mopped away and peeked excitedly and I wondered if he would offer his handkerchief to the Baron, on whose temples a film of moisture had appeared.

"Hello tha," said Miss Wilkerson. "So sorry yaw not heah, Mr. Malchen. . . . Yes, tha's a wonderful crowd heah tonight. . . . Oh, just everybody. . . . You do? . . . Oh, that's very naughty, Mr. Malchen. . . . No, I won't call you Dickie ever if you talk like that." She laughed, as Dickie apparently stepped up his campaign, and tossed back a series of arch and ambiguous gurgles. The Baron sat listening with what seemed a breathless, dreamy air. A smile twitched his mouth and he took the instrument from Miss Wilkerson.

"Will you please ask the butler to fix you a drink, until I get there?" he said. "Oh, it's no trouble at all for him. And I'm sure he has some sandwiches ready. . . . He did? Well, I'm delighted. . . . No, no, no. . . . Please, say nothing about that till I get there. And give him all the time he wants. A great art connoisseur loves to be alone with his quarry. . . . And I'm sure he'll find the paintings quite worth his attention. . . . Yes. . . . We'll finish our drinks and be over. . . . And my apologies for forgetting the hour. . . ."

He hung the phone up and looked at his wrist watch. The moisture had spread from his temples to his chin and glistened now on his shaking fingers. His voice, however, was smooth enough as he said, "Mr. Albert Malchen is at my apartment looking at some paintings I own and am not averse to selling."

Morty stared at him blandly.

"It really upset me." The Baron removed his own handkerchief and mopped his face. "I cannot bear to be unpunctual. Punctuality is perhaps my defense against a completely disorganized mind. At least, I often think so. But no harm's been done. Shall we have another bottle of wine?"

"Ah don't think we ought to leave Mr. Malchen alone," Miss Wilkerson pouted.

"But I cannot desert our new friends here so abruptly." He smiled. "Particularly Dr. Briggs, who is still curious as to why I sought the honor of his company. I am an exile from a country that I once loved. There is nothing pleases me as much as to tell stories about that country. It is the same as one feels toward an old, old friend who has died. One loves to recall him and speak of him to others."

I had an impression the Baron was babbling and waited for Morty to say as much. But Morty had grown dreamy and I knew his mind was far away from the Baron's words. He was thinking like a steam engine.

Baron Corfus spoke for another five minutes, chiefly of a dinner party at which Mussolini had recited an ode to himself. He then ordered the check from Ganzo. He was still lingering over its payment and finishing another tale of Nazi intrigue in Warsaw—the details were reminiscent of a movie I had seen a few months ago—when the waiter appeared, bearing a telephone.

"For you, sir." He nodded at the Baron, as he plugged in the wire.

"Hello," the Baron spoke into the phone. "Yes. . . . What? . . . I don't understand. . . . Oh, I see. . . . Oh, I'm terribly sorry. . . . Yes, I have one in my pocket. . . . Yes. . . . Oh, I'm sure nothing has happened. . . . Yes, indeed, I'll be right over."

He hung up quickly and rose. Morty followed him to his feet.

"Has something happened?" he purred.

"You look awfully upset." Miss Wilkerson put her hand on the Baron's arm. "Is it something about Dickie?"

"I'm sure it's nothing," our host sighed, starting toward the vestibule. Morty was at his side and the Baron added, "Mr. Malchen says his uncle locked himself in my drawing room. The door has a spring lock and I have the only key."

"Why doesn't Uncle Albert open it?" Morty asked softly.

"Apparently he is so enthralled by my paintings," the Baron smiled, "that he cannot hear his nephew's outcries."

"I am a doctor," said Morty quietly, "and will go home with you. In case one is needed."

The Baron's apartment was five minutes away by taxi. The four of us rode there in silence. The most mystifying thing in the taxi was the fact that Morty had stopped perspiring. He was cool and contented.

The butler who opened the Corfus door for us looked like Voltaire— a puny and electric old gentleman. Dickie gathered Miss Wilkerson to him and begged her not to worry, because he had already sent for Dr. Kenneth O. Bishop, the heart specialist and his uncle's chief personal physician. Miss Wilkerson patted the mariner's cheek, and was certain everything would be all right.

In the meantime Corfus unlocked the door, at which we were all looking. We saw a large, softly lighted room with a number of paintings on the walls. At the far end of the room stood an easel with a large painting of a woman on it. The easel was an imposing affair with velvet drapes on each side.

A third look revealed Albert Malchen on the floor, his face flattened against the rug. The fabled Malchen was dead. In this room hung with too many paintings, he looked like a child collapsed amid its toys.

We stood like a little group of mummers who had not learned their lines for the death scene. Particularly Morty. Morty had turned his gaze away from the mighty Malchen crumpled on the rug. He was looking at another figure—the one on the easel. It was a full-length portrait of a woman of twenty. She was a proud and fragile lady done chiefly in greens.

Dr. Kenneth O. Bishop found us with highball glasses in our hands. He was tall, learned and expensive-looking, and obviously of the Supreme Court of medicine. No M.D. had taken his diplomate in cardiology or been elected to his academic society without appearing first before this haughty face. It was apparent at once that dead millionaires were no novelty to him. Mr. Malchen's death held no surprise. He had been treating the financier for a bad heart for a number of years, he said.

Dickie, removing his arm from the Wilkerson rib cage, explained the events preceding the demise. He had accompanied his uncle into the room, and they had just started looking about when Baron Corfus had telephoned. Dickie had followed the butler to the phone, which was in another room, and asked the old fellow to mix him a drink. The butler had prepared the drink while Dickie talked over the phone. Then he had sat drinking and giving the butler his favorite recipe for mint juleps. Going back to join his uncle, he had found the door locked. Mr. Malchen had closed the door himself, Dickie imagined, because he wanted to look at the paintings without interruption.

Morty, who had been listening blandly, added the question: "Were the drapes on the easel painting open or closed when you left the room to answer the phone?"

"They were closed," said Dickie, frowning.

Morty nodded agreeably.

The more expensive-looking scientist then made a curious statement. Some seven years ago Albert Malchen had specified that he should not be buried without an autopsy. This was a request not uncommon among his extremely wealthy patients, who were evidently haunted by a fear of foul play. Of course, this phobia did not mean anything, but he would let Dr. Briggs know any interesting findings, he added graciously, favoring the gleam in Morty's eye.

He paused and sighed.

"Mr. Malchen was a very dear friend. It's obvious that he became overexcited by these paintings, particularly the one on the easel."

"It is a beautiful thing," said Corfus.

"Well, it was too much for him," said Dr. Bishop. "Poor Albert, he always loved art above everything else in the world."

"A wonderful theory . . ." Morty whispered in my ear sarcastically. "That painting never excited anybody—except me."

I saw the Baron nod to the old butler as we started leaving the room. Voltaire remained behind and slowly drew together the drapes.

Morty telephoned me the next afternoon. I asked him if he had seen the Baron.

"No," he said, "but don't worry about him. We'll see him tonight at El Granada."

"You think he'll be there?" I asked.

"You *are* a babe in the woods," Morty chuckled. "He'll not only be there but he'll be alone."

I asked my Sherlock how he deduced that.

"Because he's expecting me," said Morty. "I hold a great fascination for him. Much greater than he ever held for me."

I assured Morty that I was completely baffled by the whole thing and asked about the autopsy.

"Mr. Malchen died of a bad heart," Morty said happily. "No contributing factors in the way of bullets, poisons or blows were found. It was a perfect crime. Twelve o'clock—and don't be late. I don't want to keep the Baron in suspense."

Baron Corfus was there, and alone, poised as a bit of old statuary, his steely hair polished, the long glazed face riveted in a grimace of charm, his eyes almost shut and looking more than ever like the dashes of a code, and the camellia flying. And, obviously, he was waiting for us.

I have always admired dandyism in distress—Charles of England removing the long curls from his neck and murmuring that there was no occasion for the ax man to disturb them since they had offended no one, the literary Prince of Paris listening to the pompous death warrant being read to him and interrupting wearily: "Tut-tut . . . the style of Diderot . . ."; and that Brooklyn boy swimming through the oil-flaming Coral Sea and calling out to the rescue boat: "Hey, buddy, here's a couple of hitch-hikers." The temperament that yields no whit of its style to calamity has always been my favorite, and on this night our Baron was an elegant member of its tribe. For if ever calamity signalled its presence and Nemesis bayed in the offing, it was Morty. He squinted at our host as if he were sighting a rifle on him, he perspired, leered and fidgeted like a June bride, and he gulped down tumblers of wine. But his gloat was that of the pedagogue in pursuit of truth rather than the Puritan laying evil by the heels, and I forgave him. It pleased me to know, however, that our Baron would sit unperturbed until doomsday, and that it would have to be Morty who first unmasked. It was Morty.

"Corfus," he said finally, "I'd like to tell you a story."

"That would be only fair," the Baron smiled. "You've listened to several of mine."

"Before I begin," said Morty, "I want to make it plain that I'm here not only as one who is going to accuse you of murder, but also as judge and jury."

"The court of El Granada," the Baron nodded smilingly, "a charming locale in which to be tried."

"I'll enter the evidence quickly," said Morty, "since, of course, it will offer no surprise to you. My only reason for boring you possibly with the details is to convince you they are in my possession."

"You will not bore me," the Baron said.

"I am pleased that you're not full of hostilities and contradictions," said Morty.

"I never contradict a guest who is enjoying himself," said the Baron. "Will you have some more wine?"

He refilled Morty's glass. Morty drank it absent-mindedly.

"I'll begin with the redheads," he said. "I couldn't satisfy myself about the significance of those damned redheads. I knew, of course, they were decoys for Dickie and I knew Dickie was a decoy for Uncle

Albert. But why should a man with such authentic paintings to sell go through such a hocus-pocus to meet the art-hungry Malchen? This question, of course, was among the several answered last night. You needed both Dickie *and* Uncle Albert on the scene. You, naturally, were going to be absent. And you wanted someone present at the scene of Malchen's death besides your butler. That old gentleman with the Heidelberg scar is hardly a character that would bear close questioning. And if the mighty Malchen were found dead on the premises of a stranger with nobody but that dubious creature on the scene, there would be considerable questioning. Dickie was perfect insurance against any such investigation. Hence Dickie. Hence all the hocus-pocus."

The Baron remained a picture of polite interest.

"The part I am grateful for," Morty resumed, "was that you called me over to your table last night to use me—as part of your alibi. That wasn't very nice . . . but I enjoyed it. It was fruitful. And now we come to your vital and slightly paranoiac adventure. I knew, of course, from the first that you were neither a crook nor swindler, but a man of hate."

"Hate," said the Baron, in the most amiable of tones, "is the sole diet of continents today."

Morty mopped his face and continued.

"Last night, when you spoke over the phone here, the basic nature of the adventure became clear to me. You lied. A lie, my dear fellow, is always the best signpost to the hidden. As long as a man doesn't lie, his secret is safe. My profession of psychoanalysis, as you know, is little more than a lie hunt. I'm always geared to spot a lie. When you said over the phone that you had forgotten the exact hour of your appointment with Uncle Albert, the gong sounded. A man who has devoted two months to bagging a Malchen isn't going to forget any detail of his appointment. It was also obvious, while you were talking on the phone, that you had been engaged for two months in establishing a public habit —an El Granada habit of attendance between midnight and one-thirty. This habit would serve as your alibi—this, and ourselves. Yes, indeed, El Granada had many uses for you."

The Baron glanced at his wrist watch humorously.

"It is almost one," he said, "and I am still in the grip of habit."

"We will be through in time," Morty beamed. "To return to this spectacle of you at the telephone. You showed all the signs of extreme strain. Your hands shook, and your face sweated. And I knew that the adventure—a seven-year adventure as we learned last night from Uncle Albert's long-standing fear of murder, had reached its climax. The murder of Malchen was taking place as you held Dickie on the phone."

The Baron sighed.

"I am confused," he said. "Whom are you accusing—my butler?"

"Heavens, no," Morty said indignantly, and added, "At any rate— only as a very minor performer. The thing was so clear that I was afraid that ass Kenneth O. Bishop—O for ossified—would see it."

Morty shook his head reprovingly at the Baron.

"You took a big chance killing Mr. Malchen with a Forain portrait," he said, "—a piece of painting that couldn't possibly affect his heart action—except to depress it."

"Forain is a much undervalued artist," said the Baron, and I felt that they were both mad.

"I could see you had great faith in him," Morty chuckled, "the minute I entered the room. Nevertheless, I wondered why an art connoisseur like yourself should honor a fifth-rate canvas with a draped easel. Once I had asked myself that question, my dear Corfus, I needed only to ask another to know all the details of the murder. Were the drapes on the easel closed when Uncle Albert entered the room? They were. The rest was simplicity itself."

Morty paused as if for a round of applause. "Having gorged himself on Memlings and Goyas," he continued, "an art lover like Malchen would turn eagerly to the obvious prima donna of the collection—the canvas honored by a draped easel. Now we arrive at the crime. When I left the room, I made a final observation. I saw the butler, so-called, pulling the heavy drapes closed with some difficulty. I noticed that the knob on the cord of the drape rode up to an unusual height when the curtains were closed—in fact, above Uncle Albert's head. Uncle Albert had to reach for this knob and pull hard, when he turned at last to gaze at the deadly Forain."

I felt like laughing.

"Do you mean that the extra exertion of opening the drapes ended the life of Mr. Malchen?" I asked.

"I mean nothing of the sort," said Morty. "The knob on the draw string killed him. There was a syringe in that knob, and when he grabbed hold of it, he received a deadly injection."

"Poison?" I looked at the imperturbable Baron.

"Obviously," said Morty. "But a special kind of poison, I realized, when Corfus didn't seem to be the least disturbed by the promise of an autopsy. I spent all night over a pharmaceutical volume refreshing my memory about poisons that leave no traces. Today, when that antediluvian medical freak, Dr. Bishop, phoned to assure me the results of the necropsy were entirely negative, I knew. There is only one such fooler. Insulin."

He looked at Corfus triumphantly.

"At least two hundred units of insulin were in the needle that was released into the hand of Mr. Malchen when he reached up for that knob and pulled greedily. It was perfect. Your victim received a staggering insulin shock, which nobody can distinguish from the last throes of a fatal coronary attack."

Our table became an oasis of silence in the blaring café. After several moments Morty said, rather appealingly to the Baron:

"It's your turn, Corfus."

The Baron seemed rather tired.

"An interesting story," he said softly, "but a little fanciful."

"I haven't gone to the trouble of digging up any proof," said Morty coldly, "but if the police were told to look at Uncle Albert's right palm, they would find a perforation. Also, an analysis of the draw cord on the easel would show insulin, and would also show, I am sure, that a new and more innocent knob has been substituted for the one I have described to you."

The Baron seemed to have fallen asleep. I realized with surprise that he was talking—quietly, and without emphasis.

"Perhaps it will satisfy the judge and jury of the court of El Granada if I reveal my true name. It is Count Eitel von Lichtenfels. This name is my only defense."

Morty beamed.

"Naturally I've heard the name. I studied in Berlin, you know. It was one of the big banking families of Germany. But it doesn't shed any light."

"I am sorry," said the Baron. "It would have saved us time. That portrait by Forain that you failed to admire was of my sister—Marie von Lichtenfels."

"Why, of course," said Morty. "Forain didn't do her justice at all. She was a famous beauty."

"Yes, the gods were lavish with her—too lavish. They added one gift too many around her cradle. They bestowed on her the honor of being part Jewess. I don't know the exact percentage but it was a sufficiently large part to aggravate Dr. Goebbels. And being perhaps the richest of the undesirables, our family fled Germany in 1935. We escaped without any casualties—except that laceration of the heart which the exile feels when he must choose the world instead of his native land.

I went to Russia. My father, brother and sister went to London. In London my sister, Marie, received a cable from the American financier, Albert Malchen. He was in Austria and wished to buy a castle she owned in Salzburg. My father knew Malchen. He had tried for many years to buy a Rembrandt that was the pride of the Lichtenfels collection."

The Baron sipped his wine and looked dreamily at the dance floor.

"It is a difficult story to tell," he resumed, "because it has lost none of its horror. Mr. Malchen's death has improved it only slightly. The death of one scoundrel does not lessen the inhumanity in the world. I am sure"—the Baron looked again at the dance floor—"that there are dozens of Albert Malchens enjoying themselves around us. But if I talk like that you will think I am mad, doctor. And that is untrue. I am world-poisoned, nothing more."

Morty nodded and we waited for Corfus to continue.

"Malchen asked my sister, Marie, to meet him in Austria," the Baron resumed. "But Austria was dangerous ground for her. It had not yet been gobbled up by the Nazis, but they were sitting at its banquet board, knives in hand. Marie arranged with Malchen to meet him in Zurich but Malchen failed to appear. He sent her a letter explaining that he was bedridden in a sanitarium just across the Austrian border and he begged her to visit him and close the deal for the castle there. My sister, who was brave and eager to improve the family fortune— for we had fled with little of our wealth—my sister crossed into Austria and arrived at the sanitarium. Mr. Malchen was not waiting for her. Instead a group of Gestapo agents seized her and took her to Berlin. You see, it was known to the Nazis that our family, on fleeing Germany, had buried the bulk of the Lichtenfels art collection somewhere in a forest in Saxony. We had left fifty paintings, very famous ones and worth millions, underground to await our return when the Nazis had finished their day."

Baron Corfus sighed.

"It is a long day," he said; "longer than we imagined."

He paused.

"In Berlin," the Baron resumed, "the Nazis tortured my sister for three months. They disfigured her face and broke her hands and legs. And they were able finally to learn from her the hiding place of the Lichtenfels collection. Mr. Malchen was rewarded immediately for his part in the affair. He was allowed to buy the Rembrandt he had so long coveted for a comparatively small sum. It hangs in his own collection now. Mr. Malchen had evidently heard that the remaining members of the Lichtenfels family had sworn to avenge Marie. My father was not among them. He shot himself after Marie died. Friends in Berlin were permitted to bury her. They wrote us that they were unable to recognize her. Last night my butler, who is my older brother, Frederick, and I were able to fulfill the vow."

The Baron sighed.

"Last night," he said, "my sister watched Mr. Malchen die at her feet. If you will pardon me now"—the Baron smiled faintly—"it is one-thirty."

He stood up.

"The check has been paid," he said, "and thank you for an interesting evening. I hope we shall see each other again."

"Good night," said Morty, "and don't forget to burn the cord on that drape."

Baron Corfus bowed and walked toward the vestibule.

"My conscience," said Morty, "doesn't bother me at all. Justice of a very high order has been done."

"It's still murder," I said.

"Murder, my eye," Morty mopped his face. "The whole thing was a fantasy of mine. You can forget about it. Very pleasant fellow, Corfus. Too bad he's not long for this world. I made a close study of his physical signs tonight. That cachexia. It can only mean an advanced and pretty well metastasized cancerous condition. The man is probably in constant pain. I give him six months listening to El Granada music. It's a great place. . . . Best in town." Morty beamed, and I followed his eyes around the crowded tables.

They were all there, all the toy faces of the city's night life. Fame, wealth and beauty sat huddled like a flock of bedizened sheep come in from a storm. Outside, the world was exploding on a hundred battle-fronts. Around us the God of Trivia was still in his heaven with his votaries yawning at their devotions.

And the most elegant and ennuied of them all was Baron Corfus, bowing his good night to Ganzo in the doorway.

The Champion from Far Away

I AM VERY FOND of this story. Not because it's any good, necessarily; but because Vanya Kovelenko is my favorite hero. And Vanya's friend, Gaspodin Charash, is my favorite villain.

Whenever I get confused from reading too many books, or depressed by the return of an old insolvency trouble, or merely bored by the innocent reiterations of existence—in short about once every month, I look up Mr. Kovelenko (which must be done around 3:00 A.M.) and we sit down and discuss.

And listening to Mr. Kovelenko's slow and faltering saga filtering through as humpty-dumpty an accent as was ever brewed in the melting pot, a deep, philosophical calm takes hold of me. The hula-hula canyons of new Babylon, the electric hemorrhage of its Broadway, the fizz and pop of its nightmarish windows and Aladdinish geometries—these become phenomena of small import. Which is because my hero, for me at least, is a creature of such dignity, mood, and humor, of such Homeric troubles and earthly smell as restore man to his lordship of the Universe and reduce his handiwork—from the Battery to the Bronx —to a sort of mechanical little toy.

As for Gaspodin Charash, him I have never seen. I have only my friend Vanya's word that he exists at all. But the Charash cannot be doubted. He is as inevitable as the Wolf in *Little Red Riding Hood* or the strange gentleman in red tights who is known to have conferred with Dr. Faustus.

I shall begin long ago, skipping, however, many vital but unrelated incidents in Mr. Kovelenko's saga, and introduce you to my hero under the most conventionally heroic of circumstances—to wit, in battle.

Perhaps you will remember that famous German victory over the Russians in the Tannenberg marshes in 1915 when a hundred thousand Germans fought a million Muscovites and slew half of them. My friend Vanya was there, standing for three days knee-deep in mud, unarmed, as were seventy-five percent of his comrades (for owing to a certain confusion inherent in the Slavic character only one gun for every four men had found its way to this battle-front). Vanya was there, feeling a trifle conspicuous in this carnage, for despite his having settled a good foot in the soft ground, he still loomed over the heads of his fellow targets. At this time Vanya was twenty-three years old, weighed 235 pounds, and stood six feet three inches in his stockings.

For three days Vanya remained motionless in this shooting gallery, nibbling on a loaf of iron-like black bread, slapping his large hands against his sides to keep them from freezing off, and blinking with his pale deep-set eyes at the Witches' Sabbath in front of him. On the third morning most of Vanya's fellow targets were down—but our hero still stood munching on his bread and facing westward as he had been ordered.

He was rewarded for his long vigil by the sudden appearance of an enemy. The curtain of fire and shell broke, the ear-splitting din subsided, and streaming across the well-churned marshes Vanya beheld the myriads of Hell, all dressed in gray and heading for him.

A slight doubt as to his ability to stem this tide that was rushing forward to lay low his country, the beloved village of Shavarov included, must have crossed Vanya's mind. However, it in no way deterred him. He felt cramped from three days' inaction and not quite at his best. His head, too, was aching and his stomach (ah, what a stomach my hero has) grinding with a hunger which ordinarily would have brought tears to his eyes. Nevertheless he did his best.

He broke four Prussian heads, choked a lieutenant to death, kicked three jaws loose and bit off as many ears as came his way. Given firmer ground and a few minutes in which to recover his breath, Vanya might have turned the tide of victory—at least so it must have seemed to the wearied Uhlans who had flushed this snorting dinosaur in their drive across the marshes.

However, Vanya fell to earth, lay for a space staring up at a rain of boots, bayonets, and rifle butts, and then closed his eyes. When he opened them again the day had gone. He was lying on his back with a sheet over him, to distinguish him from the living. It was dark. Figures moved around him. Pulling the sheet below his eyes he counted them. Only six, and six were child's play for Vanya, provided his arms were still working and his legs stood up.

God was good, for Vanya found himself, except for a few sore places, still all in one piece and able to rise. So rise he did and a monstrous-looking figure he must have been, bloodied and caked with mud as he resumed the battle of the Tannenberg marshes where he had left off. Two more Prussian heads ceased to dream of victory, and Vanya galloped into the night. During the darkness he walked, crawled, and dragged himself through the bloody marshes in which his comrades lay imbedded as richly as raisins in an Easter cake. He circled and doubled on his tracks but continued to head always eastward. The day found him still moving, albeit he was hungry enough to eat his shoes—and toward dusk he smelled, as he put it, the ranks of his comrades.

A sentinel spied him and here the incidents grow vague in Vanya's memory. He recalls some talk of his being a deserter, and the anger of some officers and on the whole a great deal of confusion during which someone removed his coat and shirt and treated him to a hundred lashes—which had something to do with discipline as far as Vanya could make out.

But whatever happened was of no great importance, for a week later, Vanya, this time with an empty pistol in his hand (through an oversight his company had been given no bullets), was again playing target and facing the west as had been ordered.

Nineteen-seventeen found my hero very little changed. He has in fact a peculiarly personal memory of these years of disaster—for it is his hunger rather than the Prussians and all their hellish antics that he remembers.

"Oh, I was 'ongry!" says Vanya and recites a list of battles as if they were no more than fast days; recalls a series of campaigns that bled a dynasty to death as a time of dreadfully restricted diet.

"Before the war," says Vanya, "I eat five, seex times evrra day. I need lots food or I get seeck. The war come. No food. I am seeck all the time. I eat graas. I eat trees. I eat mud. Oh, I was verr glad when the war finch. But no. Et ees worse. Moch."

Worse it was, for Vanya's troubles began in earnest after Brest-Litovsk and the Bolsheviki. At first there was high talk and heroic singing as the proletarian sun burst over that bloody horizon. And Vanya reared his six-feet-three in the camp and sang of Bashkiria whose women were plump and whose skies rained kumiss milk.

For two weeks my hero, as far as I can make out from his modest confessions, inherited the earth indeed, drank vodka till his neck was bursting, pillaged, plundered, and ravished, fell off bridges and slept upside down in mud holes. Altogether an epic fortnight which the world watched holding its breath and which Vanya Kovelenko dimly mistook for a high-class wedding in Shavarov.

But all this passed and famine again descended on Vanya. With ringing head and shrinking stomach (which latter phenomena Vanya assures me is as painful as childbirth and, alas, more frequent) the marching began again. Back to Moscow with plenty of bullets in his pockets, for it was Russians he was now ordered to shoot—Russians who had a monopoly on the food supply (which was Vanya's simple idea of the revolution and at first an inspiring one); and from Moscow to Leningrad and from Leningrad through mountains of ice into Siberia— so my hero fared. But shooting Russians, even fat and noble ones, brought no more filling into Vanya's stomach than making faces at the Prussians had done.

And here the revolution began to lose some of its charm for Vanya. Twice he was arrested and beaten into unconsciousness for raids on the commissar provision depots and once, overheard mumbling about the pre-war glories of Shavarov in Bashkiria where you could get a gallon of kumiss for two kopecks and where there were whole cows to eat, he was shipped back to Leningrad as a Czarist.

And here there were more beatings and less victuals than ever. And there was such talk and yelling as kept Vanya dizzy from morning to night; there was a confusion for which he would gladly have exchanged the Tannenberg marshes. It seems that Vanya had only to open his mouth in some simple, heart-felt comment on the food situation and he was at once set upon by crazy men, gabbled at, beaten and threatened with death.

Vanya still marvels at how he ever kept body and soul together during the two years he was a red menace. He still marvels, too, over the way he was being continually rushed into the streets to shoot at people, sometimes in the middle of the night when he was just forgetting his hunger in a God-given hour of sleep. And over the way he was captured five times by the enemy (whoever they were) and gabbled at all over again and enrolled in a new cause and kissed on both cheeks and called Brother and shoved behind new barricades. It was impossible, says Vanya, to tell what was going on, everything got so mixed up, everybody going crazy if you so much as contradicted a sneeze, and Brother beating Brother over the head with vodka kegs even during moments of relaxation. In short it was something, says Vanya, which cannot be described or even imagined.

However, in 1919 Vanya belonged to some sort of Group concerning which he is rather vague. He remembers that this Group used to invade restaurants and throw people out of windows; and that sometimes it would hold meetings on the highway and wait for the peasants to come driving their produce wagons to town. This Group had some sort of a name and for a time Vanya had high hopes it would bring back those first happy days of the revolution and free Mother Russia of all the elaborate and complicated troubles that were slowly making life impossible—at least for Vanya.

But no. Various other Groups, including the Police, combined against Vanya and his comrades, harried them up and down alleys and finally, after a disastrous battle in which Vanya personally covered himself with glory (he was even mentioned in the enemy despatches printed that night in the newspapers as the dangerous Hooligan Giant), scattered and drove them out of town.

And here Vanya's troubles assume a classic outline. With Mitka and Chizhik, two surviving members of his Group who were soon to perish —not of hunger, says Vanya, for if anybody could die of such a thing as hunger he himself would have been dead a thousand times, but of grief, for Mitka and Chizhik were men with souls—with these two soulful comrades my hero in answer to some primordial urge endeavored to fight his way out of an absurd and civilized world.

He recalls such days of famine in this adventure as still make his eyes roll with terror, days when there were no houses to pillage; nights when there were no farms to raid; in fact not a sight or smell of food from one end of the world to the other. Nevertheless, moving steadily northward and eastward and hardly speaking to each other, these three Muscovite giants (for Mitka and Chizhik were men of stature) clawed their way toward the arctic regions. Man was their enemy and how many murders these three silent tow-headed stranglers committed in their queer climb up the end of the world, Vanya doesn't remember.

This whole passage is dim in my hero's mind quite as if it were someone else who had made this pilgrimage into the north. But his memory brightens with their arrival at the Pechora River, which is the leading river in Archangelsk, says Vanya, but in no way—either for depth, beauty, or comfort—to be compared to the Buguruslan that flows in Bashkiria.

Arrived at the Pechora and alarmed by the condition of his two friends, who were so done in by this half-year of sorties, murders, skirmishes, pitched battles, and forced marches that they could barely drag one foot after the other, Vanya built a large raft and the trio lay themselves wearily down thereon and were borne slowly toward the northern seas. Occasionally they anchored in the shadows of some sleeping village and Vanya, half frozen though he was, fighting his way in and out of the market place, would return to share his spoils with his companions.

Tragedy, however, overtook the raft. Mitka died in a snow storm, begging Vanya to play him some music on a fife which he fancied his friend was hiding from him, and Vanya, howling with grief, rolled him into the river. And a week later Chizhik the Giant began babbling like a child and took to reading aloud a letter received two years ago from his brother Parfim. And my hero, poling the raft slowly through the snows and ice of the Pechora, learned that this Parfim, favorite of fortune, now worked in a magnificent mill in a distant place called Gary, Indiana, or as Chizhik and Vanya pronounced it, Hary, Injani. Here, wrote Parfim, was the land of milk and honey and he himself was dressed from morning to night in the finest of colored silks and, what was more, lived in a beautiful cabin with three women to serve him and vie for his love.

Chizhik, grown sentimental as his last hours were on him, hoped only to survive long enough to see Parfim and share for an hour the bounties of faraway Hary. But he followed Mitka into the river, Parfim's tale of Canaan clutched in his huge, dead hand. And again Vanya howled with grief (for Chizhik even more than Mitka had been a man with a soul) and the raft moved more slowly through the ice and snows of the Pechora.

Now the sun went out of the world, Vanya tells me, and the night sat down on the dim white ground and an iron wind swung through the endless dark. And he was all alone and the hunger that came to him was a thing that made all the rest of his life seem like an unbroken feast day.

There was no longer a smell of man or life, and Vanya, pulling his raft after him—for though it had become useless on the frozen river it was yet his home and he had grown attached to it—Vanya (such is the mercilessness of fate) was forced to live on storks alone, and not many of them. In Archangelsk, says Vanya, the stork is the only variety of food accessible to the traveler. And day and night Vanya clattered after these half-frozen creatures, kicking them to death and devouring them sometimes feathers and all, so great was his hunger.

Thus drifting and sliding over the ice-choked Pechora into an ever emptier world Vanya came all unexpectedly and to his horror upon the land of the Samoyeds, a name which Vanya tells me means Eat Himself. And here, depressed by the increasing trials with which fate harried him, Vanya would have allowed himself to be set upon, roasted, dismembered and eaten (as was related in Bashkiria of voyagers who fell into the hands of these ice-bound cannibals) but for a curious hope that sustained his heart. This hope was the memory of the promised land of Hary, Injani, discovered by Chizhik's brother, Parfim.

It is doubtful, thinks Vanya, whether the Samoyeds would have found him to their taste if they had captured him, for his skin was leathery, his tongue bitter, his flanks stringy and he would not have yielded a mouthful of palatable food, however artfully cooked. Nevertheless, girding himself for battle, Vanya and his raft moved by the dim cabins of the Samoyeds whom he saw with his own eyes roasting a plump naked woman on a spit. As he was watching this spectacle horrified but, despite his Christian soul, almost fainting from the sweet, heady odors, he heard the sound of men on the river. Grimly he approached on his raft, the waters of the Pechora opening around him.

He saw a number of small craft, filled with men who were fishing, although what the Samoyeds wanted of fish when they had so much more substantial a dinner preparing for them on the shore was a matter that still puzzles Vanya. However, with a roar that must have stood the enemy's hair on end, coming as it did out of this arctic night, Vanya shot his raft into the very midst of these fishermen and there ensued a naval engagement such as the mouth of the Pechora had not witnessed since the days of the Vikings. Vanya fought for hours, drowning how many cannibals he does not remember, and with the last of their boats smashed to splinters and the voices of the women raised in a heathenish lament from the shore, emerged victoriously into the White Sea. And here my hero, bellowing with hunger, lay face downward on his raft while cakes of ice bigger than the hills of Bashkiria pelted him like stones from the hand of God and waves higher than the trees of Shavarov tossed him about like a feather in the dark.

These days, says Vanya, were like the end of the world and he would not have been surprised if the black skies had opened and all the beasts of the beyond had rushed down to devour the land and the water. Instead a much more unbelievable thing happened. A Norwegian freighter ran over him as it ploughed through the ice floes and he was hauled out of the sea, as shrunken as if he had been dead a thousand years. And two weeks later he was landed in icebound Spitsbergen.

As after a great storm all is serene and quiet, so Vanya found his succeeding days. At least that is his description of them. He was given a pair of overalls, dropped into the hold of a ship bigger than he had imagined it was possible to build. And for two months Vanya shoveled coal into its roaring furnace. The heat, says Vanya, was so great that at night his body smelled of burned hair and his eyes took fire when he closed them. The wind blew this ship, big though it was, until it tossed and spun like his Pechorian raft and Vanya, clinging to his shovel, fought to keep himself from bouncing into the blazing mouth of his furnace. But there was food, says Vanya, in small but never-failing quantities, and an instinct told him he was moving toward the promised land of Hary, Injani.

By what stages my hero in his seed-like passage from one end of the earth to the other was finally dropped on an Ojibway Indian reservation two hundred miles north of Toronto, he has not yet revealed. But summer found him deep in the affections of these redskins, a very nice but lazy people, says Vanya, with whom he would have been content to spend the rest of his days. My hero never speaks of this time without mentioning the Pickerel or as he calls it the Peek River on which his Indian friends lived and which in a few aspects compared favorably with his Buguruslan. But despite the semi-prevalence of meals now, two wives and the admiration of an entire Ojibway tribe, an instinct told Vanya that the food and women of the land discovered by Chizhik's brother, Parfim, were more palatable. So leaving his lovely Peek River, his wives, friends and red-skinned admirers, Vanya again placed himself in the wind and was blown back and forth, up and down, until he landed in New York. And this was on a spring morning four years after the signing of the treaty at Brest-Litovsk.

"Oh, I was 'ongry," says Vanya, asked for his first impressions of Babylon. " 'Ongrier than I everr was in mine life."

Somehow in a manner he finds it difficult to detail and which I will not take the trouble to invent, Vanya encountered a Red Cross worker who spoke a little Russian and who secured him a job in a Brooklyn cemetery digging graves.

And here he stuck through spring and summer, inquiring as best he could of such preoccupied people as visited the scenes of his work, where lay the land of Hary, Injani—and receiving no information and even less attention. If not for the memory of Chizhik on the raft, reading aloud the elegant and inspiring words of Parfim, Vanya would have begun to doubt the very existence of this promised land of Hary. As it was, hope dimmed in his heart, and he dug graves day after day as if life itself had disappeared.

And here, after a long pause of time, Vanya, resting on his shovel, looks up from beside a newly made grave and sees in the dusk outlined against a tombstone a certain one whose name is Charash. This Charash is smoking a cigarette and has a very high-class way of leaning against this tombstone. And my hero, whose stout heart has never failed him, looks into the eyes of this man and something cold touches his stomach. No omens attend the one by the tombstone. No seven ravens circle his head. No dreadful lights play about his feet. But from the first Vanya is not deceived.

The stranger smiles and tosses away the cigarette, sighs, and steps forward, and Vanya, who stood motionless for three days and nights in the marshes while an army died around him, is ready to drop his shovel, turn tail and flee. But the stranger speaks, and in Russian too, and calls him by name. "One moment, my good Vanya. I desire very much to speak to you. You are a very interesting-looking fellow. I have noticed you several times. I have a friend who lies here. But today I did not come to visit her. I come only to observe you. I am Charash. This is my automobile. Step in, if you please. It is all right. You will not wish to come back here. So you may leave the shovel behind. All right, Victor, first drive us to the Piruzhnaya where we will have something to eat. My friend Vanya looks hungry."

This is a piece of pure invention, this monologue. For Vanya can no more recall the words of that first meeting than recite the Red Grimoire of Cagliostro. He trembled, perspired, felt strange prickly sensations, his ears grew cold, his throat burned as if an icicle had been thrust into it. And he sat beside Charash in this luxurious limousine as if he were riding on a broomstick with a black cat perched on his shoulders.

As I said in the beginning I have never seen this Charash. But so much the better. For, alas, it is not given to people such as I ever to behold a Charash in his true colors. We are too clever to see angels and our vanity is too great for the study of devils. We are too busy with disillusion to look up or look down.

Thus as I write I am tempted to steal Charash from Vanya and attire him in proper, sensible outlines with nothing more dreadful than a Broadway leer on his Muscovite lips. However, my respect for my hero restrains me and too, a slight, reportorial laziness. For if Charash is not the unicorn in the gray derby, the Aladdin, Jinn, Babayaga's son, dervish, Llama, and sorcerer to whom Vanya sold his soul, then who is he? A pock on the realities. This, after all, is still the twentieth century and not the thirtieth, and none of us will seem much keener or more sensible than Vanya when the archeologists come to exhume our doings and sayings. So I give you a Charash as improbable as a frog's dream, as absurd as a grasshopper's honeymoon, and as truthful as Vanya's simple heart.

When we sit down to discuss Charash, Vanya shakes his head and clucks with awe. I ask questions. What did he talk like? Like nobody, says Vanya. For Charash had no human voice. He squeaked. He uttered high-pitched, hoarsened sounds that frightened you. Did he talk Russian? What a question! All the languages—Russian, English, French, Turkish. But always in the same squeak. And very fast, as if he had no breath. He walked fast, too. He was bald-headed, with a head like a big egg. He had a long, purple face. He was not so tall but he had big feet and red hair on his hands. He wore a purple suit. Where did he come from? Vanya crosses himself and his wide cheekbones lift in a sad smile. The same place, says Vanya, to which he has returned.

But there was nothing in his smell to indicate this, says Vanya with a worried look. He smelled like a fine man, always perfumed. When he took out his handkerchief to blow his nose the air became like a garden. But when he got drunk he was very cruel. What did he do? He squeaked and gurgled like a flock of ravens and made sounds in the back of his throat enough to frighten a dozen priests. And he banged on the table and cried out in Russian, so that Vanya's blood ran cold, "Attention! ATTENTION, YOU!" Then Vanya, no matter where this occurred, had to rise and stand rigidly with his fingertips in salute against his perspiring brow while Charash lay back in his seat and squeaked with glee. But all this was nothing.

Vanya remembers this first week with Charash as almost worth the years of torment awaiting him when he appears before God minus his soul. A week of such eating as Vanya's hungriest dreams had never pictured. So many fowls, steaks, chops, soups; so many vegetables, concoctions, pies, pastries and puddings as nobody, not even in Shavarov, would have believed one man could devour, were Vanya's. Five, six times a day, whenever he woke up, a man opened the door and said, "What'll you have, sir?" And Vanya would nod and answer with the magic words Charash had taught him, "The same, please." And in less time than it takes to scratch yourself into a good, wakeful state, the steaming bowls, the crowded platters, all smelling like dreams of heaven, would be on the table before him. And beside this Paradise of dishes, one, two, three or as many bottles of vodka as one needed for a good stomach wash.

And when this enchanted week was done Charash revealed himself and his purpose. This week, he explained, was only a meager sample of what life had in store for Vanya if he would sign his name to a certain paper. So Vanya affixed his name to the document which made Charash his manager, or rather which made Vanya the tool, pawn, chattel, myrmidon and golem of Charash.

It was in this way that Vanya became a wrestler known as Kovelenko, the Mysterious Russian. What did Vanya know of wrestling? Oho, says Vanya, puffing out his cheeks and thrusting forth his lower lip, in Shavarov—my God, in Shavarov his name had been a household word as a wrestler. He had wrestled with Taras the miller, Oblomov the blacksmith, Sedukim the postman, with two farm hands whose names had slipped his mind, with Korolniki, a visiting soldier, and with a monstrous Turk named Sufi who had appeared out of nowhere and overrun Shavarov for a fortnight. All these he had conquered.

In his first month which followed, Vanya wrestled two and three times a week. At the start he was nervous. The shouts of people and the bright lights over his head confused him. Nevertheless these blubbery giants Charash sent into the ring against him were as easy to throw as so many chickens. In fact Vanya hardly needed to throw them; that is, pin both their shoulders carefully to the mat. What he would do was this—after several minutes he would embrace his opponent around the belly, lift him off his feet and hold him in a bear's hug until the man's toes became quiet. Then, at a nod from Charash in the corner, he would drop his opponent and roll him over and the opponent would lie still, like a dead man, and Vanya, at another nod from Charash, would lift his late enemy onto his shoulder like a sack of meal and carry him through the excited audience to the dressing room.

One after another they went to sleep, so to speak, in Vanya's arms. But in the few minutes which preceded each of these dénouements Vanya learned some of the more fanciful ways of the sport, such as seizing a man's toes and trying to break them off; or locking his head between one's thighs and trying to choke him to death, or spreading his legs apart and trying to split him in two, or seizing his wrist and trying to snap his arm as if it were a piece of kindling, or butting him in the stomach and trying to tumble him over so his head would crack against the floor. At first, learning these matters and hearing the crowd yell with delight as he felt his arms, legs, toes, neck and head being tormented in this picayunish and unscrupulous fashion, Vanya would bellow and curse and toss about like a stranded sea cow. However, the laughter he inspired by these antics annoyed him and finally shamed him into more restrained exhibitions of pain and rage.

But after the second month, realizing that all these bedevilments offered him in the first five minutes of his work were not as dangerous as they seemed, Vanya grew contemptuous altogether of them. He even allowed a few of his victims to amuse themselves and his public with this sort of childishness—the toe-holding, ear-pulling, and wrist-twisting—before shaking them loose and coming to serious, manly grips with them. Of what use all their nonsense when Vanya's arms closed round their middles and off the floor they went, their flesh in a vise, their ribs bending, their hearts, livers, lungs and alimentary canals slowly coming together in a jelly?

Vanya remembers them all—the Turks with handlebar mustachios, little eyes and flat cheeks; the Irish with short quick legs and stocky trunks like vodka barrels; the bullet-headed Germans with pale eyebrows and massive shoulders; the flabby, elephantine Greeks, the heavy-legged Indians, the tattooed men looking like a side of beef stamped for the market—he remembers all this bellowing, grunting, Neanderthalish race of ham-and-egg wrestlers as "verra" nice boys.

Twice and three times a week in various outlying towns Vanya applied his bear hug, received a slap on the back from the jolly, squeaking Charash and was returned by train or motor to his room above the café. At the end of the first month Charash presented him with a new suit and every Sunday morning Charash placed two ten-dollar bills in his hand and slapped him on the back again.

Thus for three months my hero, become Kovelenko, the Mysterious Russian, ate and drank to his stomach's delight; rode in automobiles; walked abroad in a suit as elegant and almost as purple as that worn by Charash; learned to carry a cane as big as a cudgel but much fancier; sat up all night in remarkable places where women sang and danced for his pleasure—and lived, says Vanya, like a lord.

His name and even photograph appeared in the newspapers. Men came to converse and drink with him. And my hero underwent changes which would have astonished his one-time raft mates, Mitka and Chizhik, hardly more than they did himself. As for the Promised Land of Hary, Injani, discovered by Parfim, that was a dream forgotten, pooh-poohed at by Charash, who would wave his hand at the glitter and rumble of Babylon and say, here, this, right around where we stand, my Vanya, that is the golden land.

But now in the sixth month of my hero's rise as a gladiator, I must intrude with sad truths and disillusioning asides. I shall be brief, for the subject is not a happy one. First, I wish it to be clear that nothing of this is known (even today) to Vanya. Vanya remembers these months with a simple and honest sigh for glories that are gone. There was a certain strangeness about them and Vanya was not without wonder and disquiet during their passing. But this was because his stout heart sometimes recoiled from the thought of Charash, the queer one. And because he knew with the sad theology of the poor that one does not receive gifts from a Charash without burning in Hell for them a thousand times. But the courage that had served my hero through his stormy Odyssey did not abandon him despite night sweats and evil dreams.

Having decided to serve Charash, he faced the loss of his soul with grim and truly heroic calm. And that was Vanya's only guilt in the matter—that he had made a pact with Charash.

But the truth, unknown to him, was that Charash had made many pacts vastly more evil—pacts with each of the blubbery giants who had melted in Vanya's bear hug, pacts with their managers, pacts with syndicates and fellow promoters. The truth was that my hero was being fed not battles but set-ups; that he was being coddled and stuffed with artificial victories and cunningly converted into a Great Impostor. All this was known only to the élite of the sport. Those who watched from in front beheld, to their delight, a mysterious Russian with murderous arms and a childish lust for battle—an invincible champion in the making.

Charash, squeaking and tireless, piloting his golem from state to state, his pockets always bulging with rolls of bills; Charash, maneuvering his merry troglodyte through more and more complicated skullduggeries, slowly converted Vanya into an important name. The sporting pages took note and began to babble about the Pleistocene mannerisms of this new boon to sport, Kovelenko, the Human Bear. And then, with some fifty bought-and-paid-for victories ornamenting the banner of my hero, Charash had suddenly catapulted him into the notice of that wider public known as the Million Dollar Gate.

The newspapers appeared one morning with the tale that Vera Nash, whose diamond bracelets, ex-husbands and vie d'amour were one of the gaudier legends of Babylon, had selected Kovelenko, the Mysterious Russian, to be the father of her Eugenic Baby. La Nash, in the throes of a maternal complex—so the tale went—had decided to mate with the Human Bear and enrich the world with a Perfect Offspring, etc., etc.

Vanya remembers this matter reluctantly. He speaks of it with his head lowered and a timorous look in his eyes. The first he knew of what was going on, says Vanya, was when they brought him to have his picture taken. And they stood him beside a Princess, so delicate, so beautiful, that he found it hard to breathe and he would have sunk to the floor in sheer bliss had not Charash supported him. As it was his ears trembled, his knees buckled and the roof of his mouth froze. For never had he smelled so delicious a morsel as this lovely woman. What nonsense to call her woman, says Vanya. Angel is the word, creature out of heaven, golden and sweet and more beautiful even than the dreams of a Turk.

The picture-taking done, my hero, still trembling, his heart beating so terribly that he was certain every step he took must be his last, was returned to his room. He spoke no word to Charash and Charash spoke no word to him. Food was brought but Vanya, miracle of love, failed to respond. How could he eat when his stomach was on fire? How could he taste anything when his soul was in his mouth?

The next morning Vanya learned from the man who served him his meals of the remarkable tale in the newspapers—that this Heavenly One had chosen him as a mate. And with his own eyes he beheld the pictures printed of himself and her. He listened, grew dizzy and then, says Vanya, "I try stand up. No. No use. My legs too weak. I try speak. No. No use. My tongue ees dead. I grab vodka. One, two bottle. I throw him in my mout. Then I stand up. I go find Charash. I grab Charash. I hold him, so. Till he grow purrrple like a squash. I kees Charash. I sing the songs of Bashkiria. I am so happy I dance. I am ready to go to this angel who waits forr me. But Charash—'No,' he say. 'No.' 'To Hell,' I say. 'No,' he say. 'What,' I say. 'Thees is my wooman. She love me.' Charash make terrible noise. 'Attention,' he say. 'Attention, you!' He bang the table. 'To Hell,' I say. I knock heem down. He roll over under the bed or I keeck him in pieces, sir. And I go out and find thees place where she is."

And here Vanya holds his head and moans with memories.

The tale of Vanya's wooing, though it lasted a short hour, filled the newspapers for weeks. How he broke down doors, cracked heads, kicked two elevator men unconscious and came hurtling into the presence of the terrified La Nash; how he sang to her, danced and bellowed around her and shattered a Sèvres chandelier and overturned an elegant Louis XIV bed in his courtship; how La Belle Nash, clad in gossamer, fled this Muscovite faun and collapsed in the arms of a Park Avenue policeman; how Vanya, realizing he had been tricked, remained behind and emptied La Nash's apartment out of its eighth-story windows, and how the police, arriving finally in sufficient numbers, clubbed the heartbroken grappler out of his misery—how all these things happened to the delight of hundreds of newspaper editors Vanya himself has never told me. His memory here is mottled. He recalls laconically that he woke up with his head bandaged and Charash beside him. And he lay with his face to the wall for two days. In vain Charash produced substitute goddesses. Vanya groaned and waved them off. And this might have been an end to all the pacts so skillfully made by Charash—for my hero had stomach neither for food, fame, nor females. But Charash persisted and was patient and set to work artfully luring his stricken golem out of his despair with bottle on bottle of vodka. And for two weeks Vanya drank himself in and out of comas. And Vanya slowly came back to sanity.

In the third week he was walking normally and ready to face the world again, the memory of the true goddess flooded out of his kidneys.

The incident, dangerous though its immediate results had seemed, swept the plans of Charash to a speedy climax. For Kovelenko, the Mysterious Russian, had by this gleefully chronicled affair of the heart become an exhilarating figure—one of the overnight celebrities of Babylon. And Charash, feeling his hour was striking, came forward with a challenge and the press responded enthusiastically. Kovelenko, the Mysterious Russian, alias The Great Lover, had challenged Hans Metzger, the world's wrestling champion, and this was news.

The ancient sport had long lain dormant. Metzger, conqueror of a hundred Slav, Greek, German, Indian, Chinese, and Anglo-Saxon champions, had been tossing palookas around for two years; finding none worthy his mettle (nor, what was worse, the price of admission), participating in dubious hippodromes, giving exhibitions of strength in the vaudevilles and praying (along with his troupe of hungry managers) for a Real Contender. Now one had risen, a fiery and passionate gentleman with a record as persuasive as Tamerlane's; with color, glamour and personality thrown in for good measure, and history was to be made for the sporting pages.

Oddly enough, the soothsayers rallied to a man around Vanya. And forthwith such a barrage of jabberwock was laid down by the oracles of the press that the public (always to be fetched by the prospect of the unhorsing of any sort of champion) began to take the forthcoming struggle to its nourishing bosom. All hands agreed that Metzger was a clever, tricky gladiator, full of science and experience, but of what avail, chortled the soothsayers, of what use this cunning against this Throw Back, this Primordial Force, this Uncle of Gorilla and Cousin of the Great Bear—Mr. Kovelenko?

And these were the days of splendor for my hero. He learned to speak English by slowly decoding the ravishing statements of his prowess, genius and marvelous characteristics. In fact he trained on these clippings. Charash, his challenge accepted, had installed his golem in a gymnasium under a considerate ex-wrestling champion with whom Vanya disported himself harmlessly for an hour each day—to the awe and inspiration of the smitten sport writers. The remainder of his time he devoted to his Greatness. He gave out interviews, posed for hundreds of cameras, laughed, blinked, would even sing if urged, grew dizzy and swallowed bottles of vodka to steady himself. These were the days of glory for my hero when he walked arm in arm with illusion and sat upon a throne.

Vanya was the favorite, the Invincible Force, yet the betting odds were against him. Metzger's record as a champion, ignored by the infatuated press, sustained his prestige in the face of the great Vanya ballyhoo. Colorless, scientific, unpopular and, compared to Kovelenko, unknown, Metzger remained a three-to-two and even two-to-one choice, and this served to increase the public's irritation with him. And the public, convinced that a cautious family man with two children and a house in Newark was no match for a Throw Back, a Rapist and a Friend of Glaciers and Mastodons, attacked this presumptuous German burgher in its own way. It bet against him.

And Charash, more active, more purple and more squeaking than ever, worked swiftly through a dozen agents gathering in all such wagers. For this had been the scheme which underlay all the connivings of Charash, and a week before the great Championship Bout, Charash and his syndicate had placed some million dollars in cash bets against their own Vanya. Through the formidable ballyhoo, through the clamorous and eloquent dissertations of the soothsayers, Charash smiled happily and knew he had builded well. Vanya, his golem, was entering the ring against a master wrestler and an honest one. Poor Vanya, whose fame was a fraud invented by Charash, whose victories were part of a carefully evolved hoax, whom Charash in the privacy of his own conclaves called an oaf, a hooligan and a palooka of the lowest order—this deluded and untutored ox of a Russian had as much chance against the brilliant Metzger as a stuffed bear.

So the night of the great doings arrived. Vanya remembers first the crowd outside the Garden, standing in a drizzle and fighting to get in. Like an army, says Vanya, besieging a fortress. Then overhead the lights of this Coliseum. And spelled out in letters of gold the legend—"Vanya Kovelenko Versus Hans Metzger. World's Wrestling Championship." What a thing to see gleaming in the rain! Like a phrase in a fairy tale. Who can forget such a thing? Vanya Kovelenko—spelled out in full for all the eyes of Babylon to read!

He grew dizzy, says Vanya, looking at it, and his attendants (ah, how many attendants Vanya had that night) had to pull him away and into the great Garden. And what shouts and cheers from the rain-soaked ones who recognized him—no King or Hero ever heard louder ones.

Vanya lingers on many details of that evening of which I will forego the telling. Such a buzz and hurrah and burst of lights, such a happy noise and wonderful sight Vanya is sure was never known in the world before. How they loved him when he came striding in his leopard skin to the ring. And how he loved them. He could have kissed each of the twenty thousand on both cheeks. And how they yelled and pointed and embraced him with their soul—him, Vanya, the peasant from Shavarov, the nobody, the hungry rider of ice cakes from Archangelsk.

And there, standing like a colossus out of another age, my hero waited in his corner. Six-feet-three, weighting two hundred and forty, and shaped like a bear. Several of the sharp-eyed ones at the ringside said later that he was drunk—but this was because they remembered tears in his eyes. It was not liquor but enchantment that dimmed Vanya's eyes during these moments.

Metzger, the champion, came and was booed and derided and quickly ignored. And the Coliseum hummed now as if full of millions of bees and crickets. The referee brought them together, spoke. Vanya remembered nothing of this, nothing of the minutes that passed from the time he entered the ring to the moment Charash slapped him on the back and whispered in Russian, "Farewell, my little dove."

Then he remembers seeing as if for the first time a man in purple tights moving toward him, with hands waving in the air like the paws of a cat. A German, says Vanya softly. A German of Germans. With a square head and a square face, pale eyebrows, wide mouth and the blond look behind which Germans disguise themselves. A shapely German, much shapelier than Vanya, with good shoulders and thin in the middle. And Vanya, watching him approach, grew angry. The cries of the Coliseum dimmed in his ears. There was something so evil and intense in the eyes of this German that Vanya grew confused. Not frightened, God forgive the word, but startled. For the weeks that had passed had been such a happy time that my hero had looked forward to this evening as an hour of superb delight. And if he had given thought to his opponent he had fancied another one of those blubbery, weak-backed creatures whom Charash was always producing for him to crush and fall upon.

But in this first moment, standing motionless and watching Metzger, the German, come toward him, Vanya's spirit cleared. There was one thing Vanya knew, one thing he had looked upon and studied in many places—and that was murder in the eyes of men. And murder in a German's eyes! Ah, there came a strange, marshy smell into Vanya's nose and he straightened up as once long ago when the smoke had lifted on the Tannenberg. A Russian curse broke from him and the crowd screamed with delight, but Vanya heard not a sound. He walked forward slowly to meet and seize this one, to choke this German sneer from his face. And his hands unaccountably missed their mark. He had instead slipped his arm into a vise that was bending it out of joint. Vanya let his arm stay in the vise to see how strong this man was. Yes, there was power in the vise, enough to bend him to his knees if he waited too long. And with a sudden growl Vanya ripped his arm free and the champion staggered away and sprawled against the ropes and the crowd boomed its joy.

And again Vanya came forward and again his hands missed their mark and this time the vise closed around his head, twisting it as if to unscrew it from his shoulders. Now Vanya, fully convinced about the general characteristics of this vise, did not wait at all. He flung his shoulders up and again the champion bounced off him like a rubber ball. Vanya pursued, as a bear lumbers swiftly, and reached out for his grip, the one grip he knew—arms around the middle, fingers clasped behind the back and then the feel of flesh and bone melting and cracking against his chest. Instead of all these pleasing events, a powerful hand smashed into his face, snapping back his head. And the champion was moving away, deliberately as if frightened, and the crowd was screaming for an early kill and Vanya, growling, his arms hungry and murderous, moved forward—just as the soothsayers had prophesied. Shamelessly the champion sidled out of his reach, keeping his body bent as if in the throes of an enormous cramp—and Vanya, puzzled at this pathetic exhibition of cowardice, cursed again and plunged. For a moment it seemed that his arms had found their mark. They were almost around this strangely elastic figure that heaved and twisted in his grip like an eel. But Vanya pushed forward, ignoring the head banging against his chin. And then, to his disgust, he found himself in another vise. The German had seized his head and was pulling it over his shoulders as if Vanya were a sack of meal he was going to carry somewhere.

Vanya tried to lock his legs in the German's, pawed furiously with his hands, grunted and thrashed but to no avail. He felt himself rising in the air as if he were a child being played with; rising, floundering in space and crashing to the ground. The champion had tossed him over his shoulder with a Flying Mare.

Vanya was on his feet. He roared with the crowd now and hurled himself forward. No man had ever done this to him. He crashed into Metzger, who gave way, who seemed to twist and slip like something made of rubber; who continued to retreat shamelessly across the ring, his arms extended limply, his hands waving slightly and Vanya after him snorting with rage. Then again the thing happened and Vanya was off his feet, bellowing and clawing the air through which he spun.

This time Vanya lay for a few seconds where he had been tossed and the champion pounced on him. The vise was on Vanya's legs now; now on the toes of his right foot. A pain brought a cry from Vanya and cleared his head. He struck out with his legs and the champion shot across the ring as if he had been tossed over a precipice. And Vanya leaped after him. He landed on an empty stretch of canvas, rose, leaped again, his arms waving before him like those of a man walking under water. But all that happened was that for the third time he found himself, as in a nightmare, rising from the ground, toppling helplessly through the air and crashing head down into the canvas. He heard a noise as he lay—a burst of human sound that shook his heart and brought him to his feet. Those who watched Vanya rise the third time knew from the clumsy way he had taken these falls that he was no wrestler; knew they had been sold again into witnessing Metzger, the scientist, toss another palooka to defeat. The champion, his opponent slightly dazed, would now begin playing medicine ball with him, would now begin bashing him methodically into unconsciousness with one Flying Mare after another, as one might club a giant fish to death by swinging his head against a post.

And these outraged ones, who a few moments ago had shouted themselves giddy with love of this Bear Man, now rose in their seats and demanded a speedy kill. Their hero had betrayed their hopes. The Invincible Force, the Throw Back, the Friend of the Saber-Toothed Tiger et al., was a delusion—and despite the millions wagered, they howled for his end and thundered for his death. And Metzger, still the cat, still sidling and waving paws before him, still crouching, leaped and landed and Vanya again felt the muscles of his leg tearing in the vise. But scissor holds and spread eagles, toe twists and hammerlocks were not invented for the defeat of such as Vanya. He tore himself free as he would have torn his leg out of a steel trap. He staggered, rose, loomed and lunged forward. As much chance to win as a stuffed bear, Charash had said, and this was true. But inside this stuffed bear was a heart that required more than science for its vanquishing. Through the air he sailed again. Crash to the canvas. Up, staggering, clawing— through the air once more. Whish, bang to the ground; dizzy, grunting. Up again and another sprawl, this time on his stomach so his wind went out in a shout. But still he rose and still the champion, leaping on him, bounced off like a terrier shaken from the flanks of a wounded bear. And Vanya, again on his feet, kept moving forward. The German was no German now but a thing of mystery that slipped and twisted continually out of his path and suddenly bent over and became an inhuman apparatus for shooting Vanyas through the air. But German or mystery, human or inhuman, Vanya reeled after it, with his heart bursting and oaths snorting from his mouth.

And now the howling ones standing on their chairs realized that they were witnessing not a wrestling match as advertised but something stranger and more diverting. They were attending the longest kill in the annals of the sport, a kill that promised to continue through the night.

Nine times, ten, eleven, twelve times this Mysterious Russian, in whom they had placed their illusions, sailed through the air, to rise again, to swing his arms, to reel murderously forward. Pounded seemingly to a jelly, tossed and twisted in vise after vise, his head lolling like a dead man's, his legs buckling under him, Vanya fought on though he could neither see nor sense where the battle was for the darkness was greater than any through which he had ever moved—even on that Pechora filled with cannibals.

There was no longer a question of victory. The arms that clutched at the champion were without power; the hands that pawed him were those of a child. All strength had been pounded out of Vanya, his bear hug hammered out of his sinews. Yet each time Metzger the champion leaped to turn him on his back the same thing happened. A mysterious strength that seemed to come from another and still untouched Vanya flowed into his shoulders, legs, and arms—and catapulted the dumbfounded Metzger continually across the canvas.

Twelve, thirteen, fourteen, fifteen, sixteen—the throng, jubilant with lust, counted the Flying Mares, watched the champion lift and smash the helpless Kovelenko to the ground with crotch holds, tumble him with leg tackles, until the scene became like some slow nightmarish murder; until a strange feeling crept into the shouting thousands that Vanya was cursed with some devilish immortality. But this was only Vanya's heart, long after the rest of him was finished, refusing to be hammered into silence.

The end came after an astonishing performance by Vanya. He had risen again, swaying drunkenly, unable for a moment to straighten his legs, his trunk, to lift his arms or open his eyes—a ruined man with a last totter in his marrow. Thus he had stood teetering on unconsciousness and then he had suddenly straightened, his eyes had opened and he had come charging into the champion again. This was unbelievable, to Metzger no less than to the screaming thousands.

It was now Metzger who felt an air of nightmare in that ring. This creature whom he had all but pounded to death, whose toes he knew to be broken, whose leg he knew to be wrenched from its socket, and whose arm he had felt snap in his grip, this Vanya was coming on again, arms swinging, Russian curses once more streaming from him.

And hardly crediting their senses the throng that had been shouting Vanya's requiem, beheld their Bear Man swing his tormentor off the ground, hoist him over his head and hold him aloft. Metzger squirmed and twisted, his feet beating a powerful tattoo against Vanya's face. And Vanya threw back his head and stared up at his inhuman tormentor and smiled and walked a few steps and then paused.

The Coliseum filled with a long roar. The Bear had him. The German was gone. One smash to the ground, one crack against the canvased flooring and Metzger was out. But Vanya, still holding the tossing champion in the air, stood motionless, a man with a strange burden. Then, waving the champion as if he were some mysterious kind of flag, Vanya lifted an agonized face to the roaring galleries and his knees bent, his head fell and he went down slowly under his burden and his flag.

Metzger lay sprawled over him, cautious and waiting. But Vanya was no longer moving. Vanya was still. And Metzger, the German, smiled and rolled him over on his back with a disdainful gesture. And on his back the Mysterious Russian lay while the crowd roared and laughed, while the referee, inaudible in the din, announced the time as twenty-four minutes and ten seconds. And Vanya's eyes were still closed when two men lifted him up and dragged him, hulking and limp, through the ropes, down the aisles and into his dressing room.

Here a doctor appeared and found a number of Vanya's bones to be broken—arm and toes broken, leg wrenched out of place, two ribs smashed, jaw dislocated and, said the doctor, finishing his examination, a serious concussion of the brain. An hour later, after the lights of the Coliseum had long been dark and newspapers carrying the story of his defeat were circulating through a hundred cities, Vanya opened his eyes.

This, in truth, is the end of Vanya's adventures. What followed has little to do with my hero. The scandal that simmered and exploded around Charash and caused him to disappear, the derisive story of Kovelenko's defeat which the press reprinted with increasing angers and accusations for almost a fortnight, the exposure one by one of the numerous set-ups by which Charash had established his palooka's reputation, the general attack on the sport of wrestling—all these epilogues were enacted with Vanya, so to speak, asleep in the wings. Charash in making his exit had sent a messenger to the room above the Piruzhnaya where Vanya lay bandaged like a mummy, and the messenger had handed Vanya five one-hundred-dollar bills. And when the newspapers learned that this paltry sum was all that Vanya had received as his share of the gigantic sport swindle in which he had so painfully participated, they turned their backs on him in disgust as an oaf and hooligan unworthy of their shafts. And in less than a month the name of Vanya Kovelenko had been buried in that limbo into which Babylon disgorges its Seven Day Wonders.

Today Vanya is the doorman at the Piruzhnaya. He stands on the curbing, a towering figure in an ornate Cossack uniform, a hetman's smock and boots, and a large flower-pot hat such as the heroes of eastern Europe affect. This finery pleases Vanya and he is sure that such another uniform is not to be found in all Bashkiria. Thus festooned and grinned at by the passing crowd, Vanya returns their amused stares with an amiable and childish gratitude and if they linger for a moment to wonder at his size he hands them a printed card, as he has been instructed to do.

Here I often come to discuss with Vanya, to hear in snatches his Odyssey and to listen over again to his account of that night of glory when Charash sent him in to fight with his Master, the Devil. And as he tells me of these and other matters, of Chizhik, Mitka, Hary, Injani, of the Pechora and its Samoyeds, and of icebergs, murders, songs and revolutions, of Homeric jaunts, great hungers and the beauties of Shavarov—as he relates these things standing ornate and idle on a curbing in Babylon, he often raises his eyes, grows silent and falls to studying the electric hullabaloo overhead with a critical and quite superior manner.

"My name," he says, "eet was beeger than that one. Beeg. Beeger than thees one. Oh, yes. Beeg as the whole night, sir. From here to there, the whole building, sir, it say, 'VANYA KOVELENKO.' I look all the time, sir, and I nevare see a sign so beeg as the one weeth my name— nevare. So beeg and so bright, people, evrrybody get deezy when they see heem that night. Yes, sir. Goo'night sir. I geev you this. . . ."

And Vanya for the tenth or fifteenth time hands me one of the cards of the Piruzhnaya on one side of which the cuisine of that excellent café is discussed in glowing terms, and on the other side of which is a full-length picture of my hero in a leopard's skin, his arms folded, his sinews abulge. And under this the rather enigmatic words:

"Vanya Kovelenko. Formerly The Mysterious Russian. Now under new management. Inquire within."

Death of Eleazer

O<small>N THIS NEW</small> summer morning the city glitters with light. Warmth is in the streets. Overhead the buildings loom like plate-glass trees. The spokes of the sun turn in a thousand windows.

The hearts and bodies of people seem full of this new summer. In the shop-lined avenue there is an unaccustomed air of personality about the half-sauntering figures. In their open-throated, bareheaded salute to summer there is a smile of festival, and honeymoon in the passing faces. The smell of the ocean, whose vast and idle waters are only a few miles away, brings a truant glint to the eyes of the younger walkers, and the older ones, who no longer smile at each other, smile at memories.

This pleasant morning, without grasses or trees or trilling birds, is still lush with summer languor as if the bright warm sky were full of the odors and phantoms of river lands and rolling meadows. Nature, routed by the city, seems to creep back into its stone streets and gleam out of the eyes of these strolling citizens.

On such a day the history of the world and all its achievements seems useless. All the travail of the many centuries of conquest and progress is hardly a footnote in the heart of this summer crowd. Life, innocent of its thousand and one nights of politics and science, sways gracefully and luringly still in the bodies of the young and sighs tenderly still out of the eyes of the old.

There was on this morning one who walked this street and whose thoughts were far from rejoicing over the innocence of life. This was a reddish, square-faced man, elderly, broad-shouldered, and dressed in heavy dark cloth and thick-soled shoes which, like the rest of him, made no compromise with the season. He was James Malloy, Captain of Police. His flat blue eyes looked unwaveringly ahead of him as he strode, for Captain Malloy considered it part of his technique as a man-hunter to seem as uninquisitive as a sleep-walker.

But the captain's eyes, though immobile, were remarkably sensitive. Not only did they see what apparently they were not looking at, but they evaluated, diagnosed, and sorted all that they saw. This they did automatically, for, whatever the rest of Captain Malloy was, his eyes were two tireless and very able scientists at work in an endless clinic. They looked at faces with an instinct for character that was subtle and accurate.

Captain Malloy's greatest annoyance during his thirty years as a detective was the knowledge that of all the faces moving in any street his was usually the most transparent and the most easily to be diagnosed. He would have liked very much to be a bloodhound with the talent of the hunting beetle, which lies in wait for its quarry with its legs drawn in so that it resembles a stone. Instead, he was a reddish, square-faced man with flat blue eyes, stiffened chin, bushy brows, and taut cheeks, and there was no concealing from the stupidest of criminals what he was. There was a trained, aggressive air and a hound's keenness and an aura of detachment and righteousness to the captain, which no haberdashery or feigned mannerisms could becloud for a moment. Dressed a bit defiantly in his formidable garments, his black iron derby, his heavy blue suit and ponderous shoes, the captain was, within and without, the man-hunter.

On this morning what Malloy saw in the sauntering crowd was for the most part not worth the seeing, from any policeman's point of view. Cluster on cluster of faces bobbed past with no message for the captain's eyes. They were the faces in which moods had idled rather than foraged, and left little behind for hound senses to sniff at. And the captain noticed, though he was little given to poetical thoughts, that all these nondescript faces were a little in love with the bright morning as if the outside of the world today were of more importance than its inner stories.

But in these clusters of faces the captain's eyes now and again located the Devil's spoor, the faint but never-ending trail of crime that marked the faces of every crowd for him. Had you asked Captain Malloy what it was he saw, he could have answered only hesitatingly. For the captain's mind worked much too slowly to reveal its contents to anyone but himself. His lightning-like ability to correlate the lines of a mouth, the glint of an eye, the tautness or tremble of a muscle with the extensive rogues' gallery he carried in his memory was far beyond his power of explanation. But just as he was able by his memory to identify several thousand known criminals at a glance and to know their names, records, and predilections without recourse to any memoranda, so he was able to identify parts of these faces in the anonymity of the crowd.

He saw the quiver of the pupil that told of guilt; the white-skinned, gaunt temples and extra bony structure of eye-sockets that told of drug addictions and hidden depravities; the fleshy ears and over-lidded eyes that told of sadism and all its sleeping deeds of violence. All the conflicts and complexes out of which crime is born, all the over-greeds and under-controls that return the human to the animal, spoke to Captain Malloy out of a hundred little matters sometimes of no more significance than the placing of a wrinkle. So minute, in fact, were the signs of the trail at which the policeman sniffed that you might have agreed with some of his envious colleagues that there was more instinct than science to his work. Proud though he was of his power for noticing things, Captain Malloy would himself have agreed, in part. For he had also noticed that there was another spoor to crime than that to be seen by the eye and catalogued by the swift, microscopic work of memory. There was an aura to the malignant and the maladjusted that brushed the captain's spirit. He could have sensed a murderer in the dark and smelled a dishonest soul through a burlap bag.

Such, omitting a great deal of other matters, was the character of Captain Malloy as he strode this morning to take a train for the outskirts of the city. He was intent on visiting a Dominican monastery and consulting an old man called Father Dominic, who, he had been told, was a great authority on crucifixes.

The captain was on duty and had been so without rest morning or night for two months. During this time four murders, committed apparently by the same maniacal hand, had provided excitement for the newspapers and presumably for the millions who read them.

Captain Malloy often wondered what it was about crime that so fascinated everybody. Like the scene-shifter manipulating the worn and stupid-looking props of the backstage, the captain could not quite understand the "ohs" and "ahs" of the audience applauding the spectacle from the front. He knew, however, that they applauded and that the corpse along with the killer stirred a remarkable exuberance in them. And that the tedious business of the hunt, the arrest, the trial and conviction, was full of glamour for those who watched.

Captain Malloy had more theories about these watchers than he had about crime. For his cunning told him that in this fascination exercised by the guilty on the innocent, by the cruel on the kindly, by the mad on the sane, lay a trail deeper than the tell-tale Devil's spoor. Hidden away even in these placid faces that offered no criminal signature of lips, eyes, or ears, was a kinship for crime which to the captain seemed almost like crime itself. It seemed to him that crime was a seed in the whole of humanity, and though it came to flower in only the two percent, as figured out by the statisticians, it lay dormant everywhere. It needed but a little extra stir of grief or hunger, or often merely some accidental shifting of the glands, to set it flourishing.

And being on the way to interview a man of God, Captain Malloy wondered if it was this seed of crime lying at the bottom of all souls that was indicated by the phrase, Original Sin. The priests said Adam's deed had put it there, and his medical friends maintained that all sorts of wolves, apes, and other monsters from whom man was descended had left it there. But however it had arrived, out of Hell or from our tree-top sires, Captain Malloy knew better than most philosophers how firmly and universally this seed was present.

In Captain Malloy's pocket as he marched there lay a curious antique crucifix, which had been found clutched in the left hand of a man named Joseph Franks, who had been murdered in Central Park the night before. Joseph Frank's belly had been ripped open, and by this the police knew that Franks was the fourth victim of the sadist killer who had signed three previous deeds with a similar sign manual. But this time a clue had remained. The dead man's fingers had been pried from around a crucifix of strange workmanship that they had evidently snatched from the neck of the murderer. The fastening loop at the top of the crucifix was broken.

The first authorities Captain Malloy had consulted had said the red half-circle beneath the Saviour's feet was a partly obliterated D and obviously stood for Dominic.

Captain Malloy looked nervously out of the train window and, being a good Catholic, tried with difficulty to forget that monks wore around their necks crucifixes such as the one in his pocket and that they dangled away from their robes when they leaned over.

The gardens of the Dominican monastery on the edge of the City of New York were extremely beautiful. They occupied two acres and were enclosed by high weather-stained and vine-covered walls of stone. Within these walls grass-overgrown slate tiles made a rambling walk through clumps of pine, oak, linden, butternut, and mulberry trees. The walk disappeared into shrubberies of syringa, lilac, and magnolia and trellised towering wistarias. It emerged to circle carved oak benches and lily-covered pools of water. At one end of the garden, under a little forest of heavily-leafed maples, a young colony of ferns raised darkly-glowing serpentine heads. The ground sloped to various levels and the walk became steps by which one climbed into unexpected rock gardens half covered with vari-colored mosses and a-twinkle with diminutive blooms. Against one of the stone walls ran a series of grape arbors made of undressed cedar boughs and under their canopies the cloistered ground was covered with the flashing foliage of periwinkle, arbutus, and other creepers.

Along the walk where neither tree nor shrub cast shadows, grew the flowers. These borders were clustered also with peony and rose bushes. Verbena, lilies, phlox, cornflowers, petunias, delphiniums and scores of other early summer celebrants ran beside the walk and circled the bushes in flurries of color.

All of the garden, including even these cultivated blooms, seemed half a wilderness as if it had come tumbling capriciously out of the earth and scattered itself exuberantly over walls and hillocks. It was only when one noticed on second look the rolling areas of clipped grass, the bowered shrines and little fountains, the lilied pools and always navigable lanes curling through trunks and foliage, that one knew this was a garden carefully tended.

In further proof of this labor one saw, too, the black-robed Fathers whose duties kept them hovering like huge beetles under the shrubberies and crawling among the plants with trowels, baskets, and pails of bone meal. There were always three or four of these figures stirring in the leafy corners. And on the carved benches others were to be seen doubled like dark question marks over yellowed books, or sitting straight and contemplating the tree-leafed spaces above the garden walls.

Of these black-robed figures the most industrious was usually that of a shriveled little ancient with a weatherbeaten bald head and the face of a moldy faun. This was Father Dominic, who for sixty years had lived in this garden as attentively as any of its squirrels, aphids, or coleoptera. The Order was proud of Father Dominic as its botanist and had published some nine volumes compiled by the little Friar during the months of winter when he sat evoking garden memories in his bleak cell.

These books were among the most curious in botanical literature, being full of quaint admixtures of science and religious meditation so interwoven that it was difficult to distinguish data from piety. Indeed, some of Father Dominic's more cautious readers considered his literary work full of heresies and the product of a mind nearly divorced from the God worshiped in the monastery chapel. But even these critics,

troubled by the pagan pages printed by their Order, hesitated to condemn them. For there was in Father Dominic's nine books the distilla-
tion of a soul so gentle, so humble in its knowledge, and so full of some
mysterious love, that none who read could restrain a smile evoked by
his musing. And Father Dominic's superiors, in discussing the whimsical and somewhat disorderly meditations that fluttered like pagan bees
and butterflies among the data of his pages, remembered proudly that
the most learned of scientists, including the celebrated Hindu, Chandra
Bose, had written enthusiastically of their weatherbeaten little Friar and
found in his work secrets beyond their own talented but worldly
intellects.

Nearing eighty, Father Dominic remained to the oldest of his colleagues as unchanging as the vegetation he haunted from dawn to
sunset. Sun, wind, and earth had long ago claimed his face as their
handiwork. His eyes had come to peck like birds at what they saw;
his lips were baked into a smile as unwavering as the curl of a leaf
almost dead; his long fingers had grown hardened into a chitinous
surface resembling that of the bugs they were forever pursuing. Yet
with all his digging and floundering around in a half-century of rain,
wind, and blasting sun like any farmer, Father Dominic's senses had
remained as acute as those of a recluse. The fragile instruments by
which he measured the reaction of flowers to the passage of a cloud
across the moon, or the puzzling movements of the Oscillatoria plants,
or the quantity of oxygen exhaled by a cornflower in its modest efforts
to keep the world alive, or the beat of the soft and watery engines of
life that caused the garden to bloom, smell, quiver, and die—these required the delicacy of a surgeon's touch. There was no tremble in the
little Friar's ancient fingers. Daily he moved with his chemicals and
minute electrical devices through the enchanted factory of the garden,
catching the hidden whispers of its toil, studying the digestive apparatus of trees and shrubs, and the half-animal heart throbbing beneath
the static face of vegetation.

Not only his eyes and fingers toiled, but his nose also was as busy
as a grasshopper among the thousand scents of earth and foliage. To
Father Dominic these scents were the gage of death rather than
pleasure, and by them he measured, as by the sighs of an invalid, the
speed of the rose's decomposition and the lily's farewell.

Long ago he had written: "The odors of flowers are the sweet
signals of their mortality. They are the sweat on Nature's brow given
off in a cloud of fair smells as each of her green children toils and sinks

exhausted into her lap. The decomposition we dread so in life is the glory of the plants. And by some subtle pact with God those that die the swiftest smell the sweetest."

On this bright morning that found Captain Malloy en route to the Dominican monastery, Father Dominic was awaiting another visitor also. This was his old friend, Rabbi Eleazer, with whom he had been discussing God for more than half a century. Father Dominic's friendship for the Jew Eleazer had, like his writings, been aired now and again in the Councils of the Order. It had been given out then, by those who thought the friendship needed defending—this was long ago, when the Friar was still young—that his interest in the pale and dark-eyed Jewish youth was a call to proselyte among the most ancient and stiff-necked of unbelievers. And when it had become evident, with the passing of the years, that it was to this same Jew, now a Rabbi, that Father Dominic gave the full gift of his greatest friendship (his only friendship), these same defenders had excused the irregularity by the fiction that the conversion was proving difficult. They had even cited precedents on record when the saving of a single Jew had taken as long as twenty years, for this was a race whose history showed that it was easier to send a thousand of them to the Devil than to persuade a single one to go to Heaven. But once saved, they said, there was none like the Jew for expiating the error of his former life. Scores of Torquemada's ablest lieutenants had been lured from the stiff clutch of Israel. There was also the fact that Christianity had been created by a Jew raised up by God, even as their very Order had been launched by the son of a Jew.

Such were the considerations that marked the talk at the beginning of the friendship, for those were more pious days fifty, and even thirty, years ago, than today.

The continued visits of Eleazer to the monastery's gardens and library came finally to be accepted without remark, or even passing thought. Now, even the most holy of the Fathers had come to smile on the tall, pale Jew with his deep-set eyes and long Arab nose, and to pilot him gladly to where his friend Dominic awaited his coming, as he did this morning.

Sitting on a bench beside a pool of waterlilies, Father Dominic had the fancy that, on such a lovely day as this one provided by God, a man felt more like a plant than a human being. On a day like this, if one sat still, one was able to drink of the golden breast of the sun like any suckling cornflower in the garden. One knew, too, how the petunia balanced the whole of summer on its eager and expiring petal. And when one looked up, as Father Dominic did, one beheld the tree leaves motionless, like hands arrested in benediction.

Waiting for his friend Eleazer to come, the Father experimented with a notion he had often longed, but never dared, to incorporate in his works. The weatherbeaten old man pretended he was a plant, exhaling oxygen rather than carbon dioxide and full of that mysterious tingle of kinship he had noted and measured among the various blooms in the garden. The old man knew there was danger in this game, for at a certain point of it certain ideas came into his head for whose presence he always fasted the rest of the day by way of penance. Nevertheless, with the small sigh that innocence utters on expiring, Father Dominic gave himself over to the pleasant but guilty business of being a plant this summer hour—a hardy little shrub abloom on an oak bench. His soul communed with other shrubs and he felt the faint roar of the earth at his roots. God stepped out of the tortuous theologies and became a wind that brushed his cheek, a warmth that lay like a mother's kiss on his heart. No mystery remained to haunt the old man's head. All was serene and beautifully related. Life and Death were brothers in the garden exchanging their secrets gently with each other, and in the flushed face of the petunia, Father Dominic the shrub beheld his sister.

For timeless minutes the figure on the oak bench sat thus absorbed by Nature, so that the very bugs and gnats and toiling snails whose existence came brightly into his senses flooded him with delight. The cloudless sky descended to his eyes and entered his veins, and his nose became a door through which trooped all the mysteries of the ketones and esters, the acids and aldehydes of color and odor. When for some time he had tasted, like a plant, the perfect food of God, Father Dominic's mind awoke in the midst of this sweet dream and spoke to him like a very serpent in the garden.

"It is thus," thought the Friar, who seemed to have fallen asleep among his pleasures, "it is thus men once worshiped Nature, especially the ancient Germans who believed themselves to be descended from the trees . . . particularly those of the Black Forest in their southland. Yes . . . they used to bind and tie themselves when they came to pray in the wood so as to resemble their ancestors a little more closely. And if they toppled over while praying, they rolled out of the forest like logs and it sometimes took them weeks to get to the edge of the sacred wood. . . . There is no doubt that many of them died pretending too long they were logs in transit.

"It is easy to understand that there were people once who thought themselves descended from plants," he mused. "Much easier," he sighed, "than to figure out why nearly all the savages worshiped some animal as their ancestor. Well . . . well . . . there is really nothing in the world or above it that grows or moves or stands still, that is to be seen, heard, smelled, or even imagined, that has not been worshiped by somebody as his origin.

"I wonder wherein the totemism of the ancient races—which beheld in the bird, the cat, the bear, the ape, and the horse their original selves—where that differs from the modern theories of man's evolutionary descent? These ideas, since Darwin, say that Man is evolved out of those very animals which the most ignorant savages also identified as their earliest sires. . . . It would almost seem that the early people of the world, groping about in their memories of where they came from, and the scientists of today, groping among the skeletons and fossils for the secret of Man's beginnings, came to the same conclusions. Is it possible . . . that all of science today . . . is a faint, resuscitated echo of the knowledge that was once innately a part of Man?

"For instance . . . that myth shared by so many of the early races as to how life came to our planet. In Syria, Babylonia, far China—yes, and a hundred different places—the early peoples used to believe that a Giant had fallen from the skies, cast out by enemy Gods, and in falling was smashed to bits. And out of these bits emerged Man, Plants, and Animals. Even the Osiris of the Egyptians was a cousin of this Giant. Only . . . as I remember ⸱ . . instead of smashing to bits by himself, he was cut up into tiny segments.

"Now in what way does this myth differ from the theories of modern biology?" pursued Father Dominic. "The new and most accepted theories have it that organic matter fell to the earth from the sun. A part of the sun broke off, it has been figured out, and crashed through space. And in its long fall was ground to dust. And out of this dust, Life emerged and finally Man.

"Even in the Bible the language of the old myth continues; only there Man does not fall literally from the skies, but from the grace of God. Ah! But it is still to be noticed that he falls! The thought that Man had fallen physically from on high obviously lingered for ages in his mind. Then as he grew more intelligent, it was replaced by the thought that his fall had been a spiritual one. And now that he has become even more intelligent, he is back again to the original theory of a physical fall."

The little Friar came to himself and murmured a brief prayer.

"What does it matter . . ." he said, directing his thoughts sternly into the proper channels, "what does it matter how Life was created or where—since, wherever the deed was done, whether in the moon, sun, or in Eden's garden, it was God who created it, as is believed by all good Christians? We are His children. . . . Amen."

Opening his eyes, he smiled to see the flowers emerging as from a dream and beckoning him again to their vari-colored altars leaning tipsily above the earth. With a smile still lingering on his faun's face, he lifted his eyes and saw the tall, pale Eleazer approaching beneath the shadows of the arbor.

Rabbi Eleazer was a proud and difficult old man who gave the impression to those who knew him that he was a reluctant part of this world. Spare and pale in his old age, the body and face of Eleazer suggested some large-eyed bird that had been plucked of its plumage and robbed of flight. But doubtless one thought of birds only because it was obvious that his soul had soared so high. When one listened to this man one felt that his mind was a rickety ladder leaning against Heaven, and that while his soul soared, his thought climbed exhaustedly after it.

Unlike the screwed-up faun's eyes of the old Friar, the eyes of Eleazer were wide, placid, and unused, for they had never looked on anything that was to be seen. They were brown and full of a spaciousness left behind by dreams. His long whitened face seemed ironed out with study. Only in his full lips, whose redness had turned to russet at seventy-nine, was there any hint that he came of a tribe that had once written the Song of Songs.

Of Eleazer's outward activities as a Rabbi there was almost nothing to tell, except that his manner for fifty years had baffled the little flock of Jews whom he led in their patient pursuit of God. In his synagogue he had stood these years beneath the Torah and, with a zeal so perfect that it appeared almost like abstraction, had performed the offices prescribed by the ancient law. It is true that his flock had dwindled, and his synagogue, once elegant, had become a shabby place. And probably it was only because the Portuguese Jews who had founded this congregation are among the most unchanging of all Israel's tropisms that the doors of his synagogue had remained in use at all.

And yes, helpless though he was in many ways, Eleazer was more to his congregation than a Rabbi who presided over them with a piety amounting to indifference. He was the last of the one hundred and ten Rabbis of his name (D'Amie), who formed an unbroken line into the dark ages of Portugal, and beyond these dim centuries to dimmer ones still, when Israel had walked clothed in royal Visigoth trappings and lighted its holy candles in Iberian castles. Because Eleazer was a candle out of this Past with which a handful of Portuguese Jews still stiffened their dreams, they came to worship at its cool and hidden light. They heard the correctly enunciated Hebrew, and listened to the echo of the dreamer's hidden visions, his body's sing-song, and were content. If their hearts remained cold, that snobbery so pathetic in the Jew clinging to an ancient moment or two of manhood was enriched.

And, as time went on, they were rewarded in another way. Like a hero whose story emerges only in a long time of telling, Rabbi Eleazer came alive for them. The awkward old man, with the tired white face that had presided over their hours of death and woe or holiday peace with a courtesy that did not light up, that was not of this world, kindled a new feeling in their hearts. A new feeling vied with their foolish pride, and the awe they had felt even in his belittlement of them. They loved the old man. But this was after many, many years, when he was old, and only a handful of the former congregation remained at his feet.

Also, they understood him. Dreamer, stranger, and visionary, he was of the great line of Misnagdim who had hung their harps on the willow tree in the time of the Diaspora, and rejoiced no more. By nature he was one of those unyielding Rabbis in Jewish history, powerful in law and excommunications, who had not mingled with their people, but had kept them in their place while they communed elsewhere with God. By profession he was a mystic.

This was a study so painstaking that it could not be grasped in the presence of others. And now that his followers understood him, they knew also that his meditation and reading had taken him far beyond where they could hope to be present.

Others had been present, it is true. It was recalled that, during his years, scholars had come and gone from his house, men pale and vacant-eyed as himself. Sometimes these guests had lingered for several years and then vanished never to be caught glimpse of again, walking almost surreptitiously in and out of the brick house adjoining the synagogue.

Rabbi Eleazer's flock accepted his judgment. He had not considered them worthy of his inner light. He had been too proud to reveal it to eyes that had lost their talent for seeing God. And if he had left them cheerful worldlings, it was with their worldliness they cared now for the old man, worried about him, and took care of him in numerous ways he did not guess, while he trod, without turning, his stiff-necked path to God.

As he grew older, his faults, as faults do, increased. Serene and fanatical, he went his way as to some appointment. And yet something strange had happened in his temple. As time had gone on, he had not grown more strong to lead his people, but they, through their love, had grown stronger to follow. Perhaps he knew this. Or, perhaps, the fabric of his character wore thin with age, and he allowed them glimpses of the holy life inside him. Wonderful words sometimes fell from his lips in the pulpit, and, with tightened hearts, his people listened.

"It is not given to one man to light the soul of another by words. . . . Words that are a light for one are a darkness for another. This is true even of the words in the sacred books. I have not helped you to find God but I have been content to see that you remembered Him a little."

So he had preached on the Sabbath eve before this story opens, for that day was the Sabbath.

"Tonight in saying good-by to you I would wish to speak to you as Souls. . . ."

Over this there were some in the audience who puzzled.

"Tonight in saying good-by . . .?" they asked themselves, but many things their Rabbi said did not mean what he said, and when he said: "I shall preach no more here," they also overlooked it. A wonderful man was their Rabbi, with ways not to be known.

". . . to speak to you as Souls. But this is difficult. For it is without words that the soul must mount, and the wings of the soul lie deeper than the mind.

"I would remind you . . . of Silence . . . the Silence that has long ago passed from your hearts. I shall speak to the Temple of Silence within which the Spirit dwells.

"There is a Road that leads away from the world to God. Only turn your face toward it and shut your eyes. Shut your eyes. Look for Him under the stones of your heart. And the Road will move under your feet.

"If you would rise to His Glory, remember that you must descend first into the caverns. Return to the Silence where the world is but an evil and dimly remembered shadow, and Heaven is a light forever growing. There, my Jews, is your homeland. There, in that little heritage of ecstasy, is your Temple that no enemy can overthrow.

"Beyond the language of religion, beyond purification . . . beyond goodness . . . beyond piety . . . beyond good deeds . . . beyond all that we call ourselves . . . there is a hidden and lonely island in the soul. This is the white sand where no feet have walked. Tonight as you go home . . . begin to look. . . . Look for this sand that is dry and shining."

This, of course, they did not do, but late that night some of them awoke, here and there, and thought of their Rabbi, as they were used to doing, and, turning on their pillows, remembered the birdlike look of the old man's face and felt a concern that was like an agony gripping their hearts. They worried about his health, and if he slept well, and there were some who were still young who, sighing, would have liked to protect him with their lives.

"I am glad it's such a lovely day," Father Dominic said with a smile so golden that it showed all at once the secret of his tranquil existence. "Sit down, Eleazer. They've put the table over there. Later on, we'll have some wine and seltzer and cooked cherries and cakes. I myself am not hungry."

The Friar had a soft, almost boyish voice, and a way of speaking so unstilted that one would have known him immediately, no matter what his clothes were, for a simple man, a workman maybe, save that there was no taint of coarseness or ignorance in his talk.

"Still full of penances?" the Rabbi smiled.

Eleazer was a different being in the Friar's presence. Long ago, in his willful way, he had given his awkward and unsmiling heart to this friend and no other. Caprice and ease and many other charming ways marked his manner toward his friend.

"The smaller our sins the more aware of them we are," he quoted.

"I understand," said Dominic. It was his manner to illumine the slightest of his utterances with the rare and inexpressibly glowing smile of the happy man. "I understand, and am rebuked, Eleazer. We do penance for little sins as a boast that we have no big ones." He laughed softly. "I see now that it will be better if I eat."

"Whether you eat or not, Dominic," Eleazer said, "God knows you are a good man."

"Yes. He knows. I guess I'm old enough for Him to have made up His mind by this time."

Yet he spoke of his age lightly, as if it were a jest. For in each other's presence, the two friends felt their hearts grow younger, as if a bridge had been provided them to the Past.

Perhaps this bridge was no more magic a thing than the garden—the enchanted piece of land that blossomed and clamored with scents and frolicked like something living at their feet.

The Rabbi acknowledged it gravely, as if it were a third and beloved presence at their meeting.

"The garden grows more beautiful every year," he observed.

"Yes . . . God has been amazingly good to me," Dominic agreed, in his soft voice, and he added presently:

"It seems a shame to think how we worried, and doubted life . . . at least I did. Do you remember, I used to say to you: 'Some day we'll grow older, Eleazer, and we'll find out how grim and terrible life is'?"

"We have not found out," Eleazer said peacefully, and yet there was something in his tone that made the Friar look at him frowningly.

"Have you found out, my friend?" he asked.

"No," Eleazer said firmly. To himself he thought: "He has always been too innocent to know that I am a Jew."

The glow returned to the small face of the Friar, and he drifted back into the quietness that had been the study and the rare achievement of his life. It was good to sit here with his old friend Eleazer. Good thus . . . and presently, he knew, they would speak of God. This was the jewel and wonder of their friendship, for while it had been given to him, Dominic, to be completely happy in the presence and the creation of beauty, the Way—the very fountain at the threshold of things—he had not known. Nature had spoken to him, but God's voice he had never heard.

It had been different with Eleazer. And Father Dominic had grown content with this knowledge . . . for as long as one man is left to see the way to God, the road remains open.

Many were the wiles he had of luring his friend into these Discourses, sometimes calling himself a pagan, who did not know, invoking his friend's pity with his regrets for the hidden Source, speaking his heart in innocent praise of his friend's wisdom, and sometimes asking questions frankly like a youth, but always returning to the dear Subject.

"It's been good to know your eyes were fastened on Him, while I was in the garden chasing bugs, and it's made me almost as happy as if it were my own eyes that beheld Him," he had often said to Eleazer, in many ways.

(It was this impious turn of phrase, as well as thoughts like these, that was a concern to his brother priests.)

Or: "Without you, I would have been an utter pagan. Yes . . . You have always been able to present God to me, Eleazer. I recall three hours once long ago when you spoke to me of God in such a way that even a flower would have understood you. Oho, if the truth were told, I'm nothing better than a gardener."

Today he had spoken in this vein, while his friend soothed him, saying it was a mistake to regret one's life, and that to have given up his garden to cultivate his Soul, as Dominic often threatened to do, would have been a pity, since the one bloomed in the other. And to prove to Dominic that it was not good to seek too much, he told him this legend:

There was a Rabbi (he said) who came to the holy man Baalshem to learn from him the secret by which he understood the speech of the animals. This novice had burned to know the secret for a long time. Accordingly they went together into the forest, and the holy man Baalshem began teaching him the secret. And as the eager disciple began to master it, he heard, suddenly, all around him, the squirrels chattering to one another of places to hunt for nuts, and birds telling each other where certain little warm winds were blowing, and where the worms and snails lay hidden. He heard also the love plaints of all manner of little animals and the cries of devotion that even the tiniest and ugliest children of the forest have for one another. As the apprentice heard these things, he continued to ask the holy one further questions. . . .

He wished to know now how it was that Baalshem could understand not only the speech of the animals, but of the angels. And finally he asked the saint the secret by which he evoked the forces of God.

And Baalshem smiled sadly at his disciple and said: "Look, poor man, a while ago you heard the voices of Nature speaking, and your long dream was realized. And now, in your eagerness to learn more secrets, you are not even aware that you are no longer listening to the tongues of the forest. Of what use is it for you to learn anything when you do not love God enough to pay attention to what He reveals to you, but must always demand more gifts?" And the poor apprentice, turning his ear again to the forest to listen to the speech of the animals, heard nothing but the usual chirruping and the sound of the wind in the leaves.

So Eleazer spoke, and Dominic listened in tranquillity, as if he had nothing to do but to listen, to enjoy, to live. Sometimes the turn of a phrase lit up his face, for he loved talent, and Eleazer he admired above all men. And when his friend was done with the tale, he thought about it for a long space of time, saying gently at last:

"It was not the secrets of God that this unfortunate man loved, but his own ambition, it's clear. And when he failed in the test you speak of, Eleazer, he probably lost, not only the secret of understanding the voices in the forest, but his original desire to hear them. So that when he went away from the holy Baalshem, he was much poorer than when he came."

And he added, smiling shyly: "Thank you, Eleazer, for telling me this story. I'm going to use it in my writings, as you know." And with a twinkle in his eye toward the Friars who bent over the garden beds near by, he joked:

"Wouldn't some of *them* be surprised if they knew where a lot of my pious notions came from? Whenever my brothers feel a little doubt about my Christianity, they reassure themselves by reading the tales I have pillaged from Rabbi Eleazer."

But he spoke absently and looked before him without seeing plain the year's pristine burst of bloom. A heaviness plucked at his thoughts, and he divined that it had to do with Eleazer.

"You have dreamed something," he said presently. "Tell me what it was you dreamed."

"Yes, I had a dream," Eleazer said.

"I feel it is there in your mind—a bad dream."

"Would you say there are any bad flowers, Dominic?"

"There are one or two I don't like—the mesembryanthemum chiefly. And then of course there are the weeds."

"This was a weed," Eleazer said, sighing.

Dominic did not press him.

The old men had risen and were walking slowly through the garden. Even Dominic's stride was calm. He drifted under the garden trees, remembering how often Eleazer and he had walked in these same places.

"Eleazer and I . . ." his thoughts said—and there they paused, for friendship can think no sweeter than this phrase.

Still a sadness tugged at his heart strings, hurting.

"To live, to grow old and die in one place, to know one's roots for one's home, to wander only in one's dreams . . . why weren't these things given to my good friend, Eleazer?" he thought sadly, for he was not so innocent as Eleazer believed.

And then, as they approached the grove of maples where the table of hospitality had been set out, his eyes wandered to the ferns coiled out of the sunless earth, and his mind to its science, as was its habit. The sight and smell of ferns reminded him of a world far away in a Time unrecorded by Man . . . before trees and flowers had appeared on the earth. In that Time, owing to the content of carbon in the air, only these ferns had lived—tall ferns, three and four hundred feet high, covering the earth and massed in horrendous forests full of fabulous-looking insects larger than eagles and dogs. And of this tumultuous vegetation that had once filled the skies with its ferny-toothed towers, only these delicate scrawls of green that thrived in the half-dark remained. Nature, thought Father Dominic, has its memories just as Man. . . . The Past with silent feet walks everywhere.

The table, covered with a bright blue cloth and gay with jars of preserves, with wine bottles and earthenware dishes, recalled Dominic to hospitality, and to his friend.

Over the table, they resumed their talk. But we will not follow them. It is better to close the door on an old friendship than to listen too closely to its labyrinthian pattern, its past and present, and all its deep-springed silences. Besides, when it came to their Discourse on God— that Discourse so elliptical and high-pitched, and at the same time so pellucid and clear-souled—it is no use pretending that our ordinary ears are attuned to its overtones or that our souls are similarly attuned. Neither could words convey it, for these two were nearer the Truth than are mere words. And if the simple shining soul of Dominic is beyond our comprehension, how much more so the soul of Eleazer? For the little light of the Jew is no lamp, or candle even, but a light that flickers from hand to hand now, blown by many winds and bearing always a little nimbus. . . .

They spoke, the lover of life and he who was only a friend of life. Many anecdotes they exchanged, whose meanings are lost to us in their knowledge. And they ate, out of hospitality and a deference to hospitality, of the things set before them. They spoke of things as old as their friendship, and older, of things as old as the stones, and older, for the Light in them was older than the stones—until they came back, by the high hills and footpaths of their friendship . . . to the dream.

"Tell me how it was I knew you dreamed," asked Dominic. "Was it because you dreamed of me?"

"Yes," said his friend. "We were walking together in a field of corn —you and I. And the corn took fire. All my clothes were destroyed, and I lay uncovered, hugging the cool earth."

"And what became of me?" Dominic asked.

"You wept," Eleazer said.

Dominic pondered uneasily what the dream meant.

"Do you know?" he asked.

"I am to know soon," Eleazer replied, and smiled at his friend, whose face had grown as unhappy as a child's. And seeking to divert his mind, he spoke of other things.

"The ferns," he said, "cast a curious light on the air, as if they had once devoured the night."

Father Dominic wondered whether his friend spoke of the carboniferous era or of inner things. He decided that to a man of such spirit, knowledge and divination were identical. And this same must be true of dreams. He sighed heavily.

Two figures appeared beside the table.

"This is Captain Malloy of the Police Department," Father Francis said. "He said you had agreed to see him."

"Yes, yes, yes . . . yes . . ." Father Dominic spoke with annoyance.

Seating himself ponderously, Captain Malloy catalogued in his mind: "Old folks."

Relaxing his legs after the long walk from the station, the captain felt himself as unloved and undesired as if he had intruded on a nest of criminals. He wondered about the Father's other visitor, obviously a Rabbi. And he understood that the Father's refusal to introduce him to this visitor was a statement that his visit would be too brief for any social amenities.

It was Captain Malloy's habit, when confronted with such inhospitality, which was no infrequent matter in his life, to sit rigidly waiting until his presence had generated a sort of psychic guilt in the nerves of any reluctant host. But this time, he realized grimly, the shoe was likely to be on the other foot. It wasn't likely that the Catholic Friar would be much impressed by him. And on the other side, he felt the Rabbi's face—the distant, uncompromising, historic, and saintly face of the Jew—turned toward him, and doubtless appraising him for what he was.

An uncharacteristic shyness fell on the detective. The delicacy of his mission also confused him, for the questions he had come to ask might give the Father the wrong impression of what was in his mind, as if he were surely hunting for a monk as the murderer. It might also be that Father Dominic, being such an old man, would even conclude that he himself was under suspicion. All these considerations that lay in Captain Malloy's head unnerved him the more with his being aware that a part of his brain, beyond the control of piety or decent logic, was sniffing away at Friar and Saint with no consideration at all.

Looking up a little more reddish-faced than when he had arrived, the captain saw with some surprise that the ancient Friar was smiling at him, and that the other man also was smiling. He felt himself suddenly loved and admired as if he and not they were full of childishness. He smiled back, and Father Dominic said:

"This is my friend, Rabbi Eleazer."

"Glad to know you," said the detective.

But though he acknowledged the salutation, the Rabbi contented himself with withdrawing into a silence and behaving abruptly as if he were not present.

Father Dominic poured a glass of wine.

"You've had a long walk, Captain," he said, and handed him the glass.

The detective drank obediently, though he had a strong distaste for sweet wines.

"Well," he said as he wiped his lips, "I'll try not to take up too much time, Father. I realize a monastery garden is no place for a detective."

"You said something on the telephone about a crucifix," said Father Dominic, with a directness that startled the detective, coming from such an old man.

"Yes," said the captain, much relieved that the object in his coat pocket had finally entered the talk. "I've brought it with me. I was told you were an authority on crucifixes, Father. That's why I decided to bother you."

He produced an envelope from his coat pocket and removed from it a crucifix some four inches in length, with the figure of the Saviour sculptured on it. A small red half-circle of some inlay was at the figure's feet. Over its head, above the crown of thorns, was inlaid another crown, a wreath of tiny flowers whose colors were almost imperceptible.

Father Dominic leaned over and looked at the crucifix. An expression of surprise darted into his old face. He grasped the object and began to study it intently, turning it over, and sampling its texture with fingers that apparently began to tremble. Then he removed a small microscope from his pocket and fell to studying it through the glass, making the while strange, strangled, and incredulous sounds.

Finally, laying down the glass, he half spoke, half sobbed:

"There can be no doubt about it!"

"You *recognize* it?" Captain Malloy gasped in his turn, for he had not expected his hunch to work so perfectly.

"I know it!" the Friar cried exultantly.

"As belonging to someone in particular?" Captain Malloy asked with a tripping heart.

"It belonged to the Saint who founded the Order of which you are the guest today," the old man said with a shining face. "It was worn by him himself. It is described particularly and beyond doubt in certain papers. This crucifix never left the holy man's neck from the day it was made, and on the day he died"—here the Friar paused breathlessly —"it accompanied him to Heaven."

It was an anticlimax that hurt the captain almost physically. A crucifix that went to Heaven! No doubt it had tumbled from there, too, into the murder victim's hand.

And for all that he was a churchgoer, the decided way in which the fact had been mentioned angered the detective. And he was further annoyed by the fact that the Rabbi did not seem to doubt the cock and bull story, but listened evenly in his recess. It took the captain a full minute or two to recover from his anger. He had been prepared for the vagaries of age, and even for some of the exaggerations of religion when he had sat down with these old men, but not for this.

"That crucifix," he finally said, in his heaviest police-department manner, "was found in the hand of a man who was murdered last night. Perhaps you read about it, Father. The murdered man's name was Joseph Franks."

Father Dominic's face grew shrunken.

"No, I read nothing about it," he said.

"I heard of it last night," said Eleazer. "His wife spoke to me on the telephone."

"Was Franks a member of your congregation?" Captain Malloy inquired routinely.

"No . . ." said the Rabbi, in his faraway voice. "Perhaps I knew him, though. She said I married them."

"This crucifix," Malloy said sternly to the two woolgathering old men, "was snatched by the victim from the neck of the man who murdered him. You can see the fastening loop was broken."

"Yes . . . I see," said Father Dominic.

"The victim," Captain Malloy continued, "was the fourth man to be murdered by this same unknown hand."

"How do they know this?" Dominic asked.

"Because they were all four murdered in the same way," the detective explained considerately.

"Each of the four Jews was found with his belly ripped open," the Rabbi's voice said from the shadows.

The little Friar closed his eyes and grew pale.

"I know little of what goes on in the world," he said faintly.

"There is little to know that is new," the Rabbi's voice spoke sadly.

"Now," resumed Captain Malloy, turning to the Friar, "if you will tell me something else about this piece of evidence, something other than that miracle you mentioned, it might be of help to us in finding the murderer."

Father Dominic spoke didactically.

"It was one of eighteen crucifixes made for the Founder of the Order by Father Antonio, a sculptor who was among the first of the holy St. Dominic's followers. Seventeen of the crucifixes were given by the holy Founder to seventeen missionaries, sent by him, as is well known, to all ends of the earth. This was in 1237. The eighteenth crucifix was the one you hold so irreverently in your hand, my son. Its workmanship was different in certain details. Father Antonio, the maker, left behind a manuscript at his death giving minute descriptions of it. I will show you the manuscript."

"Later, if you don't mind, Father," the captain said. "But now perhaps you would care to tell me what church or museum might have had possession of it. That would help us track down—"

"None!" Father Dominic interrupted testily. "It went to Heaven, as I told you."

"And stayed there for seven hundred years?" The detective almost wept. "In Heaven's name, Father."

"Its seven-hundredth birthday fell on the day the first Jew was murdered," said Rabbi Eleazer's voice placidly.

Captain Malloy mopped his brow.

"Perhaps my friend knows something more that he can tell you," Dominic said, with an air of finality. "My friend is a very godly man."

Though ignoring the suggestion, Captain Malloy couldn't help reacting to the murmur of the Rabbi's voice in the background.

"I am to know. I am to know," it sighed.

"Old people . . . they talk to themselves," the captain said mentally. He decided there was nothing more to be gathered from this visit.

"Thank you," he said, and was reaching for his black derby on the ground, when another voice spoke in the little maple grove.

"Excuse me, please," said the voice, in a Teutonic accent, "I haf brought the slippers, Father Dominic. Excuse me, please, I wanted to gif them to you myself."

Captain Malloy straightened and saw a slightly stooped man of fifty with a plumpish face and the look of a strayed and eager little dog in his eyes. He was standing as if in the midst of a bow and suffused with reverence and embarrassment. He held a small bundle under one arm.

Father Dominic was smiling at the newcomer.

"In a minute, please," he said kindly and turned to the detective.

Captain Malloy bowed his head, and the old priest murmured: "Bless you, my son."

Then raising his head Captain Malloy looked quickly at the obsequious and fuzzy face of the man who was standing with the slippers under his arm. The captain stood staring for several moments and then walked away.

Dominic watched the detective walk away and then looked blankly at the man with the bundle.

"Oh," he said, as if he had forgotten his presence, "I am glad you brought them. Very glad. Sit down, my son. Sit down there on the bench."

"Thank you, Father," the man said gratefully and sat down. He began unwrapping the bundle.

"They are for you, Eleazer," Dominic said. But he was not thinking of the slippers. He was thinking in his depths of the last words his friend had spoken. Eleazer was not one to speak prophecies lightly, and he did not dismiss them lightly.

"The slippers . . ." Eleazer prompted him.

"Yes . . ." Dominic went on. "I measured your footprint in the petunia bed last month. And I had them made. They are the same kind you admired once, when you saw me wearing them. Pfefferkorn is an artist in making slippers."

The man Pfefferkorn beamed and inclined his head humbly. Rabbi Eleazer turned his eyes to the pair of colorful petit-point slippers that had come out of the bundle. He continued for several moments to look at the slippers and the workingman hands holding them. They were broken-nailed hands, soiled and heavy-knuckled from toil. Then the Rabbi raised his eyes to the shoemaker's face.

"They are beautifully made," he said, and continued to study the grateful and obsequious face of the workingman. "Have you been making slippers long, Pfefferkorn?" he asked, hesitating a half-instant before he spoke the name.

"Ever since I can remember," the shoemaker answered eagerly. "I am glad you like them."

Eleazer took them from his hands.

"Thank you for the gift," he said shyly to Dominic.

Dominic smiled to see his friend holding the slippers and examining them fondly.

"They have a curious pattern," Eleazer said. "Yours, as I remember, were a little different. These have another design woven into them.

See, there are little yellow triangles each with a smaller triangle in-side it."

"Yes," said the shoemaker happily, "it is an old design from Cologne. I haf woven it special for you, Rabbi Eleazer, special for you, please."

"It is very old indeed," Eleazer smiled. "This was the sign used by the Jews when they were forbidden to show the Star of David. They took the Star apart and laid it inside itself in the form of two triangles. And yellow," he added softly, "was the color prescribed for them by the German law as a symbol of their greed."

"Perhaps you don't like that on your slippers," Father Dominic said unhappily, and frowned on the shoemaker Pfefferkorn.

"I like it very much," said Eleazer quickly. "It was thoughtful of Pfefferkorn to embroider them so. That will give me added pleasure."

"Thank you," said the shoemaker with a sigh and stood up. "I haf worked all my life for the Fathers of St. Dominic. And I am happy always to work for them. Always to work for them."

He bobbed his head in a series of eager bows.

"Bless you, my son," the little Friar murmured.

Rabbi Eleazer held out his hand. The obsequious shoemaker looked at him with surprise in his twinkling, doglike eyes. Then he rubbed his own hand clean against his trousers and raised it slowly to the Rabbi. Eleazer's thin fingers closely firmly over the roughened palm and he stood for a moment, eyes intent and distant, holding fast to Pfefferkorn's hand. A faint color came into the Rabbi's pale cheeks and a glitter slowly lighted his look.

"Auf Wiedersehen," he said with a sigh and removed his grip.

The shoemaker bowed again and moved backward toward the walk. He continued to look with his eager grateful smile at the two old men and to make humble gestures so blind that he bumped into several trees. He murmured a little irrationally: "Excuse me. Excuse me," and continued his backward walk, saying finally: "I have some work to do up there. Excuse me, please. If anything iss wrong with the slippers, I will be there, please."

Dominic watched him move away and smiled at this skilled and able workingman who had so pleased his friend.

The two old men were again alone. They sat looking at the waning summer afternoon. Birds chirped over them. Beyond the dimly lit grove, the sky still flared white and blue and radiant with sun. But the emerging tints of the garden told that the day was ebbing. Flowers and shrubs released from the heavy hand of light were beginning to glow with their own colors. The voices of the birds were like the tender echoes of this peaceful day that lay cradled in the garden.

Father Dominic looked deep into the day with his observing eyes. He quieted the unrest in his thought by allowing the patterns of Nature to take possession of his spirit. The colors, smells, and wavering shapes of the garden, and the hidden bird throats throbbing everywhere around, overcame him with that timeless sense of life known only to the tranquil heart. His little bird eyes peering into the day felt its existence beyond himself, as if the hour in which he sat were in itself a bird note pouring from a throat overfull with song. He heard the beginning of this song far back among the fern towers and he heard its continuation in the ages and ages of summer days to come, summer days to fall endlessly out of the bursting throat of Life. And as the Past and the Future revealed themselves to him in the unchanging sigh of this summer hour, his senses tasted the wine of Immortality.

But now a change was coming subtly over the day. Wisps of gloom were heralding a summer shower.

"It's going to rain soon," Dominic murmured to his friend.

"Yes," Eleazer said. "It is getting dark."

"The rain won't touch us here," said Dominic, "and I think it won't last long either. You are in no hurry?"

"No," said Eleazer. "I am happy here."

A glow of green had come into the air, and a wind like a runner full of tidings moved over the plants and trees. The garden became bright with color as if it had turned on an inner light, and the shrubbery gleamed as if with lantern rays. A stir and a freshness were on the earth. In the deepening gloom, the garden, like a lover preparing herself with odors, arched her many bosoms for the embrace of the rain. It arrived first in the trees, pattering on the leaves. Thunder sounded and the rain rushed to the ground.

The two friends, with eager faces, watched the rain stripes in the garden and listened to the cool, wild scratch of the water on the trees above.

"It is good for the flowers," said Eleazer, and his friend smiled deeply, full of his secret knowledge of roots uncurling, soft pistons pumping, and a whole system of aqueducts distributing the rain to burned petals and parched tendrils.

"It is very good," he agreed, sniffing happily the new odors brought from the clouds.

Now the rush and surge of the rain seemed to fill the garden with a mock terror. Flowers bent and twisted about as if pretending they were being uprooted, and the shrubbery leaves danced under the beat of rain and wind as if in the throes of destruction. Beyond the standing river of rain, the sky, however, was already beginning to clear. Bright spaces gleamed eerily through the gloom of the downpour. Thunder sounded again, but more faintly. The scattered day was slowly returning. The scratch of the rain grew fainter and a halloo of light rolled over grass and shrubs. The shower had ended, leaving behind a laggard patter of water running down the leaves.

Father Dominic sighed with delight at the spectacle.

"The soul of man is a garden," he said softly, "made in the image of Nature and refreshed by tears and sighs as deeply as by the sun and fair weather. I wrote that when I was young and full of faith in metaphors."

Eleazer nodded and smiled.

"The storm is part of the calm," he said. "In the old days when God walked among men He carried His lightnings concealed in a little willow branch."

"When God walked among men . . ." repeated Dominic slowly, his eyes on the flowers.

"Yes," said Eleazer, "it was thus."

"Does He still walk somewhere with His willow branch?" Dominic asked gently.

"Yes," said Eleazer, "it is still thus."

The Rabbi rose and breathed deeply of the garden air.

At his side, Dominic thought only of how to speed him on his way happily. For when people are very old, they see in each parting the final one, and each bird song is like a parting cry.

Resolutely he put out of his mind the ghosts that had darkened the afternoon with their presence, and all the untoward shadows, and looked about him, calling on Nature for help. And just as the garden had ushered in the pleasures of their meeting, it took its part now in the farewell.

"The face of life is sweet," Dominic said, marching with loose strides at his friend's side, and calling attention with his beaming to every glowing zinnia face and every bright leaf on the way.

Eleazer understood him.

"It's hard to leave so beautiful a garden," he said.

"The twilight is marvelous," Dominic murmured joyfully.

Presently Eleazer looked up as if he had been called.

"I must go," he said, with a sudden wild note in his voice.

He leaned over and touched his cheek to his friend's face.

"Peace be with you, Dominic, and with all who are kind to you," he said tenderly. "I will wear your slippers tonight." Then, with a smile at the slippers under his arm, he walked away.

Father Dominic watched with deep love in his heart as the Rabbi moved over the wet grass, and climbed the steps of the walk into the garden beyond. Dominic remained where he was standing. Slowly the flowers clothed themselves in the veils of twilight. Bird songs rocked to and fro.

Suddenly the Friar seemed to awake to something ominous. The blood had started to beat in his temples, and he stood remembering the dream his friend had told him of, of walking in a corn field that had burst into flames and devoured him, while he himself was left weeping.

"Why did he dream that?" he cried aloud in anguish. "And why did that man come to me with the Cross of St. Dominic? And why" —he stood shivering in the dying day—"why were those miserable old symbols of Cologne on the slippers? . . . Devoured by burning corn. . . ." A name froze itself on his lips.

"Pfefferkorn. . . ."

"Oh, God in Heaven," moaned Dominic, as he began to run swiftly after his friend.

When he came to the road, his friend was nowhere to be seen.

When Rabbi Eleazer came out of the monastery gates he saw the slightly stooped figure of the shoemaker Pfefferkorn disappearing around a turn in the road some distance away. Eleazer walked after the figure.

The half-countryside beyond the monastery buildings stood intimately outlined in the twilight. Distant trees and cottages separated by swampy fields gazed out of the hollow eyes of the early nightfall. Eleazer came to the turn in the road. He saw the shoemaker again, walking now more swiftly, and Eleazer, whose muscles were weak, moved after him.

This region through which Eleazer followed Pfefferkorn was a fringe of gas stations, road houses, little truck farms, and an occasional stretch of pavement with squat, flat-roofed stores lining it. It was the far end of the city that sprawled like a scaffolding for tomorrow. In the twilight, however, it seemed old rather than new, as if it were the debris of a city long wiped away. The headlights of trucks and automobiles fled through it, leaving behind a constantly deepening silence and lifelessness.

Eleazer walked on, his slippers in a bundle under his arm. Pfefferkorn, moving quickly, so stooped that only his shoulders were visible, was still in front of him. Now the day had withdrawn, but the night had not yet come. The always unfamiliar hour that precedes the darkening of the skies occupied the flat lands. Denuded of sun and color, the trees and structures retained an ominous visibility, as if abandoned by both the day and the night and waiting within a shell for the touch of life.

Pfefferkorn had turned off the main road and Eleazer turned with him. The gloom deepened and the figure of the shoemaker dissolved and reappeared in the distance as the Rabbi followed. Through darkening fields now the Rabbi moved, through black clusters of trees looming in the shell of light, on and on in this nightless hour as if drawn swiftly over the earth by a force stronger than the muscles of his ancient legs. The wasteland smells came heavily into Eleazer's nose. The strangled watery bark of frogs and the sleigh-bell chatter of insects fell on his ears. But Eleazer was aware of none of these, nor of the swampy earth now sucking at his shoes, nor of the brambles tearing his clothes and hands. He moved on unaware of his pounding heart and the ache of exhaustion in his lungs. In his mind was a light, dim and skeleton-shadowed as the twilight around him. It was a light cast by the dissolving figure of the shoemaker in the distance. The soul of this figure, like an ominous guide, tugged at the old Rabbi's weary body and provided a secret luminescence for his way.

Suddenly the dark came and the land disappeared into the summer night. Shadows bloomed in the trees, and the road grew blind. Window lights, like distant little cores of life, lay in the wandering dark. The fleeing automobile lamps moved in faraway funnels of speed. The swampy night closed about Eleazer, muffling him with the sharp, sweet smells of decay, and encircling him with black shapes. The darkness swallowed the figure of Pfefferkorn. But there was no change in the old Rabbi's movement. On into the dark he continued, striding and plunging through bough-tangled lanes and over wet fields loud with the hissings and little trumpetings of hidden life. The dim glow of another soul swung like a lantern before his eyes and he moved panting and unseeing but knowing that the blackness before him held the running figure of Pfefferkorn.

Then abruptly Eleazer stopped. A loop of terror had halted him.

He stood trembling as if the dark around him had become another world and he had walked too far. A faint ugly odor of decay came out of the heavy tree shadows. Eleazer stood trembling in the midst of this ghostly stench and heard voices wailing far away. In the darkness the Rabbi felt himself surrounded by things rising out of the ground as if the grave of Time were opening. The night dreamed evilly around him. Eleazer closed his eyes. Then he raised his head and looked wildly at the top of the night. The deep black face of the heavens stared everywhere down on him. He stood looking up like one from the bottom of an abyss. He saw the distances increase and the night grow endless. When he had stood thus for several moments his trembling ceased. He lowered his eyes and saw he was in the midst of a thicket of fir trees. Their clawlike foliage gleamed in the starlight.

Suddenly beyond the thicket a little light winked and a window appeared, yellow and staring in the dark. Eleazer moved toward it. He saw the outlines of a dwelling hidden in a sag of shadows. The glitter of old stones uncovered a little its dimensions. It was a small and heavy house, squat to the earth. In one of its windows a candle had just been lit.

Eleazer walked slowly to the half-visible door. He stopped before it, and the things unseen that had come out of the earth to make him tremble crowded about him at this door. They struck at his old heart, and his hand reaching to push open this door halted as if seized. But Eleazer moved the terror away from him and placed his hand against the edge of the door and pushed. Slowly, with its hinges creaking, the heavy door opened. Eleazer from the threshold looked into a room. It was empty and moldy. From the window a candle spread a film of yellow light over its shadows. He saw a tall-backed chair in a corner beside a cupboard hung with a curtain. Near it was a broken couch. An uncovered wooden table stood against the further wall. On the table lay a half-dozen pairs of old shoes.

Eleazer entered the room. There were no other rooms beyond it. The night glistened in its windows. The Rabbi looked in the shadowed corners. He went to the cupboard and pulled aside its hanging. There was no occupant in the room. The candle that had been lighted a few moments ago burned lonesomely on the window sill. Eleazer walked to the candle and took it in his hand. It was still warm with the fingers of another.

Holding the candle before him, Eleazer moved about the room and found it littered with bits of leather and heavy with dust. The candle flame jumped above his hand and he stood still listening. Only the sounds of the night outside were to be heard. Birds, frogs, and insects spoke in the dark. He moved again and his foot felt an iron ring under it. By the candlelight he saw there was a door in the worn flooring. Unlike the rest of the flooring, the door was clean of dust. He lifted it up by the ring, and the wet rancid smells of a basement billowed up. The candle dimmed and flickered.

Peering down, Eleazer saw a flight of ladder steps that vanished in a pool of inky space. The steps were steep. With his back to the cellar darkness Eleazer slowly descended the ladder, holding his flickering candle close to his face. The descent took a long time, for the steps continued on and on into the dark. At length Eleazer stood on an earthern floor. A chill brushed his face and his fingers felt the moist grip of the cellar shadows.

He was in a tall cavernous room full of ugly smells. In the diminished light of his candle he could at first see nothing but its wavering yellow point before him. Currents of heavy air moved in the dark, threatening his little flame. His eyes discovered slowly that this high-ceilinged cellar was not empty. There were barrels in its shadows. His candle uncovered them and he stood watching the shadows that rose and fell around them. Then he moved toward them. He found no one. Along the wall he saw a workbench covered with odds and ends of the shoemaker's craft. He leaned over to examine what was on this bench, when the candle flame above his head leaped and stretched itself, assailed by new currents of air. For a moment it hovered between a last blue tip and extinction. Then it straightened and resumed its yellow wavering. The new currents of air had ceased.

Eleazer turned. At the other end of the darkness he saw another candle. It wavered a few feet above his own and he knew that someone was sitting on the steps and holding it. He stood still and waited. The light of this candle on the steps swelled in the stillness and he saw the face of the shoemaker Pfefferkorn. The face was watching him, its eyes glittering, its unshaven cheeks distended in a grimace. The swelling candle rays beside it fell on an ax that lay on the step.

"What are you looking for, Rabbi Eleazer?" the Teutonic voice whispered from behind the candle.

Eleazer was silent. He stood holding his candle steadily before him.

"Maybe you are looking for a cross," the shadowed face continued, "an old cross like you saw in the garden today, that the policeman brought. Is that what you are looking for, Rabbi?"

Eleazer could see the grimace increase. The grimace devoured the shoemaker's doglike and obsequious face. Peering out of an aperture of light it gleamed at Eleazer, purring and malignant. Its power filled the underground room, and the deep shadows around Eleazer became full of Pfefferkorn. From this whispering shoemaker on the steps moved a chill of terror as if the cellar had grown deeper and blacker. The darkness in which he sat with his ax at his side was like a cage sinking into the earth and bearing the Rabbi with it.

"How many such Crosses do you expect one poor shoemaker to own, Rabbi Eleazer?" Pfefferkorn's wet mouth whispered.

Eleazer did not answer, and the shoemaker sat motionless. In the silence the two candle flames wagged at each other, and the blade of the ax on the step glistened feebly. Then Pfefferkorn spoke again.

"Why did Rabbi Eleazer play detective and follow me to my house?"

"He was led," said Eleazer.

"Who led him?" asked the whisper.

"Pfefferkorn," said Eleazer.

The shoemaker chuckled. The cellar echoed around Eleazer. A chuckle came from behind the barrels and out of the dank black corners.

"I ran fast to lose him," said the figure on the steps. "I walked through swamps and woods, dark woods. I was surprised, I tell you, to see him find the way in the dark."

"Pfefferkorn held a light for my eyes," said the Rabbi.

"Liar," the whisper thickened.

"Not you," said Eleazer, "but another Pfefferkorn."

"Liar," the voice cried from behind the candle. "Jew liar."

"Who calls me that?" Eleazer asked quietly. "Not the Pfefferkorn whose soul I followed like a firefly through the swamps. Not that ancient unburied Pfefferkorn who hides today inside a little shoemaker. For he is a Jew, too. And being a Jew he knows I am no liar."

"Ah," the voice from the steps sighed, and the candle flame drew nearer the ax.

"Sit where you are," said Eleazer sternly, "for you have time, Pfefferkorn. Think of all the time you have, of the long centuries you have prowled and the longer ones to come. The deed will wait a little while."

The ax had vanished from the step and the candle moved down. Pfefferkorn's shadow leaped into the cellar and stood up wild and crooked on the wall.

Eleazer spoke as it moved.

"Why have you changed your mind," he asked, "and become afraid to hear me speak? Remember that you sent for me. You came into my dreams and pleaded that I come." Eleazer raised his voice as the shadow grew on the wall. "Why else did you embroider the yellow triangles in my slippers? So I would see them and come to you."

"Christ-killer," said Pfefferkorn thickly, "why should I want to hear your Jew voice?"

"You sent for me to save you," said Eleazer.

The shadow on the wall grew still. Pfefferkorn sat down slowly on the last step and the ax blade glistened at his side again.

"To save me!" The shoemaker's chuckle echoed from the barrels and dark corners.

"Yes," said Rabbi Eleazer. "To save you. For you are a gilgul. You are a soul, damned and wandering outside the windows of Life. A dead man lives inside you, shoemaker. And he is weary. He sent for me."

"What is this!" screamed the figure on the step. "What are you talking about! You telling me who I am! Rotten, stinking Jew! I am Pfefferkorn, the shoemaker. I work for the Fathers. You saw me in the garden."

The cellar remained full of sounds after the voice had finished. Eleazer watched the candle move from the steps to the wall and remain there as if its holder were crouching. A faint moon of light glowed on the wall. The blade of the ax dangled near the earthen floor like a glistening head struggling to raise itself.

When the echoes had ended, Eleazer resumed.

"You are Pfefferkorn," he said gravely, "who was born in Moravia five hundred years ago; Pfefferkorn who was a Jewish butcher boy in the ghetto of Moravia and whose parents were Jews and who was taught the meaning of God by the Rabbis of Frankfort. Five hundred years ago you were alive. But now you are only unburied. You are tired, and you have sent for me. Then, listen—poor, sad, accursed Jew from the synagogue of Moravia, who once stood with his people before God."

The shoemaker crouched against the wall, holding the candle before him, his other arm dangling. His eyes shone, and a grimace that exposed his teeth peered out of the little hole of candlelight. His wet open mouth growled as it breathed.

The Rabbi's voice now seemed to come from all the corners of the darkness.

"Listen—for it is the truth I speak. At night you have lain in your bed, shoemaker, listening to the voices that make covenants with the gilgul. You have lain, sweating and quaking, while the demon held court inside you, uttering cries that came not from your mouth. And you have heard a world long dead speak to him.

"I know these voices, Pfefferkorn. They are the voices of Jakob von Hochstraten, of Arnold of Tongern, of Gratius of Deventer—still moaning out of old graves for Jewish blood. It is they who speak to you."

"Holy orders they give to me!" the figure against the wall cried out. "At night!"

"Wait! . . . You have time. Lower your ax, shoemaker. Stand not between me and the gilgul, for it is to him I would speak. Gilgul, by the powers of my soul I invoke you. Come forth, demon. Pfefferkorn of Moravia, come forth!"

Darkness and silence lay in a spell about the two starry candles. The holy man did not break the silence with any invocations, nor test it with his powers. Instead he spoke presently in a whisper, as if he were merely trying out and questioning the mystery before him.

"Poor gilgul," he spoke in a voice intensely sad, "poor accursed soul. Recall yourself. Remember who it was who stole in the market-place in Moravia. Recall yourself, and it may be given to me to help you. Come, rob again your father's friend, Nathan the goldsmith. And run, thief, to the Christian monastery crying that your people punish you. Fall at the Dominicans' feet. Kiss their slippers. Save yourself from the punishment for your thieving. Cry for the Cross and Baptism. And rise, poor Apostate, poor Pfefferkorn, the Christian. Mad Pfefferkorn, baying for vengeance against your people. Pour out the false mad tale of Jewish deviltries to the mad nun Kunigunde. Hurry with her to the Emperor, her brother. And to your work, Pfefferkorn! Rekindle Torquemada's fires for the German land. Plead with kings and bishops for the scourging of Israel, the burning of Israel's holy books. Move and travel tirelessly from altar to palace, crying always: 'Death for the Jew. Let the Jew be cursed and burned and driven from the earth.'"

The figure against the wall trembled. A moan came from its lips and grew louder until it filled the darkness. The shadow of the figure loomed again, and Pfefferkorn moved from the wall.

"Let the dead wait a little longer," said the Rabbi softly. "No, do not pray, ghost and demon"—the voice of Pfefferkorn had risen, calling on Jesus—"for you know it is I who hold the mystery and the secret."

"Black Jew," the heavy, hoarsened whisper came from the wall. "There is no secret but the sweet call of Jesus Christ to save the world."

"The gilgul speaks," the Rabbi said to himself in wonder, "the ghost and demon who longs for me to save him. Pfefferkorn of

Moravia has grown tired of his accursed self. He longs to lie down among the dead and be at rest."

Long he remained silent, then he spoke in Hebrew.

"This is the Beast, O Israel, whom you cast out of our ancient soul by the first fires of Sinai. The Beast, older than the first prayers of Man. Beast—brother of the Prophets and Fathers of our first tribes—he is the Animal driven out from within the body of Israel when God placed His light in it. And because it was the Jew that first unhoused him, it is the Jew he must hound. Against the Jew he must avenge himself. Thus he has moved, Beast-Brother, through the ages, whispering to men and driving them mad with his own madness. Thus he has wandered, from age to age, faithful to his quarry, washing his hands in Jewish blood."

Eleazer paused, as though he were listening to a silence far beyond the awful silence where he stood.

"Such is the judgment," he said at last, "and such the mystery of his hands."

When he had finished, a sigh as of a dog at a closed door came from behind the candle held by the shoemaker.

Eleazer moved forward calmly to the face of murder.

"Gilgul, this I have to tell you," he cried out. "You have sent for me, but my help you shall not have. In vain you called. In vain you embroidered the slippers. It is decreed that Pfefferkorn, wearied with washing his hands in Jewish blood, must still blindly kill. No holy powers will I summon. I see no light. I do not know the way for you. Possessed by the demon you are, and so you must remain."

As Eleazer stood waiting, he saw with unchanged eyes that despair was in the sweating face before him and pain gleamed in its demon's eyes. An agony of pain came sweating out of the man.

And as Eleazer looked into this face of torment, the ax smote him, splitting through his ear. He fell to the dark floor in silence.

The voice of Pfefferkorn moaned and bleated and burst into ugly cries. Wildly the ax swung again. Its heavy blade split through the nose and the mouth. Again it swung.

Still howling, the man rushed to the workbench and snatched up a shoemaker's knife. He returned and dug the butt of the candle into the earthen floor. He remained, kneeling and cutting—his hand half hidden and moving to and fro. . . . The light of the candle mirrored itself in blood.

When Pfefferkorn, still working, looked at Eleazer, the large brown eyes were wide open. As he looked, the eyes of Eleazer moved from the right to the left. The pupils lay still in the socket corners and then moved back slowly.

Pfefferkorn sprang to his feet. The darkness swallowed him and he reappeared rolling a barrel. He tilted it and emptied the kerosene over the mutilated figure. He touched the candle to its feet.

The darkness sprang aside. A green and yellow fire mounted swiftly from Eleazer's body. It seized him in a vivid eager clutch, and the underground room became wild with light.

At the foot of the steps, Pfefferkorn looked back. In the heart of the fire that covered everything, he saw the large brown eyes of Rabbi Eleazer close slowly.

Captain Malloy had spent an irritating day in his office. His policemen had rounded up for him some thirty lunatics—shambling, timorous creatures released at one time or another from the asylums. These the captain had questioned. One after another the muttering, shifty-eyed child faces had looked from the other side of his desk, a strong light shining on them.

Puttering about at odd jobs, drifting from bedhouse to bedhouse, knowing themselves as bits of human junk that belonged nowhere, these loony ones were used to the ways of the police. When the net went out for suspects of strange and unsolved crimes, these shuffling figures with their frightened eyes and stuttering voices always emerged with the first haul.

Facing the familiar captain once again, each of them had begun with bluster his account of whereabouts and activities. But under Captain Malloy's questions each had started to shift in the chair. Captain Malloy had studied the guilt that responded furtively to his inquiries, trying to distinguish between the guilt of crimes done and crimes dreamed. The day had concluded with six confessions. Six of these shaken and beclouded souls had cried out, at the sight of the crucifix with the broken fastening loop, that it belonged to them, and that their hands had been the ones that had committed murder and mutilation. The six confessions, sprinkled with gibberish and echoing with the hosannas of mania released, were taken down by irritable police stenographers who, like the captain, knew their labors were a gruesome waste of time. But Captain Malloy had a plan in the back of his head that required the assistance of six unshaven lunatics. Accordingly, the six, wallowing in their phantom deeds, were locked away in cells.

At five o'clock Captain Malloy left his office and started once more for the monastery of the Dominican Fathers. The crucifix, so dramatically identified by the little Friar in the garden, was still in his pocket. The newspapers he read on the train were full of tidings of the lunatic round-up, of statements from eminent psychiatrists that a fourth of all the city's population was insane and in need of aid—presumably theirs; and of promises to their readers that the Police were closing in on the Mystery.

"Captain Malloy, in charge of the hunt, refused to comment on the arrests made," read one of the tales, "beyond stating that he felt certain of a solution of Joseph Franks' murder within the next twenty-four hours."

Captain Malloy, who had made no such statement and was full of no such certainty, threw down this pipe-dreaming gazette and looked out of the train window. The sultry afternoon was full of rain to come. The train was hot and uncomfortable, and outside the window the grimy streets of the city wheeled in a panorama of ugly spokes that dizzied and depressed the captain. He turned his eyes away and sat looking moodily before him. After two months of constant work, the only clue to the four murders that had come to him was the look in the eyes of a man he had seen for a moment in the monastery garden. Irritated with himself, Malloy fell to muttering inwardly that he was behaving like an old maid with the fantods, that there was no sense in this long trip after an exhausting day, that the man he had looked at for a moment was an honest German shoemaker and nothing else.

Yet this shoemaker's face, eager and beaming as he had stood beside it, had signaled something to the inner archives of Captain Malloy. The policeman had felt himself bristle, and his psychic nose with a single sniff had drawn in an ominous scent. The captain's microscopic memory tried now to reconstruct this smell for study, but he was unable to recapture its delicate ingredients. He was able to remember only that the eyes of this shoemaker had glittered as if full of desperate and hidden light as they rested smilingly on the tall, pale Rabbi who was visiting Father Dominic.

Growling at himself as the prince of wild-goose chasers, Captain Malloy sank deeper into his seat. He had come to the angry conclusion that he was wasting valuable time and behaving like a rural constable rather than a city detective. But the train continued carrying him nearer the monastery of the Dominican Fathers.

Father Francis, stocky and pink-faced, returned to the police captain waiting in the monastery's silent hall. Father Dominic, he reported, would be unable to speak to the visitor. When Malloy asked politely why, the black robe answered that Father Dominic was at his prayers and would remain so for the rest of the night.

"Perhaps you can help me then," said the captain. "I would like the name and address of the shoemaker who visited Father Dominic yesterday."

"Oh, Pfefferkorn!" The Friar smiled. "The one who brought the slippers?"

"Yes," said Malloy, and Father Francis gave him an address some miles away.

Stubbornly Captain Malloy tracked down a taxi and rode through the scattered suburb and past the stretch of marshlands. The taxi turned off into a wretched, half-passable road just as the threat of rain became a reality. The sky blackened. Gusts of chill wind swept and rattled the taxi windows. Then a salvo of thunder sounded, shaking the darkness. As the sky came swiftly close to the earth, the thunder sounded again, and the rain came down. A smear of plunging water filled the chilled and darkened afternoon, and Captain Malloy, with no raincoat, cursed aloud. In an increasing spray of mud the taxi clattered on. It came to a halt in the midst of nowhere like a raft stranded. Malloy saw a thicket of fir trees in a blank field. His driver was shouting through the window that something to the right was the Pfefferkorn house. Malloy stared into the rain-boiling field all about him, and cursed his idiot guide. Then he noticed the charred stumps of a small building. Part of a stone wall still stood, and around a blackened space lay piles of debris and soaking rubbish.

"It must have burned down last night," the taxi man shouted, as Malloy, with door opened, leaned out surveying the scene.

A blast of thunder shook the ground, and the lightning spat through the dark. There was a pause and then the storm fired point-blank at Captain Malloy in the taxi. Thunder lifted the wheels and the captain's derby and left a gasp in his throat. But his eyes caught a glimpse of the Pfefferkorn wall crumbling and the stones rolling away and he understood now how a stone house could have burned to so small an ash. Malloy settled back angrily in his seat and instructed the driver to go on. He would inquire everywhere until he learned what had happened, and if Pfefferkorn had taken refuge somewhere, or if he had disappeared. Captain Malloy was on the trail.

The rain had doubled in force when the taxi stopped before a frame house at the end of the suburban street. It was one of a score of chocolate-trimmed white wooden buildings as alike as a set of playing blocks. Captain Malloy sprinted across the pavement to its front door and stood soaking in the downpour as he waited for someone to answer the bell.

A soft-faced young woman with pale hair and pale blurred eyes drew the door curtain aside and peered out. The captain rapped amiably on the glass panel, but the young woman, with a sudden flurry of alarm, disappeared. Malloy waited stoically as the rain pasted his heavy clothes to his body. A man appeared and the door was opened. Malloy faced a pale-haired German, young and well built. He noticed the soft cheeks, the pink ears, the puffy colorless lips, the powerful arms and large hands, as he explained his presence in the hallway and told who he was. The soft-faced woman had returned and stood timidly beside the man, who was evidently her husband. Malloy's powers of observation were not too keen with women. With a quick look at her bulging youthful body, he ignored her.

"Pfefferkorn iss not here," said the young German and smiled. "His home has burned down, poor feller. He only slept here last night. My name iss Gustav Edelberg," he added, and held out his hand in stiff friendliness. "Come inside a little, if you please, Captain, and ve can talk better. I am sorry Pfefferkorn iss not here."

Malloy stood in the arch of a small parlor full of shining oak furniture. Behind a tall oak piano covered with music, Captain Malloy saw a large swastika flag, standing on the floor. Another swastika flag was tacked on the wall and under it hung a large gold-framed photograph of Adolf Hitler, the German Fuehrer.

Young Edelberg continued smiling as Malloy's eyes moved about. But behind the albino gloss of the Teutonic face the drenched but alert Malloy felt an uneasiness.

"You're a Nazi?" asked the captain.

"Yes," the young man smiled, "I am Offizier in the German-American Storm Troopers. You are welcome."

Malloy walked into the room. The soft-faced Mrs. Edelberg uttered a cry at wet shoes dirtying her polished floor. She covered her mouth quickly with her pudgy hand and stood shamefaced and cringing. The policeman leaned over a pile of large cardboard placards facing the wall.

"Ach, everything iss such a mess!" exclaimed the young wife. "Excuse it, please."

The Nazi officer looked at her coldly. She blushed and nodded her head apologetically several times.

"For parades, I suppose," said Captain Malloy.

"Yes," said the Nazi.

Malloy read a few of the lettered slogans, "Jews Are Ruining Our Country. Rise Up, Americans." "Oust Jews and Find Prosperity." "Jew Plots Kill Christian Culture."

"You know Pfefferkorn well?" the captain asked, looking up.

"Yes," said his host.

"He is a good friend of yours?" the captain murmured.

"Yes, we are very good friends."

"Is he also a member of your Nazi organization?" Malloy continued.

"Oh, yes." The wife beamed. "Pfeffy is a good member. He helped make all the signs with my husband."

The husband looked at her and spoke sharply in German.

"Get back into the kitchen quick," he said, "and concern yourself not with my affairs, please."

With a cringing, anxious look in her blurred eyes, the young woman obeyed.

"Why are you asking after Pfefferkorn?" the Nazi now asked Malloy.

Malloy said nothing. His eyes remained on the blond young man. He saw the good nature that had greeted him retreat as if behind a layer of fat.

"You are a Jew?" the German asked slowly.

"No," said Malloy, "I'm Irish."

"Excuse me, then," said the Nazi stiffly, "there are many Jews in this neighborhood. Ve must be careful."

He bowed slightly and Malloy thanked him and walked to the front door. He had learned that Pfefferkorn was alive.

"Allow me, please," the blond young man said, "I will get an umbrella for you."

"Never mind," Captain Malloy answered and sprinted across the pavement to the waiting taxi.

Careening through the rain-beaten roads, the taxi started back for the thicket of fir trees. On the way, Malloy stopped and bought a large flashlight.

The rain flung itself at the captain as he walked across the field to the remains of Pfefferkorn's house. But the spit of lightning, the blasts of thunder, the lash of water against his face and soggy clothes, were faraway matters to Captain Malloy. He walked now in an inner world, his senses on some invisible goal.

The rain steamed from the debris of the burned dwelling. Holding his flashlight before him, Malloy kicked at the slop of ashes and charred wood. His light picked out a hole in the ground. He knelt in a pool of water and looked into a cellar. There were no steps to descend. The captain returned to the taxi and ordered his driver to bring him back a tall ladder from some place. The taxi clattered out of the thicket again.

Captain Malloy waited under the fir trees. His jaws were rigid and he no longer belabored himself with criticisms of his conduct. He had found nothing new, no tangible thing to add to the trail at which he sniffed. But the trail was there, ghostly and persistent. Illogically and with no single fact to assuage him, Captain Malloy waited contentedly under the fir trees, his blue eyes looking dreamily at the house that had been burned.

In a half-hour the ladder appeared. Malloy carried it to the rain-steaming field and lowered it into the hole he had found. The hole was deep and the ladder barely reached its bottom. He climbed down its rungs, the rain pouring on him as out of a huge bottle. The black, sightless hole in which he found himself was shoe-deep with water. He splashed about in the darkness, sniffing the sharp wet ghost of the fire that had raged here. Foot by foot Malloy explored it with his light. The place was empty of all furniture. Hollow and black, it surrounded him, its odors sawing away at his nose. Occasionally the black hole turned ashen blue as the lightning stretched wildly in the outside night. The cellar flared and grew blind. The thunder blasts fired their shrieks through the hole overhead. Then quiet seized the earth and the rain worked busily in the darkness.

Malloy continued to explore. In a corner of the reeking cellar his light picked out an object. On a dry bit of earth he saw a slipper standing. Malloy stood staring at it. He saw it was made of a sort of embroidery, newly woven and unworn. Then the captain did an unaccountable thing. He looked around fearfully and crossed himself. For what he had looked Malloy didn't know. For the darkness to move, perhaps, or a thing to appear; for the muddy earth to open under his feet and the inky reeking air to become filled with pale shapes. He stood with the skin on his large body tightened. A bomb of thunder exploded over his head. Its echoes leaped around his ears. He set his jaws firmly and waited for the tremble to leave his hands. Then he leaned over to pick up the slipper. As his nose neared the ground another smell came to him. It was not the wet ghost of flames this time but an uglier smell that confused him and made him think of chickens. Straightening, Captain Malloy put the slipper under his wet coat as if it were something alive, and climbed up the ladder.

A half-hour later the captain was in a hotel telephone booth, water gushing from him as from a fountain as he waited for his office in New York to answer. He caught his breath as he remembered something.

"It was flesh I smelled," the delayed message came from the Malloy inner archives, "human flesh. Burned."

A voice answered over the telephone. Captain Malloy spoke briefly. He wanted a suitcaseful of fresh dry clothes and a raincoat brought out to him. The voice took down the name of the hotel and then said: "By the way, we got a report in that some Rabbi has disappeared out your way. It was Saturday night, and he didn't show up for services."

"What's his name?" asked the captain.

"Just a minute, I'll read it all to you," said the voice. "Here we are. It says Rabbi Eleazer, aged seventy-nine, height six feet one, weight one hundred and forty, clean-shaven, missing from the synagogue since yesterday."

"That's enough," said Malloy, "and hurry up with my clothes. I'm wetter than Monday's wash."

Malloy had intended taking a room in the hotel. Instead he walked out of the empty lobby and into the storm again. He waved his drenched arms to his taxi-driver, who had moved down the street. The taxi splashed up. Captain Malloy drove once more to the Dominican monastery two miles away. His reddish, square face, despite the long prowling in the storm, was content and peaceful.

At the monastery Father Francis, though concerned over the policeman's wretched condition, insisted that the ancient Dominic was still at his prayers.

"May I have pencil and paper?" said Captain Malloy. These were procured, and he wrote the following lines:

"Please may I see you about something involving your friend Rabbi Eleazer, the shoemaker Pfefferkorn, and the crucifix?"

"I'll wait here," he said. A few minutes later Father Francis returned. Dominic walked behind him.

"Forgive me, Father, for disturbing you again," said Captain Malloy. Father Dominic raised his eyes and said softly:

"I was praying for him."

Malloy beat back the glint of surprise in his eyes, and continued to look at the priest with his expression unchanged.

"Did you think something had happened to him?" he asked.

"I was praying for him," Father Dominic repeated. He looked pleadingly at the policeman. "What have you heard?" he whispered.

"Tell me, Father," Malloy insisted gently, "why you were praying for him. It's important that I know."

The Friar shook his head.

"It's nothing that can be told," he answered.

"Well," said Captain Malloy, "can you tell me if this slipper belonged to the Rabbi?"

He removed the slipper from under his coat. Dominic saw the yellow triangles and the familiar pattern.

"Yes," he said.

"Did he have this slipper with him when he left you yesterday?" Malloy asked.

"Yes," said Dominic. "Where is he?"

"He has disappeared," said Malloy gently. "He failed to return to his home last night. But I found this slipper in the cellar of Pfefferkorn's house. The house burned down last night."

"Burned down," whispered the little Friar.

An ashen color came into his sunbeaten face.

"It will be a great help to me and to your friend, Father," said the captain urgently, "if you would tell me why you were praying for him since he left your side last night."

Father Dominic's face twitched and the pain in his eyes was covered with tears.

"Rabbi Eleazer does not need my help," he said finally.

Captain Malloy bowed his head and turned away.

Father Dominic looked after him.

"You have done good work tonight, Captain Malloy," he said sadly, as the door opened to the storm.

The arrest of Pfefferkorn was accomplished quietly. He was taken in the morning from the house of the American-Nazi lieutenant, Gustav Edelberg. Captain Malloy placed him among the six loonies in the station cells and called his three witnesses. These were the young woman who had noticed a man following the murdered Joseph Franks, the janitor who had seen a man lurking on the street corner where Max Asher was killed, the newsdealer who had seen someone follow Irving Bronski into the deserted theater alley on the midnight he was found slain and mutilated.

Under conditions that would leave no doubt in any jury's mind, he hoped, Captain Malloy led each of his witnesses separately to the row of cells. Each looked at the seven suspects and selected Pfefferkorn as the man observed near the scene of the crime. After these identifications, Pfefferkorn was charged with the murder of five Jews. He was indicted on these counts and ordered to be placed on trial for the last of them, the killing of Rabbi Eleazer. The trial was set for a month later.

But the trial did not wait for the date that had been set. It began at once everywhere, in the streets, the cafés, the newspapers, in homes, churches, and meeting halls. Hour by hour the significance of the arrest of the Nazi Pfefferkorn for the murder of five Jews increased. All who read the first accounts of the case felt immediately that a *cause célèbre* had been born. The nation's Jews, psychically tormented by years of Nazi calumny, seized quickly on Pfefferkorn as the symbol of German Kultur. They cried out triumphantly that Pfefferkorn, the fiend, was the logical and inhuman flowering of Nazism; that Pfefferkorn, the monster, was the New Germany incarnate, legitimate spawn of a nation that had tried to strengthen itself by filling its veins deliberately with hate.

And the American Nazis, less numerous but more effectively organized, answered back that Pfefferkorn was innocent of any crime, but that he was being sent to his death as part of the cunning Jewish plot to blacken the name of Aryan. And the facts for and against Pfefferkorn were spread before the world by the newspapers and debated more and more hysterically everywhere.

In a few days the seeming innocence of Pfefferkorn began to triumph. The published facts aroused a storm of doubt. The case as revealed in the press appeared to grow vaguer and more circumstantial the more light there was turned on it. The vast jury of the public began to inquire, Where were the concrete facts of guilt? Where, even, was the body of the dead Rabbi? Police and hundreds of Jewish volunteers had dug and searched in the vicinity of Pfefferkorn's burned house day and night and no corpse or clues leading either to murder or to Pfefferkorn had been uncovered. Pfefferkorn had been identified by three witnesses as the killer of Jews. But who were these witnesses? Jews themselves. Captain Malloy, in charge of the case, refused to comment other than that he knew Pfefferkorn to be guilty and that he expected a confession before the trial.

But no confession came. Instead, heartbreaking and half-articulate stories of his life from Pfefferkorn's lips appeared in the newspapers. Rumors filled the city that the little shoemaker was being beaten and submitted to various tortures by the police in a desperate effort to force him to admit the crimes. And that behind this desperation were the Jews. The Jews were beating Pfefferkorn. The Jews were bringing their great financial powers to bear on the officials of the city, demanding that Pfefferkorn be proved guilty in order that the Nazis of the world could be convicted of inhumanity. These rumors generated swiftly and simultaneously everywhere.

And as this public trial continued, a feeling began to rise against the Jews. Their outcries that this little shoemaker was an anti-Semitic fiend hatched by Nazi hate, who had gone around disemboweling Jews, began to grow irksome and full of some alien over-emphasis, and their hysteria soon sounded offensive. This was Shylock howling again for his pound of Pfefferkorn flesh.

Swiftly the Nazi propagandists took advantage of this mood. They thrust aside the long-prized but always tenuous barriers of American tolerance, and launched an open campaign against Jews. The Hitler gibberish with all its tragi-comic naïvetés about Jew cunning and Jew dominance became new, loud fact in this public trial of Pfefferkorn.

The Jews of the nation welcomed this burst of calumny at first. Its howling and stupid accusations appeared to them to convict their accusers of every sin against reason. For to the American Jew, the racial calumny that has kept his brothers shuddering throughout most of the Christian era seemed too preposterous to be effective in the New World. As he read the virulent attacks uncorked by the city's Nazis, the American Jew was convinced that their irrationality and intolerance would prove a boomerang. Surely, he thought, the unreason and obvious disease of these German minds must arouse only revulsion wherever their cries resound.

It was this illusion that was to bring him his deepest distress, for it is always the miserable realization that anti-Jew propaganda finds immediate adherents that brings his spirit down. Noting that others believe what is unbelievable, the Jew begins to feel that all the world around him is slowly going mad, and in this madness he becomes a sort of delusion. He feels himself ceasing to be human and becoming a pariah imprisoned in the delirium of others. And there he struggles full of impotence, as one does in an evil dream.

In the second week of the Pfefferkorn controversy, the Jews found themselves slipping into this wretched fantasy in which they have immemorially lost their standing as human beings and in which everything they say is robbed of all significance, for the reason that it is Jews who are saying it. The meaning of the Pfefferkorn trial underwent a cruel change. Not Eleazer, the ascetic Jew whose face peered out of the newspapers hourly, but Pfefferkorn, the pious, hardworking German shoemaker, had become a Cause and a Victim.

And it was the Jews who were on trial, as they must always be when they so far forget themselves as to become an Issue.

Finding themselves marched into the prisoner's dock, Jewish spokesmen summoned the ideals of democracy and humanity to their defense. But the multitudinous jury of bystanders listened with increasing irritation. The appeal to their sanity and fair play angered them, for in such appeal there is always the accusation that these qualities are missing. This in itself is enough to antagonize the righteous. But there is also the fact that it is extremely dangerous to accuse any mass of people of inhumanity. It invariably sets them to proving it.

Throughout the days before the trial, the Jews continued desperately their pleas for fair play, desperately and more and more in vain. For in the long recurrent struggle of the Jew to establish himself within the bosom of humanity, it is always the same in the end. The cry for justice calls more attention to the weakness of the crier than to the strength of his cause, and the Jew ends by flushing ten sadists for every humanitarian.

The activities of Pfefferkorn's defenders, led by the pale-haired Nazi, Edelberg, reverberated everywhere. A great emotion swept the various German-American sectors of the city. Thousands of cheerful-looking men and women who sang, danced, and drank beer emerged from Teutonia's parlors in New York to heil for Hitler and Pfefferkorn, and contribute to the defense fund of the latter. These celebrants crowding the meeting halls had, however, only a secondary interest in the shoemaker's innocence. The cause to which they rallied was that of their own solidarity. Lustily and gaily, they sang songs revealing the unanimity of their thought and passion. It was this opportunity to feel the tribal rhythm of uniformity, so dear to the slave-haunted soul of the German, that brought them cheering around Pfefferkorn.

The charm and gaiety of their solidarity began to be felt everywhere. Non-Nazis looked wistfully at so much picnicking going on under their noses and began to wonder what was the secret of all this carnival spirit. They began to see that this socially enviable and humanly warming sense of solidarity had, as its welding ingredient, a hatred of Jews. And simultaneously it became apparent to thousands of outsiders that there was something not only sensible but very pleasant in this hatred of Jews.

Triumphantly the Nazi Bunds continued to color the temperament of the city of which they were so small a part. They sold its tax-bedeviled inhabitants the pleasures of hate—its anodyne of relief from petty matters and its ego-inflating joys.

Where the apologists for the Jews stuttered and pleaded and called passionately on history and humanity to vindicate their cause, the Jew-haters smiled, sang songs, drank beer, and sat happily behind their hate. The menace of the Jews to which they responded with heroic, shoulder-to-shoulder cheers was merely a piece of evil magic to be overcome by fearlessness and the waving of a Cross or the chanting of an Exorcism. That it was a fearlessness of that which had no power, of that which, horrendous though it was, would be easily crushed, made no difference. The deeper the Jew hatred grew, the braver the Jew-haters felt. For hate is the promise of courage, and when felt even against the powerless, it excites its owners with illusions of valor.

Toward the end of the month the larger part of the city stood beside Pfefferkorn in the cellar and enjoyed itself. But those who enjoyed themselves most were the inner circle, the generating storm troops of the hatred. For these, Jew hate had become more than a casual social exhilaration. It was a cult, a drug, and a sport. It set its followers apart from humanity, and welded them into that deeper comradeship which only criminals can feel. It regenerated also the German sense of self-esteem shattered by the war. In this contempt for Jews, in this embracing of intolerance and savagery, the Germans felt they were triumphing over the ideals whose protagonists had massed against them and defeated them twenty years ago.

But these and scores of other motivations were of no concern to the Germans, who are never a people for analyzing the sources of their happiness. In their hatred of Jews, shared so uncritically, they had found a rallying point, a sort of master of ceremonies for victorious mass merrymaking. This was enough for them. The Jew was the belle of the Pfefferkorn picnics, the ugly Maypole round which Teutonia, reunited and full of song, capered again.

As the fourth week of preparation for the trial began, this happy and heroic feeling of solidarity had become so great among the Germans that the possibility that their Pfefferkorn was a murderer and mutilator of five Jews was entirely overshadowed by the fact that he was one of them. At times it even seemed as if the very accusations against Pfefferkorn added stature to the man. In their mystic *Kampf* against the Internationalism and Uncleanness of the Jews, the sturdy Teutons of New York began to feel that their Pfefferkorn's deeds, though never admitted, were a mystic measure of his greatness. A man accused of murdering five Jews was a sort of phantom Napoleon around whom their own undone Jew murders rallied; a hero who by the very nature of the accusation was entitled to an Iron Cross rather than to the discomfitures of a trial for murder.

At last Pfefferkorn, now backed by the sympathy of the city, confronted his victim, not in the dark cellar but in the light of a law court. There was no ax in his hand this time, but three brilliant lawyers sat around him smiling confidently. A defense fund of several hundred thousand dollars was at his disposal. In the streets outside as the trial opened throngs of Nazis sang hymns to Pfefferkorn. And the newspapermen in the courtroom, come from a hundred centers, scribbled away on descriptions of Pfefferkorn. They had no prejudice against him. Like all greatly publicized figures of crime, he was their own—"their boy" Pfefferkorn. Gratitude for so fecund a news source as Pfefferkorn colored their scribblings, and the camaraderie between the dramatist and his subject matter animated their reports.

In the courtroom, a cordon of police lined the walls. The benches were filled with celebrities come from everywhere, avid, posturing, opinionated. The trial of Pfefferkorn, echoing through the nation and into far countries, was not only a battle front for them, but a social event. They occupied the crowded benches with the satisfied air of important people who feel themselves in a sufficiently important place.

The People's case against Adolf Pfefferkorn was in the hands of Joseph Menelli, the city's much-admired prosecutor. Short, fattish, dynamic, and bristling with a chronic buzz of conflict, Menelli entered the courtroom on the first day like a wrestler coming ominously out of his corner. He moved slowly. He looked at no one. His broad shoulders, his theatrical, self-possessed glower, his wary, provocative calm, identified him in the first few minutes of silence as more than a lawyer come to argue a case. He was the Knight in the field. Menelli, the East Side Italian butcher boy who had butted his way through a generation of politics into the metropolitan limelight, was the People's champion against Pfefferkorn. It was to be seen that Menelli, along with his law books, brought a Cause into the courtroom.

In front of Pfefferkorn at the defense's table sat Francis Cantwell, the most expensive of the city's criminal defense lawyers. He was white-haired, humorous-faced, and friendly-looking in an old suit of unpressed clothes. Behind Pfefferkorn sat John Potalski and William Emerson, aides to Cantwell and famed in their own right as the heroes of a score of murder trials. They were middle-aged men, well built, keen and driving. Unlike the friendly, humorous-looking man who captained them, they came to battle taut and restive.

In the witness rooms outside the court sat the corps of special investigators who had been toiling valiantly for the defense since Pfefferkorn's arrest. Among them were the witnesses to be called. Guards stood at the tall doors of these rooms. Guards filled the thronged corridors.

On the bench, chin sunk on his chest, sat His Honor Daniel Leak. He was a white-haired man, portentous and full of judicial posture. It was obvious even to those who had never known of this judge what his attitude would be through all the crises of the trial. He would shine as a hero of punctilio. Neither humanity nor prejudice would speak through him, but always the law and its gamelike rules of procedure.

Of dominating interest to all in the courtroom, however, was Pfefferkorn. The eyes of spectators and journalists bored at him. Their consciousness of him covered the shoemaker like a beam of light in which every twitch of his features and movement of his body was magnified into drama. His plump, good-natured face with its shaggy brows and twinkling doglike eyes radiated the magnetism of enigma.

How familiar and human he looked, this stooped, nondescript figure fished out of the colorless deeps of the crowd and landed on this high pedestal of Event; so proper, so normal, so understandable to the eye. His manner said: "I am Pfefferkorn, a shoemaker like any other shoemaker." His smile, his embarrassment, his pathetic interest in his counsel, said: "I am nobody like any other nobody. I belong at a workbench, not here. I am frightened, but hopeful. I am only what you see, the familiar, slovenly figure you have always known as a tradesman or a workman. I am one of you in a lesser way. But I am one of you."

But out of this simple and appealing humanity that spoke from Pfefferkorn came another voice, eerie and shocking. It was the voice not of Pfefferkorn or any part or grimace of Pfefferkorn, but of the five murders with which he was charged, and the one for which he was on trial. The sibilant and menacing murmur of crime surrounded Pfefferkorn. These murders spoke, saying: "We have been done. We are the brutal deeds of a fiend. Look close at Pfefferkorn. Watch him. Stare into his eyes. See if you can find us there. We are deeds that may belong to Pfefferkorn. Find us in him."

And looking into Pfefferkorn's eyes, watching, observing, those in the courtroom heard in their own heads a third voice that said: "How strange and far away is the simple thought of another. How impenetrable and dark is the life that beats in the humblest and most familiar of figures, and how perfectly hidden is the thing that we call brother. This nobody, this mild and appealing little man, this One of Us, is as great a mystery as if he had dropped from Mars."

This mystery of the familiar, this enigma that stares empty-lidded out of a neighbor's smile, multiplied the meaning of Pfefferkorn. And his simplicity multiplied it again. He sat among his counsel like a provoking and bedeviling riddle that no eyes could read, and that the short black-browed Menelli had sworn to tear open and reveal.

As the business of picking the jury started, the most experienced of the newspapermen began to sense uncertainty in the People's champion. It was too early to judge the caliber of his weapons, but Menelli himself looked dubious to these experts—fretful and curiously out of control. This was difficult to believe, for the Menelli record denied it. But this impression was discussed among the divining journalists. And it was true. Uncertainty spoke out of the very noise in which Menelli tried to conceal it. For though he rumbled and barked and seemed the most dangerous of prosecutors, his clever and violent mind was full of uneasiness. He had worked tirelessly in assembling the People's case, and had come to trial with a fevered and embittered conviction of Pfefferkorn's guilt. Behind this conviction was another almost equal certainty that the evidence of it he had to offer the jury was bleak and insufficient.

He had absorbed along with all the details of the case the mystic knowledge of Pfefferkorn's guilt that filled Captain Malloy. It was this knowledge more than any facts proving it that he found himself ready to offer as the People's side. His black eyes when they turned to Pfefferkorn lighted with hate. He felt the shoemaker's evil as if it were a stench, and his heart lifted with a will to shatter the riddle of Pfefferkorn and uncover what his senses knew.

There had come to Menelli, too, a hatred for the Nazis who were behind the defense. He saw these rabid sympathizers as so many Pfefferkorns with minds as befouled as the shoemaker's. His mind raged against them. There was in Menelli no particular love of Jews. He knew almost nothing of their history, and before Pfefferkorn's arrest had felt almost no concern for their troubles in the world. Nor had the cause of the Jew been awakened in him. He was of that sensitive but egoistic type of mind which, though incapable of surrendering to ideals, is tireless in its attack on their enemies. Injustice and not its victims trumpeted him forward. His strength must come from the ferocity of the enemy rather than the cries of the wretchedness he championed.

Preparing his case, Menelli had read through scores of Nazi speeches and interviewed the orators and leaders of the Nazi cult. His mind had sickened as if it had been inducted suddenly into a nightmare. He saw this cruelty imbedded in the German mind like the half-decayed fangs of barbarism. And he saw the ugly guilt of Pfefferkorn glowing like an infection out of the pink and white fattish faces of the Nazis with whom he talked. A philosophy based on a love of self and a hatred of everything alien to that self must end by generating in others a hate of the thing that sets itself apart. And Menelli, encountering more and more Germans during his inquiries, began to see in Germans something that grew more inhuman and preposterous with each inspection. And though he had begun with an academic dislike of their politics, he ended with a rage against their faces, accents, mannerisms, and very haircuts.

When we hate, we look only for those things in the hated one that will vindicate and increase our aversion. And as if to oblige us, the one hated seems intent on concealing all his qualities from us but those we consider repulsive. It is this psychological trick that often gives the Jews in their words and deeds the air of caricatures, as if they had been hypnotized by hate into seeming hateful. And it is as true of Germans as of Jews.

To Menelli the prosecutor, every German he interviewed added to the clarity of his hate. He saw them as a people with a spark missing, as if life were only half present in them, and the other half occupied by a corpse-like stubbornness. He saw Pfefferkorn as a German and not a defendant, or even an individual, and his hatred prepared a case against Nazidom rather than a shoemaker accused of crime. And his great forensic talents became confused and absorbed in the angry questions that crowded his mind.

How could intelligence so malformed and cast in so unhuman a pattern persist in the light of reason? How could so warped and criminal a mood seize on a modern soul and drag it singing and elated into the darkness of the past? What was there in the riddle of this chuckling, butcher-hearted swarm of Germans, full of hate and defiance, who had gleefully exchanged their humanity for the hyena philosophies of an aberrant little paperhanger named Hitler? What was there in the cries of that vengeful little eunuch whose useless sex had infected his mind with rages and phantasms that found so powerful an echo in the German soul?

These questions filled Menelli, the champion of Justice, and armed his own humanity with claws and fangs as incredible as those he had glimpsed in the Nazi cult. His intelligence cautioned him from day to day against rushing Pfefferkorn to trial, and urged him to wait until his aide, Captain Malloy, had uncovered more evidence. But his rage lured him into battle.

He appeared in the courtroom unprofessionally armed with passion, a champion thirsting for conflict rather than victory. Headstrong and dramatic, he would end floundering stupidly in the nets of the law's minutiae. His very courage and righteousness, unguided by the talent that had brought him success, would turn him into a black-browed clown as he battered at the rules of evidence. The Pfefferkorn counsel, crafty in the utilization of his emotional violence and legal weakness, would cruelly pervert this People's champion into their own chief witness. His passion would be offered the jury as part of the persecution that sought to convict an innocent Pfefferkorn of the crime of being a German. And by ludicrous but incontrovertible steps it would be the Germans and not the Jews who were in danger of martyrdom, and the victims of bigotry. Poised and amused at the futility of Menelli's onslaughts, the Nazi spokesmen would come to seem tolerant and superior, courteous and law-abiding, and, paradoxically, cast in a finer mold of reason.

These eventualities came to be. Menelli's passion defeated him from the first hour of jury picking. The procedure-haunted judge coldly edited his outbursts and outlawed his emotional attitudes. He was cautioned again and again to confine his conduct to that of a prosecutor of Pfefferkorn, not of Nazidom. As a result of these first errors, the jury, completed after four days of histrionics, was hailed as a victory by the Nazis. Not a single Jew had gained a place on it, and three of its members were German-born. The presence of these three in the jury box further undid the swarthy battering ram of a prosecutor. He took to regarding the jury as an enemy. Embittered always by the insufficiency of his evidence, he placed the jurors on trial, assailed and challenged them in every question asked and every objection offered to the bench.

The Jewish population had found immediate solace in the virtuosity of the Menelli hate. His outcries were hailed as manna by the Jewish press. But as the case progressed into its third day even the Jewish journalists saw that their first impressions had been accurate.

Hour by hour the Menelli evidence seemed to lose what stature it might have had alongside the violence of the Menelli passion. It began to appear that this volcano of a prosecutor was erupting only in pebbles, harmless and even comic-seeming because of the noise that accompanied them.

On the fourth day, which had promised the climax of the People's case in the testimony of Captain Malloy, even the stanchest of the anti-Pfefferkornites began to lose heart. Captain Malloy seated himself in the witness chair amid an expectant quiet. His rigid, square face repeated calmly the tale of Pfefferkorn's guilt as he had first felt it. He traced his work through the finding of the slipper in the cellar of the burned house. The slipper was shown him.

It was the People's lone exhibit.

Menelli had based his case on this slipper found in the cellar. Out of its presence there he had spun his theory of the Pfefferkorn crime in the opening address. Gentlemen—urged on by the thought that Pfefferkorn was the mutilator of Jews sought by the police, Rabbi Eleazer had followed the shoemaker to his house. The aged and delicate man of God had exhibited no policeman's cunning. He had walked into the Pfefferkorn cellar, sustained by the righteousness of his own soul and lured by some mystic knowledge of the shoemaker's true self. He had confronted Pfefferkorn with his crimes and under his arm he had held, as he spoke, the symbolic Jew-hating slippers Pfefferkorn had embroidered for him. And Pfefferkorn had murdered the Rabbi in the depths of this cellar. Then, exulting in his deed, he had set fire to the house. Hidden from any road, the house had burned down without attracting attention. Pfefferkorn had crouched in the glare of the flames, watching the fire continue his crime. When the fire was done, cunning had returned to Pfefferkorn. He had remembered the body in the cellar. Lowering himself into it again by a rope, for the stairs were now burned away, he had hoisted the remains out of the cellar. He had walked on in the night until he had come to the marshes he knew so well. In these marshes the body had been hidden and still lay out of sight under the muck and vegetation of the swamp. The storm that had preceded Captain Malloy to the scene the next day had removed all traces of the crime. But it had not removed the slipper. Almost miraculously the slipper had remained behind untouched by fire or criminal cunning, to speak in the absence of all other witnesses of the things that had taken place in the Pfefferkorn cellar.

Malloy, now looking at this slipper from the witness stand, nodded his head and answered yes. It was the same slipper his light had picked out in the rain-whipped cellar. Malloy's testimony ended with this identification and he was turned over for cross-examination.

And now his story under the half-humorous queries of the white-haired and friendly-looking Cantwell suffered a transformation. It became a story of obsession, devoid of fact, born of hunches and the most unpoliceman-like species of reasoning. Malloy, the bloodhound, became an irrational and hate-crazed cat's-paw of the Jews. Impervious to storm, rain, and reason, he had hurled himself at the business of fastening a crime on a Nazi, and all the subtleties that had led him to Pfefferkorn were twisted easily and even comically into the aberrations of an obsessed and melodramatic Hawkshaw.

Ridiculed and discredited, Captain Malloy stepped from the witness chair. He had left behind an impression of guilt preconceived and never proved, except in his own fevered imaginings. As he passed Pfefferkorn's chair, Malloy paused and looked into the shoemaker's eyes. They were raised to his with an expression of wonder and un-happiness so repulsive to Malloy's knowledge of the man's guilt that the captain turned crimson. The Pfefferkorn sympathizers in the courtroom, whose numbers increased hourly, tittered at the police-man's discomfiture.

All he could say when he returned to Menelli's table was: "Don't give up. He's guilty as hell."

Menelli nodded. His broad shoulders lifted and his eyes darkened. "I'll get him somehow," he said.

Father Dominic followed Malloy on the stand and again the promise of Menelli's impassioned opening address, in which the Catholic Father had figured so importantly, came to nothing. There was no evidence in Father Dominic beyond the one fact that Eleazer had left him late that rainy afternoon carrying the two slippers Pfefferkorn had made for him. Like Malloy he nodded when the slipper found in Pfefferkorn's cellar was shown him. This was his lone bit of evidence, but Menelli was not content with it. He knew of other matters that betrayed Pfefferkorn's guilt, and he plunged stupidly into the business of bringing them out of Father Dominic. Why had the Father prayed for Eleazer's safety after the Rabbi had gone? What had happened that had aroused the Father's fear for his friend's life?

Black-robed and gentle-voiced, the Friar looked uneasily at Menelli as these questions came. Menelli was wrong to ask these questions, Dominic thought. His own accurate and logical mind informed him how his words would be turned upside down by the lawyers for the defense. Still they might help. If he spoke carefully and tenderly the jurors might feel what he had felt. Carefully and tenderly Father Dominic then tried to evoke the afternoon in the garden with his friend. He told of the Rabbi's visit and of some of their talk. He repeated what had happened when Pfefferkorn had brought the slippers, and in his gentle and talented words the scene under the maple trees came again to life. Then he related the dream the Rabbi had told him. It was this dream that had frightened him.

Menelli still persisted. Why had he grown frightened? Had there been something else that had warned him, some other information known only to him and Eleazer? Here Father Dominic hesitated. His little faun's face looked helplessly through the window beyond at the summer afternoon. How tell them that Pfefferkorn was related somehow to another Pfefferkorn five hundred years ago, that Eleazer, who was a mystic, had sensed this gruesome fact, that the ancient Dominican cross found in the hand of the murdered Franks took the crime back somewhere into the hate-filled centuries of the earlier church? In what way would these curious things help the dead man he had loved? They would only bring to light the old charge that the Dominican Order had been one of the ancient breeding places of a Jew hate, and that it had burned and tortured Jews in the name of holiness, and that Pfefferkorn, the fiend who posed as a shoemaker, had the name of one of its ancient and honored sons. His little eyes, unblinking as they stared out of the window, became full of pain. He longed to raise them in prayer and to beg God to show him some way for the truth to be told so that it might be believed.

After a long pause, Father Dominic looked poignantly at Menelli and answered: "My reasons for being worried over my friend Eleazer lie between me—and Someone Else."

The cross-examination of Father Dominic was gentle but devastating. Patiently the friendly-looking Cantwell went over the old priest's tale of fears and conjectures until they lost all their poetic mood. They became the crotchety and irrational fret of age. Lawyer Cantwell was even tender toward the ancient Father's little mental quirks. But when he dismissed the witness, the Pfefferkornites had scored another great point. The aberrations of this brooding, unworldly little priest appeared to have been mendaciously summoned by the prosecution to convict an innocent man.

Facts—facts, whispered the anti-Pfefferkornites in the courtroom. And beyond the courtroom, wherever Jews were reading of the trial, the whisper repeated itself in their hearts. Facts, facts, where are the facts of the crime? Is it possible that Menelli in his fever of Nazi hatred hopes to convict Pfefferkorn only by the one accusation that Pfefferkorn hates Jews and belongs to a race that hates Jews? Where are the facts of the deed done, of Eleazer murdered, of Pfefferkorn's trail leading to his victim and away from him? Facts, facts, the desperate whisper of the Jewish elements grew louder. What had happened to their champion? How was he so unarmed? Was he betraying them? Was this another part of the Nazi plot to discredit them in the eyes of the world? Had their champion meant to lose? Were all his outcries against Nazidom no more than a noise behind which he worked for the Nazi cause?

Desperately these whispers spread through Jewish neighborhoods, and Menelli, entering the courtroom on the fifth day, found rage in all the partisan eyes that looked at him, Jewish and Nazi; and contempt in the eyes of all the others. The white-haired, slovenly-looking Cantwell alone smiled at him, as if this great battle of hatred and prejudice were no more than a casual day's work in the lives of two lawyers.

"Cheer up," said the solicitous Cantwell. "We all lose cases sometimes."

And Menelli's heart grew heavy. Throwing aside all he knew of jurisprudence, he made a last effort. He demanded of the bench that the three witnesses who had picked out Pfefferkorn in the police cells as the man seen in the vicinity of the previous murders be allowed to testify. The plea was denied by Judge Leak. Their evidence had no bearing on the murder of Eleazer. Vainly Menelli pleaded that the special quality of the case made it legal procedure to identify Pfefferkorn as the fiend who had killed others than Eleazer. The three must be heard as character witnesses, Menelli cried stupidly, and their evidence admitted. His passion irritated the bench. These alleged eye-witnesses to other crimes, said the judge coldly, might be summoned at such times as their testimony might have a bearing on the alleged misdeeds of the defendant. He added, angrily, that according to his understanding of the People's complaint, Adolf Pfefferkorn was not on trial for being a fiend but for the supposed murder of Rabbi Eleazer.

Menelli rested his case. Menelli, the theatrical battering ram, had opened no holes in the Pfefferkorn defense. The blows had spent themselves in noise and misdirection.

Calmly the three lawyers arose from the defense table and moved that the case against their client be dismissed. The bench reluctantly denied the motion. Lawyer Cantwell accepted the denial with grace. And the defense began its case.

A half-dozen character witnesses for Pfefferkorn were called, none of them Nazis. They were simple neighborhood folk who had lived near Pfefferkorn for many years. Their evidence, unchallenged by the black-browed Menelli, established Pfefferkorn as a lover of children, as an amiable and hard-working neighbor, and as a citizen respected for his honesty and kindliness.

Following these witnesses, the defense announced it had only one other witness to question before allowing Pfefferkorn himself to take the stand. Mrs. Bertha Edelberg, wife of Gustav Edelberg, the Nazi Bund lieutenant, was summoned into the courtroom. Pale-haired, timid, and full of homely fluttering simplicity, Mrs. Edelberg took her place in the witness chair and was sworn. There was a delay while defense counsel conferred. The newspapermen busied themselves with descriptions of this typical housewife and mother, shy in the limelight, with large hands that told of home chores and honest blue eyes that looked still innocent with girlhood. When counsel had permitted the quality of their witness to be sufficiently absorbed by the friendly smiling jurors, the questioning of Mrs. Edelberg began. She answered shyly, as does a woman not used to talking to strangers.

Menelli and Captain Malloy listened blankly to her answers, unaware of the direction they were taking. They had been informed that Mrs. Edelberg would be the leading Pfefferkorn character witness. Menelli had waited patiently for this single Nazi sympathizer to confront him from the stand. He had prepared a half-day of counter-questioning into the Nazi beliefs. But now Bertha Edelberg was saying things that chilled Menelli and the detective.

She had visited Pfefferkorn at his house, said Mrs. Edelberg, on the day he had brought the slippers to Father Dominic. Pfefferkorn had just returned, said Mrs. Edelberg, very happy with having pleased Father Dominic by his work. And he had told her how carefully he had made the slippers. He had even gone down into his workshop in the cellar and brought up a slipper with yellow triangles embroidered on it. This one, he said, had come out wrong because he had cut the sole too close. So he had put it aside and made another slipper to replace it.

Lawyer Cantwell held up the People's Exhibit—the slipper Malloy had identified as the one he found in the Pfefferkorn cellar. Bertha Edelberg identified it now as the one Pfefferkorn had shown her on his return from the monastery.

"He said he was getting old," said Mrs. Edelberg, smiling shyly, "because he sometimes now had to make three slippers for a customer instead of two."

Menelli stared, his eyes raging. Captain Malloy listened, expressionless.

Mrs. Edelberg finished and Menelli rose to cross-examine. This lie was the end of his case unless he could remove it. The weary expressions on the faces of the jurymen that met his angry stare told him it could never be removed by mere onslaught. It was obvious that the jurors were waiting for him to climax his hatred of Nazis by an attack on this simple and honest Hausfrau. And for the first time since he had entered on the trial of Pfefferkorn, Menelli's mind grew cool. He stood looking calmly at Mrs. Edelberg. No jury could believe that this pink-cheeked, child-like woman, so perfect a symbol of all the virtues, could lie; could lie so boldly, could invent or repeat falsely so criminal a story.

Almost pitiful in her embarrassment, she sat facing the prosecutor and waiting. Menelli studied the appealing bravery of her German smile, the doe-like flutter of her honest heart in the flush of her cheeks. As he stood with lowered head before the witness, a black-browed bull refusing the charge, Menelli weighed his chances. If he could twist the truth out of this witness, expose her lie, he would achieve— what? His lone fact, the Rabbi's slipper, would stand unrepudiated. Would it be enough to convict? For an instant Menelli marveled at the suddenly revealed bleakness of his case, this case that stood on a single slipper without another shred of evidence for support. His heart filled with nausea for his own incompetence. He could hurl himself now at this Nazi wife, torture the lie she had told. He sensed swiftly the tears that would flow from her, the cries of confusion, the pitiful appeals for aid that would break the jury's hearts. And the finish of it—when he stood discredited before this sobbing plump little matron. Menelli sighed. Already this jury hated him for his hatred of Pfefferkorn, whose guilt he had failed to prove. How much more would they hate him and how much blinder would they become to any liar's stammerings into which he could browbeat this witness if he went on now. It was not courage that left Menelli, but sanity that entered him. His own intelligence, emerging after weeks of passion, spoke to him, saying that he needed facts with which to confront Mrs. Edelberg.

"I ask permission to postpone my cross-examination for rebuttal," said Menelli and sat down.

He looked wearily at Captain Malloy. The courtroom broke into a rush of whispers. The clerk's gavel banged. The noon recess was called. The newspapermen stampeded out. They had news to flash. Menelli had struck his colors. There remained only the triumph of Pfefferkorn's own testimony. This would take an hour, and there would be a verdict before adjournment. No partisan blindness or despairing hope could doubt what this verdict would be.

In the noon streets the Nazis sang "Horst Wessel" and Pfefferkorn hymns. Of Pfefferkorn they sang that their little shoemaker was a hero sent to show the world the justice in the Nazi abhorrence of the Jew. The malignant soul behind the whimpering face of Jewry lay exposed now for the world to judge.

The crowds laughed and grew fearless of the police. They pushed Jewish-looking men and women from the sidewalks. They raised banners telling of the Plotting Jews, and marched singing through streets frequented by Jews, who stared as at a monster—that monster of their woes who had finally crossed the seas.

Menelli remained at his table in the courtroom. Newspapermen stood around him with questions. Did he still believe Pfefferkorn guilty? If Pfefferkorn were acquitted, would the state try him for the other murders? Or was the state through with Pfefferkorn and willing to let him go back to his humble shoemaking? Menelli refused to answer these questions, and the newspapermen went away. Captain Malloy appeared.

"You better get some lunch," he said.

Menelli shook his head, and Malloy sat down near him. The two men remained silent. They heard the singing and cheering through the open windows, and the cries of the newspaper extras. Malloy looked around at the vacant room. A half-dozen spectators still sat on the benches. He recognized them as members of Rabbi Eleazer's congregation. They had been present throughout the trial. Malloy saw a glint of tears in their eyes. They sat in silence, as if the court were still in session. Their faces were raised and intent, as if they were praying.

In a corner, the captain saw the black-robed figure of Father Dominic. As always, the sight of him disturbed Malloy and set something going in his head. He sniffed the secret still hidden in Father Dominic. Some day, long after the trial and its echoes were over, he would talk to the Father again. And he would continue talking to Dominic at intervals of a month, two months, a year, until he learned what it was the old Friar had locked in his head. As he stared at Dominic, Malloy knew that this case, soon over for Menelli, was only beginning for himself. He felt sorry for Menelli. Vaguely and coolly Malloy felt sorry for the Jews who would suffer from the defeat he and Menelli had brought on them. But when the detective's eyes turned to the chair in which Pfefferkorn had sat these last days beaming and eager, his face grew more rigid. Untheatric and passionless, Malloy was a better People's champion than the heavy-shouldered Menelli. He would never strike his colors.

The courtroom began to fill. The crowd brought a new silent excitement with it. There was missing the hum of greeting and discussion that usually accompanied the entrance of the Pfefferkorn audience. Judge Leak took his place on the bench. Then Pfefferkorn emerged from his door, escorted by two guards. The clerk's gavel banged, and the clerk's voice called the start of the last session of the trial. The newspapermen were already scribbling at their tables descriptions of Pfefferkorn rising and walking to the stand, being sworn, facing the crowd. These things and many others they were anticipating with their pencils. But there was a delay. Attorney Cantwell had not yet arrived. His colleague Emerson begged the Court's indulgence. Mr. Cantwell was being detained by the press at his lunch table and would be there at any moment. The judge frowned and leaned back in his chair.

The eyes of the crowd rested on Pfefferkorn. It was a Pfefferkorn grown vividly familiar. They knew every mood and mannerism of his stooped figure. But they had never heard his voice. A curious hunger to hear the voice of this over-familiar yet enigmatic figure was in the courtroom. As they had made Pfefferkorn big by their wonder and curiosity, now they waited avidly to hear him return to normal human dimensions in the sound of his voice. The suspense of a Pfefferkorn who was about to talk held the benches still, and in this silence the hundreds of eyes remained eagerly on the shoemaker.

The ticking of the clock over the judge's head became audible. From the streets below the rattle and whistle of traffic and the subdued hubbub of the crowd entered through the open windows. The pause in the courtroom deepened as if a rhythm had seized the silence.

Captain Malloy, motionless at the prosecutor's table, suddenly moved his arm as if he were about to rise. He had felt a prickling in his skin. He stiffened and his eyes turned toward Pfefferkorn. He saw nothing but a figure waiting among many other figures. Yet the prickling increased. He saw Pfefferkorn straighten in his chair. The twinkling doglike eyes widened and the thick lips parted. Malloy saw a shadow fluttering on the skin of Pfefferkorn's open throat, and knew that an artery was beating wildly.

Pfefferkorn's eyes were turning slowly toward the empty witness chair beside the judge's bench. The muscles of his jaws were set as if resisting the movement of the eyes. Yet they continued to turn. Then they stopped and stared and Malloy saw that Pfefferkorn was looking at the witness chair—staring at a point above its empty seat with terror. His mind crouching in the silence, Malloy watched. A signal, eerie and tingling, came to him telling him something was happening. This was all that Malloy could know, for the thing to be known lay beyond the world of his eyes.

Pfefferkorn was looking at the face of Rabbi Eleazer. Pale and thin and unmarked by hatchet or fire, the face of Eleazer was looking back at Pfefferkorn. The dead Rabbi sat in the witness chair. Pfefferkorn, making no sound, saw that the Rabbi's clothes were wet and out of this wetness there came to him the smell of a swamp. And though he struggled to turn away, Pfefferkorn continued to look at this pale Eleazer sitting in the witness chair and smelling of the swamp. He heard as in a dream the ticking of the clock, and felt the courtroom around him growing vague. Then as he was about to shake this phantom out of his head with a cry or a lurch from his chair, he saw the long face with the large brown eyes move. Eleazer was breathing. He was leaning slowly forward, his eyes coming nearer. Flight lifted the soul of Pfefferkorn but his body clung to the chair as if death had seized it.

"Pfefferkorn of Moravia," spoke Eleazer from the witness chair, "ancient and accursed spirit from the past, hear my words. By the power in me I command you, gilgul, ghost and demon, I summon you forth."

The Rabbi's words rang clearly in Pfefferkorn's ears and he turned his eyes slowly from side to side to see who had moved or heard. There was silence and the clock's tick. Pfefferkorn wet his lips and the grimace of his face bared his teeth. The voice of Eleazer continued wearily from the witness chair:

"Demon who was Pfefferkorn of Moravia, I have found the way for you. I have come back, gilgul, to show you the end of your road. I speak to you, tormented one, from the place of rest. Come forth, demon, and I will lead you to the grave you dream of. Deny me and you remain forever accursed and wandering outside the gates. Rise, Pfefferkorn, and let the blood on your hands proclaim you. In the name of the Almighty I summon you to tell who you are."

The courtroom suddenly moved. Heads turned. Faces bobbed. In the wait and silence, Pfefferkorn had risen to his feet, clumsily, as if being pulled from his chair. Eyes swung to him. The judge straightened behind the bench. The two defense lawyers were looking with amazement at their client. He was swaying on his feet, white-faced, and a sweat was streaming on his neck. Suddenly from the rear of the courtroom a voice cried out.

"Eleazer, Eleazer!" Dominic wailed.

Confusion filled the room, but the crowd, caught in the tension of the swaying Pfefferkorn, gaped and stayed silent as another voice was heard. It was Pfefferkorn speaking, his hands holding his head as if in agony.

"I did not make three slippers," said Pfefferkorn. "I made only two slippers."

A gavel banged. Pfefferkorn's hands rose in the air and fluttered wildly. Sweat streaming from his face, he bleated above the stir of sounds in the room.

"He brought them to my cellar. Eleazer stood in my cellar holding a candle and I killed him. Then I burned him and dragged him to the swamp. Go back, Eleazer, to the swamp. Go back. I will tell them where you lie. Go back. Wait for me. Yes—yes, I killed. I killed the other Jews. I have killed many—many others."

Pfefferkorn's voice turned to a cry that came like a sob of torment from his throat. Leaping from his seat, Captain Malloy flung his arms around him.

"Show me where he is," Malloy cried, and Pfefferkorn started for the door. Malloy clung to his arm as guards cleared the way.

Father Dominic sat in the grove of heavy-leafed maple trees and looked at the sun glistening in the garden. The foliage hung lifeless in the deep summer heat, and the inhospitable sharp light of the afternoon sun blurred the colors of the flowers. The old man frowned at the hot glare that had driven him from his work among the plants, and raised his eyes to the sky to see if clouds were forming anywhere. But the sky was empty and swollen with light, and he leaned back in his chair and turned his attention to his visitor, Captain Malloy. The detective, plagued with the heat even in the tree shadows, mopped his neck above his wilting collar, and sipped at his wine and seltzer.

"Is there any possibility," Dominic inquired of his guest, "that there will be a reprieve?"

His voice was weary and he no longer smiled when he spoke.

"No," said Malloy, "the execution takes places tomorrow morning."

"He still wishes to die?" Dominic asked.

"Yes," said Malloy. "I saw him last night. He sits in his cell covering his face and moaning for them to hurry."

"And all those friends and admirers of his," Dominic said with his tired gaze, "are they very upset?"

"Not very," said Malloy. "Their mistake seems to have brought them closer together. I heard from one of the leading Nazi organizers, who boasted proudly to me that they have recruited thousands of new members in the last two weeks."

"I am not surprised," said Dominic. "Human beings when they believe too much in themselves become always less human." He paused and sipped at his own glass. "Do they still hold meetings and denounce the Jews?" he asked.

Malloy nodded.

"Worse than ever," he said. "As far as I can make out, now they're mad at the Jews because the Jews were right. They consider that this makes them a greater menace than ever before. There's no arguing with any of them. They just hate Jews, whether they're good Jews or bad Jews, right ones or wrong ones."

"I should have liked to talk about that with Eleazer," the little Friar sighed. "He would have been able to tell us something." Looking at his guest keenly, he went on. "You have been waiting to ask me some question. Is it about why I prayed all night for Eleazer after he left the monastery?"

"I have figured that out," said Malloy, "by myself."

"What is it then?" said Dominic. "Is it about something I did in the courtroom?"

"Yes, said Malloy, "that's it."

He smiled at the Friar. "You called out Eleazer's name," he said.

"Nobody remembers that but you," said Dominic. "Why should it bother you?"

"I would like to know," said Malloy.

"The papers have been very informative," Dominic said, with the ghost of a smile on his lips. "They have explained that Pfefferkorn's guilt produced a hallucination for his eyes. You have read what the doctors said, my son. Why ask for more?"

"But you called out his name before Pfefferkorn had spoken," said Malloy. He hesitated a moment and then asked: "Did you see him?"

"Eleazer?"

Malloy nodded.

"I saw him," said the little Friar. "His clothes were wet but his face was pale and unmarked. His eyes looked a little tired. I am very sorry I called his name so loudly. Eleazer must have smiled at me in his heart for being so surprised. It has worried me a great deal since it happened—that I was so surprised."

Malloy waited for him to pause.

"Then it was a miracle," he said quietly.

"Yes," said Dominic, looking away to see some clouds forming in the sky. "It was a miracle. But not Eleazer's coming back and appearing in the court. That was only natural. It was no more than one would expect of a soul as wise and holy as Eleazer's."

"Then what was the miracle, Father?" Malloy persisted.

Father Dominic's eyes became sad.

"The miracle was," he said, "that there were twelve men in the world who believed the truth. That there were twelve human beings sitting together in a box who believed also that it was wrong to kill Jews. It must be that these twelve men were on the side of Humanity. This shows a certain progress in the world . . . which may be considered miraculous."

The old man sighed and picked up the crucifix at the end of his rosary. He made a motion of blessing, and added quietly:

"Forgive me, I have some work to do."

Malloy watched him as he moved quickly to a flower patch and knelt on the earth. As the black-robed figure leaned over the blooms, Malloy saw that his lips were moving and that the little Friar was chattering to himself. . . .

The Pink Hussar

THERE ARE many kinds of refugees in our land these days and, as is customary with people who carry too large a load of troubles, they are not among the most popular of folks. We Americans have hearts as open and unsnobbish as a drive-in frankfurter stand but we are, nevertheless, a cynical lot. We are gifted with a sort of national schizophrenia, or split personality. We will play Galahad but we know the fight is fixed.

After we have whooped with piety and brotherly love it is our habit to sit down and sneer at ourselves. And having gone to war to save Europe from losing its soul, it is natural for us, as schizos, that we should become full of carping attitudes toward this aforesaid soul of Europe.

There is, however, a tribe of refugees who are more or less unknown to our citizenry, which is unfortunate, for they are a truly charming lot and could do much to popularize the continental exiles.

These are the talents from Vienna and Budapest—the little world of song and play writers, actors, journalists and bon vivants—that has fled its beloved cafés and brought its intrigues and goulash pots intact to the U. S. A. They differ from all the other refugees because they are not refugees at all—since it is in their power to bring the best of their homeland to our shores—themselves. Their homeland is an ego surrounded by wit and good cooking. It is a Strauss Waltz and a handful of epigrams and a touch of gout. They were the hurdy-gurdy of art and letters that played in the last little charming corner of Europe, that favored anecdotes above panaceas and that, to the very end, sat polishing jests instead of sabers. Had there been enough of them, they might have laughed the Nazis out of countenance and conquest. But there were only a few cafés full and their tunes and witticisms were outnumbered by the Panzer cannon.

It is of these spritely folks I write—a task a little hazardous, for sitting among them I have heard a thousand and one tales, plots, jests and ironies—and do I put one of these on paper I will be sued for plagiarism instanter. For plagiarism suits are as firm a part of Magyar culture as double-decker pastries. In fact, the joke runs that in the golden days of Hungarian letters the first thing a Budapest playwright said to his valet on awakening with a Pilsener hangover was, "Well, Rudolph, whom do I sue today?"

Luckily the story I have to tell is one that actually happened under my nose, and do any of my Hungarian or Viennese admirers detect in it similarities to plays or novels they have themselves composed, I have a whole file of newspaper clippings to testify for me and I am certain I will escape with only a small fine plus court costs.

The most interesting thing that struck me about these famous exiles, when I first met them two years ago, was that I had never heard of them before. I had friends who sighed at the mention of their names and murmured, "Ah, Budapest—ah, Vienna." But not having been abroad since 1920 and having attended strictly to my American knitting, the galaxy of the Danube was unknown to me.

My introduction to this most amiable tribe of refugees was as unexpected and whimsical as if it had been written by one of them. I was engaged at the time in a sort of Desperate Desmond enterprise—that of raising money to produce a movie in New York. There is no reason to produce movies in New York, considering they can be done as easily as tossing cards into a hat in Hollywood. But a contrariness and a childlike fascination with high finance have urged me on several occasions into New York cinema production.

After several conferences with a bank president, I had been assured that the bank would put up half the finances needed were I able to lay hands on the other half. This is not such a bonanza as it sounds. It is exactly like being promised the Lackawanna Railroad, providing you can go out and buy the New York Central first. The sum involved, known as the second money, was $200,000 and no cents.

My delight at meeting Mr. Vinsey was thus deep and genuine. For it was Vinsey who, appearing out of the blue in my hotel-room money-raising headquarters, not only offered me $200,000 as casually as if he were proffering a bite out of an apple, but inducted me almost immediately into the ghost cities of Budapest and Vienna.

Mr. Vinsey had read my script, he told me after he had sat down and put his red-feathered green fedora on his knees, and he considered it a superb and lucrative piece of property. He begged to be allowed to place the $200,000 I needed in my hands.

I saw a smiling, relaxed man in his fifties, with a round face, a look of surprise to his fluff of grey hair, with a soothing, cynical voice and an air about him of a child playing hookey.

He sat looking at me over his green fedora as if he were at home among his oldest friends. I have seldom met a man so instantly likeable as Vinsey and, sensing he was someone of importance, I felt embarrassed never to have heard of him. Vinsey put me at my ease by reciting in an apologetic voice his list of achievements. They included the production of nine movies—three of which had won some sort of prizes—and thirty-seven plays in Hungary and Austria. I had never heard of the plays, the movies, the prizes, or of Vinsey.

"But my poor accomplishments are of no matter to you," he smiled. "What you want from me is $200,000. Am I right?"

I nodded.

"It will be very easy," said Vinsey. "We will be partners. I shall provide the money; you, the brains. It is for you an unfair arrangement. But one, alas, which the artist must always make in our mismanaged civilization."

"It's a very fine arrangement," I said happily, "and if we make it, you can have sixty per cent of the profits."

This was the statement that usually produced a snort and a string of morbid statistics from the potential second money to the effect that no New York movie production had ever grossed enough to return the hind end or second money part of the investment. Mr. Vinsey's answer was the opposite of such crudity.

"Oh, no," he said, "I could not allow that. Sixty per cent would make me your chief. I shall take only forty-nine per cent and be flattered to work under your talents in a most humble and advisory capacity."

There was an Alice in Wonderland sound to this interview, but honesty of a kind that cannot be simulated signalled from the Vinsey ego. Yet a man may be as honest as Abraham Lincoln and still not have $200,000 handy for a dubious investment.

Accordingly, I asked, "When do you think you can get the money?"

"By Monday afternoon," Mr. Vinsey smiled. "Over the week-end. You may forget about all financial problems from now on. Consider your work already in production. It is a beautiful thing and is certain to win a prize."

"Then I'll see you Monday," I said.

"Yes." Mr. Vinsey stood. "But let us have dinner tonight at a friend's house and become more acquainted."

I made inquiry before dinner time and learned that everything Vinsey had told me of himself was true. The only new fact I uncovered was that he had produced two plays since his arrival in New York and that they both had been immediate flops.

The dinner that night was in the home of Gita Lengel, the Bernhardt of Budapest and the Duse of Vienna. None of these things I knew about Gita when I met her. My first impression was that she was related in some way to Vinsey—probably his sister. The same witty smile widened her mouth, the same relaxed and good-natured tones issued from it and the same graceful buzz of personality surrounded her. She was a woman of thirty-eight and I would have called her beautiful if she had had less charm. As it was I called her delightful.

We were joined for dinner by a third refugee, a handsome and boyish man of forty. He, too, struck me as a relative, both of Vinsey and Miss Lengel.

Vinsey introduced the new dinner guest.

"My favorite dramatic critic, Janos Fulka," he said.

"Oh, no," said Gita, "novelist, essayist, and philosopher."

"He is my favorite dramatic critic," Vinsey said, "because he has given up that profession."

Fulka bowed slightly and looked very cynical as he smiled.

"I have given up none of my professions," he said. "I am improving myself secretly in all of them."

"Janos and Vinsey once fought a duel over an adjective," said Gita, "but it turned out to have been a printer's error. Something like the word compatible being changed to contemptible."

We ate chicken paprikash and Vinsey broke the news to his friends of our partnership. A great surge of excitement swept the table. Kisses were exchanged. A fresh bottle of wine was opened. I was treated for a few minutes to the joyous finale of a Viennese operetta.

When the huzzahs had subsided, Vinsey looked tenderly at our hostess and said, "It is too bad we have no part for Europe's greatest actress." Fulka immediately seized one of her hands and kissed it.

"I still live on the memory of your Nora," he sighed.

"And of Julie," Vinsey cried, "and the Princess Rividavia. You put over *The Sofa*."

I didn't know *The Sofa* was in capital letters and looked a little startled.

"Turay's *The Sofa*," Fulka explained. There was a pause and they all looked at me. "You have heard of Turay?" Vinsey inquired.

"Good Lord, yes," I said, "one of the best playwrights left in the world."

The three sighed. Their faces glowed and they nodded in unison as at a prayer meeting.

"Gita's second-act curtain in *The Sofa* was one of the greatest laughs in the history of the theater," said Fulka.

"For two seasons," Vinsey cooed. "I watched her every night."

The partnership was for the moment forgotten and both men looked at Gita with such homage as might have been given the queen of an ancient realm.

"There is nothing for me in your script," said Gita—I was to find that this delightful woman had read every unproduced script on Broadway—"but, truly, the pleasure of reading it was as great as acting in it. Believe me—and have some more wine."

"The theater of New York," said Fulka, "may be measured by this fact that Gita Lengel is not on its stage. This is exactly the same as if the United States decided to win the present war by immobilizing its fleet."

"My accent," said Gita, "and my stubbornness."

"Quite right," said Vinsey. "She has turned down excellent parts."

"A maid with a duster," said Gita, "who turns out to be the head of a gang of black marketers. And a mother who begs the governor to pardon her son from the electric chair." Gita looked pathetically at me. "Those are the two parts that have been offered—with salaries. I am not silly. I would have played them. I would play a cabbage or the hind legs of a horse—just to be on the stage again. But those plays! My dear —unbearable!"

"One of them is still running," Vinsey sighed.

"So is the war," said Gita. "Duration is no virtue for calamities."

"Tell me"—Fulka glared at me as he patted her arm—"how is it that in a city like New York with seven million adults you have a theater only for children?"

"It is the critics!" Vinsey smiled. "They are in a plot to keep the theater inferior to themselves. They like to look down instead of up— because if they look up there is too far to look."

"Worse than that," said Fulka, "the critics of New York are so old and so fat that they usually collapse before the final curtain. As a result, they do not report the play but their own symptoms."

"Schopenhauer wrote the perfect line about critics," said Vinsey moodily. "'When a jackass looks into a mirror you must not expect an apostle to look out.'"

"Poor Janos," Gita sighed, "you will never be a critic in New York.

You always admired plays that were either too deep for your understanding or too brilliant to make jokes about."

Guests began arriving as we were finishing our dinner—and as the room filled I felt as if a land of charm and curious customs was coming to life around us. I met Dr. Alper-Mayer, a portly dark-haired gentleman with a short square beard and a useless medical fame in his bow; and Stephan Holz, a thin-faced tight-mouthed painter with an overdeveloped sense of courtesy. Fulka whispered to me that his was the most vitriolic brush in Austria. A jowled and beaming playwright named Herzog appeared, and a tense young lady in a sort of peasant dress who looked as dedicated to something as an Ibsen heroine. There arrived a fragile brunette with white lace at her throat and a delicious voice that seemed to be produced by a zither and who turned out, on a second inspection, to be not twenty years old, but sixty. She was Lili Marisca, a musical comedy star with the names of Friml, Lehar, and Strauss in her diadem. And lastly, a gentleman named Lazlo with a paunch full of laughter. He announced joyfully that he was ready for a second dinner.

"Lazlo begins eating at seven o'clock," Vinsey explained to me, "and continues until after midnight. It is a difficult career in wartime. Luckily he is highly in demand at dinner parties."

"Play your new waltz, Lazlo darling," said Gita, "and I'll see if there is any chicken left."

Lazlo played and the company listened like a group of doting relatives. I heard a lilting gallant bit of music that seemed to say, "Dance with me, love with me, and forget how old and far away we are."

This was my first of many evenings in the ghost land of Budapest and Vienna. But during these original hours I learned all I was ever to know about its witty citizens. I was never to know how they kept alive, what mysterious means made possible the chicken paprikash, the wine bottles, and the pleasant apartments. Nor was I to learn until the day of the Unbelievable Plot whether failure had secretly embittered them or the memory of vanished fame left them with hidden wounds. For they apparently had only one face for life, the face of talent that remains intact whatever else has crumbled.

Vinsey spent a month trying to raise the $200,000 for our movie and kept assuring me daily that the project was a few hours from completion. I assured him in return that the delay was of no consequence and that I would not be ready to shoot the movie until the Fall.

"Ah, by that time," Vinsey smiled, "we will have twice that much in the bank. In the meantime, we remain partners without capital—but a future," he sighed. "It would have been so simple once in Budapest. I had only to pick up my telephone, and wagons full of gold drew up to my office. Here the telephone is not such a magic instrument."

The Unbelievable Plot began a few nights later with the arrival of a startling Vinsey at my hotel.

"I am very upset," he said, after downing three beakers of beer in silence, "and I have come to you to talk because I love and trust you."

"Just what is it?" I asked.

"Turay," said Vinsey in a voice of doom. "Turay is coming to America. He leaves Lisbon today. He will be in New York in no time."

I looked at Vinsey with some surprise. Turay, as the greatest living Hungarian, and perhaps European, playwright, seemed hardly a visitor to wring such groans from a fellow refugee.

"Why, that's marvelous," I said. "I'm glad to hear that Turay is alive and bringing his greatness to our city."

Vinsey groaned again.

"What's the trouble?" I asked. "Is he an enemy of yours?"

"I adore him," said Vinsey softly. "He was my God for thirty years. Since I am a boy I have sat at his feet—as have all the writers and actors and critics of Budapest and Vienna. Turay"—Vinsey's eyes grew misty —"ah, if there is a graceful soul and a fountain of wit left in the world, it wears that name. You have had many charming talents in this country. Put them all together, all the poets and lovers and brilliant playwrights and happy story-tellers—and you have, perhaps, Turay. No, not a full Turay. Such a one could only exist in Budapest."

"Then why are you beating your bosom over his arrival here?" I asked.

"Because," said Vinsey softly, "he must not come. It is wrong for him to come. He must not do what we have all done—on a smaller scale—change from a man of fame into an eccentric nobody. Dear friend," Vinsey's voice throbbed, "we all admire your country. And New York—ah, it is the last of the Ali Baba cities. But it is a curious robber—the new world. It robs the old of its glitter, its meaning, its importance. My friends whom you have met. Myself. We were all great men. The press was filled with our achievements. The public adored us. That was in Budapest, in Vienna. Here in New York, what are we?

Nobodies. We make jokes, we write plays, we paint pictures, we hold salons, we do everything we ever did—and we are still nobodies. The ear of your country is not for our jokes. Our wit dies at your feet."

Vinsey paused and handed me a cablegram. It was no climax to his eloquence. It read only, "Arrive, Dodo."

"That is the first word of English he has written," Vinsey groaned.

"Are your friends as upset as you?" I asked.

"Oh, completely," said Vinsey. "Even Dr. Alper-Mayer. Dr. Alper-Mayer is a great intellect. He was the very leading physician of Vienna. Turay's own doctor. And Schuschnigg's. The most expensive and complicated diseases sought him out. And here he is able to find neither patients nor even an office and is mistaken by everybody for a vaudevillian out of work. I spoke to him before I came to you. Turay, he said, must not come to New York. He must not be defeated here as we have been. As a result of such a thing we may all end up by committing suicide. Not Turay, mind you. But us. People, you must know, can suffer a great deal as long as a symbol of their success remains somewhere alive. Turay has been such a symbol for us. To see him fail, as we have—that would be the unbearable thing for us."

"But why must he fail?" I asked.

"Ah," Vinsey sighed, burying his nose in a fourth beaker, "the critics!"

I waited at Gita's home for the great entrance. The party was in honor of Turay and the ghost cities were assembled in full. The three rooms—including the dining room—were packed with celebrities who had lost their names.

The playwright had arrived in New York in the afternoon. This was his welcoming party, his safe-from-home-coming. During the hour I waited I learned a number of surprising things about my friends Gita, Fulka, Andri, Marisca, Holz, Dr. Alper-Mayer, and Vinsey. I learned them from strangers who, finding me in their midst, imagined I knew everything that was known to them.

Gita had been Turay's wife some fifteen years ago. Marisca had once been married to Turay thirty years ago. And Andri, the young Ibsen heroine, had been Madam Turay five years ago. Fulka had left his own wife twelve years ago and stolen Gita from Turay. And twenty-five years ago Vinsey had stolen Marisca from the great playwright. On the other hand, Turay had lured away Vinsey's three later wives from his keep. As of today, the grey-tufted Vinsey was desperately in love with Gita, who, however, had given her oath to Fulka that she would marry him—as soon as she got a job; although it was the opinion of several of the guests that it was not the job that stood between Gita and Fulka but the ghost of Turay, whom she had never ceased to love during the twelve years despite her two subsequent marriages and present betrothal.

This all seemed a little confusing but what most confused me was the fact that I had been dining almost nightly with these fanatic wife and husband snatchers and had never detected anything but an innocent camaraderie among them.

I was talking to the Countess Graudenz, a former opera star whose beauty was now a little dimmed by overeating.

"What about Dr. Alper-Mayer and Holz, the painter?" I asked. "Are they related to, let us say, Turay?"

"Dr. Alper-Mayer was married to Gita after she ran off with Fulka," said the diva, "and Holz—my God, Holz is the father of the two children Turay raised in Paris. He supported them for twenty years. But I thought you knew that."

"No, I didn't," I confessed to the Countess, and the silence of a curtain-raising came over the room. It was Turay. He stood in the doorway and smiled on the ghostland before him. And this moment of silence was like a salvo of ghostly applause. The eyes of those around me—eyes that were the connoisseurs of mockery—grew misty. And though no one wept, there was the smile of tears as if, not a man of fame, but a beloved child had returned to them.

This was true. The thing that distinguished this great man in the doorway was a quality of childishness. Or he might have been a wide-mouthed, gentle-eyed clown come to amuse other children. He was tall and plump about the waist and the sleeves of his rumpled coat were a bit too long. His grey hair slanted in a boyish mop across his forehead and his face was pink. Looking at this smiling and abstracted face, full of innocence and mockery, I realized where Vinsey, Fulka, Gita, Lazlo, and all my new friends had got their expression. They had borrowed it from Turay—for he resembled all of them except that he looked a little dreamier.

The silence was now over and there was talk and laughter as if nothing had happened. There was no rush of handshaking and no crowding of admirers around a hero. He had sat down at a table in a corner with four friends and was nibbling at a platter of cheese. The rest of the company occupied itself with the business of gossip and jest; but, though they seemed to ignore the arrival, there was a verve that had not been in their manner before. Sitting quietly in a corner, eating his cheese, Turay was among them—and all was now right in their ghostland.

Vinsey brought me to the table. Turay was telling a story, and Dr. Alper-Mayer, Fulka, Gita, and the hungry Lazlo were listening to him as attentively as if they were seated in a schoolroom.

"I was young at the time," the pink face and the grey hair were saying, "nineteen years old. I had been in the country on a vacation for three weeks and now I come running back to Budapest because my heart is breaking and I cannot endure to be away from the lady I worship. Ah, if I could only remember her name now, the story would sound a little better. I come, out of breath, to the house, the magic house where she lives. I ring the bell. I wait and I die of suspense.

"Then the door opens and a strange young woman is standing there. She has just moved in with her family. My adored one has just moved out, leaving no address. I stand looking at the young woman and I am so unhappy I begin to cry. That night I figure for the first time in my life that I will commit suicide. And I go back to say goodbye to the magic house. Here I meet the strange young woman again. And I do not commit suicide but, instead, I marry her a month later. And this is the theme of my new play—that marriage is a search for somebody who has disappeared when you are young."

Vinsey asked softly, "The new play, is it done, Dodo?"

"Yes, I finished it on the plane," Turay smiled. "You do not expect a playwright to come to market without a basket of fresh eggs."

"You have a title for it?" Vinsey sighed.

"I call it *The Pink Hussar*," said Turay, and added with an apologetic smile, "Do you think it sounds a little old-fashioned?"

"My dear friend," Fulka spoke up loyally, "Turay makes his own fashions. Is that right, Gita?"

"Yes, always, always," Gita laughed, and Turay's eyes widened innocently at the drama in her voice. Then with a smile he took her hand and, looking around the room said, gently, "We are all here. All except Immelmans, the waiter. I miss his dirty apron."

"What a play that was," Fulka cried, and explained for my sake, "a one-acter. Immelmans was the hero. Ah, his exit with the coffeepot spilling! You remember, Gita?"

Fulka laughed, overcome, and Lazlo interrupted.

"Do you remember the waltz in *A Handful of Isoldes*?" He began to hum.

"There was no music in the 'Isoldes,'" Gita said.

"Off-stage, off-stage!" Lazlo cried. "The waltz when you were dying.

During that long speech—when the little orchestra in the café downstairs drowns you out. My God, such is fame!"

"I will never forget the night you lost your voice," Dr. Alper-Mayer smiled. "The opening night of *The Sofa* when I gave you the electric shock in the larynx. It was the first time in Europe this treatment was ever used."

"She could only speak in a whisper," said Vinsey, "and I chased all over Budapest looking for Turay to make him write in the line, 'The Princess Rividavia has a cold.' "

"What a characterization that was!" Fulka sighed and added, "Of course, it was a great play."

"They were all great plays," said Vinsey. "Masterpieces."

"*The Pink Hussar* is much better," said Turay slyly, "at least so it seems to me."

I had decided to see if money could be raised in Hollywood for a New York movie production and spent the next three weeks shaking futilely at the Hollywood Christmas tree. Nothing fell from it but advice. But there was still Vinsey. Vinsey was waiting for me on my return but not with $200,000. He was in a state of shock and apparently had forgotten entirely the matter of our partnership.

"The very worst thing has happened," he told me at dinner. "No. Order for yourself. I cannot eat. Even Lazlo cannot eat. We are all very, very upset."

"About Turay," I said.

"Naturally," said Vinsey. "He has sold his play. It is going into production. It is like waiting for a massacre."

"I'd like to read the script," I said.

"It is not necessary," Vinsey sighed. "I will tell you all you have to know. It is beautifully written. Very tender. Extremely cynical. In short, Turay. And it is also as full of failure as a broken-down old actor. My God, the critics will kill it!"

"You can't always tell," I said.

"You can tell about *The Pink Hussar*," Vinsey groaned. "Four plays exactly like it—all stolen from Turay—were produced last year. By four of our best Hungarians. Did you happen to see them? They were cut to ribbons by the critics. One of the playwrights—Fodor—is still in bed moaning. Believe me, *The Pink Hussar* has even less chance. It is half fantasy. It has one speech three pages long. Guess who recites it? God. And He is not even on the stage. The stage is empty for three pages. No, there is no chance. The critics will have a feast. Turay *en brochette*. When I tell you that thirty people who love Turay better than their own fathers and mothers have read *The Pink Hussar* and all said the same thing—you will understand how there is nothing but doom ahead. Even Gita. She cried for two nights after Turay sold it. He has not sold a play, she said. He has arranged for his funeral."

"Who's producing it?" I asked.

"Jock Kane," Vinsey said, "the final black wreath on top of the hearse."

I knew Jock. He had once produced a play of mine. In those days he had been a puissant man of the Broadway theater, and hailed to the ends of the earth as a wizard. In the space of five years he had been demoted by the critics from wizardhood to oblivion, which, on Broadway, is not so far a throw as it sounds. The critics run an elevator service between these two points—with no stop-overs.

At his peak as a wizard, Mr. Kane had produced nine flops in a row. There was this, however, to say for him: Disaster had not tempered the man. In clover or in limbo, there was never a more nerve-wracking, macaw-souled figure connected with the Broadway scene than Jock Kane. With his talents and his gold petals fallen from him, and the maniacal bloom of his certainties and wizardries gone to dust, he remained a noxious weed-like fellow sticking in your eye.

"Jock used to be quite a genius," I said. "He may have a rebirth."

"When Jock Kane is reborn," said Vinsey, "it will be as a tarantula. He is a vicious, greedy, and unscrupulous man who knows nothing and has the quality of a murderer."

Vinsey watched me eat for a spell and then went on: "On top of his faults, he has a virtue which is even worse. He loves Turay. He sits around listening to Dodo and rolling his eyes like a little girl up to her neck in art. And already he has swindled him. Five per cent less royalties. A pitiful advance, only. And no say by Turay in the casting. He begged, practically on his knees, that Gita should play the lead. She would be perfect. But Mr. Kane, who loves him like a brother and Gita like an uncle, would not even consider it. Also, Mr. Kane has taken an extra twenty-five per cent from Turay out of the movie rights. But this matters nothing. There will be no royalties, no movie sale. There will be only a funeral."

Vinsey drew a deep breath and repeated his cry of a month ago, "It must not be. We must save Turay from becoming one of us—another broken-down genius from Budapest who eats chicken paprikash and tries to remember who he was. Dear friend, I have a mission. I am going to prevent the New York critics from wiping out the last bit of glory that belongs to Budapest. Gita Lengel is a bum, Fulka is a bum. Lazlo, Holz, Dr. Alper-Mayer, Fodor, Marisca, Litauer, Vinsey —we are all bums. But Turay is going to stay Turay."

Vinsey's eyes were glowing and he leaned forward with the air of a conspirator under a pier.

"Will you help in our cause and be a member of our committee?" he whispered.

I nodded.

"Then I will call for you tomorrow at seven," said Vinsey. "The producer is giving the celebration for the opening of rehearsals at Gita's home. Mr. Jock Kane dislikes public restaurants where the check inter- feres with the camaraderie."

I joined Vinsey and Fulka in the hotel lobby at seven.

"We are an hour early," Vinsey greeted me. "The dinner is at eight. We will spend the hour here, discussing the plot."

Fulka looked around, nervously.

"I think I saw the critic for the *Journal* in the dining room," he said. "He might afterward get suspicious."

"A creature who is deaf, dumb, and blind is immune to suspicious- ness," said Vinsey.

"Let me recite the plot," said Fulka.

"By all means," Vinsey said. "I will not interrupt."

"The critics of New York," said Fulka, "once loved Turay. Twenty years ago, even twelve years ago, they considered him one of the world's greatest. Even today they are willing to admire him as a museum piece. What we are going to do"—Fulka stared at me—"is arrange for the critics to hail *The Pink Hussar* when it opens, and fill the city with their love of Turay."

I stared back at Fulka and then at Vinsey. It seemed odd that two such witty men should take leave of reason together.

"What are you going to do?" I asked. "Bribe the critics?"

"In a way, yes," said Fulka. "Tonight Turay is going to be taken ill. Desperately ill."

"Dying," said Vinsey, happily.

"He is going to be rushed to the hospital," Fulka went on. "Dr. Alper-Mayer will attend him. In the morning the papers will be full."

"Turay stricken as his last and finest play goes into rehearsal," sighed Vinsey.

"And then," continued Fulka, "he will remain unconscious. His death will be assured. A matter of days. Perhaps hours."

"Wait a minute," I said. "Does Turay know about this?"

"Good heavens, no!" said Fulka. "We are not consulting him in any way."

"Then how is he going to get sick?" I asked.

Vinsey drew a small bottle out of his coat pocket.

"In his coffee tonight," he said quietly. "It is tasteless."

"What's in it?" I asked.

"I don't know the name," said Vinsey. "Dr. Alper-Mayer prepared it. Two spoonfuls will produce a heavy perspiration and also unconsciousness."

"He will have the seizure after he drinks the coffee," said Fulka. "Tomorrow when he wakes up in the hospital, we will give him another spoonful at noon. There is no danger. It is entirely harmless and even good for the nerves."

"That part of the whole thing is in Dr. Alper-Mayer's hands," said Vinsey. "We will work in another direction. The publicity."

"On the night of the opening of *The Pink Hussar*," Fulka said, "Turay will be in his last coma. Imagine the effect this will have on the critics. And the first-nighters as well. They will be listening not to a play but a swan song. Turay dying will be like an orchestra playing sweetly in the wings. The reviews will be simply sensational. And then Turay will recover slowly."

"And retire," said Vinsey. "Another deathbed would give the show away."

"You need worry about nothing," Vinsey whispered as we rang Gita's bell. "Everybody has been assigned a part to play."

"How about Kane?" I asked. "Is he in on it?"

"My God, no!" said Vinsey. "I would not trust a crook like Kane with an old shoe."

"We have saved the best news for you as a surprise," Fulka whispered. "There will be two critics at the dinner. Two big ones."

"That's a little dangerous," I protested.

"My dear friend," Vinsey smiled, "have no worry. We are the best actors in the world."

The room was filled. There were three aliens in ghostland—Jock Kane and two of the leading drama savants of the press. Fourteen of us sat at the table. Laughter rang. Witticisms bounced about like ping-pong balls. I looked nervously at the two captive critics, fearful that they recognize all this gaiety as that of a cast performing. But, no. They sat smiling politely through the great scene, hiding the discomfort of their wallflower souls in an air of tolerance and superiority. Their manner spoke that it was a noisy old-fashioned evening worthy of the museum piece who sat pensively at the head of the table. I wondered at this pensiveness and thought several times that I noted a frown on the child-like pink face.

Vinsey explained to me in a whisper as we left the table and scattered about the room for our coffee.

"Dodo is angry," he said. "He thinks we are trying too much to impress the critics with how gay and witty we are. He has an excellent sense of the theater. How he would enjoy the scene, if he only knew what it was."

Lazlo went to the piano.

"Dear ladies and gentlemen," he announced, puffing with four helpings of goulash, "I have arranged especially in honor of Mr. Turay a medley of his favorite songs—going back to when we were both boys together and in the cafes of Budapest they were singing——"

Lazlo began to play and the contralto of the Countess Graudenz sounded softly.

"Is it not beautiful?" Fulka whispered at my side. "He is going to die—with the music of his youth playing in his ears."

I looked at Turay who was frowning abstractedly over a coffee cup. The song ended and another tune was begun and then, suddenly—although I had been expecting it—Gita's voice cried out in fright.

Turay had dropped the coffee cup. He was swaying in his chair, his head rolling from side to side. Then, with a sigh, audible in the silenced room, the pink face and the grey hair slid to the rug.

The morrow found the committee gaping at victory. The newspapers showered manna. We convened in my room, behind locked doors.

"Look at this one," said Vinsey and read aloud in a lover's voice, " 'The stricken Turay's position in the theater is a high one. With G. Bernard Shaw he is the last of the Great Contemporaries.' "

"This one is better," said Fulka, and read, " 'For the past twenty-five years Turay has been regarded as one of the theater's pillars of wit and ideas.' "

"Perfect, perfect," Vinsey beamed. "We have, without question, scored a triumph."

I asked after Turay's condition.

"He was just recovering consciousness when we left the hospital," said Fulka. "Gita is with him, being very brave—for the photographers."

"She should never have gone to the hairdresser's," Fulka frowned.

"Nonsense," said Vinsey; "she is giving a magnificent performance. Tomorrow Marisca will do even better. And Wednesday, Andri. I am coaching her."

"On the whole, we have nothing to worry about," said Fulka. "Dr. Alper-Mayer remains at the bedside. At four o'clock he will administer a second dose. And the thing will grow by itself."

Vinsey read from another paper, "—a heart condition that holds small hope for recovery. As the brilliant dramatist himself has so often written—the final curtain falls slowly."

The old showman looked up.

"It is like the old days," he sighed. "Everything happens just as we dreamed."

For four days the committee sat on top of the world. The Unbelievable Plot was surpassing all their dreams of it. The press had taken the bit in its teeth and there was no need for publicity spurs. It offered interviews with Gita, Andri and Marisca, the three lovely ex-wives of Turay, and all at his bedside weeping in exotic unison—a scene the gifted playwright himself might have written. It told of messages from kings and coachmen, from big and little celebrities all over the world. It carried stories of the actors rehearsing in *The Pink Hussar* who had sent the dying dramatist a great box of flowers and saluted him with the words, "Master, whatever happens, we will make the world gay once more with your wit." Under their photograph one paper printed, "Turay's Last Cast. While the playwright lies dying, the theater he loved answers with its tender battle cry, 'The show goes on.'"

By Sunday the style of all the leading dramatic critics had undergone a change. They wheeled out whimsicalities and greeted the Grim Reaper hovering over the Hungarian genius as if they were Turays all, sprightly and wistful before disaster and never forgetting that life was a Waltz. It was all highly wonderful and the committee reeled about in its cups, giddy with the Hungarian renaissance that had smote the town—until the fifth day.

Vinsey brought me the news. He was white, his eyes were bloodshot, his hands fluttered like fans. He entered, collapsed on the couch and sat moaning.

"Something gone wrong?" I said.

He nodded.

I asked what it was.

"It is too terrible to think about," Vinsey groaned. I poured him a large drink, which he swallowed abstractedly.

"Turay is sick," he said hoarsely.

"I know that," I said; "he's dying."

"Please, no!" Vinsey cried. "Don't say that! Don't!" He clapped both hands to his head and weaved as his eyes overran. "We have done something awful. It is the judgment of God."

"I'm waiting to hear," I said.

"I am telling you," Vinsey cried. "Turay is ill. He is unconscious. He cannot talk."

"You mean honestly ill?" I said.

"Honestly unconscious," Vinsey groaned. "Dr. Alper-Mayer did not give him the medicine yesterday. We were skipping a day. The committee had agreed that Turay should regain consciousness so he could make a little statement for the press. For his sake, you understand. He would never forgive us if we did not give him a little speaking part in his death scene."

Vinsey shuddered and I handed him another drink.

"Dr. Alper-Mayer telephoned me at nine," he whispered. "I flew to the hospital. There he was. Lying there, unconscious. Turay in a coma. A real coma."

"What does the doctor think it is?" I asked.

"He doesn't know." Vinsey wiped his eyes. "He examined him for two hours. The heart is beating—but that is all. I tell you we have killed him"—he raised his voice—"the greatest mind in Europe."

"The medicine was harmless," I assured him. "I took some myself for a sleeping dose."

"It is not the medicine," Vinsey said. "It is the shock. Turay found out he was dying. Somebody must have left a newspaper by the bed. He read it while he was only half drugged. A sensitive soul like his. A mind so delicate, so open to phenomena! It reads it is dying. And it dies. It is psychological murder. We are a committee of murderers."

"What's being done?" I asked.

"Gita and Marisca have gone to church to pray," Vinsey whispered. "Fulka wants to give himself up to the police. Dr. Alper-Mayer has ordered some kind of a life-saving apparatus. And Lazlo and I have agreed to be buried on the same day with him—one on each side." Vinsey held out his empty glass and murmured, "A few last drops."

The committee crowded the hospital waiting room. Lazlo arrived last with all the afternoon papers. We listened as he read in a husky voice, " 'The scene around the dying playwright is a page out of Murget's *La Vie de Bohème*. It is a wake of wit. Each of his old cronies vies with the other in gay reminiscences of Turay's spicy sixty-two years. Jests fly and chuckles sound, but behind the mirth is the tear of a waltz ending.' "

"That was yesterday," Fulka groaned.

" 'The waltzes of Budapest play on,' " Lazlo continued reading.

"Shut up about waltzes," Gita cried from the chair. The committee breathed heavily and avoided looking at one another.

Dr. Alper-Mayer appeared. His beard glistened but his voice was calm. He bowed in front of me and said, "Mr. Turay wishes to speak to you, sir."

"He is alive!" Gita cried.

"We have rallied him slightly," said Dr. Alper-Mayer. "Ice packs. Adrenalin. The mass drip. Electricity. We have overlooked nothing."

"Is there hope?" Vinsey trembled.

"We are struggling with a hypnotic state," Dr. Alper-Mayer said. "The life force is gone."

"Think of it," Fulka moaned, "Turay should become a zombi!"

"Not quite," Dr. Alper-Mayer said. "There are left a few organs that have not become cataleptic. We are working on these."

"But if he can speak," Lazlo cried, "that means—"

"Nothing." Dr. Alper-Mayer interrupted firmly. "He will go under in a few minutes. It is only a flicker. Please remember I have had many similar cases in Vienna and Berlin. Hurry, please."

I followed him to the sickroom. He opened the door.

"I will wait outside," he said. "He wishes to see you alone. At such a time we humor the aberration."

He closed the door behind me and I was alone with the dying Turay. I stared down at the wasted face on the pillow and a distaste for Hungarian plots overcame me.

"Get me two bars of chocolate, please," the playwright whispered without opening his eyes, "and, if possible, a liverwurst sandwich. Soon as you can."

I stared.

"And be so kind to break the needle on that damn machine." The blue eyes opened and scowled sleepily at the intravenous drip apparatus. "I need a collaborator," he sighed. "It is too big a production to handle by myself."

"Your friends outside," I began, "I'll call them."

"My God, no—please!" Turay whispered. "I will explain. I am

nearly dead—but only from hunger. I have been living for five days on dew. Maybe you can bring a chicken leg back in your pocket. No. Too dangerous. I could not swallow the bones. Sit down, please. As my collaborator, you will hear everything."

I sat down and stared.

"When I woke up the first morning in the hospital," the wasted face resumed, "I knew right away what had happened. It is an old plot. Fulka and Vinsey may even be sued for using it. They were going to make *The Pink Hussar* a success by having me on my death-bed. The coffee was drugged, like in *The Juggler's Return*. I wake up. I read the papers and I understand everything. It is not a bad idea. But on the second day I begin to worry."

"You were unconscious." I stared at the child-like face. "I was here. I saw you."

"I saw you, too," Turay smiled. "I was unconscious part of the time. The rest of the time I worried. You cannot play a death scene with epigrams and gypsy waltzes. My friends were behaving like an 1890 operetta. Did you read Fulka's interview about death is like a Pierrot in a black ruffle? Very bad dialogue. It is the Hungarian failing. He writes with rouge." The voice grew fainter. "Do you know how I became famous? By not putting any jokes in my plays. I was the first Hungarian to write without epigrams. The whole world embraced me —with relief."

Turay sighed and rallied himself.

"You will bring some cheese with the liverwurst," he said.

"What kind?" I asked.

"A pocketful," he said weakly; "I am not particular. I will finish the plot for you. Yesterday, when that idiot Alper-Mayer— My God! He has been freezing and electrocuting me for thirty-six hours." Turay's voice brightened as if he were only now waking up. "Yester-day he gave me no drug. I understood at once he was going to let me regain consciousness so the public would have some hope. And then I am drugged again and the grief is greater. This type of suspense is ridiculous. It is good only in the movies. Did you see the picture *Little Women*? Very sickening. As soon as I understand, I see it is my opportunity to take over the whole plot myself. I have a bottle of sleeping pills in my pocket. Very powerful ones—from Budapest yet. I hide the bottle under the mattress and I take three. You saw the improvement in the situation immediately. Vinsey, Fulka, Gita—all of them. Now they are acting with conviction. No more epigrams. And that idiot Alper-Mayer. He is behaving like a doctor. He is confused, desperate and knows nothing."

"A sort of revenge on your friends," I said. "I can see its charm."

"No, please." Turay smiled. "It is not revenge. It is Act Two—*my* act—with a new plot turn. You will help me?" he asked eagerly. "Please, I need you."

I nodded and Turay removed a bottle from under the mattress. He spilled three pills into his hand.

"I have learned to swallow them without water," he said. "It is quite a trick." He put the pills in his mouth. "In an hour I will be unconscious. You cannot wake me up with a hammer. In the meantime, here are the principal points of Act Two. With a hint of the theme of Act Three."

Five minutes later I joined the Committee in the waiting room. They rushed toward me.

"His play," I said. "He's worried about it. He wants to see Jock Kane at once."

Dr. Alper-Mayer, followed by a nurse carrying three large ice bags, hurried to the sickroom.

"Did you tell him he wasn't dying?" Fulka asked tensely.

"He only smiled," I said. "The hypnosis is very deep."

"His soul is exiting on a wrong cue," Vinsey moaned. "I am going in there and scream in his ears. The truth! The whole truth!"

"He will only think you are treating him like a child," I said. "Call up Jock Kane. It may be wise to humor him."

Jock Kane arrived from rehearsal in a half hour. He was left alone in the sickroom. The committee discussed him grimly for fifteen minutes. One and all were agreed that he was the greatest swindler and rogue in the history of the theater, and its lowest intellect. Jock finally came out. He was oddly changed. His dark, avid face with its scorpion-like glitter looked toward us with the gentleness of a Madonna. The unscrupulous eyes were wet with tears. He sat down beside Gita and took her hand.

"You are going to play the lead in *The Pink Hussar*," he said softly. "Report for rehearsal tomorrow morning."

Gita stared.

"He asked for it," Jock continued in a purring voice. "It was wonderful. If I live to be a thousand I'll never forget that scene. A human soul stripped bare. He could hardly speak. He sounded just like a little child whispering in the dark. He took my hand like this and said softly, simply—that God was good to him because He had provided a great producer for the epilogue. Then he said to me, 'You were right about Gita. She is not ideal for the part. But with your genius as a director, she will be perfect. You will remove from her that phony Hungarian foolishness. You will breathe reality into her.' Then he smiled and said, 'When I am in my box on opening night—in my little box with the satin lining—I will feel closer to heaven if Gita is behind the footlights again.' "

Jock paused and looked far away.

"Those were his last words," he whispered.

A sob came from the window where Andri sat with two newspaper reporters. Gita's head drooped, and Jock put an arm around her.

"You must be a soldier," he said, "and forget everything. Forget your grief, your heartbreak and your Hungarian tricks. And turn in the wittiest performance of your life."

Gita nodded, and a flashlight exploded.

I returned to the hospital at midnight. Dr. Alper-Mayer was in the corridor with two internes. He seemed to have aged. The three were grouped around a large apparatus.

"I was going to try electric shock tonight," Dr. Alper-Mayer muttered sleepily, "but this *verdamte* machine is broke again. That is American equipment for you!"

I entered the sick room and slid a bag full of dainties on the closet shelf. It was dangerous but the plot called for it.

For a week I played blockade runner and my hat went off to Hungarian courage. Bedevilled by Dr. Alper-Mayer and his ice bags, electric shocks and mass drips, Turay kept heroically to his six sleeping pills a day—three in the morning and three at midnight. This allowed him a few hours of fuzzy articulation. It was during these hours that he performed his wonders.

Vinsey brought me the news of them. A second deathbed scene with Jock Kane had resulted in Vinsey receiving a ten per cent cut of *The Pink Hussar* as a gift. Turay had offered to buy this for his old friend but Jock had refused to accept any money. Three newspapermen had been present to applaud this scene of largesse. And on the following day Andri was announced as having joined the cast of *The Pink Hussar* in the important part as The Young Ghost. The afternoon papers carried news of a third substitution. Madam Marisca had been coaxed into playing The Old Ghost, another vital role in the eagerly awaited fantasy. And all three substitutions had brought only gallant phrases from the actresses who had yielded their places. Two of them had even gone so far as to tear up their run-of-the-play contracts. This was all in deference to Turay. What more fitting than that the dying dramatist should have his last play performed by the three women he had loved and made famous?

But Vinsey, Gita, Marisca, and Andri were only part of the achievements of the wily possum of Hungarian letters. One of the more emotional gazettes offered on Wednesday the opening chapter of a serial entitled, "Turay—The Last Smile of Europe." It was written by Janos Fulka, identified as the most renowned and cleverest critic in Europe. And it was illustrated by Stephan Holz, identified as the foremost caricaturist of the Continent. Fulka had launched a sprightly tale of Budapest's art life. There were enough epigrams in the first installment to stun any salon. None of them, however, were about critics. And there was, lastly, the wonder that befell Lazlo, the unemployed waltz king and mighty eater. An ent'racte score was being specially composed by him for *The Pink Hussar,* a score destined to jingle for months over the air waves.

Of how these amazing things had happened, I received only bewildered and hysterical accounts from Vinsey.

"He held the editor's hand in his coma," Vinsey reported, "and he was barely able to talk. We all thought it was the final scene. 'If I live,' he said—I never cried so much, I swear to you. Gita and Andri, too. It was unbearable. 'If I live,' he said, 'I would like to write my life for your paper. It is the perfect paper for my life. But I would be cheating your paper. Because it would not be as well written as if Janos Fulka wrote it. For drama, me. For prose, Fulka. He is our greatest genius.'" Vinsey sighed. "The same way with Holz and Lazlo. A few words he speaks. Then his eyes become glazed. His voice disappears. And the coma comes back. Death is beside him again. We hear only phrases out of a tomb—a living tomb."

I listened to Vinsey daily, read the paper, smuggled in the cheese and chocolate bars, and watched the second act unfold. The master dramatist, soggy with sleeping pills, recoiling under Dr. Alper-Mayer's scientific assaults, operated without falter.

We had a last whispered conference in the sickroom the night before the opening of *The Pink Hussar.* I suggested to Turay that he begin his recovery and so lighten the spirit of his cast.

"The girls sit and cry between scenes," I told him.

He looked at me wearily and his voice was blurred.

"No," he said, "it is better this way. They will give a wretched performance. They will overact. They will frighten the audience with their gaiety. But this hysteria will be mistaken by the critics for genius. Thank God, I will not be there to see it." The voice weakened. "My last five pills," he murmured. "I am taking them all at once in the morning." He opened his palm and looked dully at the five pellets. "I assure you I will not be nervous on this opening night," he smiled and dozed off.

The great triumph of *The Pink Hussar* is theatrical history. The three new dramatic stars, Gita Lengel, Madame Marisca, and Luba Andri are also theatrical history. The names Janos Fulka and Stephan Holz are loud in the gossip columns, dinner parties and fancy barrooms where the arts still find precarious haven. Lazlo, the new Lehar, is the toast of all radio lovers. These matters need no further comment.

The triumph of Dr. Alper-Mayer is, however, a little less known. His great work in pulling Turay back from the very brink of the grave, has resulted in medical recognition unprecedented among refugee doctors. He has not only an office crowded with adoring patients, but is busy almost nightly lecturing to psychiatric and neurological societies. The Alper-Mayer treatment for narcolepsy, so successfully practised on Turay, is certain to win the hyphenated scientist world renown.

I sat with Turay alone in his new apartment a month after the opening. It was Sunday and the dramatic sections of the morning papers were scattered around his bed. The playwright was still weak but the pinkness was returning to his dreamy face. Each time I saw him I was bowled over anew by his continued modesty, for he had revealed to none of his friends the manner in which he had toiled and suffered to reinstate them in the arts.

"The critics continue to be very kind to me," he grinned. "Did you read them today? I am the spirit of the waltz. I am the spirit of democracy. I am the spirit of the ages." He smiled. "I will tell you something secret. *The Pink Hussar* is not a very good play. I sneaked in and saw it for the first time last night. My God, the direction! It is like a ballet under water. That Jock Kane is a complete imbecile. And the acting! Even Gita. Abominable. And the play is no better. Those speeches by the ghosts and God. They are absolutely without meaning. Why didn't somebody have sense enough to cut them out? Yet everybody raves—the critics, the audience. Imagine standing room only for a Hungarian play! They applaud. They weep and laugh. It is things like that that make me love the theater. Everywhere else people see only what is before them. In the theater they see what is inside them. I am happy to be the spirit of the ages for them."

Vinsey came in.

"Ah." He embraced me. "I am glad you are here. Tonight we are having a party. Everybody will be there—including an old friend of Turay's. Did you tell him yet, Dodo?"

Turay shook his head.

"Mr. Mangriff," said Vinsey, "the munitions maker who is a refugee. But a special kind of refugee. A refugee with millions. Turay read him your script. He's mad to be the second money. Tomorrow morning he puts $200,000 in the bank. Tomorrow, also, Gita marries Fulka and Andri marries Lazlo. That is why the party. And tomorrow I am a producer again. Everybody is famous and everybody has money. How can such things happen?"

I looked at Turay sitting on his throne of Sunday dramatic columns. The pink hussar who had ridden single-handed to the rescue of Budapest's ghostland winked at me like a happy child.

The Shadow

THE MARVELOUS SARASTRO came from Warsaw although he sometimes hinted at Thibet and the Mountains of the Moon.

He was a Pole and a vaudeville magician, but given a sympathetic ear, he would fall to darkening his origins and clothing himself in such mysteries of parentage, race, and geography as gave one an uneasy feeling.

Never have I known a man to lie, boast, pose so tirelessly and childishly. But Sarastro was the true charlatan and one forgave him this. One even demanded it of him.

Often, while listening to his Mother Goose mysticism, his Munchausen adventures, his garbled and pompous chatter of genii, sylphs, and undines, I have grown annoyed at my own skepticism. How much more marvelous was the Marvelous Sarastro if one believed him! How much more entertaining this Arabian Night in which he lived, could one accept it with the heart of a child rather than the dull incredulity of a modern author.

And often, while smiling a bit condescendingly at my friend Sarastro as he unfolded his Brobdingnagian doings, I have been suddenly impressed by the thought of what a genius he would once have seemed; what a great man another age would have considered him—a savant, Magus, and dangerous kin of Lucifer. At such moments, Sarastro's somewhat humorous appearance would take on an air of distinction and authority. His small eyes appeared sinister. His thin lips seemed cruel. His plump womanish face became a symbol of enigma. His long thin nose acquired a Papal dignity. His silken brown hair, falling in a Dutch bob almost to his neck, was transformed into a fascinating and medieval coiffure.

It was with the foregoing notions about Sarastro that I called on him in his dressing-room back stage at the Palace Theater. I had sat through his turn, thrilled as always by his dexterity and pompousness. For Sarastro was no glib magician apologizing for his pretenses with aged jokes and comical patter. He performed his levitations and disappearances, his transmutations and feats of legerdemain, with the profound, unsmiling mien of one truly at work on Miracles. But I noticed, nevertheless, a change in his manner. He seemed nervous and preoccupied.

He greeted me coldly as I opened the door of his dressing-room and continued to remove his make-up in silence. I offered compliments. He nodded and said nothing. I remarked on his new feat—a disappearing cage full of birds. This was, said I, a miracle which would have astounded the great Herman.

"I am glad you saw it," said Sarastro. He was drying his face. "It is the last time."

"What is the last time?" I asked.

"The last time I perform," said Sarastro. "I leave tonight for Paris. You will never see me again. No one will ever see me again. It is the last of Sarastro."

"Why are you going to Paris?" I asked.

"To murder a man," said Sarastro. "I arrive on the 15th. On the morning of the 16th there will be one fiend less in the world."

I made no remark at this and disguised my delight with a sympathetic frown.

"What time do you sail?" I asked, as he put on his street clothes.

"At midnight."

"Would you care to honor me as my guest for supper?" I asked.

"Yes," said Sarastro. "Part of me being still human, I must continue to eat."

Twenty minutes later we entered a quiet, almost deserted café. Sarastro ordered food wearily but profusely.

"There is no hurry," he said. "My things are all on the boat. Here is my passport. Here is my ticket."

He showed me these documents.

"This is rather a new ambition," I said, "murder."

"Oh, no," said Sarastro. "I have had this ambition for twenty years."

"The same man?"

"Yes."

"I have never suspected it."

"Hate," said Sarastro, "is not an emotion which one wears on one's sleeve. It is a soul. When it enters a man he may live on, he may laugh, work, and go about, and there will be no difference to those who are his friends; but his soul has only one color, his nights have only one dream. For twenty years I have dreamed only one thing—to kill a man."

I said nothing. We ate in silence for several minutes.

"His name is Rico Sansone," said Sarastro. "Have you ever heard of him?"

"No," I said.

"On the 16th," said Sarastro, "you will hear that he is dead."

"Why are you going to kill him?" I asked.

The medieval face smiled. A dreamy look filled the small eyes.

"Because," said Sarastro, "he is the most evil man in the world. I have been waiting for twenty years for his name to appear. For as long as he chose to hide there was no hope. He is too clever. Yes, even for me. Far too clever. But I knew that his vanity would betray him and that some day I would read again the name Rico Sansone. I knew he would return to the stage."

"Is he a magician?" I asked.

"Yes," said Sarastro. "The greatest that ever lived. The most profound and evil. He has no soul."

I nodded.

"He is greater than I," said Sarastro and closed his eyes as if overcome by this statement. "He begins his performance in Paris on the 15th."

"I would like to hear the story," I said frankly.

"You will," said Sarastro. "But I must have your oath not to interfere."

"You have it," I said.

"Very well," said Sarastro. "The story begins twenty years ago. I was a young man. I traveled with a small carnival through the villages of southeastern Europe. We were a company of clowns, gypsies, acrobats, and conjurors. We traveled in gilded wagons and performed for peasants and herdsmen on the outskirts of their villages.

"My powers developed early. I was young, but I was able to cast horoscopes, foretell the future, reveal the past, and converse with the gnomes and salamanders. I wore black tights and a small black jacket that came only to my waist. There was always a sword at my side, for in dealing with the spirits that infest the darkness beyond life one must always be armed. I was known as the Black Seer, and it was not only the peasants who held me in awe. My comrades themselves feared and respected me.

"One night we came to a village in Malo-Russia. Our cymbals sounded, our music played, our torches flickered in the spring wind, and the villagers crowded around our tents and wagons. I had taken my place in the black box on the platform outside my tent. There were holes in the box through which I could watch the crowd while the barker made his announcements. He ran up and down the platform, ringing his bell and shouting, 'The Black Seer, the Marvel of Marvels, Sarastro the Magician, who speaks with the dead and reads the secrets of life. . . .'

"I saw her for the first time at this moment. Her young and gentle face surprised me among so many peasants. I said to myself, 'What a strange girl! What a beautiful child!' In a short while I began my performance in the tent. But I was restless. I kept watching the entrance. At length an old peasant led her in, holding her by the hand. I saw at once that she was blind.

"The old man led her to my side and asked that I tell her fortune. He said she was his daughter, but it needed no knowledge of the stars to see that he lied. I questioned him and learned her simple history. She had been born blind and cast aside as an infant by a tyrant-noble of the vicinity and she had been found and raised by this old man and his wife.

"I studied her face as he talked. Pure as a seraph's, her large sightless eyes calm, resigned. She was eighteen and beautiful, pale, delicate, noble. But that does not describe her. It is in the eyes that the soul of a woman is usually to be seen. Anna's eyes were empty. She could neither see nor be seen by them. But the spirit which found these eyes closed lighted the rest of her face and body. A kindly, radiant child spoke from her lips. I held her white hands which she had offered me trustingly and I cast her horoscope. A dark mist passed over me and I listened to the voices which foretell the future. 'Sorrow, sorrow,' they breathed, 'pain and sorrow. Fly . . . run. . . .'

"But I smiled and my own voice was serene as I spoke.

"'The spirits promise you happiness,' I told her, 'your hands will touch beautiful things. Love and delight await you.'

"I was rewarded for my lies by a smile such as one sees on a child's face when it is dreaming.

"That was the beginning. Her face haunted me that night and I could not sleep. I made inquiries the next morning and sought her out. We walked through the hills. She did not need my hand to guide her. She knew every stone, every turn of the paths we followed. She spoke of the trees around us. She had strange names for them. And she spoke of the flowers that were to come soon in these woods. I forgot that she was blind. I came again the next day—and the next. Her purity, her sweetness delighted me. But there was something else—a sense of disquiet. It had come to me first from the stars. I had heard a warning out of the dark mists in which the voices of the dead are hidden.

"But now more than before I felt it behind the child's smile of her lips. When her hands touched mine for the first time she shuddered and grew pale. I knew then that she was aware of her destiny. The stars had told me she would not live long and that agony and terror waited for her on the short journey.

"She was innocent, untouched as yet by life. But it is unnecessary to know the ways of the world to know how one's heart will break. Here, hidden away, she awaited her fate without too much knowledge or too much dread. Yet her soul knew it completely. Her hand, when it sought mine in the silent shadowed woods, sought the hands of a protector. In my supernatural talent, she fancied, lay a hope of escape. I understood this as I looked at her.

"We remained for two weeks in this village. When we left, Anna came with me as my wife. More than her beauty and her gentleness, the sense of her ominous future had made the thought of leaving her impossible. Thus, in seeking to save her, I fulfilled the terrible message of the stars. For it was I—Sarastro—who was the instrument fate had selected for her ruin.

"She was happy. We rode together in the gilded wagon. Her pure, trusting face was always beside me. So that she might never be lonely I instructed her in a few of the elements of magic. In a little time she was able to take her place on the platform outside my tent. Dressed in the colorful robe I bought for her she sat blindfolded—for who would believe so perfect, so beautiful a creature was without sight?—and guessed numbers, told fortunes. Everything delighted her. Everything made her smile. She was happy.

"But I was not. From the moment that I embraced her as my wife I was haunted. How can I tell you of this dread, the continual dread of knowing something, of waiting for something that one knows, of waiting for life to despoil one?

"I tried to learn more, I sought for some clue that would enable me to anticipate the thing that menaced us and so, perhaps, overcome it. But my magic could tell me nothing more. It only repeated for me the words of dread, of horror.

"Then I knew, one night as I stood in the black box outside my tent, that I needed no further word from the mists of prophecy. It was there. It had come. He stood among the peasants before our tent—a graceful figure, smiling, leaning on his cane. A man of the world amusingly out of place in this faraway little village. I looked at him through the holes in my box. As I looked a glow of fear came to my heart.

"He had turned his face and I saw his remarkable eyes lighted by the flare of our torches. They were round, colorless eyes. They were proud and smiling and yet lifeless.

"I watched him and felt afraid. He was studying Anna. Never once did he stop looking at her. When we started to enter the tent for the performance he disappeared. I said nothing to Anna. What was there to say? That a man had looked at her. She would understand too much.

"I was waiting for him the next night. Yes, eagerly. You know the eagerness with which one waits for all certainties whether they are bright or dreadful. He came back. He stood once more leaning on his cane, graceful, smiling and sinister. His eyes were on her face.

"In the wagon that night she spoke to me.

"'There is a man looking at me,' she said, as we lay side by side. Her hand crept into mine. There was nothing more to say. The same thing was in our minds.

"On the third night I decided to act. My temper was quick and fiery I came up to him as he stood watching Anna. He followed me as if my enraged demand to speak to him were a gracious request. Ah, how subtle he was, how graceful! But that is the way of those whose souls are fashioned in Hell.

"On the outskirts of the crowd I seized his arm and demanded to know what he meant by coming every night and staring at my wife. He removed my hand as if it were a child's. I can tell you there was something terrifying in his strength as I felt it for the first time. For I knew . . . but that comes later. He looked at me with his cold, lifeless eyes and he spoke softly and apologized for having given offense. He explained that he was a student of the occult traveling about the world in search of knowledge. He praised Anna as a woman of remarkable psychic powers. He said he had hoped to be able to induce her to join him as an assistant, for he was planning soon to go on the stage. But now that he knew she was my wife. . . . He shrugged his shoulders and apologized again for his seeming forwardness. Then he looked at me with a curious smile and said softly, 'She is blind, is she not?' In this moment as he smiled, I understood that he knew. Like myself, he had seen the ominous, the dreadful shadow around her.

"Yet I could do nothing. Despite my travels I was a rustic, young, hot-blooded, untutored in the ways of society. I had no words with which to resist his charm. Yes, even at that moment when I most understood him I found myself listening with interest to his talk—pleased, disarmed, moved somehow by the loneliness that underlay his eager, friendly manner. I recognized him as a genius. And he walked back to our tent with me, talking already as if I were his dearest friend.

"It was thus Rico entered our lives. Little by little, during the days that followed, he attached himself to us. He confessed simply that he had nothing to do, that he had no friends, no kin. He said he had been wandering alone over Europe since he was a boy. And he talked. Ah, his talk! We listened, Anna and I, to his tales. Yes, he had been everywhere, seen everything. He brought the world into our gilded wagon. He wooed us both as a lonely, brilliant man woos the friendship of those he likes.

"In his presence I always felt elated and flattered. But when he left and I was alone again with Anna a disquiet came. I waited darkly for her first words. You know the dangerous words a woman speaks when she finds herself interested in a man. But they did not come. Instead she would take my hands, press them to my cheeks and whisper, 'I do not like him, Sari. I do not like the way he looks at me. I feel something strange in him.'

"Then how eager I was to defend him, to remind her of his gay talk and of how he had made us laugh and feel happy. Thus does a man move in the grip of his destiny, thus do we dig with our own hands the appointed grave for our happiness. I was a fool, yes. But I was to be even a greater fool.

"For the time came when Anna took my hands one night and told me that our friend had made love to her. My heart grew black. I listened as she spoke for some telltale note in her voice. But, no. Anna's soul was as transparent, as pure as a child's. She clung to me as she had clung that first time in her native woods. And she repeated her fear of him. She told me he had come to her while she was alone, had taken her hand gently in his and asked her if she loved me and how deeply she loved me. Then he asked her if she loved me more than happiness or life. She had withdrawn her hand and answered only as a pure and noble soul can answer such questions. She had said, 'I cannot talk of love to you, even of my love for my husband. Please leave me.' And he had gone, pausing to ask her in the doorway to forgive him and to say that he understood now.

"It was late at night as she told me these things. And when she had finished and I was holding her in my arms there was a knock on the door. I opened it. It was Rico standing on the steps of our wagon. He held a heap of wild flowers in his arms.

"He entered without any word and laid the flowers on our table and I knew that he had picked them in woods beyond the village. Then he spoke. 'She has told you,' he said, and as I continued to stare at him blackly, he went on. 'It was not that I desired to hurt her, my friend.

I asked only if she were happy. Because she has grown dear to me. She is the first woman to whom my heart has turned. And I asked, because for a moment I grew weak. I knocked at a forbidden door as a lonely beggar might knock timidly and foolishly at the door of a great house within which he had caught a glimpse of feasting. Forget my weakness. Let me remain your friend. I am heartbroken to think I have brought a moment of unhappiness or alarm to either of you. . . .'

"I remember more of his words. But what are words compared to the emotion that kindles them? And I will perhaps seem like a greater fool than I was when I tell you that tears filled my eyes and that I seized his hand. For I had never before heard so deep, so melancholy a voice as his. A voice so resigned, so caressing. I poured wine for the three of us. We drank—Rico and I. But Anna did not touch her glass. She did not speak once during his visit. When he left she sat motionless for a long time. I came to her and she raised her gentle, brooding face, and her words, uttered softly, brought the dread back into my heart.

" 'I'm afraid of him,' she murmured. 'I'm afraid, Sari.'

"This was in the third month of our friendship. We were in Bavaria. Rico had come with us to Baumburg. Our carnival had planned to remain here for several weeks and Anna and I had moved into a pension. And gradually we saw less and less of Rico. He came occasionally to talk and sometimes the three of us took walks. But I began to feel it was my companionship he desired, not Anna's. He had undertaken to initiate me into the mysteries of magic and we spent long hours together—without Anna. He was learned. He knew things that are not known by many men. I was again flattered, lured, disarmed. Under his care my mind was expanding, my powers developing.

"Then one day I was sitting in my tent preparing for the afternoon performance when a curious sense overcame me. I felt a pressure on my heart as if a hand were closing around it. It was a warning. When one is close to the secrets of life and death one understands their voice, their inner voice.

"I left the tent quickly and hurried to the pension. Anna had remained behind as she frequently did in the afternoon. I tried to rid myself of the oppression as I approached our home. It would not do to frighten Anna. Yet I found myself running toward the door. I paused, waited till I had recovered my breath and then, smiling, opened the door quietly. I saw Rico standing with his arms around her, her face raised to his lips.

"Speechless, powerless, I looked at them. I heard her voice murmuring words of love. Her arms moved around his neck and she kissed him. My head grew black. In another instant I would have fallen as one falls under a heavy blow. Yes, death seemed to enter me. Then I heard his voice. He spoke her name. He caressed her with words. At their sound a horror seized me. It was my voice. It was Sarastro talking. It was a voice that seemed to come from my own throat. A horrible, familiar voice. And I understood what had happened.

"I sprang forward shouting his name . . . Rico! He turned and faced me. He pointed his finger at me as if he were an image in a mirror. 'Rico,' he echoed.

"I heard Anna scream. But murder was in my heart. I fought with this monster. I flew at him with a knife. We struggled across the room and he answered my cries with cries that echoed each note, each inflection of my voice. I saw him through my rage. His face was contorted like my own. His every feature had changed. He was Sarastro. There were two Sarastros screaming together, tumbling over each other.

"Then he held me in hands that were like steel fetters. Powerless I lay, mad with rage and terror, under him. I could not move or cry out. His hand was on my throat. I lay gasping and crazed, and it was Sarastro who was holding me. Then this horrible and familiar figure changed. It became Rico. It was Rico Sansone who spoke. The breath was leaving my body. I was strangling, dying, yet I could hear him— 'Sarastro. God! You are killing me. Sari—Sari. Have mercy. I am dying!' His voice was faint. I felt in this moment the agonies of a hundred deaths, for as my eyes grew dark I saw with horror the thing he had in his mind. He was pretending it was I who was killing him. And thus he would kill me and go to her as Sarastro. It would be Rico Sansone who was buried. It would be Sarastro who remained.

"For a moment I caught a glimpse of his cold, lifeless eyes burning now over my face as he enacted his false death—groaning, pleading for mercy. And a strength drawn from the soul filled my lungs. I cried out the name Anna—once, twice, knowing that by this she would understand it was I—I who was dying. And darkness seized me.

"An hour had passed when I opened my eyes. My head was splitting. My throat was stiffened. I raised myself and looked. He was gone. I saw her. She was standing in a corner of the room, crouched against the wall, her hand against her teeth and staring—staring into the terrible dark around her.

"'It is I,' I whispered, 'Anna!'

"She shrank from my voice. I dragged myself to her feet, calling her name, sobbing, pleading. But when I touched her she sank to the floor.

"It had come—the agonies and terror foretold by the stars. I lifted her to the bed. She recovered her senses, but the touch of my hand was enough to make her scream. I sat beside her through the night. I talked quietly of the little things that had been between us, of secrets only a husband may share with a woman. I recalled myself to her as one who has been away for years might struggle vainly to prove who he was. She lay silent, her face drawn with terror, and listened. Finally at dawn she whispered my name.

"This was the beginning. Rico had disappeared. I had frustrated his diabolical plan with my last cry. With his evil happiness a moment away he had released me and fled. But I kept this part of the horror a secret from her.

"We laid our plans. As soon as she was able to walk we abandoned the carnival and left Baumburg. We went to Munich. We were inseparable. She could not bear to have me away even for a moment. The darkness in which she had found peace and love had become filled with terror for her. I understood everything in her soul. Yes, even the trembling that would seize her sometimes when I took her hand.

"It would be folly to engage an attendant, a third one to watch, to guard. It was I alone he could not deceive. To everyone else he could become Sarastro. Even to her whose senses had learned every breath, every inflection of the man she loved, he had been Sarastro.

"Yes, we made our plans. We invented codes of greeting and secret handclasps and intimate caresses by which she might know me. Ah, how curious and terrible were these first months! With what foolish ruses, desperate childish ruses, we struggled to evade the terror that had closed around us! She was brave. She grew to smile again. The months passed. She whispered to me now as we lay together that her spirit was recovered. She was not afraid any more, she said. The thing she had feared had come and had passed. It was ended now. We were free.

"I agreed with her. I feigned exuberance, carelessness. You understand how it was. It was her soul I must cure of its dread, for in this dread alone she would go mad. When she insisted I return to work I went. I begged her to accompany me so that we might be together while we performed. But she answered strangely that she no longer felt the power in her to perform. Something had passed from her. And I understood this, too. But I would not let her see. It would not do to alarm her. I went alone. I pretended I was without fear. But it was a lie. I was still waiting. . . .

"I thought first of flying to another part of the world. But one does not escape terror by running. He would be there—wherever I was. 1 knew this, because it was given to me to know my fate. I remembered his genius. He had been made in Hell. He was a shadow from which I could not hope to hide. So we remained in Munich. I secured employment in a cabaret. Eight months passed. The dread, although it never left me, grew vaguer. And our life had become again almost like a honeymoon. Almost, I say, for there were moments in which I caught a glimpse of Anna's inner soul. I would wake at night to find her fingers tracing the contours of my face and body. I would lie motionless listening to her moan out of the nightmare whose nature I knew only too well. In the morning she would waken, tired and nervous. On such days I pretended to be ill and remained at her side. He said nothing, but we knew the shadow in each other's mind.

"These occasions, however, grew rarer. Ah, this fool's peace in which we struggled to live, this empty and ominous security we built around our love. Yes, for he was waiting. This monster, this fiend, was hovering near us and I had only to close my eyes to feel his shadow.

"I entered the cabaret where I performed one evening, feeling unusually disturbed. It was winter. The cold had numbed me during my walk to the place. I was removing my overcoat in the dressing room and it came again as I had known it would. The warning . . . the hand closing over my heart. Without a word to anyone I left the place. In the street I felt choked, dizzy. I hailed a carriage with difficulty and drove to within a block of our home. And during this ride I kept muttering to myself that my terror was only a folly of the nerves.

"I entered our cottage by a back door quietly, like a thief. And I stood listening. The room was in darkness but in the room beyond a light burned. 'She has gone to bed early,' I thought, and then, through the half-opened door of her bedroom I heard her voice. She was talking softly, happily. She was saying, 'My darling, you are ill again. We will go to sleep and in the morning you will feel better.' And a voice answered her caressingly, adoringly. My own voice it was, as before, but tender and gentle. . . .

"One does not reason in the midst of nightmare. Yet terror can wake the mind to a clairvoyance, an understanding beyond thought. I stood motionless, silent, listening. The light was turned out. I heard her laugh like a child in the dark, and this sound killed me. Yes, one is dead forever when happiness is torn from the heart. I slipped from the house like a thief. I walked in the cold streets. My thought returned. I had acted out of one clear impulse. Through the terror and agony of those moments when I heard him take her in his arms there had remained the certainty that above everything else I must save Her.

"Now I knew I had acted wisely. Had I rushed into the room, had I made a noise—she would have died. She would have known in that moment, as I knew listening to him, that he had been there before. That he had crept through our defenses as a shadow creeps. That despite our plans, despite everything, he had stolen into her soul.

"He lay beside her now embracing her, wooing her, and she with her arms holding him. I thought of this thing as I walked. And I thought again that I had only to rush back, to speak her name. Yes, and destroy her. No, I kept on moving in the cold night. I had slunk away in order to save her. And as I walked I began to understand him. Yes, we were dealing with a monster. He would manage to leave her before I was due to return from the cabaret. And if I sensed something wrong he would rely on my love for her to keep this sense a secret. He knew me well, well enough to take my place in her arms, well enough to take my place in her soul and to reason with my own thoughts. He understood I would allow my heart to be eaten away with grief and I would not make a sign lest I destroy her whom I loved more than myself. It was I who must be careful, not he. Yes, he knew me. He gambled on me.

"I returned. I undressed as he had directed I should undress, quietly. She lay with her lips parted and the faint odor of a drug was on her breath. This I understood, too, and was grateful—grateful to him. I stretched myself beside her, closed my eyes and waited. She awoke in the morning and I felt her hands caress me solicitously. She asked if I felt better and when I turned to her she started back in alarm. But I saw, thank God, it was only my cold fingers on her hand that had frightened her. I held my breath, however, waiting as one waits for death. I was ill, she cried. She must send for a doctor. Her lips covered my face with kisses and I choked back the tears. I strangled the agony in my heart. I said nothing. I pretended to be weary and I distracted her attention by continuous and querulous demands. She nursed me through the day.

"And thus it began again. My illness lasted for two weeks. I thought during these days that I would die. But I realized I must recover. She would begin to fear that there was something wrong. I left the bed finally. I postponed returning to the cabaret. But this, too, had to be done. I decided, however, to leave Munich. I explained to her that the climate was better in Berlin. We went to Berlin.

"What followed is hard to tell you. Terror leaves no memory. Yes, I no longer lived. There was only one thing in my mind. Perhaps it drove me mad. It has seemed to me always that all this time in Berlin I was able to eat, work, even sleep, only because of my desire to save her. This desire was greater than myself.

"I had determined to kill him the first moment I saw him—alone. I knew he was near us. He had tasted of the fruit of heaven and he would not go away now. I must be careful. Then I began to think he would kill me as he had at first intended and that he would go on living with her as Sarastro. She would never know I was dead. She would continue to love me in his arms, to press her kisses upon my murderer, until . . . This was the thought that contained in it the fullest measure of horror. The thought of that moment when she saw him and not me. . . .

"With this in view I wrote a long letter, sealed it and deposited it with a lawyer with instructions that he open it if I failed to communicate with him a single day and act immediately on the information it contained. For the rest I managed, God knows how, to spare her. The months passed and she felt no moment of dread. This was my reward. I asked questions, vague, subtle, disarming questions, and waited for her answers as one waits for a reprieve or a doom. Gradually I noticed that she spoke of things that were strange to me. She would continue his conversations—with me. She would speak of endearments I had never bestowed, of foolish, tender things I had never uttered.

"Do you understand the grief of these months? Yes, it is fortunate I cannot remember it. I can remember only prowling the streets like a madman, crawling into corners to weep, waking at night with my agony echoing through dreams of horror. I was like a thing in a trap, while he came and went, stealing her love, stealing my soul from under my eyes. But it was I, not he, who was afraid. It was I who held her life in my hands.

"I will pass over these months. What use is there now to remember them? They came to an end. I returned home one night after my performance. I was no longer so careful about my own comings and goings. I trusted him, do you understand—that out of his evil he would spare her as I spared her out of love. But when I entered the bedroom this time, when I opened the door of her bedroom this night, I knew he had blundered. She was alone.

"At the sound of my voice she turned. She stood facing me for a moment. Then she screamed. It is this scream I remember, it is with this voice she comes back to me. This cry of horror is my memory of

Anna. She seized her face with her hands as if she were tearing something—yes, the darkness. As I rushed to her she fell. She did not speak again. In the morning she died."

I have written the story as nearly in Sarastro's words as I can remember.

I went with him to the boat. We said good-by. Three weeks later my friend Sarastro was dead. I stared at the dispatch in a theatrical weekly with sadness and confusion. Under a Paris date line it recounted the end of the Marvelous Sarastro. He had been killed in an automobile accident. While motoring through the country his automobile had stalled on a railroad track and been demolished by an oncoming train. Sarastro, read the dispatch, had been cut to pieces. A friend who had been driving with him had escaped with slight injuries. The friend's name was given. It was Enrico Sansone.

God Is Good to a Jew

AARON SHOLOMAS' eyes were without light. This was because death looked out of them. In the street or sitting in a room Aaron Sholomas looked like a man staring at the top of his coffin.

Such a man is a troublesome one to see moving about. The people in the neighborhood where Sholomas had come to live avoided his mottled white beard and offered him no greeting when he passed. They had learned that it did not matter if they spoke, for the old refugee in the long black coat was unaware of them.

It was a neighborhood occupied chiefly by Jews who were a busy folk full of the activities of poverty. And since among these is always religion, there were many houses of worship fronting the crowded streets. They were modest temples that raised no towers but seemed to kneel over the curbings.

In one of these synagogues, Sholomas spent much of his time, but even here he attracted no companions. Other old men wearing prayer shawls looked at him, saw the gaunt face, the shaggy eyebrows, the bony hands holding the prayer book, saw his lips moving soundlessly as if they were trembling rather than praying, but, though their hearts hurt at the sight of him, none of them went beyond a silent nod of greeting. They knew his story and there was about Sholomas, still standing before God, a thing that squeezed at their souls and made them unable to speak.

When he had walked out of the synagogue, many of the pious ones hid their heads in their prayer shawls and prayed deeply for the refugee from Poland and asked God to bring him peace.

On the hot summer afternoons when Sholomas was not in the synagogue, he went to sit on a bench in the small neighborhood park. It was an arid, dusty and almost leafless park that seemed to have been coaxed into existence by the weary old men and women who came to rest in it. Here Sholomas sat in his long black coat, his black alien hat, as if he were freezing to death. No one sat down next to him. For how can you say hello to someone who doesn't know the sun is blazing?

In the evenings, Sholomas, the refugee, climbed three flights of stairs and entered a small room that had been provided for him by a family to which he was distantly related. He walked up the steps like a man in a dream and he offered no greeting to the anxious faces that opened the door of the tenement flat.

The head of this family that sheltered Sholomas was a man of seventy named Jacob Rabinowitz. He owned a small shop in which women's dresses were made. He was a robust, pink-cheeked, hearty-voiced man and would have looked well as a great captain of industry. But his heartiness had never lifted him beyond the edges of misfortune. His shop was small, his earnings were precarious, and his strong hands were twisted with fifty years of hard work.

Nevertheless, there was a sort of indomitable childish beam on his large face, and his pride as head of his tenement family was as strong as if he were presiding in a castle. He roared when he spoke, frowned autocratically on all interruption, ate lustily and was full of a gurgling love for all the faces at his table. It pleased him mightily that, despite his age, it was his hands that still provided food and a roof for his own.

Jacob had a wife who was stout, ailing and preoccupied fanatically with her kitchen stove, as if she were preparing a constant feast. Her name was Sonia and she had once been called Sonia the Beauty. With all her age and girth, her head was still tilted to one side in the arrogant manner that had delighted Jacob Rabinowitz when he first saw her fifty years ago.

There was a daughter of forty, seemingly as old as her mother, and two granddaughters of thirteen and fourteen who were fragile, blue-veined children and looked as if they had escaped the robust mold of the family. There was also Jacob's brother, a dodderer of seventy-eight named Hershel.

This Hershel was a red-eyed, feeble old fraud, full of mock piety and mock wisdom and mock suffering. He spent most of his time making sad faces and looking rebukingly at his robust brother and his other active relatives. He had given up trying to earn a living in his middle years, due to many fancied diseases and to the solvency and good nature of the younger Jacob.

Other faces had been in this tenement flat, but they had died, among them a son-in-law whose dying had left Jacob undisputed king of his roost.

In these crowded rooms, there was place for the refugee, Sholomas, because a grandson had gone into the Army. Jacob was in a continual excitement over the heroic deeds of this grandson and, though a man of great honesty, had taken to lying about his Herman.

"Mine grandson," he would boom at any guest, "is in the Second Front."

The family, knowing that Herman was in Carolina, held their tongues. Hershel alone would have dared contradict, but the Second Front and Carolina were equally confusing places to him, so he, too, was silent.

"He is fighting over there," Jacob would continue, "and getting ready to march to Berlin. We haven't heard from him for some time. Who knows? Maybe he is fighting in Germany already. Over here is his picture. Have a look at it."

Grandfather Jacob would point to the wall where hung several photographs of Herman, revealing him at ten in a white sailor suit doing a hornpipe, at fifteen still in knee pants and holding a violin moodily under his arm, and at nineteen in an Army overcoat with an unexpected humorous gleam in his eyes. Under these photographs stood a bowl of fresh flowers.

The refugee from Poland had been given the lumpy iron bedstead that had once been Herman's and that stood beside a back window looking out on a swarm of other tenement back windows.

"This is a great honor for you," Jacob had boomed. "In this bed mine Herman slept since he was a little boy. Here is where he growed up, in this identical room. I'll betchya lots of times when he is fighting the Germans, mine grandson remembers this room. I am keeping it for him." And Jacob beamed at the stark cubbyhole as if it were a holy place.

The refugee from Poland was a silent and almost invisible guest. The family saw him only when one of them brought him tea to drink at night and a plate with fish and bread. He ate so little that Jacob, whose stomach was in love with everything that grew in the sea or on the land, believed that the white-bearded one would die of famine any hour.

"I don't like to see a man in mine house should starve to death," Jacob complained. "Bring him in some *varenya.*"

This was a cherry jam that Jacob considered irresistible. Twenty jars of it had been sent to Herman in the Carolinas.

But Sholomas left the *varenya* untouched. When the tea-bearers opened the door of Sholomas' room, they asked politely, without entering, "Are you all right? If you want something, just say so."

Sholomas would look up and say nothing, so it was presumed he was all right and wanted for nothing.

Sitting around the supper table, the family often discussed their distant relative in the back room. The older ones remembered him from the time before they came to America. He had been a man of learning, and people used to travel miles to the town where he lived to consult him on great problems of piety and behavior.

"You have no idea how famous this man Sholomas was," said Jacob. "He was a great man. A fine, handsome man. Not just a rabbi, but a poet. The finest poems that was written in our language, he wrote. We were proud in them days to have a cousin named Aaron Sholomas. Hershel, tell 'em."

Jacob nudged his rheumy-eyed brother, who spoke up at once in woebegone tones, "I am t'inking of something else. Please don't interrupt me."

"Go on, tell them!" Jacob boomed, and Hershel, sighing deeply, moaned, "You are speaking from Aaron Sholomas?"

"You heard me!" Jacob cried.

"He was a dolling man," Hershel went on moaning. "He raised geese and tended beanstalks."

"Not beanstalks!" Jacob roared. "What's a matter with you? Bees! Bees, he tended."

"Beanstalks," Hershel repeated stubbornly and rubbed tears from his eyes by way of ending the argument.

"It was anyway his wife who raised geese and tended bees," Jacob said. "Because he, himself, was a student all his life. He was not only a rabbi and a poet but a wise man. In the old country, a wise man is different from here," he boomed educationally at his granddaughters. "Nobody laughs at him, but he sits around like a king, helping the people and explaining them how to live. I remember when I was leaving for America, I went to him because I wanted to make him a donation of a few dollars he could give to the poor people who was always his best friends. Because rich people don't need a wise man, either in the old country any more than over here. And he said to me, 'My boy, you keep your dollars. A man starting out on a journey must not give away presents. Because a single dollar—even a few pennies—might prevent him from arriving where he is going, you understand. After he has arrived and his journey is over, then he can give away presents.'"

Jacob chuckled at this remembered wisdom.

"I can remember exactly the words he said to me," he went on. "I was a young boy, too. He said, 'A man must not try to buy God's good will in advance. He must only give God presents out of gratefulness. The other thing is like bribing.' "

"That saying is written in the Talmud," Hershel sighed. "Yes, yes, it is everything written down—everything." And summoning a look of hauteur into his woeful face, the dodderer quoted a proverb in Hebrew.

"I remember this Sholomas very well," Jacob interrupted the quotation. "I remember he had eyebrows so big they hung almost over his eyes. And he had such kind eyes you fell in love with him the minute you sawn him."

"A dolling man," said Hershel, "and a fine swimmer. He could swim farder and longer than anybody in this room." And Hershel looked at his robust, pink-faced brother with a sneer, for Jacob had been famed in his youth as a mighty swimmer—a fame which, with the aid of Hershel's grudging corroboration, he had managed to keep alive for forty years. . . .

Several weeks after Sholomas' arrival in the Rabinowitz home, Jacob's daughter stated one evening that the old man should be coaxed into eating with them.

"It's no good for him to sit alone," she said. "He sits there like a dead man. I don't see why we keep him if he's going to sit in a hole like a dead man, day and night. He'd be just the same off in some old people's home."

"He is mine cousin," Jacob boomed, "and he shall stay in mine house. How would it look if I throwed him out after the agency went to all the trouble locating some relative of his?"

"I don't care," said the daughter. "He don't enjoy himself. He makes the whole house like a tomb. I'm afraid sometimes to open his door."

"What are you afraid of?" Jacob asked. "He don't harm nobody."

"He sits there," said Jacob's daughter and shuddered.

One evening a week later, the hearty Jacob sat at the table in silence and nibbled glumly at his food.

"What's the matter with you?" his wife demanded, her head angrily to one side. "Are you sick or something? Go on, eat! What am I standing all day in the kitchen cooking for?"

Jacob frowned at his plate and drank a second glass of brandy. The family talked loudly over his silence, but their eyes looked nervously at his unemptied plate. In the middle of the meal, Jacob pressed his brother to join him in a third glass of brandy.

"You will excuse me, please," Hershel moaned. "I am not feeling so good tonight."

The statement angered Jacob. "You've been healthy as a horse for seventy-five years," he growled, "ever since I known you."

Hershel rubbed tears from his eyes, tucked the corners of his mouth down and trembled his nose.

"What have you got to cry about?" Jacob demanded. "You sit there crying, day and night. For what?"

"He ain't crying," Jacob's wife called out. "That's how he looks naturally. He can't help it."

"Thank you, Sonia." The dodderer looked tenderly at her. "You was always mine favorite dolling."

Jacob pushed his plate of uneaten chicken from him. "I talked to a man from the agency today," he said. "I met him by an accident in Siegel's restaurant. He says to me, 'Are you Jacob Rabinowitz?' I told him, 'Yes, that's my name. What can I do for you, sir?' So we sat down, and he told me from Aaron Sholomas, mine cousin. The whole story. It's something you can't believe. You can't imagine such a thing."

The family nodded and became silent. Jacob scowled at the many platters of food around him.

"Go on, we're waiting," said Sonia.

Her husband looked at his two grandchildren.

"Not in front of them," he said. "Why should they hear such things?"

"We know, anyway," said the older of the girls. "He was in the massacre where all the people in the town were killed. All the Jews were killed."

"Quiet!" said her mother, seizing the child's hand and kissing it. "Let your grandfather talk."

"It is something unbelievable," said Jacob hoarsely. "It was written out in a report about what happened in the town where he lived."

"The name of the town was Scuzin," old Hershel spoke up firmly. "We used to go there in the summertime to swim in the river."

"Thot's right," said Jacob with a deep sigh; "but nobody is swimming on thot river no more. It's for dead people, thot river."

He half closed his eyes, and his voice hoarsened as he went on, "The Germans locked up four thousand Jews in the ghetto behind the walls. They wouldn't let them come out, and nobody is allowed to give them any food, and if they are sick, they can die and nobody is allowed to bring them medizin."

"Ai," said Jacob's wife and lowered her head slowly.

"They was starving and going crazy, them people," said Jacob hoarsely, "and finally they got so hungry they couldn't stand it any more and they start climbing over the walls of the ghetto and breaking down the doors, so they can get out. And they come out into the street looking like animals that are starving to death."

"Ai," said Jacob's wife and bowed her head over her plate.

"The Germans let them people run in the street for a while, begging for food," said Jacob. "Then they start chasing them and shooting down everybody like it was a hunt for animals. The old men, the women, the children, they are shot down by the Germans while they run in the streets begging for food."

Jacob's work-twisted hands clutched at the table edge.

"They shoot down two thousand in the street," he resumed, "and the rest keep on running. They don't even know they are dying, they are so hungry. They run to the river and jump in and start swimming. Where are they swimming to? No place. Where can they swim? They are just crazy from hunger and swimming around and around. The report says two thousand of them was in the river swimming. Them Germans stood by the side and shot every one of them until the river was full of dead people."

Jacob paused as if he were out of breath, and old Hershel spoke up:

"Simon Meyerberg used to have a mill by the river." His voice quavered. "We used to go there in the summertime and ketch pike. He was a fine man, yes, sir." The dodderer looked far away. "He died when I was a little boy," he added.

"Mine cousin, Aaron Sholomas, was in the river when Germans are shooting," Jacob went on. "He swimmed with the dead people all day and by night he crawled out on the ground and he sat by the side and pulled the bodies out of the river. He was looking for his wife and grandchildren. He couldn't find them because it was dark, and finally he fell down unconscious by the dead people. In the morning a Polish man sawn him and took him up in a wagon and saved him."

Jacob poured himself another glass of brandy. "I can't stand it," he boomed hoarsely. "That man's wife, his grandchildren and everybody he known in the whole world, butchered in front of his eyes."

Jacob's wife began to weep, and the older of the girls whispered to her, "Grandma, don't cry. Please don't cry."

"Simon, the miller, used to have a horse," old Hershel spoke up. "It was called Spilka. Three people could ride on him. I can remember to this day."

"What happened to Sholomas?" Jacob's daughter asked.

Jacob was looking at the photographs of his grandson over the bowl of fresh flowers. The humorous face above the Army overcoat seemed to straighten him in his chair, and he answered in a loud, rasping voice:

"Mine cousin lived for a month hided away by the Polish farmer. Then there was a law passed that anybody who hided Jews had to be killed the same as the Jews themselves. So mine cousin, when he heard this law, left the home of the Polish farmer and walked by night every night for weeks to Lublin. On his hands and knees, this old man crawled in the nighttime to Lublin. And what was there in Lublin for him? Only more Germans. I asked the man from the agency, 'What was he living for? What did he want to go on living for?' And the man explained to me that mine cousin was crazy now and was looking for his wife and grandchildren. He didn't remember they was all drowned in the river."

Jacob stopped, and though he looked long at the phtographs of his grandson, he was unable to go on, and the group at the table sat in silence and waited.

"I don't like to think what happened in Lublin," he resumed. "In Lublin, the Germans put twelve thousand Jews behind the walls of the ghetto. Then they killed them. All of them. They took 'em in the field in wagons. Five hundred at a time in wagons on top of one another. They blown them up."

Jacob groaned, and his large hands lifted the brandy glass. The liquor spilled over his chin.

"There was a few of them who wasn't dead," he went on. "When the Germans was shooting the ones that was lying on the ground still alive, they don't shoot Aaron Sholomas. They left him lying with the dead bodies, and in the nighttime he crawled away again. And like before, he hided himself in the daytime and walked every night. Then somebody recognized him while he was crawling in the night that he was Aaron Sholomas, the wise man from Scuzin, and they saved him."

Jacob stopped, his eyes on the doorway. The bearded figure of Sholomas in its long black coat and alien hat stood there.

"Come in," said Jacob softly. "Come in and join us. Move up a chair for him, somebody, please."

His daughter placed another chair at the table. The refugee's eyes were without greeting. They were open and staring and only the doddering Hershel was able to look into them.

"You remember me, Aaron Sholomas," said Hershel. "I am Hershel Rabinowitz, a son of Samuel from Scuzin. Simon Meyerberg who owned the mill there in Scuzin was a first cousin from mine father."

Sholomas moved a few steps into the room and then seemed to become lost. The gaunt white face under the black alien hat remained silent, and its silence struck those in the room as something terrible. There were no words that could speak to it.

Jacob Rabinowitz raised his eyes, and his pink face became chalk. Not Aaron Sholomas but all the dead Jews of Europe stood in their grave clothes beside his dining table. There were millions of them, and Jacob could hear their voices calling in the night as they died. He saw the river of Scuzin with the May flies darting over it and the frogs leaping from the mud banks, and under its willow trees he saw the water filled with dead; old men like himself floating with their arms limp and their faces hidden, old women like his wife drowned and bobbing through the hail of bullets, and many like his grandchildren clawing at the dark river as the German guns picked them off from the shore.

This river he knew and he could remember how the moon looked in it. He could see the road that led to its banks and the winding streets of Scuzin and he could remember a guitar that played and a horse that trumpeted in its stall. He knew the smell of this summer night and he knew all the dead, all the crazed figures stumbling through the little streets of Scuzin, the women with their hair streaming and their pale children locked in their arms; the old men muttering to God as they toppled over.

He knew them all, for they were people among whom he had laughed and lived and he could feel the bullets striking them down. He saw them in the river among the leaping of frogs and the hum of startled insects, spinning with the current around the trunks of the willow trees, and they called out in his heart for mercy.

Their voices that nobody heard, their helpless look at the sky as if they were dogs being slaughtered and not people—these overwhelmed Jacob, and the dining room in which he had eaten so heartily for so many years grew dark before his eyes. It became a grave in which he sat with the dead Jews of Scuzin and of all the slaughter places whose names were too many to remember. Jacob covered his face with his hands and his body shook with weeping.

His brother nudged him as he wept. "Jacob," said the dodderer, "you should not cover your face like thot. We have a guest." And in a voice full of sudden dignity, old Hershel added, "Aaron Sholomas, we are proud to have you at our table. Kindly sit down."

Jacob uncovered his face. He saw that Sholomas had seated himself next to his granddaughter. The bony hands of the refugee were resting limply on the table, his face was lowered, and his lips were moving silently.

"Shh," old Hershel looked reprovingly at his weeping niece, "he is making the prayer over bread."

Late on a September afternoon, Sholomas sat in the neighborhood park enveloped in his long black coat. The light was leaving the sky. As the glare of the sun lifted from the streets, the park in which he sat became full of sharp color and bold outline. The sudden presence of so many vivid things around him confused Sholomas. He stood up and, with his eyes to the ground, walked out of the park.

At nine o'clock Jacob Rabinowitz was worried. He had finished his third glass of tea, and his wife and daughter had cleared the table of everything but a jar of *varenya* and a plate of cookies.

"It's no use talking," said Jacob. "Something has happened to him. Where else can he be at this hour of the night?"

"You are speaking of Aaron Sholomas?" Old Hershel raised his eyes from the newspaper.

Jacob grunted. His brother was taking on daily more and more the ways of an idiot.

"Who else!" he boomed. "Nine o'clock and he ain't home yet."

"He is not a little boy," said Hershel calmly and picked the pinochle cards out of the cut-glass bowl on the sideboard.

He sat down at the dining table and started shuffling the deck. A sly look came into his rheumy eyes. Despite his trembling hands and doddering ways, he was able invariably to win a few pennies from his domineering brother.

"Don't botherin' me with the cards," said Jacob. "I'm worried about mine cousin." His large pink face scowled at the clock. "What can a man like thot be doing at this hour?"

"Maybe he dropped in some place for a glass tea," Hershel offered.

"Honest!" Jacob glared at the dodderer. "I hate to say this from my own brother. But you have got less sense than a ordinary child."

A melting look came into Hershel's woebegone face. "Don't get excited," he said softly. "There is some people got all the sense but don't know what to do with it."

Jacob shook off the insult. "I'm going to look around for him," he said.

"What is this?" Jacob's daughter peered out of the kitchen. "What is the racket for?"

"He is going to look for Aaron Sholomas," said Hershel, scowling at the cards in his hands. "You should stop him, dolling."

"You can't go running through the streets," the daughter said. "You're tired from the shop. You'll get sick. Sit down. Sholomas will come home all right by himself."

Jacob was on his feet, his head thrown back, his eyes half shut, which was his way of signaling that he was not to be contradicted further.

"Where is mine grandchildren?" he boomed. "Come on, girls. We are going to look for our cousin."

The night was warm and the streets were full of idle figures. They sat on steps, stood at the curb or tilted back in chairs placed before the dimmed store fronts. Down these tranquil streets, a thought moved furtively and painfully, as if all the idlers resting after their day's work had but one head. It was a thought of death. The idlers in these tenement streets were watching the slaughter of the Jews.

On each warm night, with their tasks done, they sat sprawled in the summer dark and looked on the great killing of the Jews and listened in their hearts to the unheeded Jewish prayers rising from the German massacre grounds. They talked to one another of many things, gossiped and complained, but their souls were fastened on a faraway stage where the strange and awful murder of the Jews was then going on.

Their sons, brothers and grandsons were in the war, and their thoughts were full of Mediterranean names where battles were happening. But these battles seemed like happy events to them. Germans were being killed in these battles. The thought of their kin, armed and fighting fiercely, brought a sigh of relief into the summer streets where the many Jews sat watching the distant slaughter of their kind.

The radios squawking in the night proclaimed the hourly deeds of the distant armies; but deeper and louder in their hearts than all the other voices in the world was the unheeded call of the millions who, without any weapons in their hands, were facing the German massacre squads.

Such was the neighborhood through which Jacob Rabinowitz, holding a granddaughter by each hand, walked in search of his cousin. The tall heavy-waisted Jacob walked proudly with an old habit of arrogance in his ungrayed head. He paused now and then before idlers on the steps and inquired in a peremptory voice if they had seen Aaron Sholomas, the refugee from Poland, who was his cousin. None had seen him, and Jacob marched on, clinging to the hands of his granddaughters.

In the synagogue where he knew Sholomas spent his days, he was told that the old man had left his prayers at seven and walked away toward the neighborhood park. Jacob led his granddaughters there. The two pretty girls were full of love for their tall grandfather as they walked beside him and, knowing that he was unhappy, they began telling him of the fun they had had in school that day and of the fine things their teachers had said to them. Whatever his troubles, Jacob always chuckled proudly when he heard tales of his grandchildren's schooling.

Many people sat on the shadowed benches of the park, and the three searchers walked for a time, looking into their silent faces.

"You sit down, Grandpa," the older of the girls finally said, "and we'll go and look all over the park."

Jacob sat down with a lordly grunt. "Ask the people," he instructed them, "if they have seen him and what way he went. You understand?"

"We will," the girls said eagerly. "You just sit still."

They walked away and Jacob sat on the bench. His large body was straight and his eyes peered into the dark. He felt tired and in his weariness he kept remembering a river in which he had once swum, and a great pain filled his heart. For no Jew would ever laugh or swim in that river again.

"It's no good thinking about such things," he told himself angrily. "It don't do you any good to suffer when you can't help something. Here is a fine park, and the people are enjoying themselves. That's enough to think about."

But the memory of the river continued to hurt his heart. He looked into the silent, shadowed faces near him, and a miserable kinship with all the park sitters came over him. They, too, were sitting with memories and staring at faraway rivers and villages filled with dead Jews.

His granddaughters returned, out of breath.

"We asked everybody," they told him, "and nobody has seen him at all."

"Maybe he has come home already." Jacob frowned and stood up. He felt the night breeze on his face and sighed.

"It's a fine night," he said, smiling at his granddaughters. "Gorgeous! Look how nice it is here for the poor people."

He took the girls by the hand, and the three of them moved through the streets again.

The family had gone to bed. Jacob sat down heavily at the dining table.

"Go on, go to sleep," he said to his grandchildren. "You got to be in school early tomorrow."

The girls kissed him on each side of his forehead and cried, "Good night, Grandpa."

Jacob remained alone at the dining table, staring fearfully at the empty chairs.

When he walked out of the neighborhood park, disturbed by the sharpened colors of the dying day, Aaron Sholomas awoke from the half sleep of a year. Since the night he had crawled away from the river of dead in Scuzin, the world had been veiled for Sholomas. His soul, like a ghost, had lived only among the prayers in his head.

He looked about him now as he walked and saw the strangeness of streets and buildings, and his head nodded as at an event. He knew that reason had returned to him and he said a prayer of thanksgiving.

I have been away, he thought softly, and his eyes looked timidly on the sights of an unclouded world.

"It is a strange land," Sholomas said softly to himself.

He tried to remember his journey to it, but, when he looked into the past, a pain seized his throat and his mind grew clouded again.

There are things not to be remembered, he thought, and remained like one half asleep and half awake.

He felt the heaviness of his legs and remembered then how old he was and was startled by the number of the years. Like many who devote their lives to thought, yesterday—even the yesterday of his boyhood—had seemed always an hour away from Sholomas.

Time had not touched his mind or altered its preoccupations during the whole of his life. Because of this, the great changes it had worked on his body had often confused him. He was confused now to find himself so old a man, and he thought that he would never be young again because his memories were gone. The road to youth was finally closed in his heart and he would never run down it again to other days.

As he moved through the new streets, he recalled the letters that had once come to him from this strange country describing its wonders and its oddities. Again the pain seized his throat and his heart felt suddenly made of dust. For the letters reminded him of the house in which he had lived and of his wife and grandchildren to whom he had read them aloud. He remembered his wife smiling at them and saying, "How can people be happy away from their homeland, Aaron? It must be they fool themselves."

The pain almost closed his mind again but he continued defiantly to think and he saw in his soul the many burning streets and the dead ones sprawled over one another in the roads and fields. That had been their homeland.

Poor little nests, Sholomas thought, that never belonged to us no matter how lovingly we warmed them.

With a strong effort he kept his thought from running to the grave where all his kin and all his memories lay—the wild grave of Poland.

There are things not to be remembered, he repeated, and busied himself thinking of a history that he knew as well as his own.

This was the history of the Jews. He looked into it now, as he had done since his boyhood, and saw the Jews of many countries and many centuries wrestling with the hate of the world. A fair world, it was—full of learning and gallant deeds. But always it darkened around the Jew and always its wisdom and its kindness vanished in his presence. Sholomas pondered the reasons for this as he walked.

It had grown dark, but the refugee from Poland continued his meditations unaware of the nightfall. He was eager to use his mind but he knew it had become like a wanderer, ready to vanish in a mist if he offended it.

A few people noticed Sholomas as he walked through their city. They saw an old Jew in a long black coat and a ceremonial hat moving slowly in the street. There was nothing in the gravity of the long thin face or the steadiness of the step to tell them that this old man was wrestling with a madness that had imprisoned him for a year.

Sholomas came to a more lighted district. He had been walking for hours and his legs had grown too heavy to move. He stood and mused. These were streets in which Jews were not hated and these were people, according to what he had heard, who were not eager to revile and slaughter them. Sholomas wondered if this were really the truth, for it had never been true in the history he had studied. There had never been such streets or such people in the world. The history he knew revealed that the Jew in moving to a new land carried among his little belongings always the gibbet on which he must hang.

It is not wise to rejoice, he thought softly, over the kindness of a new host.

He had walked far and didn't know where he was, nor could he remember the name of the man in whose house he lived.

He sighed and knew that the silence and emptiness in which he had been living were returning to him again. He thought faintly: I am in another country far from the Germans. But maybe I am only dreaming this is so. Out of much pain, the soul sometimes creates dreams for itself in which to hide.

Sholomas' head grew heavy and he murmured sadly to himself, "God takes away life because I am too weak to look into it. It is not certain that I know where I am. I am old and lost."

He stood with his eyes shut, and the mist covered his mind as it had done on the night in Lublin when the dead moaned in their graves. He began moving his lips soundlessly in a prayer.

After a time, he opened his eyes and what he saw overwhelmed him. He stood for moments trembling and a fear melted his heart. Not far away, a great fire was burning. He could see the flames and the reddened sky and the smoke winding out of windows. Then Sholomas saw there was a crowd moving toward him and he shut his eyes again.

He was bewildered no longer and he no longer doubted where he was. This was no longer a strange country but a familiar one. This was death, the homeland of the Jews. For he knew that where there was a crowd moving, there was death. Where fire burned, there Jews died. Where voices filled the night, there massacre moved with its wild laugh.

It was clear to Sholomas that his hour had come and that, around him, slaughter was raging again. He lifted his head and found new strength to stand erect and think of God.

"Though the Jews are slain as the lowest of beasts," he said softly to heaven, "it is as the children of God they must die, with His name on their lips. For if their goodness is not wanted by the world, they must keep it strong and bring it to God who will accept it."

The sounds of the night overcame him and he stood for a time without thought and waited. Figures rushed by him, jostling him and sending him against a wall. Here he remained with his eyes on the glare of the fire. There came back into his head the voices of the dying in the streets of Scuzin and the voices from the river under the willows and the voices from the fields outside Lublin and from the roads where death had obliterated his people.

He waited for the glare of the fire to sweep over him and for the shouts to bring him death, and he thought as he stood before his last hour: They continue to kill us. I must go talk to those who are dying. I must tell them that it is not we who are doomed. It is those who slaughter us who are doomed. For it is not we they are killing, but a thing in themselves they are destroying. And they must live without goodness or the light of God in their souls until they die. For it is not we who die as beasts but they who live on as beasts. It is written that the man of evil shall be powerless, though he vanquish cities. It is written that he can never vanquish goodness or righteousness except in his own soul.

Thus Aaron Sholomas spoke in his mind as he waited for the massacre to carry him to the wild grave of the Jews.

The policeman who had been keeping part of the Third Avenue crowd from breaking through the fire lines noticed a white-bearded old Jew against the wall.

"Hey!" he called. "Keep moving along there!"

The old man remained motionless, his face raised to the night. The policeman pushed through a group of enthralled fire-engine watchers and came to the old man's side.

"What's the matter, pop?" The policeman took his arm. "The fire scare you?"

A middle-aged woman, standing near them, spoke with sudden nervousness. "He's sick, officer," she said. "I think he's fainted."

"He's standing up by himself, ain't he?" said the policeman, frowning.

Other faces turned toward the stiffened old man at the wall.

"You better get him to a hospital," a second policeman pushed through and decided. "I'll put in a call."

"Poor old guy!" said a voice. "He looks all in."

"We ought to do something," another voice spoke. "We can't just leave him standing up like that."

The night around Sholomas became filled with the kindly voices of an American crowd in the presence of a sidewalk mishap. Someone brought a chair out of the building and put it under the old man. Fingers unbuttoned his odd-looking coat and removed his curious hat from his head. A hand appeared and thrust a small glass of whisky toward Sholomas' mouth.

"Try and drink this," said a voice. "It'll do you good."

Sholomas remained motionless and with his eyes shut.

The faces watching the bearded old man in the chair became silent. The fire in the building had been put out and there was more interest now in this lean, patriarchal figure who sat as if he were dead and yet not dead.

"He looks like a Jew," said the second policeman, returning. "Does anybody know how to speak Jewish so's we can ask him where he lives?"

No answer came, and the silence of a crowd that held no Jews seemed to awaken Sholomas.

"He's coming to," a voice said, and the crowd watched the old man's eyes opening.

The aged face, white with years, raised itself and the eyes looked frozenly out. There returned to Sholomas a flicker of thought, and he wondered feebly where he was and in what land he sat. Then he remembered the burning street and the shouting and he looked at the ring of faces with disbelief. There was no massacre around him. Voices were talking, and two men in uniform were beside him. One was kneeling and holding a glass to his mouth.

Sholomas sipped the liquor and his eyes continued to look from face to face with disbelief, for he saw kindness and compassion. They were the faces of a strange land, faces that grew tender when they saw an old Jew sitting helpless in the street. The liquor warmed Sholomas, and his mind grew suddenly bright.

The wisdom of Aaron Sholomas looked on this strange street in which he was to die and saw its goodness. Here was the street he had never found in the history of the Jews, the shining street in which faces smiled on the tribe of Abraham.

Many unbelievable things had happened to Sholomas, so unbelievable that his wisdom had fled from life. But none was as unbelievable as this street in which he sat with pounding heart, this promised street full of friends.

In these last moments of his life, the torn soul of Sholomas filled with love, and he thought eagerly as if he were young again and had never tasted agony: After many years and after a long journey, I have found goodness that does not vanish where the Jew stands. I have found a home. God is good!

Sholomas closed his eyes, and his lips moved in silence for another moment. Then his body slid from the chair.

The two policemen laid him carefully on the pavement and one of them placed the ceremonial hat under his head. For several minutes, the crowd stood in silence looking down at the dead man lying where people walked. Some of them removed their hats, and others shivered to see, staring up from this busy street, the end of life.

As he had closed his eyes, Sholomas had dreamed of this miracle—that a Jew would be lying dead among strangers and that the night would be filled with compassion.

The Wistful Blackguard

IT WAS FIVE O'CLOCK of a February afternoon in 1919 and Harry Gruenwall, of the *London Express*, and I were standing in the snow-covered Potsdamer Platz, Berlin, full of doubt and excitement. One of those things which belong to the day-dreaming side of newspaper reporting had actually happened to us. As a matter of fact it had only happened to me, but Mr. Gruenwall, an alert and suspicious fellow, had been looking over my shoulder at the moment of its occurrence. The letter which Mr. Gruenwall had helped me read was in my pocket now. I had found it among my mail at the Adlon Hotel. It read:

"Honored Sir,

"The undersigned begs one of the Representatives of the Entente Press to meet him at the corner of the Potsdamer Platz, side entrance, Palast Café, at five o'clock on Friday afternoon. The matter is one of the utmost importance to both parties. If the Sinn Fein influence in Ireland is to be fought in a successful manner, I am the man who will supply the material."

It was signed: "One of the Irish Brigade."

"P.S. Writer will be standing opposite the Palast Café door and will be whistling the refrain of 'It's a Long Way to Tipperary.'"

I had heard of the Irish Brigade—macabre legends relating how five thousand Irishmen had deserted from the English army in 1915 and fought alongside the Germans; and of how Sir Roger Casement had been executed for his part in this wholesale treason. The thing had been one of the most tragic and colorful of the early war incidents. I had been in Germany two months, however, and had been able to find neither hide nor hair of one of these Irish traitors.

The Germans I had talked to were invariably silent on the subject. General Hoffman, who signed the Brest-Litovsk treaty, had shrugged his shoulders and answered, "Yes, I know Sir Roger. A very fine man. But don't talk to me about those Irish scoundrels of his. Damn all their souls, is all I can tell you."

Mr. Gruenwall and I stood waiting. There was much excitement in the Platz. Sparticusten—German Reds—were bombinating from improvised street platforms. Herr Noske's government troopers were dashing about with swinging rifles. A putsch was going on—one of those nose-thumbing encounters between the gabby left wingers of Berlin and the well-fed, well-armed retainers of Herren Ebert and Scheidemann, enthroned in Bismarck's Wilhelmstrasse as heads of the new Socialist Republic. Snow fell. Figures scurried. Battle cries sounded. Hoch this and Hoch that. And Mr. Gruenwall and I, veteran observers of scores of these embryonic Bastille days in this same Platz, waited with our minds on other matters.

"It's a wild-goose chase," said Gruenwall.

"We'll stand right here till six," I insisted.

"Unless these idiots start shooting," said Gruenwall.

Reason counseled me that I was as likely to encounter one of Caesar's legionnaires whistling the latest New York fox trot as I was to come upon my musical Irish traitor. As a reporter I had kept such trysts a score of times and they had always fizzled into adventures with ambitious panhandlers.

At 5:30 Gruenwall grabbed my arm and pointed carefully. Standing a few yards from us in the midst of a street-corner argument was a tall, clean-shaven man. He wore the German uniform and over it the long gray military overcoat. He was topped by an under-officer's cap and sported the bit of black and white ribbon which identified him as having been in the Kaiser's active service. On the cuff of his coat, however, was sewn a shamrock and with an immobile face he was whistling "It's a Long Way to Tipperary"; whistling it softly, with his eyes far away and a bantering smile in them.

"That's a nice song you're whistling," I said to him in English.

He continued the tune without looking at us.

"It's an odd song for you to be whistling here," said Gruenwall.

"It is that," said the whistler in a gentle Irish voice. "Let's go over to the café yonder."

The three of us walked into the Palast Café. A waiter with a shaved head pounced on us.

"We'll take another table," said the Irishman. "I don't like the fellow.

He spotted the shamrock on my coat when I came in. They watch us pretty close now in this God-forsaken city of swine."

We moved to another table in the rear. I asked him what he would drink.

"So you'll drink with me," he said, smiling. "Well, you're an American and an American will drink with the devil, the liquor being good. But how about your friend? He's English. I can tell by the supercilious way he holds his nose. The English can do a lot with the nose, denied to lesser peoples."

"We are three men doing business," said Gruenwall and smiled. "What's your order?"

The Irishman looked at him amiably. This was a few months after the Armistice and patriotism was still a major matter in the world.

"A strange people, the English," said our guest. "Well, if you'll drink with me, the both of you, that's encouragin'. Even though the liquor's no good. Nothing's worth a damn in this hell-hole of a place."

We gave our order. Shots sounded in the Platz.

"Do you hear 'em?" said our guest and chuckled. "Poppin' away at each other like a lot o' ducks in a shootin' gallery. God aim all their guns straight and keep 'em from wasting good ammunition."

Our drinks arrived.

"Well, to begin at the beginning," said our guest, "my name is Quinn Lusk. And here's luck to you and me. I see," he turned to Gruenwall, "you're studyin' my uniform. Yes, take a good look at it. There it is. It's the sort of uniform that fits a traitor and a blackguard, eh? That's what you're thinkin' now. Well, I don't usually parade around in it. But I put on my full regimentals for the rendezvous. Gentlemen, you are studyin' the uniform of the Irish Brigade, that bunch of high-minded cut-throats who fought for old Ireland in the war—on the Kaiser's side."

Gruenwall sputtered.

"I told you the liquor was no good," said Quinn Lusk. "Or is the business not to your likin', sir?"

"Go on," said Gruenwall.

"If it's not to his liking," said I, "there's always the door and a droshky back to the Adlon."

Gruenwall grinned at me.

"I'm a newspaper man first," he said.

"That's fine," said Quinn Lusk.

"Go on about the Irish Brigade," I said. "And I'll order some more drinks."

"Oh, we were a fine lot, we were," said Quinn Lusk, "and so were the ladies and gentlemen who enlisted us in the holy cause of Irish freedom, damn their souls, under the Hun flag, the dirty swine."

Gruenwall, grinning like a Chessy cat, was fumbling with a pencil stub.

"Never mind taking the notes now," said Quinn Lusk. "I'll write it all out in a formal document myself. I'm a pretty good writer. And I'll get you legal documents, letters to Roger Casement and letters from Sir Roger; and I'll load you down with all the existin' data there is on the famous Irish conspiracy, I will. And all that for a paltry few hundred dollars."

He paused to smile at the machine gun trilling a few blocks away.

" 'Tis music," said Quinn Lusk. "It rocks me to sleep every night. Do you suppose there's any likelihood of them blowin' the whole town to bits, swine and all?"

"I doubt it," said I.

"Before we can get down to prices," said Gruenwall, "we'll have to hear a sample of your story."

"Here's lookin' into the bright eyes of the future," said Quinn Lusk, raising his glass, "and here's the sample of the story without any doo-dads thrown in. First, I'll tell you that I was a member of the Royal Irish Regiment stationed at Raglan Banks, Davenport, England, when the war broke out. And that for six months I fought beside my comrades against the Huns. And if you'll come to my room I'll show you my real uniform, the uniform, sir, of the Royal Irish Regiment that I've kept like a mother keeps her baby's shoes."

Quinn Lusk swallowed another drink—we had ordered a bottle brought to our table—and turned his bantering eyes to the snowfall outside the windows of the Palast Café.

"The liquor, bad though it is, makes me mellow," he said. "I'm sittin' here thinkin' that there was only one rotten low-down trick left for me to do that I haven't done; and that was to sell out the people who have kept me fed and clothed for the last year. But that's what I'm doin' now or goin' to be doin' so it's perfectly all right. Me character is intact. If you'll pay me money, I'll give you the story of the Irish Brigade. I've stolen a lot of letters and documents incriminatin' everybody that's been good or bad to me."

"How much?" said Gruenwall.

"Well," said Quinn Lusk, "I'll leave it to you and your conscience."

I suggested five hundred dollars. Gruenwall frowned.

"Your friend is right," said Quinn Lusk, "that's too big a sum to pay for anything except my appearance on the gallows."

"Three hundred is plenty," said Gruenwall.

"I'm in no position to haggle," said Quinn Lusk. "I'll trust you for the amount in case you haven't got it on you. I know you newspaper men, English or American. You'll buy drinks for blackguards and deal honestly with the devil for the sake of a story. You're a fine sort and here's to you. So that's settled. Three hundred dollars, American coin, it is."

We waited while Quinn Lusk indulged himself in a reverie.

"I don't feel just right about it," he said, "for even a scoundrel like myself has his fine feelings and his better moments."

"You'd better forget them," said I.

"Not a hard thing to do," said Quinn Lusk. "I'll tell you somethin'. I'm a traitor and I turned traitor because I believed a lot of lies. Or, to be honest, maybe I didn't believe 'em so much. I'm wastin' my breath exoneratin' myself and I know it.

"You're English, Mr. Gruenwall, as I saw at once from your supercilious nose, and you'll maybe get red under the collar. But the English have always been dirty dogs to me. They turned my grandmother out of her home in Ireland and they've ridden my country for a century like she was a spavined nag fit only to be whipped. Ha, listen to me wave the green flag! Me, a dirty louse in a turncoat."

Gruenwall continued to nod amiably and sip his brandy.

"Well," said Quinn Lusk, "when the opportunity came, if you wish to call it by that fine name, I was ready to meet the Hun halfway. I'll tell you all about that as soon as I have swallowed me next drink. You've got to be used to this cognac to drink it for it ain't fit to wash the feet of a pig in. Now you lads keep sober and let me do the drinkin' for it's a small bottle, be damned to you. First, gentlemen, I wish to say that if I had it to do over again, I wouldn't be doin' it for a fortune nor would any of the boys—the worst of them—not that there were any good ones, I assure you.

"Some of us joined because of the wine and women they gave us and the high-class food; and some of us went over because we were dirty scoundrels. But we all had something in us that made it seem right—when we got enough liquor under our belts—a love for old Ireland and a hate for England."

Quinn Lusk leaned back in his chair and whistled softly his theme song, "It's a Long Way to Tipperary," and we waited patiently for the end of this musical interlude.

"Well," said Quinn Lusk, "I was thinkin' this while whistling. When you come to write the story be sure you make one fact certain and outstanding—that there were only forty-nine Irishmen in the Irish Brigade. That with all the thousands of marks the boches spent, with all the women they dragged into our beds, with all the fine, dirty promises they made, they could only get forty-nine of us. Not another soul. Just a damned forty-nine. They claimed one thousand and five thousand, but damn their eyes, forty-nine is the number; forty-nine creatures like meself.

"Oh, it was a black day for me when I listened to Casement. But Sir Roger was a man. Don't mistake that. A fine man with a big soul. The only man in the whole lot of swine who was working for Ireland at German expense. Working for Ireland, indeed! A lot they cared about Ireland. A lot they cared about freedom and all the fine words they talked. A pack of double-dealing swine they were, with nary a spark of soul in them, makin' traitors out of half-starved Irishmen in German prison barracks. Lyin' to them and cheatin' them worse than any English landlord. All except Sir Roger. Nary a word against Sir Roger from me. I was a boy of twenty when I joined. And it wasn't till later that I saw that poor Sir Roger was bein' played with, cheated and lied to by the Huns. He was never a scoundrel was Sir Roger, but a gentleman and a patriot with a silly head on him. I'll drink his health now and damnation to all the rest of the Irish Brigade, meself included, and every man and woman who had their dirty fingers in the mess."

By himself Quinn Lusk drank his bitter toast and then grinned at us.

"It's an old story to me," he said, "rattlin' around in my head for four years. But it gives me a queer feelin' to be tellin' it to gentlemen like yourselves. You see, I was one of the first to succumb to the Hun blarney. I was in prison barracks and when they come after me I thought they were the salt of the earth with their Kultur and their fine manners and their words of love for Ireland. And recognizin' my merit, they made me recruiting sergeant among the Irish prisoners in Germany and gave me my pick of a dozen gals for me escort. I was the silver-tongued little flag-waver who talked Ireland to the boys. And to help me along in their conversion, my polite friends, the Huns, held up their rations and beat them when I wasn't looking. And when they were rollin' on their beds with pain and hunger I would come marchin' in spruce as a Darby winner and begin promisin' them countesses and duchesses and feather beds the like of which they'd never even seen, let alone slept in with their dirty hides. 'Kisses and wine, money and victuals,' said I to them, 'and a noble cause to fight for.'

"And they only got forty-nine of us, with all of it. Forty-nine of the blackest-souled scapegoats in the army, including your humble servant, meself. By God, we'll drink to old Ireland that had only forty-nine traitors in her ranks—silly, empty-headed blackguards though they were."

Again Quinn Lusk drank his toast alone. He continued seemingly none the worst for the half-bottle he had swallowed.

"Well," he said, "we cost the Huns a pretty penny and we killed more of them back of their lines than we ever did fighting them from the Allies' front. We gave them plenty, I tell you, even though we did march up and down Unter den Linden like a lot of geese under an Irish-German flag. There was Malone who broke the neck of Unter-Offizier Baumgarten in the football game at the stadium. And Paddy who cut the throats of two sentries in the Danzig guard house. And Tim who knocked the life out of a Prussian Hauptmann with a monocle and a lisp. And our Sergeant-Major who stole the wife of a Bavarian Colonel and then finished the irate fellow off with a club. The Colonel's lady was a wild one and before we got through with her she was havin' fits at the sight of a green blade of grass.

"Oh, we've done our bit back of the Hun lines, fighting everybody, including ourselves. For we were a fine pack of patriots after Sir Roger left us—drinkin' and ravishin' and murderin' up and down the country."

Gruenwall interrupted.

"Did they put you in the trenches?" he asked, softly.

"Put us in the trenches," Quinn Lusk laughed. "Eh, now you should know better than to be askin' that. They knew better than to be askin' us that, they did. No, they didn't stick us in their lousy trenches, nary once. They knew what we thought of them and there wasn't a man in the Brigade who wouldn't have sold what was left of his soul for the chance of emptying a brace of guns into a Hun dugout. No, they paraded us in our fine uniforms with the shamrock starin' woefully from our sleeves and the poor flag of Ireland over our heads. They used us as propaganda. And the girls leaned out of the windows to cheer us and pelt us with roses. There were forty-nine of us in the propaganda and there were forty-nine hundred who got paid for the job—Americans among them: Irishmen livin' on the fat of the land while we starved in our traitor barracks—after Sir Roger left us.

"Yes, sir, a lot of fat rogues collectin' their thousand marks a month as the price of our shame while we had to knock a man down in an alley to pick up the price of a drink. That's how the thing turned out, you see. We sold our souls to the devil and he double-crossed us."

We ordered another bottle of the raw cognac and our guest shook his head to clarify it and agreed he would eat some eggs.

"I feel better now," he said, "about sellin' them out. When I come to think of it in the full light of me reason it's not so bad a deal I'm doin'. Perhaps I'm doin' Ireland a good turn after all, by handin' them over, names, letters, documents, and all kinds of fancy proof. And that was all I wished for once when I listened to poor Sir Roger. Here. I brought one of the letters—as a credential of me villainy. I'll read it to you before I go on with the story. But another drink. Because I'm sellin' out one of the few women that was good to me. A very fine Irish lady and a traitor like meself. Mrs. Fannie G—— of Munich. A lovely woman and a traitor but she meant well and she was an honest friend to Sir Roger."

Our guest removed the letter from a wallet and read it.

"Dear Sir Roger,

"Just a line to cheer you up with the news that thanks to the generous assistance of Mrs. R——, Mrs. T—— and Mrs. S—— where you dined one evening, I will be able to send a very nice Christmas present to each of your Irish volunteers.

"I wish you could see the things because I am so pleased with the result myself. Each one gets a green satin bag filled with some cakes and candies—a tiny sample of tea tied up in green. A box of fifty cigarettes and what else remains to be decided tomorrow, but I thought best to let you know lest you might be getting things in Berlin when they are provided here."

"I repeat," said Quinn Lusk, "I have a room full of papers and documents and such. It is the whole history of the Sinn Feiners and their connection with the German Irish plot."

"We've settled for three hundred dollars," said Gruenwall.

"That we have but I've changed my mind," said Quinn Lusk.

"For instance?" I inquired.

"You'll be surprised," said Quinn Lusk, "but I'm for giving it all away free. Not a shilling asked or taken."

"Don't be a fool," said Gruenwall.

Quinn Lusk's eyes, a bit reddened with the liquor, grinned at the two of us.

"I'm not that," he said. "Never that. Do you happen to know the British Colonel stationed in Berlin?"

"Yes," said Gruenwall.

"Then I'm a lucky man," said Quinn Lusk. "For if you'll arrange for me to meet that gentleman I'll give him all the evidence I got against the traitors of England—free without a shilling changin' hands."

"To square yourself for going Hun?" asked Gruenwall.

"To Hell with that and with the British, all of them," said Quinn Lusk. "I'm feeling this moment like I always have for the British. A pack of lyin' tyrants that have ruined my country, if I can be said to have a country, which I doubt. I bear them no love, mind you. And I hate the Huns, mind you. And I hate the Sinn Feiners for gettin' me into this mess. I hate them all impartially. But if you'll arrange the matter I'll hand the documents over to this Colonel providin' he agrees to let me go back."

"Where to?" asked Gruenwall.

"Dublin," said Quinn Lusk.

"No other perquisites?" asked Gruenwall.

"None but that," said Quinn Lusk. "I would like to walk on God's earth again in Dublin, daffy though it sounds. I would like to sit in an Irish pub and get drunk again with Irishmen. And I would sell out me own grandmother for the privilege. Take me over to his nobs the Colonel after you have spoken with him and he can have everything I've got. Enough evidence to jail a thousand Irishmen and hang as many if he wants. And all I'm asking him is safe passage back to Dublin and he wash his hands of me once I land there."

We made the pact, interviewed the Colonel and waited for word from Quinn Lusk. We learned after a week that he had been arrested in Riga for drunkenness and fighting. And while he was languishing in some Baltic jail the March revolution broke out in Berlin. This interfered with our using the Quinn Lusk story. And in the excitement of workingmen fighting behind barricades, of aeroplanes bombing our hotel and of rumors that Trotzky and his Red Hordes were about to sweep westward across Europe, Gruenwall and I almost forgot our Irish traitor.

He appeared late in March, bleary-eyed and in tatters.

"I broke jail," he said after we had taken him to my room. "I thought sure they would be makin' an end of me. I was in for two years and I was almost tired enough to stay there. But I gave me promise to the British Colonel and I'm here to keep it. I've moved the documents to a place outside the city. Come along and I'll get them. And trust to the honor of an Englishman to keep his side o' the bargain."

At this point I was pushed into the background of the negotiations. British officers appeared. There was considerable palaver and scurrying and Quinn Lusk, in a new suit of civilian clothes, seemed a busy man. A week passed and he arrived again with Gruenwall in my room.

"I'm for saying good-by," said Quinn Lusk. He was half drunk and beaming. "My friend Mr. Gruenwall and the British factotums, God bless their dirty souls, have arranged for my returnin' to Dublin. Only I have had to promise the Colonel and so has Mr. Gruenwall that we will not be using the story I told you—for some time."

Gruenwall rather sheepishly corroborated this.

"I've given my word," he explained, "not to use the yarn until the British intelligence department gives me permission. I'm in rather a fix. You have half-rights in the story and it's up to you. If you want to print it go ahead and Quinn stays here in Berlin. If you care to hold off publication Quinn goes to Dublin."

"Sure you'll hold off," grinned Quinn Lusk. "What is a story more or less to you, you havin' the fine brain you have for figurin' out so many o' them. It'll be as good tomorrow for printing as it is today. Hold off," he stared intently at me, "and I'll drink to you every night wherever I am, in good Irish whiskey. And to you, too," he turned to Gruenwall. "I'll toast the both of you from one end o' Dublin to the other. What's more it'll only be a question of months. A few of them, I tell you. The Sinn Feiners, who are a nosey lot, will be finding out what I've done and be after me. I'll have an alias and take care but they'll come on me when I'm least expecting them, the filthy dogs, and make an end of me. And once I'm out of the way you can print the story as long and as wide as you please."

I succumbed to the sentimental project of preserving the worthless life of Quinn Lusk. Gruenwall gave me my share of the documents, although the cream of them had gone to the British Colonel. Two days later Quinn Lusk came to say a final good-by and drunker than ever.

"God damn their dirty green souls," he cried. "I'm goin' to Dublin tomorrow and there's no race as cruel and vengeful as the Irish. Swine they are but me own kind. They'll cut me to pieces as soon as they find out who and what I am. But I'll drink enough of their liquor and listen to enough of their talk to last me for a long time in Hell, before they rend me to bits."

Quinn Lusk left Berlin and the subject was dropped. Gruenwall and I commiserated with each other one evening on the sentimental trap into which we had fallen and went about our business for our papers.

I returned a year later to New York. Quinn Lusk went out of my head along with other curious anecdotes that had occupied me in post-war Germany. Another year passed and then the story received its ending. A letter from Gruenwall arrived containing a short clipping from the *London Express*.

"Maybe this will interest you," wrote Gruenwall.

The clipping read:

"The body of a man riddled with bullets and outrageously beaten was found on the West Road outside of Dublin. A hint of mystery was aroused by the discovery of the crime when it was learned that the dead man was one Quinn Lusk, active for some time in the Sinn Fein movement. Lusk had been living in Dublin for two years under the name of Timothy Frees and leading a disorderly life. No clue to his murderers has been found by the police."

Specter of the Rose

I HAVE TO MAKE up much of this story because it's something that happened inside of a man's head. I knew the man well. But knowing a man and knowing the inside of his head are separate matters. A Russian once wrote, "The soul of another is always darkness." This is true about most people we know, even those close to us. The human mind, including the one we use ourselves, is an eternally unknown land.

But in writing of my poor dead friend I'm not dealing entirely with matters unknowable and unseeable. For there is a tribe of people whose secrets are more apparent than those of the rest of us, and whose mental underworlds are to be glimpsed by the veriest of strangers. These are the people who are medically identified as mad. My friend was one of them.

His name was André Sanine. He was young, he was handsome, he was a ballet dancer, and he was mad. He had the muscles of a tiger or a truck driver, the endurance of a sea gull, and the face of a smiling boy.

When I first knew him his madness had not progressed beyond the stage of charm. His character consisted seemingly of a single quality. He desired only to please people—not only people he knew, but everybody. A taxi driver, a waitress, a newsboy, a hotel porter, a property man, anybody's wife, mother, or uncle—André wooed them all as if he were a child plotting to locate the good graces of the world and snuggle in them. You would have sworn that this powerful and gentle youth owned a heart as innocent and overflowing with love as a valentine. You would have sworn it, and wondered why it was necessary to argue a thing that seemed so obvious. But that was always an interesting thing about André—he failed to convince you entirely that he was the André you knew. Yet my friend was so graceful, so reserved, and his eyes were so selfless and so full of a happy interest in everything they looked on, that people felt refreshed on meeting him, and when they got to know him better were ready to forgive whatever secret evil might lie hidden behind so pleasing a manner. For you could smell this evil.

There was about André's youth the faint and bitter smell of decay that you can detect in some flowers when they are at their prettiest. Long before he became mad and revealed the evil that was in him, it was to be sensed. It lay somehow coiled away in his boyish smile, and you could get a glimpse of it moving dimly under his very wooing of you.

I doubt if any one was bright enough to see through André when he was the talented darling of the ballet. I know I wasn't. I found him at times a little disturbing, as too much charm often is. And I wondered at times why it was that, if André loved everybody and everything, he had nevertheless managed to avoid falling in love with one particular human being. This was curious, since many exotic young women I knew were always swooning at the mention of his name. Yet no scandal of any sort had ever attached itself to that name. I thought this not only curious but surprising. For André inhabited a world where scandal was the rule, where passion, hysterics, and intrigue were the commonplaces of every hour. This was the world of the ballet—whose inhabitants seemingly devote themselves only to grace and disaster.

The people of this exuberant world are to be seen in the rehearsal halls toiling like the damned in the development of every one of their fifty-odd sinews, leaping about bathed in sweat, paling with exhaustion, breaking their toes, ankles, and kneecaps—a little race of men and women incredibly dedicated to the pursuit of ruptures, of heart enlargements, and of major bruises. All these exhausting rehearsals flower a few evenings a year into a dance. On these few evenings the toilers are to be seen drifting about in colored spotlights as rose petals, autumn leaves, sylphides, peacocks, and genii made of smoke and magic.

Yet these people who have learned to move as if music and not blood flowed in their veins engage in amours often as graceless as those of the most backward of savages. Their matings, infidelities, and reprisals are full of scream and cruelty. It may be there is a connection between their austere and backbreaking labors and their sadistic romances, but I will forego prying into it. I hint at all these matters only because they were André's background, and if you knew this background you could understand the glint of evil that touched his most boyish of smiles and the cruelty that seemed to sleep in his gentlest of words—and ignore it as only natural.

André's position as a dancer was, in these first years I knew him, more a matter of promise than fact. He was expert in all the leaps and sudden flashes of strength and balance the art of the ballet demands of its children as a matter of course. He knew the myriad steps and pantomimic movements that went with the various great tunes to which the ballets are performed—for these maneuvers are seldom left to the inventiveness of the dancer. They are usually a ritual handed down by the choreographers. André was alive also with that extra gleam of personality which, more than any other factor, ultimately separates the champions from the chaff in the ballet as everywhere else. And underlying all he did, even to the smallest of his day's details, was a love of dancing—a love so obsessive as to make him seem either less or more than human as do the yogis and lamas and the ancient saints.

Whenever I was with André where music played, were it only a barrel organ or a taxicab radio, he danced. He danced sitting still and with every muscle motionless. He danced inside himself, his mind moving about in leaps and convulsions. At such times André wore a sleepy and abstracted look and gave the impression that he had turned into a statue.

Thus equipped, this fragile-faced youth with the constitution of a truck driver might have made that skyrocket leap out of the ranks of promise but for the thing that happened to him—madness. It was a long time—a year at least—before I or anybody, except one person, had any idea of the mania that had come to roost like a vulture in André's head and to feed upon him, to devour his charm, his talent, and his bright smile. During this year that he had gone mad behind our backs, as it were, André worked hard and danced well, and continued to woo those he met, to beam upon and refresh hundreds of strangers. And the first rumor his friends had of his coming darkness was entirely unrecognizable as such an omen. Talk came to me that André was in love with a pretty dancer named Maria Ivonova, who was not nearly as foreign or exotic as her name, having been hatched in Trenton, New Jersey, and raised in the home of a warehouse employee and an ex-stenographer—her parents.

André finally achieving a love affair was, in fact, pleasant news to his many friends, all of whom immediately considered the girl lucky beyond her deserts, for she was neither particularly beautiful nor greatly talented. As the year progressed I saw André and his Maria a number of times. I saw always a smiling youth who treated his blond and rather innocuous sweetheart with the same grace and politeness he might have lavished on a dancing partner behind the footlights. But after several dinners with the couple I began to notice that André's Maria had acquired a wary look, that her manner toward my friend was too eager, too uncertain. And I began to suspect there was an André I didn't know at all, a behind-closed-doors André who was as far removed from a valentine as a war communiqué.

I read of this André one morning in the papers. He had choked Maria Ivonova to death in the middle of the night, and been found sitting quietly at her bedside in the morning and smiling to himself.

There was no doubt whatsoever from that morning on that André Sanine was a maniac. Even the police did not contest this fact. And André's trial as a murderer never got beyond his examination by the medicos. The doctors all agreed that André was insane, and supporting their finding was the diary poor Maria Ivonova of Trenton, New Jersey, had kept. In these almost childlike pages was found a record not of a lover but a monster. They revealed that since the first month of their marriage—a fact André had kept secret from his friends—he had been intent on only one thing: the murder of his bride.

He had begun with a series of jealous rages which had startled Maria into writing that André was unreasonable and that she would do everything she could to convince him that she loved nobody but him and was entirely true to him in all her thoughts as well as deeds. But apparently André's jealousy, so groundless and yet so necessary to him, was not to be reasoned with. It bloomed, it flourished on all of Maria's protestations and proofs of innocence. It grew big and dark and engulfed them both in something that could barely be written about—at least, not by Maria Ivonova. There were innumerable pathetic entries in the diary recounting nights of violence, screams and sobs.

She wrote in the third month a frightened cry of understanding. He was not responsible, she put down. He wanted to drive himself crazy, so that he could scream and mistreat her, because there was something in him that made this necessary. And after he had hurt her he would fall at her feet and weep and ask to be forgiven. Then his face, grown strange in the night, would become familiar again. In the fourth month she wrote that he had begun begging her to leave him and save herself from his craziness. But she had refused because she loved him. And he was trying hard to cure himself. He worked so long and so hard that when he came home he could hardly sit up. He would fall into bed and go to sleep scowling at her and trembling as if something were shaking him.

Toward the end of the year she wrote a dark little cry of love that I have never forgotten.

"How can he be so nice to everybody else?" she put down. "He must be two different men. I am afraid of him. I ought to leave him now. He cries all the time that I am ruining him with my badness. He says I am not to be trusted out of his sight and that I run after every man who looks at me. This is so untrue. But I can't tell him that any more. It only makes him worse. All he wants is that I should confess something to him. And when I have nothing to confess, he goes crazy and he loses control of himself. I know he will kill me, because that's what his craziness wants to do. But I can't bear to leave him even if he is a monster. Because sometimes he is still André. He still kisses me sometimes."

André was sent to a state institution as a man criminally insane. I visited him there occasionally, as did many of his friends. For a long time—years, in fact—these visits were more or less perfunctory. They were of no service to André—he was unaware of them.

I would come to his ward and watch him for ten minutes or so as he sat immobile before a long wooden table, his arms hanging limply, his head turned rigidly at an angle. He never moved. At such times I remembered how he had used to sit almost like that when music played and he danced inside. I wondered if this melancholy rigid figure were still dancing inside; for there was always music playing out of the ward's radio.

Many of his friends forgot André, for his fame had not been enough to make a legend of him. But a few of us continued to come to the institution to take note of his condition. And after five years we began to see that André's melancholia was loosening its violent fingers from his soul. André began to look at us and to remember us. He emerged slowly, as if he were afraid of the light into which he was moving again. He spoke and smiled once more—a little timidly. The doctors told me, however, that he had no memory of his crime and that the name Maria Ivonova was gone from his mind. It had sunk somewhere into the depths of his soul, together with the monster it had evoked.

I was glad about André's improvement. I called more often. And he took to showing me drawings he had made of dancing figures or of curious whirling patterns which he explained shyly were the essence of dance movements. He drew them always while the radio played.

The authorities finally allowed him a phonograph and I was permitted to bring him records of his favorite ballet music. He asked only for three—*The Faun, The Blue Bird,* and *The Specter of the Rose*. I was told that his condition had improved basically and that there was some chance of his being released. The doctor explained to me, however, that as long as his crime remained hidden from him and the name of Maria Ivonova out of his mind, André could not be considered sane, no matter how plausible all his speech and actions seemed.

André's charm began to reassert itself. Every one who came in contact with him now began to feel, as of old, refreshed by his presence. Innocence was again returning to his smile, and the authorities grew eager to help him. Thus encouraged, he began to plan his return to the world. These plans consisted at first only of daydreams and drawings. He dreamed and he drew dances. He had selected the three ballets —*The Faun, The Blue Bird,* and *The Specter of the Rose*—to practice and to dream about.

"I am," he said to me, "going to be like Nijinsky was. I am going to dance his ballets. They are letting me practice now. My elevation is better than ever and my beats are a great deal improved. I am very good. I dance very well. I never get tired. And besides," he added, smiling sadly, "I have something else in me."

I asked him what that was.

"Atonement," said André. "I must atone for what I have done. I can only atone by dancing. I am unfit for living. I have learned this. I am fit only for art. I will atone for having been so bad by dancing better than anybody ever did in the world. Wait and see!"

When André told me this, I knew for the first time he had remembered Maria Ivonova.

He was thirty-six years old when the doctors, who had come to adore him, declared that he was sane enough to return to the world. And after fourteen years of exile André returned. Many things had happened in these fourteen years—among them the fact that the world had gone mad. Wars had swept nations out of existence and shaken the soul of man into a rage and a confusion almost unparalleled in all history.

But none of these things had happened to André. He returned to the world he had left. Neither politics nor cannon had touched it. It was an inner world so serene and pretty that André, living in it again, seemed madder than he had ever been. Still, it is unfair to consider a man a lunatic because he refuses to participate in the lunacies of others. Just the same, I was worried about André from the first night we dined together in our once favorite restaurant. I watched him go to work in the rehearsal hall and went to concerts with him, and tried to assure myself that André was sane. Nothing had aged in him except his smile. His face was still a boy's, his body still leaped like a cat and a sea gull and seemed full of smoke and magic.

But his smile appeared to wear a little crutch. It appeared to lean on his mouth.

"You mustn't worry about me," he said one night. "I am entirely better. I understand myself. There was something bad in me. But it's gone. Or anyway it's buried so deep it will never rise again. I won't let it."

Then he leaned over and whispered with a smile, "I won't let it."

André delayed his return to the ballet. He rehearsed constantly, bought costumes, and spoke of nothing else. But I began to feel that André, with all his rehearsing and planning, was never going to dance again. It is that way sometimes with artists who dream too deeply and aspire too high. They outstrip their talents. They sit like birds dreaming of the moon which is too far away to reach, and their wings, accordingly, remain folded. I don't know if there are any such birds, but there are such artists—rehearsal halls and attics full of them. André had become one of this tribe of "not good enough yet to start" geniuses. Other dancers dropped in to watch him practice. They clucked with excitement over his work, pronounced him head and shoulders above all his contemporaries, but seemed to understand perfectly his need for more practice.

After five months André turned up one evening at my studio with his new partner. Her name was Nina. She was young, blond, shy, and shapely. We sat for an hour trying not to show our nervousness. I was nervous because Nina reminded me of Maria. André was nervous because he knew what I was thinking. And Nina was nervous because she was obviously entranced with André and hoping that his oldest friend would approve of her. I didn't. I wouldn't have approved of Genêt or Pavlova as a partner for André. I would have preferred never to see him smiling gracefully on any woman again.

"Would you like to see a performance?" André said, after we had talked for an hour.

I turned on the phonograph. It played *The Specter of the Rose*. This is a ballet in which a young girl returns home from a ball, falls asleep in a chair, and dreams of a beautiful man dressed like a rose who arrives through the window and dances for her. She rises in her dream, dances with him, and returns to her chair. And the beautiful man spins and soars about her, and then, to a final burst of music, leaps out of the window and her dream.

I was full of admiration for the performance. There was no question about it—André was that thing apart, a body made to dance. His technique was invisible. He leaped as if he were floating, and he still seemed to float as he returned to his feet. He gave you the confusing impression that his body was so light it had more difficulty remaining on the ground than capering in the air.

That was the last time I saw André dance. It was also the end of my friendship with André. After this visit he became fugitive and mysterious. He took to rehearsing in out-of-the-way halls. Tracked down in one of these, he vanished again. He moved from his small hotel and his address became unknown. He was to be seen occasionally dining or making a purchase in one of the special shops dear to the ballet people. He had not disappeared out of the dance world but removed himself to its edge. And here he hovered like a shade—but not a lonely shade, for Nina was always beside him.

I thought several times of notifying the doctors who had become so fond of André about his new love affair. But I knew that André saw them every month. If he had lied to them about Nina, my uncovering the lie would mean his return to the asylum. This stopped me. I remembered also André's whispered promise that he would not let anything happen.

This is the part of the story now that must be made up—the part that happened in André's head. He married Nina as he had Maria—in secret. They were married the night they danced in my house. And Nina loved him even more than had Maria. For she was simpler and had no inkling of the inside of André's head. She failed to see the vulture return and the darkness come again.

She has told me since of how deeply André loved her. She remembers his love as something rather mad but wonderful. She lived with him as if they were two people alone on the moon. And to the end she never knew that it was not love but murder that lay beside her.

He used to spend the night trembling and weeping, with his body curled into a ball beside her and his hands clinging to his strong ankles. When she asked him why he wept, he answered her always that it was because he loved her.

All day he danced in various dusty rehearsal halls. She danced with him, performing over and over again the three ballets he was forever preparing. He wore out dozens of phonograph records, bought new ballet shoes, went into debt for fresh costumes, and sat up half the night drawing pictures of figures leaping and of whirling patterns. And when he was so tired that his head fell forward, he came to bed and curled himself up in a ball and lay trembling beside his bride. And of all this struggle with the vulture come to feast again on his sanity poor Nina had only one memory—a memory of being loved.

André was keeping his promise. He was not letting it happen again. But why did he remain with her when the thing began? Why did he keep her at his side when he knew that murder was again in his hands?

He must have seen the strangeness of his face in the mirrors before which he practiced constantly. He must have felt the evil back in his heart, and unreason, like a goad, tormenting him. His need to cry out the hatred he felt must have eaten at his throat.

The answers to why he remained are difficult to make if you think of André as he seemed—a smiling, eager lover of life, full of charm and gentleness. But there was another André. This other André lay for months locked away in a ball, and the André I knew wept and trembled with the agony of keeping him there. The André I knew lay in the dark, night after night, saying to himself that he was a dancer and not a murderer, that he was meant to dance and not to kill.

And dance he finally did. I have the story of his performance from Nina.

Due to a lack of money, they had moved into the servants' quarters of a large midtown hotel. André knew one of the managers. The room they occupied was small and furnished with only a bed and a dresser. It was directly under the roof and forty stories above the street.

They lived here on the management's bounty for a month. During this month André's nights had increased in horror. Even Nina had begun to feel there was something wrong with him; for, though he still loved her and wept at her side and trembled, he no longer spoke to her. He had fallen into a silence that nothing could break, not all her pleas and kisses. And, what was worse, he had stopped practicing.

On awakening each morning now, André would dress himself in the costume of the Rose, and he would remain sitting all day on the edge of the bed in his tights, his flower jacket, and his ballet shoes. Nina found a job clerking in one of the small stores in the neighborhood. She would leave André in the morning costumed for his ballet. At six o'clock she would return to find him still sitting in his lovely costume. The phonograph stood on the floor at his feet, but she learned from the people in the next room that it never played while she was away. It never played when she was at home.

But its music was in André's head. It never went out of his head. It played constantly to him, and he danced constantly to it—as I used to see him doing long ago—sitting still without a muscle moving and dancing inside himself.

It was on a spring night that Nina came home with the news that she had spoken to a doctor about André. The doctor was coming to visit him in the morning. André looked at her with tired eyes and said nothing. He sat motionless beside the silent phonograph.

Nina was weary that night. She sighed herself to sleep, dropped some tears silently on her pillow, and managed to sleep, although she knew *he* was still sitting on the edge of the bed. Something woke her— a sound, a sense of danger.

She opened her eyes and saw André standing over her. He was still in his costume—otherwise she would not have recognized him. His face was contorted, his eyes were another color. His mouth was stretched wide open and a strangling sound came from his throat. Nina's heart almost stopped as she saw the figure leaning over her. She saw the hands rise from his sides and reach toward her throat. She was unable to move or cry out. The hands came slowly around her throat. Their fingers tightened—and her terror was such that she was able only to whisper, "André."

The fingers remained, but their grip grew weaker. They remained for a number of minutes, and during these minutes André's face bending over her did not belong to him. Then the hands fell away and André stood up straight. He held his arms out rigidly. He raised one foot, bent his knee, and spun in a pirouette. Watching him from her pillow with eyes still terrified, Nina saw that André was dancing.

There was barely space in which to move, but André danced in it. And she recognized each of the long practiced turns and leaps of *The Specter of the Rose*. She recognized even the part of the ballet he was dancing. It was the part where she had returned to her chair and her dream was leaving her.

André's face was his own now. She recognized the gentle gleaming smile with which he had always performed the finale, and although the room was silent she knew he was dancing to music. It was a smile only music could bring. And then Nina's heart grew cold. For Nina knew the finale, the famous leap to be made out of the room—and out of her dream.

André was spinning like a top beside the bed. He came out of the spins. His eyes smiled gently on her. They were the eyes of a lover who was a rose, a dream, a thing of smoke and magic. And suddenly, coiling himself into a ball, he made the leap. His body crashed through the window.

Nina was on her feet. She rushed to the broken glass. She looked and saw him. He was falling straight as an arrow, his arms lowered, his hands folded in front of him, and his feet were making entrechats. His head was tilted gracefully to one side.

She saw him only for a second or two, but she was able to tell me this: He was dancing as he fell.

The Bull That Won

BEHOLD THE ANCESTORS of Pepe Santoyo, very prominent and spectacular people. Aztec priests and princes walking in gold shoes wearing mantles made of many-colored feathers; stately, childlike and sadistic. Gilden barbarians, say the historians, a race of murderous peacocks who once presided over an ornate little nightmare in the hills of Mexico. Grandfathers, these, of Pepe Santoyo.

Then come Cortez, the Great Captain, with his little group of helmeted cronies and earth shakers. A greedy, dauntless troop, say the historians, of Castilian Vikings; an iron-hearted crew called Conquistadores that hacked its way through the wedding-cake forts of Montezuma. These are also the grandfathers of Santoyo.

Then come the Colonial Lords, the Dukes and Hidalgos with their gibbets, bonfires and snickersnees. Horrendous bloodletters who vivisect an Empire and perform a hundred years' autopsy on its twitching cadaver searching for gold. And among these elegant monsters and Epicurean ogres of New Spain, more grandfathers for Pepe Santoyo.

And here our hero's lineage takes on complications. The sacrificial stone atop the Temple of the Sun no longer runs a river of blood down the pyramid steps into the gardens of Teotihuacán. The Aztec peacocks, plucked and scattered, chirp sadly in the hills. Pepe Santoyo's second crop of grandfathers rule but undergo mysterious alterations. Their skins slowly darken, their voices soften, their eyes grow velvety and a third yield of grandfathers enters the Santoyo lineage.

These are known as Mexicans, a moonstruck race of harlequins, heroes, and barefoot generals. Blood runs, death gallops the deserts and the purple hills; new flags and slogans fill the air—but the historians smile. These new grandfathers of Pepe Santoyo are full of glory and garrulity. They make war like happy children and die like stock company actors. They bow to firing squads, sing between volleys, fight like lions and argue like geese. They laugh at blood and weep at sunsets. But out of the hurdy-gurdy sounds of their battles and powwows the Republic is born. New government buildings rise and become full of statesmen in frock coats. And a lusty counter party known as The Revolution entertains the world with a mysterious series of Lost Causes.

And among these are the immediate forebears of Pepe Santoyo. They include a wagon-load of generals—General Inez García, grandfather and patriot who spent twenty-five years capturing people in the hills of Chihuahua and who in his dotage took to collecting the ears of his enemies; General Fierra, grandfather and patriot, who blew up the first, second, and third railroads between Monterrey and Saltillo as non-conducive of the honor of his country and the liberty of his people; General Manello, uncle and patriot, who seized the City of Vera Cruz and declared war on England, Germany, and America, in which unequal contest he died gloriously; General Santoyo—but the list is too long for detailing. Suffice that all these patriots who combined in the creation of Pepe Santoyo met death with a flourish, fell before the white wall smoking cigarros and smiling contemptuously upon the antics of their executioners. All, that is, with the exception of Santoyo père, whom destiny favored not only with a civilian temperament but an attack of the influenza, and who died (to the astonishment, no doubt, of innumerable ghosts) at the ripe age of forty-nine in a Louis XIV bed in the midst of more collateral than glory. Señor Santoyo, head of a Tampico oil company, was mourned by a board of directors, a widow aged twenty-eight, and a son turned eleven.

When he was eleven, Pepe was an undersized, sallow arrangement of skin and bones such as would have broken the heart of any Nordic mother. His manners seemed to hark back to a first-run ancestor, Ixtlxochitl by name and Lord of the Sun, who at the age of four fought and vanquished his nurse, drowning her in a deep well. When asked for an explanation the youthful Ixtlxochitl replied coldly that he did not relish somebody always telling him to blow his nose and that the defunct attendant had failed on the whole to treat him with proper dignity.

This same precocious sense of lordship had run in the veins of Pepe Santoyo almost from his birth. He had grown from a fragile but domineering baby into an egomaniac of eleven. At this age he conceived the world as revolving around him and its chief inhabitants—beginning with his mother, her fourteen servants and his three uncles—as slaves dedicated to his whims.

His father's death had made no impression on him. He had nothing in common with this puffy, methodical old gentleman and he received the news of his passing with a shrug whose heartlessness actually frightened the youthful and grieving widow. Some ancient impulse gave Pepe the impression at this moment that he had succeeded to some throne and after the funeral he worked quickly and ruthlessly in establishing himself. For a year the Señora Santoyo allowed herself to be bullied and harassed as his chief subject. But at the end of this year her brother, Felipe Ortiz, observing her rapid decline under the rule of her beloved tyrant, stepped in. Pepe, his four personal servants, his two wagon-loads of toys, devices, souvenirs and loot, were moved to the vicinity of Guadalajara and installed upon his uncle's extensive ranch. Uncle Felipe had expected this new and more primitive environment to curb the extravagances of Pepe's spirit and make a man of him.

"My men," said Uncle Felipe, in conference with his now hysterical sister, "are a very hard lot, half-bandit, half-centaur. They will soon take all this babyish nonsense out of Pepe and in a year he will change into a fine, healthy, sensible youth—like his father."

"But they may hurt him," the Señora protested. "They won't respect him and he suffers so. My poor little one is so proud."

Uncle Felipe snorted.

"They are honest, simple fellows, my men," he said, "and they will respect Pepe as much as is good for him. And no more."

"Take care of him," wailed the pretty Señora in farewell.

"I will, mucho," smiled red-faced Uncle Felipe, rancher and stock-breeder. And the train pulled out of the Tampico station.

None of the things Uncle Felipe had expected happened. Pepe, from the moment of his arrival, annexed the thousands of acres, crops, stock, bandits and centaurs, and set himself up as their new lord. Neither his spirit nor physique underwent a flicker of alteration. The bandits and centaurs struck no awe in him, and the boiling sun, the cold winds, the hard riding in the hills, trudging through deserts, hunting, sleeping under stars—all these numerous physical forces and activities left him as sallow as before, added apparently not a muscle to his undersized and spindly body.

But among these half-wild folk who worked the Ortiz ranch and defended it against other half-wild folk in the hills, Pepe Santoyo came into his own. They were of a race that had always responded to lords and heroes. In this arrogant, contemptuous little one, they perceived with a vision much more romantic than Uncle Felipe's, the blood of kings and captains. Nor were they misled, as Pepe's previous retainers had been, by the spindly legs, bony hips, flat chest and sallow face. They beheld under this anemic exterior a grace that delighted them, a mysterious strength that seemed to come from neither muscle nor sinew, and a courage that was noble. He would tire quickly, this little one; he would fall suddenly to the baking earth exhausted from his chasings, and there he would lie white and spent like a stunned fledgling. But he was up and on his feet in a few minutes, as good as new, as arrogant and contemptuous as ever and as ready for more hardships as the toughest of them.

Then, too, they admired his ugliness, his long nose and slightly malformed mouth and jaws. He was no pretty boy of the towns such as came to visit in the hills sometimes—but a muchacho who, with all his lordly airs and riches, bore the stamp of race on him such as their own ugly brats exhibited—the true mongrel look of one whose grandfathers came from thrones at different ends of the earth.

In the second month of his visit Pepe Santoyo discovered old Barrera, the ex-matador, and his stable of bulls. Barrera was an assistant overseer on the Ortiz ranch, but twenty years before he had worn the coleta in the bull rings of Spain and Mexico. Fame, riches and the love of many fine ladies had been his, he explained to Pepe. But he had been forced to retire and to turn his back upon glory because of a hernia. He could for that matter, he insisted, despite his gray hairs, and his hernia, go into a bull ring today blindfolded and with a penknife vanquish the kind of moth-eaten bulls with which the present worthless tribe of matadors engaged in Mexico City. Two years ago he had attended one of these disgusting exhibitions and wept over the collapse of the great sport.

"In the old days," said Barrera with a sad and modest snort, "there were matadors. Today there are little clowns in red and gold."

Pepe Santoyo, when he heard these statements, sneered and nodded. There was born in him immediately a great contempt for all modern bulls and all modern bullfighters.

Barrera from time to time had added to his staff certain cronies who came drifting through Guadalajara—toreros and picadors who had in the old days played the bull-ring circuits at his side. These joined in bearing out the tales of the hernia-ridden matador.

In the third month of his guardianship. Uncle Felipe, busy with a roundup and far from his hacienda, despatched messengers for Barrera and his riders. They were needed in the hills. The messengers returned in three days with word that Barrera and his men were deeply engaged by the little one who had refused to release them from their work. They were, said the messengers, training the young Señor to be a matador. Uncle Felipe fumed and rounded up his herds and galloped back for a showdown with Pepe. But on the long ride Uncle Felipe began to think this over. His sun-bitten bandidos riding behind him were already improvising songs of the future glories and triumphs of their muchacho.

"The finest bulls will die of fear
When they behold our boy come near,"

they sang:

"Their eyes will roll, their blood will freeze
Before the nephew of Ortiz."

And Uncle Felipe, for whom this nephew's charm had been always a waste product, mopped his red face and pondered as his saddle creaked. Never had he had so little trouble with these rascals behind him as since Pepe had come. Who knew but what it might turn out for the best? If not a matador what else in the name of many saints was this nasty youth good for? An ugly, irrational, and idiotic child, mused Uncle Felipe, but decided there would be no showdown.

The training of Pepe Santoyo was from the start an unconventional business. Before he had learned to tell a bull from a heifer Pepe demanded a matador's suit. After it had been constructed, he wore it on Sundays between the hours of three and six, parading the cattle pens so that his uncle's bulls, in case any of them ever found their way into some bull ring, might remember at such a time how a real matador looked.

Under the guidance of Barrera and his erstwhile troupe of toreros and picadors, Pepe chased young bulls with a stick, learned their mannerisms, studied the language of their eyes, hooves, and tails. Within nine months he had mastered the repertoire of Barrera and his cronies, learned in theory all the passes, gestures, and genuflections of the great art. Never had Barrera beheld such precocity. Never had he seen anyone, even in the great days, so at home with the cape, so graceful with the sword. But more than this was the thing that could not be taught—the courage that shamed the bull and filled his heart with despair long before the steel entered it. This his protégé possessed beyond all his predecessors in the arena.

Pepe listened to the praise of his instructors and nodded kindly at them. Praise, even then, did not embarrass or elate. It inspired a passing friendliness. But brilliant pupil though he was, Pepe became a great trial to Barrera. He disdained certain invaluable rules. He was indifferent to the play of the cape which makes a good show and delights the crowd. He was disinterested in the thousand and one ballet gestures and flourishes which are the pride of the matador. He refused to handle the banderillas and confined his practices more and more to lunging with his new sword at a mark and to chasing and being chased by bulls.

"I care nothing for all that other," Pepe explained coldly. "When I enter the ring, I will not act. There will be no make-believe. I will kill the bull, immediately."

"But," argued Barrera nervously, "the people will not like that. They like a good performance. Believe me."

"Good," argued Pepe, "then let them send in bulls clever enough to perform against me. For when I am matador the bulls will perform, not I. I will kill."

The bandidos and centaurs roared at these replies and Barrera grew thoughtful. This mania for killing in his pupil impressed him. It was a sign, he whispered to his cronies, of greatness. Not a day passed but Pepe brought down a half-dozen chickens and a stray dog or two with his agile sword. His marksmanship with this weapon delighted his admirers. One old Zapatista watching him one night climb the roof of the hacienda, sword in hand, and give battle to the bats swooping around his head, crossed himself and swore to his friends that there was devil's blood in this princeling.

The feats which most delighted Barrera and his cronies were those in the bull pastures. One bull did not suffice but he must venture with three and four. He would stand still, wooden stick in hand, staring calmly at the animals while the horsemen lounging in the vicinity looked on and held their breaths. Then he would approach one of the beasts, smiling almost lovingly into its eyes as he drew near. And when the animal charged, with that swift, head-lowered rush of a locomotive, Pepe's face would brighten, his eyes would glisten, his body would stand poised as if arrested in a dance measure. And with the death-dealing horns lifting to toss him he would move aside with neither leap nor scurry in his step. His manner at these vital moments thrilled the very stomachs of his tutors. His movements, as quick and unexpected as those of some fish, were a delight to watch, but more than these, for Barrera and his cronies, was the sense of mastery which stamped the performance. With two, three, and sometimes four of the beasts hurling themselves at this fragile and seemingly motionless figure, bellowing and thundering by him with their horns grazing his arm as they lifted for the kill, it was the bulls and not Pepe who appeared full of troubles. Uncle Felipe, observing Pepe's daily flirtations with death, noting how he delighted in teasing the most ferocious of the beasts, maliciously plucking their tails when they had failed to murder him, whacking them with his wooden stick as they wheeled to renew their goring efforts—noting these blood-curdling antics of this sallow whippersnapper of a nephew, Uncle Felipe would shrug his shoulders and observe calmly that he was witnessing either a great matador or a young corpse in the making—and that personally it was a matter of small importance to him which.

During the three years that followed, Uncle Felipe, at the insistence of the Señora Santoyo, engaged other tutors than his horsemen for Pepe—gentlemen of learning from the capital who were given the task of educating his ward. Pepe waved aside their theories of education, their books and their lessons and suffered them to remain on the ranch only as long as they had stories to tell him, historical tales to recite, or new and unforeseen facts concerning life in general to impart. As soon as they ran out of these pleasing informations Pepe dismissed them and waited coldly for their successors.

At sixteen Pepe killed his first bull and this was in the bull ring of Durango, a sun-baked town some hundred miles from the Ortiz ranch. Uncle Felipe and all his horsemen, friends, and neighbors were in the stands. Barrera, acting as sword valet for his pupil, was as nervous as a dog with a bone. The bull lumbered into the sun, the toreros turned him in circles, placed the banderillas; a picador's horse was gored, the trumpet sounded, and Pepe stepped forth in his gold braid and gleaming red silks. Nothing to speak of happened. He approached the bull disdainfully, for he had seen at a glance what a stupid beast it was. He stood looking into its eyes with contempt for a few moments and then with a single flourish of the cape lowered its head and thrust home with his sword. The bull's legs buckled. He sank and died. Pepe withdrew his sword, wiped it clean, and bowed first to the dead animal who, though unworthy of his steel, had yet the honor of sharing his début, and then to the President's box.

Uncle Felipe's horsemen cheered and old Barrera leaped up and down and was for rushing into the bull ring to embrace his pupil. But the crowd remained unimpressed. They saluted the youth of the matador with a few good-natured vivas. That they had witnessed the début of a great bull-ring hero never entered their heads. And leaving the arena, Pepe sensed his failure with the crowd and smiled.

"They are a pack of stupid fools," Pepe confided to his uncle that night.

To which Uncle Felipe answered, very pleased with his nephew's chagrin, "They are the audience you have chosen to impress."

"They are not," Pepe answered.

"Oho!" said Uncle Felipe, "you are already dreaming of Mexico City and Madrid and Lima. Hey! Hey! Hey! Well, let me tell you now, my young one, you'll find the same audiences there as in Durango."

"I am not dreaming of audiences," said Pepe.

"Then why," pursued Uncle Felipe, "why waste your time becoming a matador if you are so nobly indifferent to audiences."

"I do not need audiences," said Pepe. "I would just as soon kill bulls by myself. I am all the audience I need."

"You are a young fool," said Uncle Felipe, growing red. "You make me angry."

Pepe was silent and as his uncle's face reddened and his head lowered he regarded the rancher with very much the same look in his velvety eyes that he had turned on the stupid bull who had shared his début a few hours ago.

"You are not worthy my attention," Pepe answered slowly, which was also what he had said to the beast in the bull ring of Durango.

Two days later Pepe left the Ortiz ranch, taking with him his many swords, his dozen matador suits and Barrera. The bandidos and the centaurs rode with him to the railroad station, singing:

> "The palm trees will weep with every dawn
> When they wake to find our hero gone."

And prophesying to another clanking tune that within a short time the most beautiful women in the world would be groveling at the feet of their muchacho for one of his smiles:

"Farewell," they sang, "O prince of matadors. If you get into troubles call us, send for us and we will come and strangle your enemies with their own whiskers."

A few days later Pepe embraced his mother in Tampico, demanded an advance on his inheritance, listened politely to her maternal cries of love—and departed.

There are now many journalistic legends about Pepe Santoyo's beginnings in the bull ring, tales recounting his early prowess and fame. But these are, alas, apocryphal. Pepe's stubborn antics in the bull ring that first year almost finished him. For it was audiences he fought more than bulls, audiences and toreros, picadors and sport officials.

In the Puebla arena he stood regarding a knock-kneed bull by the name of Diablo for five minutes without moving, then walked up to the chicken-hearted beast, slapped its nose soundly and killed it with a single thrust—all this after the toreros had leaped about the ring in fine exhibitions of courage and agility in the face of this same death-dealing Diablo.

In Jalapa he tossed aside his sword at the signal for the kill, snatched a stiletto from Barrera's kit, returned to the wobbly and meditative beast and despatched it, exactly as he had seen it done in the slaughter house in Tampico.

In Monterrey he actually pulled a doddering old fake of a bull around by the tail, dragging the discouraged animal to the President's box and killing it while holding its nose to the ground with his foot.

Toward the end of the year, however, word trickled into the capital of a very youthful matador whose integrity was disorganizing the bull-fights in the provinces. Disgruntled toreros helped launch the Santoyo legend. Barrera, who knew his way among the sporting groups of Mexico City and who was almost beside himself with the unrecognized genius of his protégé, finally secured the big managers. There was always the likelihood of news in a newcomer. The capital boasted a number of bull-ring favorites, fellows full of grace and daring. But since the retirement of Juan Belmonte, there had been no greatness in the arena, no one to release that curious ecstasy which lay in the public bosom for the true master of the bull.

Under Barrera's eye the fight was properly planned to show off his protégé at his best. First a noble bull, if there was such a thing left in Mexico; secondly, very little business from the toreros; thirdly, small business by the picadors. Señor Santoyo desired to reveal his skill against a ferocious and untired beast.

On the appointed Sunday, Pepe emerged, bowed, and walked across the glaring ring to engage the murderous attention of El Fino—and the stands beheld almost immediately their new idol. For there is in every type of champion the unmistakable signal of destiny—unmistakable, that is, to eyes trained for its existence. It is the inner strut of the hero, the aloofness and precision of the artist who offers not himself but his performance for the vivas of the crowd.

The fragile figure of Pepe Santoyo in its gold and scarlet silks, facing the bull on this first afternoon, filled the veteran spectators with that strange vibrancy which the virtuoso, known or unknown, must generate before he can perform as one. It is this pause before action, this arresting and secretive evolution of the human into the promise of hero under the very eyes of the spectators that raises their spirits and prepares them for doings on a higher key. In these first moments before El Fino, not all the ancestors of Pepe Santoyo marshaled around him could have added a whit to his boast of courage and prowess.

The stands applauded, the señoritas smiled excitedly, the newspapermen, who in Mexico resemble old-fashioned bartenders, nodded appreciatively to one another; the scattering of American tourists marveled unprofessionally at the youth of this gladiator and his lack of physique and his ugly face; and the occupants of the President's box leaned forward expectantly.

Pepe Santoyo's joust with El Fino passed into bull ring history that afternoon. For twenty minutes he stood without breaking ground, gliding and turning before the charges of the beast with the sudden, imperceptible agilities of a fish evading a blow. Time and again it seemed that El Fino, head lowered, horns tossing, had rushed right through him as if he were a phantom in red and gold; which is probably what the distracted animal complained about to its gods as it swung its empty horns and bellowed at the blinding sky.

One of the newspapermen described the performance as a thing of such exquisite beauty as to move the dullest member of the anti-administration forces to tears. It was, he wrote, superb, and restored bullfighting to the estate from which, owing to the confusion in Mexican life created by these same sinister forces, it had fallen in recent years.

The public that had actually witnessed the début of the new idol grew more mysterious and inarticulate as its raptures increased. It remembered the details of Pepe's performance through the haze of hero worship and was ready to proclaim each of his gestures a grace unknown before, and each of his movements a feat unparalleled. As for the young matador's courage, that was beyond the power of mere words—even Mexican ones—to describe. He had not fought but danced gravely with a bull more ferocious than any ever seen in an arena. He had waltzed the beast to death, never missing a step, and despatched it in a single gesture so rhythmic that El Fino himself must have felt its grace.

The cafés buzzed with the advent of this new hero. And of these matters Pepe Santoyo, dismissing the fawning and garrulous Barrera for the night, had only to say: "It was a fine bull, my friend."

The fame Pepe won this afternoon was his beginning. Within six months Lima and Madrid had enrolled themselves as captive cities. There too he inspired raptures and rode on the shoulders of idolators. But it was in Mexico that he was loved. Was he not descended of Cuauhtemoctzín, King of Kings; of Ixtlxochitl, Prince of Princes; of Captains and Generals, Heroes and Saviors too many to mention? It was truly as if all these potentates in feather mantles, all these conquerors in steel and silver, all these noble and spectacular sires of Pepe

Santoyo had collaborated to produce one supreme human being. And in these flourishes of adoration with which they surrounded his name, Pepe's countrymen were stating indeed a biological and racial truth.

For Pepe's secret in the bull ring was that he held himself not as matador but conqueror and priest. It was the smell of death that stirred his senses as he approached each beast and its blood that gushed after his sword was the symbol of a mysterious consummation. The battle with the bull became for him more and more a delicious ritual in which his pride was crowned not by the plaudits of the stands but the death of the beast. As his countrymen sensed he was in truth the perfection of a breed. Out of a double lineage drenched in blood, whose sadistic deeds and valor incarnadined two worlds, had been hatched this murderous little goldfish of a matador who loved to kill bulls.

Three years passed and Pepe progressed from the position of idol to that of national institution. He made his home in Mexico City, establishing himself in a great house surrounded by lovely gardens. He appeared weekly in the bull ring and made trips to Spain and Peru when the Mexican season was at an end. Despite the fabulous success that had come to him, he remained unchanged. His egomania was more than a match for his fame. As on his Uncle Felipe's ranch, praise failed to impress him. He had the air of one who wanted nothing, least of all the plaudits and ecstasies he inspired. Fame, his manner proclaimed, was an accident unnecessary to his greatness.

The caprice and cruelty, the fanatic pride in self and disdain of the world which his new friends mistook for the results of a turned head, the bandidos and centaurs of the Ortiz ranch had known years before. Uncle Felipe, after a brief visit to his nephew's palace in the capital, testified, in fact, that he had found the young man altered by not a hair, but the same bad-mannered peacock he had tried in vain to make a man of on his ranch.

The only change which distinguished Pepe, the national idol, from that spindly, sallow boy who had chased his Uncle Felipe's bulls with a wooden stick was his attitude toward the women who fell like exhausted moths at his feet. It was an attitude which would have stunned a moralist and outraged a lover. The señoritas who achieved his favors found themselves reduced in his arms to a species of toys. Their sighs, swoons, cries of love and fealty were to Pepe a very natural and pleasing form of play they had to offer. He was gallant and lavish. He returned vow for vow, kiss for kiss, fire for fire and passed from adorer to adorer with hardly a consciousness of change. He loved gracefully and at times his spirit softened to a kindly, almost childlike excitement.

But however ardent his arms and lips, his heart never dreamed of to-morrow or remembered yesterday. His heart, in fact, had no existence in his amours.

When he was twenty Pepe succeeded, with small effort on his part, to the affections of a vixenish nymph of the theater known to the public as Venida. The liaison contained a slight novelty for the national idol. Venida, scratched and dented from the hands of his predecessors, was still a brighter toy than Pepe had yet acquired.

She was to begin with a very odd creature to look at. A few inches less of height and she might have been classified as a dwarf, or rather as a miniature adult. Unlike so many undersized women, her head was small and perfectly proportioned, her body and features exquisitely re-lated. She gave the impression of a full-blown, beautiful woman seen through the wrong end of an opera glass. Despite the jet coiffure and the high instep she was neither Spanish nor Indian to the eye, but that perfect neutralization of the racial atom which produces a breed iden-tified in all countries as exotic.

Pepe, listening to her sing at the vaudeville theater one evening, felt the stir of interest which as a child he had always experienced before a rare toy. Her voice, full and robust, as it issued from so fragile a mold, delighted him, and never ceased to delight him for three months.

Barrera, now factotum to the nation's idol, was less delighted. The nature, name, and color of Pepe's conquests were matters which he re-garded with the indifference they deserved. But this little doll woman who came hardly to the shoulders of the great matador was with all her airs of this and that a vixen, a bawd, and a wolf at heart. She filled the great house into which the amiable great man had introduced her with such yowlings as belonged in the fishmarkets. A strumpet, said Barrera, a female to be handled with a brass-studded belt. There was nothing in the world worse for a man than this breed of wanton, not even a diet of cactus or a pocket full of rattlesnakes.

"She's not for you," pleaded Barrera; "you can never understand such a beast as this. She is worse than a bull with six horns."

Pepe waved his factotum aside. He understood the grounds of Barrera's complaint. Venida was the first of his conquests who neither swooned in his arms nor sang hymns to his glory. But Pepe was tired of embracing señoritas with a matador's suit and bored with being em-braced in return as if he were some public shrine on the loose. He pre-ferred this, at least for the remainder of the bullfight season.

Accordingly, for three months Venida wheedled gifts out of the national idol as if he were a Tampico oil man with a roll; stole from him, lied, cheated, and indulged herself in such infidelities and hysterias as her position at the theater offered. And all this delighted Pepe. She had for him the mystery and charm of the heretic.

One Sunday night Venida came home in an astonishing mood. Pepe was in the garden awaiting her. He was half asleep. The bullfight season had closed that afternoon and he had been carried out of the ring on a thousand shoulders and almost murdered by adoring salutes. There was also Señora Morales, a proud and beautiful lady who was languishing with love for him; and her fifteen-year-old sister Teresa who had threatened to return home and hurl herself from the top of the highest pyramid in Yucatan unless he kissed her. The great matador had spent the evening in the home of these two admiring and swooning women. Thus he awaited the charming Venida under the tropical stars, with that good nature and detachment which only a rake can bring to the problems of love.

She arrived two hours late, walked the garden for fifteen minutes and then threw herself on the ground at Pepe's feet, embraced his legs and fell to sobbing. Pepe grinned in the dark. Such homage had never been his from Venida. And what pleasanter finale to a crowded day than this—the surrender of a heart that had so long mocked him? He listened, however, a bit dubiously. Venida was a talented actress. He listened and studied each note of grief, each arpeggio of pain and then closed his eye contentedly. The tune was perfect. He had never heard it better sung, or more sincerely. What a fool Barrera was. A bull with six horns, indeed! This little one with head lowered, as all the rest, for the coup de grâce! Ask nothing of a woman, be content to kiss, smile, and wait and her heart broke for you. He was pleased. It was in these moments of heartbreak that Pepe found, connoisseur fashion, the caress of pride he most desired. And surfeited though he was by the sighs, kisses, and hosannahs of the day, Pepe felt grateful for this exhibition in the garden. He stroked the grief-tumbled coiffure and felt very wise and gallant, even though no thoughts were in his head.

Venida's sobs ended but her tears continued to flow as she spoke, as if there were two voices coming from her. Pepe listened, his hand making tender comment on her hair. She did not expect to be believed, the poor little one insisted. She had been so wicked, done so many naughty things; even laughed at him in her heart. But look at her now. Weeping. She had never wept for any man before.

Briefly, Venida's tale concerned an American, Señor Lewis, a mighty theatrical producer from the city of New York, who had been swept from his feet and enchanted by her talent, and who had offered her a contract, three thousand pesos a week, her name in electric lights bigger than the Montezuma Beer sign opposite the Regis Hotel, to return with him to the States. Confronted with this golden opportunity, Venida had shuddered and found herself unable to seize on it. All this because she could not bear to be parted from her matador. She had never suspected it before, but the tragic incident had revealed to her that she adored him. She had refused riches and a career for love of a faithless man. But she was content. Love had made a fool of her, as she had so often done of men. This was justice. She asked no more than to be allowed to remain at the side of her lover until he tired of her and cast her away.

With this tale of sacrifice concluded, Venida, overcome anew by its significance, resumed her sobbing. Pepe, looking down on her in the silver-lighted night, considered her for the moment a creature of infinite charm.

There is a gallantry in heartlessness that lovers can never hope to achieve. To the lover, sacrifice is a reward for pains and desires. To the gallant it is a challenge to his pride. Pepe, receiving this unexpected gift, reached for his own superior pocketbook.

There were perhaps other forces that moved him to the gesture— the bullfight season was over, the capital was hot, Barrera was becoming a bore, Doña Morales and her juvenile sister had insisted he spend a month with them on their estate, and, as happens to all monarchs at times, his domain this night under the monotonous moon seemed to have grown small and airless. He thought, however, of none of these things. Speaking casually, as befits the bestowing of a truly royal and superior gift, Pepe pointed out that her grief and sacrifice were unnecessary since he had decided to go with her to the city of New York.

He was delighted with the result of his announcement. With a cry, the little one stared at him an instant and then sank to the ground quite as if she had fainted. Pepe accepted this gesture. He was, himself, pleasantly overcome by his own sense of largesse and with a tired and amiable grin he raised the little one to his side.

"Broadway—the heart of the world," sang the chorus boys who have rouged and asymmetrical faces. The chorus girls waved their bodies and squealed in unison of love and the summer moon.

New York, tall, glittering, and hot, drifted like a plate-glass galleon through the summer day. At night there was a Chinese actor full of grave and incoherent passions and a German pugilist with a promising right-hand wallop. At night there were Africans who leaped to a chant called Black Bottom, a Spaniard who strummed the guitar as if he owned four hands, an English lady with a Hamlet face who sang ribald Cockney songs. A cannonade of lights proclaimed these and other novelties in the Broadway dusk. Jazz bands played, clowns sobbed their griefs, courtesans bewailed their broken hearts. Semites moaned for the Carolinas, gigolos hurrahed for the Open Road, and from a thousand stages came the strut and whinny of the evening's makebelieve. New York, tall, daft, and cosmopolite, cakewalked with a Roman candle in its hand.

Pepe Santoyo, moving in these gaudy streets, felt a sting of desire in his heart. He was no longer an alien. New York colonizes its admirers quickly. Seven weeks had made Pepe a New Yorker.

He knew where the loudest bands played, where the prettiest girls danced, where the best liquor was sold, where the finest people went. He had learned the names of the funniest comedians, the most exclusive hostesses, the biggest gamblers, the best prize fighters, the leading baseball heroes and the current sophisticates. He was already a familiar and accepted figure in the whirligig of the town's night life. His name was inscribed in the shifting roster of celebrities that meet like some secret society in the cafés, theater lobbies and hotel suites.

He had learned to pass under the charging traffic without quickening his step, to drink ten cocktails without falling asleep or making arrogant remarks to strangers; to distinguish between the regulars and the upstarts, the Giants and the Yankees, the head waiters and the diners, the wives of Caesar and the cuties of Pan. He knew his way blindfolded from the Savoy Plaza to the Forty-fourth Street theater where Venida's name was raised in burning letters above the crowds. He spoke a broken but determined English and could whistle the chorus of the Maine "Stein Song." He had met the Mayor, week-ended on a magnificent yacht, raided the Fifth Avenue haberdashers, presented a tall, blond and internationally famous hetaera with an extravagant keepsake, been fêted by the Spanish-American Society and given a movie test at the Paramount Studios in Astoria.

These experiences and accomplishments, which had crowded the seven weeks in their acquiring, had generated a queer excitement in Pepe Santoyo, had disrupted that character which so many kings and captains, presiding over his inception, had bestowed on him; and had planted a nettle in his heart.

Amid these gaudy streets, surrounded by these pale, glib people,

Pepe felt the impact of a stronger land. Here, in Broadway, was that bull with six horns of whom Barrera had mumbled. And if his mind, never an instrument for analyses, failed to visualize the scene in the dramatic terms of the Great Sport, his spirit responded with an eagerness which reminded him of his early days in the bull ring. Ambition filled him, for what he did not know. Desire kept him awake, for whom he could not tell. He was, as he explained it to Venida, full of new life.

He was admired and sought after. He plunged from revelry to revelry, sporting his coleta amid Hindu turbans and Montparnasse haircuts. He offered side-splitting imitations of Venida, using a lampshade for a hat and a phonograph record for a fan. He laughed more in one night than he had in a year, and his gay, vibrant manner overcame, wherever he appeared, the handicap of his long nose, his prognathous jaw, his sparrowlike physique and his rapine tendencies. He was regarded by his new friends and hostesses as a distinguished youth of precocious poise and energy, as a dangerous satyr and an amusing type of Mexican.

Yet, with his blood tingling under this bombardment of jazz bands, cocktails, social and amorous triumphs, which seemingly made him master of this new and fantastic bull of the six horns, Pepe woke each noon clamorous and unsatisfied. There was too much fame, too many heroes, too many ballyhoos to drown out the vivas he won. It was a land that consisted of too much; of too much play and work, too much money, too much noise and light; a land that was lost behind too many. This was its lure for Pepe and the nettle in his heart.

He laughed at Venida's capers. Her infidelities, now signalled by the appearance of jewels and shining automobiles, amused him no less than in the capital. He reminded her ironically, during their infrequent tête-á-têtes, of how her great love for him had almost caused her to sacrifice all these delights. And arriving one night in her dressing room, sleek as a Pomeranian, ugly as a cuttle fish and bristling like a seltzer bottle, he told her he was returning to Mexico in four days for the opening of the bullfight season. He inquired, with mock tenderness, whether she could bear to stay in New York without him.

"Yes," said Venida, "I am no longer a child."

Sitting in her dressing room, watching her change from a Mexican into a Broadway cameo, he smiled coldly at her answer. He preferred the Venida who had burned and swooned at his feet in the silver-lighted garden a few months ago and for a moment this unruffled Phoenix angered him. She seemed suddenly part of that New York which one held and lost from day to day. Pepe studied her and whistled the Maine "Stein Song."

"I have called to take you to my party." He came out of his favorite musical practice with a smile.

"Your party," Venida laughed.

"Yes. It is in my honor," said Pepe, "to wish me good-by."

"Who will be there?" Venida inquired, for no less than Pepe, she was now a connoisseur of parties.

"Everybody," said Pepe.

Pepe had looked forward to this revel arranged in his honor by a visiting ambassador as a climax to his New Yorkhood. Very prominent people would be present, representatives from all the electric-lighted courts of fame that flourished in this land.

Pepe beheld them as he entered the buzz and glitter of the drawing room, the bull with six horns decorated for the coup de grâce. They had assembled to honor him with a farewell and he beheld them with a proud heart—sportsmen, financiers, aviators, aristocrats, journalists, gilded idlers, a renowned philosopher on a world tour, a British peer famed for his horses, a sprinkling of high-priced actors and opera stars; polo players, gamblers, and Casanovas all occupied like a well-trained chorus, bowing, nodding, chattering, drinking, laughing, and with an easy, unyielding egoism in their eyes; and illumining the corners and divans of the room the consorts, conquests, and courtesans of these assorted heroes.

Venida disappeared from his side. For a few minutes his entrance rippled the scene. Butlers balanced trays before him, celebrities turned bright welcomes on him. Journalists paused in their interminable anecdotes to shake his hand. Paunchy little men with tight red faces whom he recognized as members of the mysterious tribe called lords of industry offered him cigars and cigarettes and inquired with youthful winks after his friend Venida. For an hour he drifted from group to group swallowing another cocktail every time a butler caught his eye. He wandered into the room where the music played and made love to all the women he danced with but one. Her he treated to a whistled accompaniment to the orchestra playing the Maine "Stein Song."

But despite these familiar exertions the sense of revelry died in Pepe's bosom. Despite the music, liquor, kisses, and laughter, Pepe found himself being pushed by something very mysterious, out of the scene. It occurred to him that this farewell party in his honor had nothing to do with him. New York had nothing to do with him. He tried for several minutes to assemble his pride and greatness and he stood, as had one of his third-yield grandfathers, blowing a bugle to charge to troops that had fled.

He surveyed the scene, closing one eye to see it better, twisted his mouth into a remarkable sneer and spat at a passing butler. The servant paused and glowered. Pepe, as if challenger to a sneering competition, twisted his mouth, this time including his nose, into an even more horrible grimace. The butler gave up and hurried away.

What did these gringos know of bulls and the fine business of blood and death? What had he, Santoyo, been doing, wasting his time with such ignorant and lowly ones! (The troops, a bit disheveled, were shuffling back to the battlefield.) Did they think they were as fine and noble as Santoyo? Well, he would settle that matter right now. He was through with them. Closing one eye, he surveyed again the blur of gringos laughing and chattering around him with another fearful contortion of his face, this time abetted by a contemptuous noise half hiss and half belch, then he turned his back on them and moved to a corner. There he sat down and waylaid drinks whenever they passed, scowling until his jawbones stuck out at unbelievable angles. A stupid race, the gringos, who did not even know how to smile. Give him the hearty laugh of the bandidos.

Pepe opened his mouth wide and a sudden penetrating cackle rang out. A lady nearby dropped her drink and squealed. Pepe made a sickening face at her.

"Oh—but they're dangerous, these Mexicans," said the lady who was too old for kissing and moved hurriedly away.

Pepe fell to dreaming of better company. A smile hovered over his sour face and his eyes rolled up in a melting look as if he had drifted abruptly into a trance. Ay, Mexico! he was hungry for that Mexico whose dust lay white and tender on his heart. He began to fancy in the midst of this stupid gringo scene, the sun-baked roads of Jalisco. The acid sweat of bulls came into his nose. And over the deserts rode the black-browed, the strong-hearted, and ever-smiling bandidos. He saw them, himself in their midst, and heard them singing as he left them at the little depot, a matador on his way to the bulls.

"Farewell," they sang, "O prince of matadors. If you ever need us call for us and we will come and strangle your enemies with their own whiskers."

A cry broke from his mongrel, exiled heart.

"Ay—y, muchachos. Here I am. Pepe!" He held up his hand.

"Very good for killing bulls," someone laughed behind him, pointing at the fist he shook.

"Yes!" screeched Pepe. "No good for punch. No good for baseball, tennis ball, football. No good for here. But for keeling bulls, the best in the world."

A chorus of cheers stopped him. He looked drunkenly around, his heart sick for the little red and yellow kingdom of the bull ring, for the vivas of his empire. Now was the time to go. The muchachos had come and rescued him. He felt the calm and smiling faces insulting him for the last time. On the way to the door, staggering from figure to figure, he saw Venida. She was gringo scum. He was going back to Mexico. She would never go back.

"Good-by." He lurched past her, making a nasty sound under his long nose.

In the next three days Santoyo continued to drink and to grow more Mexican. In restaurants he demanded eggs with garlic and at the Savoy Plaza, where he lived, he required chili sauce on his chicken. He discovered a group of Mexicans in a Fourteenth Street speakeasy and dragged them with him for a new round of farewells to celebrities. He sought out also Cubans, Puerto Ricans, and Venezuelans as well as Spaniards. He slept without undressing, sang Mexican songs till his voice cracked, and on the fourth day, still drunk, was lifted aboard the New Orleans flier, embraced by a hurried Venida, deposited in a drawing room and started back for the land of his fathers.

On the second day, approaching New Orleans, his head began to clear. On the way to Laredo, he shaved himself three times during the day, drank several gallons of ginger ale and investigated the contents of his five suitcases. He recalled dimly the crew of flunkies who had attended his packing at the hotel and marveled at these Americanos anew. A strange people, in all ways. Not a shirt stud was missing. He alighted at Brownsville and telegraphed $300 to the Savoy Plaza to be distributed as tips.

And at Laredo, his face once more growing asymmetrically hand-some, or at least dignified and purposeful, he presented himself to the Mexican customs for inspection and was recognized. The crowded station broke into cheers. "Santoyo . . . Pepe!" they cried. Men leaped to their feet and rushed to embrace him. Women smiled and clasped their hands and offered him their babies to kiss. He drew a deep breath and raised his arm to them in salute. He felt strange and confused—but he was going back to the bulls.

The three-day journey to the capital thereafter was a triumphal sweep through hills and deserts. News of Señor Santoyo's return preceded the train and produced mobs of ragged barefoot Indians and

Mexicans at the smallest depots. Bands played as the train pulled into the larger centers. Gifts were raised to the opened car windows. Scores of cooked chickens, pastries, bottles of wine, and silver ornaments poured into the drawing-room where the great matador sat, smiling and silent. Occasionally he emerged, let himself be seen on the steps of the train for a moment, and the bright air filled with shouts.

At Mexico City the national idol was greeted by a cavalry band, a troop of policemen, five senators in frock coats and silk hats, all the journalists the capital owned, and a mob estimated by the giddy narrators of the event as the largest ever seen in Mexico during a time of peace and plenty. Pepe was driven through the boulevards, cheered from thousands of windows and finally deposited in his home. Here Barrera wept on seeing him, kissed his cheeks, and screamed orders at the servants for an hour. It was Wednesday. The bullfight season was scheduled to open the following Sunday.

For three days Pepe lolled about his gardens, receiving the homage of admirers and answering the questions of the journalists.

His visit to the great capital of the north, they announced to their infatuated readers, had done more than a hundred treaties to cement the friendship between the two countries. Señor Santoyo had been fêted as a prince from the moment of his arrival to the moment of his departure, and the great sportsmen of New York had been filled with envy and chagrin at not being able to behold the beauty and skill of their Santoyo in the bull ring, since, owing to a complete absence of torero talent in the Anglo-Saxon, bullfighting had no home in the land of Washington. However, their idol had by his own personal magnetism, despite the handicap of the absence of bullfighting, won the hearts of the Americanos and the journalists felt certain that now that the Yankees had beheld this flower of Mexican manhood the immigration question would soon be satisfactorily settled. Señor Santoyo, modest as always under the new glories he had won, had returned eager for the bullfight season and had spoken with his old fire of his love of the great sport.

Barrera busied himself for the three days to insure a heroic opening for the season and return to the ring for the great matador. With the advent of this day, however, a nervousness came over the veteran. The lethargy he had smelled in the mood of his idol from the moment of their first embrace, appeared to have increased. Riding beside Pepe to the bull ring, he cursed himself for an old fool, stared desperately at the silent hero and grew heavy-hearted. He repeated to himself that he was father and mother to this young one, that it was he who had taught him every twist and move which had made him the greatest bull-fighter in the world—and that he had a right to know what was clouding the Señor's eyes, what made his hand so listless, and what his thoughts were. But with high masculine insight for the dangers of such talk Barrera guarded his tongue and sat making angry faces at the chauffeur's head. Halfway to the bull ring his worry would no longer be denied.

"What are you thinking about?" Barrera scowled at the abstracted face.

Pepe's eyes glinted and a half smile came to him.

"The bull with six horns," he answered.

That was it! Barrera cursed silently. His warnings had been ignored and the Venida, snake of a woman with a pepper box for a heart, had crawled into his muchacho's soul and was devouring it. Let her show her face around him again. He would know how to deal with her this time.

"El Chico, your bull, is a fine one," he said.

El Chico was indeed a fine bull. The stands applauded as he came snorting into the ring. The toreros shrugged their shoulders and wished their part of the show over. The bulls Santoyo engaged were all of a stripe, cruel, swift, and unreliable. Fortunately the idol preferred to do his own cape-playing and the sooner they retired from the ring and the fresher they left the beast, the more pleased the President and all the officials. As for the stands, they had no eye for these preliminaries when Santoyo was awaited.

The band blaring gayly in the bright afternoon became silent. El Chico charged, wheeled, pawed the earth and charged again. The spectators smiled and, as if under a hypnosis, waited for Santoyo, their hearts remembering the incomparable spectacle of man, beast, and death he always provided.

A roar of delight greeted the familiar little figure in gold and scarlet silks as it stepped into the bull ring. They cried his name, threw their hats in the air, clapped their hands, and laughed joyously. Pepe heard these sounds of happiness and drew a deep breath. He had stood waiting like a man in a dream for the ovation—and for the first glimpse of the shining beast to awaken him. He saluted the President's box and moved forward slowly as was the tradition of his style. He took his stand in the center of the hot glaring ring and waited for El Chico to begin the performance.

With the first charge of the bull, a curious alien sense came over

Pepe Santoyo. His cape made a perfect flourish, his lean body turned gracefully and precisely from the thrust of the horns. But his heart had not experienced that quick throb of delight by which he knew himself master of the beast. He waited coolly for the return charge, his instincts warning him that this was another of his favorites—those bad ones who charged the smell of the man instead of the enticing swirl of the cape. Again the animal rushed, again the horns missed and again Pepe turned coldly and without elation for the next maneuver.

Now he knew that something had happened to him. He flashed the cape, pirouetted, kneeled and swayed before the plunging horns. The stands filled the bright day with shouts of joy. Their Santoyo was better than ever, quicker than ever and even more courageous. He was taking greater chances, allowing the horns to come nearer and nearer. But with each new burst of cheering that drifted to him Pepe felt this alien sense deepen. He had felt it first when his countrymen had cheered him in the little custom-shed at Laredo and the sensation had grown stronger as he had ridden farther and farther into the deserts and hills of his native land.

As if to shock himself into a livelier mood, he rose from his knee and approached the glowering beast, walking the path between its horns. El Chico rushed. Pepe did not twist aside. He remained in the path of the bull, stepping nimbly back before its charge. The horns framed his arms, the animal's head butted his thighs. Pepe slapped its nose and El Chico fell back with a snort. The stands rocked with excitement. There was no hero in the memory of the oldest and fattest of the journalists who had ever allowed this caress of death in the open. Señor Belmonte had let the beast pin its horns into the fence, standing between them. Never had this been seen in the open ring before.

Their Santoyo was greater than ever. Their Santoyo transcended all men's dreams of glory and courage. But these wild cheers coming to him in the glaring, lonely bull ring filled Pepe anew with that curious sense of alienism. He pirouetted, flourished the cape once more, and felt confused.

He was not frightened, his body moved with precision, his eyes were cool. There was nothing to be seen by even Barrera, watching with his heart in his mouth, that told of change or waver in the great matador. But to Pepe this always exalting dance with the beast seemed to have undergone a dismal disenchantment. He stood poised as if in a dream of himself. He saw the bull as an unreal monster and the very color and sounds around him, the blaze of sky and the burn of the sand were part of a phantom scene. There was no reality in this, no familiar ritualistic urge in his heart. His soul, it seemed to him, had changed and become a stranger to the spectacle he was contributing. He was viewing it with strange eyes, performing with a stranger's skill and senses. Reality lay elsewhere and, fronting the beast whose horns continued to graze him in their thrust, whose fetid breath burst again and again in his face, Pepe's thought wandered to that other Bull of the Six Horns, to the umbrellas of light that hung in the sky, to the clamor and throb of that greater land he had visited. The roars from the stands came to him like the murmur of a handful of children. The blur and flutter of faces that caught his eyes filled him with derision. He seemed suddenly engaged in childish antics before a group of nobodies. Even El Chico appeared a fool.

Amid those gaudy, far-off streets, surrounded by that pale glib and superior folk, Pepe had undergone a mysterious evaporation, as if the ghosts of Cuauhtemoctzín and Cortez and all the first, second, and third yield of grandfathers had departed his loins. The smell of death and the business of blood and sacrifice no longer delighted his soul. He had outgrown them. This was no longer an inner ritual that related him to the murderous peacocks, the Temple of the Sun, the helmets of the Conquistadores and the gibbets of the Colonial lords—but an alien and dangerous exercise. He stood now in the bull ring like some strangely disinherited one.

El Chico charged. Pepe smiled wearily at the persistent beast. The bugle signaled the kill and, drawing his sword, he approached, poised himself on his toes as if he were going to take flight, extended the glittering weapon and lunged. He felt the sword point sink and stop. Stupidly he pressed harder, refusing to believe in this vital moment that he had missed the mark. The ground suddenly swept away. He was on the horns. He fluttered a moment in the air like some flapping, ornate bird. He had been tossed. He came down on one of the points. There was a sickening burn in his groin. The horn sank in deep, wrenched at his flesh and thrust him high in the air. He had made no cry but from the stands came a high-pitched moan. Vanquished, that exquisite mechanism of courage, grace, and skill. There it was to be seen for another unbelievable moment, spinning like a broken plate on the sharp horns, falling to the earth like a bit of bright fabric. It lay without moving. El Chico nudged it with his reddened horn, sniffed, nudged again. It remained motionless.

The toreros were out, fluttering capes, and in front of them was Barrera. Tears poured from his eyes. He cursed as he ran. The stands were groaning as if in the midst of some slow disaster.

It was Barrera's cape that turned El Chico. The beast charged and the hernia-ridden veteran leaped clumsily from its path and rushed to the bleeding figure in the sand. Pepe moved. The stands bellowed their relief. Their Santoyo was up, his hands over his wound. Barrera seized him. Pepe squirmed loose. El Chico was running with the sword dangling from his neck and beating his sides like a silver drum-stick. Pausing, the beast tossed his head again and the weapon sailed through the air. It fell at Pepe's feet.

"Thank you," he cried. He picked up the weapon and wiped it on his dry side, waved Barrera and the toreros away.

"Go away—go away," he screamed. The stands drowned his cries.

Barrera wavered. El Chico had turned, his sides running blood, blood dripping from his mouth. But his eyes were still unclouded. He sniffed, trembled and gathered himself for the charge. Pepe stood swinging the sword at the toreros. They cursed him and sprang aside.

"Come on. Hurry if you want to be killed by Santoyo," Pepe cried to the beast.

His head was spinning. His groin burned. His stomach was heavy and faint. The sky was darkening for him. He could see only the black mass of the bull coming forward.

The stands saw him reel as the beast came on. They watched the point of his sword waver, the toes on which he tried to rise for the kill refuse their burden. Then, abruptly, as if a new life had been granted him, they saw their idol rise, stand in perfect balance, and thrust forward. Man and beast, both running blood, came together. The horns lifted, the sword flashed and vanished, disappearing to the hilt inside the body of El Chico. The beast stopped. Pepe Santoyo closed his eyes and the stands, screeching as if they too were under the horns of El Chico, saw bull and man go down together. They fell face to face and El Chico, as his legs buckled, slipped forward till his dead nose lay nuzzled like a dog's against the body of the matador.

The din continued as the figure of Santoyo was lifted over the fence by a hundred hands and rushed to the hospital a block away. He was dead! Santoyo had died. The horns had ripped his body to death! The band hesitated, started to play. A great wail silenced the musicians. The President's box was empty.

To the hospital! The spectators tumbling over each other rushed for exits. In the streets men and women seized each other to weep, cry out their grief and hurry on. Where was he? Dead in his dressing-room under the stands. No. In the hospital. Men came running toward the bull ring waving their arms. Santoyo was alive. The doctors said he would live. A bad wound but no arteries severed, no vital parts torn. He would never fight again. No five, ten such wounds could stop Santoyo. He would be out in a week, in two weeks. The crowds scurried the streets in panic. Police formed around the hospital doors. Throwing themselves tearfully against the guards, the crowd demanded news. Was he suffering, their little one, was he in pain? What were the doctors doing now?

The story of Santoyo's injury swept through the capital. Shops emptied. Stores closed. The streets filled with clamorous citizens hurrying to the newspaper offices, to the bull ring, to the hospital. People screamed to each other the details of his glorious deed as they ran, how he had stood dying, sword in hand before his murderer El Chico and with his own last breath sent the point home. What a man! What a matador! God save their idol, the saints give their glorious Pepe strength. The newspapers arrived. Santoyo lived, said the headlines. The prince of valor and idol of Mexico was undergoing an operation with every hope of recovery.

Inside the hospital six surgeons and a dozen nurses crowded the operating room. Pepe Santoyo lay on the white table. The wails of the crowd came dimly through the closed windows. The surgeon in charge nodded. Barrera, standing with half-shut eyes in the doorway, watched them wash the lean body of his pupil.

"Not a bad wound," said the head surgeon with a happy sigh. "Give him the ether a little."

The anesthetist placed the cone over the great matador's mouth. Pepe, closing his eyes, inhaled deeply. The cone was lifted. The surgeons studied him closely.

He was going under. A sleepy smile shone on his face. His lips pursed and he was whistling faintly the chorus of the Maine "Stein Song."

Actor's Blood

THE DEATH of a famous actress is the signal, as a rule, for a great deal of maudlin excitement. The world that knew her rushes up on that last stage where she lies with her eyes sincerely closed and joins, as it were, in her death scene, posturing and poetizing around her bier like a pack of amateur mummers. For a few days everyone who knew her is a road company Marc Antony burying her with bad oratory. The stage is a respectable and important institution, what with its enormous real estate holdings, but we still patronize an actress, particularly a dead one.

Marcia Tillayou's death let loose an unusual amount of "Alas, poor Yorick" poses among the laity because she was found in her apartment one summer morning with three bullets, all of them through her heart. This struck everybody as almost too rich a scenario to believe, that so glamorous, beautiful and witty a woman should add murder to the excitement of her dying.

We who were her friends were not exactly delighted. But there's no denying the thrill that lay in that dénouement. Even to her intimates the whole business of mystery surrounding that dead and beautiful body seemed more dramatic than real, seemed more a performance than the ending of a life. Not Marcia lay in this bed of death, but another of those exotic and witty characterizations for which she was famous.

As for the Press, it was honestly and naïvely grateful. It is seldom that an interesting, let alone famous, woman gets murdered. Our murder victims are in the main the dullest and most depressing of stooges. The best that tragedy has to offer the city editors is an occasional chorus girl and more rarely someone sufficiently well dressed to warrant the word Society in the headlines.

Marcia's exit kept the presses roaring. There was inexhaustible color to the mystery, and there was more bad writing and idiotic sleuthing than had distinguished the news columns for some time—a month at least. A life-sized portrait of Marcia as Pierrette hanging over the "murder bed" had been slashed across the middle. The furniture of the

413

gaudy room had been smashed. Her satin-hung dressing table with its glass top and hundred perfume bottles had been demolished. All in all it looked as if Marcia had been done to death by a herd of bison. But the police and the newspapers chose to regard the attendant ravages as the work of a Love Fiend.

Since these matters and all the clues and surmises of that first week came to nothing there's no point in dwelling on them. My story of the Marcia Tillayou mystery is, as a matter of fact, not part of any police record nor is it to be found in the newspaper files.

At the time of Marcia's death there was one who wept more than all the rest, who ranted more, postured more and seemed more humanly objectionable than any of the mourners who carried spears to her funeral. This one was her father, Maurice Tillayou, a Thespian hero of other days, an ancient theatrical windbag with a soul still full of grease paint and obsolete bravado.

Old actors are perhaps the greatest bores in the world, particularly old actors whose day is past and whose very agents no longer carry their telephone numbers in their records. Tillayou was of this tribe, and so much the actor still that he could never seem the man again on the stage or off.

This rubbery-faced son of bombast had had his heyday at the turn of the century. He had strutted his little hour as one of those barrel-voiced, fur-collared, blue-skinned tragedians of whom our fathers, forgetting their names, still mumble with pretended delight.

Unlike many of his generation, old Tillayou had never adjusted himself to the growing realism of the theater, never tried to soothe his grandiloquent antics to fit the more prosaic tempo of the modern stage. As a result, at fifty, he had almost vanished from the boards; at sixty, he had become one of those myths who cling to some dimly-lighted corner of a theatrical club drinking bitterly to the death of art and the venality of managers.

He who had played all the Great Rôles—Hamlet, Lear, Romeo, Jekyll, Monte Cristo, Richelieu, Ben Hur, St. Elmo and Quo Vadis among them—sat in the shadows without a part, as if not he alone but all the swaggering, thundering heroes in whose shoes he had paraded shared his exile. He was given, because of this quaint delusion, to rolling his eyes, working his shaggy brows with mystery and wrapping himself in a peculiar sort of phantom dignity. He spent the day in sonorous complaints against destiny and like all discarded actors was full of an offensive and useless egoism.

There was nonetheless a slightly exciting air about Tillayou, soiled and musty though he was. His wispy gray and yellowish hair rose from his mottled scalp like the whiskers of a cat. He wore an old-fashioned stand-up collar into which he could have retreated turtle fashion had he so desired. His clothes were as ill-fitting as a waiter's or perhaps a philosopher's. His massive face seemed in repose to be folded up and able to open like an accordion. But bore though he was, didactic and misinformed on almost every human topic, his mind as disheveled as his garments, he had about him the charm of authenticity. He seemed more "theater" than a hundred electric signs. He seemed with his tiresome boasts, his rumbling voice, his pompous mannerisms and overplastic face like some lost puppet playing truant from those theatrical storage houses in which the thousand and one forgotten kingdoms of the stage are stacked away.

During the years I knew him I saw him in harness but three times. A restoration drama revival brought him before the public for a few weeks and once, under the wing of a profit-sharing actors' enterprise, he blossomed briefly and rather foolishly as Richelieu. For, removed from under its bushel, the old Thespian's genius, alas, set no rivers afire. Tillayou emerging from the shadows of exile brought with him all his retinue and was never content with the mere acting of the rôle on the program. He sought to dazzle as well with a dozen other remarkable characterizations of which he was equally master.

The third time I witnessed his performance was the occasion of the anecdote I've set out to relate.

Marcia Tillayou became a star when she was twenty-five. This means a great deal in the theater. It is, as a rule, the reward more of personality than of talent. You must be distinctive and have a new pattern of vocables and gestures to offer. You must have a peculiar voice, it may be inaudible as a conspirator's or incoherent as a train announcer's, but this matters very little providing it has any peculiarity at all—barring adenoids. You must have a set of mannerisms to keep you from being submerged in any characterization, and a certain high-handed way of playing all your parts alike, whatever the dramatist has written or the director demanded.

Marcia had been playing Marcia Tillayou for some eight years, most of them on Broadway, playing this peculiar young lady consistently and with infatuation, when rather abruptly one evening her persistence was rewarded. She had stumbled upon a part even more Marcia Tillayouish than herself—a waspish-tongued, brittle-spirited creature of disillusion invented by Alfred O'Shea—a woman whose green eyes shone with wit and despair, whose gestures were tense with ennui and who, in the play, loved, jested and died like a glass of champagne going stale.

Through the medium of that particular drama which was called *The Forgotten Lady,* audience and critics beheld Marcia Tillayou for the first time as dozens of intimates already knew her, and this enlarged recognition of her personality made her a star. It was a tremendous début and all who witnessed it knew that ever after, whatever fortunes befell, however many bad plays and adverse criticisms came her way, her stardom was fixed, she would always be one of that handful of women of the stage who are an Electric Sign in fair weather or foul.

Marcia Tillayou's emergence as a star was not the only dramatic event of that evening. There was also Maurice Tillayou's emergence as a father. This happened shortly after the last curtain fell.

There was a reception in Marcia's dressing room. Nobody in the world, except perhaps nursery dolls, receives such concentrated and overwhelming flattery as does an actress on the night of a Great Success. The theater touches off the facile emotions and its heroes and heroines come in for blasts of adulation which would terrify more realistic souls.

Maurice Tillayou was present at this backstage coronation in Marcia's dressing room. He stood in a corner, a soiled and musty unknown, his eyes glittering at the sight of the make-up boxes, the mirrors, hangings, strewn finery and heaped floral offerings; his ears tingling with the praises showering the head of his daughter. He lurked silently in the corner until the ecstasies had subsided and the last of the bandwagon soloists drifted out of the room. Then he came forward and, for the first time in the memory of either, kissed his daughter. He pressed her hands. His eyes shone with tears and he added his gift to the triumph of that evening.

"You are a great artist," he said in capitals, "you have taken your place tonight in the great tradition of the stage beside the immortal figures of Rachel, Siddons, Bernhardt and Modjeska. May I have the honor to congratulate you, my child?"

He said this all very glibly and sonorously as was his habit, but in a strange way this pronouncement of her hitherto boring and negligible parent excited Marcia. Regarding the old windbag with her tired but always witty eyes, she felt the deeper meaning of his words. He had come offering her his egoism, that battered, offensive and useless egoism which had sustained and applauded him when all other palms had grown silent. He too had undergone a transformation this night. He was no longer Maurice Tillayou, the star, albeit in temporary eclipse;

but old Tillayou, father of a star newly risen. Holding her hands and kissing her, the old gentleman seemed to Marcia to be letting go forever his treasured career and passing on to her, twenty-five years after her birth, some gaudy, hereditary talisman of genius.

The story of Marcia's nine years of stardom is a tale that wants a longer telling than this. It was the career of a high heart in a higher mind. To those who kept pace with her or contributed to her life she seemed as complicated as music by Stravinsky, as troublesome as a handful of fine but broken glass. She owned an acidulous mind and a schoolgirl's heart. She was ironic and disillusioned, yet ineptly romantic. She was always beautiful. Her hair shone as if a light were concealed in her coiffure. Her green eyes were never without comment—amusement, derision. Her skin was pale, her mouth wide and mobile, with restless lips. And, as in women of personality, her face seemed bolder, more strongly modelled than suited her taut, slender body. Her crisp voice was an instrument for wit rather than sighs, and her beauty, despite her reputation, was a thing of which men seldom thought lightly. There was too much character and epigram behind it. Clever people have a way of seeming always gay and this was Marcia's manner—to jest at scars, her own or others'. Her sprightliness, however, was disconcerting, not only because of the cruelty it contained but for the fact that in her very laughter lurked always the antonym of weariness. She was like one of those fragile chemicals that burn too sharply, giving off a curious and vicious light.

Throughout the nine years of her stardom Maurice Tillayou hovered in the background of her affluence, intrigues and follies. He lived elsewhere but was to be seen often at her dinner table, drinking his wine with a faraway happy stare at the Maestros, Savants, Journalists and Heroes of the Pen and Stage who graced his daughter's board. He was still a musty old dodo but full of punctilio and reticence.

What there could be in common between this ghost of the theater and the glamorous daughter whom he haunted no one was able to make out, except that she obviously supported him and that he doted on running errands. Marcia's life seemed hardly fit for such continual parental observation, but there he was peering continually from behind his high, stand-up collar at this legendary world of which he had always dreamed. He lingered in the background, saying nothing that anyone heard, through Marcia's hysterical marriage with Alfred O'Shea, author of her first success, *The Forgotten Lady,* and through that scoundrel's subsequent hegira with Reena Kraznoff, the dancer; and through a dozen liaisons and entanglements, all of them full of heartbreak and hysteria. For Marcia was one whose heart clung to illusions that had no place in her bedroom, and who bought her counterfeit pleasures with genuine coin. Like many of the stage she bargained desperately for beauty and took home tinsel.

Old Tillayou was somehow involved in all these unfortunate doings of his daughter. And though Marcia suffered no social blemish from her wanton antics, her father seemed to lose caste, to become a sort of paternal gigolo.

Yet however bedeviled by her wit, reduced by her sins or made the butt of her reminiscences maliciously remembered from childhood, Tillayou remained always charmed by her presence. She treated him as if he were some eccentric toy to which she was playfully attached. Yet this once most touchy of Hamlets seemed immune to her belittlements. He would smile at her sallies and add a bit of trenchant data to her tales and remain, in a way that touched the hearts of those inclined to notice him at all, respectful and idolatrous. He was, in short, a musty old spectator basking in a corner of his daughter's glamour.

The year and a half which preceded her mysterious death had been a troublesome time for Marcia. A reverberating set-to between herself and Phil Murry, her producer, had resulted in the closing of the play she was in. There had followed a shortsighted jump to a rival producer, a hasty production under his banner and an equally hasty flop. A second appearance under the management of the gifted Morrie Stein had resulted in another failure. And Marcia found herself verging toward that second stage of stardom in which the star, unexpectedly and as if bedeviled by witches, develops play trouble. Still glamorous, still a great box office draw, she floundered through productions that set critical teeth on edge, her colors flying valiantly above a bog of theatrical bilge.

That alchemistic combination which makes for success on Broadway is a tenuous one. Its secret often evaporates, leaving no visible change in the ingredients, except that the gold is gone. And sadly there rises for these stars confronted with empty seats the first bewildering breath of limbo. All this was beginning to happen to Marcia. There was no belittlement of the name Tillayou. It was still an Electric Sign but growing ghostly, slipping, still aglow, into the side streets of fame.

At this time, too, Marcia's finances came in for ill luck. Yet with a falling market and diminishing salary checks, her extravagances continued. Credit took the place of money. To the clamor of friends and lovers on the telephone were added the appeals of tradesmen, dressmakers, bootleggers, landlords and even servants. It was a stormy period and full of those thunders and lightnings with which temperament, thwarted, manages to circle its head as an antidote.

During these months old Tillayou's importance increased. It was he who led the talk in the dressing rooms after each new disastrous first night. He was an encyclopedia of alibis. Where, he wanted to know, had they got such a Leading Man, so horrible and unpractised a fellow? He had, said Tillayou, ruined the two major scenes. And where, he wanted to know again, had they discovered the Character Woman? How could a play mount with such a bungling amateur hanging on to it? The set, he was quick to point out, had killed the third act completely. And the rain, he was certain, had depressed the audience. The lighting in the love scene had been atrocious; the director had garbled the first act curtain. But Marcia had been and was always wonderful, superb as ever, giving the best performance he had ever seen any woman offer on the stage. Moreover, he was quick with that final solace —that it was weak plays such as this which made the best vehicles for great stars, that it was in such as these that they personally triumphed.

Papa Tillayou stood at the pass like some valorous Old Guard. He knew, alas, all the thousand and one excuses for failure, all the quaint, smug, fantastic box-office circumlocutions which in the theater deaden the sting of defeat. And his voice rumbling, his eyes glowing with their best Hamlet fires, he fought these dressing room Thermopylaes, a veteran forsooth.

In the excitement of Marcia Tillayou's murder, Maurice Tillayou lapsed into complete shadowiness. He had been observed at the funeral carrying on like a Comanche, bellowing with grief and collapsing on the wet ground not once but a dozen times. He had ridden back alone to his bailiwick in Washington Square. And here Maurice Tillayou had remained in seclusion while sleuths and journalists played bloodhound through Marcia's life in quest of the villain who had sent three bullets through her heart.

This made fascinating reading and sophisticated dinner-table talk for the Broadway cognoscenti. Theories were as plentiful as jackrabbits in May and as elusive. We who had known Marcia felt the thrill of tragedy and mystery on our doorstep and we spoke guardedly of the matter, for there seemed always present, or closely represented, some one on whom our choicest suspicion was for the moment centered.

Although the police were baffled, God knew and so did some hundreds of New Yorkers who are nearly as omniscient, that there had been material enow in Marcia's life for a whole series of murders. Marcia's career had been interwoven with the careers of equally electric names, names which live in a sort of fidgety half-public undress and seem always but a jump ahead of the thunderclap of scandal. We waited excitedly for the hand of the law to fall on one of these—for who could have murdered Marcia more logically than one of those who had been part of her life?

First in our suspicion was Alfred O'Shea, who had married her once and who at her death was still legally her husband. This tall, dark, prankish chevalier, Don Juan, playwright, wit, over-charming and malicious, full of grins, bon mots and moody withal as a beggar on a rainy day, was a most obvious suspect to us, his friends. His strong Irish-Castilian face held a jester's nose, pointed and a bit awry, held cold, centered eyes and a gaunt muscular mouth and a promise of high deeds —murder among them. We knew his story well enough. Absurdly infatuated with his Reena, a dancer with a lithographic face and an accent full of charm and faraway places, he had abandoned Marcia and set up a clamor for divorce. Marcia had refused, loathing, she said, to hand him over to so belittling a successor, and we remembered hearing of times this over-charming Celt, drunken and vicious, had broken into Marcia's bedroom threatening to have her heart out unless she released him. What bourgeois trait, what subterranean wiliness inspired Marcia to step so out of character and thwart this man whom she had so desperately loved, I could never make out. She had only jests for answers.

But O'Shea was in a goodly company of suspects, those first weeks of the mystery. There was also Phil Murry, the producer—cool, round-faced, paunchy with a homely chuckle and a little piping voice, all very deceptive qualities, for Mr. Murry was as treacherous as a cocklebur to wrestle with. He was a maestro as famous for his unscrupulousness with women as for his hits.

Marcia had been his mistress until supplanted by Emily Duane, long considered her closest friend. La Duane, an Electric Sign in her own right and a vest-pocket edition of Duse, cello-voiced and full of a deceptive ingénue wholesomeness, had jockeyed Marcia completely out of Murry's life—his theater as well as his arms. We remembered poor Marcia's to-do over Murry's faithlessness, her involved campaign of retaliation—a matter of social ragging and continuous public baiting which had driven that paunchy maestro out of his mind on a number of occasions and reduced Emily to a sort of humorous female Judas in our eyes. How these two had hated Marcia and what vengeance they had sworn against her poor, sad wit!

There was also the grayish, Punchinello-faced Felix Meyer, theatrical lawyer de luxe as he called himself—glib and of the old school as his redundant phrases and ancient cravat testified. This elderly bravo was a species of liaison officer between Broadway and a mysterious world of reality called the Law. But to that world he found it seldom necessary to resort. For, immersed in the thousand and one secrets of the theater, his practice was in the main a species of affable blackmail and counter-blackmail—his activities as arbiter, backer, judge and Don Juan being only dimly sensed by his intimates, and not at all by his wife.

His affair with Marcia had been an unusually gritty one, based on her inability to pay him an exorbitant legal fee for services rendered. It had lasted several months and left both of them with a horror of each other. Lawyer Felix went about in terror lest Marcia, out of spite, betray him to his wife, to whose name he had with foolhardy caution transferred all his holdings. And Marcia, aware of his craven fidgets, had time and again promised to do just that. How relieved this glib and accomplished fellow must have felt that first moment reading of her death, and how full of disquiet he must have sat while the blood-hounds scurried through Marcia's life sniffing for clues.

There was also Fritz von Klauber, who had painted Marcia as Pier-rette, a dapper gentleman of the arts with a mandarin mustache and a monocle to help him intimidate the less fortunately born theatrical producers (a rather numerous set) for whom he devised unusually expensive scenery. Von Klauber's relations with Marcia had ended more unprettily than most. We knew that he had borrowed thousands of dollars from her while her lover and refused to recognize the debt after discovering or pretending to discover her in the arms of Morrie Stein. Mr. Stein, a purring, monkish Semite with over-red lips, upturned eyes, a grasshopper's body and a prodigious sneer flying, flag like, from his lips, had been Marcia's last substitute for love. We knew little of this adventure, but our suspicions of Morrie were quickened by an aversion which all his intimates seemingly held for him.

There was slightly down on the list of suspects, but still qualifying for our gossip, Percy Locksley, a Pickwickian fellow minus, however, all hint of simplicity or innocence—a journalist with a facetious but blood-curdling cruelty to his style who had figured disturbingly in Marcia's life. He had been rumored as her possible husband, which rumor Marcia had scotched with great public cries of outrage and epigram at Locksley's expense. And though this might seem small motive for murder, to know Locksley was to suspect him of anything, from homicide to genius.

And there was also Emil Wallerstein, the poet, who had hounded

Marcia's doorsill for a year, smitten, drunken, vicious, bawling for her favors and threatening to hang himself with her garter (like Gerard de Nerval) if she refused; who had made quite a show of going to the dogs (at his friends' expense) as a result of her coldness; and whom Marcia, for reasons hidden from us, had thoroughly and always cleverly despised.

Also further down the list was Clyde Veering, a charming, faded roué, once a font of learning and now a fat little Silenus in oxford glasses clinging to a perpetual cocktail. Veering was known amusingly as a connoisseur of decadence. His tasteful bachelor apartment was at the service of his friends of both sexes provided their intentions were sufficiently abnormal or dishonorable. It was a bit difficult to conceive of Veering as a murderer, but like a number of others we held suspect, it was more his possible secret knowledge of the crime than participation in it which excited us.

However, none of these, nor anyone else, came under the hand of the law. There was some surreptitious questioning, a great deal of libel-cautious hints in the news columns, but no arrests. Nothing happened despite the baying of the bloodhounds. A peculiarly gallant reticence seemed to surround Marcia, dead. No letters were found among her effects, no voice from the grave gave direction to the hunt. And the mysterious ending of this charming and famous woman slowly embedded itself behind other local excitements.

It was four weeks after the murder, when its mystery had subsided to an occasional paragraph, that Maurice Tillayou emerged from the shadows and in a spectacular manner.

We who had known Marcia well, or too well, received an invitation from the old gentleman. It was strangely worded. It read: "May I have the honor of your company at a dinner Friday evening which I am giving in memory of my daughter, Marcia? I strongly urge you to attend, for matters vital to yourself as well as to the mystery surrounding my daughter's murder are to be revealed in my house. I am asking you in all fairness to be present—or represented."

A few of us were amused and touched by the old actor's melodramatic summons. But there were almost a score of others whom I found to be filled with disquiet. The matter was guardedly discussed over a number of telephones. Efforts to reach old Tillayou in advance for further information availed nothing.

It rained on that Friday night. Thunder rolled in the sky and the streets were full of that picnic-like confusion which storm brings to the city. I rang the bell of the Tillayou roost and waited in the unfamiliar old hallway until the door was opened by an amazingly senile fellow, stooped, cackling and practically mummified. He was obviously the servant and obviously in a state of complete mental paralysis. For behind him in a large studio-like room, buzzing, clattering, laughing, was as browbeating a coterie of celebrities as the theater had to offer. They had arrived, and this was odd for these chronic dinner wreckers, on time. I noticed that a number were already on their third cocktail and that the babble which greeted me was completely lacking in those overtones of ennui, disdain and bad manners which usually marked their get-togethers.

I looked vainly for a glimpse of Tillayou and learned from several sources that the old windjammer was still lurking in the wings, building up his entrance. It was a familiar enough group, a rather morbid round-up it seemed, of men and women who had loved Marcia Tillayou, cheated her, quarreled with her, lied to her, drunk with her, amused and betrayed her and been part of that strident, characterless treadmill which is the Broadway Parnassus. So reminiscent were they all of Marcia that she seemed almost present, almost certain to appear and join them, as they stood about maliciously guillotining absent comrades and exchanging those tireless reminiscences which Celebrities always have for each other.

I was rather thrilled at the spectacle, for old Tillayou's intention was plain. He had assembled a company of suspects and was obviously going to climax the evening by some formal accusation of guilt. There was a handful, like myself, who could look forward to no such distinction, but who knew what the old actor had got into his addled head. We had all been part of Marcia's world and we might all be presumed to have had some insight into the mystery that had climaxed her life.

This little world Tillayou had summoned out of its orbit into his humble old actor lodgings made a uniform picture. Its members were as alike as the decorations on a Christmas tree. There was about them an identical air, a similarity of inner and outer tailoring as if they had all been finished off on the same loom. Success was in their names and New York, the New York of the roman-candle signs, of Ballyhoo and Ego, Merry-go-round Achievement and Overnight-Fortune hung like a tag from their words and manners. They were the cream of a certain electric-lighted firmament—its satraps and its nobles—and if you liked this world you liked them; if you revered this world, as old Tillayou once had, these were gods for your genuflections. A swift and glittering world it was, a bauble of a planet, out of which were hatched nightly the ephemera of art, the fireflies that masqueraded as beacons for an hour.

I joined Veering, always a source of rich information. He was pouting childishly over his fifth cocktail, cackling that he was much too bored by old Tillayou's banality to talk about it and regretting he had wasted an evening, when so few (virile) ones remained. I moved toward Locksley and fell to studying the half-hundred costume photographs of Tillayou in his heyday that decorated the wall.

"He played all the parts," I said. "He could illustrate a full edition of the Bard."

"Yes," said Locksley, "he had that talent for bad acting which made him a natural and tireless Shakesperean."

Von Klauber, joining us, remarked, "Marcia always called him that Old Davil Ham."

"We saw him once as Richelieu," O'Shea said, coming up to us. "I'll never forget Marcia's delight when he went up in his lines in the third act. She said it saved the play."

Wallerstein, the poet, not yet drunk, stood glowering at von Klauber.

"The destruction of your Pierrette painting of Marcia," he veered, "was a great blow to the world of art."

"Thank you," said von Klauber, "I didn't know you had ever had the good fortune to see that painting."

Veering chuckled.

"Marcia always loathed it," he said, winking at everybody. He had, mysteriously, a distaste for artists.

"It was painted under handicaps," said von Klauber calmly. "Miss Tillayou must have been a very difficult subject."

Lawyer Felix had joined us.

"Not difficult to paint," said von Klauber, "but difficult to please."

"And very ungrateful," Locksley chuckled. "She always secretly believed that the portrait had been painted with a cake of laundry soap. Or so she said."

Veering stared morosely toward the door of an adjoining room.

"That," he said, "is presumably the old gentleman's lair. Do you think if we applauded violently, he would come out for a bow, at least? I'm slowly perishing of hunger."

The rain rattled on the windows, the thunder rolled, our babble grew tense and nastier with a growing undercurrent of mutiny, a large contingent beginning to murmur of bolting the entire farcical business, and then Tillayou appeared. He was dressed in a combination of evening clothes and a black velvet jacket and looked surprisingly younger. None of us had ever seen or dreamed of so vibrant a Tillayou, or fancied so dominant a figure would crawl out of that old cocoon.

We stopped talking and listened to Tillayou as if the lights had gone out around us and he alone stood in brightness. He had brought a stranger into the room. He introduced this new guest, identifying each of us unctuously by calling and achievement. The guest was Carl Scheuttler which was a name as striking to us at the moment as Sherlock Holmes. Mr. Scheuttler was from the District Attorney's office. He had led the futile hunt for Marcia's murderer and had promised, in the news columns from day to day, "important developments before nightfall." His presence in this room surrounded by this round-up promised definite entertainment. Marcia's murderer was among us, or at least so Tillayou thought, and was going to be served us for dessert.

We started for the dining room, all grown very formal. A long, improvised banquet table was set for us. Tillayou ordered us to find our place cards and under no circumstances change them. Mr. Scheuttler was eyeing us professionally, at least so it seemed, holding himself aloof from our sallies and making no compromising friendships which might embarrass him when the great moment of accusation and arrest arrived.

As we seated ourselves we noted a number of odd things, which then dropped at least out of my mind because of what happened immediately. Locksley was the first to speak after the chairs had stopped scraping and we were all in our places.

"Who," inquired Locksley feelingly and pointing at the empty chair at the foot of the table, "who is that miserable miscreant?"

From the other end of the table where old Tillayou and his velvet jacket were presiding came a slow sonorous answer.

"That is for my guest of honor, sir."

Locksley reached over and examined the place card.

"Well, well," he chuckled, "this seat has been reserved for one not entirely unknown to all of us."

"Who?" inquired Morrie Stein.

"Marcia Tillayou," said Locksley, "who has gone out for the moment to fetch her harp."

"Serve the dinner, Mr. Harvey," said our host to the old mummy, "we are all here."

Kraznoff, the dancer, who was seated rather near the empty chair, rose nervously.

"Please, I like change my plaze," she announced.

There was laughter.

"Come, come, sit down," Morrie Stein grinned. "Marcia was much too sensible to turn into a ghost."

Locksley was beaming at our host.

"This is marvelous," he said. "Mr. Tillayou, bless his old heart, will turn out the lights and little Marcia will dance for us with a tambourine."

"It's an insult to Marcia," said Emily Duane.

"You're mistaken," von Klauber smiled at her, "the insult is to us. But a very stupid one. So it doesn't matter."

Lawyer Felix, sensing troubled waters, grew oily.

"Perhaps Mr. Tillayou isn't serious," he said. "It may be just a sentimental gesture. You do not really believe she is here, Mr. Tillayou?"

To this Tillayou answered softly, "There are more things in Heaven and earth, Horatio, than are dreamed of in your philosophy."

"Very good," said Locksley.

O'Shea, who had been staring sadly at the empty chair, suddenly leaned across the table and addressed it.

"Hello, darling," he said softly. "You look quite stunning tonight. Who gave you those beautiful lilies?"

The thunder rolled outside. Emily Duane gasped. But Locksley, not to be outdone in sallies by thunder or screams, cooed politely.

"Pass the olives, will you, Veering," he said, "before Marcia makes a pig of herself."

There being no olives and since there was no Marcia, this struck us as doubly droll. We laughed. Von Klauber turned his monocle on the "Representative from Scotland Yard."

"Do you believe in ghosts, Mr. Scheuttler?" he asked.

"I'm sure they're out of his jurisdiction," said Veering.

The elderly Mr. Harvey was tottering around the table filling wine glasses. Wallerstein, his dark, angry face intent on the empty chair, announced abruptly:

"Death is not a final word. We do not die so quickly. Marcia was never more alive than she is in this room tonight. Her innermost secrets are at this table. We are a compendium of Marcia."

"That's quite right," said O'Shea moodily. "We all loved her, in our varied fashions."

Tillayou, silent and queerly aglow, repeated under his breath the words, "loved her," and stared around the table, his eyes flooding with tears.

"Now that's rotten taste," Veering murmured, "calling us here to stage an exhibition of table rapping—and tears."

"A little grief over Marcia's death wouldn't be so amiss," said O'Shea, "particularly among her friends."

The aged Mr. Harvey, who, Locksley had been quick to decide, was the famous Santa Fé provisioner, was bringing in soup plates, sparsely filled and almost cold, and clattering them down one at a time in front of the guests. Indignant requests for spoons rising from one end of the table confused him and brought him to a standstill, shivering in his tracks and regarding his master unhappily. Tillayou nodded reassuringly at him, dried his eyes, beamed, pushed his chair from the table and stood up. This unexpected gesture brought quiet. I noticed that Mr. Scheuttler had lowered his head and was frowning severely at the tablecloth.

"I am an old actor," Tillayou began in measured tones, "and with the audience seated and the curtain up, I find it hard to wait."

He favored us with an engaging, almost cringing smile.

"'Art is long but time is fleeting,'" he continued, "and there is one who bids me speak." However, he didn't speak, but fell once more into quotation. It was a poem this time.

> "Love, hear thou! How desolate the heart is, ever calling,
>   Ever unanswered, and the dark rain falling,
>   Then as now. . . ."

This mystic invocation done with, Tillayou struck a pose that showed the oration itself was about to begin. But how describe such an oration! How bad it was, and how illumined afterwards with a grandeur we never knew was in it. Yet to betray its climax would be somehow to deprive it of the quality belonging to it during its delivery, the bravado with which he spoke it into the sharpened teeth of perhaps the city's most finicky raconteurs, the clownish humors which it achieved unconsciously as it went on, the boredom, the suspense which seemed to promise only the cruel laughter of the audience.

There were, alas, sad lapses of logic in his speech, when the old actor's mind failed to provide the correct transition, ironies which would have seemed far-fetched and inexplicable were they not so obviously borrowed from Marc Antony's funeral address; and there would have been more pauses in it even than there were, had Tillayou not helped himself to the language of the Bard. We heard *King Lear,* and *Macbeth* and *Romeo,* in whispers and inflections that sounded to our kind like rather hilarious caricatures. We listened with distaste, sneers, and apprehension for what might still follow, to Shylock's unctuous tones, and the cries of Spartacus before the Roman populace. Altogether, it was a performance that would have required more than a little indulgence on the part of the politest audience, and one which only O'Shea among us, his head leaning on his hand in one of his idle postures, seemed mysteriously to enjoy.

"You are my guests," it went, "very distinguished guests, and if I offend by what I am going to say, I ask your indulgence as the father of one who was admirable to you. I am the ghost of Banquo come to trouble your feasting.

"These, Mr. Scheuttler, are all very honorable and distinguished citizens who have gone out of their way to gratify the whim of an old actor by supping in his home. They are the great names of that world I have so long served with my humble talents.

"You asked, sirs, if I believed my daughter Marcia was present in this galaxy of her friends. It may be the wandering wits of an old man but I see her there, sitting tragic and beautiful, about her the sound of rain and of sweet bells jangling out of tune. Smiling at those who loved her. Yet she looks with cold eyes at one who sits here, with accusing eyes at one whose heart shouts, 'Avaunt and quit my sight! Let the earth hide thee!'

"Sweet and fair she was, the brightness of her cheek did shame the stars as daylight doth the lamp. But I won't bore you by asking you to recall those charms you once admired so, those virtues you once held so highly, almost as highly as myself.

"You have not come here tonight to hear a doting father spread his miseries before you, but for sterner business which from your courtesy and attentiveness I feel sure you have guessed.

"Mr. Scheuttler asked me to tell him this matter privately but I refused. For you were all her friends, her honorable friends, and I wanted you present.

"Who killed my daughter? Who took her life? There's the question. I have the answer. But I'll not merely give a name and cry 'murderer!' No, I have the proofs.

"You all loved her and admired her, helped her through the years of struggle, made life sweet for her with your tenderness and understanding and unselfishness. Yet one of you murdered her. Murdered her!

"He is here. He came to my humble house, fancying himself too clever for detection. He sits now at my table. Mr. Harvey, close the doors! Lock them! So he can't escape. Lock us in! The windows, too.

Ha—good man, Harvey. He has served me well. He was with me through those years when I too, like my daughter, was a star; not as bright or shining as she. But Maurice Tillayou was a name, sirs, that belonged to the grand days of the theater. Thank you, Harvey. You may go to bed now and sleep sweetly, and may angels guard thy dreams.

"Where was I, Mr. Scheuttler? Oh, yes, the doors are locked. Is this not like a play? Your faces waiting for the name—the name of Judas. All of you waiting, each edging from his neighbor. I keep my promise, Mr. Scheuttler. I have the proofs, all of them, enough to send that one from this table to the gallows. The man who killed Marcia, who murdered my Marcia, is looking at me. Ah, the terror in his eyes. His name is——"

Thunder had been rolling through the last of his words. Now it crashed outside, drowning out his voice. And at the same time the room in which we sat turned black. The entire scene disappeared as in a dream. The lights had gone out. The women screamed. Chairs toppled over. There was a moment of mysterious confusion, consternation, with cries and even laughter in the dark. But we were riveted by a voice calling wildly in the black room. It was Tillayou.

"Let me go! He's killing me! Help! Help! Oh, my God! He's killing —killing——"

The voice shut off as if hands were choking its sound. There was a flash of lightning and in the phosphorescent glare that lay in the room for a moment we seemed to see something mad—Tillayou sinking to the floor in a corner, his hands over his heart, and blood flowing over them. The tableau vanished.

An awkward, nightmarish and foolishly restrained commotion followed. We seemed to think it was something unreal we were witnessing and we were not a crowd to scream, to throw down chairs or believe in murder at a lightning glance. Reality is a far cry from those forever writing about it. Emily Duane inquired in a polite voice for lights.

O'Shea was the first to hold a cigarette lighter over the old man in the corner. On his knees, gasping, one hand on the floor and trying to crawl somewhere, we made out Tillayou. In the same moment Mr. Scheuttler, who obviously knew his way about in such dilemmas, was on O'Shea with a flashlight and apparently convinced he was the murderer. Now at last there were screams from the women and a rather hysterical calling for lights from the men and over it all the groans and gasps of a dying man whom Mr. Scheuttler was hounding professionally for a dying statement.

In fact we, Mr. Scheuttler and Tillayou seemed to be acting in a play—one of those Broadway melodramas full of darkness, murder, suspects and all the unconvincing trappings of theatricalized mystery. Some of us lit matches, others cigarette lighters, others searched for lights or joined in hounding the dying man alongside the frantic and barking Mr. Scheuttler. O'Shea provided a minute's extra excitement by kicking in the door and reappearing in the face of Mr. Scheuttler's drawn gun, this official having forbidden anyone to leave the premises, with a candelabra. This he lit and the candelabra illumined with its mellow beam a scene that seemed as operatic as *Tosca*.

"It's dark," Old Tillayou was moaning. "Marcia, where are you? My little bright-haired girl. Marcia, my child."

Now we all leaned over him, urging him, like a mob of earnest supers, to tell who had killed him, and eyeing each other the while askance. Mr. Scheuttler, in particular, convinced that the old man was about to name his murderer, waited with his gun still drawn.

But the old actor was raving.

"Blood," he said, lifting his hands and staring at them. "My blood." And again asked to speak out, he started crying for Marcia. "Listen," he said, "listen to her. Ever calling . . . ever unanswered." There was more of it, heartbreaking and somehow unreal.

Then there was the awful moment when the old man seemed to search for someone. Now his eyes were calm. He recognized Mr. Scheuttler.

"Let me whisper the name," he murmured eagerly, and so faintly we could hardly hear. "He—he mustn't escape. Closer, my friends. Lend me your ears. . . ."

"Who was it?" someone couldn't help saying desperately.

Mr. Scheuttler roared for quiet, only to repeat the question himself in the next moment.

"Ah," said Tillayou, "it was . . . it was . . ." and lapsed into a silence. There was a babble of questioning as the silence grew prolonged, and then hysterical. Mr. Scheuttler no longer seemed to be watching his suspects. He was looking at the old man who appeared to be quietly crying. Some tears rolled down his cheeks. And then an incredible thing happened. Tillayou died.

There had been some coughing, the rattle that is so unmistakable even to those who have never heard it. But no one somehow had expected death.

An even more melodramatic pandemonium followed Tillayou's passing. Police were called for. We were ordered about. Mr. Scheuttler flourished his gun. Mr. Harvey was sent for from his sleep guarded by angels and, as he stood moaning over his master's body, questioned about the switch for the lights which hadn't worked all this time. O'Shea took a lead in this questioning, despite Mr. Scheuttler's violent orders addressed to one whom he now regarded firmly as a murderer. Mr. Harvey was incapable of any answers but O'Shea suddenly went down on his hands and knees and began crawling under the table while Mr. Scheuttler, fancying this an effort to escape, threatened loudly he would never get out of the room alive. But suddenly, in the midst of these threats, as O'Shea fumbled under the carpet at the table's edge, the lights went on.

"If you will allow me to be a bit oracular and put that gun away," O'Shea said, poking his head up from under the table, "the mystery is a very simple one. Tillayou turned out the lights himself. The switch was right under his foot. And then he killed himself."

It was dawn when Locksley, O'Shea and I entered O'Shea's rooms. We had spent an active and rather noisy evening as guests of Mr. Scheuttler and two police officials. Mr. Harvey had finally told his story. Tillayou had had the switch under the table installed the day before and this vital clue had been quickly verified from the electricians who had done the work. Mr. Harvey related that Tillayou had ordered him not to cook any food for our banquet, saying it wouldn't be necessary, and had also said that dishes and silverware would not be needed at his dinner. The absence of these items had been one of the odd things we noticed when we had first entered the dining room. Mr. Harvey also identified the dagger removed from Tillayou's body as one that had seen service in an ancient production of *Macbeth* and one which his master had spent the hours before the arrival of his guests sharpening in his bedroom.

There was no doubt that Tillayou had killed himself. But Mr. Scheuttler and the two police officials remained confused by the manner of his suicide. O'Shea persuaded them, aided by Mr. Harvey's tears and tattle, that the old actor's mind had been unhinged by grief over Marcia's death, and that the whole matter could be explained only by the poor man's insanity. We were all allowed finally to go, after assuring the officials we would appear any time they desired us for further questioning.

In O'Shea's rooms, Locksley and I waited patiently while that moody Celt opened bottles and prepared us drinks. After he had accomplished these rites he went to a drawer in a desk.

"I'll let you read this letter," he said. "It's from Marcia. It was mailed the night she was found dead."

He handed us a scrawled piece of note paper. We read:

"Alfred, I'm bored, tired, hurt, sick, full of nasty things. You were always the nicest. So take care of my father, like a good boy, will you? I'd stay a while longer but death seems easier and simpler than life. What are a few pills more or less to one who has swallowed so much? Good-by and do you remember the first night of *The Forgotten Lady*? For the last time,
"MARCIA."

O'Shea smiled at us moodily as we finished.

"That's the truth," he said. "She committed suicide."

"What about the bullets?" I asked.

"Guess," said O'Shea.

"Tillayou," said Locksley.

"Right," said O'Shea. "He found her dead with the poison still in her hand, very likely. And he couldn't bear that."

"I hate to think of it, too," said Locksley.

"He worshipped her," said O'Shea. "She was his star. But stars don't commit suicide. Only failures do that. Only very miserable and defeated people do that. He tried to keep her a star. So he set about slashing the painting and wrecking the place. It was all done very bravely so that the world might never guess that Marcia had died so ingloriously.

"At least," said O'Shea, "that's what I thought it was at first. And I decided to say nothing. What we saw tonight has got me all excited." He smiled and drank again.

"It was terrible," said Locksley.

"It was marvelous," O'Shea grinned at him. His gaunt, muscular mouth trembled with the mood of eloquence. "I read the signs wrong," he said. "Do you know what happened?"

"No," said Locksley, "except that the old boy was madder than a Hatter, poor soul."

"He wasn't mad," said O'Shea, "he was sane. You see, my lads, the old polliwog never thought of Marcia as having killed herself. He found her dead by her own hand. But that didn't mean anything. He saw her as murdered—by all of us. Murdered, gadzooks, by all the lying, cheating, faking rabble of friends that had danced around her including your humble servant, Alfred O'Shea. We'd killed her," he said dourly.

"Do you remember what he called us—all honorable and distinguished friends, all full of sweetness and unselfishness toward her? That was cute of the old windbag. Looking at us whom he hated so and rolling those juicy sentences at us. We were a flock of vampires that had fed off her. That's how he saw us, all of us. When he found her dead he thought of her as murdered, by us, by Broadway. It was all our hands that had lifted the poison glass to her mouth. And he went cracked with the curious idea of somehow bringing all these phantom murderers to justice."

We nodded. O'Shea drank again.

"That was a great performance tonight at the table," he said. "And a cold house. But he went over big."

"What made you think of another switch?" I asked.

"I knew that something strange was on the boards," O'Shea grinned. "I wanted to interrupt. But I hated to break up his show, whatever it was going to be. I'm kind of glad I didn't, aren't you?"

We said we were, but looked blandly at our host for further explanation. O'Shea drank again, grinned, his eyes filling with admiration.

"Do you realize," he said softly, "that the old barnstormer was playing his death scene from the moment he came into the room, with Sherlock Holmes in tow? He had the dagger in his pocket. He'd figured it out, rehearsed it in his bedroom for days, sharpening away at Macbeth's old toad stabber. He had his lines down pat. He'd planned to kill himself with the name of the supposedly guilty party almost on his lips. He was going to go as far as saying who it was that had murdered Marcia and then, out with the lights and the dagger in his heart. Suspicion would be turned on all of us. We'd all of us be clapped into jail and raked over the coals, not for his murder alone, but for Marcia's. That was the main thing. Whoever had killed Marcia had snapped out the lights and done him in, just as he was about to reveal the name. That was the plot. What a grand old boy! I'll never forget his dying."

"Nor I," I agreed.

"Dying and remembering his lines to the last," said O'Shea. "What a memory. That was my favorite poem he kept quoting—*Rain on Rahoun,* by Joyce. He heard me recite it once—on my honeymoon. You remember when he lay in the corner with the knife in him—acting, by God. All that waiting and mumbling about Marcia—do you know what he was doing? Ad libbing, like the good old trouper he was, filling in because death had missed its cue. Lend me your ears—it was the grand manner—grease paint and blood. And do you remember how he gurgled finally in that old ham voice of his—'It was . . . it was . . .' and died exactly at the right moment? What timing!"

"I remember how he said good-by to Mr. Harvey," said Locksley, "that was pretty."

We sat silent, overcome by the memory of old Tillayou's oration, hearing it anew with the mystery out of it.

"None of us will die as gallantly," said O'Shea, "and so much in the full sanctity of love—and art."

Locksley rose and shivered. A wry smile came into his Pickwickian face.

"A lovely piece of old-fashioned miming," he said, "but as fruitless a drama as I ever had the misfortune to witness."

"You're right," O'Shea said, "the plot was full of holes. I could have helped him a lot with the construction. But—it was a great Last Night."

Crime without Passion

MR. LOU HENDRIX looked at the lady he had been pretending to love for the past six months and, being a lawyer, said nothing. Mr. Hendrix was a gentleman who could listen longer to female hysterics without unbending than was normal. This, he would have said, was due to his aloof and analytical mind. Then, also, the events which were taking place in this boudoir at the moment were of a familiar pattern. Some eight or nine times Mr. Hendrix had been the hero of just such climaxes as this, when new love had entered his life, and necessitated similar farewells.

The young lady who, this time, was doing the screaming was a nymph of the cabarets known as Brownie. Her full name was Carmen Browne. She danced, and very effectively, at the El Bravo Club where, devoid of plumage as an eel, she led the Birds of Paradise number. In this she was ravishing as a Dream of Fair Women.

Why so young and delicious a siren as Brownie should be so disturbed over the amorous defection of Mr. Hendrix would have confused anyone who knew this gentleman or merely took a one-minute look at him. He was not Romeo nor was he Adonis, nor was he even such a male as one associates with the general practice of seduction. He was a little man with that objectionable immaculateness which reminds one, instanter, of sheep's clothing. He was one of those popinjays of the flesh pots with the face of a tired and sarcastic boy. His sideburns were a wee too long, his smile unduly persistent (like a ballet dancer's), his voice far too gentle to have deceived anyone, except perhaps a woman, as to his spiritual composition. But one can always depend on the ladies to misunderstand the combination of gentleness and sideburns.

Brownie, who among her own kind was considered not only quite a reader of books but a sort of practical authority on masculine characteristics, had misunderstood Lou Hendrix amazingly. Carry on as she would now, she was no match for this caballero of the law who, out of a clear sky, was engaged in giving her what she called "the go-by." As her monologue of screams, epithets and sobs progressed the lovely and muscular girl understood it all. She perceived, much too late for any use, that she had to do with as purring a hypocrite, rogue and under-handed soul as one might flush in a seven-day hunt on Broadway, which, according to the chroniclers Brownie most admired, is the world's leading water hole for human beasts of prey.

Looking around at the pretty apartment in which Mr. Hendrix had installed her and in which she had lorded it over her friends for the six months and from which she must now exit, love's dream being ended, Brownie spread herself on the couch and filled her Sybaritic diggings with a truly romantic din. From the more coherent utterances of this tear-stained beauty it seemed that she was innocent of all dally-ings with a certain Eddie White, an ex-college hero, and that since leaving this same Mr. White, whose love interest she had been before the Birds of Paradise number was staged, she had never once permitted him to lay a finger on her. She was, wailed Brownie, being wrongly accused. Then, sitting up, her greenish eyes popping with rage until they looked like a pair of snake heads, Brownie laughed, as she would have said, scornfully, and declared that she could see through Mr. Hendrix and his so-called jealousy. He was getting rid of her because he didn't love her any more. He was tired of her and putting her on the escalator—that was all there was to it.

To this, Mr. Hendrix, thoroughly seen through, made no reply and Brownie, announcing that she was not going to be made a sucker of, fell back on the couch, beat some cushions with her fists and shook with grief. The telephone rang. Brownie straightened on the couch.

"It's probably for you," she said.

"More likely it's Mr. White," said Mr. Hendrix.

The taunt brought Brownie to her feet.

"If it's for me, by any mischance," said Mr. Hendrix, "say I'm not here."

Brownie spoke into the phone.

"Who?" she asked. "No, he's not here. No, I don't know when he'll be here. No, no, I don't expect him." Hanging up, she looked bitterly at Mr. Hendrix. "Your office," she said. "Always making me lie for you."

"You might have been a bit more polite," said Mr. Hendrix.

The heartlessness of this suggestion sent Brownie back to the couch and her grief. She resumed her sobs. Mr. Hendrix continued to regard her with creditable, if villainous, detachment. His heart was in the high-lands with another lassie. But even discounting that factor Mr. Hendrix felt he was pursuing a wise course in ridding himself of so obstreperous an admirer as lay howling here. He had no use for overemotional types.

They were inclined to drive diversion, which was Mr. Hendrix' notion of Cupid, out of the window with their caterwauling.

Mr. Hendrix' soul, in fact, was a sort of china closet and he was firm in his aversion to flying hooves. He belonged to that tribe of Don Juans, rather numerous at the Broadway hole, who never hang themselves for love. Tears he regarded as bad sportsmanship and heartbreak was to him plain blackmail. Beauty—and by beauty Mr. Hendrix meant chiefly those delicious and agile Venuses of the cabaret floorshows—beauty had been put into Broadway (if not into the world) for man's delight; certainly not for his confusion and despair. And this little barrister lived elegantly, if rather villainously, by this conception.

A number of things, all obvious to the analytical Mr. Hendrix, were now operating in Brownie's mind and making her wail—Eddie's vengeful delight at her getting the go-by from his successor; the tittering of the little group of columnists, hoofers, waiters and good-time Charlies whom she called the World; the lessening of her status as a siren—she might even be demoted from leading the Birds of Paradise number, and through all these considerations—the Nerve of the Man, throwing her down as if she were some Nobody! As for the more passional side of the business, the pain in her heart at losing someone she had so stupidly loved and misunderstood and at losing the foolish Broadwayish dream of wedlock she had cherished for half a year, Brownie chose not to mention these in her ravings, being too proud.

Mr. Hendrix, still preserving his finest courtroom manner of Reason and Superiority, watched on in silence and fell to wondering what he had ever seen in this red-headed, almost illiterate creature with her muscular legs and childish face to have ever considered her charming or desirable. But he was given small time to meditate this problem of idealization. Brownie, with a yell that set the base of his spine to tingling, leaped from the couch, stared wildly around and then, emitting a series of shrill sounds, had at the furnishings of the Love Nest. She pulled a portière down, hurled two vases to the floor, swung a chair against the wall and smashed it, beat Mr. Hendrix' framed photograph to bits against the edge of the piano, seized a clock from the mantelpiece and bounced it on the floor and was making for Mr. Hendrix' derby, which he had placed on a chair near the door, when he, with an unexpected shout, headed her off.

The barrister, defending his derby, received a blow on the side of his face that sent him spinning. A thrown object caught him behind the ear. Brownie's pointed shoes belabored his shins. He retreated. But the hysteria to which he had been coolly and analytically listening seemed suddenly to have been injected, like a virus, into his bloodstream. It had started with the tingling in the base of his spine. Smarting from blows and full of some sort of electric current which gave off oaths in his head, the little lawyer began to outbellow his now ex-paramour. He came at the lady and in his hand he held, almost unaware of the fact, a large brass candlestick.

What it was that made this popinjay, so renowned for coolness, strategy and cynicism in his twin professions of amour and the law, so completely shed his character, God alone, who was not at Mr. Hendrix' elbow at the moment, could have told; and perhaps a psychiatrist or two might also have made a guess at. But here he was much too far gone for analysis, his own or anyone else's, charging at the lovely Carmen Browne like a bantam cave man, screaming and swinging the heavy piece of brass in the air.

There was no precedent in Mr. Hendrix' life for such a turn of events and no hint in any of his former love doings that passion could so blind his faculties and hate so fill his heart. Yet blind he was and full of a clamorous hate that demanded something of him. From the oaths which escaped Mr. Hendrix during this preliminary skirmish with the brass candlestick, it seemed that what he hated was women; loathed and hated them with a fury out of the Pit. Announcing this he swung the piece of brass and the second swing exhilarated him more. It had struck squarely against Brownie's head dropping her to the carpet. Mr. Hendrix, out of breath, stood cursing and grimacing over her like a murderer.

Slowly the little lawyer's rage melted. His heart swelled with terror and the nape of his neck grew warm. Brownie lay as she had fallen. He leaned over. Her skull was cracked. Blood was running. Her eyes were closed. Her legs, exposed in an incongruously graceful sprawl, were inert. He put his ear to her bosom. There was no heart beating. He stood for several minutes holding his breath and listening automatically for sounds outside the door. The choking sensation in his lungs subsided and the cool, analytical mind that was Mr. Hendrix returned like some errant accomplice tiptoeing back to the scene of the crime.

Carmen Browne lay dead on her hearthstone. No more would she lead the Birds of Paradise number at the El Bravo Club. But Mr. Hendrix wasted no time considering this sentimental phase of the matter. He had committed a murder, without intent, to be sure; even in self-defense, looked at factually. But no, self-defense wouldn't hold, Mr. Hendrix was thinking swiftly. There rushed through his mind all the angles, holes, difficulties, improbabilities and prejudices of his case and in less than a minute the little lawyer had put himself on trial on a plea of self-defense and found himself guilty.

Since a young man, Mr. Hendrix had always been close to crime. He had had that unmoral and intellectual understanding of it which helps make one type of excellent lawyer. In action, defending a criminal, Mr. Hendrix had always been like some imperturbable surgeon. Guilt was a disease that could be cured, not by any operation on the soul of its victim, but by a process of mental legerdemain which convinced a jury that no guilt existed. Mr. Hendrix might have said that he served a cause beyond good and evil, that of extricating the victims of fleeting misadventures from the unjustly permanent results of their deeds.

Thus, far beyond most men who might have found themselves confronted by the strange and ugly dilemma of having unexpectedly committed a murder, Mr. Hendrix was prepared for his new role of criminal. He knew all the ropes, he knew all the pitfalls of the defense of such a case as this. He knew the psychology of the prosecution. And with an expert, if still slightly fevered mind, he knew the perfect details by which his guilt might be cured, the ideal evidence, persuasive and circumstantial, by which a jury could be cajoled to the verdict of not guilty.

In less than a minute, Mr. Hendrix had a full grasp of his case, seeing far into its convolutions and difficulties. He set about straightening these out.

But like some dramatic critic who, after observing plays for years with subtle and intimate understanding of them, is summoned suddenly on the stage and with the strange footlights glaring in his eyes told to perform the part whose words he knows, whose ideal gesture and intonation he has always dreamed about, Mr. Hendrix felt the panic of debut. To know and to act were phenomena surprisingly separate. This was what delayed the cautious barrister for another minute, a minute during which Mr. Hendrix' client, with beating heart and white face, mumbled for speed, chattered even of flight.

But at the end of this second minute Mr. Hendrix had elbowed this ignominious client into a far corner of his mind, seated him, as it were, at the counsel's table with orders to keep his mouth shut—and taken charge of the case. He leaned over and looked at the clock on the floor. The dial glass was broken. The clock had stopped, its hands at two minutes of four. Mr. Hendrix' thoughts were rapid, almost as if he were not thinking at all but knowing. He could move the hands forward to five o'clock. He could leave the premises undetected, if possible, and attach himself for the next two hours to a group of prospective alibi witnesses, remain with them during the hours between four-ten and seven and this would be the proof he had not been in the apartment at the time of the murder. Mr. Hendrix examined the watch on Carmen Browne's wrist. It too had stopped. It registered one minute after four. The two timepieces, evidently synchronized by their owner, told a graphic and substantially correct tale. At 3:58 the struggle had begun. At 4:01 the woman had been killed. He would have to set the wrist watch forward a full hour to preserve this interesting discrepancy in the stopped clocks.

The telephone rang. Mr. Hendrix straightened, not having touched either of the hour hands. He had actually anticipated a telephone ringing, and in this anticipation known the ruse of the forwarded time hands was stupid. At 3:50 Carmen Browne had answered a phone call, a record of which was with the switchboard man in the lobby. Now at 4:03—he consulted his own watch—she failed to answer. Other phone calls might likewise come before five o'clock, all of which Carmen Browne would fail to answer, thus establishing an important series of witnesses against the fact that the murdered woman had been alive between four and five o'clock; thus rendering his alibi of his own whereabouts during that time practically futile. There was also the possibility that the neighbors had heard their quarrel and noted the time of the screaming. And more than all these the chance that someone, a maid or the building agent (Carmen Browne had been consulting him about sub-letting her place) might enter the room before five o'clock.

It was the hour preceding 4:01 for which Mr. Hendrix needed an alibi. He already knew its vital ground work. At 3:50 Carmen Browne, alive, had told someone on the phone—probably Tom Healey of his own law firm—that he was not in her apartment. Mr. Hendrix' eyes had remained on his own wrist watch as his thoughts slipped through these pros and cons. It was 4:04. He glanced at the sprawled figure on the floor, shivered, but stood his ground. Another phase of his case had overcome him. He smiled palely, shocked at what had almost been an oversight. He must not only provide an alibi for himself but fortify it with evidence tending to prove someone other than he had done the deed. He must invent a mythical murderer—leave a trail of evidence for the sharp eyes and wits of the prosecution leading to Another—a never-to-be-found another, but yet one always present in the Case.

Carmen Browne's fingerprints were on the broken clock, the

smashed chair, the battered photo frame. This was wrong. It would reveal that it was Carmen who had been in the rage, smashing things, demanding something that had resulted in her murder—and this sort of a situation, brought out by the prosecution, might easily point to Lou Hendrix, known to have been her lover. No, said Lawyer Hendrix swiftly, it must have been her assailant, demanding something of Carmen Browne, who had been in the rage and done the smashing and struck the fatal blow. Mr. Hendrix established this fact circumstantially by wiping Carmen Browne's fingerprints from the objects in question with a silk handkerchief. He wiped also and more carefully the brass candlestick. The absence of fingerprints pointed to a certain self-consciousness on the part of the assailant after the deed but that was both legitimate and normal. Men of the deepest passion, and there was precedence for this, remembered to obliterate evidence.

At the door, Mr. Hendrix, in his hat, overcoat and gloves, paused. He repeated to himself carefully, Carmen Browne had been attacked by some suitor, jealous of her real sweetheart, Mr. Hendrix, as witness the destroyed photograph of the latter. But why hadn't she used the gun the police would find in the desk drawer two feet from the spot where her body lay? There were of course normal explanations to be put forward. But Mr. Hendrix did not admire them legally. For fifteen precious seconds Lawyer Hendrix balanced the issue. During this space Mr. Hendrix listened rather than thought. He listened to the prosecution pointing out to the jury that the reason Carmen Browne had not reached for this available weapon with which to defend herself was because she had not expected an attack from the assailant, because the assailant was one familiar to her against whom she had no thought of arming herself; and even further, because the assailant, all too familiar with the premises, knew where this gun was as well as did Carmen Browne, and prevented her from reaching it. All these values pointed shadowly, Mr. Hendrix perceived, at his client. He removed the gun from the drawer and dropped it into his coat pocket. He must be careful in disposing of the weapon and Mr. Hendrix' mind dwelt stubbornly on a dozen cases in which an attempt at post crime evidence disposal had been the connecting link with guilt. But Mr. Hendrix assured his client firmly that he would be more cautious in this regard than any of his previous defendants had been.

With the gun in his coat pocket Mr. Hendrix stepped out of the apartment. Now he was, he knew, purely in the hands of luck. A door opening, a neighbor appearing, would ruin his case instantly. But no untoward event happened. He had three floors to descend. He listened at the ornamental elevator doors. Both cages were going up. Mr. Hendrix walked quickly down the three flights and coolly, now, like a gambler rather than a lawyer, rehearsed the possible permutations of Luck.

He had entered the apartment at three o'clock that morning with Carmen Browne. But because it was his habit to preserve a surface air of respectability toward the attendants of the place, though he fancied they knew well enough what was going on, he had walked up to the apartment with Brownie. The switchboard operator concealed in an alcove in the lobby had not seen them come in, nor had the elevator boy on duty, as both were out of sight at the moment. If now he could leave the building with the equal but vitally more important luck of not being seen, his case would be more than launched.

The lobby was empty, but Mr. Hendrix did not make the mistake of slipping out too quickly, and coddling the presumption that no eyes had observed him. He knew too well the possibility of the unexpected witness and he paused to study the premises. The switchboard attendant, half hidden in the alcove, had his back to the lobby and was reading a newspaper. Both elevator cages were out of sight. There was no one else. Mr. Hendrix stepped into the street.

Here again he stopped to look for that unexpected witness. How often, he remembered grimly, had the best of his cases been tumbled by the appearance on the stand of those aimless, incalculable human strays who had "Seen the Defendant." Mr. Hendrix saw two of just that type. Two women were walking, but with their backs to him and away from the apartment. A delivery truck was passing. Mr. Hendrix noticed that the driver was talking to a companion and that neither of these passers looked in his direction. There was no one else. Mr. Hendrix turned his attention to the windows across the street. Only the first three floors mattered. Identification was impossible, or at least could be sufficiently challenged, from any greater height. The windows were empty. As for the windows of the building directly over him, if he kept close to the wall none could see him from these.

Satisfied with this rapid but concentrated scrutiny, Mr. Hendrix started walking toward the corner. If the triumph of intellect over nerves, of reason over the impulses of the senses, may be called heroism, then this smiling, casually moving little popinjay in the black derby and snug overcoat might well be called a hero. Innocence, even aimlessness, was in his every movement; and in his refusal, despite a driving curiosity, to look at the time on his wrist—a tell-tale gesture were it recorded by anyone—there was something approaching the loftiness of purpose which distinguished the ancient Ascetics. As he turned the corner, Mr. Hendrix, still unruffled, still amiably rhythmic in his movements, looked back to make sure no taxicabs had entered the street. None had.

He was now on Sixth Avenue and he moved more briskly. He had four blocks to walk and habit sent his eyes looking for a taxicab. But, alert to every variety of witness, he shook his head and stayed afoot. He smiled, remembering that his own bed in his own apartment was unmade. He had just turned in the night before when Brownie had telephoned and asked to meet him. Thus his housekeeper, who never arrived before noon, would establish simply the fact that he had slept at home. This was unnecessary, to be sure, unless some passerby had seen Brownie and a man enter the former's apartment at three this morning.

Mr. Hendrix arrived now at a Sixth Avenue cinema palace. He looked carefully over the small crowd waiting for tickets and then joined the line. In a few minutes he was being ushered into the roped enclosure at the rear of the auditorium. He slipped away quickly, however, and walked in the dark to the other side of the theater. He approached one of the ushers and demanded to know where he could report the loss of a pair of gloves. After a brief colloquy he was led to the office of the Lost and Found department and here Mr. Hendrix, very voluble and affable, explained his mishap. He was not, he smiled, usually so careless with his belongings but the picture had been so engrossing that he had forgotten all about his haberdashery. Then Mr. Hendrix gave his name, address, a description of the missing gloves and watched with a glow of deep creative satisfaction the time being written down on the blank form used for cataloguing such matters. "Four-eighteen," the man wrote and Mr. Hendrix, consulting his watch, pretended to be startled. Was it that late? he demanded. Good Lord! he had had no idea of the time. It was quite a long picture. And the Lost and Found official, drawn into chumminess by Mr. Hendrix' affability, agreed that the film was a little longer than most, but well worth sitting through—to which Mr. Hendrix assented.

Emerging from the movie palace, Mr. Hendrix rehearsed his case to date. The main body of his alibi was achieved. He had spent the time between two-thirty and four watching a movie. His continued presence at four-eighteen in this theatre was written down in black and white. He had also taken care that it should be a movie he had already seen so as to be able to recite its plot were he questioned in the next few hours. And he had also provided a motive for seeing this particular movie. The film had to do with the character and career of a mythical state's attorney, and a newspaper friend of Mr. Hendrix who conducted a gossip column had asked him to contribute a few paragraphs from a legal point of view carping at the improbabilities of the scenario.

Mr. Hendrix' next port of call was an elegant speakeasy. Here he had a drink, engaged in an exchange of views with the bartender, who knew him, asked the correct time so he might adjust his watch. At 4:50 he stepped into a phone booth in the place and called his office. He inquired whether anybody had been trying to reach him that afternoon. The law clerk on duty for the firm, Tom Healey, answered as Mr. Hendrix had expected. Mr. Healey said he had been trying to find him in relation to a disposition but had been unable to locate him. At this Mr. Hendrix feigned a light anger. Where had the incompetent youth called? He had, said Mr. Healey, tried everywhere, even Miss Carmen Browne's apartment.

At this bit of information Mr. Hendrix, in his mind's eye addressing one of his future star witnesses, changed his voice. He grew angry and very obviously so, for he knew the laziness of people's memories and their slipshod powers of observation. He inquired sourly if Mr. Healey had spoken to Miss Browne. On hearing that he had, Mr. Hendrix said:

"Do you mind telling me how she seemed when you asked if I was there?"

"Well, I don't know," Mr. Healey said.

"Try and think," said Mr. Hendrix. "I'd like to know."

"Well," said Mr. Healey, "come to think of it, she struck me as a little curt or upset about something."

"Ha!" said Mr. Hendrix and, to the surprise of his office underling, called the young lady a villainous name.

"I don't want you to call me up at her place any more," he raised his voice. The clerk, Mr. Healey, said he would never do it again, but Mr. Hendrix, as though too enraged to notice this promise, continued, "I'm all washed up at that telephone number. Understand what I mean? You can just forget about it. Any other calls?"

"No," said Mr. Healey.

"O.K.," said Mr. Hendrix and hung up the phone with an angry bang.

He walked from the speakeasy with the light step which to Mr. Hendrix' office colleagues always characterized a Not Guilty verdict in sight. Now that the tingling at the base of his spine as well as the annoying warmth on the nape of his neck, as if a Prosecuting Staff were actually breathing on him, had gone entirely, Mr. Hendrix was beginning to feel not only relaxed but even amused. He could hear the Prosecution falling into this little trap he had just laid.

Question: So Mr. Hendrix told you that you needn't try to reach him at Miss Browne's apartment any more?

Answer: Yes, sir.

And Lawyer Hendrix looked winningly at the jury that sat in his mind's eye. Gentlemen of the Jury, consider this. As if, having committed a crime, the defendant would be so gauche as to give himself away by some such oafish remark to a law clerk—a type of person trained to remember what he hears. Not a casual stranger, mind you, but a man with sharp and practiced wits.

Mr. Hendrix, skittering happily along the street, cleared his throat, beamed and felt a desire to laugh. He had never quite so enjoyed a case. What subtle and yet vital psychological proof of his innocence was the fact that he had just said to Tom Healey what he had; what perfect proof of the fact that he had been the victim of an obvious coincidence in saying he was washed up with Carmen Browne when she lay dead in her apartment. No guilty man would ever have said that.

From a drug store he was passing, Mr. Hendrix made another telephone call. He called Carmen Browne. Inquiring for her of the apartment switchboard operator a sharp excitement stirred him. Before his eyes the image of her body, sprawled gracefully and awfully on the floor at his feet, swayed for a moment. He hoped the crime had been discovered, although there were still chances to improve his Case. But the switchboard man calmly plugged in for Carmen Browne's apartment.

"She doesn't answer," he said after a pause.

"This is Mr. Hendrix calling," said Mr. Hendrix. "Has she been in at all? I've been trying to get her all day."

"Hasn't come in while I've been here," said the man.

"How long is that?" said Mr. Hendrix.

"Oh, about three hours," said the man.

"Thank you," said Mr. Hendrix and hung up.

He had told Tom Healey he was washed up with Carmen Browne and now he was trying to reach her, and Mr. Hendrix considered this paradox, in behalf of his client, with a smile. It revealed, Gentlemen of the Jury, a distracted man; a lover full of confusion as a result of —what? Of the fact, gentlemen, Mr. Hendrix purred to himself, that my client was jealous of the attentions he had found out someone was paying to Carmen Browne; that he did not believe the poor girl's protestations of innocence and, driven from her side by suspicions, was yet lured back to her by his deep love. Jealous, Gentlemen of the Jury, of the attentions being paid to Carmen Browne by this creature who that very afternoon had entered her apartment and against whom Carmen Browne had defended herself until struck down and killed.

To augment this phase of the case, Mr. Hendrix returned now to the apartment building in which Carmen Browne lay murdered. He approached the switchboard operator, who greeted him by name. Here Mr. Hendrix controlled a curious impulse that whitened the skin around his mouth. He felt impelled to ask this man whether he had noticed Mr. Hendrix in the building before, whether he had seen him during the few moments he had walked from the lobby an hour ago. Astonished at this impulse, Mr. Hendrix held his tongue for a space, aware that the switchboard man was looking at him with curiosity.

Question: How did the defendant seem?

Answer: Confused.

Gentlemen of the Jury, and how would a man consumed with jealousy seem while inquiring, against all his pride, if the woman he thought was wronging him, was home?

"Has Miss Brown come in since I called?" asked Mr. Hendrix.

"I haven't seen her," said the man. "I'll try her apartment again."

There was no answer.

"Give her this note when she comes back," said Mr. Hendrix.

He wrote on the lower part of a business letter from his pocket:

"Darling, if you are innocent, don't torture me any more. Give me a chance to believe you. I'm willing to forget what I heard or thought I heard over the phone. As ever, Lou."

He placed this in a used envelope, scribbled her name on it, and sealed it.

Gentlemen of the Jury, can you imagine any man who had killed a woman he loved or had loved, so lost to all human reaction, so fiendishly wanton as to have written that little plea when he knew she was lying dead at his hands?

That was merely a rhetorical overtone, the human rather than evidential side of the note, but Mr. Hendrix filed it away in his memory as a bit of decoration. His alibi, Lawyer Hendrix murmured to himself, was now complete. But the secondary phase of the case needed further effort. The beauty of a case lay always in the elaborateness of diverse but corroborating detail—as if the world were crying the defendant's innocence from every nook and cranny. And happily at work, Mr. Hendrix had lawyer-like so far forgotten the human existence of his client as to whistle cheerily the while he turned over and re-turned over the major psychological problem in his mind.

Defense—Carmen Browne had been murdered by a man to whom she refused, after perhaps leading him on, to surrender herself. Also it might be that the killing had been one of those passional accidents which the sex instinct, run amok, precipitates. It might be that Carmen Browne had led a double life and was discovered in this double life by her slayer.

Ergo—Lou Hendrix, sharp-witted, observant, a veritable connoisseur of women, must suspect the existence of this other man. And Defendant Hendrix must also be jealous of him.

Witness to this—his talk to Tom Healey; his note to Carmen Browne now in the hands of the switchboard operator.

And Lawyer Hendrix, with the thrill of a gambler rolling a third lucky seven, remembered at this point a third witness—a veritable star witness, beautifully, if unwittingly, prepared for her role a few days ago. This was Peggy Moore.

Miss Moore danced at the El Bravo Club as a member of the ensemble. She had been Brownie's confidant for a year. Mr. Hendrix smiled blissfully recalling his conversation with Miss Moore less than a week ago and recalling also her general character, one made to order for the part he was to assign her.

This young lady was a tall, dark-haired Irish lassie with slightly bulging eyes and an expression of adenoidal and not unpleasing vacuity about her face. She was, as Brownie had frequently confided to him, a veritable love slave, a dithering creature incapable of thinking or talking on any subject other than the emotions stirred in her bosom by love or jealousy.

Some days ago Mr. Hendrix had selected this almost congenital idiot as the opening pawn in his decision to rid himself of Brownie. He had confided to Miss Moore's ears, so perfectly attuned to all tales of amorous agony, that he suspected Brownie of being still in love with his predecessor Eddie White. Miss Moore's eyes had bulged, her mouth opened as if to disgorge a fish hook and simultaneously a shrewd, if transparent emotion, had overcome her. Miss Moore, the victim of so much perfidy, had been convinced instanter of her chum's guilt and had launched at once into a series of lies, all defending Brownie's integrity and offering idiotic details of her devotion to her lawyer lover. Mr. Hendrix, intent on laying some foolish groundwork for his subsequent defection, had persisted, however, and, for no other reason than that he delighted in playing the human fraud whenever he could, had feigned sorrow and talked of woe.

Now Mr. Hendrix summoned Miss Moore on the telephone to meet him at the speakeasy he had recently quitted. He spoke guardedly, hinting at a lovers' quarrel, and pretending he needed her to verify some evidences of Brownie's guilt, just unearthed. Miss Moore, full of a laudable and loyal ambition to lie her head off in Brownie's behalf, as Mr. Hendrix had foreseen, arrived in a rush. And the two sat down at a table in a corner, Miss Moore to invent innocent explanations and alibis for her chum, at which like all over-tearful addicts of passion she was amazingly expert; and Mr. Hendrix to weave her artfully into his case.

But first Mr. Hendrix, aware of the lady's sensitivity toward all matters pertaining to love, proceeded to get himself drunk. He must be the lover stricken with jealousy and seeking to drown his pains in liquor, a characterization which this simple child and student of amour would remember only too vividly on the witness stand. Three drinks were consumed and then, honestly befuddled from such an unaccustomed dose, Mr. Hendrix launched into cross examination. And despite his thickened tongue and touch of genuine physical paralysis, Lawyer Hendrix remained as cool and analytical as if he were in a courtroom. He was not one to betray a client by any human weaknesses.

He put himself at Miss Moore's mercy. He must know the truth and she alone could tell him. Otherwise with too much brooding and uncertainty he would be sure to go out of his mind. His law practice was already suffering. He would lose all his money. Miss Moore nodded tenderly and understandingly at this saga of love woes. In reply she could assure Mr. Hendrix that he was being very foolish to be jealous of Eddie White because Mr. White wasn't even in town and besides Mr. White was engaged to marry a society girl in Newport. Mr. Hendrix sighed appreciatively at this walloping lie.

"It's not Eddie," said Mr. Hendrix; "it's somebody else. You know that as well as I. You're in her confidence. Don't try to lie to me, dearie. I caught her red-handed, talking over the phone. She hung up when I came into the room. She was making a date—and not with Eddie White."

Miss Moore paled at the thought of this dreadful contretemps, but kept her wits. Her chum's guilt frightened her but at the same time she saw through Mr. Hendrix' effort to lead her astray. Of course it was

Eddie White of whom he was jealous. Miss Moore was certain of this and Mr. Hendrix, listening to her somewhat hysterical defense of Brownie, sufficient to have convicted that young lady of a hundred infidelities had he been interested, realized exactly what was in his companion's mind. He considered for a moment the plan of involving Eddie White in his case. He had thought of it before—Brownie's previous lover, a known hot-headed young gentleman given to nocturnal fisticuffs in public places. But for the second time he dismissed this phase. Eddie would have an alibi and the establishing of Eddie's physical innocence, however psychologically promising his guilt might have looked, would embarrass his client's case.

For the next hour Mr. Hendrix drank and discussed his jealousy, pleading with Miss Moore to be kind to him and reveal what she knew; and hinting at gifts in return for such service. But Miss Moore only increased the scope of her lies.

"Have you seen Brownie today?" Miss Moore finally broke off, winded.

Mr. Hendrix weaved in his seat and looked at her with bleary drunken eyes.

"No," he said. "I don't trust myself to see her. God knows what I would do—feeling this way."

"You're just worked up about absolutely nothing," said Miss Moore and rose. She had to toddle off to the El Bravo where she performed during the dinner hour. Mr. Hendrix accompanied her to the door.

"Tell Brownie," he whispered, "I'll be over to the club tonight. And . . . and give her a last chance to prove her innocence."

"I'll give her the message," said Miss Moore and sighed.

Alone Mr. Hendrix returned to the phone booth. He sat down heavily and put in a call for Carmen Browne. His case was ready. He desired to hear the news of the finding of the body. An annoying tingle touched the base of his spine as he waited for the apartment switchboard to answer. He wondered how drunk he was. Drunk, to be sure, but sober enough to know exactly every phase and weigh every nuance. The moment he heard of the crime he would rush over, be detained by the police and with the aid of his intoxicated condition act thoroughly irrational and grief-stricken. He would hint at no alibis, reveal not a shred of his case until the coroner's inquest.

The switchboard operator finally answered. Mr. Hendrix inquired thickly for Miss Browne. He was told Miss Browne was not in. He hung up. Rising and swaying for a moment, Mr. Hendrix, thoroughly at peace with the world, except for this intermittent tingle, decided on the best course. He would go to the El Bravo Club, order his dinner and wait there till Brownie's absence was noticed and a search started.

The El Bravo orchestra was rendering a dance number. The dance floor was crowded. Mr. Hendrix looked dizzily at the circling figures. He had selected a table far to the side, one of those at which the performers and their friends grouped themselves during the evening. The stuffiness of the air made Mr. Hendrix feel drowsy. Looking up, he beheld a familiar figure approaching. It was Eddie White, whom he had pleased to style the ignorant drop-kicker. Mr. Hendrix smiled. He noticed tiredly that Mr. White seemed a little drunk.

The ex-college hero, still a sturdy tanned and muscular product of the Higher Education, greeted Mr. Hendrix calmly. He dropped into a chair at the table and inquired, with an eye roving over the place, how tricks were. Mr. Hendrix said they were fine.

There was a pause during which the music filled the café with glamorous and exciting sounds.

"Didn't know you were such a movie fan," said Mr. White apropos of nothing and Mr. Hendrix felt himself sobering up as if in a cold shower.

"Just what do you mean?" Mr. Hendrix managed to inquire and very casually.

His companion was busy looking them over on the dance floor and offering a roguish eye to a few of the tastier numbers. Mr. Hendrix stared at him in silence and felt the tingle return to his spine.

"Saw you going into the Roxy this afternoon," Mr. White resumed.

"You did," said Mr. Hendrix and then added, as if he were looping the loop, "What time was that?"

"What time?" Mr. White repeated, looking at the little lawyer with a dull, athlete's stare. "Oh, a little after four, I should say."

"You're crazy," said Mr. Hendrix, "if you think you saw me going into the Roxy after four. Why, I came out about twenty after four, after seeing the whole show."

"I don't care what you saw," said Mr. White. "I saw you going in at about a quarter after. I was gonna say hello but I thought the hell with it. How'd you like the picture? Ought to be in your line—all about one of those crooked legal sharks."

In the brief space during which Mr. Hendrix was now silent his thoughts were very rapid. Mr. White, God help Mr. Hendrix, was that most objectionable of all humans known to a legal case—the aimless stray that the Prosecution was wont to drag, rabbit fashion, out of its hat with which to confound the guilty. And Mr. Hendrix knew without thinking the full significance of this witness, Eddie White. If the defendant had been seen entering the movie theater after four, he had been seen entering after the murder had been committed. But that was the least damaging phase. The defendant had left the movie theater at 4:20, having lied to the attendants and told them he had spent an hour and a half in the place. With the fact of this lie established, the prosecution could take apart piece by piece the obvious mechanism of his alibi. There was no alibi. There was no case. In fact, to the contrary, Eddie White's simple statement of the time of day—after four—revealed all of the defendant's subsequent actions as those of a thoroughly guilty man, and Mr. Hendrix leaned across the table and put a hand on the athlete's arm.

"It must have been somebody else you saw," he purred.

"Listen, don't tell me," said Mr. White. "I saw you looking around, buying your ticket and ducking in."

Mr. Hendrix winced at the damning phraseology.

"I know it was about a quarter after four," pursued Mr. White, "because I had a date outside. And don't get so excited. It wasn't with Brownie."

The tingle at the base of the Hendrix spine was almost lifting him out of his seat.

"That's a lie," said Mr. Hendrix thickly.

"What's that?" Mr. White demanded.

"I said you're lying," Mr. Hendrix repeated slowly. "You didn't see me."

"Oh, that's what you said, is it?" Mr. White was unexpectedly grim. "Listen, I never liked you and I don't take talk off a guy I got no use for. Get that."

And for the second time that day an unprecedented mood overcame the little lawyer. He made an effort to stop the words which suddenly filled his head but he heard himself saying them and wondering confusedly who it was who was drunk—he who was listening or he who was speaking. He was telling Mr. White what a liar, numbskull and oaf he was and Mr. White stood up. Words continued, Mr. Hendrix aware that he and Mr. White were both talking at once. But the music made a blur in his ears and the El Bravo Club swayed in front of his eyes. Then Mr. Hendrix realized, and darkly, that the towering Mr. White's hand was on his collar and that he was being lifted out of his seat. The El Bravo orchestra was rolling out a jazz finale and nobody seemed to have noticed as yet the fracas taking place at this side table. As Mr.

Hendrix felt himself being hoisted to his feet, a sense of nausea and helplessness overcame him. He thrust his hand into his coat pocket.

"Calling me a liar, eh?" Mr. White was growling in the Hendrix ear. He added a number of epithets.

The little lawyer saw for an instant a fist pull back that never landed. Mr. Hendrix had removed a gun from his coat pocket, a gun of whose existence in his hand he was as unaware as he had been of the brass candlestick. The gun exploded and Mr. White with a look of suddenly sober astonishment fell back into a chair. The music at this moment finished with a nanny goat blare of trumpets. No heads turned. No waiters came rushing. Shaking as if his bones had turned into castanets, Mr. Hendrix stood looking at the crumpled athlete and watched his head sink over the table. The mouth was open. The athlete's fingers hanging near the floor were rigid.

Music started again and Mr. Hendrix turned his eyes automatically toward the dance floor. Blue and pink floodlights were shining on it and out from behind the orchestra shell came a line of almost naked girls. White legs kicked, smiles filled the air. Leading the chorus line Mr. Hendrix saw Carmen Browne. She was dancing.

The little lawyer grew sick. He shut his eyes. Then he opened them. They were full of pain and bewilderment. It was no hallucination. It was Brownie. Extending under her ear at the back of her head he saw strips of court plaster. She was alive and restored.

Mr. Hendrix knew exactly what had happened. The last time he had called her apartment, the switchboard man, failing to recognize his liquor-thickened voice, had withheld the information he might have offered Mr. Hendrix—that Carmen Browne was alive, that she had summoned a doctor, that she had left the apartment.

And even as he was thinking of this tiny detail, a hundred other details crowded into the Hendrix mind. He remembered his accusations to Brownie that she still loved Eddie White; his statement to Peggy Moore last week and this afternoon that he was too jealous to trust himself; his attack on Carmen Browne, his subsequent drunkenness, his idiotic antics in the movie theatre—as if he were shadowing Eddie White—what else could his rushing in and rushing out mean? Everything Mr. Hendrix had accomplished since 4:02 this afternoon pointed only at one conclusion—that he hated Eddie White, that he had almost killed his sweetheart out of jealousy over White, that, still burning with this emotion, he had tracked White down and murdered him in cold blood.

Mr. Hendrix, during these brief moments staring at the crumpled athlete, wanted to scream, so macabre did all these events strike him, but his voice trailed off into a moan. What was this insane thing he had done for his client! Exonerated him! Mr. Hendrix, still shaking, slipped down into his chair. He, Lou Hendrix, the shining legal intelligence, had like some Nemesis convicted himself—and not of manslaughter, which might have been the verdict otherwise—but of premeditated murder in the first degree. There was no case. No defense was possible. There was nothing left to do but to flee like some thug.

Mr. Hendrix looked at his wrist. He had twenty minutes to make the ten o'clock train for Chicago. From Chicago he would travel to New Orleans and thence into Mexico. He had a wallet full of bills. The side exit of the El Bravo was ten feet away. But Mr. Hendrix, struggling to get to his feet, swayed and fell forward. The dozen drinks he had so shrewdly tossed down his gullet to help him act his part joined the hideous plot he had hatched against himself. He was too drunk, too dizzy to stand up and move quickly.

They found the little barrister hunched in his seat staring at the murdered athlete. The gun was still in his hand. Mr. Hendrix was mumbling passionlessly:

"Guilty. Guilty. Guilty."

The Rival Dummy

I WAS DINING in a place where vaudeville "artists" congregate to gossip and boast, when my friend Joe Ferris, the booking agent, pointed to a stocky little man with a gray toupée, alone at a table and said:

"There is, I think, the strangest, weirdest, craziest man in New York."

I looked a second time, and noted, despite this identification, nothing more unusual than the aforesaid gray toupée, a certain bewildered and shifty manner about the eyes, and a pair of nervous sensitive hands. He reminded me—this solitary diner—of some second-rate Hungarian fiddler worn out with poverty, alcohol, and egotism.

"That," said Joe Ferris, "is the man who ten years ago used to be known as Gabbo the Great—the world's most famous ventriloquist. I guess he heard me"—the booking agent lowered his voice—"but it doesn't matter. He'll pretend he didn't. We're not supposed to know who he is, you know. That's what the toupée is for. Disguise. Mad—madder than a cuckoo. It gives me the shivers just to look at him.

"I'll tell you his story," continued Ferris, "and maybe you can figure it out. That's more than I can. But being a newspaperman, you won't call me a liar. I hate to tell stories to people who are always certain that anything they never heard of before is a lie.

"This particular yarn"—Ferris smiled—"began way back before the war. He came over from Belgium, Gabbo. That's where a good percentage of the best performers come from. God knows why. Jugglers, contortionists, trapeze acts, strong men, and all that kind of stuff. Belgium and Lithuania, sometimes.

"I booked Gabbo when he first landed. The best all-around ventriloquist that ever played the big time—if I do say so. And nuts, of course. But you got to expect that from the talent. I never see a first-rate act that wasn't at least half nutty.

"The first time I met him I ask him what his name is.

"'Gabbo what?' I ask.

454

" 'Gabbo the Great,' is the answer. And then he adds very seriously, 'I was born Great.'

"I thought at first this was the foreign equivalent for a gag. But there was less humor about Gabbo than a dead mackerel. He used to sign his letters G. G. Imagine. And—to give you a rough idea of what kind of a loon this baby was—he always opened his act with the *Marseillaise*.

"He used to come out in the middle of it, stand at attention till it was finished, and then, in a low, embarrassed voice, announce: 'Ladies and Gentlemen: I have the honor to present to you tonight the world's most gifted ventriloquist—Gabbo the Great.'

"And he would take a bow. That's pretty cuckoo, ain't it? But it always went big. You'd be surprised at what an audience will swallow and applaud.

"Well, the first time I came to the conclusion that there was something definitely cockeyed about Gabbo was when I called on him one night after his performance at the Palace. It was up in his room at the hotel. He'd just got in and was taking his dummy out of its black case. It had velvet lining in it, this case, and was trimmed in black and gold like a magician's layout.

"Let me tell you about this dummy—if I can. You've seen them. One of those red-cheeked, round-headed marionettes with popping, glassy eyes and a wide mouth that opens and shuts.

"Well, Jimmy—that was the name of this wooden-headed thing— was no different than the rest of them. That is, you wouldn't think so to look at it. That thing haunts me, honest to God. I can still see its dangling legs with the shoes painted on its feet and—let's forget about it. Where was I?

"Oh, yes. I go up to his room and stand there talking to him, and just as I'm making some remark or other, he sits Jimmy up on the bed, and all of a sudden turns to him—or it or whatever you want to call the thing—and starts holding a conversation.

" 'I suppose,' says Gabbo, angry as blazes and glaring at this nutty dummy, 'I suppose you're proud of yourself, eh? After the way you acted tonight?'

"And Jimmy, the dummy, so help me, answers back in a squeaky voice, 'Aw, go soak your head. Listen to who's talkin'.'

"Then this nutty ventriloquist speaks up kind of heatedly. 'I'm talkin',' he says. 'And I'll ask you to listen to what I have to say. You forgot your jokes tonight, and if it happens again you get no milk.'

"Well, I thought it was a gag. You know, a bit of clowning for my benefit. So I stand by, grinning like an ape, although it don't look funny at all, while Gabbo pours a glass of milk and, opening Jimmy's mouth, feeds it to him. Then he turns to me, like I was a friend of the family, and says coolly: 'This Jimmy is getting worse and worse. What I wanted to see you about, Mr. Ferris, is taking his picture off the billing. I want to teach him a lesson.'

"I've had them before—cuckoos, I mean—and it didn't surprise me. Much. They come pretty queer in vaudeville.

"Remind me to tell you sometime about the prima donna I had who used to come on with a dagger and throw it on the stage. If it stuck, landed on its point, she'd go on with the act and sing. If it didn't she wouldn't. Walk right off.

"She was pretty expert at tossing the old dagger, so it usually landed right—they ain't ever too crazy. And on that account of the dagger always landing right, I never find out what it's all about for weeks. Until one night she up cold and walks out on herself. On an opening night at the Palace, too, where she's being featured. And when I come galloping back, red in the face, to ask her what the hell, she answers me very haughty: 'Go ask the dagger. He tell you.'

"Well, that's another story, and not so good, either. About this night in Gabbo's room, as I was saying. I took in Gabbo's little act with the dummy, and said nothing.

"But I started making a few inquiries the next day, and I find out plenty. I find out that this nutty give-and-take with the dummy is just a regular routine for Gabbo. That he keeps up a more or less steady conversation with the dummy like he was a kid brother. And not only that, but that this idiotic dummy is the only human being—or whatever you call him—that Gabbo ever says more than hello to. Barring me, of course.

"Look"—and Ferris snorted—"can you imagine him sitting at that table now and looking at me and pretending he don't know me? And, what's more, that I don't know him? On account he's got a nine-dollar toupée on. Well, that's part of the story, and I'll come to it.

"The way I figured it at the time—and I may be wrong—was that Gabbo was such an egotist that he could only talk to himself. You know, there's lots of hoofers, for instance, who won't watch anybody but themselves dance. They stand in front of a mirror—for diversion, mind you—and do their stuff. And applaud it. That's vaudeville for you.

"So I figured Gabbo that way. That he was so stuck on himself he got a big kick out of talking to himself. That's what he was doing, of course, when he held these pow-wows with Jimmy.

"As you can imagine, it kind of interested me. I got so I'd always try to drop around Gabbo's dressing room whenever I had time, just to catch this loony business with the dummy. I didn't think it exactly funny, you know, and it never made me laugh. I guess it was just morbid curiosity on my part. Anyway, I sort of become part of the family.

"The fights they used to have—Gabbo and this crazy dummy; fighting all the time. Usually about the act. Gabbo sore as the devil at Jimmy if anything went wrong with the turn—if one of the gags missed fire, for instance, he'd accuse him of stalling, laying down on the job, and honest to God, once he sailed into the damn thing because he was sure it wasn't getting enough sleep. Believe me or not, they were as quarrelsome as a team of hoofers.

"And after I got used to these spats—you know you can get used to anything—I got to thinking of Jimmy almost the way Gabbo did. I got to imagining it was him answering back—squealing, kidding, and swearing. And not Gabbo talking with his stomach—or whatever it is ventriloquists talk with.

"But with all this fighting between them, you could see that Gabbo had a soft spot for Jimmy. He fed him milk. There was a can or something fitted up inside. That's where the milk went.

"For instance, just to show you the pretty side of the picture, about three months after I change the billing and take Jimmy's name off the one-sheets, Gabbo arrives in my office with a demand that I put the picture back and the name too, in twice as big lettering as before.

"And one other time he comes to me, Gabbo does, and says Jimmy isn't getting enough money. Well, as you can imagine, this sounds a bit phony. There's such a thing as carrying a gag too far, is my first reaction. But so help me, he meant it. And he won't go on with the act unless I come through.

"Well, I learned long before that it don't pay to win arguments with the talent. It's worse than winning an argument with your own wife. Costs you more.

"So I finally control my temper and asks, 'How much of a raise does Jimmy want?'

" 'Five dollars a week more,' says Gabbo. And Gabbo was pulling down four hundred dollars for the act; so you can see the whole thing was on the square—asking a raise for Jimmy, I mean. Then he explains to me that he has been paying Jimmy ninety-five dollars per week right along, and he wants to make it an even hundred because Jimmy has been working very hard and so on.

"So much for that. Here's where the plot thickens. About three weeks or so after this conference, I get wind of the fact that Gabbo has fallen for a dame; and that the thing has become quite a joke among the talent.

"I can hardly believe my ears. Gabbo never looked at a dame ever since he was on the circuit. The loneliest, stuck-up professor I'd ever known. He used to walk around like Kaiser Wilhelm. Grand, gloomy, and peculiar. And with a mustache. Don't look now—he's shaved it off. Part of the disguise. But in those days it was his pride and joy.

"Well, the next thing I heard about his love's young dream is from Gabbo himself in person. He comes back to New York, and comes walking into the office with the information that he is adding a woman to his act; Mlle. Rubina. I look at him and say, 'What for, for the love of Pete? What do you need a jane in the act for, and why Rubina?'

"'For the water,' he answers. 'To bring on the glass of water which I drink. And take it off.' And he scowls at me as if to say, 'Do you want to make anything out of it?' And when I nod sort of dumbly, he goes on: 'She is willing to join me for a hundred dollars a week.'

"Well, this is pretty nuts. Rubina was a bowlegged wench working in a juggling act. Fetched plates and Indian clubs for Allen and Allen. And worth all of fifty cents a year as talent. Not even a looker. But go argue with Gabbo. I tried a little taffy about his going over so much better alone—that is, with his pal Jimmy to help him out. But he waves his hand at me, pulls his mustache, and begins to jump up and down with excitement.

"So I agree, and he then becomes the gentleman. He'll stand for a fifty dollar cut in his salary—that is twenty-five dollars out of his take and twenty-five out of Jimmy's. That's the way he puts it. And I should kick in with the other fifty for Rubina's graft.

"That's how this Rubina joined the act.

"I went over to catch it three nights later and see what was going on. I came right in the middle of Gabbo's turn. There he stood, with Jimmy sitting on the table, and this peroxide Rubina all dressed up in red plush knickerbockers with green bows on the sides of the knees, hovering around and 'acting'—registering surprise and delight every time the dummy made a wise crack. It almost ruined the turn.

"But what I noticed most was that Gabbo was a changed man. His whole attitude was different. He wasn't making his usual goo-goo eyes at the audience or shooting over personality—which had been his long suit.

"He was all wrapped up in Rubina, staring at her like a sick puppy with the heaves. And calling her over every half-minute, between gags, and demanding another glass of water. And bowing like an idiot whenever she handed it to him. He must have drank fourteen glasses of water during the act.

"And that, my friend, was just the beginning. The circuit thought it a big joke—Gabbo's crush on Rubina.

"And what everybody considered the funniest part of the racket was that Rubina was as fond of Gabbo as if he had been a rattlesnake. She never had anything but a sneer and a wise crack for him, and, when he got too fancy with his bow, just a low-down scowl. She would have none of him. Why, God only knows. Except perhaps that he was a little too nutty even for her. And she was no picker, believe me.

"In about two months things begin to grow serious. It seems, according to reports which come in from every town on the circuit, that Gabbo has carried his anger against Jimmy to such lengths that he'll hardly talk to him on the stage, mind you. Keeps sneering at his jokes and trying to trip him up, and bawling him out in front of the audience.

"And then, after the act, he sits him up on the table in his dressing room and starts in hurling curses at the dummy and screaming. It scares people out of their wits. The actors back-stage, I mean. You know, it's kind of woozy to pass a room where you know a man is alone and hear him yelling at the top of his voice. And, what's more, answering himself.

"And all this excitement, it seems, is due to jealousy. That was the whole point. It seems that this Rubina valentine had tumbled to the fact that Gabbo treated Jimmy like a living person. So, out of sheer cussedness, she had taken to patting Jimmy's wooden cheeks on the stage. Or winking at him during the turn. And the blow-off came, I learned, when she slipped Jimmy a caramel as he was sitting on Gabbo's lap in the dressing room. This was just downright morbid viciousness on Rubina's part.

"After that there was nothing could straighten the thing out. As soon as Gabbo lands in town, I go back-stage with him. He's in his dressing room, and he stands there—the turn being over—just motioning me away and raging at this maniac dummy of his.

" 'That is the kind of a one you are,' he screams. 'That is the way you show your gratitude. After all I've done for you. Trying to steal the woman I love from me. The woman I love above everything.' And then I listen to Jimmy answer, and, so help me, for a minute I thought it was that damned wooden image speaking.

" 'My life is my own,' says Jimmy, squealing wilder than usual. 'I can do what I want. And I'll ask you to mind your own business, you big tub of lard.'

"At these words Gabbo jumped into the air and pulled his hair out in handfuls.

" 'Viper,' he howled at the dummy.

" 'Idiot,' Jimmy squeals back at him.

"What could I do? I just sneaked off and left them calling each other names like a pair of fishwives. I crossed my fingers and hoped that the act wouldn't split up—that's where I was chiefly concerned, you understand.

"Then came the second stage. I don't know whatever got into this Rubina dame. She'd never pulled down more than thirty dollars a week in her life. And here she was getting a hundred. For doing nothing. And yet she writes me a long misspelled letter, that she's quitting the act on Saturday and for me to find someone to take her place.

"I was of course tickled silly. Fifty dollars is fifty dollars. And, besides, I sort of liked Gabbo and I felt this Rubina was dangerous to him. It's best for lunatics to steer clear of women—or for anybody for that matter.

"But my satisfaction didn't last long. I get a telephone call the following Monday to hurry over to the Bronx where Gabbo is opening—being starred, mind you. My great ventriloquist, it seems, has gone out of his head.

"I get there just as the bill has started. Gabbo has just told the manager he won't go on. He won't act. He knows what he owes to his art and his public, but would rather be torn by wild horses than to step out on the stage alongside of that black imp of hell—Jimmy.

"And as he says these things he walks up and down in his dressing room, cursing Jimmy and glowering at him like a maniac. They're having an out-and-out bust-up, like a team. Calling each other hams, among other less repeatable things.

"The house manager and all the actors were frightened silly at the noise. But I was used to Gabbo by this time, and began trying to calm

him down. But I got no chance to get in a word edgewise—what with
the way these two were going after each other. Gabbo thundering in
his baritone and that damned dummy squealing back at him in his
falsetto.

"I saw at once that Gabbo had really sort of gone over the edge.
This time there was a murderous rage in his voice. And in Jimmy's,
too.

"I got so mixed up I began to worry—for Gabbo. Dummy or no
dummy, I began to think that . . .

"Well, anyway, it appears that Rubina, his adored, the light of his
life, has flown. And Gabbo's idea, nutty as it sounds, is that Jimmy
knows where she is. That she and Jimmy have framed against him.
That Jimmy, the dirty hound, has stolen her love. Can you beat it?

"There's no use trying to reason under such circumstances. Any
more than getting logical with a man who has the D. T.'s. Gabbo won't
go on with the act. And he don't. He's through. And I stand still, and
say nothing, and watch him hurl Jimmy into his black case, grab it
under his arm, and start out with it.

"And I follow him out of the theater. He starts walking peculiarly,
like a man half stewed. Then I see that he's doubling on his tracks, trying to elude somebody. Me, I figured. But I kept on. Finally he goes
into a store, and I watch him through the window. It's a hardware
store, and he stays in there for five minutes, and then comes out and
makes a beeline for the hotel.

"I got to his room almost as soon as he did. But the door was
locked. I stood there listening, and all of a sudden I hear screaming.
In English, French, and several other languages. I swear to you, it
scared me silly.

"I started banging on the door. But it's no use. Finally I beat it
down after the manager. We're back in five minutes. And we open
the door.

"Well, the room is silent and empty.

"I stood staring for a minute. Then I saw something. The floor is
covered with pieces of wood. Splinters, sticks. It's Jimmy. Chopped
to pieces, cut to smithereens. He'd murdered Jimmy, honest to
God.

"We looked all around the room, and found the ax he'd bought in
the hardware store. And then found that he'd lit out through the window. Made his getaway down the fire-escape.

"And that's the last trace we could pick up of him. We hunted
high and low. I had two men scouring the town. But he was gone,

leaving everything behind him. Fled—like a murderer, a murderer fleeing from justice, so help me.

"I'd gathered Jimmy up and put him in a piece of wrapping paper. That's how confused I was. And I carried him to the office and finally threw him in the wastebasket. And then I went home, and was unable to sleep for six nights.

"That's almost the end of the story. Except that two years ago I come in here one night after the show, and I see somebody familiar sitting at a table. I can't place him for a few minutes, and then all of a sudden I see it's Gabbo—Gabbo the Great—with a gray toupée and the mustache shaved.

"I rush over to him and begin talking. And he stared at me— highty-tighty like.

"'My name,' he says, 'is Mr. Lawrence. I am sorry you make a mistake.'

"Well, I'm not unusually dense, and as I stood there it dawned on me that Gabbo didn't want to be known. That he'd come back after fleeing from justice for eight years—come back disguised and with a different name, so that the police wouldn't pick him up for his great crime.

"And here he sits." Ferris looked at me with a mirthless smile. "Everybody knows his story in this place, and we all kid him along, calling him Mr. Lawrence and keeping his secret. Yeah, and when we get funny we call him the Ax Murderer. You know, just a gag among ourselves.

"Wait till he leaves"—Ferris picked up his glass—"and I'll take you over to the table where he's sitting."

This struck me as a rather empty offer.

"What for?" I inquired.

"So you can see what Jimmy looked like."

Ferris suddenly laughed. "He always draws a picture of that damned idiotic dummy on the tablecloth—every night."

In the Midst of Death

THERE IS A WORLD of which little sensible gets written and if I too now add another of those childish and unconvincing chronicles of ghost land to its white-sheeted history it will be a sorry reflection of my talents as a reporter.

But before setting down the experience from which I have only recently recovered, I will answer the questions which every reader, arrested in his workaday world by some sudden frightened whisper of hobgoblin, werewolf or ghost, is entitled to ask. To wit, I have no romantic notions tucked away in the back of my head that corpses rise from graves to walk the earth, that curses survive the foolish mouths that utter them. I have no belief in the survival of living things after they have died, whether they be trees, dogs, cats or foul old misers. If there be banshees and leprechauns, vampires and a company of wailing disembodied souls floating in the night I have never seen such gentry nor had any commerce with them.

Yet I believe, or rather I have for several months lived, in a world as evil and unnatural as any the voodoo worshippers go hunting in the dark jungle. That I escaped from that world alive I attribute more to chance than to the superiority of reason over unreason.

I will start my story with no other description of myself than that I am a writer. I had planned to write a book and because of the nature of this book I had moved myself and my favorite belongings into a strange and little known part of New York City. I had rented a house in Cherry Street, a battered, almost obliterated survivor of a street on the East Side.

In this street the island of Manhattan comes to a sad and ragged end. There are no tenements. There are half-dismantled houses that resemble packing crates more than domiciles. There are empty lots used as dumps and very little left to dump in them. There are a few sagging warehouses, much broken glass and tottering fences and a handful of rather mysterious folk, who, like the street to which they cling, seem

463

more survivors of some past era living on scraps wrested from a wasteland than residents of today's New York.

A few blocks to the west the tumult of the slums and the ghetto
begins. But Cherry Street, idle and decrepit, is not part of these. It is
as dormant and faraway, despite the noises that drift over it, as any
collapsing row of houses in those abandoned mining towns that dot the
western desert.

The house in Cherry Street into which I moved had been built in
1800. It had the look of a house that had been stormed and taken again
and again by hosts of vandals. Its sides gaped. Its stoop had been
wrenched away, its rear undermined, its roof shelled. It still boasted its
Adam doorway intact, and inside, the walnut floors and stairway survived. But from the odors which struck me when I first entered this
house I felt these could not survive for long.

I stood that first spring morning inhaling so bitter and dominant
a reek of decay that it seemed this derelict house must at any hour give
up its architectural ghost and collapse into a heap of refuse. Yet in two
weeks' time, with its windows restored, its odors banished or at least
neutralized by grate fires and aromatic smokes, its walls repainted,
beams repropped and its thousand spiders crushed, this ancient house
took on a persuasive if shabby dignity.

Sitting at nights in its lamplighted living room, now filled with
books and such comforts to which I cozen, I felt rather smug over
my domestication of this tramp of a house. I forgot the abandoned junk
yard that was my north neighbor and the tar-paper shanty on the south.
I had cleared away and spaded up the plot of ground in the rear and
done some spring planting, thrilled to find the soil into which I dug,
once the overlay of refuse had been carted off, full of evidences that a
garden had once thrived within the dismantled brick wall which still
outlined the little area.

As for the odors of this castaway street, within a month the mingled
scents of rust and sea, of decaying wood and stale walls, had grown
downright pleasing to me. Here on the edge of the thundering city I
found a stillness, sudden and ominous. This street, no longer useful, no
longer more than half alive, seemed like one of those half-sunk barges
rotting at a wharf and threatening to drift away and disappear.

Although I was charmed by the neighborhood, I found sleep difficult at the beginning, owing to the noises I seemed to have rented along
with the house. Rats scurried in the dark and the quick, furtive shuffle
of feasting and exploration was at times frightening. Likewise the
babble of rotted wood, of creaking fibers, dripping plasters, warping

beams which became audible in the night's stillness was disturbing. Behind the new paint and all my improvements, decay, like some restless ogre with a thousand tongues, continued its monologue in the dark.

I would get out of bed a half dozen times a night, and lighting a candle, walk through the house expecting to find God knew what ghosts, or acrobats at least. But there was nothing ever to see but empty rooms and shadowed walls. There was nothing to find but the continued creaking, grunting, pitter-patter and moan of the dying house. Reassured, I would return to bed, pleased, although not for long, with this romantic and vegetable symphony of corruption around me.

However, after a month I found these once disturbing sounds of no consequence. I grew pleased with the mood of loneliness the house gave me. It enabled me to work. And at night, feeling as if I were adrift on some derelict ship, I would fall asleep despite a sudden running on the stairway or a half strangled cry from the cellar.

But one night after having become thus inured to this house, to its peculiar sounds and smells and its musty, shadowy walls, I was awakened by a sense of shock, by some trembling response to danger that had penetrated my sleep. I sat up in bed chagrined at this return of my original nervousness toward what I now considered a charming and friendly old house.

The room was dark. A faint moon outlined my little garden beyond the window. I realized as I reached for the box of matches that I was listening too intently, that an odd sharpness animated all my senses and that it was not for the familiar noises of this old house my ears were straining but for some other unknown and yet psychically expected sound.

I was about to light a match when this mysteriously awaited sound came into the room. It was a soft footfall. That quick chill with which the heart signals its terror, its desire for flight while the mind lags behind in confusion, entered my blood. But in a moment I knew I was listening to nothing more alarming than a cat. A cat was in the bedroom and in my relief over this fact I conceived an immediate love for the animal regardless of its color, shape or degree.

I settled back and, growing used to the dark, made out its silhouette. I watched it move slowly across the floor and with a silent agility that made it seem to take flight rather than leap, mount the window sill overlooking the garden a few feet below. Here it remained crouching and staring. Again the tremble of premonition that had awakened me returned, as if all were not as well as my cat had led me falsely to believe. Once more I found my heart chilling and my senses strained and full of expectation, that undesirable expectation which fear kindles and which devours one's will like a fire. I moved uneasily to the edge of the bed and looked out of the window in which my visitor crouched.

There was another visitor. In a far corner of the garden a figure was standing. The face was not visible. I could make out only an outline of someone stooped and motionless. As I lay looking it moved and shuffled off and I saw that my trespasser was a woman, old and bent and barely able to walk.

A rumble brought my eyes to the window sill. The cat had risen on its legs. Its back was arched, its fur pointed. It spat and leaped from the window into the garden, vanishing after the departing figure.

I lit two candles, picked up a book, but was unable to read. The presence of the old woman in the garden had not particularly alarmed me. But the antics of this cat appeared to have affected my nerves.

Of my half-amused and half-hysterical conjectures that night I will say only there is hardly anyone so sane, so realistic but that somewhere lingering in his brain lobes may be found the lore of cats and witches and the whole childish paraphernalia of forgotten fairy tales.

The morning brought a rich sense of absurdity—to my relief. There is nothing quite as absurd as the supernatural in the bright morning sun, and the memory of witches and evil cats made me smile. I went to work on my writing with the incident thoroughly digested and disposed of. Returning from dinner, which I ate in a restaurant a mile or so from the old house, I discovered a souvenir of my night's disturbance. The cat—I knew it at once for the same animal that had invaded my room—had obviously adopted me as a source of board and lodging. It was an unsightly creature, a bit too long and cylindrical to stir the enthusiasm of even a promiscuous cat lover. And it ate the food put before it with a remarkably unfeline boldness and relish. Also, after its meal it went to sleep in a manner which was rather surprising. Instead of curving up and settling gracefully into slumbers as became the tradition of cats, this eccentric and stringy animal fell over on its side, its legs outstretched like a dead horse, and in this stiffened posture closed its eyes and slept. I watched it for a time, thinking perhaps it had died, but the twitching of its legs reassured me and I returned to my work.

In bed, having put out the candles, I thought of the other garden trespasser and lay staring out of the window hoping she would appear again. The night was brighter and the garden pleasantly visible. I looked forward to my witch's return with a sense of entertainment.

But I fell asleep and wakened as I had the previous night full of that same tremor of disquiet and expectancy. My friend, the stringy cat, was in the room. He was moving toward the window, and he struck me as a rather tense, electric fellow. I could feel a wave of feline disquiet. Looking out, I saw again the figure in the same far corner of the garden, but this time visible in its details.

It was, as I had surmised, an old woman with a face almost destroyed by age. In the moonlight I could see plainly the senile and malformed features. Shrunken, ashen, it frightened me as the faces of the very aged sometimes do—those faces too close to death out of which the corpse already peers and on which a mold already seems to be gathering. The long, bulbous nose that almost covered the mouth, the toothless, stiffened jaws, the hollowed eyes half overgrown with flesh, the wrinkled, baggy skin that seemed ready to fall away from the bones, became in the moonlight so startling a mask of evil that I turned away. She was shawled and wore a heavy black skirt. Her hands were hidden.

I watched, wondering what strange inner errand could bring so old a woman into my garden after midnight. As I continued to look, the sense of alarm increased. This crone standing so still appeared to me suddenly as someone engaged in some dreadful activity. I found myself quivering, my senses bristling with fears and full of a wordless ugly conviction that something was going on in the garden.

I held my breath, fearful of attracting those hollow brooding eyes to me. All that I saw was this motionless figure in the night, this mummy in the shadows. But now it struck me that it was too motionless. It was watching something. The thought came to me, like a spider crawling through my head, that there was something in the night of which this visitor was a part. My ears and eyes strained themselves for a hint of hidden things. I could detect nothing, but the night grew ugly and unfamiliar, and I lay staring with the sick taste of fear in my mouth.

What was it I felt, what did I expect? What was this motionless one with hidden hands doing? Why did she come to my garden to stand and stare? Then, as on the night before, I heard a rumble from the window sill. The old woman had moved and was shuffling away.

I saw the cat arch its back, spit and leap into the garden and, to my horror, an almost uncontrollable impulse to jump out of the window after it laid hold of me by the hair. I lay clinging to the bed, gritting my teeth against this sudden compulsion. My legs already felt in flight toward the garden. I could already smell the dank half-flower, half-refuse odor of that little plot of earth as if I were walking across it. But

I remained in the bed resisting this flight of my senses, and after a few minutes found myself rid of this inexplicable and shocking inner command. I lay covered with perspiration, too weak to light the candles and cursing myself for a neurotic and an imbecile.

In looking back over the subsequent events I marvel over nothing as much as my own weak will, my inertia and my mysterious submission to the thing which that night brought into my life. That the hidden selves of a sane man may respond to the eerie, the magical, the unknown is in a manner natural. But that sanity itself, the surface of logic and practicality which we proudly identify as our ego, should so easily become stricken and impotent to direct one is a sorry indication of the paper thinness of our wills and pretenses.

I made no effort the next morning to explain my curious impulse to jump into the garden after the crone. Stupidly I shelved the memory as belonging to another set of circumstances, as having no particular point in them for sanity to discuss with itself. I fed the cat, noted once more its peculiar methods of slumber, grinned at its unsightliness and resumed my writing.

But even that first day an enervation had begun to rob me of both facility and ambition. I idled about the old house. The arrival of Mrs. Hanse, my elderly and amiable charwoman, threw me into a burst of temper. I felt her presence hostile and alien. This stout and busy old woman did not belong around me. I ordered her off, to her surprise as well as my own. Toward evening I took my daily walk to the restaurant. I had no appetite. I was too eager for an event—the night. There was no doubt in my mind. My visitor would return. I knew almost the hour she would appear. I knew she would stand in that same garden corner and that my friend the cat would again be on the window sill.

I recall a moment or two of wonder during this day. What was this eagerness? Why was I so excited? What was it I was expecting and what had stirred in me this strange mood—half furtiveness, half anger. I answered these questions smugly enough. My desire for another glimpse of my garden visitor was merely proof of my courage. Most men would have been quaking at the prospect of such another little spectacle. But I was one whose cynicism enabled him to enjoy such hints of the supernatural. This explanation pleased me and I noted nothing strange in my behavior.

On this third night the sky was dark with clouds. I walked back from my dinner, which I had hardly touched, and as I entered the dreary, broken street in which I lived, a sense of pleasure came to me. I stood looking up and down this forlorn and castaway street so devoid of life in the dark. No lighted windows with blinds insufficiently drawn to reveal little bits of human scene, no vehicle clattering cheerily on human errands, no sounds of music or argument came to disturb my mood, my strange appreciation of these empty derelict sidewalks. Alone I remained, sea wind blowing in the night. Something less than life seemed to exist in the half-visible shanties and battered fences. At the end of the street a few figures moved but these with their furtive, pre-occupied air seemed part of the meaning of this scene just as the figures of mourners walking among old graves add somehow to the significance of death.

I went to bed and lay grinning and full of fancies. The garden was almost too dark for objects to be seen and, despite my vigil, it was not until the cat had again mounted the window sill that I became aware of my visitor.

There she stood again in the corner, a blur of black against the crumbled wall. But though I could make out nothing I could feel her motionless. She was some cracked old beldame, I began to think, some eccentric crone that belonged in this castaway street, a pothering grannie dizzied with the approach of death and shuffling aimlessly through the dark. But my thoughts dwindled. More powerful things than words were talking to me.

They came out of the garden, messages so confusing and so sickening to my sense of reality, of self, of the worldly practical intellect that was still I, that I lay breathing as if running uphill. An intolerable duality seemed to be taking possession of me. I was aware of things my senses were denying me. My ears and eyes straining again for a hint of hidden matter in the night detected nothing. But an odor was slowly filling my nose, an odor of roses in bloom—heavy, sweet, evilly romantic. And I felt the night air on my face as if I were outside. Wind rushed on my skin as if I were running and I heard myself panting as if with some unimaginable activity. This was hallucination for I still lay in the bed, the me I knew lay clutching the sheets as if fearful of being swept from his place. In the far corner of the garden I could still see the motionless old woman.

An anger made my head hot. This anger was strange. It seemed to sweep something out of me. It propelled me as on the previous night to the garden, but this time with so violent and blind an impulse as was almost irresistible.

I saw the cat leap again and I rushed from the bed to the window to throw myself into the dark, my mouth full of bitter unintelligible curses. I stopped at the window. The garden, a few feet below, was an instant away. But an unexpected glimpse of myself saved me. I saw myself in the dark windowpane—a dim image with wild, staring eyes. This image seemed to hover unreal as a ghost in the night. But it was I. And clinging to the sill with trembling hands I shrank from it. It halted me, and sent me cowering back to the bed. I fell exhausted on the pillows and slept soundly.

When I awoke I knew from the unlightened mood which dawn and supposed rationality brought that I was in the midst of some experience deeper than I had bargained for. I felt a depression as of danger waiting. Yet more than on the previous day I desired no company. This perverse longing for loneliness, for fear, surprised me faintly. I know dimly now that I was behaving in a manner foreign to my intelligence. Finding myself about to enter the garden that afternoon to do some weeding, my feet lagged. I started mumbling to myself that I was too tired to work outdoors and that the earth was too damp. I returned to my living room with a wretched impression of danger averted.

I made no investigations in the neighborhood or, what was worse, in my mind. I sat about the old house reading and scribbling ineffectually and allowing something to drift, as if I had become too much like this street that had once seemed to me a half sunken and rotted barge moored to a wharf and threatening to disappear. I felt a character change but thought or rescue were impossible. I had escaped my will.

My antics and agonies during the weeks that followed have left no special memory. I recall nights when I watched, my friend the cat beside me on the sill, and no visitor came into my garden. And other nights when she appeared. I recall seeing her sometimes plainly, too plainly, as if her miserably aged face were pressing against mine. There is the memory of her motionlessness, of her never-varying, lifeless vigil in the dark and of the sense deepening in me that danger, horrid and nauseating, threatened me. But chiefly there is the memory of the growing need to join her in the garden. Against this strange and ugly need I struggled each night she appeared. Although my sanity, the I of my ego, dwindled and I became nightly more and more an oblivious actor in some evil and infuriating scene transpiring in the dark, yet I clung to my side of the window with inexplicable resolve, exhausting myself with the effort, finding myself the next day often unable to leave the bed, as if drained of all will and vitality by the night's struggle.

I made several half-hearted attempts to leave the old house. I telephoned friends. I paid visits. But the thing happening had fastened itself to me. I did not desire to avoid it. I was pleased to lie trembling in this dying house. I seemed to have become a plotter against myself, a secret ally of those forces which were pulling me out of the window each night to join something in the garden.

Those friends who saw me during this time commented on my gauntness and bad temper, advised fresh air and new diets and usually departed angrily. As the summer grew hotter visitors stopped calling and even my few intimates, repelled by my unfriendliness and uncharacteristic bursts of anger, left me alone. I lived with the stringy queer cat that I had never fondled nor given a name, but that I continued to feed eagerly each day as if it were part of the mystery into which I was soon to be inducted.

I knew days before it happened that I was going to join her in the garden. There was no longer anything that could stop me. I was aware of a secret in my heart, mind, senses—a duality that still evaded my thought but to which I must surrender. Inside my identity, burrowing through what I had deemed my sanity, a new person, a new set of moods, desires, had taken shape. I had something to do with this half-dead crone who came haunting my garden at night. I had something to do with her vigil. What, I didn't know. But even in the brightness of the day I found myself scowling, moving about my lonely house full of truculence and loathing. What was it I hated, what was it I loathed? There was no answer to this, yet I knew the answer. It lay in the garden. An impulse was overwhelming me as if hands were fastened in my hair dragging me outside myself.

I remember of the final night few actual sane details. That there was a bright moon I recall. Yet I mistrust even that memory. I seemed aware during the day of a storm over the sea, of a heavy wind blowing and the old house creaking and moaning as if it must collapse any moment. I locked myself in, refusing to admit the amiable and persistent Mrs. Hanse. I sat waiting in the bedroom. At twilight a desire to undress came to me and I grew frightened at this. I did not wish to undress. But my hands, obeying an inner command, began removing my clothes. I did not desire to sleep, yet I crawled into the bed, naked and shaking. As I lay I remembered with an odd distress that the cat was not in the room. The absence of the cat filled me with violent disquiet. I jumped from the bed and unlocked the door. The cat was outside waiting, but it remained on the threshold, refusing to enter my room. I whispered to it, coaxingly. Finally, angered by its obduracy, I reached to lay hands on it. It rose stiff-legged and spat at me.

I smiled and returned to the bed. There was no need to coax this cat. I knew that it must be in this room this night and I laughed aloud at its futile hesitation. It kept watching me and then slowly, its legs stiff with fear, it came in and slunk into a corner. I saw its eyes burning like two fiery discs in the dark and, appeased, I fell asleep.

When I woke it was after midnight. I slipped furtively from the bed and moved barefooted to the window. She was there, motionless in the far corner of the garden and the sight of her brought so deep a rage into my heart that I bit my lips to keep from cursing aloud. A mood, furious and blinding, lay hold of me. Standing in the dark window watching the figure in the corner near the garden wall, I knew who she was. I screamed and hurled myself into the garden. Rage lifted me from the ground as I fell. I heard another shout. It was I running through the garden toward this figure, toward this motionless one. I was gasping something in a hoarsened voice, a name—"Jenny, Jenny!" I never reached her.

A pair of arms seized me. They came out of the dark, enfolding me, crushing me against a body cold and violent. I fell and the arms clung. I heard my screams. A cold as of death gripped my throat. I was being choked. I fought. A tall, heavy man panted in my ear, cursed, growled and kept tightening his hand on my neck. I felt death and murder in the dark. My senses were almost gone when, opening my eyes, I beheld something so strange as caused me to gasp and cry out.

I beheld around me a tall brick wall with flower boxes arranged along its top. Against the wall dahlias bloomed and in a sudden flood of moonlight I saw garden beds teeming with asters and gladioli. Under the window of my bedroom rose clumps of towering bushes and the smell of roses flooded the air. In the far corner stood a great tree. In the instant I beheld this unnatural sight that was part of the hand choking me to death, a pain, ghastly and intolerable, wrenched at my head. I lay in this non-existent garden, crushed under the body of this non-existent murderer, feeling life grow back and I heard myself cry out crazily, "This isn't true!" With these words, as if I had waved some holy talisman in the devil's presence, the walls and flowers, the heavy garden scents, the great tree in the corner and the moonlight vanished and with them the cold hand disappeared from my throat.

I recovered consciousness in the dawn. Barely able to move, I crawled into the old house. My neck was stiff and sore. In the hallway I saw my cat. It was lying stiff-leggedly as if in its peculiar sleep. I bent over it. Its head was crushed and it was dead.

I remained in bed for two days nursing bruises and too weak and stiffened to move. Mrs. Hanse, buxom and spry beyond her years, took care of me. She was of the opinion, as she applied remedies to my bruises, that I had been in a nasty fight, and this reminded her of what she called the good old days of Cherry Street when homeric combats between Celt, Teuton and Semite had livened the neighborhood.

I listened to her reminiscences with crafty, flattering interest. I was afraid to be left alone in the house. I induced her to take one of its rooms for a bedroom. Yet though I lay cowering at night, fearful of looking into the garden and listening almost hysterically to the pitter-patter and moan of this dying house, I refused to leave it. A sense of violent shock lingered in me and my mind was beginning to torture itself in a search for explanations, reasonable explanations of all that had happened. I was myself again, weak and convalescing from something that haunted me as if it had been a dream. But to leave would be to leave behind only half of my disease, whatever it had been. My mind, unsatisfied and tortured, would keep alive these dormant fears. Cherry Street with its forlorn and castaway stare, with its night noises and unknown figures would follow me wherever I went. And the garden would follow me.

On the fourth day, feeling stronger, I asked Mrs. Hanse the question that had been rolling furtively over and over in my head.

"Do you know any old woman in the neighborhood named Jenny?" Mrs. Hanse nodded.

"Aw, she's a funny one, that one," she said. "Old Jenny. Sure, she hangs around yet."

"What do you know about her?" I asked. And Mrs. Hanse told me the first part of the story. A few days later, able to leave the house, I visited the Public Library and rummaged for hours through old newspaper files. By the end of the week I had pieced together Old Jenny's history.

The old house I had rented had been the home seventy years ago of a man named Philip Massover. Jenny had been his wife. They had lived there but a short time, less than a year. In that day this old house had been a likely and dignified residence and Cherry Street a tree-shaded, charming avenue. The Massovers had moved into this house immediately after their marriage.

This marriage had been an unhappy one. Jenny had loved another man whose name was John Tell and who was captain of one of the sailing ships her husband owned. A drawing of John Tell I located in the *New York Times* of September 10, 1860, reveals a tall, heavy man with deep-set eyes. Of Jenny or her husband Philip I could find no likenesses.

One day in the summer of 1860 the police, urged on by worried neighbors, visited the Massover home in Cherry Street. They found it deserted. The beds were unmade, the dishes lay unwashed in the sink. Husband and wife had vanished. Inquiry revealed that Philip Massover had not been at his shipping office for five days. Eager neighbors introduced the name of John Tell into the mystery and four months later Captain Tell was arrested as his ship docked in the harbor of New York. With him was found the missing Jenny Massover.

Both were charged with the murder of Philip Massover and a hunt for the remains of that deceived husband instituted. Captain Tell and Jenny related what seemed a straightforward and, for that day, dreadful story of sin. Jenny had run off with Captain John one night, leaving her husband asleep and unsuspecting in his bed. His subsequent disappearance was a surprise to her. Neither she nor John knew aught of what had happened to him.

The police investigation dragged through the autumn and was finally discontinued. I could find no hint of where John and Jenny went on their release, whether they married and settled down or took to the seas in one of Captain John's boats. But this was the Jenny who came to visit my garden. She had returned from God knows where to the home of her youth. Mrs. Hanse explained that a few old-timers who had the story from their parents had recognized her but that it was impossible to talk to her. She was deaf and almost blind and lived on scraps.

But there was no need to talk to Jenny. Once I had gathered her story my own participation in it became clear to me. I knew what the police had never found out and what the legends of the neighborhood had never contained. I knew that Old Jenny, blind and tottering, had come back from somewhere to the scene of a crime committed a summer night some seventy years ago. She had come back to stand under the tree that had once filled the far corner of the garden as she had stood one night in the arms of her lover, Captain John, while her husband slept in the room I occupied.

But on that night her husband had wakened, perhaps through the noise of a cat creeping through his room. He had looked out the window, seen her embraced. Rage had filled him and he had jumped into the garden to attack the scoundrel and despoiler of his happiness. And this scoundrel, Captain John, had met him half-way, his arms reaching out of the dark to seize him. They had wrestled until Captain John, stronger and burlier, had choked the life out of Philip Massover. Jenny had stood by watching. Philip murdered, the lovers had worked swiftly to dispose of him and then hurried to the captain's ship in the harbor and disappeared.

This was what Old Jenny, motionless night after night in the garden corner, had been watching—the murder. Her half-blind eyes looking out of another self had stared at this scene of passion and death in the garden, had watched night after night a man come leaping out of the bedroom window over the rosebushes, rushing through the aster beds and coming to grips with another man and dying.

It was this memory of murder done in these same shadows, this vision in which Old Jenny lived, that had come scratching at my senses like some phantom at the doors of life. Old Jenny, lost in her memory of that wild night, watching that scene of terror relive itself, had cast a telepathic spell over me. I was sleeping in the bed where Philip had slept. I was watching from the window through which Philip had watched. And I had finally become Philip!

This was the secret I had felt but been unable to understand, this the change of character that had slowly overtaken me as I stared night after night out of the window. I had become part of Jenny's hallucination. I had slowly caught her madness as one might catch a disease. I had experienced a disintegration of self and will and become dominated by a vision creeping like some mist through my senses into my soul. On the night I jumped from the window I was Philip, a phantom Philip. I was Philip seen by Jenny in her trance, Philip running to be murdered in the garden seventy years ago.

But here I pause. The marks on my neck, my bruises, the crushed head of my cat—these were real. What hallucination could have this power to squeeze life out of my throat, injure my flesh and wrench my shoulder?

I answer this cautiously. It was not a ghost that assailed me in the dark, but a dream. Our bodies, I discovered that night, respond not only to those things we glibly call realities. Our imagination can also create images with the power to destroy us, can people that inner world of hallucination with monsters of no substance that nevertheless can wound the flesh, break the body and crush life from us. Our senses, our organs, can respond with a mysterious logic to the assault of chimeras and bleed when phantoms strike, die at the touch of shadows. This is the secret of stigmata, of those physical disorders which hallucination produces.

But this phantom that tried to strangle me in the dark was no figure hatched by any dream of mine. It was a thing of mist risen out of the memory of the crone who stood dreaming in the night. It was Jenny's past playing ghost in the garden, Old Jenny's dream, that assaulted me

The answer then is that our hallucinations have power not only over us but over those who can be reached by them. These shades generated by obsession are residents of an inner world in which time, space and life are unknown and yet in which we may live and die. This is the world of death that lies dangerously at the bottom of the mind. Of this inner world we carry in our heads we know almost nothing. We are as unaware of its dimensions and powers, of its disasters and ecstasies as we are unaware of the universe beyond the skies. And in this world which will some time be opened and explored by man dwell today those forces of which we get glimpses in the guise of banshees, vampires and ghosts.

On the night I rushed into that non-existent and blooming garden I was Philip Massover, and out of the past, out of this inner world into which I had been lured, strong hands rose to murder me again.

Two weeks after I had recovered from the assault I saw my garden visitor for the last time. She was waiting motionless in the garden corner, half hidden by the night. I stood in the window trembling, a curious memory agitating my senses. But I knew the exorcism necessary. I cried out to Jenny and ordered her to go away. When she failed to move I threw a stone. It fell near her feet. Startled, she raised her half-blind eyes to me, glared at the old house and shuffled off.

The next morning an idea filled me. I began digging in the garden. I dug for two days. At nightfall of the second day I uncovered with the help of a laborer two skeletons. They lay a number of feet under the earth where my visitor had kept her vigil. One of them was that of a man. The other was that of a cat.

The Ax

ZELLER PUT the ax behind the furnace out of sight, the head of the ax on the cement floor, the long handle leaning against the side of the furnace.

Still it wasn't hidden. It showed if you stood in certain places in the basement. Zeller nodded. He would take care she shouldn't stand in those places.

Then it seemed to Zeller suddenly that he was lying, that he was not going to kill Mrs. Lansen. The whole thing was a fake. Coming down in the basement to wait for her, hiding the ax and emptying the barrel in the corner so it would be ready for her—he was making believe. It was a lie. The thought that he was lying to himself became intolerable to Zeller.

He had lain awake all night enjoying the death of Mrs. Lansen. The way she would come walking into the dark basement, angry and proud and sneering as always, calling, "Zeller, Zeller." And he would step out of the shadows and listen to her. Her complaints. They would be the last complaints she would ever make. The house was cold. Why did he let the fire go down? As if he could help it overnight. A fire went down by itself. And why hadn't he shoveled the snow off the sidewalk? She didn't want any lazy bums around.

For five years he had never answered her. Just a mumble, his head hanging. This time he would look right at her, straight into her eyes while she hollered at him.

Everybody was afraid of her. How many times he had heard that daughter of hers getting her head banged against the wall and crying, "Mother, mother, don't!" And how many time he had heard that husband of hers whining like a dog that was being whipped while she hollered at him. The whole neighborhood was afraid of her. The way she held her head and sneered, as if people were dirt under her feet, as if she was right all the time about everything.

But he was lying. He wasn't going to kill her. He was going to hang his head again and mumble. He knew this because his stomach was like ice.

Zeller walked to the ax and picked it up. He could hardly close his fingers on it. It seemed alive, as if it would jump away. Suddenly he swung the ax through the air. There was a metallic crash, a terrible bang of sound that filled the basement. He had cracked the side of the furnace.

He threw the ax to the ground and stood staring at it. He was crying. The tears ran from his eyes down his cheeks into his large black mustache.

He remembered how he had come home eight years ago and there was no supper on the kitchen table and his wife was gone. Gone, the rooms empty, all her clothes gone. Gone with some man, loving somebody else, and how he had lain in the empty bed hugging her pillow and crying—just like he was crying now.

He picked up the ax and held it against him. It made him feel weak. He wanted to kiss it.

A voice began speaking in his ears. It said, "What do you tell yourself lies for? You're such a big liar you ought to be ashamed of yourself. You ain't gonna kill anybody. You're a liar."

Zeller caught his breath. His body quivered and a soft broken wail, guttural and low-pitched like the last sob of a child who has wept itself into silence, came from him.

"Zeller! Zeller! Where are you? Come right here!"

Mrs. Lansen. She was coming down. Her heels banging on the stairs made him wince.

He tried to put the ax back quickly out of sight but the air seemed to have thickened around him so that he had to push against it to move. He was putting the ax behind the furnace—but slowly, slowly as if he were bewitched. What if he didn't get it hidden in time!

"Zeller! Zeller, where are you?"

He was waiting for her.

"Good heavens, why don't you answer me? Standing there like an idiot!"

She was coming across the dark basement. His eyes were on the ground, but he could see her, the sneer, the angered face, the proud head that called him dirt.

"You lazy fool, letting the fire go down! On a cold day like this. And the walks unshoveled. What am I paying you for? To stand around and do nothing! Wake up! Don't look so stupid. Look at me! What was that noise down here a few minutes ago?"

Zeller shivered and hung his head.

"I heard something smash."

Zeller mumbled.

"My God, haven't you any common, ordinary sense? Look up at me. I'm talking to you."

Zeller's stomach felt like ice. He lifted his head slowly, fearfully. There she was with her face with rouge on it, an old woman with rouge and her hair done fancy. Hollering at him.

Why was he so frightened? She would see him trembling and the sweat on his face rolling into his eyes. Why couldn't he breathe through his nose instead of keeping his mouth open and panting—so she could see? He hung on to the side of the furnace. It was hot, burning his hand. But if he let go he would fall down. He felt limp. He wanted to scream something. Go way! Go way quick, Mrs. Lansen. He wanted to scream this at her, at her rouged old face, at her finger with rings on it shaking under his nose. He was a liar. The ax, the barrel, the banging on the furnace—these were lies. He stood staring at the angry rouged face, shivering, sweat covering his body, his stomach like ice.

Then he heard a noise, a very faint noise behind the furnace. The noise made his heart stop beating. It was the ax. The ax had fallen down. Somebody had knocked over the ax. No. Not somebody. He had done it himself. He wasn't standing here. He was behind the furnace knocking over the ax and pushing it out so the handle showed. This made him feel queer . . . that there should be two Zellers in the basement.

He could hear that other one behind the furnace breathing—or it might be the fire in the grate making that noise. He must go see what was there. She wanted to know what the noise was. What noise? What noise? That was himself mumbling. But wait a minute—there was somebody behind the furnace.

Zeller leaned over slowly and touched the ax handle. He was afraid it would jump away. But it came into his hand.

Again the air seemed to thicken so he could hardly move. He was moving as fast as he could, yet between each of his movements, between putting his hand on the ax and picking it up; between picking it up and turning around to look at Mrs. Lansen, there were terrible pauses as if he were paralyzed. Something began to whimper in his ears, "Faster . . . faster. . . ."

Then everything stopped. Mrs. Lansen stopped. He was looking at her.

A strange feeling was in him, a warm flood that melted the ice in his stomach. There wasn't time for her to run away. She was just as paralyzed as he was. The air was too thick for her to move in. She was waiting for him, giving him plenty of time, with her eyes raised looking at something in the air and her mouth wide open.

Through this stopping of everything Zeller saw Mrs. Lansen for an instant and this instant seemed longer to him than his whole life. The Mrs. Lansen he saw filled him with so great a happiness that he shouted. A queer Mrs. Lansen with red spots on her withered cheeks, like an old clown; a Mrs. Lansen whose face was twisted into such a frightened, imploring expression as nobody had ever seen before.

In this instant Zeller forgot about the ax. He was going to say something but he couldn't speak fast enough. The ax kept moving, flying. He was killing her.

Zeller closed his eyes. He was flying with the ax, flying in circles up and down as if in a marvelous dream. Then his arms grew tired. The flying was over.

There were noises in the basement. The fire roared. Boards creaked. Lumps of coal slid over each other in the coal bin. Rats were gnawing. Zeller looked around. There was the barrel. He hadn't lied. It had all happened. He felt proud. He pulled Mrs. Lansen along the cement floor toward the barrel and was surprised at the way she looked.

Zeller came out of the basement smiling sleepily. He blinked at the sunny winter morning, at the bright, peaceful street. He started walking away and it seemed to him his heart would break with this sense of peace and brightness that was in the world.

Then when he had walked several blocks Zeller stopped. A voice was calling behind him.

"Zeller! Zeller! Where are you?"

He stood still.

"Zeller!"

How could it be that thing in the barrel calling him?

"Zeller! Zeller! Come here at once!"

Yes. Mrs. Lansen! My God, he was a liar. He had only made believe. It hadn't happened. He had fooled himself. The ax, the barrel, hadn't happened. Again his stomach felt like ice.

"Zeller! Zeller! Where are you?"

The voice screamed in his ears. Violent, raging, like he was dirt under her feet. Sweat covered him. A sob such as a child gives who has cried too long, came from him.

Then as his name repeated itself over and over in his ears, Zeller began to run. He ran wildly, his legs waving under him.

He was running back to the basement. He would show her if he was a liar. He would show himself who was a liar. He would grab the ax and chase her through the house and keep his eyes open this time.

A crowd of men and women stood around the basement door. At the far end of the dark basement policemen with searchlights were looking into a barrel.

Zeller stood for a moment bewildered. A boy was screaming and pointing at his reddened hands.

The Lost Soul

IT WOULD BE DAWN SOON.

The man in the cell was unable to sleep. He had dressed himself. He stood looking out of a small barred window at the waning night and the winter stars going away.

Two heavy-set men with tired puffy unshaven faces were also in this cell. They stared at the cell walls with a remarkable ox-like persistency.

Then, as if overcome by a secret curiosity, they turned their eyes on the man at the barred window and looked shyly over his shoulder at the first colors of dawn.

Yet a fourth man appeared.

The two heavy-set men greeted him with unexpected dignity in their voices.

"Hello, Doc," said one.

"What time is it?" said the other.

The cell door was unlocked. The doctor came in. He took a small silver pencil out of his vest pocket and began rolling it back and forth between his thumb and fingers. Then he cocked his eye at the unshaded electric light burning high up in the cell. He was very nervous.

"Hello," he said.

The one at the window turned. He was smiling.

"How do you feel?" the doctor asked, continuing with the silver pencil.

The one at the window shook his head with a rather queer good-humored politeness.

"I didn't sleep well," he answered. "I suppose it doesn't help any to worry. But . . . well . . . I was just talking to these two men here who have been good enough to keep me company. You see, I'm in a very awkward predicament. . . . I don't know who I am."

The doctor blinked. Then he turned and stared at the two heavy-set men. They looked remarkably inscrutable—even for oxen. The doctor put the silver pencil away and removed a black leather case from his coat pocket. He opened it and took out a stethoscope.

"Just a formality," he muttered. "Open your shirt, please."

He put the instrument on the man's chest and listened.

"Very remarkable," he spoke after a long pause of listening. "Normal. Absolutely normal heart action."

The two heavy-set men nodded mechanically but correctly. There is a certain etiquette of nodding and staring which the laity proudly observe in their relation with the professions.

"I don't know who I am," the man at the window resumed in a slightly high-pitched tone, rebuttoning his shirt. "I feel all right, doctor. But I haven't the faintest idea"—the queer, good-natured smile played apologetically behind his words—"I haven't the slightest idea what my name is. I presume the officials are working hard and doing all they can . . . to determine. But it's getting a little on my nerves. It's lucky I have a sense of humor. Otherwise. Well. Imagine finding yourself in jail. And just not knowing who the deuce you are or where you come from. I suppose I was picked up roaming around. Nevertheless it doesn't seem right to me to put a man in jail. They might have been decent enough to think of a hospital. Or a hotel. I unquestionably have a family who are worrying. You know, I've been trying to figure out what sort of man I am. It's very interesting. For instance, I'm obviously educated and unused to jails."

The doctor turned to the two heavy-set men. They shrugged their shoulders. The doctor looked at his wrist-watch hurriedly.

"What time is it?" one of the heavy-set men asked in a shy voice.

The one at the window sighed and went on talking as the doctor, with a secretive gesture, held his wrist-watch for the two heavy-set men to look at. They looked and nodded.

"I've searched through my pockets," he was saying from the window, "and not a shred of identification. No pocketbook or handkerchief or any marks. Of course—my hands. Not those of a workingman, I should say. And—a—"

He stopped and began rubbing the back of his head.

"Don't you remember coming here?" the doctor asked, looking intently at the man.

"No, I can't say I do," he answered. "I feel quite aware of everything in the present. But the past. Well! The past—"

He closed his eyes and frowned. A slightly bewildered and contemptuous chuckle started his words again.

"Of course, efficiency is more than one has a right to expect from the police. Or they would have had me photographed. As I was telling these two men. And my picture put in the newspapers so that my family would see it and sort of claim me. Obviously"—he stared at the doctor with some anger—"obviously I am somebody of importance."

The doctor drew a deep breath.

"Don't you remember," he began.

"Nothing," the man at the window interrupted irritably. "Pardon me. I don't mean to get angry. But it's damned awkward. You know, I might be somebody very important—with all sorts of people dependent and worried. There's some medical term for this condition, isn't there, doctor? I forget at the moment. The sensation is decidedly queer. And amusing."

He was staring at the beginning of morning light beyond the barred window.

"I don't know why I should feel amused," he chuckled. "In reality what it amounts to, I suppose, is that I have lost my soul. Or, that is, misplaced it for the time being. A most serious matter, it seems to me. But, damn it, I must be a humorist or something. Because the situation makes me want to laugh. I'm sure most men would be wailing and tearing their hair if they suddenly lost their soul. But really, I—"

His face spread in a grin and he began laughing softly.

"By God, what a beautiful morning," he murmured, his eyes again on the world outside. "Doctor"—he crossed to where the doctor stood regarding him, the silver pencil again working between his thumb and fingers. "Doctor, if I could only get hold of my name," he whispered, "who am I . . . who . . ."

The doctor cleared his throat.

"Your name is," he began, "is—"

He stopped. There were footsteps in the corridor. People were coming.

A group of six men came walking toward the cell. The two heavy-set men stood up and shook their legs. The doctor grew excited. He stepped into the group and began talking hurriedly and in a lowered voice.

"Don't read it," he repeated, "it'll just give us a lot of trouble, sheriff. He's amnesic. It'd just be borrowing trouble to wake him up. Let him go this way."

"Well, he'll find out pretty soon," said the sheriff.

"I doubt it," the doctor whispered. "Anyway, by the time he does you'll have him strapped and—"

"All right"—the sheriff thrust a sheet of typewritten paper in his pocket—"let's go."

"Come on." The doctor returned to the cell.

The man at the window nodded good-naturedly. The doctor took his arm and led him into the group.

They fell into place around him—two on each side, two in front, the two heavy-set men behind and the doctor still holding his arm and watching his face.

"You see," the man in the center began talking at once, eagerly, quickly as if a dizziness swayed the edges of his words, "I haven't the least idea who I am, gentlemen. But if you'll be patient with me, I'm sure my family or some other clue . . . I dislike being such a bother. Is that a clergyman? Where, by the way, are you taking me? Please . . . I insist! I must know! Where are you taking me? Good God!"

Silently, without answer to this amazing question, the marchers escorting James Hartley to the gallows continued on their way.

And in the tall, gloomy death chamber a hundred or more spectators sat waiting for the hanging of the creature known as the Ax Fiend who a few months ago had murdered his wife and two children in their sleep.

A group of marchers stepped through an opened door onto the gallows platform.

A confusion ensued. Figures moved about on the platform. Then, out of this bustle on the high platform, an amazed face looked down on the spectators. The mouth of this face was opened as if it were about to scream. Its eyes moved wildly as if they had become uncentered. Gasps came from it.

A shining yellow rope was being tightened around its neck.

A man was adjusting a voluminous white wrapper about the figure under the rope.

Another man was stepping forward with a white hood in his hands. Suddenly the face screamed.

Three words filled the smoke-laden air—three words uttered in a sob so pitiful, so agonized, so startled that the sheriff paused with the white hood.

"This ain't me!" screamed the face. "This ain't ME!"

The spectators held their breaths, and stared.

A white bundle was swaying and twisting on the end of a long thin yellow rope.

The Heavenly Choir

Y ou will remember that God once sent a flood to remedy certain matters He found distasteful in the world. I have here the account of another such Miracle. And if you have, mysteriously, heard nothing about it to date, I am sure this will in no way interfere with your believing it. It is as easy to believe in Miracles that haven't happened as it is to believe in Miracles that have. Only the most quibbling would dispute this.

But you will have to be patient and allow me a Prologue. Since the Miracle is to destroy a sector of civilization which you possibly, at this very moment, admire, it will be to your advantage to attend my preliminary catcalls, however involved-seeming or divergent. They may woo you from certain unthinking Loyalties and Admirations and kindle in you a bilious eye for these very matters you consider, heedlessly, so pleasant. And such new aversion will enable you to enjoy the Miracle and applaud rather than shudder at its havoc.

There is a certain Mr. George Woodyard who catches my attention as I assemble the data for this disaster. I behold him hanging by his suspenders from a chandelier in his impressive office, the suspenders being around his neck and he as wry-faced and out of wind as any highwayman I saw pendent beneath the Cook County gallows in my youth.

As I look at this dangling Mr. Woodyard, it occurs to me that here is a proper hero for my tale and that, if I begin with him and end with him, there will be a certain unity which is usually lacking in Miracles. I therefore remove his suspenders from around his bruised and sausage-stretched neck and with a false comradely slap on his shoulders restore him to his Heyday. He blinks at me a moment, straightens his vest, and then smiles as gently and reassuringly as if his presence were a Cathedral, likely to overwhelm any stray worshiper. Whereon he returns to his desk, slowly, as if he were approaching another Mr. Woodyard almost as remarkable as himself. It is obvious that he has forgotten the grisly matters that took him to the chandelier, for he sits himself down with air-cushion pomp; he regards sternly the Documents, Calendars, Inkstands, Push-Buttons, and Photographs on his desk as if he were reviewing a battalion of heroes passing in salute; and he then looks up at me and inquires with a sort of modest good-fairy humor:

"And what can I do for you, sir?"

This is a silly and even pathetic question, for it is I who intend to Do for Mr. Woodyard—and without further delay.

Mr. George Woodyard's kith and kin regarded him, very likely, as a Human Being—that is, as a Citizen full of distinctive appetites and odd little habits. They most probably saw in him constant, if minor, evidences of that caprice and illogic that convince one School of Psychologists that Man is a product of some Inner Deterministic Creation—a Blossom painted on Nature by a spirit brush. It is an old contention that the Breath of God blowing from the inside molds the human soul, and not the breath of platitude blowing from the outside. The truth lies, I suppose, with God, but I, for one, have an open mind in the matter.

I must insist, however, that as far as I could see there was no Inner Man to Mr. Woodyard. He was put together by contemporary winds like a sort of jigsaw puzzle blown together, and very inaccurately. His mind, his soul, his dreams, were made out of little vari-colored pieces of cliché and current bombast and slightly larger pieces of sky-blue Space. The whole thing didn't fit at all, though it was immediately recognizable as the Picture of a Leading Citizen.

Leading citizens have been immemorially, I am sure, like Mr. Woodyard. Nevertheless, they are difficult to describe. For how describe people who seem always on the side of Error and Bigotry when you look back at them, and on the side of the angels when you shake hands with them? It can't be that they are all villains. I prefer to think that they are the Cautious Ones, the Slow Ones, who make more money than sense, and who delay the world while they wring a last dollar out of its Yesterday.

Factually, Mr. Woodyard was the president of the Woodyard Advertising and Radio Service Company. This was an organization that spent some fifteen million dollars a year in pollination work for a score of Toothpastes, Automobiles, Laxatives, Tobacco Products, Beautifying Creams, and certain Life-Giving Cereals. I shall go into this more fully later.

Enough for now that the Woodyard agency was one of the largest and shrillest of the Pied Pipers in the land. Mr. Woodyard, under whose baton its varied choir of salesmanship assailed the earth and the skies, was in his fifties. He had a square jaw and bushy eyebrows, seemingly borrowed from an illustration for the *Art of Ruling Men*; pale Sunday School superintendent eyes, narrow shoulders, and a large pear-shaped paunch. His long legs tapered like a Brownie's into childish calves and small feet. He had warm, soft hands and artistic nails. His mouth was wide, his lips thin, his cheeks loose, and some wattles hung, statesman-fashion, from his chin.

He covered this fat-padded, old-womanish body with perfect tailoring, a little on the archaic side. His linen was starched. Gold-studded detachable cuffs protruded from his pressed sleeves, hinting of an elegant but cautious soul. He wore a stiff detachable collar and his ties never ventured beyond maroon. But more than by these impeccable draperies, Mr. Woodyard was clothed in an aura of Right Thoughts.

Success had robbed Mr. Woodyard while he was still in his teens of whatever intelligence or Inner Man he might have possessed. Like all weak men who find themselves in positions of leadership, particularly in the leadership of Finance, which rolls its captains out like dice from its wantonly rattling box, Mr. Woodyard had one definite mental characteristic. He was opposed to Thought. Since no thinking had landed him on the throne he occupied, it was natural that he regard cogitation as an alien, dangerous factor.

However, Mr. Woodyard was not opposed to what he called "understanding people's needs." In serving the People—as all Rich Men piling up their dividends insist they are doing—Mr. Woodyard was never tired of saying, at banquets and board meetings, that you must give the People what they want and what is good for them.

What Mr. Woodyard meant, in a coarser manner, was that the easiest way for a peddler to get rich was to carry only a Line of Necessities. But this was no explanation of Mr. Woodyard's success at all. He carried no Necessities. He had nothing to sell that the Public needed and little of what was good for people. Although he talked like one, Mr. Woodyard was no honest peddler knocking on lonely farmhouse doors with packages of pins, thimbles, and beeswax. And when he pretended he was, he wasn't really trying to deceive, but merely being part of a pretense larger than himself and as beyond his talents to question as the Laws of Matter. This is, in fact, the secret of the non-Inner Man and his villainy. Having no contradictory vision of any sort, he has no need for pretending. The hypocrisies of his day, which he finds plastered on his tongue like circus posters on a fence, are for him the Truth. Success speaks out of him, glibly and innocently, like a Prince of Barnums. The great significance of Mr. Woodyard lay in that he was no peddler at all, though his entire dream of life was concentrated in salesmanship. He was a sort of mystic evolution of a peddler or, rather, a peddler's aide. Since the Peddler, whom I will now put in capital letters by way of promotion, had taken to selling things that were no longer necessary to the world and to hawking nuances rather than commodities; since he had burdened his pack with more gewgaws and gadgets than there were customers, more utilities than there were users, and more panaceas than there were ills, he had found it necessary to create an Assistant, even in the Pre-Radio Era. The duties of this Aide were simply to invent desires in the human soul, hitherto absent, and to inflame it with greeds hitherto dormant.

Abetted by brigades of Circes and Psychologists, Mr. Woodyard and his fellow-Aides had remodeled a generation. Theirs was a task to the horrid nature of which everyone closed his eyes, since in the emptying of the Peddler's pack, by fair means or foul, was said to lie the rainbow's end of prosperity for all. Unchallenged even by the most carping of sages, these Aides went about their work of palming off the overenterprise of an economic system whose trimmings had outstripped its necessities.

Under cover of Art and Poetry and the great Democratic Credo that every man had a right to blow and market as many soap bubbles as he desired, the hawking of superfluities became the soul of the nation. Nobody attacked our Peddler's Aide. Even the Anarchists, who needed an advertisement or two to keep their Red Sentinels going, ignored him. Where find an editorial egg to throw at the golden goose who was apparently laying them for all? Unheckled, this drum-beating, fife-tooting, tambourine-banging, and whirling dervish of an Aide, leaping about with a million tin cans tied to his tail, devoted himself to reshaping the human innards.

I shall attempt no orderly survey of Mr. Woodyard's work, but touch briefly on some of his more obvious wiles and conquests. A cigarette habit, to begin somewhere, according to some doctors a habit almost as injurious as dope addiction, had been injected into the national consciousness by an appeal to the bounderism of the masses. Cigarettes had been revealed on a million walls and billboards as being the diversion of exquisite gentlemen, presumably young and old Dukes, lolling about on Yachts or attending the most exclusive of Social Events. And the opportunity to improve their own social status by aping the vices of their betters at the cost of a few pennies had proved irresistible to the masses. They took to smoking like mad, fancying themselves with their cigarette holders and snapping cigarette cases and mysterious preferences for this cigarette over that cigarette as a part of a very dashing world.

Later, with the cigarette well launched and half the nation suffering from dry throats and jittery fingers and on the verge of realizing the cause of its troubles, a secondary campaign had been rushed into the field. Marvels of male and female athletic prowess, huntsmen, parachute jumpers, wrestling champions, lion tamers, racing drivers, and tight-rope walkers had been revealed as grateful devotees of nicotine who owed their steady nerves to the chronic use of the weed, and the tobacco industry had been saved from threatened collapse.

Other inflammatory psychological campaigns had been placed behind Automobiles, Washing Machines, Bathing Suits, Oil Heaters, Wrinkle Removers, and nearly all the rest of the content of the Peddler's pack. Bawdy wenches with breath-taking contours postured for attention from billboard and printed page, with deodorants, laxatives, and hair restorers in their hands—for the Peddler's Aide had discovered Sex. Whereupon, in addition to the bamboozling implication that he would share in the glories of his Superiors if he bought certain brands of Underpants, Whiskies, Shoes, Canned Soups, or Mattresses, the market Bo-Peep known as the Consumer found himself the butt of such a phantom attack on his libido as might have signaled the rebirth of Sodom instead of the mere rise of Mr. Woodyard.

Bacchantes gamboled now on the billboards in juicy and provoking poses; glistening stockings drawn over Fragonard legs, eager mouths moist and red and apparently hissing with passion, bosoms bulging with concupiscence and eyes lurid with lechery battered away at the sales resistance of the masses. The Psychologists had discovered not only Sex but one of its most pathetically fraudulent uses. Unable to embrace the superb strumpet offering a new Sedan, a Kitchen Stove, or a Bottle of Pop, the Consumer's libido—always a blind force in human history—was very likely to embrace the objects themselves.

This salesmanship worked in another way but even more effectively on the women than on the men. To women it had the deeper appeal of sympathetic magic. The plainest of housewives was inclined to feel she partook a little of the seductiveness of the lovely nymphs whose stockings and bloomers she wore and whose deodorants and laxatives she used.

But this cunning business of selling not to the needs but to the bounderisms, libidos, inferiority complexes, etc., etc., of the simple-minded Consumer was only part of the shambles. Over and beyond all these odoriferous ruses to set a public whinnying for wares it did not want was the main drive of reiteration. Although he was willing to experiment with clever lures and psychotechnic baits, the Peddler's Aide knew (as all great forces for the confusion and belittlement of mankind appear instinctively to know) that success lay less in the exercise of his wits than in the basic ninnyism of his victim. Accordingly he let loose a propaganda of signs, layouts, panegyrics, and beacons, the only purpose of which was to beat with some sort of hypnotic rhythm on the always available eye.

The process of wigwagging the public and shooing it like a brood of hens to a thousand and one bargain-counter corn cribs gave the land a false literary glow. Newspapers and magazines multiplied fantastically under the largess of the Peddler's Aide, to whom all periodicals became pretty carts carrying his pigs to market. As a result the Republic wore a rash of printed matter that would have looked like a Belles-Lettres Renaissance if it hadn't looked so much and so transparently like the drool-and-dribble partner of a sales campaign.

By this monstrous coaxing the Peddler's Aide succeeded in perverting the buyer into a giddy spendthrift. A restlessness overtook his pocketbook and an echo of this restlessness filled his soul. His fancies, lashed by Duchesses and Bacchantes, began to poke feverishly at the Peddler's pack. Be-advertised into a state of economic somnambulism, he bought where he needed nothing. And then, obedient fellow, he bought duplicates of what he needed not at all. And then he bought improvements on these superfluous duplicates. And then he developed a whole set of extra and exotic appetites and nibbled delicately away on every newfangled product, with not hunger but a hawker in his stomach.

As he had been hornswoggled into the cigarette habit, he was decoyed and nose-ringed into the automobile habit, into the gadget and thingumabob habit; into the redecorating his home with daffier and more strawberry-box grandeurs habit; into the medicating himself like a chronic scurvy victim habit. He was tobogganed into the new hats, new shoes, new pants, new dresses, and new buttons for every change of weather habit; into lotions, creams, shaving, muscle-building, dieting, fattening, hair-restoring, flavored-slop drinking and chewing gum habits and other habits too vague and too pervasive to catalogue. He bought not to have but to have the right thing, which was constantly being changed by the savants, scientists, and seers a-toil in the Peddler's backyard; not to possess but to be in style.

And though at first our Consumer had been a resisting victim of the sorceries loosed by the Peddler's Aide, he became now, together with his wife, who is always ninety percent of the American picture, a creature of fretful and wry-brained acquisitiveness. He blossomed as a sort of dumping ground and he wriggled proudly and patriotically under the accumulating hill of his gaudy refuse.

It was only by developing this stunned and capricious Customer that the Peddler's system based on the overstuffing of his pack could continue. And continue it did. But there was no joy in the Peddler's camp. There were, instead, doubt and apprehension and a group of Handwriting-on-the-Wall experts. The Peddler and his backers became alarmed. It became apparent—and not only to malicious and unpatriotic eyes—that a system whose outlets depended on a perversion of human instincts was likely to lose its shirt, its pants, and its Stock Exchange.

Thus it was decided even among the Manna Makers that something would have to be done. Since it was inconceivable to the Peddler that anything so subversive and unhuman as a curtailing of his pack be attempted by way of remedy (such tactics led straight to Bolshevism, Cannibalism, and the Antichrist), there was only one other road open. This was to inflame, confuse, and behowl the already reeling Consumer into a more staggering materialism and connoisseurship.

And, lo, the new road was revealed to them quite as if God were a Stockholder. The Radio, blooming overnight like the dragon-teeth-sown army of the Mongols, offered its hydra tongue to the worried Peddler.

Among the first to discover this new road to riches was Mr. Woodyard of the pink face and yet unsilvered hair. But, like so many who later became Radio Kings, Mr. Woodyard did not so much discover his Kingdom as find himself seated in its midst with no knowledge that it was a Kingdom or even a Duchy.

Mr. Woodyard was at the time in the Advertising business and busy as a flea on a cow's tail plastering the land with pornographia and proverbs in behalf of the Peddler's pack. He was, presently, of the opinion that radio was a silly medium for his Service and that money spent hollering at people over the air to buy things was futile and undignified. Would that he had been right.

It is usually the way with men who gibber-jabber of Vision and Progress that they are devoid of any instinct for either and that if you left the world in their hands it would still be flat and full of icebergs. Not that, as you will discover in detail very soon, I consider the radio the measure of any movement forward of anything. To the contrary, I greeted it in its crackling infancy and held it to its dramatic death as the ugliest of the inventions by which man had managed to bedevil and corrupt himself. This hydra-headed megaphone attached to man's greed, his vulgarity, and his infatuation for error had in my opinion already howled half the Arts out of existence as well as belittled the very source of wisdom—the human word—before God smote it. But more, much more of this later, for my tale, when I am finished with this drum-rolling and get to it, concerns itself with the Miracle that squelched forever this newly hatched brother of Bedlam.

Mr. Woodyard quickly altered his views, proving that the simpler the parasite, the more nimble he is at changing his spots. He became a Pioneer. He began to build up Radio Advertising. It would have been impossible, in the year 1923, to have imagined that the Peddler's Aide had only scratched the surface. He was already scribbling away with smoke in the sky, hanging bargain banners from balloons and dollar signs from flagstaffs. He had already plastered all the available fields, fences, walls and rooftops with his visual tom-toms, and he already owned, spiritually at least, nine-tenths of our publications. (For the Consumer's stubborn inability to read only Advertising Matter still made necessary a sugar coating of magazine literature.) What other fields, indeed! we might have scoffed.

We had reckoned without physiology. Nothing more was possible for the Eye, but the Ear was virginal. The great American Ear, heretofore the property chiefly of snake-oil doctors and can-can spielers, was promoted to a place in big business. And what had seemed to such sensitive fellows as myself the last vulture cry in greed-propaganda seemed now to have been no more than a mannerly bit of buttonholing. The Peddler's Aide, howling up and down the air waves, became loathsome where before he had been merely objectionable.

The reason for the difference was this. There is a chastity to print that even greed does not dare bespatter too much. The written word grown hysterical loses its meaning, and to whatever idiotic enterprise or bargain it seeks to lure one, it must retain not only its grammar, but also some sign of dignity. The spoken word has no such handicap. It does not exist, aloofly, within its own content. It is not merely a symbol. Behind it the speaker can moan, gurgle, rumble with passion, sough with righteousness, and play the whole shameless orchestra of human emotion.

Mr. Woodyard was among those early Radio entrepreneurs to invest in vocal mountebanks to cry his clients' wares. He bought orators, elocutionists, and spellbinders to carry the message of his clients' Good Will to All into the American ear. Venal and sonorous charlatans proceeded to invade the bedrooms, living-rooms, and other hideaways of the Consumer. They dumped their gewgaws on his bed, spread them on his dinner table, and pumped away at his poor little money bags with a suction that was irresistible.

There was immediately a major boom in panaceas, those investments most dear to the addle-headed. The Peddler discovered it was much easier to frighten the Consumer vocally into believing himself a vat of horrid odors, a creature endangered by a thousand decrepitudes, than it had been to convince him of these things in print. Where print, usually in shamefaced agate type, had been used to inform the victim of his wretched status—muttering pimp-fashion out of the corners of newspapers about all manner of magic salves and purges—now there came into his ear no mutter at all, but tones as firm and holy as any ever heard in the Vatican. Print is always print, but the voice can sound like Galileo that has only a truss to sell and echo like Pasteur that has no more than an itching powder to peddle.

Every box of cheese, bit of fabric, bite of food; every lotion, vehicle, toothpaste, cigarette, liver poker, colon swabber, electrical doodad, screw-on appliance and screw-off appliance—all the contents of our Peddler's bulging pack now augmented by a world of new fiddle-faddle discoveries—became forthwith the Heroes of Hymns. Cardinals (seemingly) intoned the vitamin wonders of cabbages. George Washingtons lent to hitherto humble hair-restorers a dignity of utterance unknown outside the pages of history. Sindbads panted of diamond valleys lurking in every neighborhood store and Ciceros declaimed the triumphs of stink-removers. There was turned loose such a quiver-quaver of piety tones, brotherly love tones, straight from the shoulder tones, America for Americans tones; such a throbbing of cello calls and swooning love cries, that one would have expected the entire nation to fall victim to a mass attack of *mal de mer*.

But the wheedling and bombastic voices fell on the Consumer's ear and sent him spinning to the markets. And as these nauseating histrionics began to lose somewhat their power, the Peddler whistled for his dancing girls. And now came a renaissance of entertainment—an irruption of jesters, yodelers, banjo players, thespian bawlers, and star gazers. A thousand gullets poured revelry hourly into the Home and a thousand orchestras all going at once in various glass-enclosed chambers bombarded and enfiladed, sniped and barraged at the Consumer's castle.

Parnassus was wheeled to the microphone and the apoplectic hawkers found themselves augmented by Beethoven, Brahms, and Orpheus himself—and what an Orpheus!—by braying bands with their machine-gun rhythms; by Stars of Screen and Stage knee-deep in goo; by Philosophers whose quivering tongues seemed more to lick than to speak; by pun pluggers, wit sockers, hilarity uhlans; by skits and sketches and comic-strip dramas out of the largest swill barrel ever to emerge from the alleys of Art; and chiefly, and to a point of Walpurgian horror, by ballad sadists and aria flayers enough to strangle the whole of song.

And all this free fun and melody released by the Peddler, become suddenly a Cuckoo-Clock Maecenas, yielded wondrous dividends. For it was a simple psychology, as apparent as flies in a milk pot, which the Peddler's Aide had discovered or had wished on him. He would sell his wares by appealing to the gratitude of his victim. There being no other reason to buy a toothpaste, Mr. and Mrs. America would buy it because it had made them laugh, rendered their home a cave of echoes, or reminded them of their mother.

This abrupt raid on the Arts had effects other than the emptying of the Consumer's pockets. What it emptied most amazingly was the Arts themselves. The eclectic music of the world, long preserved for the high ornamentation of human mood and long but sparingly used as a ladle for stirring the soul of man, came pouring now out of several million cuckoo clocks, preceded and followed by voices chanting the virtues of Headache Remedies and Corn Plasters. And where we had once listened to the Great Composers in the hush of auditoriums, our very souls attuned to the mystic language of notes, we heard them now with ears only. They cackled like geese out of the Peddler's pond who had once sung like cherubim out of Heaven. Their nobilities grew less with the lessening of our moods as audience. And though it was Genius that still played beside the Peddler's pack, it was eventually only Simple Simon who listened.

For a time the Peddler's Aide covered himself with bay leaves. He was hailed as an Evangel by those sages who see in the democratization of anything, whether it be Bach or the Bastille, a step forward. He was, it was eagerly stated by authorities who should have known better, colonizing the Ivory Towers. He was bringing about, they decided, the long-awaited liaison between Beauty and the Beast. Not alone for the few would the loveliness of great music exist, but for the All. Well, this is a fine theory, but like most Samaritan-hatched ideologies, it exploded in the face of its theorists. It was not the Beast that underwent any marked alterations, but, as always, Beauty. For Beauty lying down with the Beast too often grows a bit cockeyed and contemptible herself. And though she still hummed and fiddled for us her homeland songs, we knew her for an exile from that homeland. She had lost her power over us. It was in this way that the Peddler's Aide gutted the art of music.

There were other as morbid results. The manufacture of tunes was speeded up beyond the penny-whistle talents of the tunesmiths. Ballads crowded on ballads until not garden larks but magpies sang. A boiler-factory jamboree of jingle and heartbreak assailed our ears, such a pother of yearnings and bedroom-frustrations that we soon stopped learning and remembering songs.

And finally, in this desperate feeding of our glutted senses, the cuckoo-clock maestros began to run amuck. They invented pompous and classical orchestrations for the rankest of hill-billy tunes. They laid hands on the Classics and twisted the great tonal pillars of art into penny pretzels of sound. Visigoths of the air, calling themselves by such titles as Jam Kings, Swing Kings, Jazz Kings, Jive Kings, continued razing and firing the Orphic domains, and ravishing and hamstringing their deities, to the delight of a growing mob of followers. These capered after their heroes, whooping and jiggling like a rabble on its way to a lynching bee.

I shall conclude with only one more phenomenon. This was the intimidating of the Consumer by the radio Cassandras. News commentators came leaping out of the loudspeaker like bogey-men. Voices, trembling and ominous, dinned war scares and political warnings into the Consumer's masochistic ear, appalled him as he lay in his barber chair, hounded him in taxicabs, and disorganized his liver with terror at the dinner table. It began to seem to this brayed-at and goggle-hearted Consumer that he no longer lived in a civilized world, but in a house of cards. The effect of such subtle terrorization was all too obvious. Jumpy nerves began to generate a jumpy national and international politics, and politicians, wrestling with their immemorial scraps of paper in the high winds of the world, began to feel that disasters were demanded of them. Hysteria, an ally they had been able to evoke at the proper time for their own ends, sat now in an opera box demanding encores before the show was on.

How now with Mr. Woodyard, prime master of these Peddler Revels, Chancellor of Cacophony, and Boy Scout Monitor of Bedlam?

Does he flourish, does he smile benignly at the millennium in his lap?
Is he Prince of Cornucopia abroad in a Toga and has he found the
Philosopher's Stone? Verily, all these happy augmentations of the
Woodyard soul have so occurred. He is all the Arts. He is Ibsen and
Pavlova, Bizet, Epictetus, and Shelley. He is Demosthenes and Harle-
quin and Cyrano. He is the wind in the trees, the eagle on the wind,
and the feathers on the eagle. He is the Mandarin sage of the Hwang
Ho; the thunder is his sigh and the lightning is his fan. But all these
avatars are only his side line. It is with his left hand that he takes
over the tasks of Barnum, Ziegfeld, Albee, Gatti-Casazza, Diaghilev,
and Toscanini. With his right hand he still fills orders. His Consumer,
saturated and pulpified by the maniacal cuckoo clock, now sashays to
work covered with Glass Beads, bristling with Feathers, Pomaded,
Physicked, Deodorized, and Pedicured and Lord of all the Rubbish
Heaps under his nose. He is now Prince of Consumers, a Village
Idiot snooping about after shiny pieces of tin, and Mr. Woodyard is
his Guiding Star.

So we come on Mr. Woodyard this particular evening, Novem-
ber 27, 7:45 P.M., bestriding his Castles of Caterwaul. Truly the pride
that goeth before the fall was Mr. Woodyard's. As he sat at his dinner
table this ominous evening, he seemed as devoid of cares as a toad
of feathers. His pinkish face glowed and twinkled like an altar and his
wattles were as commanding as a cluster of Field Marshals.

This being, all unbeknownst to its millennium-drunk head of the
table, a sort of Last Supper, I shall linger on its last few minutes and
reveal who were present. At the other end of this shining stretch of
silver, glass, linen, and mahogany, loomed Mr. Woodyard's wife—a
plump décolletée and bedizened matron with the chop-licking purr of
successful matrimony. Of such wives as Mrs. Woodyard one can say
little more than that they are a sort of appendage, a tail wagged by the
husband; or a third leg sharing the pomp of his stride and contributing
no more than a freakish look to it.

There were present also the son of the house and his youthful
madam. This son, whose name was George Woodyard, Junior, was a
vacuous and beefy youth, almost completely stunned by his sire's lordli-
ness. A protracted education had passed through him like grain through
a goose. His head was as hollow as his father's, but lacking the bay
leaves. Where success had wreathed the parent, its shadow had reduced
the son to a mushroom. George, Junior, hated nothing and loved
nothing, and beyond lying in bed figuring out some practical joke he

might play on some one of his semi-conscious friends, he had no plans for his tomorrow.

His wife, Madeleine Woodyard, unable to become a tail or a third leg to so negligible a biped, contented herself with a limbo-like glitter. She had once been in the chorus of a night club, where, parading her nudity under an Egyptian headdress, she had appealed to some mysterious mating instinct in George Woodyard the Second. Two years ago she had discarded her career with her headdress, and a year of concubinage followed by a year of marriage had given her that sloth-like and decorous look with which beauty reveals the vacuity of its keeper.

Of more interest than these family members were the other two diners, Mr. and Mrs. Charles Chaley. Mr. Chaley, a roly-poly abstracted gnome man with mustard-colored hair and a freckled, somnambulistic face, was the manufacturer of the Chaley Beauty Products. He had made several millions of dollars by persuading several millions of women to inflame, erode, and macerate their skins with nightly applications of his products.

Success, however, had only provoked Mr. Chaley, since it had made further expansion of his beloved industry more and more difficult. Behind Mr. Chaley's almost idiotic stare lurked a veritable business satyriasis. His huge income from his innumerable and worthless beautifiers left him as restless as a bankrupt. He had apparently no interest in money and was monastically indifferent to all the pleasure it might have bought for him. He disdained leisure, was contemptuous of possessions, lived as unornamental a life as a Pullman-car passenger, and appeared, like some coral-obsessed polyp, to have only a single reason for his existence. A fever such as sometimes seizes the gambler had burned away in Mr. Chaley all interests beyond that of increasing the number of jars and bottles bearing his name.

Just what satisfaction Mr. Chaley derived from this form of expansion is hard to fix. There was, obviously, something alive and bewitching in the continued increase of Chaley jars and Chaley bottles, and had they come out of his loins he could not have been prouder of them. He daydreamed continually of ingenious sales campaigns, and after twenty-five years of strenuous familiarity with the ins and outs of every Chaley jar and bottle, there was still nothing so beautiful in the world for him as a window display of Chaley products.

Having determined to increase his output beyond its present colossal, but to him doldrumish, proportions, Mr. Chaley had turned to Mr. Woodyard—that peerless Peddler's Aide—for assistance. This evening, as a result of scores of conferences and months of artistic travail, was to hear the inauguration of a new Coast-to-Coast radio hour sponsored by Mr. Chaley and offering one of Mr. Woodyard's most masterly ensembles of wit, melody, and Peddler Cries to the Public.

Mr. Chaley sat beaming abstractedly over his coffee. He was thinking of the ten million homes into which, in a few minutes, the wonders of the Chaley products would be brought on the wing of song and jest.

As for Mrs. Chaley, nobody at the table had yet addressed a word to her and for the good reason that as far as it was possible for anyone to be non-existent, Mrs. Chaley was more mist than matron. She was a delicate-voiced, gray-haired little woman with an intimidating abstraction in her gentle eyes. She had, shortly after her marriage, endowed a Theosophy Center in her home city of Cleveland. Her subsequent preoccupation with the Occult fitted in nicely with Mr. Chaley's qualities as a husband. She sat now, facing the Lotion King, but looking thoughtfully, as was her habit, into certain problems of Transmigration which she carried like a menagerie in her head.

Mr. Woodyard put an end to the sporadic tittle-tattle by announcing that the Chaley Hour was at hand. The diners entered the Woodyard library, and, except for the coffee, the Last Supper was practically at an end.

The picture of these six folk agog in the Woodyard library, eyes focused on the little silk-covered hole of the Woodyard de luxe radio, is one which has already become a nostalgic part of the world's yesterday. And as the years festoon it with the charm of Things-No-More, it will gather further those nosegay qualities which so improve the looks of the world in retrospect. As one of those who found the reality always irksome, I can report the scene with no fiddle music beclouding it. And not this scene alone, but the millions of similar scenes which at this hour dotted the land, unaware that they postured before a final curtain.

In the Woodyard library a gong now sounded out of the radio, such as summons lamas to their devotions, and a voice trembling with joy sang out like a rescue party on a mountain peak: "Chaley! Chaley's Beauty Products are on the air! Chaley! The name that all the world over stands for feminine loveliness! Feminine Charm! Feminine Desirability! Chaley presents to you tonight the first of a series of all-star broadcasts featuring Mr. Willie Watts, King of Swing, and his Merry Andrews, Madame Olga Sweitzer, the world's highest-paid prima donna, and last, and by no means least, the great comedian Jimmy Carter, famed favorite of stage, screen, and air."

Dropping from these exuberant tones to one of vibrating intimacy, the Voice continued, in a rush of *sotto voce* passion:

"Chaley means Beauty. A Chaley bottle in your boudoir means an enticing skin on your face and bosom. A Chaley jar in your hand means ten years off your age. Use Chaley lotions and Chaley creams to smooth, liven, and beautify your skin. Chaley Products remake the Face of Womankind."

Whereupon the Voice returned to its Mountain Peak. "Introducing," it cried, "Mr. Watts, King of Swing! And remember, folks, Beauty is as Beauty does. Swing it, Henry."

Mr. Watts's orchestra, timed to the instant, dashed upon the ether like a cavalry charge.

The six in the library listened like relatives at a Confirmation, or rather five of them so listened, for Mrs. Chaley seemed not to be listening at all. To Mr. Woodyard the music, like all music under his auspices, seemed very personal, a series of glamorous sounds given off by the Woodyard Advertising and Radio Service; and to Mr. Chaley the whole thing seemed a hymn to his jars and bottles. He was very happy and nodded approvingly at his host and took to winking at anyone who caught his eyes.

Mr. Woodyard's pulse beat a little more rapidly. He thought of the ten or twenty million ears listening throughout the land to the delicious sounds of Mr. Watts's troupe, and a sense of mystery stirred his vitals. It was not the mystery of how this cuckoo clock worked that touched the Woodyard depths, or any wonder by what devilish legerdemain Mr. Watts's orchestral ravings were emitted in a sort of invisible dust to settle instanter on myriads of ears. It was the Mystery of these Ears that held Mr. Woodyard spellbound—of this Kingdom of Ears cocked in rabbit-like salute. Whatever troubles there were in the world and whatever tragedies and confusions, here in these ears lurked the True Humanity—the man or woman Ready to Buy.

The music ended and Mr. Woodyard beamed at the group as if it were he who had just laid aside the talented baton, for it is the ancient delusion of Entrepreneurs, even the dumbest of them, that they are the show. Mrs. Woodyard was about to wag vocally at her husband's achievement, when he arrested her with a good-natured finger of warning.

"Quiet, please," he cautioned, and just in time, for the Voice of the Mountain Peak filled the room.

"Chaley!" it cried out, so passionately that the owner of that name blushed to his toes. "Chaley!" it repeated, shaking with excitement. "The Name that belongs in Every Woman's Life!"

And at this moment the Unbelievable happened; a thing happened that opened Mr. Woodyard's mouth wide and left it open—in fact it was never really to close again—and that lassoed the woolgathering Mr. Chaley out of his daydreams. As for the others, they heard it too, and stared first at the little silk-covered hole and then at Mr. Woodyard's open mouth.

What had happened was that Another Voice was on the air, speaking in a kind of idiotic duet with the one on the Mountain Peak. And though this Other Voice was gentle and flute-like and wondrously tender, it was nonetheless horribly distinct.

"I am so happy," it said, wailing the words like a faraway peanut whistle. "Oh, so happy." Then it added a faraway little laugh by way of corroboration.

"So very, very happy," it continued while the Mountain Peak, as yet unaware of this competition, thundered on about the Chaley Products.

"Pure!" it cried. "One hundred percent Pure! No deleterious chemicals to leave their marks on Milady's face."

Which serious misrepresentation even a jury of scientists would have ignored, for the Other Voice continued like a nightingale.

"It is wonderful here," it quavered tenderly. "Oh, wonderful, wonderful. And I am so happy. So happy. I wanted you to know."

Mr. Woodyard, mouth still open, was now on his feet.

The Mountain Peak had evidently now been signaled that he was not alone on the microphone, for a tremble hinting of protruding veins and beads of sweat had come into his tones. "Chaley," he quavered, "waits for you like a Friend in every Drugstore, like a Magician in every Beauty Parlor, like a Lover in . . ."

"Can you hear me?" wailed the Other Voice wistfully, and brought a bellow of rage from Mr. Woodyard by this offensive question. "I want you to hear me," it explained gently, "because I am so happy. Oh, so very happy."

Mr. Woodyard was at the telephone. The rest of the group gaped, wrinkled their brows, squirmed in their seats, glowered and perspired in embarrassment; all except Mrs. Chaley, on whose blank face a little smile had bloomed. Mr. Chaley had removed his watch from his vest pocket and was twirling it dangerously by its chain.

The Mountain Peak Voice had teetered for a moment on its last metaphor and then toppled into silence. The Happiness Boy was left alone on the air.

"Everything is so beautiful here," his swooning voice continued, and slid moodily into a whistling solo.

"There are smiles that make you happy," it whistled, "there are smiles that make you sad . . ."

The whistling trailed away and there was nothing to be heard on the radio but blurred sounds and some crackling indicating an impromptu studio conference, and in the room Mr. Woodyard's voice shouting into the telephone to be connected immediately with a Mr. Aikens. The others in the library, excepting Mrs. Chaley, sat as if under the first breath of calamity. Mr. Chaley was the grimmest.

Then a crash of melody came out of the silk-covered hole, signifying that Mr. Watts had rushed his men into the breach. They played "La donna è mobile."

Mr. Woodyard, thrusting a finger into one ear, cried into the telephone: "What do you mean, sir, you don't know who it is?"

Mrs. Woodyard tiptoed to the radio and lessened its volume.

"It's some joker," Mr. Woodyard continued savagely, "or it may be somebody from the Eversweet Hour." This was a rival Beauty Products Program.

"Call the police," went on Mr. Woodyard, "and have them comb the building. Get the head engineer on it. You have? Well, where's Mr. Aikens, then? Indeed! I see. Hold the wire a moment." Mr. Woodyard turned and listened to the music and then replied over the instrument. "There's no interruption now. No, not a sound of him. It's coming over fine."

Mr. Woodyard hung up and smiled on the company as he mopped his face.

"The situation is in hand," he said. "It was either a pitiful attempt at a joke or pure sabotage. We don't know which yet. We'll have a report on it in a few minutes."

Above the orchestra now rose the siren-like and tobogganing tones of Madame Olga Sweitzer, the world's highest-paid soprano. The great warbler was singing with that added exuberance that characterizes the artist in action against odds. She filled the library with a veritable festival of melody, raising the old hurdy-gurdy tune of fickle womanhood into a compelling aria.

"Everything will be all right now," Mr. Woodyard whispered at the brooding face of his client. He was lowering himself into his armchair as into a throne of Normalcy when the Unbelievable thing hap-

pened again—and just as Mrs. Woodyard had increased the volume
of the radio by turning a little wheel. Mr. Woodyard remained
crouched in midair, his bottom for the moment abandoned by his
brain. The Voice of the Happy One, gentle, far away, but incredibly
distinct, had joined Madame Sweitzer in song, albeit of a different
genre.

> "Sweet Genevieve, sweet Genevieve,
> For you I pine, for you-oo I grieve,"

sang the Voice as the diva's throat hurled rival cadenzas into the field.
"Ta taa ta tumm, tum taaa ta tummm," continued this Other Entertainer, who had evidently run into a memory snag and was now
merely baying after a lost melodic trail. Then, with a triumphant lilt,
the eerie Voice doubled on its tracks and located happily the beginning
of its ballad once more.

"Sweet Genevieve, sweet Genevieve," it resumed, "for you I pine, for
you-oo I grieve."

But again it floundered, revealing a haunting but diminishing
knowledge of the ballad's structure. Throughout its efforts Madame
Sweitzer's voice remained a-soar above the whoopings of the orchestra.
But in vain were all its rafter-shaking powers. In vain she sang the
little Verdi tune as if a herd of Valkyries were hallooing it at the Fire
Gods; that is, in vain, if her intention was to drown out her quavering
colleague and his faltering but nostalgic cries for Genevieve. Madame
Sweitzer achieved volume and tonal beauties such as had never before
come pouring from her larynx. But by some astonishing twist of sound
perspective, the Voice of Genevieve's mourner remained brilliantly
audible. It continued in its fragile but indelible tones to sing, having
for a third time become re-entangled in the opening of its ballad.

"For you I pine, for you I grieve," it inverted the couplet by way
of emphasis, "sweet Genevieve, sweet Ge-hen-evieve."

Mr. Chaley, with a cold look at his open-mouthed host, marched
across the library to the de luxe radio cabinet. He snapped off the
current. The silence that followed was truly golden.

"That's not going to do my Product any too much good," said
Mr. Chaley stiffly. "I'm kinda disappointed in the Program, Mr.
Woodyard."

But Mr. Woodyard was glued to the telephone, where he had been
hoarsely at grips for several minutes with a busy signal.

"You can't blame Mr. W. for that nasty fellow," said Mrs. Woodyard.

"Keep it going," Mr. Woodyard commanded; "we don't want to miss any of it. It's all evidence."

"I don't enjoy it, whatever it is," said Mr. Chaley angrily.

The Woodyard daughter-in-law, finding herself confronted by the Lotion King, who was pacing swiftly from one end of the library to the other, made a sweet effort to distract Mr. Chaley from his troubles.

"I wanted to talk to you ever since we met," said the young matron, "about that new Boudoir Cream of yours."

"Some other time," said Mr. Chaley and continued his pacing churlishly.

George Woodyard, Junior, always a fascinated student of practical jokes, sat with his nail tapping his lower teeth and his eyes raised in meditation. He was trying to figure out from a cursory knowledge of radio construction how the thing could be done.

"I keep getting the busy signal," Mr. Woodyard said raspingly.

"Hang up," Mr. Chaley flung back; "the whole thing's a filthy mess."

"Somebody evidently pulled a secret hook-up," Woodyard, Junior, offered, removing his finger from his mouth. "I've been figuring it out."

"Oh, do tell us!" his pretty wife cried. "Georgie has figured it out," she added, tapping Mr. Chaley's elbow. Mr. Chaley paused.

"It was a hook-up from outside the studio," said George, "because you will remember that the voice of the Main Singer, what's her name, was the furthest off, although it was the loudest by far. Whereas the little Voice, the one that we heard doing the Genevieve number, was in reality closer, almost in our ears in fact. By God"—he beamed suddenly—"I wouldn't be surprised if it was somebody in this room—right here!"

"What the hell are you talking about!" Mr. Chaley demanded.

"One of us"—the junior Woodyard lifted his beefy frame out of the chair with difficulty—"that's it! By God, one of us is a ventriloquist!"

He looked searchingly at the little gray-haired figure of Mrs. Chaley and inquired boldly: "How about it, madam?"

"Don't be a fool, Junior," his mother spoke sharply. "It came over the air. I heard it."

"She hasn't answered," said Junior.

"Listen, young man"—Mr. Chaley dropped his hand on his wife's shoulder—"we'll have no insults."

"Sit down, George," Mr. Woodyard commanded, still jiggling his telephone bar. "Besides, they heard it at the studio, so it can't be just in this room."

Junior was silenced.

"Whoever it was," Mr. Woodyard went on, enunciating distinctly from the telephone, "they will be arrested and prosecuted to the full extent of the law."

"I hardly think so," Mrs. Chaley said quietly.

The others looked at her with surprise.

"Go on, darling," Mr. Chaley answered with unexpected deference; "I'd like to hear what you have to say on the subject."

"I'd rather not," Mrs. Chaley smiled, after a pause.

"Please," insisted Mr. Chaley. "Why do you think they won't be arrested, sweetheart?"

"Well," Mrs. Chaley sighed, "it's really something I very seldom talk about, as you know, Charles. But if you insist . . ."

"I do," said Mr. Chaley.

"Well," Mrs. Chaley went on, smiling at the company, "the reason they won't arrest anybody is that there's nobody to arrest. You see, it's not a human being that did that—I mean, as we understand people to be human beings."

"I don't follow you," said Mr. Chaley.

"It's a ghost, Charles, very likely an earth-bound spirit caught between Transmigrations. It frequently happens."

At the end of this flow of words Mrs. Chaley sighed and looked eagerly at the radio.

"I wish you would turn it on again, Charles," she said. "He may still be hovering. And—it's really very instructive."

"Why, the idea!" exploded Mrs. Woodyard. "A ghost on the radio! Did you hear what she said, George?"

But Mr. Woodyard chose to ignore the vaporings of his client's wife.

"Listen," he snarled into the telephone, "it can't be busy all this time. I demand to be put through."

The library door opened and a visitor, pale and out of breath, strode into the room. This was Mr. William Aikens, president of the Trans-Continental Broadcasting networks, used by Mr. Woodyard for all his major programs. He was a thin, witty-looking man.

"Hello, folks." Mr. Aikens nodded automatically at the group. "Hello, George. I got here as fast as I could. Almost wrecked my car. Had to run the last two blocks on foot. Never mind the telephone, George." He waved at the instrument still in Mr. Woodyard's hands.

"You won't be able to get the studio for a month. There are at least twenty million people on the phone. The biggest drawing power I ever saw any program reveal," he added with a clever look at Mr. Chaley.

"What in God's name . . ." began Mr. Woodyard.

"Let me get my breath," Mr. Aikens pleaded and slid into a chair.

"Well, Mr. Aikens"—Mr. Chaley stared at him—"so that's what you call radio advertising, is it?"

"Listen, I'm as much at sea as you are," Mr. Aikens answered adroitly between gasps.

"I want this distinctly understood, gentlemen." Mr. Chaley raised his voice. "You've made a laughing stock out of Chaley Products. And that's unforgivable."

"Nonsense, Chaley," Mr. Woodyard said. "The whole thing will react in your favor. It always does."

"What always does?" demanded Mr. Chaley. "Gentlemen, name me one possible way in which this doesn't make a fool out of Chaley Products."

Mr. Woodyard mopped his face and turned to Mr. Aikens.

"What steps have been taken," he inquired, "for the arrest of this fellow?"

Mr. Aikens had now recovered his wind and wanted a drink.

"It's the Goddamnedest thing," he said, pouring himself one. "I put the whole engineering force on it, the minute it started. They've gone over the entire system. Not a screw loose."

"The Eversweet Hour," Mr. Woodyard interrupted.

"I thought of that," said Mr. Aikens, nodding. He swallowed his drink and, with a glance at his wrist watch, walked to the radio. He snapped on the current.

"I left orders to resume the program at exactly 8:30," he said. "Our experts will have been all over the machinery by then."

The radio remained silent.

"Three more minutes," said Mr. Aikens apologetically.

"Can't we try some other station?" Mrs. Chaley suggested quietly. "He may have switched over to some other studio, you know."

"Who's that?" asked Mr. Aikens.

"The ghost," said Mrs. Chaley.

"She has a theory it's a ghost," Mrs. Woodyard explained and patted the theorist good-naturedly on her arm. "There, there, dear—there's no reason for any of us to get hysterical."

Mr. Aikens stared at the little gray-haired woman as he poured himself a second drink.

"A ghost, eh?" he chuckled. "That's very funny."

"I don't mean to be funny," Mrs. Chaley answered. "I would never have mentioned it if Mr. Chaley hadn't insisted on hearing what was in my mind."

"Baloney!" Mr. Aikens exploded, his nerves severely tried by the evening's confusion. "That's what's in your mind, madam."

"That's my wife." Mr. Chaley came forward.

Mr. Aikens blinked.

"Terribly sorry," he said, and extended his hand. "Glad to meet you, Mrs. Chaley. You must forgive me."

Mrs. Chaley nodded and shook hands.

"Oh, it's all right," she said. "I never expect to find any believers."

"She's up on those things," Mr. Chaley explained proudly.

"Well." Mr. Aikens took a deep breath, ignoring this hint of Mrs. Chaley's erudition. "Eighty-thirty. Here it comes."

As he spoke, the Mountain Peak Voice charged into the room. But now it was a voice full of good humor and quivering happily as if but recently recovered from a round of merry laughter.

"Ladies and gentlemen, members of the radio audience," it cried gaily, "there has been a slight delay in our program due to an absurd and highly amusing mishap. I will not bore you with the details of what happened, good folks. I hope you have all been as amused as we have by our amateur friend whose pathetic efforts at entertainment tangled themselves in our wave length. Highly diverting though his contribution to our program proved, it will not be repeated. I thank you for your indulgence. And now"—the Voice clambered back on its Mountain Peak—"on with the Show! Introducing Chaley's Master Mind of Fun and Prince of Comedians, Jimmy Carter."

The orchestra, accompanied by a storm of studio handclapping, played the first bars of a song called "Here Comes Cookie" and the voice of the hilarious Jimmy Carter, familiar to the radio millions, uttered its zany chuckle like a tinkling of caps and bells. Mr. Woodyard, who was quivering, sat down slowly and shot a heroic smile at Mr. Chaley.

Jimmy chuckled again as if wrestling himself out of a blissful state of idiocy and then began to call eagerly for some comrade called Herman.

"Herman," he cried gleefully, "I know who done it. I know who done it."

"Who did what?" demanded Herman, none other than the Mountain Peak in a more artistic vein. "Who did what?"

"Made all that Genevieve twouble," lisped Jimmy. "I met him. He's a midget, the most terrible, blood-thirsty midget alive."

"A midget?" repeated Herman. "Well, that doesn't sound possible. Are you certain?"

"Am I certain! Ha!" Jimmy screamed in falsetto excitement. "I seen him, I tell you. With my own eyes. He was pointed out to me as the only midget gunman in the world. He's called," said Jimmy almost out of breath, "he's called Public Enemy Number Three-Eighths."

The studio laughter covered Jimmy's guffaws.

"Did he have anything to say to you by way of explanation?" demanded Mountain Peak Herman, apparently struggling unsuccessfully to keep serious.

"Yes," cooed Jimmy, imitating the tone of the recent interloper. "He said: 'I'm so-o happy. So very, very happy.' And I said: 'What are you so happy about, silly?' And he said . . .'"

But whatever it was that Jimmy had learned was never heard by the listeners in the Woodyard library. For at this instant the Unbelievable returned with reinforcements. A Quartet of Voices, all flute-like and far away as the original's and singing in wavering amateur harmony, came valiantly out of the little silk-covered hole.

"Sweet Genevieve, sweet Genevieve
For you I pine, for you-oo I grieve,"

sang the Quartet.

"Turn it off!" Mr. Chaley cried. "By God, that's too much. I cancel my contract."

"Just a minute." Mr. Woodyard was on his feet and as out of breath as if he had been run over. "We're all in this together."

"I never ordered a Quartet!" cried Mr. Chaley. "It's a distinct abrogation of contract. I bail out here and now."

"Hold your horses, Chaley," began Mr. Aikens, who was unable to take his eyes off the little silk-covered hole. The wailing Quartet was now a-flounder in mid-ballad. "We are not responsible for any acts of God."

"That Goddamn Quartet is no act of God!" Mr. Chaley shouted. "Any jury will bear me out."

Far away, Jimmy the comedian was still hard at work with his chuckles and his jests. But none of those in the library heard him. Panic entered their voices as the Quartet continued its wistful uncertain harmonizing.

"It can't be *four* ventriloquists," George, Junior, was saying reverently to himself.

"Please, everybody," Mrs. Woodyard cried out, "my husband will take care of it. Let's all keep our heads. George"—she scurried to his side and tugged at his arm—"there's no time to lose, darling. You must simply do something."

"Kindly mind your own business!" Mr. Woodyard bellowed and looked wildly for the telephone.

"Listen to them," Mr. Aikens demanded. "If that ain't the God-damnedest most mysterious thing I've ever heard."

"There's nothing mysterious about it," said Mrs. Chaley gently. "He just went and told some friends."

"Who did?" asked Mr. Aikens, off his guard.

"The ghost," said Mrs. Chaley. "He brought his friends back and organized a Quartet. It's entirely understandable. There's nothing to be alarmed about. They're doing their best to entertain us. I doubt, however," she added, critically, "whether they were singers in *this* Vale."

"Sweet Genevieve, sweet Genevieve, for you I pine, for you-oo I grieve," the Quartet was reopening the ballad. The zany chuckle of Jimmy Carter deserted him.

A babble of voices followed, Jimmy's growing fainter as if he were being dragged from the microphone. In the confusion the Mountain Peak Voice appeared to be battling its way forward. Finally above the crackling and blurred sounds it boomed ecstatically out of the little silk-covered hole: "Chaley! Chaley! The Name of Beauty! Loveliness in every Chaley jar. Charm in every Chaley bottle. When you visit your neighborhood drugstore ask for . . ."

Silence fell on the Mountain Peak. The station had gone off the air. The Woodyard radio, an instant before an outpost of bedlam, stood now in wooden innocence before the eyes of Mr. Woodyard and his guests.

The newspapers the next morning carried accounts of the matter under various headlines. One reported: "Air Squatter Wrecks Broadcast." Another announced: "Hooligans Rout Chaley Program in Mystery Joke." Another stated: "Man in Moon Takes Charge of Radio Station. Angry Advertiser Investigating." A fourth maintained, though in a joking vein: "Stage-Struck Ghost Raises Ruckus as Wave-Length Stowaway."

The narratives beneath these headlines were all written in that broad vein of whimsy affected by newspaper men when dealing with matters a bit too strange for belief. For there was no one like the Press, in those Pre-Debacle days, for poking fun at Mysteries. Although it occasionally reported a Miracle or a Miraculous Cure with a sober face and an eye to its devout Catholic circulation, it did not then regard God and His doings, or the secrets beyond the grave, as legitimate news items.

I know it is the fashion now to look back on the newspaper columns of the Radio Era and marvel at what seem the venality and cynicism of the then Fourth Estate. But the cynicism of the Press in such a crisis is not difficult to understand. Having to report from hour to hour with straight face and stern tongue the idiocies of the current politicians, having to ladle out in demi-tasses the Niagara of buncombe roaring around its ears, having to give credible dress to the decomposing and disheveled platitudes by which we manage to trick ourselves into a fairly orderly society, having to play usher to all the Political, Social, Artistic, and Industrial jackanapes whooping for front seats, is it any wonder that Journalism grows full of subterranean laughter? Not that its sons all rise above the litter of their columns or toil like Sages in Chains. But this constant flying of flags for Error, and keeping an endless twenty-one-gun salute going for the crackpot parade of existence, breed in them a need for sneering.

And yet this brings us face to face with the question: What can they afford to laugh at? What phase of existence is there sufficiently remote from their advertising columns and partisanships for them to vent this giddy cynicism on? Artists and poets, naturally, a few poor goats who pose as Casanovas, a Personality now and then with a feather too many in its cap; but chiefly it is the Supernatural that wears the safest motley. The Press, prostrate like a street Arab before every Altar, can usually afford a snicker for the miraculous.

In the case of the radio ghosts there was also in the happy chortling of the Press on that first day a less complex ingredient. This was a natural jollity regarding any misadventure that might befall an Advertising Rival.

Still, one might ask the newspaper gentry sternly how it was that they, as well as the millions who heard the Genevieve crooners, failed to know the truth at once. And worse, having heard these contented ghosts yodeling so benignantly of their condition, how could they ignore this tale of other worlds, as if by their indifference to that phase of the affair they outlawed its very existence?

I fancy I have answered as well as asked the question. It is by this

Indifference that we survive. It is this Indifference that is our chief strength, our dike against the avalanche of the Unknown. The indifference of the public to the first whinnyings of the Radio Miracle was no greater than its heroic indifference to the numberless other Mysteries, Muddles, and Miracles that lie beyond each of its moments. Of the world we live in we know hardly more than the turtles; of the world that lives in us we know less the older and more complex we grow; and of the world beyond us, all we know is that its immensity is woefully unflattering, and that men have immemorially lost their wits merely from trying to describe it.

In short, though the Miracle had signaled, business went on as usual the next day, but not Mr. Woodyard's business—not quite. Mr. Woodyard appeared in his office the next morning apparently fully recovered, outwardly. Somewhere inside him, close to his solar plexus, however, his mouth was still open. He had received a great shock. Arriving, he skimmed through the reports of the Engineers, Electricians, and Physicists who had labored all night under Mr. Aikens's direction. They had been unable to figure out any possible way by which the Hooligan Broadcasters could have tapped the wave lengths of the Chaley Hour. This did not, however, cause them to alter their finding that such tapping by such hooligans had taken place. Being Scientists, they were a little more pompous about knowing nothing than ordinary people. They very nearly convinced Mr. Woodyard that the whole delicate investigation would soon end in the arrest of some hinterland playboy with a trick aerial in his barn.

Somewhat encouraged, Mr. Woodyard turned his attention to the Press reports of his troubles, including a daring editorial in the *Morning Inquirer* on the hazards of Air Advertising. As he read, Mr. Woodyard opened his dictograph and spoke sharply to his secretary.

"Get me the Advertising Manager of the *Inquirer*," he said. "Tell him I want him in my office between three and four this afternoon."

Then he closed the instrument, smiling for a moment at the retraction he anticipated. That Newspaper Ned would think twice before he ever plucked again at the Fabric of Society. He continued to smile, despite the nervous pulse that appeared near his liver as he read the data prepared for his morning's attention. His underlings seemed all to have been stricken overnight with an annoying jittery zeal. He learned that twenty thousand calls had been reported by the Telephone Company as having been made, unsuccessfully, to Mr. Aikens's broadcasting studio, and that five thousand more consumers had simultaneously besieged the Chaley Main Office in New York, that forty

thousand derogatory postcards had already been received from trucu-
lent and sarcastic listeners, and that these reposed already in files on
Mr. Chaley's desk. Mr. Woodyard felt that he was being annoyed by
Superfluities. There were a dozen departments for the consideration
of such matters, and Mr. Woodyard called in his general manager, a
Mr. Isaacs, and gave him hell.

Let it be said for Mr. Woodyard that he rose above all those tel-
ephonists and postcard writers at this stage. Like all leaders who mold
Public Opinion, Mr. Woodyard knew there wasn't any.

A few hours later he tried to explain this phase of the situation to
Mr. Chaley, who had arrived just as the repentant Advertising Manager of the *Morning Inquirer* was leaving. Mr. Chaley had brought
with him a suitcase full of the more unnerving postcards, which he
could hardly lift, and which he insisted on regarding as so many death
warrants for the Chaley Products.

Mr. Woodyard smiled at these alarmist views.

"You are welcome to withdraw your account," he said, "and leave
the Eversweet people in sole possession of the field. That's up to you,
sir. I will interpose no legal difficulties."

Mr. Woodyard calmly opened a drawer in his desk and removed
a gold-sealed document as thick as a time-table.

"Here's your contract, Mr. Chaley," he said. "Tear it up if you care
to. It's my only copy."

Mr. Chaley accepted the ponderous document and stared thoughtfully at his name, flickering in every tenth line as a sort of clue.

"What I would like to say to you, Chaley," went on Mr. Woodyard
as casually as if he had handed his visitor a blotter instead of a million-
dollar contract, "is merely this. The Consumer Always Forgets. That
fact is the soul of all advertising. If the Consumer were able to remember anything, we wouldn't have to spend these millions reminding him hourly of things he already knows, now would we? I can
sum up all I have found out in years of studying the Advertising Problem, in these few words—the Consumer can't even remember his own
name. That's the long and short of it. He not only forgets *what* he
wants to buy, but *why* he wants to buy it. He has to be reminded
constantly. As for remembering the virtues of any Product, I assure
you that's ridiculous. If you asked the most intelligent Consumer you
could lay a hand on why he smoked a certain cigarette that spent
twenty millions a year advertising itself, that Consumer wouldn't be
able to tell you. And if he did tell you, ten to one he would be quoting
some rival cigarette product. Well, it stands to reason, Chaley, that

if they forget the good, they must forget the bad. In a few days not a single listener who heard that trouble last night will remember whether it happened to you or the Eversweet People or the lamppost. I sincerely think you're frightening yourself with a molehill."

Mr. Chaley hummed a few minutes and then tapped the suitcase at his feet.

"I brought these over," he began.

"I know, I know," smiled Mr. Woodyard, "the usual flash-in-the-pan resentment. It means nothing. I've been through it too often. If you're wise, you'll just burn them. They're a side of the Public you'll get nowhere listening to. They don't mean a thing by the time the ink is dry on them."

Mr. Chaley sighed with hope. He had been unable to sleep, convinced that the Chaley Products were ruined and that laughter would forever dog the aristocratic heads of his bottles and his jars.

"Tear up that contract, if you want to," said Mr. Woodyard coolly. "You're your own boss. I don't think I can advise you any further."

Mr. Chaley looked at the many-paged document and hesitated.

"Woodyard," he said slowly, "I couldn't afford to have another of those joke programs. I didn't sleep a wink."

"Well, that's one thing you'll never have to worry about again." Mr. Woodyard beamed, aglow with his victory. "We'll start over again tomorrow night and——"

Mr. Woodyard looked up in surprise. General Manager Isaacs had come through the private door at a run.

"Turn on the Magic Coffee program," Mr. Isaacs panted. "Something's going on."

"I must ask you not to come running in and out of this office as if it were a lavatory," Mr. Woodyard began, but the whiteness of his general manager's face and the glitter in his eyes halted him. "What are you talking about?" he added nervously.

"Turn it on," gasped Mr. Isaacs and stood pointing at the radio behind Mr. Woodyard's desk.

Mr. Woodyard's hands had grown cold. Magic Coffee was one of his Key Clients. He wheeled slowly in his chair and snapped on the current and dialed quickly. Paul Whiteman's orchestra was playing handsomely a medley of jive favorites, but Mr. Woodyard failed to hear this part of the entertainment. What he heard was a Voice wailing, not the Voice of the Chaley disaster, but a brother to it—a little hoarser and less tender.

"Hello, everybody," the Voice was saying in that maddening faraway sing-song these hooligans appeared to favor. "How are you, everybody? I want to say something. Don't go away. I want to say something nice."

Mr. Whiteman's bandsmen, although apparently aware of the new welkin squatter, continued with fine musical indifference, being made of sterner stuff than the entertainers who had lost their heads on the Chaley Hour. Mr. Whiteman, himself, ad libbed gaily to the audience during a pianissimo passage.

"Pay no attention, folks, to our little unseen friend," he said and then, addressing this Ether Pirate, added: "How are you anyway, brother? Are you very, very happy this evening?"

Mr. Whiteman's first violins were heard to chuckle at this sally of the maestro. To Mr. Woodyard's horror the peanut whistle Voice replied:

"Oh, yes. I am so happy. But I want to know how Irma is. How are you, Irma? Are you happy, Irma?" And without waiting for any reply from either Irma or Mr. Whiteman, the Voice slid tenderly into song.

"When it's apple-blossom time in Normandy," it sang, "in Normandy, I long to be."

Mr. Woodyard snapped off the current and looked foggily at Mr. Chaley and then at his general manager.

Mr. Chaley said: "Say, that's kind of serious. What are you going to do, Woodyard?"

Mr. Woodyard looked accidentally at the ornamental chandelier in the center of the ceiling. It had come out of a Florentine palace.

"Have the police been notified, Mr. Isaacs?" he inquired weakly.

His phone rang and he lifted the receiver.

"Hello," he said, "this is Mr. Woodyard speaking."

An expression of pain, which gave him suddenly a childish look, spread over all the Woodyard features as a voice crackled in his ear. It was the voice of Andrew Watterson, head of the United Cereal Products Company, and even more than Magic Coffee, a Key Client.

"What the hell is the meaning of this, Woodyard!" Mr. Watterson was demanding. "There's some Goddamn buttinsky on the Golden Flakes Program hollering and singing like a lunatic."

"Just a minute," said Mr. Woodyard. "I'll see what the trouble is." Turning, he said hoarsely to Mr. Isaacs: "Golden Flakes."

Mr. Isaacs dialed the program in. Mr. Woodyard knew in a way what to expect. Nevertheless, his mouth opened again with shock. A Handel oratorio was being beautifully chanted per schedule by the

St. Peter's Episcopal Choir, Mr. Watterson being religiously inclined in his sales campaigns. It was not these soul-stirring tones that Mr. Woodyard heard, however. What he heard was a woman, obviously a Negress, wailing away tenderly and, like the other hooligans, wonderfully distinct.

"Oh, Joe," she said, "why did you shoot me, Joe? Ah neveh loved nobody but you, Joe—so help me, Joe. That other fellah neveh got to fust base with me, Joe. Neveh got to fust base, Joe. Neveh got to fust base; honest, honey. Why did you go and shoot me, baby?" And with a little faraway sob, the speaker slid into a song.

"Who broke the lock on the backhouse door?" she wailed tunefully. "Who let that wind come blowin' in . . . blowin' in . . . ?"

Mr. Woodyard heard the telephone crackling on his desk and picked it up.

"Hello," he said.

"Tell them to take off that program!" Mr. Watterson screamed. "I ain't sponsoring any Southern harlots. Shut off that program and keep it shut off, or I'll throw you and your whole Goddamn organization into jail."

"My God!" said Mr. Chaley softly. "I got off lucky. Just listen to her."

"I'm putting through a call to the Federal Radio Bureau," said Mr. Woodyard into the telephone. "Personal messages are absolutely against the new code. We can get them on that."

"Get who?" Mr. Watterson howled so loudly that Mr. Chaley could hear.

"You better tell him the truth," he whispered.

"Just a minute," said Mr. Woodyard into the telephone. "What truth?" he demanded shakenly as he covered the mouthpiece with his palm.

"That it looks like ghosts," said Mr. Chaley quietly, "as you were informed right off the bat last night. If you had followed Mrs. Chaley's suggestions you might have gotten somewhere by this time."

Mr. Watterson had disappeared when Mr. Woodyard removed his palm from the instrument. Mr. Isaacs silenced the radio.

"Well," said Mr. Chaley. "I guess that's that."

Mr. Woodyard sat glassy-eyed as Mr. Chaley began slowly to tear up the contract foolishly placed in his hands a half-hour ago.

The Press on the following morning was divided between jolly descriptions of the two wrecked Programs and a stern curiosity as to the future of Radio as an advertising medium, now that irresponsible and malicious amateurs had found a way to join the entertainment personnel of the broadcasting studios.

"There is no telling where this unfortunate discovery, which evidently enables any Tom, Dick, or Harry to tap the wave lengths, may lead," one of the Editorial pages observed soberly. "From what has happened, however, it begins to look as if no Artist or Advertiser will be safe from the vicious, if often amusing, raids of these new Ether Pirates. The matter calls for immediate action by the Federal authorities if the great field of radio diversion and propaganda is to be preserved."

In its news columns, however, the Press controlled its alarm over the radio's future. It dealt with the situation aloofly and with a beady eye for all its comic values. The thousands of inquiries asking for explanations and the thousands of explanations put forward by the more active-minded students of the phenomenon were a rich lode for the News Gatherers. And by noon the Press had, as if under some common baton, uncorked its full gale of laughter at the Supernatural. For out of the explanations advanced, the notion that ghosts were responsible for the confusion appeared to be gaining ground. Seemingly the entire lunatic fringe of news readers had taken to bombarding the editors.

This lunatic fringe, which includes the never-failing crop of Phantasts, Seers, Voodoo- and Spook-Mongers, Alchemists, Rosicrucians, Perpetual Motion Machine Inventors, crime witnesses and confessors, Hermits, Nudists, Whiskered Prophets, White and Colored Messiahs, Table Tippers, Frustrated Writers, and those who maintain there never was a Jesus Christ—this little but devout army of Unreason was generally ignored as a news source by the daily papers. A firm prejudice in favor of the utterances of the sane, or at least the pretenders to sanity, had been an ancient editorial dictum.

On this day, the Press, however, acting the facetious Master of Ceremonies, opened its columns to the crackpots. Interviews with basement savants, ferreted out among their witcheries, filled the papers. Members of Ectoplasm Societies and Swami Circles and End of the World groups were quizzed with mock seriousness, and the great body of confused but normal readers was treated to a Mark Twainish holiday.

It is sad to relate that this laughter and calm, so rare a team of Editorial horses, remained but briefly in the field. For by seven o'clock on the third day the Press, with a *volte-face* more spectacular than any in its swivel-minded history, was on the streets baying the wild truth of the story. Headlines with less humor in them than a hangman's noose announced in fat slabs of ink that "Ghosts Rout Radio," that "Mystery Voices Fill World," that "Dead Orators Invade Air Fields," that "Heaven Speaks to Earth," that "Souls Stampede Radio." And there was one Editor who, finding the *mot juste* for the sudden rush of piety to the headlines, proclaimed: "The Heavenly Choir Is on the Air."

But these headlines were hardly news any more. For the news had already burst over every radio in the country. Beginning at five o'clock, thousands of voices, obviously under a sort of faltering organization, had joined the regular earthly programs. One group, seemingly numbering a thousand throats, came over WZX in a truly stirring version of "My Old Kentucky Home." Another group over WJY wailed in mighty chorus "Put on Your Old Gray Bonnet with the Blue Ribbons on It." Another calliope-like ensemble of heroic proportions took possession of WMX with "Old Black Joe." There were other units, evidently less rehearsed and only vaguely organized, that offered little but false starts and rallying cries from overzealous leaders.

Before a half-hour had passed, all efforts at any organized performances appeared to collapse, and the choirs seemed to grow out of hand both in numbers and in energy. Conflict obviously broke out in the wildly multiplying ranks of these unscheduled entertainers and a sort of anarchy overtook the whole Venture. Swarms of voices concentrating on a single tune were still to be heard, particularly one vast and dominant section which kept offering "It's a Long Way to Tipperary" in fine rhythm. This old tune came over station WOL and for ten minutes its swinging melody echoed sturdily out of the Other World.

By six o'clock the celestial program had degenerated into a hairraising shambles. Over all the networks, drowning out the last desperate efforts at human competition, these increasing faraway hordes now whimpered, thundered, whistled, screeched, and hallooed, in a terrifying caricature of entertainment. All that was audible was a deafening surf of whooping and hilarious sound—and this surf rolled over the Great Dike.

This senseless booming and whistling out of Nowhere had the immediate effect of bringing half of Humanity to its knees to await the End of the World in the posture it had been taught was most pleasing to God. The other half of the world, which kept its feet, engaged just as earnestly in the various enterprises that bloom always under the nose of great disasters, such as Looting, Arson, and Rapine, while a minority who obviously did not believe in a Future Existence took to their beds in more concrete devotions than those of prayer.

And as in all routs, the horrible imaginings outstripped the present fears. For disaster is never disaster enough for the human mind, and whatever horrors chase it down the night it will multiply them by ten and recaparison them with the largess of hysteria.

By eight o'clock that species of hair-streaming information that travels the currents of mob thought had spawned the tale that an incalculable horde of wailing Dead had captured the radio stations; that vast troops of white-sheeted Spooks were marching through scores of cities and causing them to dissolve under their graveyard breath; and that it was only a matter of hours before these myriad Visitors would have reduced the world to a guttered candle. Harassing each other with these tales, droves of people came bounding out of their homes in quest of that last refuge against calamity—the touch, sound, and shiver of one another.

Now that we have come to accept the presence of ghosts as no more mysterious than that of other interstellar Gases, it is a little difficult to understand the wave of universal horror that swept these first hours. Apparently any modicum of Truth is enough to shake the world into insanity, as witness its behavior on first hearing that the earth was not flat, and on being apprised, more recently, that Man had not been pulled rabbit-fashion out of the Garden of Eden hat by God but was a creature evolved with heroic patience by Nobody in particular from some sort of Oyster.

The proof that Life existed after Death should certainly have come as no thunderclap to a race which had maintained just that since its earliest babblings. But there you have the weakness of human thought. However real it is, it never prepares us for reality.

By dawn the apex of the Rout had been passed. Most of the radio broadcasting stations had been burned and razed by mobs engaged in the traditional way of dealing with Truth by the stamping out of its mouthpieces. The churches in the morning were still doing a terrific turn-away business and streets were still full of demented groups hugging each other and bellowing hoarsely for the sight of Kingdom Come. But there was a recession of panic. For one thing, most of the radio receiving sets had been destroyed, thus removing the actual sources of the terror. And for another thing, the Press began to take the situation in hand.

"Life after Death is not physical," one Editorial announced boldly. "We have nothing to fear from our Heavenly companions. We should, indeed, be overwhelmed with joy to learn that They are all happy and full of Song in their Home beyond the skies."

"They are still singing," stated another Editorial occupying half a front page, "and seemingly full of the comradely delusion that they are delighting the living by their efforts. Let us not tremble, but rather sit back and know that we are merely listening to Another Program, and one very close to God."

On the second day the Press bristled with statements from scientists and savants of every hue offering theories concerning the electrical composition of the human soul and its obvious affinity with other forms of electricity. And though these theories were too abstruse for the understanding of ninety-nine percent of their readers, they were greatly reassuring—as is anything that is couched in scientific words.

A statement from Washington revealed that the government, too, had not been idle. It announced that only one of the nation's broadcasting stations would be allowed to remain open and this only for the further study of the life-after-death phenomenon. A bill was rushed through both houses of Congress prohibiting all human radio broadcasting. The possession of radios was declared illegal. A special arm of the law was quickly created to confiscate all privately owned radio apparatus, with power to arrest and imprison citizens caught using radio sets.

And on the third day the debacle had spent itself. There was, apparently, no period of convalescence. Man recovered as he always does from these blows to his ignorance, instantly. He revealed, as he has so often done, that the basic meanings of human as well as divine activity by which he lives are of no actual importance but a sort of pretty scenery in front of which he playacts. Shift the scenery and he continues to perform the never-changing comedies and dramas of his daily life.

But no sooner had the Dead lost their status as a menace than they became the object of embittered controversy almost as menacing to the peace of the nation. The streets became full of men and women arguing in behalf of rival Interpretations. Innumerable Societies were hatched, each proclaiming itself the custodian of the Real Truth. Soul Worship Sectarians, crowding thousands of rooftops, took to howling back at the Invisible Ones in pious efforts to entertain Them. Their singing provoked the less demonstrative elements who were already back in office and shop. Police were finally called to dislodge these rooftop minstrels. Pitched battles were staged high in the air and hundreds of the Sect showed their determination to amuse the Dead by leaping from cornices to join the Heavenly Choir beyond the reach of infidel police clubs.

Driven finally from the building tops, the survivors took to parading the streets in the wake of large brass bands and singing frenziedly. For several days the racket set up by these worshipers threatened to disrupt the communities almost as much as the musical blasts of the Dead had done. Police and militia managed after some difficulties to scatter them into basements and other hideaways.

A tenderly worded but nonetheless stern document from the Vatican helped quiet the Holy Singers. The souls of the Dead, said the memorable announcement, must certainly be regarded as remiss in their duties to God and the Glories of Heaven in wasting their time listening to the profane music and questionable comedy of the world. The Living, it concluded, must not further their fall from grace by offering them tawdry secular entertainment and luring them from the superior bliss awaiting them at the feet of God.

Of the countless individual fanatics who took to chartering balloons and, equipped with mandolins, fiddles, accordions, and mouth organs, sailed off into space as pilgrims to Nowhere, never to be seen again, a great martyrdom literature is already extant.

More touching, however, than all these tales of aberration and confusion are the first accounts of the disillusion that overtook the nation. From the very beginning the knowledge that Heaven was no more than a raucous amateur hour began to depress the more thoughtful laity. Science, however, held out the promise of a great cultural renaissance. A process by which the myriad voices of the Dead still pouring out of the skies could be filtered through a sort of electrical sieve had been perfected in the first week. The achievement was heralded by the Press as opening unlimited vistas. It was eagerly announced that the boon to human knowledge from such orderly communication with the Dead as had become possible would be immeasurable.

In a few days, though, the Press began to abandon some of its first optimism. It became obvious that the Dead appeared either unwilling to contribute a mite to the reservoirs of the world's information or that they knew nothing. In reply to the most tender and patient questioning by a corps of scientists, priests, rabbis, and literary lights nominated for the task by the President, the Voices isolated by the electrical sieve offered only snatches of old songs or some pardonable but purely selfish interest in the status of some relative. A few of the fanatics who had leaped from the city's rooftops to join the Heavenly Choir were located and fruitlessly questioned.

The theory soon began to afflict even the most hopeful of the world that Heaven was as full of imbeciles and irresponsible souls as earth. And with this growing realization the great era of atheism in which we live today came upon the world.

But to return now to Mr. Woodyard, whose failure to survive the collapse of his Radio Empire I have already revealed. If you will recall, it was as a casualty hanging from the chandelier that I first introduced him. But before Mr. Woodyard was driven to this end, he struggled violently and with some heroism to restore Radio to the high estate from which it had been dashed and to rope and tie the vanished Consumer again. He threw his entire fortune into the laps of certain wizards and charlatans who were attempting to weed out what they called Ethereal Static—the new scientific name for the Dead. At the end of the first month of his labors he was joined by an unexpected ally, Mr. Chaley, who, it appeared, desired once more to advertise his products on the air.

"We'll show her," Mr. Chaley remarked slyly, referring apparently to his wife, "who's running the world—us or the ghosts."

For several weeks Mr. Woodyard, as is the habit of deposed monarchs, found solace in garrulity. He issued long interviews to the Press which were never published.

"In our rejoicing over the discovery of life after death," said Mr. Woodyard in one of these interviews, "let us not forget the Consumer. The fact that the Consumer has been deprived of that world of Music, Art, and Culture which he has come to regard as his fairest heritage, is indeed, a sad one. Personally, I shudder when I think of the silence in the American home."

In another unpublished interview a week later Mr. Woodyard "stated" a little more hysterically:

"It surely cannot be the will of God to wipe out the spirit of industrial enterprise which has been the greatness of America. But this is exactly what will happen if He allows the Souls who are His charges to overrun the radio. The falling off in national purchases is appalling, and forecasts inevitable depression and panic. Who are these so-called Dead that they should be permitted to fill the air lanes with their insane noises!"

Thereafter Mr. Woodyard, although he spoke to his few remaining employees of million-dollar war-chests, became subdued. He lacked any further capital for demonstrations. He was practically penniless toward the end. With his last seventy-five dollars Mr. Woodyard, abandoned by his friends as well as his family, hired a hall where he lectured to seats empty but for the loyal Mr. Chaley. What he said was that Mr. Roosevelt had shown himself a wretched coward in surrendering to the Radical Element in Heaven. In 1940, he roared at the happy Mr. Chaley, the Republican Party would put the Dead in their place! Mr. Chaley applauded wildly.

Shortly after this episode, Mr. Chaley, who had contributed two hundred and fifty thousand dollars to the radio war-chest, disappeared, having been committed to an upstate sanitarium on the plea of his wife. Mr. Woodyard lingered on. One of his last acts was to stop a taxicab in the middle of Seventh Avenue traffic and inquire pathetically of its occupants whether the Dead ought to be allowed to interfere with American business to the extent they were doing. At the end he wrote a letter. It was addressed to Mr. Chaley in the upstate insane asylum. It declared fervently that when he, Mr. Woodyard, reopened the air waves to industry, the Chaley products would be the single commodity advertised for thirty days. Alone and without competition of any sort he, Mr. Woodyard, would put on a new and greater Chaley program for twenty-four hours a day without pause.

It was at this point that Mr. Woodyard surrendered to the great beyond, via the office chandelier.

On the day that Mr. Woodyard joined the Heavenly Choir the scientists in charge of the Electrical Sieve succeeded in isolating three Soul Voices. Their report was submitted to the Congressional Committee for the Investigation of the Dead and added to the already voluminous archives of that body. It recorded that one of the three Souls had sung for several hours selections from *The Chocolate Soldier* and refused to answer any questions at all. The second was summarized as an obvious schizophrenic case unable to assemble into any coherent pattern whatever intelligence it possessed. The third Voice was discussed at length and quoted in full.

"We isolated this interesting Voice shortly after 2 P.M.," says the report, "and were pleased with its unusual clarity. It is one of the few Voices we have contacted that preferred expressing itself in speech rather than song. When caught in the Electrical Sieve, it was wailing loudly:

" 'Can you hear me? I am addressing the world of the Living. Can anybody hear me? I have something of vital interest to say.'

"We were able to assure the speaker of our attention. No sooner had we answered than the Voice uttered a curious shout.

" 'Chilly!' it cried. 'Chilly.'

"'Tell us about it?' we inquired soothingly. 'What makes you chilly?'

"The Voice repeated with excitement: 'Chilly!' and for several minutes disappeared out of our Sieve. It returned, however, and began exclaiming violently:

"'Chilly! Loveliness! Loveliness and Beauty! If you want to be beautiful be chilly!'

"Aware from experience of the confusion which overcomes the dead Souls, we spoke cautiously to it, pretending to understand its message and to be fascinated by all it was saying.

"'Unearthly beauty!' it cried. 'Please don't interrupt me. Listen! Fairer than any dream of Heaven. Chilly! Am organizing Dead to be chilly. Stand by for announcement.'

"After some minutes of incoherent babbling which we were unable to decode, the Voice slid gracefully into song, as is the habit of the departed. It appeared to favor the old ballad 'Sweet Genevieve.' It was still singing its haunting notes when it fell out of our Sieve and joined the indistinguishable uproar of the Other Side.

"'Vale, sweet singer of Heaven's mysteries,' we called after it.

"As if in reply, we were able to catch a faint, faraway repetition of the word 'chilly.'

"At least this Soul has revealed to us," concludes the report, "that our old conception of Heaven has not been entirely false. From its happy cries Heaven seems to be, as we have always fondly imagined it, a white and snowy chaste domain. That the newcomer to its glories considered it a trifle chilly need not affright us. We must remember that the fevers of earth were still clinging to him."

There are, of course, still many who speak with nostalgia of the Radio Era, and there is always that crop of essayists for whom the past is tender copy. One hears and reads these unscrupulous romanticists moaning away about the Parnassian days of Soup Hours and Cigarette Programs, of the wit, melody, and drama that once throbbed ceaselessly in the ears of our citizens. And remarking these moony historians it would seem that another Golden Age had been snatched from under our noses by the abolition of the radio.

All of which, as every semi-enlightened reader knows, is a thumping lie. Considered from the medical viewpoint alone the death of the radio is perhaps the greatest boon that has been contributed to the world by science. Statistics for the past decade show a fifty-percent lessening of gastro-intestinal ailments, particularly those due to distention, inflation, and subsequent dehydration by catharsis of the thirty-odd feet of bowel inherent in each human being. The public has slowly been weaned away from its wanton use of physics, deodorants, corn cures, pain killers, and nerve stimulants, with the happiest of results. The millions who were terrorized into alkalinizing their kidneys with proprietary medicines now report sanely to doctors when the occasion warrants, and feel better immediately. Our ladies, also, have taken to hormonotherapy, the latest of medical achievements, rather than to searching for youth in fancy bottles, beribboned salve boxes, and electric belts. Whether they have found it or not is beside the point. At least their faces have become cleaner.

The falling off in smoking, coffee- and pop-tippling, gum chewing, and other semi-pernicious habits has in general helped restore the public health incredibly.

With the disappearance of the impassioned hawker and his thousand and one dehumanizing gadgets and inventions the consumer has lapsed into comparatively human activities. Cooking, for instance, has been restored to the American home. In short, benefits too numerous to itemize have fallen like manna on the Republic.

But more than these concrete advantages has been the improvement in the mood of the world. The silencing of dictators and political dervishes has stabilized our governments. The return of music to the theaters and auditoriums has brought that oldest art back to itself. And there has been restored to man, particularly the workingman, whose leisure hours are precious, some measure of reflection.

A sort of peace has descended on earth. In the very first spring following the miracle many strange and unheard-of things began to happen. People picked flowers again, sat in the grass, read books and poems, or let their hands lie idle in the sun. And Youth took again to walking abroad in the night and raising to the skies that duet of silence which is most acceptable to love and the orderly propagation of the race.